THE ROAD BUILDER

BLUEHEN BOOKS

a member of Penguin Putnam Inc.

New York

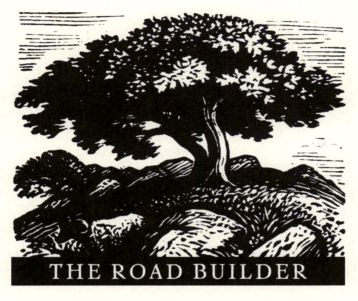

THE ROAD BUILDER

NICHOLAS HERSHENOW

BlueHen Books
a member of
Penguin Putnam Inc.
375 Hudson Street
New York, NY 10014

Library of Congress Cataloging-in-Publication Data

Hershenow, Nicholas.
The road builder / Nicholas Hershenow.
p.   cm.
ISBN 0-399-14754-3
1. Americans—Africa—Fiction.   2. Uncles—Fiction.
3. Africa—Fiction.   I. Title.

PS3558.E7766 R6   2001   00-065081
813'.6—dc21

Printed in the United States of America

1   3   5   7   9   10   8   6   4   2

This book is printed on acid-free paper. ∞

Book design by Marysarah Quinn
Title page and part title page artwork by Reynolds Stone

ACKNOWLEDGMENTS

I'm grateful to the many people who gave me support and helpful commentary during the writing of this novel. Specifically, I'd like to thank Anidelle Flint (my mother), Keith Smith, and especially Eberle Umbach for reading early drafts.

Greg Michalson, my editor at BlueHen Books, through careful reading and patient, insightful critique, helped me shape the final form of the book.

From the inception to the completion of this novel, my wife, Phoebe, and my good friend Mike Kane have provided many critical insights. The book would not be what it is without their contributions.

I'd also like to thank the Idaho Commission on the Arts for a grant that gave me financial support and a great deal of timely encouragement.

Most of all, I want to express my gratitude and love to Phoebe, Max, and Cassia for providing encouragement, motivation, forbearance, and distraction, each in appropriate measure.

CONTENTS

BOOK ONE

UNCONFORMITIES

1

DEATHBED, TEA, WIFE

This morning Uncle Pers rose out of his deathbed to join us for tea.

We hear him shuffling out of the dark cluttered recesses of his house. We hear the slow thumping of his walker in the hallway, and when the thumping pauses we hear his rattling breaths. Then he emerges into the sitting room, blinking and squinting like some pale wrinkled creature of the underground, stopping to shade his eyes against the light reflected off the pastel buildings and the bay and the arid blue sky.

"His will to live is phenomenal!" Aunt Mavis says emotionally, though exactly what emotion she is expressing is hard to say.

I should clarify "deathbed." He has been lying there for weeks, but it became clear some time ago that he was not about to die in it. And now he is up and coming to tea. But no one is fooled into thinking that the deathwatch is over. Uncle Pers is old and very sick, and any recovery he makes will be short-lived; within days, weeks at best, he'll be having tea in bed again, and it can't be long before he dies there.

Pers stops, leaning hard on the walker and glaring at Mavis. "And why do you assume that my will has anything to do with it?"

"Because you have reason to live. Because you have work to finish!" She glares back, nods shortly, smoothes his shock of thin white hair, and gives him a pat, or a slap, on his unshaven cheek. Mavis is old too but you have to look closer to see it. She's fit and ruddy, and always dressed as if for some special occasion, if only a costume party. Today she's wearing a slithering kimono thing and a sort of headdress streaming silk and ribbons, and the scent of some exotic woodsap hangs in the air in her wake. She helps Pers into his chair and joins Kate in the kitchen preparing the things for tea.

I should clarify "tea." We have tea twice a day, at ten o'clock and three o'clock, but in fact we never actually have *tea*. We have coffee, mineral water, juice, wine, beer, gin, brandy—almost anything *except* tea. But tea is what we call it. With tea we also have food, though not the kind that satisfies hunger, that nourishes bodies and sustains life. We eat delicate things, the foodstuffs of ritual and illusion: tiny sculptures and still lifes that crunch once or twice, then disappear in the mouth like vapors and resonate in the stomach like dreams.

The old man stares out the window toward the brown hills of Marin, the hazy refineries of Richmond.

"Well, it's all still in place, I see. And it still hasn't rained, has it?"

He seems to be addressing me, but Mavis, coming into the living room with the tea tray, answers instead. "Not a drop! One gorgeous day after another, drying us up. It's *so* gorgeous out that Kate and Will and I are planning a sail."

"Good for you. Of course, there isn't any wind, is there?"

"The wind will come up."

"It could. And if it does, you may have a gale by afternoon."

"Katy will captain. She's very competent. After all, she was taught by one of the world's finest sailors."

Pers has gin, Mavis sherry, and they argue about the wind. Kate and I sip coffee and wait for the argument to run its course. Such arguments also are part of the rhythm of life in this house, as ritualized as tea, as impossible for an outsider to comprehend.

I wonder if the tea thing comes from Mavis' side of the family—people with old money, is my impression, and plenty of time on their hands. Or maybe it's a Flemish tradition from Pers' childhood, or one of his Anglicisms, acquired in his youth along with his mastery of the English tongue. In the years before he began to make his way in the colonies he studied in England— prep school, university, reform school, I'm not sure exactly, though I ought to know. It's my job to know. I'm paid well to get such details in order. And I'm not bad at it, actually. I can be systematic and analytic and efficient. I can click my way through a few icons of Pers' computer, and the screen will light up with lists of folders and files, diagrams, indexes, outlines: essential organizational tools, because there are an awful lot of details.

But away from the computer the details of Pers' life blur; he is a frail figure now, in the long shadow of corporations, consortiums, cabals. Somewhere behind him there are sweatshops and plantations, venture capitalists, con-

THE ROAD BUILDER   5

tracts and kickbacks, a legacy of transported earth, diverted water, engineered landscapes. Uncle Pers blurs, but behind him are solid things: the infallibility of Science, the harsh laws of Commerce, the power of Money, the unsentimental knowledge of how the world really works.

It's probably obvious to him by now that none of these things is anywhere behind *me*. He sips his gin, eyeing me over the top of the glass. He seems to find something humorous in the sight. But under the gaze of those pale and watery eyes I blink and look away. What is he seeing when he looks at me like that? Something that isn't there, I keep thinking.

"So. Where did you spend the morning, William?"

"Well, here in the house. Kate and I were in the study, working."

"Still working, eh? I thought you'd finished. Well, then. Your body was in my study, your fingers were flipping through my papers, you were reading. So, where did you spend the morning? Where were you *transported*?"

"Oh. Well, Indonesia mostly, I guess. After the war, when you were up on the Indragiri. We've still got some big gaps and discontinuities in the manuscript, and I went back through some journals to see what we might have missed."

"Well, that sounds tedious. And haven't you already done that? Incidentally, I finished reading that manuscript last night."

"What did you think?"

"Well, *I* wasn't transported anywhere. That's not your fault, of course. You and Katy have certainly improved on my organization. Which is what I asked you to do."

"I imagine your editors will have some more suggestions. But at least we've got the structure in place, we know when things happened. We've got things lined up in some kind of order."

Mavis looks up sharply from her conversation with Kate and wags a finger at me. "That can be a trap too, Will. Remember that time is circular. The present is woven into the past. That has been his trouble all along: this urge to impose linear structures. To impose arbitrary, man-made distinctions on things."

Pers nods, still looking at me. "The distinction between past and present, for example, eh? Between memory and imagination. Between symbols and the thing itself. Arbitrary, William, but nevertheless I keep imposing. A long habit, I suppose."

He and Mavis give each other one of their looks, while Kate and I give each other one of ours. The women renew their conversation. I eat a rusk draped with a paper-thin slice of cheese, a thing so insubstantial I might leave it floating in the air beside me while I flick the crumbs from my hand and sip my coffee.

"Do you have a passport, Will?"

"A passport? No, I haven't—"

"You'd better get one. Your, um, *wife* has one, you know. And you put yourself in a precarious position, if you are married to an impetuous girl with a passport and you haven't got one in hand yourself. Ha-ha!"

"Well, I think—"

"What about immunizations? Yellow fever, typhus, cholera . . . I don't know what's required anymore, but a young man in your position needs to be current on such things."

His gaze drifts past me and he falls silent, seemingly lost in a study of the wooden figurines on the windowsill—fertility or sex icons from somewhere like Cambodia or New Guinea, which Kate says have perched on that windowsill in the same position for at least twenty years: poised for copulation but perpetually distracted by the view. But what is the old man talking about, my position? I have no position. Though there's no point in reminding him of that, and certainly no point in contradicting him, arrogant and sardonic and knowledgeable as he is. Still, I think he's wrong about Kate. It's true she's full of surprises and prone to act on sudden impulses. But my wife is not the type to light out with no warning for Rio de Janeiro or Madagascar or someplace. My wife—

I should clarify "wife." Well, no. Wife is unequivocal, and wife is what she is to me, in the full meaning of the word. To love and to cherish, to have and to hold, in sickness and in health, et cetera, et cetera—though no one has ever said as much, in so many words. Nevertheless, my lawful wedded wife she is, or so she claims. And who am I to doubt her? I love her, and what do I care for the lawfulness of it, anyway?

Still, like Uncle Pers, I sometimes choke on the word. Not that Kate's an inadequate wife; far from it. She's a beautiful woman, though you might not notice that at first, because her beauty isn't conspicuous but rather part of a complex mix of female vitality. It's one of the qualities I might check off, in a stunned, disbelieving assessment of my good fortune: beauty, intelligence, grace, lust, kindness, humor, good education, good prospects, good family— good enough, anyway, to harbor serious reservations about her husband.

Or maybe I'm taking their reservations too personally. After all, they do seem to like me. Probably they're just disoriented, as I am, by the timing, the suddenness of this marriage. Wife and husband, husband and wife. Kate and I have no common history to support the solid weight and implications of these words. They are just difficult words to pronounce, when you haven't had a chance to get used to them, when there's no background behind them, no foundation beneath.

Even from his sickbed—that is, his deathbed—Pers saw this at once and took advantage of it. It's as if he got one look at us, husband and wife, and said: "So—you have no history; I'll make you historians. You are living in the present; I'll transport you to the past. You have no story of your own; I'll give you mine."

2

ROAD TRIP

But we do have our own story, however short and inconclusive. It lacks structure, and it's hard to say where to begin. The first encounter, the courtship, the wedding, the abduction, the reconciliation, the honeymoon? Well, why not the wedding? An arbitrary point, and hard to place exactly on a time line, but no more so than any other particular beginning. Which is to be expected. After all, we were on the road, where time lines don't function well. The normal chronology of events breaks down, confounding cause and effect, skewing proportion. Small things take on unexpected significance, and large things are obscured behind these looming details. And the roadside is littered with symbols, with omens and portents, though none is fulfilled; everything, even the moment of revelation, is sucked into the jumbled past and quickly forgotten.

This must have been one of the effects that humans feared, when we first began to travel at speeds faster than the gallop of a horse. It's unnatural, people said; the mind will spin out of control; the heart will shudder and weaken from the strain; the established order of the world will break apart. And their fears have been borne out. Kate and I, traveling at unnaturally high speeds down from the plains and mountains of Montana, into the forest canyons of Idaho, found that our minds and hearts were strangely altered. Everything was open-ended, magnificently unstructured. We were exalted and fearful at once, and easily seduced by the portentous nature of things.

Late afternoon, gray light, waves of rain, and between the highway and the river a little mill town, narrowed by the steep canyon and a dense second-growth forest. An outpost that had lost its bearing and purpose, bypassed by the concerns of the world. Half the buildings were boarded up, but there were a few pickup trucks parked outside the café/video store, and a "Vacancy" sign glowed, no doubt perennially, on the riverside hotel. And the mill itself still smoked sullenly, saws idle but vital organs rumbling, brooding on the days when the forest stretched unbroken clear to the Montana plain and the big trunks of white pine and cedar jammed the river.

"I'm sure they don't expect anyone to stop, Kate."

"I'm sure they don't. It's been years since anyone's stopped."

"So why are we breaking with tradition?"

"This place is under some kind of enchantment, Will, don't you see? Don't speak to any of the inhabitants or the spell will be broken. Just mutter under your breath a lot. Use a lot of consonants. Make Slavic sounds. We'll pretend we're foreigners, from some country nobody heard of until it didn't exist anymore."

But in the tiny hotel lobby, ringed in by walls hung with musty animal heads, the proprietress studied my credit card and signature on the receipt without speaking. She pushed the guest register across the counter and kept watching me while she shuffled for the key. Perhaps we really were the first guests in years. In any case, this was her turf, some inbred enclave in the bottom of an Idaho canyon, where all the locals had guns in their pickups and animal heads on their walls, where resentment smoldered in the old sawdust piles and the cavernous shadows of the mill. You don't want to play games, you don't want to offend people's moral sensibilities in a place like that. The hotel woman didn't take her eyes off me, and I signed the guest register: "Mr. and Mrs. Will Haslin." Kate jabbed me in the ribs and snorted. The woman looked up sharply and reluctantly handed over the keys.

I could have explained our alien presence, if she'd opened her tight lips and started asking questions. Sure we were on the loose, heading south like wild gypsies, but we weren't really gypsies. Kate—my wife—was actually a scientist, in the process of writing a dissertation. Rewriting it, in fact, for the third or fourth time. A complex research design, a highly technical analysis, and a set of advisors who perceived new flaws each time she submitted her work to them. As for me, you might say I also was doing research, or at least experimentation. But my experiments lacked scientific credibility. They lacked focus, hypotheses, quantifiable data. Also I lacked a discipline, or a career. Or even, for that matter, a job. I'd had all sorts of jobs in the past— hard labor, soft labor, no labor to speak of, bureaucratic jobs, jobs in the woods and in restaurants and research labs and out on the open sea, jobs where you had to think quickly to survive and jobs you couldn't survive if you thought about them at all. Jobs that had given me what I thought I wanted: a life of freedom and spontaneity. Though lately I'd begun to wonder if perhaps the conventional wisdom didn't have it right—if this improvised life, while tolerable for a young person, simply did not age well. Its early promise of infinite possibility was already broken, in its place an unpleasant diffuseness, the sensation of the world accelerating away from me. And now I wasn't even sure I had the stamina for spontaneity anymore, though I was only thirty-two.

"That bed was especially uncomfortable, didn't you think?" I said to Kate the next day. "All night I felt like I was about to get skewered by a bedspring. I didn't really sleep."

She was driving. It was my truck, but she was very comfortable driving it, right from the start. One hand rested on the steering wheel and the other hung out the window, pushing against the seventy-mile-an-hour wind as we crossed the basalt scablands and alfalfa fields of southern Idaho, skirted the columnar canyons of eastern Oregon, then turned down the long fault lines of the Nevada mountains and valleys.

"That place was a dive." She shrugged. "Nobody goes to a place like that to sleep. You have to wonder how a respectable couple like Mr. and Mrs. Will Haslin ended up in such a dive."

"They must have misread the signs."

"I guess. What exactly *were* you thinking, Will? Putting me down as Mrs. Haslin?"

"Well, I wasn't thinking of anything. I just didn't want a scene. That woman's righteousness cowed me."

"Her righteousness!"

"Yeah, along with the mood of that town and everything. Sex before marriage is a hanging crime in a town like that."

"In a town like that, the only punishment for sex before marriage is *marriage*."

"For homegrown teenagers, maybe. For transient adults, it's hanging."

"Your paranoia is quaint, Will. But I think that place was a whorehouse. That's why that bed was so awful: it's been ruined by decades of trashy sex."

She grinned at me, then looked away, out the window at greasewood, sagebrush, piles of blasted rock. It was one of those empty places in Nevada where you have to refer to the road only occasionally as you drive. "Mrs. Haslin!" she muttered, as if the words were distasteful, or comical at any rate.

After a while she looked over at me again.

"Hey, what are you doing?"

"Reading your dissertation. Shouldn't you be watching the road?"

"You're not actually *reading* it."

"Sure. What's wrong with that?"

"It's just not the kind of thing a normal person would pick up and read, unless somebody was holding a gun to their head."

"It's good. I like it."

"Nobody *likes* this kind of thing, Will. There's nothing to like. It's just a question of whether I jumped through all the hoops, followed the procedures properly. Which I haven't, apparently."

"Well, I like it. It's so focused and precise. There's an austere beauty here, Kate. And the language of the text! It's so, so—"

"Incomprehensible?"

"Well, yes, but—"

"Does it make any sense at all to you? Because it doesn't make sense to me anymore."

"Well, no. I mean, I don't understand it on a rational level. It's like poetry. You have to make some leaps. The connections run deep beneath the surface."

"Oh. Well, it's supposed to be like science. And science is supposed to be understood on a rational level, by definition. You don't understand it any other way."

"I'm not so sure. There's all this symbolic power in the language of science. Metaphorical power. Especially in the language of statistics. Degrees of freedom, standard deviations, multivariate linear regression . . . That's suggestive, mysterious stuff, Kate. Yet tangible. *Quantification.* I'd like some of that in my own life. Some linear regression in my life."

Ahead of us we could see twenty miles of straight symmetrical road. A long descent through the juniper and the sagebrush, across the alkaline flats, a long climb through the sagebrush and the juniper to the shoulder of the next range. On the black road the November sun seemed unnaturally bright, and the distant mountains shimmered as if in the heat of summer. We were silent until we reached the middle of the basin.

"You have a beautiful life, Will."

"Thank you, I guess. But—"

"Sometimes you get kind of nervous and agitated around the edges. But there's a calmness at the center of your life that's very beautiful."

"Oh. An appearance of calmness, maybe you mean."

"No. I think it's genuine."

"It could be something that just looks like calmness, you know. Something more like . . . paralysis, for example."

"Most people are ground under. Boxed in. Their jobs are killing them. Their routines are stifling. It makes a perfect regression line."

"Yeah. Whereas me, I don't even have a job. So I guess that's not killing me."

"We can find you a job, if that's what you want."

Who's we, I wondered, but I didn't ask. It wasn't the right time for that line of inquiry. She might have connections, she might already have more of a plan for my future than I did, but right now we were operating without a plan. We both were renegades, floating along the Nevada highway at seventy or eighty miles an hour. The situation was unsettled even by my current standards. Kate and I had known each other for only a few months, and it had been little more than an impulse that sent us out on this road trip together. We seemed to be in love with each other, but there was not necessarily any structure or stability in that. Maybe I was just in love with the idea of her dissertation; maybe she was just in love with all those degrees of freedom I seemed to represent. But we both were unstable, and neither of us was to be trusted. Possibly we were heading in opposite directions, and converging for only a brief moment.

Still, it was a rare feeling, a highly charged dream, and we both understood that what the dream needed was this highway momentum and the insulation of the truck cab. If we stopped, if we made contact with the desert inhabitants, if we renewed our connections to the world we had left behind, the dream would short-circuit and die.

So it was necessary to keep moving, to go south. We would go deep into Mexico, a country that nurtures this kind of dream, or once did. We would explore the back roads. We would stay in cabañas on the beach and swim in the ocean, snorkel the reefs, drink beer and tequila in open-air beachside bars. That was about all the plan we had, though there were little pieces of structure attached to it. In Chiapas and Oaxaca we would buy jewelry and blankets, which we would stash in the truck and smuggle back across the border. That would pay for the trip, at least. I'd done this several times, many years before. I called it smuggling, though there was nothing surreptitious about the method. You didn't try to hide anything, you didn't sneak, you just drove through customs at Tijuana or Juarez in the middle of the day in a multilane flow of traffic and hoped the customs agents didn't look, or if they looked you hoped they didn't notice, or if they noticed you hoped they didn't care, which was the bottom line, because after all they weren't looking for trinkets and blankets, they were looking for drugs and illegals; in the great northward flow of drugs and illegals, what did a few blankets matter?

That was the plan, but we never carried it out. In our dream state we wandered for a week in the Southwest, driving fast, but only indirectly making our way south. Finally we arrived in Nogales, bought Mexican car insurance, and filled the gas tank. Then Kate said she had to check in with her family, and went to make a phone call.

She was in the phone booth for half an hour. I waited in the convenience-store parking lot, watching her make four or five separate calls, and getting nervous. She was making that connection, violating the insularity of the dream. Maybe she just assumed she could step back into it, but I knew it was a big risk.

She returned to the truck and sat silently. I waited, looking down the street toward Mexico, a vision that receded as her silence stretched on. Finally she looked at me and said that her uncle Pers in San Francisco was dying, that he was asking for her, that they'd been trying to locate her for more than a week, and that she had just made a reservation on a plane leaving Tucson in four hours.

"It's been real fun, Will. And I was really looking forward to Mexico, the beaches, the smuggling thing, all of it."

I said nothing.

"Maybe we'll get another chance. Maybe you can go down alone, and if things work out after a few weeks I could fly down and meet you. Depending on how things go."

I shrugged, and started the truck. "Tucson, then."

"It has been real fun," she repeated. "This isn't the kind of thing I've done before." She sat far away on the other side of the cab, suddenly reserved and awkward, which is how she sat the whole way up to Tucson, as if she couldn't wait to get to that passenger drop-off zone, shake my hand, and disappear into the terminal.

"We could go out, have a nice meal, a bottle of wine," she said unenthusiastically. "I'll have a couple hours before the plane leaves."

"I'm not hungry."

"We could get a motel room, if you like."

"I'm not sleepy."

"Look, I'm sorry, Will. But—"

"It's not your fault. You have to go."

Of course it wasn't her fault. Of course she had to go. But as I drove north, the fear and then the conviction grew in me that this sudden change in direction must be the beginning of the end. That destiny was shifting out of my favor, that our dream was still too tenuous to endure the jolt of awakening, and that the airline terminal ahead of us was exactly that: the terminal, the *end*. That the plane coming for her was a shining evil machine that would take her away from me forever.

It was dusk on the outskirts of Tucson.

"So, what exactly is wrong with your uncle? I mean, is he . . . imminently dead? They think he might die tonight, for example?"

"I don't think so, Will. My aunt gets overwrought; it's hard to judge. He'll probably hang on for a while. Days, weeks, months, who knows? But he needs me now."

"*Right* now?"

"I guess so. Yes. He wants me to help him finish putting his memoirs in order. So it's important for me to get there fast. While he still has the strength to work."

"Well, I'm thinking that maybe I should just drive you there."

"What? No. I'm flying, Will."

"But it's not really an emergency. He's not really dying."

"Oh, he's dying, all right. We just don't know when. So I want to get there fast."

"I don't like our trip ending like this."

"I don't like it either. But that's what's happening. You have to adapt."

"Take the next exit," she said.

I stayed in the center lane.

"Coming right up, Will. The airport exit."

We were in the midst of a great flow of traffic, still seventy miles an hour but now packed together like a parking lot. A weaving pattern of cars, some of them breaking off onto the airport interchange. But we kept heading north.

"What are you doing, Will?"

"I'm taking you to San Francisco."

"I'm flying to San Francisco. I told you, I need to get there right away."

"He's not dying right away. But if you need to be there, then I need to be there, too. So we'll go eighty all night long, and we'll be there by morning."

"I have a plane reservation, Will!"

"I'll pay for your plane ticket."

"You don't have any money."

"I'll get a job. As soon as we get to San Francisco, I'll get a job. Believe it or not, I'm very good at getting jobs."

"Will. Take me to the airport, goddamnit."

I kept driving.

"I just can't believe this. You're *abducting* me."

"Well, sort of. But I'm taking you where you want to go."

"I want to go to the airport!"

"The hell with the airport. We're on a road trip, Kate."

"This is incredible. I had no idea you were such a . . . such an *asshole*."

She argued and even screamed at me, and then she was silent. For an hour and a half she was silent, just sitting there in the darkness, no longer awkward but rigid and fierce. I drove fast, hoping there were no cops, hoping she wouldn't suddenly lean out the window and start screaming for help, or leap across the cab and wrench the wheel out of my hands. Hoping that the ambivalence I heard beneath her anger was not purely a product of my imagination.

Somewhere east of Needles she broke the silence. Her voice came harshly out of the darkness, startling me.

"I don't have to let you into their house, you know. I can get out on the corner, slam the door, and adios. You won't even be able to find a parking place."

"I'll double-park. And I'll get in, don't worry."

"Your truck'll get towed. And they've got about forty dead bolts on their door."

"They'll open them for me. I'll charm them. I'll seduce your aunt."

"That's disgusting. She won't be charmed by you. *She's* not so easily deceived."

"I'll lay siege. I'll sit on the porch steps and wait. I'll sleep on the sidewalk."

"They don't let people do that anymore, not in that neighborhood. It's not 1974, Will. Just because *you're* still bumming around Mexico in a beat-up old hippie truck."

"You making fun of my rig?" I nudged the accelerator and the speedometer moved up to ninety. The wind howled, the windows rattled as if about to shatter. "Hey!" I shouted. "This old hippie truck is taking you to San Francisco, faster than the speed of sound. I can't even hear your threats and insults."

We crossed the Mojave in darkness, without speaking. I stopped once for gas, and took the keys with me when I went to the bathroom. Kate remained silent as we went over the mountains, though I could tell she was awake. The signs and portents were still out there. Windmills looming out of the shadows, indecipherable as the monuments of lost civilizations. They were motionless; perhaps the night was windless. But along the ridges stretching out beyond the edges of our vision they seemed to whirl madly. A stillness not quite believable, a motion not quite apprehended. But we made no comment. We dropped into the Central Valley ahead of the dawn and raced the low streaking sun rays west until the full morning overtook us.

In the coastal valleys mists rose off the fields. The plowed earth was black and damp from irrigation, or from long-awaited rain showers. In shaded places on the brown hills there was a hint of green: new winter grasses promising a transformation of the desiccated range. Horses stood with their heads down and tails still along the walls of a collapsing barn, and a line of cattle moved out of the misty bottoms into the sun.

"It reminds me of Italy," Kate said suddenly.

"I didn't know you'd been to Italy."

"Mists, fields and vineyards, overgrazed hills. It's all so Mediterranean. You're right, I've never been there. But I've seen a lot of Italian movies."

"But you grew up here. California should evoke California for you, not Italy."

"No, it makes me nostalgic for Italy. A couple of telephoto shots into a hazy sun, peasants in the vineyard, chinks of sunlight in an old barn—that's all it takes to overwhelm the real experiences of my childhood."

Were we so easily reconciled? But she wouldn't say anything else, and when I glanced at her she didn't look back at me. Obviously she was still angry, but maybe she wasn't even thinking about me. Maybe she wasn't even angry anymore. Maybe I was already out of her mind, nothing more than a means, if not the preferred one, of transporting her to her dying uncle.

I tried to remember what she'd already told me about this uncle. Raised in Belgium, or maybe Holland, he'd been some kind of engineer, working all over the world in colonial industrial and agricultural ventures, eventually becoming a director of his company himself. As a child she'd hardly seen him, and he was a kind of legend to her—an explorer punching roads through the jungle, subduing barbarians, bringing the bounty of modern industry and the Green Revolution to the ignorant and starving primitives.

When she was a teenager he retired from the field and returned to live permanently with his wife in San Francisco. Kate spent several summers with them and got to know him well. She'd told me she admired him as much as anyone she knew, in some ways. But for a long time now she'd felt disillusioned about him. He'd been one of the last colonialists, really. And though the details were sketchy and she knew the morality of it was not always black and white, it did seem that Uncle Pers had always been there, on the wrong side, when the empires were falling apart and oppressed native people were trying to get the Europeans off their backs.

Sometimes she'd wanted to challenge him, but she'd always felt too in awe of him to really argue. And too naïve. Her opinions seemed infallible to her until she tried to express them to him—they just disintegrated into knee-jerk formulas when they collided with his experience. But he never said her criticism was wrong, and beneath the irony and sarcasm she could never tell where he really stood.

We crossed a wide plain in fog and silence, skirting dunes. Behind the dunes was the ocean. I rolled down my window to listen for the surf, but heard only the howl of engines and the swirling of air along the border of our wind tunnel. The fog thinned; the plain steamed as if from the heat of extinguished fire. We climbed above it, speeding over low hills and looking out on fields where long straight rows stretched into the distance and disappeared in the lifting haze.

"Farmworkers," said Kate.

They were far out in the fields, some of them gathered around their cars, others dispersed among the rows.

"My God," said Kate. "They're hoeing."

"Well? They're farmworkers. Wouldn't you expect them to be hoeing?"

"That field's immense. It's built by huge machines, constructed, not cultivated. What use is a hoe in a place like that?"

Soon after that she fell asleep, curled up on the seat beside me. When I was sure she was sleeping I put my hand on her cheek. She didn't stir, and I kept my hand there while the last of the farmworkers and the Italy-evoking fields and orchards flashed past, interspersed now with housing developments and shopping centers. It was an improbable juxtaposition, or collision, of worlds. But on the freeway we were part of no particular world. The freeway cut through everything impartially, a neutral medium that tied the whole awkward continuum together, linking it all—suburb and field, orchard and mall, industrial park, international airport, and row after row of little box houses—to the city by the bay where Pers and Mavis' house shone in the sun on the crest of a hill.

I parked my truck right in front of their house, in a drop-off zone. And so our road trip ended. Kate sat up and looked around. She got out of the truck and went around to the back and took her bags out. Then she stuck her head inside the passenger door.

"Thanks for the ride," she said. Like a hitchhiker: emancipated, independent, needing nothing more from me. *Thanks for the ride, mister.* And yet, with the shadow of a sleepy grin on her face, her tongue pushing the corner of her mouth. Ambivalence, definitely. Maybe even an invitation. But then she shut the door and was crossing the street, hurrying up the steps and around the corner, out of sight.

A meter cop's cart was double-parked at the end of the block. But I left my bag in the truck and bounded up behind her, past the ivy and the geraniums and blooming impatiens, the wrought iron and the algae-stained brick, onto the porch where she had just a second to glance at me—a complicated, turbulent glance, and I couldn't begin to say what it signified—before the dead bolts slid back and the door swung open.

3

MUSEUM LEGS

In the early evening the wind dies and the sailboats return across burnished water to their harbors. The sun hangs low over the ocean, the city glows, and the towns nestled in coves and valleys across the bay are like whitewashed Greek villages, vanishing into the shadows of dry hills. The world is made of simple and harmonious elements: sails going slack, light softening on the water, tankers and container ships moving unhurried and radiant past the islands toward the East Bay, plowing up the shipping lanes we crossed in a sailboat a few hours ago.

Afternoon tea is over. Mavis is shopping for dinner, Kate has returned to the study, Pers remains seated in his overstuffed chair at the tea table with his second glass of gin. And I stand at the window, sipping my third or fourth glass of wine and glowing as incongruously as the tankers.

This is the hour of relaxation. Pleasant and casual conversation, an excellent wine, through the window glass a shining watery world, and behind me a vigorous outing and a good day's work for generous pay. Yet I am not relaxed. Ever since Pers got out of bed this morning I've been feeling increasingly nervous. As if he's pursuing me, edging me into some trap. His voice is mild; his words pass soothingly over the surface of things. But I can tell he's leading up to something. Moving in for the kill.

I think he's grown fond of me, in a patronizing sort of way, but at the same time it's obvious he's disappointed in me. It's clear to him now that I lack education, training, conviction, sense of purpose and direction; that I am stunningly unqualified to be standing at his window drinking his wine, wandering through his library perusing his books, and sitting in his study editing his memoirs. Not to mention raging about in heat in his guest room, naked with his precious niece.

In fact, his niece is precious; in fact, I am unqualified. And though I'm sure I must have *some* convictions, in his presence they seem to evaporate. If he were suddenly to demand that I tell him what I believe in—which is just the sort of question he seems to feel he has every right to ask me—I imagine I would be struck entirely dumb.

"Notice that all those boats are sailing past San Francisco, Will. Going over to Oakland. A port that still ships and receives *things*, a city where work in the traditional sense is still performed. Lifting heavy objects, ratcheting steel cables, that sort of thing. A dirty and greasy business, and we don't do it here. Our port is only for tourists, our only product is nostalgia."

He leans forward, peering intently at me, and says something in French. His tone is aphoristic and conspiratorial, as if he expects me not only to understand but perhaps to parry with some italicized remark of my own. I've told him that the only foreign language I speak is a rudimentary traveler's Spanish, but apparently he can't accept this. He himself has mastered any number of languages, though he claims not to know exactly how many. They come and they go, he says. "There's no point in speaking more than four or five at a time. The others one just forgets until one needs them, and then they come back, you understand?"

I don't understand, having spent the longest hours of my life in college language laboratories, a set of headphones feeding incomprehensible sounds into a brain unable to absorb them, while a tape recorded the sporadic grunts and gargles I forced through my throat in response. I could not imagine the French I studied in those labs coming back, not in a form that would convey meaning to anyone.

Still I can't fall mute simply because I have nothing to say and no second language to say it in. I have to make some charmless monolingual response.

"Well, the city seems to be getting along fine without the shipping. I mean, there's lots of activity. People are . . . well, they're drinking a lot of coffee. They're out shopping, out in the parks jogging and doing their Tai Chi and so forth. They seem affluent. So I guess there's still *some* industry. Money must come from somewhere."

"Yes. That is a vast mystery, isn't it? Where does money come from? And the obvious answer is: from the affluent people, the ones drinking coffee.

Tourists, though in this case many of them live here. You see, this city has at last been turned entirely into a theme park. And the theme is—the city itself! It's a wonderfully profitable tautology."

I point across the room, out the south windows toward the downtown sky-scrapers. "Are those part of the theme park too? Is there something nostalgic about them?"

"Well, no. I'm forgetting half the formula. I should say: our port is for *two* things—tourists, and money. Here we also ship, receive, and transform money. We *process* money—make it vanish, reappear, take on disguises, swell to unnatural dimensions. We perform innumerable alchemies on it. Of course. Help yourself to more wine, Will. I'm afraid dinner will be quite late."

"Well, we did just finish tea."

"Yes, that was late as well. It's because you were out sailing for so long. Mavis was being such a good sport."

"She said it felt like a holiday to her."

"Yes. She doesn't enjoy holidays either. Too unpredictable, too inconvenient. No. She went sailing not for her pleasure, or yours, but for my therapy. For my vicarious stimulation. And I indulged her, I watched you with my spy-glass from high in my turret. Ha-ha! But it wasn't long before I fell asleep. I love sailing, I love my little boat—I built it myself, you know, and sailed it for twenty years—but it's a poor entertainment, watching it sail back and forth in a light breeze far across the water. It made me wonder why I'd bothered to get out of bed this morning."

"Well, I'm sure it wasn't just to watch us go sailing."

"No? Well, then. Why do you think I got out of bed, Will?"

I don't know why he got out of bed, or why he's asking me to explain it. Maybe he just wanted to tell Kate and me that we've done a lousy job with his memoirs and we may as well go to Mexico now. But he could have done that lying down.

"Well, I guess you got up because you're feeling better."

"Better than what? Better than a corpse, is that what you mean, Will? All right. Different, anyway. I'm not dead yet, in spite of having spent all this time dying, so I got out of bed. I suppose Mavis is right. I got up—because I have work to do. Because I have reason to live! No good reason, perhaps, but so what? The body requires very little reason at all. Say to the body: The memoirs must be finished! The work is entering a new stage! Your attention is required! And the body gets out of bed, trots—well, all right, hobbles, creeps—out to visit with young Will, young Kate, who have done such an admirable job of organization, against impossible odds. Five thousand pages of journals to sort through, William! Such a tedious scribbling of detail. Such a headache to go through it all, especially for young people, anxious to get on with their own future, eh? No wonder the end product is not what we might have hoped for."

"Actually, the work has been kind of fun. Not at all tedious."

"Fun." He pronounces the word slowly, running his tongue along his gums as if something unpleasant is lodged there. "Fun. I forget . . . this is your honeymoon, isn't it? So you will have fun, no matter the circumstances. And you have been paid quite well for your time, which adds to the fun, doesn't it? Still, it's not the usual moonlit romantic frolicking, not at all. What kind of honeymoon reading is this, Will? The stale gossip of a bush engineer! The story of how a little swampland was drained, a processing plant built, a four-wheel-drive track cut through the jungle, leading from one place no one has ever heard of to another. Spiced up with a little name-dropping, a bedroom revelation here and there."

"Well, there's more to it than that. The detail's fascinating. The historical context."

"Yes! This is what Mavis says, you know. It is all history, and all history is equal, all history is interconnected. Linkage! One of her favorite concepts. Everything is linked to everything else. Of course, who can argue? So, although these are only small events, they are critical, because without them the big events would never happen. Here are the butterfly wings that spawn hurricanes, eh, Will? Small permutations triggering famines, sparking revolutions, leading us to the ineluctable syllogisms of war, the cruel archetypes of oppression and occupation and colonialism. Ha! Which reminds me, I have thought of a title for the book: 'Confessions of a Colonialist.' And a subtitle: 'Forty Years Between the Twenty-first Parallels.' What do you think?"

I think I should have another glass of wine. I think this is the first time anyone has ever used the world "ineluctable" in a conversation with me. I think—but what does it matter what I think? Pers talks on, without waiting for a response.

"You will object that it's not really a confession at all. I agree. The title is a ploy, intended merely to placate my agent, who is trying desperately to squeeze glamour and titillation from my humble account. But I don't mind such a title, either. Perhaps it will help sell more copies at the mall bookstore. Yes, why not the mall! Come to think of it, maybe it's not bad reading for the honeymoon. Inspirational, eh? It could fire you up, you and your wife. Maybe someday you'd like to try something similar, do you think? I mean, if no one's going to finish a dissertation or do anything productive. You might go on a different sort of honeymoon instead. By the way, I thought you got off to an excellent start, refusing to drop Katy off at that airport in Phoenix or Albuquerque, wherever you were. That was good judgment, good improvising. A little flush of passion seizing the wheel, eh? But since then, what? You haven't followed through. You ought to throw out your script entirely. Improvise, Will!"

"Well, I thought I was. I mean, I don't know what script you're talking about. And as far as doing things you did—most of that isn't possible anymore. The stuff you write about is . . . well, it's history. Things were totally different then."

"Oh? What do you mean?"

"Well, the world's changed."

"Has it?"

"Well, yeah. I mean, you just don't have the same situation anymore. Everything changes so fast now, you know? The world's so precarious, overpopulated, overrun with refugees and disease and terrorists and weapons and ecological disasters. Controlled by huge alliances. Technocrats, technocapitalists, huge mafias. Except there's no real control, because the systems are so complex, evolving too quickly. Nobody understands them. The acceleration of Time. People feel trapped by it. There's all this *energy*, but no frontier to expend it on."

I'm suddenly aware that my voice is too loud, and abnormally high-pitched. But Uncle Pers gazes at me calmly, blankly, even, as if I haven't yet completed the argument or for that matter said anything that makes the slightest sense. I blunder on: "Every place has been discovered; the native cultures are overwhelmed. In fact, everybody's overwhelmed. Disoriented, disengaged. And tourists are everywhere; every place is a theme park now, not just

San Francisco. It's a global village, right? You can't go to a remote, foreign place anymore. You can't operate like you used to."

"Well." Pers takes a long drink of gin, making a gurgling sound that seems to come from his lungs. "Times have always been bad, if that's any consolation, Will. Help yourself to more wine. In this sense the past is not so remote from the present. In this sense Mavis, who is always trying to mix the two up, might have a point. These memoirs somehow must be brought out of the distant past, into your exploited, terrorized present. That's the next step, don't you agree? Or don't you have an opinion about this? Never mind. As far as the memoirs go, you've done your job. It's no longer your concern. You don't actually need to have an opinion."

He empties his glass and sits back in his chair, coughing quietly. I sip my wine, peer into the depths of the house, turn again to gaze out the window. I suppose he's right. I'm the nephew-in-law, without a job, without qualifications. I don't need to be expressing opinions. I need to be deferential, humble, nervous. I need to study my surroundings, to adapt, to watch for veiled omens and sudden shifts of light and shadow.

Here on the outer edge of the living room we are caught in a strange light. This is a border strip, illuminated by the tranquilized glow of the outside world. But that glow doesn't penetrate the darkness filling the house behind us. From those interior shadows come machine sounds: the old refrigerator humming, the firing of the furnace deep in the basement, the faint sound of a keyboard clicking. Beside me Pers rumbles and hacks softly, another ancient motor firing. He's looking past me now, or through me, which allows me to look more closely at him: his shock of wispy hair a radiant white, the lines in his face deepening and increasing in the low-angled light. He's like an old painting, a Dutch Master hung in a forgotten room in some obscure museum, oils cracked and deformed, fractures multiplying, but the glow of late-afternoon drawing-room light enduring for centuries.

Abruptly he reaches for his walker, and with a grunt heaves himself upright. He says something about a nap before dinner, shakes my hand and nods—still without really looking at me—and then begins the low slow shuffle toward the shadows of his bedroom. He moves so painfully; shouldn't I help him in some way? But how do you help someone who's shuffling along in a walker? And hasn't he just dismissed me in any case? Hasn't he just told me:

it's time for a different sort of honeymoon? Over the bay the glow intensifies, as if the light is amplified by some other radiation, as if some kind of charge is building between the water and the sky. Hasn't he just told me: *this is no longer your concern?*

I turn away from the window and move along the mantelpiece, picking up treasures and trinkets, turning them in my hand. Polished malachite, rosewood smooth as soapstone. The keyboard is silent now. The house hums with the mindlessness of its machines. Uncle Pers, vanishing now into its deeper recesses, is impossible to read. Though I suppose he made it clear enough that my services are no longer required. *Throw out your script. You don't actually need to have an opinion.* The museum is closing.

The murmur of voices rises from the back bedroom, as if people are drifting from one exhibit to the next, offering a veiled critique here, a cautious observation there. I stand, pour myself more wine, rock back and forth on my heels. A stifled yawn, the sleepy weight of time, a heaviness in the legs that moves slowly up the spinal column, spreading into the brain. Museum legs, metastasizing into a systemic toxicity.

Kate emerges from the hallway and stands close behind me, her voice low and soft, telling me about something she has just discovered in the journals, some connection, dates and events that have unexpectedly fallen into place. A small gap closed, a minor mystery solved. I guess she doesn't know the job is finished. But I don't interrupt her. Her words are not aural so much as tactile: currents of warm, moist air blown into my ear, vibrations of her chest and throat on my back as her arms slide beneath mine and encircle me, reminding me that we are not a part of this decay, that we carry life and fire into these musty chambers. That we are only visitors to this old museum, and its decorum and codes of restraint exist to be shattered.

At the appointed times we have tea; we wander through the rooms, making a little hushed conversation, studying the books and collections, emulating the dry civility of our hosts, the torpor of their old age. But in the narrow passages between rooms we brush against each other, in alcoves and corners we softly collide, and the collisions produce new sounds: the slow rustling of cloth, soft breathing only slightly quickened, the barely audible parting and moistening of lips. Muted sounds, almost reverent. Museum sounds, at first. But then a sudden muttered gasp, zippers and snaps coming open, hoarse rumbling as if from the throats of animals. Sudden heat and moisture, new ripe smells rise among the porcelain and ivory. We drop to our knees, and in a moment we are rolling on the Kashan rug, our skin pressed into dense fibers no one has lain on for years. We bump the Delft vase, pull away, slam into the coffee table, and Kate breaks loose and slithers away beneath it, suddenly giggling. Then she's out the other side, up on her feet and fleeing for the stairs just ahead of me. She slows after a few steps and my fingers move up the backs of her thighs, across her butt, and hook over the tops of her pants, so that when she tries for another step the pants, already unbuttoned, come down easily in my grasp. They fall to her ankles and I move up another step, letting my own pants slide down my legs. In a moment she's gripping the banister, swaying, dropping to her knees on the steps and now the light is finally coming through, that evening glow reflected off the yellow pine steps and Kate's arching back, flexing haunches. Suddenly our room is impossibly far away, how could we leave this fantastically lewd glowing place on the stairs, with all these impotent fetishes and brittle old artifacts looking on? Kate clings to the banister, tossing her head, and the blood pounds so loudly in my ears that only when she stiffens and hisses an alarm do I hear the sound of Mavis' key beginning to fumble its way through the dead bolts in the front door behind us.

Then we're in desperate flight up the stairs, our half-nakedness suddenly ridiculous, my state of arousal mortifying. But the pants at our ankles frustrate a quick escape. Kate pauses to pull hers up and I break out ahead of her, hopping and dragging myself up several steps at a time with my arms. But at the landing I slip and lose momentum, and she bounds past, goosing me as she takes the turn. She's safely out of sight but I'm still floundering around the landing when Mavis steps into the house, fussing with her packages and trying to extract her keys from the lock. I do a kind of seal flop onto the second flight of stairs, a difficult if graceless maneuver, and Mavis turns her head. She seems to be looking straight up at me, but she doesn't react. Either she mistakes me for another priapic artifact brought home decades ago from the jungle, or else she has seen so much of the world that she's no longer shocked by anything, even the sight of her niece's husband squirming up the stairs with his pants around his ankles, taking his deflating erection up to the honeymoon suite where it belongs.

4

THE FIRST MUTATION

The first time I heard those dead bolts slide open I was on the other side of them, standing on the porch with Kate, and I didn't know if I was ever going to see the inside of the house. I was a kidnapper, not easily forgiven, and when the door opened, Kate might well turn to me with a poisonous smile, another cool "Thanks for the ride," and slip into the house, leaving me facing a closed door and listening to a row of dead bolts click shut one after the other. When they finished clicking I would be trespassing, unshaven and unwashed and alone on a porch on the edge of the continent, with my truck in a five-minute-parking zone below and the meter cop working his way down the hill.

So when Aunt Mavis opened the door I didn't wait for either an invitation or a dismissal. I went right inside, nudging Kate ahead of me and stumbling in on her heels, figuring that the look of delight on Mavis' face at the sight of her niece permitted a semiforced entry. And I got away with it, though Kate glared openly at me and Mavis seemed momentarily baffled. But she remembered *her* manners. "Come in! Come in!" she said, though we were already standing in the foyer.

She and Kate pretended to kiss each other's cheeks, and Mavis squeezed Kate's hand. "He's been waiting," she breathed. "We were sure you'd be here this morning at the latest. Every time I called the airport they had a different story. One young man had the nerve to suggest you weren't coming. They're so *presumptuous* at airports nowadays. Anyway, you're here. He'll be so happy to see you."

While she talked she led us down a hallway and into a bedroom. We passed through several different bad smells, as if separate air masses hung like invisible curtains in the passageways. The shades in the bedroom were drawn, and the television was on without any sound. In that dim and inconsistent light I couldn't make anything out, but Kate went directly to the bed, where she lifted a clawlike hand from among the sheets and bent to embrace the shape that rose from the pillows. That gave Mavis and me a chance to look more closely at each other. She was old, but it was hard to guess *how* old, looking at her—so disconcertingly alert and vital-seeming, and certainly well decorated, with her face extravagantly drawn and painted and her eyeglasses glittering with tiny cut stones and a host of brooches and bracelets and necklaces dangling from her clothes and body. She smelled of some strange earthy perfume, better than the smell of the room but still an acquired taste. I smiled at her as warmly as I could, and she smiled back, not warmly at all. But what kind of smile could I expect? I hadn't slept for a day and a half. I'd just abducted her niece and driven a thousand miles without stopping and shoved my way into her home without introduction or explanation. I'm sure I looked like a madman, and perhaps I was.

Finally Kate stood up. Now all three of them were looking at me. "Aunt Mavis," Kate said, "Uncle Pers, I'd like you to meet Will."

I shook Mavis' hand and went over to the bed and shook the same claw Kate had lifted. I could make Uncle Pers out a little better now—white wrinkled head, gaping mouth, a dark hint of bloody gums and thrusting reptilian tongue. And bright intelligent eyes looking hard at me for a moment, then turning again to Kate, expectant. There was an awkward silence.

"Right." She giggled nervously and took a breath. "Will Haslin. My . . . my husband."

"Really!" gasped Mavis. In fact, we all gasped, and a heavier silence fell.

"We'd better drink to it," croaked Pers weakly.

Naturally I assumed she was making some kind of joke. And she was, in a way, though in another way she wasn't at all. My wife is a playful woman, and she can get a lot of mileage out of a joke. Sometimes she doesn't even try to separate her jokes from the not-so-jocular part of her life; sometimes she tries for strange blends of joke and solemnity, impiety and reverence, nonsense and meaning, revenge and reconciliation.

"Was that really necessary?" I asked her after Mavis had shown us to our room.

"What do you mean?"

"You're a grown woman, Kate. An independent woman. And I thought you said they were broad-minded. Bohemian."

"Well, they are. Bohemian, but stodgy bohemian."

"I don't understand why you had to tell them I'm your *husband*."

"Well, I guess I didn't have to. But it wasn't like I *planned* to tell them. It just came out of my head, it seemed like the right thing to say. Like you battering your way into their house, I guess that just seemed like the right thing to do? But anyway, why not tell them the truth?"

"What are you saying?"

"Well, that is the truth, Will. You are my husband."

I stared at her. "Ha-ha. Only we are not married, Kate."

She shrugged. "There are lots of ways to get married, you know. Some people make a big deal, throw rice, stuff cake in each other's mouth, promise each other the moon. It depends on where you happen to be, for one thing. In Las Vegas, you can get married and divorced in the same night, over and over like feeding a slot machine, if you have the cash. And in some places, like Idaho, for example, money doesn't matter: all you have to do is represent yourself as being married, and legally you are. It's a common-law statute, kind of archaic, I guess, but still in effect. If you publicly claim you're married— like, for example, if you check into a hotel room together and sign 'Mr. and Mrs.' on the register—then for legal purposes you *are* married. As long as both parties agree, of course. If you decide you don't want to be married, you're free to state that you didn't really mean it—that is, that you were lying. That's how common law works, I guess. It's imprecise, it's accommodating. No preachers, no lawyers."

"Where'd you hear about this?"

"I read it somewhere. Or somebody told me about it. I don't remember. Look, I don't even know if it's true. The point is, what does it mean to get married? It's an understanding between us and nobody else, right? An act of faith, Will, not a contract."

"A few minutes ago you were telling me thanks for the ride, get out of my life. And now you're telling me that in your mind we're as good as married."

"That's right. Unless you're telling me that in your mind we're as good as not."

"Well . . . it's irrational, Kate. Not just imprecise. Irrational."

"It's no more irrational than any other way to get married. And it's not as if it's something absolute and final, and suddenly everything is cut and dried. Love isn't cut and dried, friendship isn't, sex isn't. Even abduction isn't cut and dried, is it? So why should marriage be? Things evolve; it's not like you can expect to just carry somebody across a threshold and there you are. I mean, for some people I'm sure the threshold works. But for people like us, marriage is evolutionary. This is only the first mutation."

It seemed like an awfully random mutation. There was no decision made, no stated commitment, no plan for a common future or declaration of love and fidelity. The only thing this mutation really had going for it was that we were truly in love. And yet it was adaptive, in a strange way. It got us a niche in the static ecosystem of Pers and Mavis' house. Right away, before the meter cop made it down the hill, it got my truck off the street and safely parked in their garage. And in spite of her reservations about me, it got Mavis to take us upstairs and show us our room: a suite of glass and light at the very top of the house, in the midst of buildings and sky.

That room was filled with light, even at night. Wide windows on three sides let in the moon and the lights of the city and the bay. We lay on the hideaway bed in an electric twilight that lasted until dawn, with a brighter pulse every twenty seconds as the rotating searchlight on Alcatraz Island swept for a moment along the walls of the room. We could have pulled the blinds, of course. But Kate slept soundly, and for my part I never longed for the dark. That room at night seemed like a place where sleep and dreams were already in progress, and the searchlight only deepened the hypnotism. We slept to the rhythm of its rotation, and if I woke I always found it easy to return to sleep between slow flashes, as the beam made its wide, soothing sweep of the bay.

Here are some other things our first mutation got for us: a house, a job, a book of memoirs. We didn't possess these things but we used them as if they belonged to us. Ever since she was little, Kate had been enchanted by this house, and I soon came under the same spell. It was a place of multiple dimensions, a building that connected the earth to the sky and allowed a person to occupy both simultaneously. From the garage, a dim cavern that smelled like mushrooms and underground rivers, a passageway led past the padlocked treasures of the forbidden basement into the house itself, past closed doors and small secret rooms, up long flights of wooden stairs, through alcoves and dormers and out into rooms filled with light, rooms with high ceilings and deep mirrors and huge windows of old rippled glass that opened on equivalent expanses of sky and land and water.

The house was like a museum, full of objects to be looked at rather than used. Because its inhabitants were so old, I thought, but Kate said it always had been like that. She remembered standing on a chair to reach for those same objects, running her fingers over smooth figures cut from jade or ivory, or from a black wood as hard and heavy as rock or metal, and feeling as if she were drawing close to the strangeness and remote distances of the world. She'd studied the pictures woven into tapestries and blankets, and wondered at the myths and dreams encoded there. She remembered staring back at fierce masks of cracking wood or cut and hammered tin, at demonic puppets and freakish dolls and grotesque carved figures that flaunted huge phalluses and breasts, as blunt and massive as war clubs, as pointed and sharp as spears.

She remembered summer nights when she was fifteen or sixteen, lying in her downstairs bed while the fog rolled in, and hearing through the thin ceiling the clatter of Pers' typewriter in his study, the shuffle of papers, and the floor creaking when he moved in his chair. Occasionally his door was left open, and when she passed in the hallway she caught glimpses of papers scattered everywhere, rows of old books, and piles of notebooks on the desk and the floor. She knew that the stories that he parceled out so frugally at the dining table were contained in abundance in those papers and notebooks, and she assumed that the book he was writing would finally make those stories available to her.

But the years passed, and the book did not materialize. At one time or another it was to be a novel, a short-story collection, a volume of critical essays. But nothing was completed. Pers never acknowledged failure; he merely shifted his focus, working toward the most appropriate form. In those days he still traveled and was occupied with more pressing responsibilities, and the book seemed like a hobby, a diversion.

But now in the final years of his life it had become his obsession. It had evolved into a memoir—the most logical way, he'd decided, of transforming his massive collection of journals and drafts into a publishable account. He had an agent and a publisher and a contract, and the book itself was practically finished.

But his health was deteriorating. He suffered a small stroke, his kidneys were failing, he was plagued by intestinal problems and strange infections he'd picked up decades before in the tropics. He was running out of time, and in fact losing ground. By the time Kate picked up that convenience-store telephone in Nogales, papers were scattered all over his study and he couldn't get out of his bed. When he asked her to come at once and help him complete the memoirs, it sounded like a last request. So of course it had been cruel and selfish of me to delay her arrival. But because I had kept her off the plane, because we had mutated, the stories were now also offered to me.

Almost immediately, Pers hired me as Kate's assistant. He said that would lighten her workload and give her time to work on her dissertation as well, that I probably had some qualification for the job. I'd admitted I had no real editing experience, minimal computer skills, and only scattered knowledge of the places and events discussed in his journals. But there I was, attached to Kate, and he had to do something with me. "You'll do fine, I think," he said. "You were a kind of clerk once, you said? Well, the job is mainly clerical. Taxonomy, not discovery. Organization, not invention."

I suppose this was a way of warning us that things were massively *dis*organized, though we didn't fully appreciate his meaning until we spent time in the study. Mavis had cleaned it before our arrival, but Pers did not permit her to rearrange his papers and she was able to remove only the most superficial layers of dust and grime. In any case, cleaning seemed futile. There was a mold embedded in the wood, and a dry dust that could not be shaken from the curtains and the rugs. Ragged yellowing notebooks and stacks of paper overflowed the filing cabinets and the desk and chairs. A confetti of scribbled notes covered the walls—messages Pers had written to himself in a code he no longer could read. Among the papers we found unfinished drafts, outlines, indexes, and chronologies, none consistent with the others, none imposing order on the mess. Rather, each, in its incompletion and eventual abandonment, seemed a testimony of defeat in the face of an undisciplined torrent of words and memories.

It was in the journal entries themselves, often undated and hastily scribbled almost beyond any hope of deciphering, that the chaos of his study seemed to originate. There was no dependable chronological order to the entries; apparently Pers had moved from journal to journal according to some inconsistent scheme of his own, a now forgotten idea of theme or mood that at the time must have seemed to unify a particular journal. Often small things were described and analyzed in meticulous detail, while more significant events were dismissed with a few vague sentences. And for certain periods of his life we could find no account at all.

There were thousands and thousands of pages of this, stuffed in folders and scattered throughout the study. Only Pers' computer seemed to defy the triumph of chaos. It sat beside a neat row of software manuals and a box of diskettes on an otherwise empty table—an alien presence in that room, an invading power. But if so it had managed only to establish a beachhead, like the fenced compound of the colonialist in a jungle clearing. And even the beachhead seemed abandoned. We found no data files at all on the diskettes or hard drive, and when we questioned Pers, he complained that the machine's capabilities had been vastly exaggerated, that he'd been tricked into buying it. So we turned again to the papers: first the various drafts, and when they proved inadequate the journals themselves. We read and catalogued and eventually came to suspect that for Pers this computer was not a modern tool but a primitive talisman, like something from a cargo cult. He must have bought it out of an impulse of superstition and magic, dimly imagining a technology that would impose order upon all the scattered words he'd written over the decades.

Kate and I at least understood this much about the technology: that the algorithms capable of processing such jumbled recollections had not yet been written. Still, after weeks of reading, we did begin to use the machine, as well as her laptop. We transcribed drafts and journals, typed in diagrams and outlines and time lines and indexes. Beginning with a skeletal outline of Pers' life, we worked our way through the journals. Gradually we put the flesh on his childhood in Brussels and adolescent exile with relatives in the Dutch colonies; his war experiences in Indonesia and postwar travels and business dealings throughout Southeast Asia; his work in Asia, Africa, and Latin America as an engineer and field-operations manager for Jucht Brothers, the Belgian agricultural and construction company; his experiences as Belgian consulate in a small South American republic; and finally his return to

Europe and ultimately the United States, where until his retirement he sat on the board of directors of Jucht Brothers.

His expertise was broad, his accomplishments diverse. He helped design and build agricultural processing plants, survey plantations, and construct roads. He managed and administered, studied and experimented. He wrote and sporadically published economic and foreign policy analyses, travel accounts, articles for technical journals, even a few poems. He was a competent amateur violinist. He invented some kind of valve used in industrial pumps. A mushroom he described in a botanical journal was named after him. And he and Mavis collaborated on a collection of primitive art and Asian antiquities, much of which they donated to American museums.

But such a summary says nothing about the true value of his journals. Here were crumbling empires and lost worlds, evoked not by an account of celebrated historical events but rather by the small peripheral details of their dissolution. And sometimes we sensed we were about to stumble onto something less peripheral, something hidden in the blank spots, in those periods of time that were unaccounted for, except by the occasional allusion that tantalized but remained unfulfilled. Unconformities, Kate called these empty spaces, using a geological term that referred to a missing layer of deposition between younger and older strata of rock.

Pers, lying in his bed reading the drafts we compiled, was intrigued by her analogy. But he could fill in no gaps. "You want me to remember something else? But that's no longer possible, thanks to these journals. A journal is an insidious thing. It draws the blood out of memory. The living tissue has long since rotted away, and now even the bones have been replaced by other substances. Real memory is extinct. These fossils are all you get. Anything not recorded here has ceased to exist."

In the gloomy sickroom, with the old man's ghostly hands trembling atop the bedcovers and his voice quavering and the television flickering interminably, this talk of things ceasing to exist sounded doom-ridden and tragic. But back in the study the perspective was different. There the future seemed to be opening up, even as we immersed ourselves in history. Someone else's history, yet between Kate and me something of our own was crystallizing: the dream that had almost died at the Mexican border rebuilding in intensity and taking us in unexpected directions, the way a dream will do. Together we began to experiment with the journals. We tried making unlikely connections, sliding a new layer into the unconformities, putting disparate pieces together to see how they fit. It wasn't detective work so much as make-believe. An irreverent diversion from the sometimes tedious clerical work, but also an intimate game we played with each other. We sat back at our computers and traded scenarios, or just let our fingers run over the keys, shamelessly sensationalizing the places where documentation was thin, where the small mysteries persisted. We made Pers into a secret agent, an arms merchant, a money launderer, and even a saboteur: blowing up a bridge, blocking the movement of rebel troops, shifting the balance of power in the civil war, leading to the toppling of one despot, the rise to power of another, instability shifting to chaos, his half-finished factory going up in flames, the shattered road choked with refugees, Pers fleeing with the sachet of smuggled diamonds, hanging from the struts of the bush plane as the government troops burst into the clearing with their automatic weapons firing.

And what was his American wife, Mavis, doing during all this? That was another hole in the story. In most of the journal writing he made only the briefest acknowledgment of her seemingly inconvenient existence. Here she was accompanying a shipment of furniture from Jakarta into the Sumatran hinterlands; there she appeared in the Orinoco wilderness with a case of whiskey, a box of marzipan, and a round of well-aged Gouda, vanishing quickly again after a whirlwind buying spree of art and artifacts. She detested the tropical climate; she could not bear the constant sight of sick and hungry children. But what if *she* were the secret agent? No, not likely. But what were they doing apart from each other all those years? Mavis shuttling between museums and galleries, a house in San Francisco and an apartment in Brussels; Pers surrounded all day by servants and foremen and peons but left alone each night, scribbling away in his journal with the self-discipline and compulsion of a Victorian explorer. Did his concentration waver when the native women passed his tent on their way to dance in the open yard to the humming drum and the wailing flute, with the moonlight and lianas streaming through the trees? Did he think for a moment of Mavis roaming through their great creaking house in that same moonlight, running her fingers along the mantelpiece, feeling the settled dust on the fetishes and amulets she had brought back from the far corners of the earth? He seized his pen again and wrote on, feverishly recollecting everything but denying the relentless drum and the cries of the women and the image of Mavis coming into her bedroom, standing at the window staring hazily at a book in her hand, deaf to the sounds of traffic and sirens and the pounding of running feet on the pavement. She moved to the bed, reached for the covers, and was startled by the low voice coming out of the darkness just beyond the reach of her hand, because she had almost forgotten she was not alone.

Pers slammed his pen down on the desk and swore against the heavy heat of the night. He stood in the black doorway while outside the drum went silent and the rain fell and the invisible women moved past, spread out along the muddy road in the darkness. He could smell their sweat in the rain; his lungs drew in air saturated with the vapor coming off their bodies. He held it as long as he could while they passed below him their soft voices calling their glistening eyes their bare feet stirring the mud and rustling the shadows of his tent until he blew the air out into the night in a long howl of desire and invocation.

But if something like that had ever happened, it was not the kind of experience he wrote about in his journals. In fact, I made the whole thing up, sitting in front of his computer one day. I made it up, typed it on the screen, read it to Kate. "That's so beautiful, Will," she said, and she got up and came over and stood behind me. She put her arms around me and bent to kiss the top of my head. "Now delete it," she whispered. I deleted it, and went back to transcribing journals. After all, this was a job. We weren't paid to screw around, to dabble in historical fiction and romance. We were paid to create chronologies, to put the known facts in order. Solid lines of words, telling what actually happened; blank dates and empty spaces, telling what might as well never have happened at all.

"But we should consider the possibility," said Mavis, "that sequence may be the least meaningful connection between things." She wafted into the study, streaming her ribbons and taffeta, papers fluttering off the desk in her wake. The room was infused with her scent: herbs and tree saps, astringents and essential oils, roots and leaves and a smell from the heart of the soil. "Essence of mycorrhiza," Kate muttered, and Mavis said: "We should consider the possibility that these empty spaces give us freedom. This is what I tell him, Katy.

Freedom to finish the book, and then move on. Freedom to seek out the stronger connective tissue. To go beyond this *drudgery*, Will. Classifying things, numbering chapters. As if memory were nothing but a linear progression, ending in death!"

Her shadowed eyes were fixed on me. I had no idea how to respond. Kate, though, turned in her chair and gazed up at her. "But Aunt Mavis," she said, "he *is* dying."

"Oh, yes." Mavis quivered. Her perfume seemed to increase in potency, coming over us in suffocating waves. "He's dying, he's an old man. And old men should finish the business of their youth, and look onward. 'Old men should be explorers'!"

She left the room, but her smell lingered in the air, heavy, sweet and sour. We worked through it, drinking coffee, typing, shifting our eyes from the yellowing journals to the bright glowing screens, seemingly transfixed by an old man's story, absorbed into his past. Maybe we *were* connecting things, moving in new directions. Or maybe we were just sanitizing, making the past palatable to the present. Maybe I felt an unexpected passion for the work I was doing, or maybe the work was just the incidental object of other passions.

We finished our first draft and brought it to Pers in his bed. He read it with the TV on, and while he read we went back to the study and kept working, already tinkering with revisions, still poring over the journals in search of the enhanced detail, the missing connective tissue.

In the suite of glass I slept against the cool skin of my new wife, lying in a strange half light, the electric glow of the midnight city. Not the banishment of darkness from the human dominion, not the triumph of light but its defeat, the night mocking the day. And all night long the searchlight came and went. It must have influenced my dreams, but when I awoke in the morning I remembered, as usual, no dreams at all. But Kate said she'd dreamed of Uncle Pers blazing in the doorway like a patriarch of the Old Testament, scattering his journals in a terrible wind, heaving his walker at the computer and driving us from the study amid thundering prophecies of fire and flood, of war and disease, of mutation after mutation after mutation visited upon us like an unending torrent of blessings and plagues.

5

A PLACE OF NO SIGNIFICANCE

"Oil, Will."

"Excuse me?"

"Just one word, Will. Oil."

The old man and I sit side by side on the couch with cocktails and hors d'oeuvres. We began several feet apart, but his upper half is getting closer and closer to me, slowly tipping in my direction. Either he's lost his equilibrium and is gradually falling on his side, or he is trying to emphasize his point, whatever his point may be, or he just wants me to get a really good look at his face: the obliterations and excavations; scars, eruptions, and depositions; patterns of blood running in tiny threads on the surface, barely contained by the sloughing cells of his skin.

"I don't know much about oil."

He stabilizes, his face inches from mine, and dismisses my ignorance with a wave of his spidery hand. "You know more than you think. There are opportunities, Will."

"In oil? Well, I'm sure there must be."

"Technicians, systems analysts, consultants. I receive newsletters, memorandums. I hear about openings, unusual situations. And I have influence in the selection process."

"I see. I guess it must be a tough industry to break into, even for somebody with the right background—mining engineering, petroleum geology, or whatever. Or an MBA or something. And of course, you can't be picky about where you live—Saudi Arabia, Houston . . ."

Pers snorts. Tiny particles of food appear on his lips, and a mist of saliva showers the narrow column of air between us, sparkling in the candlelight like the falling embers of a fireworks explosion. It may be that he is laughing.

"Excuse me, Will. I misspoke. Not one word. Two words. Palm oil."

"*Palm* oil? I don't know anything about palm oil."

"No? It's a tropical oil, of course, extracted from the orange fruit of the oil palm. It has a number of culinary and industrial uses. At one time it was among the great commodities of the world, at the center of trade routes and empire expansion. But now it's much diminished in importance. We've developed cheaper substitutes for many of its uses, and it's full of saturated fats, implicated in heart disease. So here in the Free World, where it was once in great demand, we now fear and despise it. And because we enjoy such bountiful freedoms, we are able to reject it, and lubricate our gullets with less objectionable oils. In this house I'm sure there's never a drop of palm oil on anyone's plate. Mavis would just as soon smear her cooking pans with mercury. I'm not mocking her, Will! No doubt I owe my continued survival, for whatever it's worth, to her vigilance in these matters."

"You said there are opportunities. Yet you just described a situation of shrinking markets, falling demand."

"Yes. Perhaps you haven't yet learned to recognize Opportunity in all of her disguises, eh? Now, Will, have you finished your drink? Here is Mavis to escort us to dinner. I believe we're celebrating something or other."

"Certainly we're celebrating," says Mavis. "You got out of bed. You finished your book."

Pers raises his glass. "To my resurrection!" Our glasses clink together with a pure tone, light gleams off the silver and the china, and the wine glows, a deep intoxicating red. The food too is beautiful, arranged on our plates like a few isolated rocks artfully placed in a Japanese sand garden. In fact, it makes more sense to think of it as Art and only incidentally as food. Art, not life. I'm sure there's more organic matter in the centerpiece than on all our plates combined.

But right now I don't care about the food, or the job I seem to have just lost, or whatever Pers was getting at with his talk about palm oil. I'm basking in a beautiful glow. We all are, even old Mavis; even Pers no longer looks half dead, now that his face is distant enough so that the shadows and scars of wasting disease are neutralized by the candleglow and the ambient light of the city. His hair is so white it seems to be the source of its own light, and his pale eyes glitter. But everything glitters, like Pers' eyes with a restrained and subtle rather than a dazzling light: the wineglasses and silverware, the chandelier, the women's jewelry, the treasures of glass and stone and metal, and the windows that reflect all this and simultaneously open beyond it onto a glittering city and sky, and bridges strung in glittering chains across the bay.

Everything glitters, but Kate is radiant. I can't help but stare at her. She smiles back across the table at me, and I know she too is thinking of our own private celebration, of late-afternoon light falling on the Kashan carpet, on the slippery stairs, across the hideaway bed in our honeymoon suite of glass.

But perhaps I exaggerate. Perhaps I mistake the flush of wine in her cheeks for afterburn; perhaps she's only drunk. Perhaps I'm only drunk. Well, yes. I *am* drunk; a pleasant drunkenness is a requirement of the choreography of this dinner. The whiskey was excellent, the wine is even better, and so I suppose I'm an unreliable observer.

Still, I do begin to sense that something might be wrong with all this glowing and glittering light. I'm wondering if maybe it isn't in some way a betrayal of beauty, a warped and poisoned beauty, like a sunset enhanced by polluted skies. Already the choreography is falling apart. Mavis, trying to orchestrate a blessing, wants us to join hands and create a circle of healing energy, but Pers will have nothing to do with it. He raises his glass to propose another toast instead. For a moment there is a stalemate. Bemused, Kate looks from her aunt to her uncle and back again, but she neither lifts her glass nor takes Mavis' outstretched hand. My glass is already in the air and my other hand extended across the corner of the table, where it lies, awkwardly stranded, in Mavis' warm palm. And perhaps because the circle is not completed and no blessing is pronounced, what I am aware of is not healing energy so much as the strange physical reality of Mavis' hand: a thing made of intimate soft folds and creases, coated with powders and suffused with lotions and oils.

"To the engineers of my miraculous recovery," says Pers, beaming around the table. Mavis gives up on the blessing, sets free my hand, and raises her glass as well.

"And to my editors, who have completed the first stage of an ambitious work." Pers smiles at Kate and me. We drink again. "Did you have a toast to propose, Mavis?"

"No. You go on. I can see you've got several bottles' worth."

"Well, yes." He winks at me. "You see we celebrate much more than one small and short-lived resurrection here, Will. Ha-ha!"

He refills our glasses, and we keep toasting. To the imminent completion of Kate's dissertation. To a promising career move. I'm not accustomed to guzzling expensive wine like this, though it's not difficult to do and there seems to be plenty of wine. But I'm not sure exactly what these toasts refer to. If we've completed the first stage of something, then what's the second? When is Kate finishing her dissertation? Who's made a career move; who even has a career?

To the resolution of unconformities, toasts Pers. To the explorers of the future and the past. We keep drinking, except for Mavis, who now only toys with her glass and watches her husband with a faint smile on her face, as if she's observing the antics of a slightly amusing, mostly annoying child.

"Your toasts are all very ambiguous, darling."

"Are they? You know I don't approve of ambiguity. Well, let's be straight-forward. Let's drink to my death, and to the rejuvenating promise of your widowhood."

This time only Pers drinks, and Mavis stops smiling. "Now you're merely being morbid."

"Morbid! No. I am looking to the future, to new life. Because there's no question that you will flourish as a widow, dear. Finally marriage will provide some benefit to you, when you become a widow."

"You shouldn't talk to her like that," says Kate. "As if she's just waiting for you to die. As if you don't appreciate all she's done for you, how hard she's worked to get you healthy again. And it's only her encouragement that's kept you going on your memoirs."

"Encouragement! Why, Mavis has been quite obsessed, Katy. And yes, her obsession seems to be contagious. It's true we never would have gotten this far without her inspiration. We should drink to that! As a corollary to the toast I have just proposed. To widowhood, which is immeasurably enhanced by the publication of a dead husband's memoirs! And certainly you deserve a book of memoirs, dear, as some compensation for so many decades of marriage. Though perhaps we should observe, in passing, that there are other approaches a widow might take with respect to her husband's journals."

"Are there?" says Mavis. "I'm sure we should like to hear about them."

"Well, as an example, Richard Burton's wife burned his."

"Liz burned Dick's journals?" I laugh. "The tabloids must have had a field day!"

Kate looks pained, and Pers takes a deep breath. "*Captain* Sir Richard Burton. Of the nineteenth century. The explorer, the linguist, the ethnographer. Not a damned movie star. When he died, Isabel Burton put thousands of pages of his journals in the flames. She wasn't concerned about a few blank spaces. And perhaps she was right. We lost some details, we are left with some mysteries, but we have a clear picture of Captain Burton. Clearer, perhaps, *because* of the widow's fire. We see the point of his life. In obvious contrast to my journals and my life. I have data, yes, reams of information, yet the point eludes me."

"A point is dimensionless, dear," says Mavis. "It has no property except location. So it will always elude you. But that doesn't mean it isn't there."

"I'm not speaking in goddamn geometric analogies, darling, I'm referring to the meaning, the essence . . . damnit, yes, I mean the *point* of all that scribbling. Is that too much to ask?"

"Well, I think you are being ambiguous again," says Mavis. "And you don't make things any clearer by always changing the subject, or swearing at me. Are you suggesting that I put your journals in the fireplace?"

Pers squints down the table at her. "No, I suppose not. The smoke might cast a pall on your widowhood which we have just been toasting. But perhaps there is a timely lesson to be drawn from Isabel's example. Perhaps she is showing us that we ought to concentrate not so much on the data as on the holes in the data. The unconformities, eh, Katy? Places where the fire has already burned, so to speak."

"Like the Kivila Valley, for example?" says Kate.

"Exactly." Pers smiles.

I am still holding my wineglass aloft, stupidly waiting for the next toast. But everyone has begun to eat now. I drink in the absence of a toast, then set the glass down and pick up one of my forks. I have been fooled. The atmosphere seemed so intoxicated just a short while ago, a benign and charmed drunkenness. I felt a part of it, and I got drunk. But now I see I'm at a great disadvantage.

Suddenly everyone is sober and serious, and things are proceeding according to a logic I can't grasp. I am missing connections and information. Information that Kate has, apparently. Why should she now mention the Kivila Valley, a place in Africa where Pers lived for several years? I remember the name because it's associated with one of the largest gaps in his narrative. We thought perhaps entire journals were lost. And when we asked him about it, of course he claimed he couldn't remember anything.

But now, raising his wineglass again, he says: "To the Kivila Valley. A place of rivers and rain." He speaks slowly, as if the words are evocative; as if he's recalling the rush of water, forest blurred by heavy rain, the smell of leaves and saturated earth. But then he continues: "Rivers and rain. That's all I remember, that and the names of the roads. The Bumba Road, Ngasi Road, the Mission Highway. Nothing else. But maybe that doesn't matter, these memories are not much of a loss. Because after all it's a place of no significance. Nothing that happens there has any effect on anything elsewhere. It's right in the center of a continent, but outside the flow of events in the world. Which is why I thought of you, Will."

"You thought of me?"

"Yes. Because you feel . . . what did you call it? Marginalized. Disengaged. The pace of events accelerates, the world unravels, and you are only a witness, lacking passion for the heroic if futile gesture, as well as endurance and conviction for the longer commitment, the sustained effort."

"It's normal, dear," says Mavis sympathetically. " 'The best lack all conviction, while the worst are full of passionate intensity.' "

"Well-quoted, darling! So you count Will among the best."

"Well, he's certainly not full of passionate intensity, are you, Will, dear?"

"He has his moments," Kate says, kicking me softly under the table.

But Pers says: "Oh, well, that's just poetry. It can be depressing, but I wouldn't take it to heart. And I wouldn't worry about being disengaged, Will. After all, what motivates people to engage? Money, glamour, power, fame. Victory over others. Status. You are rightfully scornful of such aspirations. Yet perhaps you wonder if some of this scorn might not be the product of something equally contemptible: envy. In fact, sometimes you wouldn't mind feeling powerful, glamorous, maybe a little famous yourself, isn't that right?"

"Well, that's not—"

"Let's say you just want a little public respect, that's all. A modest glory, or at least recognition of your superiority. After all, you lack conviction; you are one of the best. You deserve greatness, in some form or other. And greatness is actually quite easy to come by. We will simply take you out of this place which marginalizes you and put you in a new place, where you are rare and exotic. And powerful, because there you will be seen as the embodiment of all the superior power of your native land."

"Excuse me." My voice is weak. "Where are you putting me, exactly?"

"Why, the Kivila Valley, of course. Haven't we just been talking about it?"

"I'm not sure we explained everything," says Kate. "Will's a little vague on the details still. You see, Will, Uncle Pers has offered us a job."

"*I* didn't offer it, Katy. I'm merely facilitating. Providing a little nepotistic nudge. I can't guarantee the outcome."

Kate leans across the table toward me, her eyes glistening. "Will, it's an incredible opportunity. Uncle Pers just found out about it. They want consultants for a palm oil operation in the Kivila Valley. Where Uncle Pers used to work. It's a contract thing. A Jucht Brothers concession, but we wouldn't be working directly for them."

"As consultants? But we have no expertise. We don't know anything about palm oil."

Uncle Pers smiles. "You raised that objection earlier, Will. Yet already you know far more than you did when you raised it, assuming you remember what I told you. And as for expertise, well, that's merely a matter of context. I will arrange for you to get hired, if possible. It's up to you to come up with whatever expertise is necessary. Use the materials at hand. It's impossible to predict what will be required."

Mavis has been sipping her wine distractedly, but now she abruptly sets down her glass and peers over her spectacles at Pers. "I think we ought to clarify something for Will. A place of no significance, yes, but Will . . . are you aware that at times in the past it has been considered a place of great significance? When *he* was there, for example. I think he remembers *that* much." She arches her penciled eyebrows in Pers' direction, and he lifts his head and gazes at her own over the long rugged promontory of his nose.

As for me, I feel like I'm running out of air, trying to claw my way to a surface where conversation is concrete and intelligible. I look at Kate, then Pers. "What about this 'contract'? I mean, where's the money come from?"

The old man laughs softly. "Who knows where money comes from? Corporations form and dissolve, agencies proliferate, loans materialize, then vanish. . . . Money moves through a vast structure, altered at every exchange. A great deal of higher mathematics, amounting to sleight of hand, comes into play. None of which should concern *you*. Enough money will come your way. Take care of the palm oil mill, the palm oil trees. I have no idea what you'll be expected to do with them, but I doubt the work will prove taxing. I anticipate that you'll have time for other things. Exploration. Research. Finishing a dissertation, perhaps."

Kate wrinkles her nose at him, and Pers leans over to pat her hand. "Hypothetically speaking, Katy, dear. Just one of many possibilities. But then, it's all hypothetical, isn't it? You don't have the job yet. You haven't even applied. This is merely a means of considering possibilities. Which become quite numerous and intriguing once you have abandoned my study, with its—what did Mavis call them?—'arbitrary distinctions,' 'linear arrangements of facts.' Once you begin to explore the blank spaces."

Kate leans toward me again, her face close to the heat of the burning candle. "I know this seems totally out of the blue, Will. But that's part of what makes it so right for us. I mean, so far everything's been out of the blue, hasn't it? This is a natural evolution, a way of continuing what we've started. With Uncle Pers' memoirs, and with other things, too."

She looks so beautiful, gazing into my eyes as if we're alone at the table, enclosed in the intimacy of candlelight. But of course we're not alone. Pers and Mavis are gazing at me, too; the whole family's got me in its sights, three pairs of eyes boring in on me. Pers sitting back now, mellowed and pleased with himself, admiring the webs of abstraction he has spun around me. Kate glowing, a heat kindled inside her, only apparently it isn't afterburn lighting her up but this crazy idea of going off to a palm oil mill in Africa. And Mavis radiating something, too, though her glow is mainly exterior and artificial, the product of putty and paint and a half hour of meticulous work in front of the boudoir mirror. Yet some kind of mysterious fire burns inside her, too, fueling strange eruptions, the sudden convergence of all her scattered energies on me.

"A paradox, Will!" she cries. "You continue with the memoirs, in a sense. At the same time you leave the memoirs behind, completed, ready to publish. And yes, it's a natural evolution for you, precisely *because* it's completely out of the blue. Just as the significance of that place lies in its lack of significance. More paradoxes!"

"Yes, well, what's your point, dear?" Pers growls. "Are you still *clarifying* something for Will?"

"There you go, looking for a point again! Fine, then, here's one: You talk of expertise, but you don't make it clear to Will that the reason he's the perfect expert is precisely because he has no expertise. See, Will, another paradox! Showing you that this is a journey for which you can't prepare. Or rather, the best preparation is to not prepare! Because you must go with a completely open mind, an empty mind, even. So you won't seek out the wrong things. Things that never existed, or that are no longer there, that have already vanished. Poof!" And she throws her arms in the air as if invoking a disappearance or a transformation: commanding the glass to shatter and crumble into sand, the artifacts to return in an instant to their homelands, all the electric lights to blaze together and then fade into the native darkness of the earth.

BOOK TWO

THE BAMBOO AIRPLANE

6

THE BAMBOO AIRPLANE

Outside the airplane window the African earth reared up from below, while all around the sky reeled with unnamed terrors. The airplane descended on a purposeful, programmed course, but in the cabin I felt untethered and radarless, paralyzed and doomed and somewhat drunk. Especially I regretted the drunk part. I wanted to be sober, I'd wanted that ever since that candlelit dinner in San Francisco when Pers and Kate first spoke of the Kivila Valley. At the time of course I was truly drunk, but in the weeks since I'd often had that same longing for sobriety, whether or not I'd had any alcohol. Though in this case I had. Kate and I each had drunk several cocktails during the flight from Brussels, and for a while we'd collaborated in sustaining a kind of giddiness, a euphoria I knew all along was hollow, founded purely on crude chemical manipulations of our brains. At least that's all it was for me; maybe Kate's euphoria was more complex and genuine. She had real enthusiasm for this undertaking, a conviction that we were embarking on a great star-crossed adventure, with all the planets aligned, all the Fates and Muses poised to accommodate. Whereas my thinking went more like this: we were in love, and not entirely without resources, so why was it necessary to throw ourselves off the first cliff that presented itself? It wasn't as if we were desperate, in flight or forced into exile. Sure, somebody eventually needed to get a job, but this going off to the palm oil plantations of Africa seemed ludicrous. It was dramatic, but there was no logic to the drama, though Kate acted as if it were perfect, as if everything had fallen into place. But why palm oil? Why Africa? We hadn't even made it to Mexico yet. Couldn't we at least have begun with Mexico?

In spite of all my anxiety I did feel liberated. We were free of Pers and Mavis. In fact, it was unlikely I would ever see old Pers again, for which I felt some sorrow, because after all I was fond of the old man; in certain ways we had connected with each other, and I wondered if he didn't yet have some wisdom to impart to me, and I some comfort of innocence to offer him. It had been a strange and desolate farewell in their living room, to grip his hand and look into his eyes and realize that we had come to the true end of something, that the life would surely go out of those eyes before I returned. If I ever returned.

Still it was a relief to leave him on the ground, the old schemer, up to the last minute working his secrets and intrigues. He motioned us close when Mavis went off to the bathroom. "That book isn't published yet! And it might not go off to the printer as quickly as Mavis hopes. Meanwhile, I'll wait to hear from you. One of your duties is to keep me informed. Ask questions. Continue the research! But be discreet! Don't mention my name or your connection to me."

He gave us a long, meaningful look, but I had no idea what the meaning might be. What ancient intrigue might he still be nursing? What did he care if we mentioned his name to anyone? Fine, I'd be happy enough not to mention him, to just forget about him for a while. To be free of his obsessions and fossilized memories and sharp wit and scrutiny. His arthritic finger shaking in the air, pointing and stabbing, skewering every twisted inconstancy in my soul. Let the unconformities in his memoirs gape, or fill in of their own accord, if there really was something there, in the places where the fire had already burned. In the meantime, we could think of this as a fresh start on the honeymoon, if we wanted to think that way. There would be southern stars, there would be tropical breezes, there would be palm trees. Of course, they were not the honeymoon kind of palm trees. They were industrial palm trees, and what mattered to us was the quantity of palm nuts they produced, their oil content, the distance from the plantations to the mill and the mill to the market, the type of machinery used to extract the oil from the fruit, the cost of labor, the availability of fuel, road conditions, demand for the product . . . . What mattered to us was how all these things might be manipulated to increase palm oil production, market stability, and profits, because that, according to our contract, was what we were going to tell people how to do.

I knew all these things were important considerations, or at least that they'd once been important considerations, because I had already read about them in the book that lay open on my lap and that I now turned to again, as Kate's gaze drifted out the window and the chemical reactions of euphoria sputtered out in my brain, replaced by the more familiar chemistry of anxiety and doubt. The book was a 1961 publication called *Products of the Oil Palm* by a C. W. Lindquist, a professor of agronomy or something like that in England, and also in a sense my predecessor, since he too had been a consultant to the palm oil industry in Africa. I'd found Professor Lindquist's book on Pers' shelf a few days before we'd left, and notwithstanding Mavis' admonition to empty my mind and prepare by not preparing, I'd resolved to read it cover to cover before I reported to work at my new job.

But it was tough going. The most readable part was the introduction, where I learned that the palm-oil industry had gotten its initial boost from the suppression of the slave trade by the British, which left intact an infrastructure of international commerce but denied it its principal merchandise. Palm oil flowed into the vacuum, becoming the commodity that replaced human flesh. Demand was driven at first by the need for an oil for soap making, a booming business in those days, whether in response to higher standards of hygiene or to the dirtier world of the Industrial Revolution, Lindquist didn't say.

I learned that today, or at least as of 1961, palm oil was used as a cooking oil and to make soap, margarine, livestock feed, candles, glycerine, and detergents. It had some kind of application in the steel industry, and a few other uses as well. And for many of these applications, Lindquist wrote, less expensive and better substitutes were available, and so the palm oil markets, and the value of the product itself, were in decline.

Lindquist slogged through endless statistics documenting falling production, decreased plantation acreage, closures of processing plants. He made it clear that way back in 1961, long before it was indicted as saturated fat—bearing sludge, palm oil had become a second-rate commodity. If it vanished from the face of the planet, the industrialized world, which once had built empires on it, might hardly notice. Lindquist himself might hardly notice, he seemed so depressed. Yet it seemed to me that having so forcefully established the irrelevance of his subject, he might have had the decency to admit there was little point in writing a book about it. He might have closed out his short narrative and faded humbly into the obscurity that posterity had arranged for him and his chosen oil. Instead, as if in bitter contempt for the indifference of the world, he turned to the heart of his book—a long, highly technical description of a palm-oil refining mill. He held forth for long chapters on sterilization, stripping, digestion and mashing, extraction, clarification, and fiber separation. He waded deep into chemistry, mathematics, engineering, and went on for pages about the relative merits of oil extraction with a hydraulic press versus a centrifuge. I sincerely tried to follow his discussion because apparently I would be required to know this stuff. But I couldn't help but notice, beneath the neutral monotone of his professional voice, Lindquist's disdain for his subject, and his boredom. Occasionally he roused himself from his torpor to issue a dryly disparaging remark, or even to openly ridicule palm oil in his humorless and pedantic style. I began to wonder if some of his scorn might not be directed at me, his reader. Don't you have anything better to do, Lindquist seemed to sneer, than fill your head with dull industrial facts about an obsolete tropical oil? Well, what about you, Lindquist? I shot back. Just because you devoted *your* life to acquiring this obscure expertise, does that give you license to burden the world with this incredibly tedious book?

Kate pulled on my arm and pointed out the window. The plane banked, a long spiraling descent, and a green world wheeled below. Ribbons of sun-flashed water, strips of red road, scatterings of settlement in the green undulating plain. And in the airplane vertigo and nausea, cocktails sloshing in my stomach, a sudden claustrophobia even here in Business Class, with those wide seats and ample leg room. G-forces pushed *Products of the Oil Palm* oppressively against my guts, and I hurriedly stuffed it into my bag.

"God, it's beautiful." Kate breathed, still looking at the window. Then she glanced worriedly at me. "You've got a really weird expression, Will. Are you okay?"

"No. I think I'm mutating again."

Yes, that was it. It was all part of the evolutionary process, along with the contracts we'd signed, the assignment notice we'd received, the checks we'd already cashed. Yet the whole thing seemed improbable and strange. We'd still had no direct contact with Jucht Brothers, the operators of the palm oil concession. All our employment arrangements had been made by mail through the contractor, a firm called Global Interconnect. G.I. (I had to wonder about the abbreviation, especially now with my guts already roiling at the mere sight of African water and soil) had promised us an orientation program and a four-wheel-drive vehicle when we arrived in the country, issued us an extravagant travel and resettlement allowance, and paid for these spacious plane seats and regrettable cocktails. So the money was real; the job, which had seemed to materialize out of innumerable half-drunken toasts in Pers and Mavis' living room, seemed to be real, too. We were now consultants, descending on Africa with presumed stores of knowledge.

We spent several days in Kisaka, the capital city, waiting for our instructions and our vehicle. While we waited we wandered about, trying to get a sense of the city. But that wasn't something to be done in a matter of a few days. This Kisaka was not like other cities I had known. What was it I had said, ranting disjointedly in Uncle Pers' living room? *Every place is a theme park now.* But there was nothing of the theme park about Kisaka. No sense of nostalgia or romance, no illusions or simulations, no façades even of institutional culture, of history or architectural identity. It all seemed an improvisation, a mass of displaced people swarming through disintegrating streets, having converged there for reasons they no longer remembered. There was commerce, of course—that must have been the reason for the convergence—but it was mainly a commerce of desperation, sucking people out of their far-off villages into the spreading shantytowns, with their open streams of sewage and mazelike streets blocked by rubble and excavation and constructions of scavenged tin and lumber and cardboard—harsh and miserable in the daylight, yet only a shadow behind the night streets with their intensity of music and sex and laughter and talk and dancing, a collective will to obliterate the images of the day.

Certainly there were social intricacies interwoven below the surface, new cultures brewing, a sharp impact of languages colliding, and out of the collisions entirely new sounds and meanings reverberating down the streets, new hybrids rising from the poverty and clichés of the shantytowns, maybe even the embryos of new civilizations spawned in the obvious wreckage of the old. But Kate and I, buffeted about the city on pure strangeness, were unable to recognize such things. We penetrated nothing, and we made no distinctions, overwhelmed as we were by our own distinction: the whiteness of our skin. People stared, welcomed us, cursed us, tried to steal from us. And we couldn't tell the thieves from the Samaritans, couldn't distinguish among officials, loafers, muggers, artists, scammers, beggars, cops, entrepreneurs, smugglers, cab drivers—everybody hustling or milling or lounging about to no apparent purpose, but with a predatory edge on them. Police and soldiers were everywhere but imposed no sense of order. They were unpredictable and impulsive too, just a part of the anarchy.

We went in and out of the Jucht Brothers office in a gated and guarded compound downtown. The secretary found a file on us, confirming our assignment to a town called Ngemba, in the Kivila Valley. But no one seemed to know what to do with us, and the promised four-wheel-drive vehicle was not available. The vehicle was the director's responsibility, the secretary explained, and the director was gone to the field. En brosse, the secretary said, where it was impossible to communicate with her. Eventually it came out that she would not be back for a week at least. Finally someone arranged for us to get a ride with Père Andrés, the père superior of Bumba Mission, which was the largest Catholic mission in the Kivila Valley region and only a few miles from our post.

"Père superior" seemed a grand title for this pasty Belgian, with his choppy improvised English and a button-down shirt gaping open across his pale hairless belly. He had an unnerving and persistent chuckle, which at odd moments modulated into an unclerical giggle. When we shook hands I was struck by his anemic grip and the softness of his skin. But he seemed experienced and capable just the same, and sardonic in spite of appearances.

"So, you gonna live at Kivila Valley," he said. "But no camion. Just walking forth and back among the jungle, eh?" He giggled.

"They'll send our vehicle out in a couple of weeks."

"Send? They mail it? Postal? Okay, sure, ha-ha! Tell me something. You *see* this camion yet, with your eyes?"

"No. What, do you think we should wait here for it, to make sure?"

"What is this meaning, to make sure? Sure? How long to wait? One week, two week, a month? Maybe camion is existing. Sure! Who knows this? Maybe they give over the keys, you are driving it upon the road for Ngemba. Sure! Who knows? But I will advice you for one thing: there are many, many camions here, and the most of them constructed out from everybody's dream. But you want to make for sure, it is better for you coming with me, because this one"—he slammed his pudgy fist down on the hood of his Land Rover and let out a guttural giggle—"they making of steel and grease."

We stood on a rise in a long narrow peninsula of savanna that divided two river valleys. Behind us tall sharp-edged grasses waved in the wind. At our feet the escarpment fell away, and a steep path descended the slope through scattered trees toward the valley bottom, where the unseen river wound through a deeper forest. "You are seeing Kivila Valley," said Père Andrés. He took off his glasses, wiped the lenses on a handkerchief, and shoved them back on his nose. He giggled. "Your new home."

"It's like Mongolia or something," said Kate.

"Mongolia!" I said.

"Yes. The steppes, you know. The emptiness. The immensity of grass. A green desert. I mean, I've never been to Mongolia or anything."

"No. But maybe you've seen a lot of Mongolian movies."

"Maybe I've had a lot of Mongolian dreams."

The père waved his arms at the forest, apparently pointing out landmarks—his mission, the palm oil mill at Ngemba, the route we had followed across savannas and valleys. Kate and I nodded, but really the place looked uninhabited. In the valley there seemed to be only jungle, broken by sporadic clearings that barely implied human settlement. Père Andrés pointed at clumps of trees along the sinuous savanna peninsula behind us and intoned the names of villages we already had passed through. They were the villages of his parishioners, and he, no doubt, had some reason to distinguish among them. Perhaps we would also, someday. But to me they seemed identical in their poverty, to all appearances devoid of innovation or creativity or any elaboration on the basic functions of human existence. From a distance they were picturesque, and there was grandeur in the setting. But that is true of any large expanse of earth and sky. And people don't occupy these vast spaces—they live in small clearings hacked out of the forest; they huddle together beneath clumps of trees on the savanna.

It was impossible to imagine Mavis living in a place like this. No wonder she had stayed behind in Brussels and San Francisco when Pers had come out here. Disappeared out here. And now we were looking straight into the blank face of one of the gaps in his memoirs. Insignificance—not an abstraction now but a physical reality, given shape by the burned-out colonial buildings, the highway littered with broken-down trucks, the eroded and overgrown roads leading into the bush, the crumpled thatch villages where men loafed in the heat and ragged round-bellied children stirred from the dust to make a game of chasing the père's truck. Beyond the villages, in the fields of charred stumps, gullied red earth, and scraggly shoots of corn and manioc, women in bright cotton wraps—pagnes—straightened up from their hoeing to watch us and wave. The sweat shone on their faces, and sometimes a baby still latched on to a floppy breast as its mother bent again to scratch at the earth.

"What about wildlife?" I asked, and Père Andre snorted. "Sometimes a little—how you call? Ant-lope. High in the tree a monkey, a squirrels. People shooting at everything. Making a fire in all the bush. Only a small animal escape. So we have many mouse, oh yes, great herds of bush mouse, ha-ha!"

Back in the Land Rover, we slammed into a rut, and the wheel spun out of the père's hands. "The superhighway!" he chortled as we swerved up on the embankment. "This road for crossing the continent, do you know what? The autopiste, ha-ha! Following this direction, my friend, for making the drive to Indian Ocean!"

We came to a roadblock—a long pole laid across the rutted track. Soldiers sauntered to our windows with rifles slung on their shoulders. The père spoke to them fiercely in their own language, and cut off their replies with an abrupt gesture. Then he drove up to the roadblock and pressed his horn. The soldiers, looking confused, snatched up the pole and waved us on.

Once we were past the soldiers, Père Andrés giggled and pushed his glasses up on his nose. "Of course, I don't behave so strong," he said, "if I am suspecting bullets in the guns."

A hot wind thundered through the Land Rover. Away from the escarpment the landscape diminished; now there were only the fields of grass leaning into the road, whipping through the open windows as we jolted through. Over the noise of the wind and the engine I strained to listen to the talk in the front seat but soon gave up, growing drowsy in the heat and the long corridor of grass. Père Andrés jerked the wheel back and forth and we swayed in the deep sandy ruts, catching and losing a rhythm. I was almost asleep when we came over a rise and saw an airplane soaring in the clear sky.

We dropped off the rise, and the plane vanished behind the low ridge ahead of us. We climbed, and it appeared again, banking along the rim of the savanna. The airplane seemed magnificent to me, swooping into and out of view as the road dipped and climbed. And strangely it lost none of its magnificence when we came out into a clearing, a small farm or settlement, and found ourselves suddenly abreast of it: a *very* small plane, a model airplane with a wingspan of perhaps two feet, constructed not of metals but of bamboo and raffia, like the huts below it. And not flying but attached to a bamboo pole maybe sixty feet high, stabilized by long vines stretching to the corner of the compound. Except for the plane, the compound was as barren as any other we might have passed, and now in the heat of the day empty of movement and life.

Kate had been watching the plane as raptly as I was, and as we passed the compound she turned to Père Andrés, whose blinking eyes were still on the road.

"Do you know anything about that plane?"

"I know the man who builds it. Ndosi. Monsieur Rêve. Dream Man, you may say."

"Does he belong to your church?"

"Oh, well, sure. A believer, okay, maybe. The church here is very big room."

"What is the meaning of that plane?"

He shrugged. "Maybe a toy. Maybe symboling something. Who knows? It maybe is a fetish of some kind. Ha-ha!"

"Like a rosary or something, you mean?"

"Excuse?"

"Never mind. How long has it been there?"

"Long time. Months, perhaps a year." He laughed again. "It is the most strong construction on the lands, have you notice?"

I felt a sudden urge to be in the cockpit, looking out over the curve of the world, rocking at the center of the sky. Far below, this land we had bumped so tediously across would be brought into a truer perspective: no longer rutted roads connecting small fields and huts and patches of bush, but a great green savanna inlaid with forest valleys of a more saturated green, a pattern of contrasting shades and textures extending north to the unbroken rain forest, south to the pure savanna.

We turned off the transcontinental highway and skidded down a gullied broken track into the forest. Soon we were in cooler, shadowed places, speeding on a hard clay road. Chickens and goats scattered before us, and people with baskets and jugs on their heads stood on the side of the road, shouting and waving, or just staring. This forested world was where we were going to live, but I kept thinking of the airplane up on the open savanna. Some kind of talisman, something to cling to in a desolate and confusing landscape. Or, as Père Andrés had suggested, a symbol, in which case you had to wonder what it represented: whether a spirit of invention and play or the will and the hope to escape.

7

THE OIL MILL

The chef de poste was friendly and accommodating right from the start. He showed us around, made introductions, and sent people bustling here and there on our behalf, and I only vaguely sensed that he wasn't entirely certain who we were or what we were supposed to do for him. But I don't think his expectations were high. I do know that after five minutes of conversation with us he didn't expect to understand anything I said.

"Your French is terrible," he said to me. "Lucky for you hardly anyone around here speaks French. My advise to you is: learn Kituba, and in the meantime let your wife do the talking."

The chef de poste was the boss of Ngemba station—the chief. He was a fat man with white hair and a deep, hoarse voice. He kept taking a handkerchief from the pocket of his grease-stained coveralls to wipe the sweat, from the folds of skin in his neck. But fat or not, we all were dripping sweat, because it was ungodly hot. I wanted to jump in the river, or at least sit in the shade, but the chef insisted on showing us the camp.

We walked up a road above the mill, which rumbled and whined and spewed a greasy orange smoke into the air. The chef de poste talked all the time, in French. Sometimes I more or less understood what he was saying, and sometimes I got tired of concentrating and just let his talk blur. He pointed out the company store, and behind it the houses of the camp—two rows of identical crumbling brick and cement buildings on either side of a rutted muddy road. People stood in the dirt yards of the houses and stared at us. A few of them waved, and some approached to shake our hands. But the chef moved us along, past a spacious and well-kept building with a large veranda and a cultivated flower garden. This was the guest house, the chef explained. It had been the chef de poste's residence years before, when the chef wasn't expected to run the entire operation. But now as chef de poste he lived across the river, because if he stayed on this side he would never get a moment's peace, and anyway the guest house was needed for important visitors like the chef de collectivité, the commissaire de zone, and the director, if the director ever came.

Beyond the guest house a small cement-block building with a tin roof and dirty whitewashed walls overlooked the river.

"The consultants' house," announced the chef de poste, and we mounted the broken and eroding steps to a small porch. He unlocked a padlock and we entered a tiny cement cubicle, one of three rooms, identical barren chambers holding stale and sour air. Kate threw the shutters open, like rolling stones off a long-sealed tomb. She smiled grimly, stepping from one room to the next.

"Kitchen, living room, bedroom, voilà!"

I tried my French again. "Ou est l'eau?"

"Lo?" said the chef, puzzled.

"C'est a dire, le tuyeau," Kate explained. "The plumbing. The water tap. The bathroom."

The chef stared. "The water is in the river," he said patiently. "Your boy brings it up. You pour it on your head. That's it, a shower."

"Our boy?" I said.

The chef hustled us outside, and we stopped in the full glare of the sun on the porch, where he lit a cigarette and pointed toward a tumbledown out-house across the yard. "The waysay. Of course, it may be in some disrepair. We'll fix it."

A small breeze came up, providing a bit of relief from the heat on the porch. It also blew the smoke from the mill across the compound, and we smelled for the first time the heavy industrial odor of a palm oil mill. The chef, inhaling deeply on his cigarette, did not seem aware of the orange smoke. We stood together on the porch and looked out on the yard and out-buildings. The cook shed, the shower shed, the garage, the gardens, the chef said. In the flower bed below us a few scraggly daisies fought their way out of the weeds and through a mulch of broken concrete, decomposing plastic, and rusting steel cans. An expanse of barren red earth, compact as pavement, formed rills and gullies as it sloped toward the fruit trees, vines, weeds, and wild saplings that grew entangled beyond the outbuildings. Beyond that was the road, and the river glinting through the strip of forest that lined its banks.

"Well," I said to Kate, "the porch is nice. I mean, it's not the bougainvillea-draped veranda I was maybe thinking of, but at least it's a porch. I could hang out on it. I mean, in the evening, after the sun goes down."

Kate was looking at the raw, eroded yard. "I guess we'll plant some grass," she told the chef.

The chef was horrified. "Grass? No, madame. Jamais! There are snakes down there in the forest. You understand? Les serpents! Always looking for grass!" His fat arm slithered in front of our faces. "Be sure to tell me if you see a snake. But your boy will keep the yard clean—no grass, no bushes. No snakes."

"Our boy?" I said again.

He laughed. "You don't understand French. Your wife knows what I said. Anyway, this house is her concern. Men can live anywhere, in the forest if we have to, but women need a house. So, madame. You'll be comfortable here? You see that I've made all the arrangements. Security, maintenance, everything. You need something fixed, just ask me. Je suis chef de poste! I'm in charge of everything. The mill, the camp, the coupiers who cut palm nuts in the forest, the cantoniers who keep the road repaired, the boat that takes the oil down the river—I'm responsible for it all. That's the duty of the chef de poste. And now, I'm responsible for the consultants as well."

He stared at us—friendly enough, accommodating, as I said, but proprietorial, and maybe wondering what we were up to here, and whether we were looking to challenge these territorial claims. Then, as if realizing that part of his responsibility included not letting us collapse of heatstroke on our own porch, he led us across the yard into the shade of trees, offered us seats on a couple of benches, and scattered the crowd of children that had gathered by the gate of the guest house to watch.

We sat down. Kate said something to the chef about how pleased we were to be there. "But the house needs some work. The walls are filthy. The floor is full of holes, and somebody's bound to break a leg on those stairs. These outbuildings are going to collapse in the next thunderstorm. I can smell the waysay from here. In fact, the whole place stinks. And the yard's a jungle, except where it's a desert."

The chef nodded, gazing at Kate with admiration. "You speak French so well. At least as well as I do. Of course, French isn't my strong point. I didn't go to school for long. I'm a mechanic, not a bureaucrat. They made me chef because I work hard, I keep things running, but I got my education on the job. I need French to talk to soldiers, to the commissaire, to politicians and to consultants like you. But I prefer Kituba. My secretary speaks real French. He's been to school, and traveled. My French is full of mistakes. Maybe you can tell. Your husband can't. But who can remember all the damn rules in French? Naturally I make mistakes—it's not a sensible language. We have hundreds of languages in this country, and we end up trying to talk to each other in French. That's why we have so many problems—politicians are worrying about verb tenses instead of trying to say something that makes sense. Tell your husband he isn't missing out on much; he should learn Kituba if he wants to talk to people. In the meantime, if he wants conversation he can visit the priests. They love an excuse to talk. Or he should try Monsieur Tom in Malembe, just down the road. He's an American too, and his French is nearly as bad as your husband's, even though he's lived here for years."

"I'll tell him," said Kate. "What about the house?"

"Well, we'll fix it up. Frankly, madame, we weren't entirely prepared for your arrival. A communications failure. People in Kisaka don't communicate well with those of us out here in the field, doing the work. But here, things are different. Here, I'm the chef: I tell people what to do, and they do it. Those things you mentioned are all very easy to deal with. And I've already taken care of the security problem for you."

"What security problem?"

"Right, madame. It's very peaceful here. Yes. But maybe there are dangers you can't recognize. In any case, you need someone watching the place. You need a nightwatchman to protect you and your house, your garden, your camion." He waved his arms in a wide inclusive gesture that made me wonder if he were suffering delusions, if he saw bountiful crops in the garden and a mud-splattered Land Rover cooling in the driveway.

Kate wandered off toward the garden, and the chef turned to me. "She wants a bigger house. Women always do. But I don't have one for you. I couldn't give you the guest house even if the commissaire weren't coming. It's because of our history, which maybe you haven't studied. The overseers used to live there, back when we were colonized. Sometimes a director, sometimes a chef de poste, sometimes a crew boss or an engineer. White people. But now we're independent, and I can't put you up there, in the biggest house on the river, as if we were still your slaves. As if we were still working for you, and not the other way around."

Pushing through weeds as tall as herself, Kate called to me from beside a collapsing wooden structure on the edge of the garden. "Look, Will. A chicken shed!"

"Of course, you will have some people working for you," said the chef. "The sentinel at night, and by day, your boy."

"Right. Our boy."

He slapped me on the shoulder and laughed. "Your wife understands French," he said. "But you—you don't know what I'm talking about." And he shook his head silently, as if to say, what's the point of talking, and offered me a cigarette, which to my own astonishment I accepted. It was the first cigarette I'd smoked in years, and it made me sick to my stomach, but for a couple of minutes before the nausea hit I achieved a lightheaded sense of camaraderie and power, smoking in silence with the fat chef as we stood together on the hard red earth, in the shade of unfamiliar trees.

At night we had the sentinel: Placide the nightwatchman, padding around the compound silently, on bare feet that were cushioned with calluses like the paws of a cat. Small and dark and quick, with an affinity for shadows, Placide was capable of remaining still for very long periods of time. In the evenings I sat on the porch and looked out into the unfamiliar darkness, but I never knew where Placide was, until he spoke to me suddenly, close at hand but still invisible in the shadows, or until he appeared in the fireglow down by the cook shed to warm himself or feed the fire he kept burning in a small brazier.

Next to his fire he had a cement block to sit on, and inside the cook shed he kept a pile of old cardboard. On cool nights he sometimes dragged the cardboard out beside the fire and crawled beneath it for warmth. But he didn't fall asleep, or if he did it was an alert sleep, because he would instantly emerge, bow and arrows in hand, at the slightest sound.

At first Kate and I were merely amused by Placide. We thought he was cute, maybe because he was so short and had a pug nose and an implacable deadpan and wore a watch cap and tattered overcoat in the tropical night. Because he had a hoarse piping voice and spoke a light and syncopated language that sounded charming to us, accustomed as we were to the guttural rumbling tones of English.

It took only a few sleepless nights inside our claustrophobic house, with Placide skulking around the compound with his machete or his little bow and arrows, to shatter that sentimental illusion. I couldn't decide which was more unnerving: to see him huddled in his overcoat by the fire, casting a flickering and deceptively large shadow against the cook shed; or to *not* see him yet know he was there, peering from the darkness at my pale and nervous face. The chef de poste claimed there was a security problem, but Placide's sober vigilance seemed extreme. There was scarcely a passerby to challenge. What did he think about all night, stalking the yard in his overcoat, tending his minimalist fire, watching over a garden of weeds and a Land Rover made of dreams? Yet I was drawn to him—in some strange way his presence made sense, fit perfectly into the night. I sat on the porch and studied him, felt his tension and watchfulness, even shared a little his sense of purpose, though I had no idea what that purpose might be.

By day we had Dimanche, our boy. Everyone else called him that—"your boy," using the English word without any qualms or self-consciousness. Self-consciously, we called him our "helper," a seemingly innocuous title that always sounded calculated, like a euphemism—more patronizing, in a way, than calling him our boy.

Dimanche was about twenty years old, a big fleshy kid by local standards. "Because he converts all his calories to mass and storage," said Kate, "instead of squandering them on work." It was his job to wash our clothes and dishes, clean house, carry drinking water from the spring, maintain the yard and gardens, and help with the cooking. But each morning when he arrived he greeted us with a lifeless handshake and immediately sat down on the living room couch, staring at the wall until we asked him to get to work. He never took the initiative on his own. And as soon as he finished one job, he'd head for the couch again. He'd come in from washing dishes (he carried them off in a basin to a water spigot somewhere in the camp, I presumed) and drop the dish basin in the corner, flop the dishrag on the rim of the basin, and collapse with a heavy sigh on the couch, as if he were a dishrag himself, as if there were nothing to be done with such a weighty body but let it sink into the gravitational field of the couch.

Kate generally broke the uncomfortable silence. "Did you get water, Dimanche?"

"No."

"Do we need water?"

"I don't know."

"I think we do."

A grunt. A pout. The continued weight of his dense flesh on our couch.

"Could you please get some water, Dimanche?"

Silence. The continued blank averted gaze. A smell in the still air, venomous and corrupt; a bodily smell, but coming from someplace deeper than sweat glands or hormones. Finally the almost imperceptible stirring, the slow labored rise to his feet, the sighs of—what? Exhaustion? Exasperation? Despair? He took up the empty plastic jug and went down the porch steps. And then it might be an hour or more before he dragged himself back up the path with the full jug of water balanced on his head. I never complained, since I wasn't sure how far he had to go for it and anyway it was such a relief to get him out of the house. But when the chef de poste asked us how we were getting along, we told him we were unhappy with Dimanche.

"What's the problem? Is he stealing from you?"

"Not so we'd notice," said Kate. "He's just lazy. But the real problem is, we don't like him."

The chef laughed. "What difference does that make? He's your boy—you don't have to drink with him or sit around and talk with him. Why like him? Why dislike him? It's all the same so long as he does his work. And maybe you don't notice everything he does for you. You might be lost without him. Sure he's lazy, a big zero, but maybe his duties aren't clear to him either. How do you talk to him, Monsieur Will? In French? Ha-ha! Maybe he gets tired just trying to understand you. Maybe he's confused."

No doubt that was true. Kate and I were still mutating, and constantly trying to figure out where the mutations left us in relation to each other. It didn't help to have this stranger moving incommunicado through the territory of our private lives. And neither of us was comfortable giving orders, but Dimanche, apparently, required them: he did not respond to hints and polite requests.

Tom, the American who lived in the neighboring village of Malembe, said it was no wonder we resented him. "He won't comply with your cherished egalitarian principles. Or do you think they might be myths? Look, Dimanche is stupid, okay, but he can still see the writing on the fucking wall you're wishing he'd wash. He can see that life has mainly screwed him over, and he wants to be sure you understand it, too. See, I don't think Dimanche's miserable personality is actually the issue here. Sure it's a drag to have a farceur like him hanging around your house, but we're looking at something deeper than that here. We're looking at racial fear, class warfare, you know what I'm saying? Don't laugh. You ought to be crying. Dimanche is helping you peel back a few layers of self-deception, and the process should hurt."

"Oh, I see," said Kate. "He's *enlightening* us. It's the sulk of enlightenment. Well, I still want to fire him."

But it seemed too complicated, sorting through the social and political repercussions. After all, wasn't he the chef de poste's man? And wasn't his family dependent on his income? And besides, it was hard to fire somebody for doing a bad job when we weren't doing much of a job ourselves.

Early on, we decided to divide our responsibilities. Kate would be agricultural consultant, concerned with raw-materials production and the oil-palm plantations themselves; and I would concentrate on processing. The chef gave me an office next to his secretary's in the building across the yard from the mill. It was an airless cement cubicle with one window, a desk, a chair, and a photo of the president of the republic on the wall. And out the open door a view of the mill, a huge building of faded yellow brick, spewing smoke and steam, howling and grinding and steeped in that strange heavy odor. I could see it, smell it, hear it, and all the evidence suggested that it was a very horrible place indeed. And I was the consultant, here to tell people what to do with it.

From the edge of our yard I had a view of much of the operation: the mill itself, the offices and warehouses, the old Mercedes trucks, the ferry, the riverside quay where the decrepit oil boat docked once a week, and the power lines coming from the small hydroelectric plant on a nearby creek. I could see the porch of the company store, and the broken tile roofs of the company houses—smoke-blackened hulks looking out on expanses of dirt and rutted roads and paths. These were not ancient ruins, not in the usual sense. They might have been fifty years old. But they looked and felt like antiquities. The rounded, algae-stained brick and cement block of the camp houses were like the old rectangular stones of a Mayan city, decomposing in a jungle clearing. Yet a few decades before, those houses must have been immaculate, well furnished, and landscaped, with neat lawns and walkways delineated by rows of whitewashed rocks. The whole place must have bustled with orderly work crews, wielding shovels and machetes under the stern eyes of pith-helmeted Europeans, among them Uncle Pers. They built roads and factories, cut down trees, planted different trees, poured cement, moved whole villages, eradicated pestilence. And to at least some of the participants it may well have seemed wonderful: industrious and purposeful, a miraculous link to a world of wealth and ambition, though the pith helmets, if they really did wear them, must have given to the entire enterprise an underlying tinge of lunacy.

Now the mill and its environs struck me as an absurdly elaborate, if shabby, apparatus to produce something that much of the world seemed determined to no longer consume. What kept it going? What compelled someone to send that rusty diesel-spewing hulk upriver every week to collect the processed oil? Who conjured up those stacks of bright-colored bills that the chef dispensed every payday and that each day were worth less than the day before? And speaking of conjurations, how did anyone account for the thousands of dollars deposited in our bank accounts every month? Where did money come from, anyway?

Expertise is merely a matter of context, Uncle Pers had said. *You build it out of the materials at hand.* I considered the materials I had at hand, at the time when the secretary and I crossed the bright hot yard and penetrated the hotter shadows of the mill. There was my self-imposed title: technical consultant to the Ngemba mill; there were pieces of technical jargon and theory passed on to me by bitter old Professor Lindquist; and now there was this deafening racket of the mill, further insurance that no one could hear me say anything that would reveal the depths of my ignorance. Here in the mill I could speak freely, with confidence and authority, shouting unintelligible words into the secretary's ear. And indeed the secretary nodded, looking thoughtful: the consultant had spoken, his expertise was confirmed.

But in fact I was having trouble keeping my head. I tried to remember what I had learned from Professor Lindquist, to apply his diagrams and long-winded explanations to these bursts of steam and fire, bubbling cauldrons, and howling machinery. But Lindquist's despondent prose had not prepared me for this. The world of *Products of the Oil Palm* was theoretical and schematic; it could not stand up to the heat of the blast furnace, the shriek of resistant bearings and corroded flywheels. Confronted with this cobweb of machinery, I could recall nothing of Lindquist's careful and logical diagrams. Instead, as I followed the secretary through swinging doors and into the bowels of the mill, I found myself thinking again of Uncle Pers—though not exactly of Uncle Pers, or anything specific that he had said. I was thinking more of the strange low rumbling that I had heard so often coming from deep within his house, nearly drowning out his frail voice. The sounds of old furnaces and water heaters, pipes groaning in the dark room behind the basement door we never opened. A room of buried treasures and secrets from Kate's childhood, a great mythical room like a catacomb beneath the asphalt of the city, filled with nightmare machinery, issuing muffled and monstrous industrial sounds.

Now I followed the secretary through a shadowy maze of extruders and compressors, pumps or centrifuges—who could distinguish among them?—past vats of boiling oil and the open door of a glowing furnace, up stairways and greasy ladder rungs, and onto a platform in the high open spaces near the roof, where the rising heat was trapped. Shafts of daylight entered through gaps in the roof, and the light from below was reflected by the oily aluminum sheeting. Below us half-naked workers moved among the pulsing machinery, but I was thinking again of that old house in San Francisco. This dim light among the girders and cables and pipes was like the unreal midnight light in our honeymoon suite of glass—only not like it at all, because that had been an illumination that penetrated the night, while this was a diminishment of the full light of day, a reversal, a negative image of that city glow.

The secretary and I no longer pretended to talk. Yet it seemed that voices were cutting through the layers of machine noise, though the workers were far below us. Trying to locate the voices, I looked across the building and saw Uncle Pers, crossing the air on a high swinging catwalk. He leaned over the rail as if to shout across at us, but of course he couldn't be heard. And of course it wasn't Uncle Pers at all, just an optical trick of false light, an effect of heat and noise on the gullible brain. I looked again, and saw the black skin of a mill worker glistening through the holes in his shirt. Then he straightened, crossed the catwalk, and vanished into the unnatural light and shadow, the day mocking the night.

When the tour ended I shook the secretary's hand and went straight home. I was sweat-drenched and heat-exhausted, my ears rang and my head throbbed, but I stopped for a moment at the top of the driveway and looked back again at the mill. It *seemed* like some medieval allegory of hell, the oldest terrors fused with industrial technology but still relying on elemental and primitive forces and devices—steam and fire, grinding iron, boiling oil. But really it was just a big room full of machines that beat, mashed, cracked, stripped, steamed, boiled, spun, and poured. Acts of violence, every one of them, but the point of it all was only to get the oil out of the palm nuts. There was no mystery or terror in that. Any mystery in the place came from outside, I told myself: just random associations and surges of memory, escaping from my own undisciplined imagination onto the swaying catwalks.

8

THE FISH THIEF

I told Tom I must be getting assimilated, because I was starting to hallucinate like everybody else. He looked at me unsmiling.

"What do you mean by 'hallucinate'?"

"Well, nothing unusual. I guess that I'm projecting my own peculiar associations and impulses onto the physical world."

"You *saw* that old uncle on the catwalk. Now you want to write him off as a misfiring neuron?"

"Oh. You mean it *wasn't* a misfiring neuron? That really *was* Uncle Pers up there?"

"I didn't say that. I'm only saying: don't take all the credit for your own hallucinations. Don't assume that your illusions are your personal property."

I laughed, but Tom just stared at me, as if this time he meant what he said. And maybe he did. You just couldn't tell with Tom. He had odd ways of making a joke, and sometimes it was hard to take him seriously anyway, when he was peering out at you through cockeyed black plastic glasses that were patched together with wads of duct tape and always sliding down the bridge of his nose, in the style of Père Andrés. His clothes were haphazard and disheveled, and it was obvious he cut his own hair. I didn't know what to call the patchy growth on his face, more than just unshaven but not exactly a beard. He always wore boots: big heavy mud-stomping leather work boots. He was muscular but only of average build, yet the boots, and maybe a sense of manic strength and energy held barely in check, made it seem as if something large and powerful and dangerous were in the vicinity.

"People hallucinate all kinds of things, including the truth," he said. "Sometimes they hallucinate what's already right in front of their noses." He turned to Kate. "So here's your husband, hallucinating a reminder that you didn't come here totally out of the fucking blue. There is a connection: your uncle, who used to pace the catwalks in the mill like old Captain Bligh, keeping the whip on the palm-oil niggers."

"I don't know that he kept the whip on anybody. He worked here for a few years. I think mainly he built roads."

"And now, thirty years later, when the roads and the palm oil and everything's pretty much gone to hell, a couple of high-priced consultants show up. And it turns out the wife is this old road guy's niece. Only they don't mention to anybody this relationship. Now, don't you think it's going to freak people out when they make that connection?"

"I don't know," said Kate. "I don't know what freaks people out. And I don't expect them to ever make the connection."

"Oh, they will. You can totally fucking depend on them to root out a connection like that. And it will freak them out, I can assure you. The longer it takes them to figure it out, the more they will freak. But what the fuck. You're going to freak them one way or the other no matter what. May as well go for something heavy, the big mojo. You want some beer?"

"For breakfast?"

We were in Tom's hut in the village of Malembe, a mile or so downriver from Ngemba, waiting for Mr. Sticky Tree to serve us breakfast. Mr. Sticky Tree was Tom's helper. His real name was something multisyllabic and difficult to remember, and when they'd first met three years earlier, Tom, hoping for something to use as a mnemonic, had asked him what it meant. Sticky Tree had told a long, confusing story about the circumstances of his birth. Somehow a tree with sticky sap had figured into it, and as Tom understood it, his parents had named him after that tree.

"I was trying to make things easy on myself, so I asked him if I could just translate the name and call him Sticky Tree, and he said sure. But later, when I spoke Kituba better, I found out his name wasn't actually a tree but more like a branch or a stick, and the sap wasn't sticky but slimy. Only by then it was too late, the name had—well, it had stuck. Everybody called him Sticky Tree. Anyway, I couldn't very well go around calling my worker 'Slimy Stick,' though I guess that's what everybody else thinks they're saying when they call him Sticky Tree."

Tom had originally come to the Kivila Valley with the Peace Corps, to teach farmers a method for building ponds and raising fish. He wanted to stay on when his two-year service was up, but the Peace Corps wouldn't grant him an extension. "We'd drifted apart," he said. "No, that's not what happened. It was like a lot of divorces: over time it became apparent that we had nothing in common. It seemed like we started out with the same noble vision, but there was no way the relationship could last. Those people are bureaucrats and social engineers, and hey, I'm an anarchist. So what do you expect? We split. That's fine, no hard feelings. Who wants to work for Uncle Sam anyway? Who wants to be a chickenshit underhand tool of U.S. corporate foreign policy? So I just stayed on my own, without the sanction of any government or organization. An independent operator, which is a total fucking anomaly in this place, I'll tell you. I had enough money saved to buy my own motorcycle and pay the bribes and kickbacks you need to get a visa and keep the soldiers and government bullies off your back. People in Malembe gave me a house, they feed me. I help them with their fishponds, their gardens, and screw around with all sorts of small-scale appropriate technology applications. Basically I'm just another consultant, like you, only with different compensation: I get free rent and all the luku, saka-saka, and palm wine I can hold."

Mr. Sticky Tree set three empty glasses down on the table. "Excuse," he said, and slammed a beer bottle on the edge of the table. The cap flew off, the beer foamed on the floor, and Sticky Tree poured our breakfast beer.

"Of course, I got other responsibilities too," said Tom. "Welcoming committee. Ad hoc consul. Make the rubes—no offense—feel like somebody's looking out for them. 'Course, you're the first fucking rubes to show up in years."

Sticky Tree reached over us, set a pot on the table, and removed the lid. "Luku," he announced.

The luku steamed, a pale yellow mound. Luku is a dense porridge of manioc and corn flour that you dip in a sauce and eat with your hands. "If there ain't luku," said Tom, "there ain't food. You'd get it three meals a day around here, if anybody ate three meals a day. Do you like it? You will; you'll get hungry and then you'll like it. You'd better like it. Some mamas went to a phenomenal amount of work to get it to you. This stuff looks simple, elemental, but do you know how they make it? They had to grow the manioc, obviously, and when we get out to a farm I'll show you how much work that is. Then they have to dig it up, put it in a basket, and carry it to the creek, where they soak it for days, because manioc is loaded with fucking cyanide, believe it or not, and you have to leach out enough so you can eat it. Then they squeeze out the water and put it in a basket and carry it up to the house and put it outside on racks to dry for a few weeks, and keep a kid posted to chase off the dogs and chickens and take it in out of the rain. Then they pound it up in their mortars to make flour—that's what you hear every morning: the village alarm clock. *Then* they sift it. Finally, they cook it. And now we can practice eating it."

Mr. Sticky Tree set another pot on the table. "Bima," he said, removing the lid.

The bima steamed too, so much that we could not see precisely what it was. Sticky Tree's announcement didn't help, since "bima," roughly translated, means "things." Things are what you eat with luku, things in a sauce, generally: greens or mushrooms or vegetables or bits of fish and meat, or even bugs, often given more zest by the liberal addition of pili-pili—hot chilies.

Sticky Tree brought in a basin of water, which he held out to each of us while we washed our hands. Then he set the basin down, bowed, and joined us at the table.

"This is kind of embarrassing," said Tom. "You know, my egalitarian principles and all. But he insists on serving like that when I have guests. He says it's just the way things are done. So I say, hell, do what you have to do. Mr. Sticky Tree has a precise sense of propriety. Ceremony is critical, even the ceremony of servitude. Especially the ceremony of servitude. I mean, let's face it, he's a fucking servant, right?"

"The bima's good," Kate said.

"Oh, yeah, Sticky Tree knows how to do Things. This is just saka-saka, you know. Fucking manioc leaves, loaded with vitamin C. C for cyanide, huh? But Tree's a good cook. He knows that with a big enough squirt of palm oil and a few spoonfuls of pili-pili he can make almost anything palatable."

"That's what make it so . . . orange, I guess." I was just kind of nibbling, actually. None of it tasted very good to me—the luku was sour, the Things were harsh and bitter. "Kind of Day-Glo. That palm oil is something else, isn't it?"

"Yeah." He scooped up a wad of luku and looked at me thoughtfully. "The fifty-thousand-dollar-a-year lubricant. Or I don't know, maybe you earn a lot more than that. Whatever. Most people make about fifty cents a day around here. But you know, you two don't look much like real consultants, have you ever thought of that? You don't have the aura. I know, I've seen a lot of consultants; they're crawling all over this country. They run the place, to the extent that it gets run at all. At least they dispense most of the cash. And you can generally recognize them. They project self-assurance. A well-developed sense of their own importance. They got opinions, credentials, they speak three or four languages. I'm not saying they know anything of substance, or that their expensive advice is valid. I'm just saying they got a certain look."

Sticky Tree stood up and turned on the radio, a shortwave unit. He crouched next to it, fiddling with dials, giving us blasts of static, a few blurry chords of rock music, news in French, more static. Tom raised his voice.

"You want me to tell you what kind of look *you* got? No offense. You got a look of complete and utter fucking confusion. So it's a good thing the ad hoc American consul is right up the street from you, with time on his hands, to get you oriented. But you'd better pump me while you can, because I'm not going to be around for long. Come the dry season, I'm out of here."

"Well, weren't you going to show us around the village now?" said Kate. "I'd kind of like to get going."

"Sure." But Tom was already refilling our beer glasses. "Another thing that's weird about you: you're walking. You don't have any wheels."

"Nobody around here has wheels," I said.

"Yeah, but you're white. You're supposed to have wheels. Especially since you have a real job. White dudes with real jobs *always* have wheels."

"Technically, we do have wheels," said Kate. "I think we have a Land Rover. Only there was some kind of screw-up with the paperwork or something and we don't actually *have* it yet. I think they're going to deliver it or something."

"You think?" said Tom.

"So you're going home soon," I said. "After three years here, I guess you're ready."

"I didn't say I was going home. I said I was leaving. But it's not because I'm homesick. Definitely not. No. Let's just say . . . I'm tired of the food. Don't tell Sticky Tree, but I've had enough saka-saka to last me and all my descendants for eternity. An unfathomable shitload of saka-saka. But that's only a metaphor for everything else I've had enough of. I mean, this place is a fucking backwater, have you noticed? I liked that about it at first. But eventually you have to broaden your horizons. I mean, *I* have to broaden my horizons. I've been to two places in my life, basically: the Kivila Valley and Thanesboro, Pennsylvania, where I grew up. I bet you never heard of it."

"It doesn't ring a bell."

"'Course not. But it's a great town, people are great. Provincial, which is a great quality in a town. People don't overreach, and they're only mildly dissatisfied with their lives. They realize some of their dreams. And I was on that track. I went to junior college there, I fell into a job for life, I could have got married. But I panicked. I joined the Peace Corps, and they sent me here. And in some ways it's as if I never traveled at all. I feel at home here, among people with a limited worldview."

Sticky Tree was still twisting the dial. He stopped on a BBC news broadcast, listened for a moment, and looked over at us, grinning. He hissed. "Mputu," he said.

"Right, Mputu," said Tom. "Europe, America, whatever. White-man's land, generic and borderless. Not unlike Africa, as conceived in the minds of most people in Mputu."

I wondered if Sticky Tree distinguished between England, represented by the BBC announcer, and the U.S., represented by Kate and me. Maybe he did. Now he crinkled his nose, pursed his lips, and did a passable imitation of a British accent, though he was speaking only gibberish, no recognizable English words at all.

"Change the channel," said Tom. "We need music, not news from a fucking time warp." He spoke English, but Sticky Tree laughed and turned the knob. He soon settled on another station—jangly Afro-pop, drifting in and out of static. As if to compensate for the poor reception, he turned up the volume and then began to clear the table. The rest of us fled to the yard.

Tom pointed to a palm tree. A raceme of orange fruit hung below the fronds. "That's an oil palm, in case you're wondering. They get palm oil from it. By a process of dyslexia. Ha-ha." He pushed his glasses up on his nose and studied us for a moment. "You really don't know a goddamn thing about palm oil, do you?"

"We didn't," said Kate. "But we're fast learners. Almost instantaneous. It's a mutation thing."

"A mutation," Tom repeated thoughtfully, then shook his head and laughed. "You know, pretty soon everybody in Ngemba is going to be hallucinating your old uncle up on the fucking catwalk. Just so you understand: nobody has a problem with nepotism around here. People expect nepotism. They understand it, a lot better than they understand credentials, certificates, masters degrees in palm oil extrusion, whatever dreary bits of technical expertise you might have showed up with instead."

"Well, you're right," I admitted. "We didn't show up with any of that. We were told to create expertise out of the materials at hand."

"That's it! And there's a shitload of material. But you still need direction. You need training, mentoring. You need . . . a consultant! Everybody needs one. It's an infinite hierarchy, an endless chain of knowledge, or at least the pretense of knowledge. So, you're especially fortunate to have me: a consultant who in fact does know something useful to you. And I'm a bargain, at least compared to you. Just pay me in beer and gas money. Fucking good value. I'll help you learn the language, and I can explain the inexplicable, up to a point. I mean, it'll always be weird here. You'll always be a stranger, but eventually you can feel like strangers who aren't sure they want to leave."

So for a while Tom took us under his wing. Not a particularly comfortable or nurturing place to be, but it was good for an education, if only by exposure and contrary example. Kate especially went around with him a lot. She was the field consultant, and he took her out into the field—sometimes on the back of his motorcycle, sometimes walking, touring farms and villages, meeting people, and learning the language. She usually returned from these outings shaking her head, telling me how much Tom had angered or embarrassed her or just made her crazy. But a few days later she'd go somewhere with him again. "I'm learning what I need to know," she said. "I'm seeing some incredible things, Will. Besides, Tom makes me laugh."

I was the mill consultant, and what I needed to know I would have to learn, presumably, inside the smoke-spewing industrial relic a hundred yards down the hill from our house. An incredible thing, in its own way. But most days the closest I got to the mill was my office, where I passed the time writing letters, practicing French and Kituba with the secretary (whom I'd hired as my language tutor), and reviewing the files he brought me when one or the other of us lost patience with my thick tongue and inability to remember verb conjugations. Then he would return to his usual work, whatever that might be, and I would open the files and go through old records of oil production, income and expenditures, payroll and maintenance. These all were in French, and I often required the secretary's assistance here as well. But slowly I was compiling facts and statistics: dull bureaucratic fodder, mainly, but it gave me something to focus on, material to include in the report—my "Consultant's Assessment"—that I had decided to prepare and submit to the Jucht Brothers office in Kisaka.

Every once in a while I wandered over to the mill and looked around. I had no more visions of Uncle Pers, nor any revelations about what might be done with all that grease-blasted hell-evoking machinery. But I compared what I saw with the diagrams in *Products of the Oil Palm*, and eventually arrived at a general understanding of the way it all worked, though to what use I might put such knowledge I could not imagine.

I also went out with Tom on his motorcycle a few times, or with him and Kate together, walking. "On tournée," Tom said. "Part of your training. You know, like a field trip." He took us to a farm near Ngemba, a mile's walk on an old road and then a trail through the forest. The farmer, Telo, a sturdily built man wearing a ragged T-shirt, shorts, and plastic sandals, met us in a clearing at the base of a grassy hill, the first rise of the escarpment that sloped up to the savanna. He shook our hands gravely and led us past an empty stick corral and mud and thatch huts into an immaculately swept dirt yard, where an old woman lay on a mat in the shade, a few naked children played listlessly, and two old men sat in silence beneath a palm-frond veranda, rousing themselves occasionally to berate the children or kick at a dog.

"This is a pretty nice farm," said Tom, straight-faced. "Telo himself is not a lot of fun and games. I mean, I like him, but just look at him. A grim-faced motherfucker, isn't he? That's what honest ambition does to a person in this place. He's always worrying about something or other, always trying to figure some scheme for digging himself out of the hole that keeps expanding around him. For a while he had this plan: he was going to come to Mputu with me when I leave. He said he'd be my boy for a couple of years, and save enough money to buy a tractor. I try to tell him that the boy thing wouldn't fly in

Thanesboro, and that anyway he wouldn't fit in, he's way too ambitious for that town, and back in Mputu I'm just a poor boy, nobody's patrón. Naturally he doesn't believe me. The guy's sober as hell, full of Calvinist virtues, but still kind of a fucking nut, in his own humorless way."

All this time Telo was standing right next to us, looking the part: intent, unsmiling, heavy-browed. And Tom flaunting his English, our private exclusionary language, though I thought his gestures and expression made his meaning fairly obvious. Still, Telo's expression didn't change. He spoke to Tom in a slow, rumbling voice, took up his machete, and went down the path toward the forest. His wife emerged from one of the huts with some chairs, and we sat down near the old men in the shade of the veranda.

Telo would return shortly, the men told us. "What they mean," said Tom, "is that they have no fucking idea where he's gone or when he'll be back. Well, we'll wait. That's part of your training, for sure—you learn how to wait. You want to create some expertise, well, here's one thing you're gonna get good at, or else."

He sat back in his chair and closed his eyes, as if he were settling in for a nap. Kate tried to strike up a conversation with the kids, and then disappeared into the hut to talk with Telo's wife. We waited twenty minutes, half an hour. The day's heat built up around us, moving in on the tenuous comfort of the shade. I must have dozed too, I don't know for how long. When I opened my eyes I was staring at a pair of blindingly white bell-bottoms and a paisley polyester shirt. Telo had changed his clothes. Another man stood beside him, holding a large dried gourd with a white liquid foaming from its open neck.

"Oh, Christ. I should have known that's where the sonofabitch went to," Tom grumbled. "He won't let us off his farm without making us drink some palm wine."

But Tom drank the sweet, slightly putrid sap with far more enthusiasm than I could muster. "You don't like it?" he said. "Don't worry, you just lack training. You just haven't got uncomfortable enough yet, to where you fully appreciate the numbing effect."

The man with the palm wine laughed. "Ah, Monsieur Tom," he said, slapping Tom on the shoulder. Tom squinted up at him.

"What do you mean, 'Ah, Monsieur Tom'? You don't understand a fucking word I'm saying." The man broke into another peal of laughter and topped off our glasses.

"Fucking Mr. Dream," said Tom. "Ndosi. You met him yet? Fish farmer, coupier, palm wine tapper, and mind fucker extraordinaire."

"And aviator," said Kate.

Now I remembered the name. It was Ndosi who had built the bamboo airplane we'd seen soaring over the savanna when we drove in with Père Andrés. Kate told him in her shaky Kituba how much we admired his plane, and asked what its purpose was. He laughed again, and spoke slowly and clearly for our benefit, mixing French with Kituba to clarify his meaning.

"What's the purpose of any plane, madame? To fly, of course! Oui, il faut voler! But I have no gas. Pas de tout. Monsieur Tom is the only one with gas, and he won't give me any."

"Not a drop," said Tom.

"Est-çe que vous avez d'essence, madame? Maybe you and monsieur will share with me, and I'll take you flying."

"We don't have any gas. We don't need it, we walk everywhere. Which reminds me: what happened to our farm tour, Tom? Do we still have time?"

"Time?" Tom slouched in his chair and stared thickly at Kate, looking as though the numbing effect had already taken hold. "We got time for a trip to fucking Alpha Centauri, Kate. Time is never the issue. The question is, do we have the will?"

"Well, I do," she said. "I'd like to see the farm."

"Sure," said Tom. "The problem is, there's nothing to see. I mean, this is what they do: they cut down trees, burn them, stick some seeds in the ground, and hope it rains enough so they grow, but not so much that the whole damn thing washes into the river."

"Slash and burn," I said.

"Slash and burn," Tom agreed. "Hey, it works, sort of. It's worked for Telo." He switched to Kituba. "Telo, tell the consultants how rich you are."

"Oui, I'm the richest farmer in the valley," said Telo obediently. His thick, rumbling voice smothered the crisp inflections of the Kituba language, and Tom had to clarify or translate most of what he said. Glumly, he ticked off his assets: his wife's fields, a small coffee plantation, a number of fruit trees, several fishponds he had built under Tom's direction, one of the few cows in the valley, a half dozen sheep and goats, and at least a dozen chickens. And there were lots of oil palms around, of course; like many men he augmented his income cutting palm nuts to sell to the mill.

So he was making progress, building up wealth. He would have built up more, except prices were so low; the Company paid poorly for all this produce, but there was nowhere else to sell it. Still, his fishponds, his coffee, and especially his cow made him a rich man, though he was losing money on the cow. She had yet to calve, and in the meantime she ran wild, always getting lost in the forest, trampling people's fields, knocking holes in their huts. He had spent many days in the bush hunting her down, and had been called to a tribunal three times to pay trespass and damage fines. Now he kept his son home from school so he could watch her.

Though he maintained his vision of a livestock empire, Telo had owned the same number of stock for several years now, and hadn't slaughtered an animal in months, because he was trying to build up his herds. But his animals were slow to reproduce, and when they did he generally sold the offspring as soon as they were weaned, because he needed money.

"Well, at least they keep you in milk and eggs," Kate said.

"Ç'est ça, madame." He coughed. "Milk and eggs, except that the cow and the goats are too wild to milk, and of course I try to hatch out the eggs, because who wouldn't rather have a chicken than an egg?"

"But you still have only a dozen chickens."

He coughed again. "Yes. Because in fact these chickens don't often lay eggs. And then, sometimes the eggs don't hatch. Anyway, there isn't much point in having lots of chickens, because if you have a lot of chickens, you just have to pay them in taxes."

"Chicken taxes?"

"Ç'est ça, taxes. Or fines. Sometimes fees, registrations. They call them different things, it depends on which chef or soldier. But chickens are usually what they like to collect. Last week, for example, the commissioner's inspector for public health was here, at my farm. He inspected our waysay and wrote me a citation because the door was improperly installed. I had to pay two chickens."

"You see what I mean about the hole expanding?" said Tom, pouring the last of the palm wine into our glasses. "The more chickens you have, the more inspectors come poking their noses around your shitter."

"He sure coughs a lot," Kate said.

"Yeah, I guess he does. I hardly notice it anymore. It's not like he's sickly or anything—in fact, he's strong as a fucking rhino. He just coughs all the time."

"Maybe he's allergic to his farm," I said.

One morning, the three of us climbed a footpath out of the valley, crossed a narrow savanna ridge, and descended into the next valley, where Ndosi was harvesting one of his fishponds. At least fifty people were gathered along the dikes of the pond, waiting to buy fish. Telo, wearing his paisley shirt and with his white bell-bottoms rolled up to his knees, stood with some other men with a net stretched across a narrow cut they had made in the downstream dike, watching water flow out of the pond. Ndosi came up to greet us. It would be an hour before the fish were actually harvested, he said, and in the meantime he had something to show us. So we set off on a trail up the valley.

Ten or fifteen ponds ran in a chain along the narrow valley bottom. The pond Ndosi was harvesting was open to the sun and bordered by thick dikes covered with close-cropped grass. But farther up in the valley the dikes were low and full of rotting debris, the ponds shallow and dark beneath huge trees. Tom explained how Ndosi's uncle, a sorcerer, had built these ponds decades before. He kept crocodiles and snakes there, people said, and the ponds were a source of his power. After he died no one dared come here, for years, until Ndosi cleared the old trails and started rebuilding some of them, for raising fish.

Ndosi nodded. "I worked here for a while, then I asked Monsieur Tomás to come help me. He said I should build canals, so I did. He said make the pond deeper, the dikes bigger and stronger, cut down the big forest trees so the sun will come in. I did all these things. Tom said: Il faut faire de compost! Fertilize the pond with leaves from the forest, ash from the fires, shit from your goats. Oui, merde de chevres! Okay, I did that. Then Tom gave me some fingerlings, and I put them in, and soon I began to harvest lots of fish, big fish, from this pond. So I built another one, and now I'm working on a third. But my uncles come down, they see my harvests, and they say: Petit, give your family some fish. I give them fish. Each harvest they ask me for more, and now they are saying: These ponds were built by our brother. They were passed down to us, not to you. They belong to us."

We came to the pond that Ndosi was rebuilding. He had removed the old dikes and partially constructed new ones. But large sections still needed fill, huge amounts of fill, impossibly out of scale to the tools that lay next to them: a battered shovel and a basket he used to carry the dirt on his head. And in fact, Ndosi said he had not worked on the pond for weeks, though it was not the labor itself that discouraged him. "That's only earth," he said. "If we keep working, it will yield. But look!"

A stick protruded from the mud in the middle of the pond. Tied to it by strips of raffia was a messy-looking wad of material. Kate touched Tom's arm.

"It's a fetish, isn't it?"

"Right, a fetish. Feathers, grass, hair, bones, and who knows what. The idea being to frighten Mr. Dream away from this place." He turned to Ndosi. "You're hoping I'll do something about this?"

"Yes. That is, I want your advice on what I should do. You're my fish consultant."

"Sure. You consult me about fish. I don't know anything about this, whatever it is. It looks like a bunch of feathers and hair and crap hanging from a stick."

"That's what it is."

"But it has the power to keep you from working on your pond?"

"No, Monsieur Tom. The fetish has no power."

"So. Is there a problem? Grab your shovel, man. Show Madame Katie your big muscles. Show her how you can move dirt."

Ndosi laughed. Tom laughed too, and Ndosi slapped his hand. "Ah, Monsieur Tom," he said, still laughing. Then he squatted on the unfinished dike and sighed.

"What are you worried about?" said Kate.

"Just hair and feathers, madame. Sticks. It's true what we say, it has no power. It's an old thing, from our past, and its power is defeated. I'm a young man, looking forward, with modern ideas, and I believe this. But the old men who put it there still have faith in its power, and that's where the danger lies—in defying their faith."

The harvest was disappointing. With the pond nearly drained, Tom took off his shirt and boots, rolled up his pant legs, and joined the men in the muddy pond bottom, grabbing fish and tossing them into baskets. But the yield was less than half of what Tom had expected. Ndosi climbed up on the dike, mud-splattered, grim and muttering, and began a fierce argument with the old men in the crowd. He glared and shouted at them, and one after another the old men stepped forward to deliver short, angry speeches. It seemed a tense and disturbing turn of events, but no one paid much attention. Children searched on their hands and knees in the pond mud for fingerlings the men might have missed, and Telo and some other men wrapped fish in banana-leaf packets to sell. Mud was splattered everywhere, and Telo had been in the midst of it, but his bell-bottoms remained miraculously spotless. The crowd pressed in on him, and Ndosi and the old men continued to argue. Kate bought a packet of fish and joined Tom and me on the dike.

"What are they so upset about?"

"Ndosi says he's been ripped off," said Tom. "He says these old uncles stole his fish."

"Do you think they did?"

"Somebody did. This was a good pond. It shouldn't have been empty. But I can't really follow the argument. Some of it's by rote, and some is improvised insult and slander. These old bastards are masters of innuendo and double entendre. They got about a million grudges to sustain, and you have to be as paranoid and deceitful as they are to crack their code."

Telo joined us on the far dike. Kate asked him what the argument was about.

He shrugged. "Somebody stole Ndosi's fish."

"The old men?"

He shrugged again. After a while he said: "The old men say Ndosi is selfish and greedy and looks out only for himself. They say he forgets his elders and ancestors and is corrupted by strangers. And that he stole his own fish."

"Why would anyone steal his own fish?" said Kate.

Telo shrugged once more and turned away, and Tom, bare-chested and mud-flecked, grinned at Kate. "Well, it might be the only way he could keep them for himself. See, half the people down here are related in some way to Ndosi. At least four or five of them have made some kind of claim on these ponds, and all of them figure he at least owes them a couple of fish, just out of family loyalty. He worked his ass off rehabilitating these ponds, and had to defy some bad mojo to do it, and now if he gives everybody a fish who thinks they got one coming, his hands are empty. And if he does the little red hen thing and blows them off—hey, where were *you* assholes when I was digging these holes and humping this dirt?—it'll create some real bad blood. It's a dilemma, and maybe one way out of it is to make sure there aren't many fish in the pond when the water drains away."

The pond was empty now, all the children gone up on the sunny dike with their tiny scavenged fish, leaving small bare footprints across the muddy bottom of the pond. They kindled a tiny fire and squatted on the high bank away from the adults, skewering their fish on grass stems and laying them on the fire to roast.

"So, you also think Ndosi took them himself," said Kate.

"He *could* have. Actually, I have no fucking idea what happened. Those old bastards are perfectly capable of ripping him off. Lots of people are. Maybe *I* ripped him off. I've been accused of that too. Anyway, you can see how people get addled. You can see how they get some whacko ideas, hanging out in a place like this. I mean, look up there. It's a godforsaken haunted bogeyman swamp."

The crowd dispersed, people going up the trail into the late-afternoon sunlight, back to their villages and farms. Ndosi and Telo were nowhere to be seen. The high voices of the children still echoed across the valley, but the sound was subdued and the children themselves had disappeared below the downstream dike. The commotion of the harvest subsided almost instantaneously, and now it was just the three of us, Tom and Kate and me, alone on Ndosi's dike.

"Let's go," said Kate, but she didn't move, she just stood looking across the drained pond. I touched her arm but her skin was sticky with sweat, and I let my hand drop to my side. Suddenly I felt queasy, nauseated. A strange biting smell—acidic, organic—rose on the air, as if from the exposed mud. As if from something that had a history there, some gas escaping, a decomposing by-product of witchcraft worked long ago. I sniffed the humid air, and Tom raised his nostrils and sniffed too.

"Yeah, we stink," he said, and I sniffed again and understood that he was right. What I smelled was us, the mingled odors of our three bodies, our sweat, the pond muck drying on Tom's bare arms and chest.

Ndosi and Telo returned from wherever they had gone. We climbed the steep path out of the valley, into the brightness and heat of the sun, while below us the shadows of high-buttressed trees fell heavily over the shallow ponds of Ndosi's sorcerer uncle, with the small stream trickling through and the birds silent and the sterile water opaque, acid-stained.

THE FIRST TOURISTS

"I worked out a diagnosis for my condition," said Tom.

"I didn't even know you had a condition," I said.

"Of course you didn't know. You're fucking oblivious, Will. Naïve. Starry-eyed. I mean that as a compliment. You probably don't even know *you* have a condition."

"Okay, what's *my* condition? Besides being naïve and fucking oblivious?"

"Sorry, I can't tell you that. I only do self-diagnosis."

"Fine, then, what's yours?"

"Fucking agoraphobia. Fear of expanse and exposure. Fear of movement. Fear of travel and the wide-open world."

Naturally I wondered why, if that were his condition, he had traveled halfway around the world to live for three years in a primitive village on the edge of a remote savanna in Africa, but Tom said there was no contradiction there, because, as he'd told us, in fundamental ways the village and his hometown in Pennsylvania were the same: parochial and inbred societies, little clusters of small-minded people. But at least their minds were on a scale with their lives. There was a certain rare harmony in that, he said, and so he'd huddled comfortably in that African village for three years, nurtured by a constricted but strangely familiar vision of the world.

I pointed out that at the moment he wasn't huddled in a village; he was out in a savanna wilderness, taking a piss break on the roadside beside an overheated motorcycle. Out in the open. *Exposed.* And Tom said that was the point, for him if not for me. I was merely in training, an obscenely overpaid consultant casting around for expertise and purpose. Whereas he, thanks to the agoraphobia diagnosis, was practically feverish with a sense of purpose.

"I'm out here for the therapy, Will. Trial by fire. Hair of the dog, you know what I'm saying? That's why I have to keep moving, seeing the back-country. The remote stations. Kilala Mission. Kivila Falls. Mafemba and the trans-African highway. Each destination pushing the envelope a little more. Each arrival a small taste of victory."

I gave him a skeptical look, though what I really questioned was not Tom's self-diagnosis and treatment but my own wisdom in getting up on the back of a motorcycle driven by someone who felt that he needed this kind of therapy. I wondered: did the therapy really require that he accelerate through blind curves and keep the throttle open even when the roadway was crowded with animals and people? But Tom said you need momentum if you have to make sudden maneuvers. He was a great believer in momentum—essential for crossing bridges of questionable structural stability, for powering through sandy ruts, for navigating potholes of unknown depth and solidity, for overcoming doubt on all levels, he said.

"It's a Zen thing, you know? Perfect control through recklessness. You couldn't achieve that level of control being careful. Anyway, people *expect* me to blow past them. They like standing close to the road like that, close to the moto wind, where they can wave and shout, proposition me, flip me off, whatever. Where they can feel like they're *participating*. But that doesn't mean they want me to slow down, unless I'm going to be fool enough to stop and give somebody a ride. They just want to be close to my speed. If I slow down it'll confuse everybody, and somebody's liable to get hit. And if somebody gets hit, we got trouble."

"Yeah?"

"Oh, yeah. They kill us. What, you don't believe me? I know, they don't *seem* like killers. Just simple villagers, right, innocent, pure-hearted. Did you hear them yelling back there? *Monsieur Tomás, Monsieur Tomás, beto ke zola nge!* They do, they love me. I'm a demigod to these people, man. Someday you will be too, Will. We just made their fucking week, driving past and polluting their village with this stinking greasy motorcycle. But if I were to hit one of them . . . Well, they'd have to put aside their love for me long enough to torch my bike and cave our skulls in. That sort of roadside retribution happens fairly often out here. It's almost an instinct with these people, know what I'm saying? Like killing a snake."

"I see. They're genetically programmed to do this."

"Genes, ancestors, social circumstances: however you want to put it, Will. That's not what's important. What's important, if anybody ever gets hit, is to remember the African Bad Samaritan Rule: don't stop and render aid, don't exchange insurance information with anybody, just get the hell down the road and don't look back."

Late in the morning we came to Kilala Mission, a collection of low buildings set back from a small savanna river. Scattered huts and sparse sandy manioc fields surrounded the colonial structures, yellow brick stained with smoke and algae. Few people were about. Children watched us from a gutted school-room, women in a manioc field stared silently and did not return our waves, and an old Flemish priest peered from the garden and padded out from between beds of bolting lettuce to greet us.

"You see us in our decline," he said. "You must imagine this place as it was: a garden spot, an oasis of culture and civilization." But we saw little and he said nothing to evoke such a place. Instead he seemed obsessed with mar-tyrs and the details of ruin, the day thirty-five years before when the rebels had come out of the east to destroy the memory of the white presence. He showed us the old convent where the nuns had prayed before they were raped and murdered, the tiles in the rectory still stained with the blood of decapi-tated priests, and the rubble where the old chapel had been dynamited. He pointed out the marks left by ricocheting bullets on the wall where the village men had been executed. He himself had been off in a neighboring village, and the women had hid him in a cornfield, where he remained until the rebels left.

After the rebels the government soldiers and mercenaries had come. Again he had fled to the cornfield, and had returned this time to smoking ruins—everything combustible had been put to flame, more women raped, more men tortured and killed.

Finally a rescue plane arrived, but he had chosen to stay on—to bury the dead, comfort the survivors, to rebuild and continue the work of God. "And you can see"—he waved his hand at the piles of old brick, the smoke-tinted rooms, and the weed-choked gardens, and spoke in a voice miraculously drained of all irony—"that the work is not yet finished, and we are still rebuilding."

He served us coffee. Sighing deeply, he wondered if we wished to stay for lunch, or even spend the night. Occasionally travelers did, though the lodging facilities might not meet the standards to which they were accustomed. He and the sisters were satisfied with a simple diet, but he had noticed that most guests ate very little. And this time of year they seldom slept well, having to choose between stuffy chambers or, if they dared crack a window, swarms of mosquitoes and blackflies. And guests who were in spiritual conflict might find the chambers uncomfortable for other reasons. For his part he was not morbid; he honored the dead and indeed considered that they had died a fortunate death, martyrs in the service of God, but travelers, he had noticed, sometimes had difficulty sleeping in beds where people had been hacked to death.

We declined the invitation. He waved us off and faded into the shadows of his rectory, and we rode out into a treeless country, with sharp grasses and sterile, sandy soils. Villages were widely scattered and very poor. People rarely smiled or waved when we passed, and children didn't chase the motorcycle the way they did in the villages to the north. Still, everyone stared at us. They came out of their houses or put down their hoes and stood up in the fields to watch us, because it was unusual, an event, the passing of two white men on a motorcycle, but they understood that it was an event that would have no impact on their lives. Here people regarded us dully, without hope or desire. They expected nothing from the outer world. They knew they were on their own, laboring under some curse in a haunted land.

We pulled up near a couple of old men who sat on a bench outside a hut. Tom kept the engine idling.

"What way to the falls, Papa?" he called out in Kituba.

The old men stared at us wordlessly. Were they stunned into silence, amazed at the terrible smoking apparition that had come out of the wilderness, or did they just have no use for people like us? Tom cursed and revved the engine, but before he could let out the clutch a younger man hurried up, followed by several others.

"How can I assist you, monsieur?"

"Do you know the way to the falls?"

"The falls. Ah, oui, the falls!" The man conferred with his companions. They began to argue, and Tom shifted impatiently and twisted the throttle again. The first man stepped forward and began to give directions. He talked rapidly, mixing French and Kituba, pointing and waving his hands about. After a minute Tom held up his hand. "Merci, citoyen. We'll find it. Mambu ve. Which means, 'Fuck it,'" he said over his shoulder. "I mean, the sonofabitch hasn't even got me out of the fucking village yet." We started to move forward, but the man grabbed his arm.

"You'll get lost," he said. "Baka mono. Take me with you, and I'll show you." "Baka nge? Wapi? What the hell do you mean, take you with me?" Tom shifted again to English, punctuated by an occasional Kituba word. "You're gonna ride with me. That's a brilliant fucking idea, isn't it? Mpila ve! Where do you think you're gonna sit, on Monsieur Willie's lap? You gonna straddle the fucking tailpipe? These fucking people. They can't just give you a simple piece of information, you know? They can't *communicate* a simple piece of information, not without making a goddamn endless *ritual* out of it. *Baka mono.* Well, what if I were crazy enough to let this farceur get on? Next thing we know he'd be inviting us into his house for a meal, we'd have to drink his palm wine, meet his wife, fuck his daughter, *then* we'd have to let him ride on the goddamn handlebars out to the goddamn falls, only I'm certain he's never been to the falls, he doesn't have the slightest idea where the falls are, but he still ain't gonna rest until he personally gets us all hopelessly fucking lost looking for them in this godforsaken fucking savanna. And that won't be the end of it either, because the sonofabitch is gonna show up at the door of *my* hut six months from now, aren't you, papa citizen brother? Remember me, monsieur? Your brother, your guide from Kivila Falls? Now give me a meal, monsieur, I'm hungry, give me some palm wine, can I have your Nikes, I want your radio, take me with you to America, brother. I mean these fucking people make me crazy."

We didn't see the falls until we were there beside them. Upstream the river meandered in an open plain, and downstream it churned in a narrow gorge that we didn't see either, looking across the rolling savanna that bordered it on either side. So it was a surprise, after riding in a kind of rattling trance over miles of unsigned road that seemed to lead nowhere, to come into a parking lot, a patch of weedy asphalt in the hot grasslands, and then to follow a trail of cracked and overgrown pavement down to the overlook, with its cement bench and foundation and its view up the canyon, where, squeezed between black cliffs, the Kivila River poured over its falls. That was another incongruous sight, as much for the rock as for the great plunge of water: black burnished rock in a land where the eye grew accustomed to sand and clay and soft plant tissue. A wind churned in the canyon, and squalls of spray swept over us, a relief from the afternoon heat and the swarms of small biting flies. Above the opposite cliff, hooded buzzards roosted in the sun, hunched in short frail trees on the edge of the gorge.

"Incredible!" I shouted.

"Yeah. Big falls. Still, it's nothing really special, just water falling over rock. But what the hell is this?"

Tom squatted, peering at the base of a guano-splattered brick structure. At one time the brick apparently had served as the foundation for a monument; we could see where the statue once had stood, and the marks of the tools that had chipped and pried it away. "They shouldn't have made it out of metal!" shouted Tom. "They should have known that people would melt it down and reforge it into something useful."

But in the base of the foundation a plaque had been left behind, possibly because it was so algae encrusted that no one had noticed it. Tom wiped the algae off with a wad of stiff grass so that we could read the inscription, in French, which explained that the monument was built to honor the Tourist. The Tourist, who comes with an impressionable mind and an eye attuned to Beauty, who speaks for the unity of Man and the universality of Culture, who is made welcome by an emancipated people to walk their garden paths, to explore the high meadow trails of the flowering patria. It went on to extol the virtues of a landscape that sounded alternately like an English country garden and a cirque in the Swiss Alps, but never like this cleft of churning water cut into a bright and empty savanna. Finally the inscription became illegible beneath a veneer of black algae too thick and encrusted to yield to Tom's scrubbing.

"Now *this* is incredible!" yelled Tom. "I mean, the Tourist! Who the fuck are they kidding?" Strands of wet hair pressed against his forehead. He peered at me over the top of his misted glasses, waving his arms at the thundering falls and the clouds of river spray sweeping across the sky.

This time I understood what he meant. What tourist, after all, had ever sat on that wet bench? Who in this wild and barren country had even seen a tourist? People were familiar with consultants, technicians, missionaries, project administrators, but what villager, skirting the fearful chasm on the sandy road, carrying a sack of manioc or herding a few scrawny cattle, even knew what a tourist was?

We climbed back up the path to the parking lot, where we could converse at a normal volume. "Still," said Tom, "maybe it's not as ridiculous as it appears. So what if a flesh-and-blood tourist has never actually come here, until now? Maybe we're looking at it backwards. Maybe that monument's not intended to *commemorate* anything. Maybe it's looking the other way: a prediction, an artist's conception of the future."

"Does that make it any less ridiculous?"

"Maybe. Maybe we shouldn't laugh at that kind of vision. I mean, the people who wrote that plaque, they came out here, they saw how bleak and isolated the place was, but they understood that to be an illusion. They knew the world's not really like that anymore. They knew that humans are evolving away from being hunter-gatherers, farmers, herdsmen, manufacturers, and so forth, and instead becoming—what? Tourists, man. They understood that tourism is very much where it's at, even in the totally fucked-up countries. A tourist just ain't all that absurd anymore, anywhere. Or else the absurdity of the tourist is so commonplace that nobody hardly notices it. You just expect it, even out here. Which means this monument is actually farsighted, futuristic. Prophetic. And you and me, Will, maybe we're the fulfillment of the prophecy. The First Tourists."

"Oh. And the flowering meadows and garden trellises are next?"

"Well, that part *is* ridiculous, sure. But look, Will, that's just derivative poetry. Fallout from cultural imperialism, right? Somebody ended up reading nineteenth-century Brit poets when he should have been deciphering the ravings of his own elders. You know how literature can warp your sense of reality. But that doesn't really contradict the tourism vision. What does tourism care for a sense of reality? A tourist just wants to fulfill his expectations, right? Meaning, he wants to sustain his illusions."

"Not like the agoraphobic, I guess."

"That's right! The agoraphobic is paralyzed, because he fears reality. But the tourist has no use for reality at all. He moves freely, penetrates nothing, skims the surface, encounters no obstacles. And this landscape is perfect for him."

"It is?"

"Sure. I mean, look at it. Wind in the grass, silver river, groves of trees, puffy white clouds, waterfall mists. If you got a postcard of it you'd think it was beautiful. You'd think it was a vision of paradise."

"It *is* beautiful."

"Sure. Pictures don't lie. They just leave out some detail. Like this brutal fucking heat. Like these miserable little gnats, drilling for human blood. Or those vultures waiting for whatever carrion is going to come flushing over the falls. Like the fact you can't even touch the grass without slicing your hand open, or that the soil it's growing in is nothing but Kalahari sand, sterile, porous, won't hold a drop of rainwater. You get a postcard from this place, you can consider it a total grand illusion. It looks like paradise, and it's a green desert hellhole. God is twisting His knife in the poor bastards who try to live off of this land."

Kate, Tom, and I sat drinking warm beer in an open-air bar in Mafemba. The trans-African highway was right at our feet, a rutted dirt road lined with corrugated-metal shacks and thatch huts and the hollow, blackened hulks of cement buildings. Bars and bodegas, machine shops and brothels and gas stations and warehouses: an indistinguishable architecture of commerce and squalor. Piles of garbage and the rusting skeletons of stripped vehicles lined the roadside, and the road itself was flooded, a chain of stagnant pools that glittered with the iridescence of oil slicks. Pigs, goats, and chickens wandered among the piles of garbage and in and out of the buildings. The crumbling cement was blackened by smoke, grease, dirt, and algae, and also grimmer, unidentifiable stains. Perhaps that cement had never been washed; once deposited, layers of grime remained until they eroded away with the buildings themselves. You could probably read the human history of the place in the stratigraphy of its filth.

Or you could study the humans who inhabited it now. Drunks and lunatics, truck drivers, destitute children, lounging soldiers, hustlers, petit commerçants with their tiny inventories of cloth, watches, cigarettes. Travelers with the look of refugees piling into already overloaded trucks with goats, chickens, babies, bundles of clothing, and sacks of manioc and peanuts. Boisterous market women in bright pagnes, laughing and shouting. And prostitutes, exquisitely coifed and wrapped, sitting sleepy-eyed and bored in the bars.

"My God, so many of them are so beautiful," said Tom. "Incredibly beautiful, and they live in this shithole and fuck drunk truck drivers for small change all night. And now every last one of them is toxic—a hundred percent infestation in a place like this, you know? Beauty and death. The spectrum is full in a place like this. It blows me away, if you want to know the truth. I get this feeling of heightened spirituality, you know what I'm saying? There's so much beauty, such *purity*, in the heart of all the shit and slime and decay and stinking bodily secretions."

"Fine," said Kate. "But right now my body's hardly secreting at all. I'm just trying to enjoy this beer, okay?"

They had to shout over the Afro-pop that jangled and buzzed from overloaded speakers behind us. The place did stink of urine, and when the music paused for a second I heard a man pissing in the stall behind me.

"You smell death here," yelled Tom. "All the time. Randomly stirred in with all these smells of life. It's a potent mixture. But therapeutic too, in it's own way."

"All I smell is old pee," said Kate. "But it's not so bad, you get used to it. Anyway, I like my beer. So shut up, Tom."

That was Mafemba. The edge of the frontier, Tom said, and it did seem that we'd arrived at some culmination of our explorations. Or at least the practical limit of them. It was as if we'd come to Mafemba in increments, each motorcycle excursion a logical extension of the previous one. And now, looking back, they seemed to merge into one long tournée leading to Mafemba, though in fact we hadn't come to Mafemba on Tom's motorcycle but rather in the cab of a flatbed truck driven by Tom's friend René, a Belgian who managed a tree farm somewhere in the province. And we'd driven out from the Kivila Valley in less than three hours—a short distance, really, when you just drove and were done with it. On a clear day, from the top of the bamboo pole

Ndosi had raised beside the road in front of his house, you might almost be able to see Mafemba: 100 kilometers away as the bamboo airplane flies, or dreams of flying.

René danced with a prostitute on the dirt floor. René had lived in the country for fifteen years, married to a native woman. He'd come out to Mafemba to get a part for his tractor, and we'd come along for the ride. For the training, or the therapy. René did not seem surprised to find the part unavailable; he cursed softly, suggested a beer, and shifted the focus of his mission to the prostitute.

"He needs that tractor part," Tom said. "He ordered it a long time ago, and he got a call on the radio saying it was here. Now nobody knows anything about it."

"He doesn't seem to be taking it very hard," I said.

"He's been here a long time. This is a minor setback—not even a setback, it's normal. In fact, in a sense it's a successful venture. A small victory. Because now he's liberated from his tractor. Now he can drink beer and be with this girl."

"She's beautiful," said Kate.

"René knows her," Tom explained. "He comes out here every once in a while."

"For tractor parts?"

"Sure. I don't know. Yeah, she is beautiful. Thin, like a model, huh? Of course she's thin, she's got AIDS, right? He doesn't talk about AIDS. He acts like he doesn't believe in it. I doubt he uses a rubber. Maybe he thinks he'll get used to it, like he's gotten used to driving a hundred and eighty clicks across the savanna for a tractor part that's not there."

"Maybe he's had a lot of Mafemba therapy," said Kate. "Beauty and death."

A truck piled high with sacks of produce, people, goats, and chickens made its slow way over the ridges and through the flooded troughs of the trans-African highway. This was washboard on a scale I hadn't seen before—a full five feet or more between the tops of the ridges and the bottoms of the troughs. The truck splashed through the pools, climbed the ridges, and dove into pools again. People and animals clung to the swaying load. The boy chauffeur—a kind of driver's assistant, de rigueur on all trucks—jogged ahead, shouting, and people scattered from the road. "Pas de freines! Pas de freines!" the man called out. The truck whined and rumbled toward the east, rising and falling, leaving town. Children and ducks returned to the pools it had disturbed, and in the dirt yard the beautiful girl in her elegant pagne danced automatically, looking up with unfocused eyes over René's slouching back. Her body was very thin, and I saw now that the disquieting beauty of her face was derived from its shadows and angles, from the deep sockets in which her eyes were set, staring out as if from two holes in the earth, watching a small oval-framed piece of the sky.

Tom gazed after the truck. "Jesus. A truck with no brakes on the trans-African highway. Does this place blow you away, or what? Warm beer, people pissing in the street, no brakes, no condoms. All these *smells*. I don't know, maybe you two are getting homesick for some civilization. I mean, that's why we've got civilization, right? To filter out our own stench. Or at least disguise it."

"So *that's* what it's good for," said Kate.

"I don't know. Sure. To cover the running sores. Flush away the excrement, sop up the secretions, and wash everything down with Lysol and feminine-hygiene spray when we're finished. A noble fucking achievement."

Kate made a face at him, half disgusted, half amused. "Well, there is something to be said for flushing excrement, Tom."

"Sure. And there's something to be said for Mafemba. For women who are sexy in such an apocalyptic way. For warm beer and trucks without brakes and a road that could take a person right to the edge of this stinking continent."

I finished my beer and wandered out into the intense bright heat of the street. In the marché, a makeshift band was playing—guitar, bass, drums, and a percussion set made up mainly of what looked like automobile parts. A tiny battery-powered amp sent the music out through a single buzzing speaker, but it sounded good to me. People were dancing, and I began to rock a bit with the crowd—it was one of those times when I felt that I had the beat. A young woman called to me, beckoning with spreading arms and rippling fingers. I stepped forward, and the crowd pulled back, leaving an open circle for the woman and me. She smiled. People hooted and called out, and the ring of spectators thickened. The guitar fired rounds of high-pitched staccato notes, the bass rippled and slid, the clutch plate sustained an oddly harmonious drone. I studied my partner's face—flaring cheeks, remote smile, steady brilliant eyes—and the muscles in her arms and shoulders, the sleek body rippling beneath her pagne. Her movements were simple, something I could do myself, and watching her I heard clearly the basic tempo underlying the syncopation and polyrhythms. She had taught me this simple, essential movement, and now everywhere I looked on her body I saw that movement compounded, amplified, expanded. And my own body understood. I felt the same looseness in my limbs, the same deep tension that controlled them. She danced close to me, her eyes looking straight into mine. I hadn't noticed her mouth change, but now her smile was gone. The rhythm rolled out, intensified. There was a big crowd now, a rising noise around us, but still I was not distracted. The woman took my hands in hers, her hips, her whole body, pumping and swelling. We pressed together like that, hard against each other, grinding. Through the thin damp fabric of her pagne I felt the contours and temperatures of her body. I felt the heat and moisture where her stomach and pelvis pushed against me, and I felt her breasts, soft and cool against my chest. Her legs still moved with the music, even as they seemed to climb on me. Her eyes locked on to mine. The sounds of the crowd, the music, and my pumping blood all blurred together, and the rhythm was lost.

The woman kept grinding but I broke free of her. She reached out, but I shook my head and backed away, and she turned from me with a strange cry, a laugh or a howl, and kept dancing, calling, maybe, for another partner. Suddenly drenched in sweat, my temples pounding and my face flushed, I pushed through the laughing crowd.

What had happened? One second I was dancing, astounding myself with my sudden miraculous comprehension of rhythm and movement, and the next second the rhythm had propelled me into some kind of sexual frenzy in the arms of a stranger, out on the street in front of a hundred people. Such a thing was so unlike me that I felt more puzzled than embarrassed by my behavior; it was as if some other white man had been bumping and grinding out on the public square.

As I returned to the bar, a boy chauffeur, curled up beneath an overhang of flour sacks in the back of a truck, gave me a sly, knowing look, conspiratorial almost. In the shadows of the flour sacks he was rolling a fat cigarette— marijuana, presumably—with a sheet of notebook paper. I hurried on, mindful of the soldiers loitering on a nearby corner. Then I heard Kate's voice at my elbow. Suddenly I *was* embarrassed—what if she had seen me dancing?

But she wasn't talking to me. Standing by the driver's door of that same truck, she was conversing in Kituba with the man behind the wheel. I listened for a moment—they seemed to be talking about trucking routes, produce transport, something like that. Kate always acted interested, she always found something to talk about with whomever she happened to meet. It was admirable. But what, after all, did she care for the cost of shipping manioc? Was no detail too arcane for her? She noticed me watching her and stopped talking for a second, momentarily flustered. Maybe she *had* seen me, and what would she think, to look up from a conversation about trucking to see her husband grinding pelvises with a strange woman in the streets?

I ducked into the restaurant. Tom sat at a table with René and the prostitute, opening a beer bottle with a spoon. He brought a hand down hard on the handle of the spoon, and with a loud pop the bottle top flew off and hit the ceiling. Tom cheered. René's laconic smile did not change, and the prostitute's eyes were still unfocused.

I picked up the spoon and tried to open another bottle using the same technique, but I couldn't figure it out. I fumbled for a minute with the bottle and the spoon, and then the girl reached out and took the bottle from me, put it up to her mouth, and popped off the cap with her incisors. Now she smiled at me, saliva glinting on her straight white teeth. I smiled back, but I didn't drink the beer she poured into my glass. After a while she got up and wandered away. We left a big pile of money on the table, went out to find Kate, who was still talking with the truck driver, and climbed in René's truck to drive home.

Just outside of Mafemba we got a flat tire. René cursed expressionlessly, but he was cheered to find that he had a jack and a tire iron, and a spare with some air in it.

"Another victory, in a way," said Tom, and he opened a beer. Not a single one of the lug nuts was so rusty that we couldn't get it off, and quickly we changed the tire. "A *great* victory," cried Tom. He jumped up on the back bumper, grabbing hold of the railing. "I'm gonna be boy chauffeur for a while," he said. So we set off in high spirits, at high speeds, across the savanna. Tom yelled and hooted and kept up some kind of running boy-chauffeur chatter in the back. But twenty kilometers down the road he started banging the side of the truck. René slowed and leaned his head out the window. "The fucking jack!" Tom yelled. "We left it on the side of the road!" Without answering, René veered out into the grass, whipped the truck around in a shuddering, sliding maneuver that turned out to be a U-turn, and drove even faster back toward Mafemba. Tom made his way up the bed of the truck and stuck his head around by the passenger window. "It's not gonna be there!" he shouted. "They already got it; they were hiding in the grass, waiting to scavenge it. Now they'll try to sell it back to us. Unless they already melted it down and turned it into a cooking pot. Or put it on a stand and made some kind of musical instrument out of it."

"Who are you talking about?" I shouted back. "We're in the middle of nowhere. There's nobody out here."

"Nobody out here?" Tom laughed bitterly. "Are you kidding? There's *always* somebody out here. You think somebody's not out here watching us, every fucking second of the day, no matter how far out in the sticks we think we are? Well, somebody is. And they lifted the fucking jack, you can goddamn well count on that."

But the jack was still lying in the sand on the side of the road, and Tom's bitterness evaporated. "We've prevailed!" he crowed. "A *total* victory."

We got out of the truck to retrieve the jack and empty bladders strained by beer and the bumps and jolts of the road. "What a day, huh?" said Tom. "We successfully changed a tire, and *we didn't lose the jack*. We experienced Mafemba. And now we've got a million acres of grass to piss in. Feeling victorious, Will?"

I looked at him but made no answer. A hot wind swept down the long corridor of grass. Suddenly I felt very weary. Tom stopped grinning and looked hard at me, and for a moment, in the low glaring sun and with the shadows of windblown grass playing across his face, something new was revealed: not an expression or physical feature but a strange chemistry made visual. Something radiating from him, a field of intense energy lost, diffusing into the empty savanna. And what remained was like an acid burning in his belly, exposing some hard truths for a moment, and then dissolving them.

Kate came around from the far side of the truck. Tom glanced at her, and sighed. "Sure, Will. I know this is a passing euphoria. As soon as we get home we'll all be overwhelmed by randomness and contradiction, agoraphobia, whatever. We'll be failures. Participants in a grand failure infinitely larger than ourselves. But that's got nothing to do with what we are out here. Out here we're the First Tourists. We've done Kilala Mission, Kivila Falls. And today, we did Mafemba. Today we know the taste of . . . *victory.*"

1 0

THE BOY

Kate thought I was taking Tom too seriously. But I told her that I saw the point of his jokes too clearly to just laugh at them. I understood that Tom's facetious celebrations of victory were merely expressions of defeat, and I wasn't prepared to join him, not yet, in those days before we fired Dimanche, before I began to experience firsthand the defeats and humiliating victories that were the daily regimen of the boy.

Dimanche worked for us for three months. At first we hoped he would adjust to us, then we thought we might adjust to him, and eventually it became apparent that we had to get rid of him.

"Get rid of him?" said Tom. "Aren't you even curious about what further developments your relationship might take?"

But Kate said that she had absorbed all the moral instruction she could from Dimanche and it was time to move on. She said that with Tom's help Dimanche had shown her the hypocrisy at the center of her stinking bourgeois soul, and she was comfortable with that, as long as she could find a servant who didn't rub her face in it every time he took a rag to the tabletop.

"You mean you want the work performed invisibly," said Tom.

"Sure. That'd be great."

"Like back in the States, huh? Dishwasher, microwave, washing machine, food processor . . . Technology has eliminated the poor downtrodden servant, I guess."

"I guess so. And we like that about technology."

"Except that it doesn't really work like that, Kate. Technology has just removed him from your kitchen is all. Put him out in the assembly lines and mines and sweatshops, still working for fucking peanuts to get madame's clothes clean, to fetch water for madame's bath. You turn that dial on your washing machine, you're sending a message out to the world, and what it's saying is this: 'Dimanche, get down to the river, boy, and beat my fucking clothes against a rock.'"

"Okay," said Kate. "But what would *you* do in our situation?"

Tom grinned at her. "I'd fire the sonofabitch."

And so eventually we did, though when we finally sent Dimanche home for good, we softened the blow with two months' severance pay. He'd probably never heard of severance pay before, and maybe it wasn't even a blow; maybe it was as much a relief to him as it was to us. He took the news like he took everything, with a couple of sullen grunts, a glowering stare at the wall, and a long period of immobility on the couch.

It was a relief when he finally got up. He put the money in his pocket, gave us each a clammy handshake, and shambled off. But the problem wasn't solved, because of course Tom was right: the real problem was not Dimanche. The problem was the inherent inequity of the situation, the impossibility of resolving high-sounding principles of human dignity and equality with the actual circumstances of human society, which require that many people devote their lives to menial and degrading tasks in order to sustain the comfortable existence of substantially fewer people.

But Kate, tired of these paralyzing ethical dilemmas, was ready for some realpolitik. "Jefferson had slaves," she said. "Gandhi had servants, right? The world is made of patróns and boys. People have to make a living. Somebody has to do the dirty work, and some contradictions you just have to live with."

"Unless you can resolve them," I said.

"How?"

"Mutation, of course. Mutation by fusion. The patrón and the boy become one."

So I turned down the many applicants—suppliants, in fact—who came inquiring about the job. "We've already hired," I said. They looked around blankly, but the boy was standing right in front of them, and when I had sent them on their way I began to straighten and sweep the house and the yard. Then it was down to the river to do the dishes. Sometimes I'd cook up a pot of beans or a stew, and once a week I took the laundry down to the river and beat, scrubbed, soaped, and rinsed for as long as I could stand it, though the laundry never seemed to get very clean.

All these jobs were potentially humbling, though nothing like going to the spring—the source—to get water. When I got water I created a public spectacle of humility. The source was only a kilometer away, but I had to walk through the camp with my plastic bidón in hand to get there, which meant everybody knew I was going. I always picked up an entourage of kids along the way—everyone was eager to join the freak show, to be part of a procession led by Monsieur Will. "Led" in the sense that I went first, but if they didn't tell me which way to go, I'd be sure to get lost every time on the confusing forest paths.

The source was beautiful: a gush of clean, sweet water in a grotto of mossy rock and the foot-worn clay. I might have liked to spend some time just sitting there, except for the children watching me and the anxiety I felt about carrying the water home. They all carried their bidóns on their heads, even the five-year-olds, but that was out of the question for me. Aside from the problem of balancing it, the weight of a five-gallon container of water on my head for a kilometer might well have made a lifelong hunchback out of me. Sometimes I would hoist it to my shoulder and stagger along for a hundred feet or so with the water sloshing out on me as I walked, since the bidón invariably had lost its cap. Mostly I carried it like a suitcase, though it wasn't easy descending slippery paths with a forty-pound suitcase in hand, and I had to stop and rest frequently. The kids would wait, watching me solicitously, bidóns balanced on their heads, and eventually I would break down and let them take turns carrying my bidón the rest of the way home, although then I couldn't in good conscience run them off the property when we got back, so I had to put up with them loitering around all afternoon.

Many of the boy's duties revolved around getting and preparing food. A few groceries were available at the company store behind our house, but once a week I went shopping at the nearby Bumba Mission, which had a general store and a small marché. It was less than an hour's walk, but these shopping trips lasted most of the day, since I was generally invited for lunch and beer with Père Andrés and his partner, Père Michel, and often I stayed for coffee and cookies with the sisters as well. And I was never in a hurry to leave the spreading parklike grounds of the mission—those acres of open, close-cropped lawns, the clean and sturdy colonial buildings, the anomalous air of order and prosperity.

Even on days when I didn't go shopping, the boy's chores took up most of the morning, and I seldom sat down at my desk in the mill office before afternoon. Which was fine. Never mind egalitarian principles, the best reason for being the boy was that as long as I was sweeping and fetching and scrubbing, I didn't have to be the consultant.

The boy at least knew what he was supposed to do, even if he showed little aptitude for doing it. But the consultant was still adrift, possibly because he had yet to be consulted about anything at all. Still, everyone was very polite to me, and made a point of calling me "Consultant," which, once I got used to it, probably helped me feel some affinity for the role. And I guess I clung to the hope that if I went through the motions of having responsibilities and carrying out duties, actual duties and responsibilities eventually would manifest themselves.

So nearly every afternoon I went down to the office, and for at least an hour or two I worked. The chef de poste, poking his head in the office to check on his consultant, or the secretary, barging in with another pile of records or a pop quiz on French verb conjugations, might have gotten the impression that my work was deeply absorbing, that already I was producing documents of importance and insight. Often enough I was writing furiously, bent over my notebooks, filling page after page with my indecipherable English scribblings. What they couldn't know was that very little of it had anything to do with palm oil. I did manage to finish a draft of my Consultant's Assessment, and under the secretary's direction I compiled long lists of French and Kituba vocabulary. But most of the time I was writing journal entries, or letters home.

One of your duties is to keep me informed, Uncle Pers had told us, and dutifully I sent him information. Factual stuff, at first, businesslike or newsy, and a little impersonal. But it was impossible to sustain that reserve, and gradually my writing took on a different tone. The vast physical distance that separated us, Pers' proximity to death, the likelihood that we never again would meet face-to-face, the glaring whitewashed light and deranging heat of my office (that had once, perhaps, been his office)—these things all worked on me as I wrote, and made my writing uninhibited and emotional, even confessional. I described to Pers the unreal vagueness of my job, the strangeness of the forest and the separate strangeness of the savanna. I described Tom, Placide, Telo, and Ndosi; the haunted fishponds, the bamboo airplane. I told him of Kate's growing enthusiasm for her job; her energy and her wildness upwelling while I grew meditative and isolated in my office, the house, the front porch. In detail I described our house to him, and wondered: did he remember it? Had he perhaps lived in it once himself? Certainly it was different now, run-down, no electricity in spite of the chef's continued promises to run a power line from the mill up to our house. Kate finally had told him not to bother.

"But he promised us electricity," I said. "We should have held him to his promise."

"Why? Have you noticed how weak and sporadic that electricity is, what a morose, shabby light it sheds on everything, turning a room into a prison cell? What good is that? Personally, I *like* the way things look in a kerosene-lamp light."

"Well, yeah. It'd be nice to have a fridge, though."

"Why? What would we put in it? Besides, Will, I don't like the idea of a power line coming from that mill, with the chef's hand on the switch."

"What about running your laptop?"

"The laptop! Why?"

"I'm thinking of your dissertation."

"Oh, *that.*"

She'd never said the hell with it in so many words, but she hadn't mentioned her dissertation in weeks. She was on to a different kind of study now, working off of instinct and impulse and pursuing something other than the careful, tedious replications of scientific method. She had plenty of hypotheses, she was tangled up in hypotheses, but she wasn't quantifying anything, she wasn't about to graph correlations or record measurements of incremental change. She was poking and probing, and seeking a catalyst to shift some balance in the world.

Always she was *doing* something. She seemed almost feverish at times, going off on tangents, inspired, obsessed with sudden odd enthusiasms for things like laying hens, varieties of manioc, compost. She spent entire afternoons at the mission, dogging the sisters with questions about hog raising or

marketing coffee beans or the difficulties of fertilizing tropical soils or transporting corn to market. And nearly every day she went out in the fields and
the villages, talking to farmers and to the women who didn't call themselves
farmers but who did most of the work in the fields. She asked about their
planting and their harvesting and how much money they would get for a sack
of coffee or manioc; she ate luku and Things—bugs in a sauce, caterpillars,
monkey meat; she followed the coupiers into the deep forest and waited while
they went up into the trees with their machetes and calabashes. Squatting on
the ground with sweating, crazy-eyed men, she drank palm wine out of a cup
folded from a forest leaf and nibbled on the grimy kola nuts they pressed into
her hand. Occasionally she spent the night in a village, sleeping in a stuffy
room on a hard pallet with mosquitoes whining in her ears. But more often
she came home late in the day, muddy, sweaty, and sometimes half drunk on
palm wine or jittery from too many kola nuts. Sometimes she didn't arrive
until dusk, when Placide was already kindling his fire or patrolling an imaginary fence line. It distressed him that she would go to the river to bathe at
such a gloomy hour, but she laughed, and said that at the sight of her terrible
white belly the crocodiles would flee or go blind.

Nearly every day people came by the house claiming to have some business with her. All kinds of people: the little bands of ragged village children,
of course, but also women loaded down with babies and baskets of manioc;
coupiers with foaming calabashes, raggedy shorts, and bleary drunken eyes;
high school students or teachers, well-scrubbed and a little stiff in their neat
clothes, with their formal, polite French. They'd stand at our gate calling for
her—*Madame Caterine! Madame Caterine!* Often I'd have to go to the porch
and tell them she was away at some village or farm, or gone to the mission, or
ridden away on Tom's moto to look at fishponds. "Ah," they'd say regretfully,
and stand at the gate for a very long time, waiting, while I remained on the
porch, waiting.

Sometimes, in the interest of ending these standoffs with some grace and
expediency, I'd yield a bit to the etiquette of small talk, offering up some
comment or question, whether or not I had any interest in the answer,
whether or not the answer was self-evident. "You're taking manioc to sell to
the commissary, Mama? A-ha." "Where are you off to with that piece of
soap? Yes, of course, to the river to bathe. I see." "What are you up to, Papa?

Oh, tapping palm wine. *That* explains the climbing harness, the machete, the calabashes."

Before long they would sigh, shake my hand, and depart, obviously disappointed. After all, everybody knew Kate was capable of expounding on all these themes, going on in the same vein for ten or fifteen minutes until by chance a richer lode of conversation might be struck and something truly interesting revealed. But for me these vacuous exchanges were simply lubricant for social encounters, enabling me to slide past people with a minimum of friction and snagging. I wanted to avoid complications, or any revelation that might be too personal or unpleasant, and I wanted to do nothing that might increase my chances of being invited into somebody's house to drink fermented tree sap and dip luku into a sauce of Things that might be made of any kind of thing at all.

So the field consultant wandered in her fields, and the mill consultant sat in his office flipping through files and writing letters. And when the letters were finished the boy took them to the mission to be mailed. But that was like sending something off the edge of the earth. For months there was no response. Maybe letters got lost; maybe some were never delivered. Maybe the mail was just impossibly slow.

That must have been why my own letters became so unrestrained. What did it matter what I revealed when my words simply disappeared into the vast emptiness that lay between the Kivila Valley and the cities of America? It was as if Pers really did dwell in the vague Mputu of the African imagination, inaccessible and remote, not a dark continent but a blindingly bright one, so bright that from where we stood in the center of Africa no detail or distinguishing feature could be made out, and no line of communication opened. Kate said she felt connected to him as never before, but to me the old man in San Francisco seemed to be receding, becoming as remote and dim as the man who had built roads and cleared jungle in the Kivila Valley thirty-five years earlier, with revolution and independence bearing down on him like an obliterating storm.

We did receive a few letters here and there, from family and friends. We got a Christmas card from Mavis, telling us that Pers' health had improved, that they might even manage a small vacation, and that although Pers remained obstinate about certain details, she still expected to deliver the memoirs to the publisher within weeks.

But we'd been in Africa for months before we heard from the old man himself. A boy from the mission came by with a letter; I sat in the living room and opened it, and suddenly Uncle Pers, with his insults and his flattery and his uncanny insights, was back in our lives.

You say you are hungry for news from home, so I will oblige, though I'm afraid my news is not likely to satisfy your appetite. What news can I offer, other than a report on the state of my internal organs? A tedious subject, very nearly the only one left to me. Though there is a certain affectation of drama about the whole business, and it's possible to be fooled into thinking that it is something real and important. My doctors, for example, are lately triumphant, because their tests indicate that I have, against all odds, recovered some semblance of health. Indeed, they now act as though they no longer expect me to die at all. This has long been Mavis' game, though I always assumed it was only an expression of her credo of enforced optimism, with its requisite denial of mortality even in the immediate presence of Death. But now these doctors, who one might think would know better, seem to be conspiring with her. Do they expect me to be cheered by such a notion? Are they cheered themselves? Mavis seems cheerful, which is good evidence that she believes nothing of her own playacting.

These doctors! They also pretend that my alleged improvements have something to do with the medication regimens they have concocted on my behalf. This seems unlikely, since each month they invent a new theory and a new strategy, which is to say a new combination of drugs. My prescriptions have been changed often enough now to render absurd any pretense that there is logic or method to their pharmacology. I told one fellow as much. I told him that in my presence at least he is free to abandon all conceit and acknowledge what we universally suspect: that the practice of medicine is fully as capricious as the progress of illness and death.

Mavis, reading over my shoulder, informs me that this isn't what you mean by "news." She says you want to hear about my memoirs.

Is that true? Perhaps. Well, there isn't any news about the memoirs, if by news you mean fresh information, because at this point news must come first from you, the researchers. Everything I have is old and stale, surely you're aware of that by now. In the absence of fresh information, the unconformities remain, the story is incomplete, the moments of significance continue to elude us. The only change is that Mavis grows increasingly impatient, anxious, difficult. And I grow increasingly convinced of the essential emptiness of what I have written to date.

We haven't heard much from you, Katy; you seem to be out and about a good deal, and that, I suppose, is a good thing. Perhaps in your wanderings you will come across a bit of news that might be useful to me. You see now how huge the place is, how easily one can get lost in it. Yet it must also be clear to you what I mean by "a place of no significance." Though what Mavis said is true as well: that it was once a place of great significance. A Cold War flash point. In America the papers were full of it, and people were very excited and anxious, until they grew tired of it. Yet even while they were making it significant, the newspapers somehow created something very small in their readers' minds. The secretary general's plane went down, and I received cables wondering if I too had been killed—I think people had the idea it might have come down on me!

That's the trouble with our idea of significance: We focus on one thing, and lose all sense of vastness and possibility.

I am making inquiries, but so far no one has been able to explain why you have not been provided with a vehicle. However, my influence over the matter is limited, since the vehicle is the responsibility of your employer—this Global Interconnect, the contractor—and Jucht Brothers has little to do with the day-to-day execution of their contract. You see how loosely such things are managed there. So you must be walking for a little while longer. I, at any rate, am encouraged, because at least some of the roads I built must still be there, if you are asking for a vehicle to drive on them. This is a hopeful sign—one of many in your very encouraging letters. Well, one must read between the lines, one must judiciously interpret your abundant descriptions of ruin and decay.

I enjoy those letters immensely. In fact, I can now say what I never could about my own accounts: I am transported. Your letters suggest that while the memoirs may be solid and lifeless, the story itself is only beginning to unfold. You are stirring things up for me. Not memory, exactly, but evocation, let us call it, of something still beyond my grasp. No gap is filled, no mystery solved, but what is intensified is the sense that in fact there is mystery, that the unconformities are not so barren as we might have guessed.

Of course, you haven't yet given me anything substantial in this regard. You haven't buckled down and begun the actual research. But I think, for example, of your description of that man's model airplane—so beautiful, the plane dipping and swaying above the savanna grasses, the entirely convincing illusion of flight. Mavis was quite taken with that image. In fact, she has decided that she must have this bamboo airplane for her display shelves here at home. She wants you to buy it for her. I assured her that you won't, and in any case it wouldn't work. In the living room, the beauty will die. There will be no sense of flight.

I don't care about the sense of flight, she says. I desire the innocence. I want to contemplate the purity of that man's innocence.

The idea of displaying a man's supposed innocence in a model airplane on your living room shelf! And drawing from it some sustenance for one's own jaded soul. But as usual there is a kernel of insight in Mavis' impractical vision. She recognizes, as you have, that this bamboo airplane is something significant, something more than the fantasy fetish of a primitive man.

In any case, your descriptions of your various absurd dilemmas are often quite amusing, Will. The boy, the consultant, and so forth. And yet . . . it's all rather trite, isn't it? Inadequate. Like that fellow with the bamboo airplane, you need a vision of something larger. Something significant, Will! You need to quit indulging yourself in these farcical identity crises and come to an understanding of who you really are. Then act upon it.

You're a bureaucrat, Will. Maybe you don't like the sound of that, but it's true. And under the circumstances, it's not so bad. After all, there are different species of bureaucrat. There are the common species—the cynical, self-serving, or stupefied bureaucrats. And there are the rarer ones—the bureaucrats with a sense of mission, the noble bureaucrats.

So don't think I'm saying that you're merely a cog in some overgrown, self-perpetuating institution that can't find its way out of the dense organizational structures it keeps creating. In fact, your situation is the opposite! The

structures have all collapsed, or are so rotten they sustain only savage para-
sites and scavengers. You are the bureaucrat unburdened of bureaucracy, the
pioneer bureaucrat, unhaunted by the ghosts of his predecessors. They (all
right, we) made a mess of things, surely. But they've long since fled, or been
corrupted and warped beyond recognition by the decay of their own institu-
tions. And now you've come to reopen their old clearings, to build on the
rubble they left behind.

An enviable position, Will! Because although they curse him as a lowly,
emasculated, amoral creature, the fact is people now look to the bureaucrat as
a beacon of hope in a chaotic world. People understand that it is only our insti-
tutions which oppose the looming chaos, and that we need the bureaucrat to
guide us through the labyrinths and catacombs he has created to defend us.

Yes, Will! There's opportunity for nobility here, for honor and even a
modest heroism. I confess to feeling jealous of you—though obviously all this
is well beyond my reach now, and my time for nobility and heroics is passed,
unless there is some shadow of these things in the writing of autobiography,
which I doubt.

—Pers

The day we got Pers' letter Kate came home just before dusk. She bathed in
the river and then read the letter on the porch, while I fixed dinner and
Placide made his evening rounds and built his fire. Then we ate our rice and
beans and went into the living room for tea, because the mosquitos were getting bad on the porch. Kate had done some decorating in the living room.
She'd had someone build us a rough coffee table, and she'd draped a piece of
brightly printed fabric over the couch, and hung some masks and carvings,
purchased from local artisans and dealers, on the wall. The room was somewhat transformed, though not necessarily improved. Certainly it wasn't an
effect of domestic tranquility that she'd achieved with those masks, glaring
out at us from the shadows through hollow eyes, while the ancient sound of
drumbeats rose and fell in the camp above us.

"Seems like those drums have been beating all day," I said.

"A little girl in the camp died today. The women told me about her. She
came into the dispensary a couple of days ago with a fever and some sores on
her leg. They treated her with something, and two days later she's dead."

"So now they're having some kind of wake for her?"

"Yeah. I promised some of the women that I'd go up there for a few minutes. You could come too, if you want."

"I don't know. Maybe I'll stay here and do some paperwork."

"Oh, right. The noble bureaucrat. Gosh, do you think Uncle Pers' intellectual standards might be slipping a little? Or is this another one of his obscure jokes? A pioneer bureaucracy! What have you been telling him in your letters? Did you tell him there are plenty of bureaucrats here already, it's just that they don't get paid? That what they've got here is bureaucracy *instead* of public services or political organization, bureaucracy that's nothing but an institutionalized thievery? Not quite the tool of a police state, if only because the government is too dysfunctional to operate a police state?"

"Well, I didn't tell him *that,* exactly. Who knows where he gets his ideas? Not from me, I don't think."

"Don't be so sure. Uncle Pers really likes you, Will."

"I guess I amuse him, at least. I'm sure he thinks I'm hopelessly ignorant and uncultivated."

"Oh, he thinks that about everybody. Including me."

We sat in silence for a while, close together on the couch. There was something cozy about the living room after all, in spite of the masks. She was right to reject the chef de poste's electricity, anyway, right about the kerosene-lamp light. I liked watching her face in that light, and hearing her voice break the silence of our sealed house, with the buzz and hiss of the forest beyond, and the brown river whispering against its banks.

"If it wasn't for you I'd know nothing of this life, Will."

She took up my hand, stroked my fingers, sighed.

"You liberated me. From my dissertation and everything it stands for. Tameness, predictability, drudgery."

"I'd say it's more your doing than mine. We're here because of your uncle, anyway."

"Sure. But you know, Uncle Pers always kept me separated from this part of his life. Even though we were so close in other ways. All his adventures, the exotic places he lived, the history he was a part of . . . I could only experience it from a distance, as a story. Well, the outline of a story was all. But ever since you've been with me, the partitions have been coming down. I'm *connecting* to that story now, more and more."

She swung her leg over mine and straddled me, kneeling, her weight on my thighs while she slipped her hands under my shirt and kissed me deeply: a surprising kiss, full of gratitude and passion. Then she stopped kissing and straightened up and started talking again, her eyes shining down on me as if she were gazing on something wondrous and beautiful. She was always thinking about Uncle Pers, she said. Whatever she did—shaking the old people's hands in the villages, cruising the roads on Tom's moto, holding her breath and crossing those old log bridges—she was aware of him, she felt his presence. People talked about him too, she was starting to pick up on that. As if he were some kind of mythical figure, though she hadn't figured out what the myth was yet. But she had this sensation of some discovery beginning to unfold, new worlds opening up. And sometimes this *thrill* going through her body, that had to do with having immersed herself in Pers' memoirs, and now being in this place with these people who had known him, and living in this little house, with me.

I gazed back at her. There she was on my lap, I had no choice. And yes, I was struck with my own sense of awe, my own sense of gratitude and passion— for her liquid eyes, her ripening smile, the unrestrained pressure of her thighs on mine. At the same time my response wasn't quite right. I was a little overwhelmed. All those *words* right in my face, that full-grown female body clambering all over me, desire for her stirring in me but also some other force, something turning in my stomach that made desire weak. Also I was thinking: if what drew her to me was a sense of liberation, how well could that connection hold? A sense of liberation: how could anyone depend on *that* to work as a force of adhesion?

Her expression changed. The eyes solidified a little, the lips tightened.

"Why are you looking at me like that, Will?"

"Like what?"

"You're looking at me exactly the way you look at Placide."

"Placide!"

"The way you look at him when he comes up to the porch and says something totally off the wall, that you have no idea how to respond to."

She sighed again, and swung her leg off me. But she remained sitting close beside me, and after a minute she started stroking my hand again.

"You and Placide do have an amazing relationship, Will."

"Amazing in what sense?"

"Well, I don't know. Intense. Mysterious. Whenever I'm out lying awake in some hut in Kasengi or Bulolo or one of those places, I like thinking about you. How you're probably sitting on the porch, and Placide's out in the yard, and every once in a while you bump into each other but you never really make a connection. But just like him you're watching the night, right in the flow of it. As if you were made for Africa. While I've spent the evening floundering, still searching for my niche."

"Are you saying I've found my niche?"

"Oh, definitely."

"Spacing out on the porch? Missing connections with Placide? That's my niche?"

"Well, a niche is never entirely a positive thing, Will. Just because you've got one doesn't mean you're purposeful or productive or even content. A niche can be very confining, almost by definition. But for me it's comforting to know that's where you are. I guess I just like the image: Placide hunched by his little fire, you up on the porch, and all that darkness between you."

11

SENTINEL

Across the river the chef de poste turned up his boom box, and frantic and repetitive music crossed the water. A noise to shatter the serenity of the tropical evening, except we were already plenty agitated, all of us, each in his own niche: the insects buzzing and shrieking and clicking in the strip of forest by the river, the bats scuffling and snarling in our attic, the mourners chanting to drumbeats in a clearing in the camp. And the consultant standing on the porch looking out on the night, rocking and swaying to that radio music.

The first time I heard it I thought this music might eventually make me insane, but I had since learned how to channel it, along with a lot of other noxious stimuli, to passive background regions of my subconscious. This was not easy, since this music was always played at the highest possible volume, as if to emphasize distortion and accelerate speaker damage. But I watched the chef de poste and tried to listen to the music like he did—to take it in with my entire body, without filtering it through any analytical brain tissue. When I did this right the music no longer bothered me, and sometimes I even started dancing myself. People laughed and stared, but this inhibited me less than I might have expected—they laughed and stared anyway, no matter what I did. Why not make a spectacle of myself by dancing, since I achieved the same effect by reading a book or tying my shoes?

Placide didn't laugh the first time he saw me dance. He came close to me and watched, a look of wonder on his face. I smiled, but he didn't smile back.

"I've seen this before," he said when the music ended.

"What?"

"I saw it often in the capital, when the whites danced. Le Jerk. It must be a very difficult dance, monsieur."

He spoke gravely and did not respond to my laughter. But he must have been kidding me. It was hard to tell with Placide, who came up with outrageous statements, devoted his life to an absurd duty, yet comported himself always with serious and measured dignity.

A wind came up, fanning the coals in his brazier down by the cook shed, sending a few sparks skittering across the garden and carrying the smell of the fire up to the porch. A strange, sweet smell, the burning charcoal of a tropical wood, a smell unknown in higher latitudes. The glow of the fire illuminated the corrugated-tin siding at the corner of the cook shed, and in the faint reflected light I could make out a couple of scraggly goat-eaten tomato plants in my vegetable garden. But away from that glow the Kivila Valley was completely dark, and its sounds—drums and thunder, insects, boom-box music—came to me across invisible spaces.

Like me, Placide stood in the shadows and looked out on those spaces. The difference was that he could see something. He could see me jittering up on the porch, dancing my inscrutable Jerk. I stopped myself. Placide didn't care, or at least his sense of professionalism prevented him from passing judgment, but maybe I still wasn't entirely free of self-consciousness. And Placide's dignity inspired me. I wanted to learn to move through the night with a hint of his grace and stealth, and convulsive responses to music were not compatible with that goal.

So I stilled my quivering muscles, though the radio music was really wild now, accelerating as if to a climax. But in fact those hysterical and redundant riffs were not going to stop anytime soon. Those songs went on and on, and they were never formally concluded. After countless repetitions each song was finally just chopped off, which made me wonder what actually happened in the studio or bar where the music was recorded: beyond the patience of the sound technician had there at last been a conclusive ending, or had the musicians played on until they collapsed, one by one, in exhaustion and madness?

There was a sudden commotion over my head in the attic, some pushing, and the indignant squeal of a bat. Then a flurry of flapping and snarling, and silence again as the bats drifted back into a resentful sleep. Out of the darkness at the foot of the porch steps came Placide's quiet voice, startling me as always. How did he come so close, so silently?

"Monsieur Consultant."

"Placide. What's going on?"

"Nothing. Peaceful. Will Madame Kate be home soon?"

"Probably. She went to the funeral with some women. I imagine it'll end soon."

"The women will dance all night, monsieur. Our child died today. She was sick, and then she died."

"Yes. It's sad. I don't think I knew that little girl."

"You knew her, monsieur. You shook her hand many times."

An accusatory tone underlay Placide's flat statement, as if he were suggesting that the repeated touch of my hand was somehow linked to the child's death. Or that I should have somehow intervened to prevent her death. Or that I wronged the dead by not remembering her. But how was I supposed to remember her? There were a thousand children up there, all of them grimy and undernourished, feverish and afflicted, thrusting their filthy hands at us every time Kate and I ventured into the camp.

"I've got crickets to ignite," said Placide.

"Good." My response was automatic. I had no idea what he meant. Maybe he didn't say he had crickets to ignite at all. My mastery of Kituba was still shaky, creating plenty of opportunity for miscommunication. On the other hand, people do some remarkable things. Possibly the ignition of crickets had something to do with the performance of Placide's duties, which I still understood only vaguely.

"Why did that little girl die, Placide?" There was no answer. Placide was gone, vanishing as silently as he had appeared. It was a wonderful thing to see, or rather to not see: a nocturnal man, blending so artfully with the night. But he was wasting his talent, watching our little house night after uneventful night. He should have been something else—a hunter, a guerrilla warrior, a spy, a thief.

The fire flared and a shower of sparks went up, though there was no wind. Placide hunkered down, poking at his coals with a stick, his face visible in the fire's glow. He stirred the coals and stared into the fire. Now I was the silent one, the invisible watcher, trying to comprehend a waking life centered on a small fire in an iron pan, with a great darkness over half the world.

That was Placide by night. By day, he didn't seem like much: a small, polite man, a little shabby. But people were afraid of him. Maybe they saw a man who had spent too much of his life in the world of spirits. Maybe they were afraid of what he had seen peering into the shadows every night, or what he had imagined.

He sat on his cement block, hunched by the fire with his back to me. Dozing, perhaps, though when I stepped off the porch he was instantly on his feet.

"You're not sleeping tonight, monsieur?"

"Not yet. What time is it?"

He pulled back his overcoat sleeve and stared at the glowing numerals on his digital watch. Crunching something in his mouth, he showed me the watch. Twelve-seventeen.

"What are you eating, Placide?"

"Cricket." He held up half the charred body of a cricket. Of course. *That's* what he said he was going to do—roast, not ignite, crickets. As usual, my translation was flawed.

"Would you like one, monsieur?" He handed me a cricket, still warm from the coals. He popped the other half of his cricket into his mouth, and I slipped mine into my shirt pocket. I had yet to eat a cricket, though Placide, who stalked them by night and tossed them live onto his coals to roast, often gave them to me, ever since he somehow got the idea from one of our garbled conversations that I considered them a great delicacy.

The distant thunder rumbled and the drumbeats rolled on, as monotonous and repetitive as the clicking and buzzing of insects. But the chef de poste's radio, I realized suddenly, was silent. How long had it been off, and how did it go off without my noticing it? How could that intrusive noise blend so easily into the soundscape of the night? Insects and water, thunder and drums, a soft song of mourning rising in the camp. And the chef's radio going silent, as unremarked as a night breeze dying out in the leaves of the palms.

"I'm going for a walk."

Placide stared at me, uncomprehending. Maybe I used the wrong word. Maybe there was no way to express the idea of "going for a walk" in his language. It was too frivolous a concept, perhaps, a pointless squandering of limited energy, especially at that hour. The spontaneity, the carelessness, the pure nuttiness of going for a walk at *night*—Placide could hardly respond to it.

"I'll check on Kate," I added. Now Placide nodded gravely, and squatted in the glow of his coals to decapitate another cricket with his careful little fingers.

I went out the gate with my flashlight in hand, switched off. Lately I'd been walking around at night without using a flashlight. This started on moonlit nights, when I realized the light was superfluous at best. But even on dark nights like this, the flashlight didn't really illuminate the night; it only lit up a cone of space, and changed everything that occupied that space. I suspected some night objects of becoming invisible when the beam hit them, and outside the beam the night became entirely opaque.

Without a flashlight I might begin to penetrate the actual night, like Placide. I scrambled up the path, conscious of my eyes adapting to the darkness, of my brain deciphering night shapes, of vision itself becoming irrelevant as other senses were brought into play. Then I lost my footing on the wet clay and slid heavily into the narrow ditch that ran above our house, soaking a boot and a leg in muddy water, and slightly twisting my ankle.

"Monsieur!" Placide was already at the gate, heading up the path.

"It's okay. I just slipped into the water a little."

"You should turn on your flashlight, monsieur."

"I don't like my flashlight. It keeps me from seeing the night."

"Oui, monsieur. But it helps you to see the ditch."

This advice was irritating, coming as it did from Placide, who never turned on *his* flashlight to see the ditch. But I said nothing; I just flicked on my flashlight and followed the beam away from the river, into the hotter night and the camp.

On the old river terrace above my house, hidden from Placide behind the dispensary and the store, I stopped and turned off the flashlight. Immediately the sky blazed with stars. A sky we've lost back home, with our extravagance of electric light. And even here I could extinguish most of those stars just by flipping on the flashlight. Which kept me from stumbling in the ditch and also shackled me to the earth, made of me a dumb, myopic beast, blind to those infinite layers of heavenly light. Of course, I say they're infinite layers only because that's what I've been told. They didn't actually *look* infinite. They looked far away, sure, but I couldn't say that the galaxies or stars looked any farther off than the satellites.

I sat on the ground, taking the weight off my throbbing ankle, and tilted my head back. Which of those twinkling lights were huge galaxies, sprawling for a billion miles across space, and which were tiny satellites, smaller than a meteorite? And what were the satellites up to? Some of them deciphering stellar chemistry, others bouncing images around the globe, measuring elemental half-lives in the atmosphere, tracking heat and motion on the surface of the earth. And there, that blinking light must be an airplane, moving off toward the dark horizon to do its work of hybridization—binding the great cities, churning the human blood.

Finally I craned my head back so far that I ended up just lying on the path. It would be upsetting for some traveler to come along and see my pale arms stretched across the ground, a pale face rising suddenly from the path. But it was unlikely anyone would come. And I really did like lying there. I felt a deep sense of satisfaction, the source of which I couldn't really trace. It wasn't as if I'd accomplished anything that day. I'd gotten up early, as always, read a little, and then done some chores—yet the house was still a wreck, laundry scattered and piled all over, and there was still no food to speak of in the pantry. I'd meant to go shopping at the mission marché, but I kept putting that off and finally decided to go the next day. In the afternoon I'd sat in my office and gone through some papers, trying to work up something for my Consultant's Assessment, but I couldn't seem to focus. All I'd really managed to do was read Uncle Pers' letter, which, come to think of it, mainly expressed *dissatisfaction*, impatience, a demand never quite articulated. A hint, nothing more, that I still wasn't measuring up.

Well, what if he could have seen me lying on the ground in the middle of the night? Six months in Africa, Uncle Pers, working the territory of my niche, and I still hadn't figured anything out. My job, my wife's job, how to carry on a coherent conversation with my nightwatchman. Certainly nothing that might resolve the unconformities in your journals. Your niece seemed to be on to *something*, but I couldn't say what that might have been. In fact, I couldn't even say for sure where your niece was at the moment, though it was after midnight, and the night was pitch black, and the land wild. I was just going up to look for her, only I decided to lie down on the path instead. And I couldn't deny the pleasure in lying there, the feeling of tranquillity and well-being. I felt *grounded*. Well, okay, I was lying on the ground. But I felt a connection with that ground. Not the pull of native soil, surely, but some affinity, the conformation of my body to the contours of eroded and compacted dirt, trod upon daily by hundreds of plastic sandals, rubber boots, hookwormed feet. God knows what other parasites and pathogens it could harbor and transmit. But really I hardly considered that, because I was basking in my achievement, which was this: to watch the sky without apprehension, and to be at peace with the ground I lay on at the end of the day.

It was a little peculiar that I still should be lying there, though, listening to the distant thunder and the nearby drumming and singing of mourning villagers, long after I told Placide I was going up to look for Kate. Probably I was hearing her voice as I lay there, part of that homogenous chorus. After all, she'd proven herself a master of assimilation, engineer of her own mutations. I didn't doubt her ability to navigate out there, even in a night like that, among mourners stirred up by the mysteries and superstitions of a child's death.

I was less confident of my own navigational skills. Still, I did have to go check on her at least. I stood up, though I couldn't bear much weight on my ankle. Probably it needed to be put on ice, but there wasn't any ice. I flicked on my flashlight and hobbled up the road, into the camp.

In a circle on the edge of a fire the women danced, swaying, their arms around one another's hips. The sweat glistened on their arms and faces. Their eyes were closed, or unfocused. They sang, a murmured chant in the language of the village, incomprehensible to me. They leaned on one another as they danced, and the circle rippled but never tore. No one stumbled, though they must have been dancing for hours.

Only one man was drumming, and the drums and the chanting were the only music. The drummer sat in the shadows on the edge of the circle of dim light; eyes shimmering, sweat glinting, the palms of his hands flashing with his intricate beat. A few men stood near him, watching the dancers and talking quietly. Other people gathered in small groups here and there, or lay on mats in the clearing, or watched from the doorways of huts. The fire and a few candles and palm-oil lamps gave off a dim flickering light. People ducked into a hut; there was conversation, even laughter, and several men greeted me as I approached the outskirts of the gathering, though in the darkness I recognized no one. I stood stiffly, my pant leg clammy against my throbbing ankle.

"Monsieur Consultant."

It was the storekeeper, Kukonda Mayele, or something like that, I could never remember his exact name.

"Storekeeper." That was a neat trick I'd learned recently. A title could be used in place of a name. People were flattered, and it made me feel colloquial, as though I'd lived there a long while.

"Are you looking for your wife, monsieur?"

"Yes. I don't see her here."

"She was here earlier. She danced with the women."

"I wish I'd seen that."

"She dances well, Consultant! Vraiment! Pas comme vous, eh? Not at all like you."

"Really. That's interesting, Storekeeper. Do you know where she is now?"

"She left a while ago, with her friend the nurse. I'll ask where they went."

While the storekeeper made his inquiries I remained on the outskirts, suddenly awkward, a voyeur. Lying on the ground, I'd heard the drumbeats and the women's voices as ambient, exotic sounds of the night, harmonious with insects and thunder and radio music, part of what kept me out on my porch in the night. But suddenly here were sweat-streaked, tear-streaked faces in a grainy orange light, people wrapped in *pagnes* lying on the hard ground, and the circle of women swaying deeply, holding one another up. The dance was simple and monotonous, yet hard to follow. Each individual woman seemed to be going down, but the circle remained erect. They yielded to the pull of gravity without falling, and somehow their dance helped everyone bear the sorrow of putting a small body into the ground.

I asked a man what the child had died of. He shrugged. A change in atmosphere, another man said. The rains had been hard, and she was not a strong girl. The men nodded. The girl's father had an argument with her uncle, one said. The uncle hired a fetisher, and the fetisher killed her. The men nodded once more.

The storekeeper was at my side again. Kate had gone to the nurse's house at the far end of the camp, he said. He offered to take me there.

"That's all right. I just wanted to know where she was. I'm sure she'll be home soon."

The storekeeper rocked and swayed to the music, leaning toward me, sour palm wine on his breath. We stood together for a couple of minutes, swaying, but we kept bumping shoulders and knocking each other off balance. Was the storekeeper drunk, or was I having my usual problems with the rhythm? But I *felt* that drum music, it was coming through to my bones. I even felt the grief it conveyed, in some way that was not entirely abstract. I wanted to sway like the women, smelling the woodsmoke, with sweat on my neck and the dim orange light of fire and lamps falling on my closed eyelids. But again we bumped shoulders, and though my eyes were closed I could sense the storekeeper looking sideways at me. The next time we collided, I pretended I was nudging him.

"I'm going home now, Storekeeper. Good night."

"Ah, oui. Bonsoir, Consultant." Still swaying, the storekeeper shook my hand, and I turned away into the darkness and followed the tunneling beam of my flashlight home.

"I see you've got your flashlight on, monsieur. Very intelligent."

It was impossible to gauge the irony implied in Placide's compliment. In some ways Placide must have thought I was fairly stupid—for example, in my inability to handle a flashlight—but in other ways I know he thought I was extremely intelligent—for example, in my ability to build a jet airplane. He said as much to me once, that jet airplanes were proof of how much smarter I was than him or any of his countrymen.

"What are you talking about? I don't have any idea how those things work."

"But you build it, monsieur. It flies."

"Look, *I* don't build it. I couldn't build a plane any more than you could."

I saw that he didn't believe me and tried to explain with an analogy. "It's like in the village. Somebody knows the best wood for making a boat, the best way to make it. Nobody else has this knowledge, you just go to him if you want a boat made. Or maybe some old woman knows the plants in the forest that cure a fever. Other people have no idea, so they go to her when they're sick. It's the same with us and airplanes. A few people understand them. If the rest of us want an airplane, we go to them."

Placide shook his head. "In the camp we eat the plants the old woman gives us, but the fevers keep killing us. As for you, your airplanes fly."

"I don't have anything to do with those planes, Placide."

"You belong to the knowledge, monsieur." How could such a high popping voice sound so somber? And why did conversations like this always leave me feeling naïve and foolish, while Placide turned away with his dignity intact?

But the question for Placide was how to deal with somebody who knew how to make airplanes but didn't have the sense to turn on a flashlight in the dark. You might speak ironically to him, and you might not. You might find him ridiculous, and you might find him awe-inspiring. So I never knew how Placide was taking me, how straight he was playing me.

Now he huddled by his fire and gave me a sidelong look. I couldn't quite make out what he was asking me. Did I or do I like something? The funeral dance, maybe? My walk? His uncharacteristic grin and enthusiasm indicated that he wanted me to say yes. Okay, I liked it, I said politely, and his grin broadened, his head bobbed.

"It was good, Placide." A cautious elaboration that might not betray my incomprehension.

"Try again!"

Try what again? A different adjective, maybe? But I knew so few. "Beautiful, Placide. It was beautiful."

"Oh, beautiful, monsieur, yes!" Placide was actually laughing. "Tasty, eh?"

I nodded and broke away, heading for the porch. Tasty? It must not have been the dance or his fire he was asking about. I sat in my chair, trying to figure out what Placide and I had just said to each other. Again we were on that shifting ground where it was impossible to distinguish between irony and incomprehension, between servility and ridicule. Again we had bumbled our way through a conversation that began with an unintelligible premise. But we both knew it wouldn't do any good to try to clarify what we were saying. With Placide and me, clarification was just another means to further muddle the sense of things. Anyway, clarity of meaning is only one of many possible attributes of conversation. We also valued mystery, allusion, tone, momentum, and the camaraderie we were building—all things that couldn't withstand the interruptions required by a dogmatic insistence that we understand what we were talking about.

And in fact what Kate had said was true: Placide and I, with our brief and inconclusive exchanges throughout the long nights, had forged a kind of bond, transcending our difficulties with the language and the insubstantial ground on which we encountered each other: he the nightwatchman who guarded me from nonexistent terrors; I the consultant who transferred to him the intangible knowledge. Together we smelled the smoke of his fire, watched the flicker of lightning, heard the thunder roll down off the savanna, and listened for the smaller sounds behind the thunder and drums and insects—the river, the wind in the palms, the soft songs of grief in the camp. I saw that Placide was a man at some peace with his place in the world, and when I sat on my porch and watched him huddled on his cement block, I felt something of his love and fear of the night. When he slipped off to stalk crickets or make his rounds he taught me the theory, if not the practice, of moving in the dark; and when he stopped and bent his head I listened with him and learned to make some sense of the racket I heard each night, to focus with him on distinct sounds: the paddle in the water, the frog in the ditch, the footstep on the path, the cricket on the leaf.

The cricket again. That's what he was asking. He wanted to know if I liked the roast cricket he had given me earlier, which was still in my pocket, intact and untasted. And I told him it was good, it was beautiful, and yes, tasty.

Well. Perhaps it was time to taste it then, if nothing else so I could retract my statement before he stuffed my pockets with barbecued crickets. I pulled the cricket out. It was squished a little, and damp with sweat. I ran my fingers over it, feeling its burnt little legs, its carapace, antennae, thorax. These were not body parts I was accustomed to eating. Still, it was only another arthropod, it might as well have been a shrimp or a crayfish, and I'd peeled the little boiled legs off many a shrimp without a second thought. And so, thinking of shrimp, thinking Arthropoda rather than Insecta, I popped the cricket into my mouth.

It was delicious. The flavor really did remind me of shrimp. Shrimp, only with terrestrial overtones—the smoke of Placide's fire, the forest leaf the cricket was wrapped in, the wet grass where it hid and sang, the night wind that blew off the river and carried its song up to Placide. I'd expected to choke it down, but instead I chewed slowly, savoring the texture and flavor, the unexpected pleasure. There was something exciting in the taste of that cricket, uplifting, and yes, even beautiful. At the same time an involuntary shiver went down my spine and into my stomach, because after all it wasn't a simple business, eating my first cricket and contemplating the beauty and dread of the equatorial night, where a little girl lay freshly buried, where my wife had mysteriously vanished.

The thunder rumbled, leaves rustled, a warm damp breeze rose up—too warm, too damp. Suffocating, actually, and carrying out of the forest the smell of rot and putrefaction. The half-swallowed cricket suddenly gagged me. Jointed legs caught in my throat, a prejudice rooted deep in my guts rising to overrule the spontaneity of my tastebuds. Swallowing hard, I managed to get the cricket down, but by now that prejudice had me firmly in its queasy grip. I hurried inside for a drink of water, and ended up lying on the couch, breathing fast, pulse racing, sweat cold on my skin.

So here again was that force churning in my stomach: the sudden triumph of nausea, overwhelming the mystery and sensuality of the tropical night. But that's not exactly right. Nausea, I knew by now, *belongs* to the mystery and sensuality of the tropical night. Nausea *is* sensuality, carried to its fullness. In our northern winter we have a dream of sensuality unleashed, a euphoria of the senses in some southern country. But in reality the border between euphoria and nausea is unsecured, and out in the jungle, where life bursts forth and decays in equal abundance, agents of nausea are at work in every province of the senses, infiltrating even the central objects of desire.

And so honeymoon passions founder, mired in sensuality. I thought of Kate, wherever she was, and sure I got a tender feeling, my heart swelled with true love, and also I was mildly anxious for her safety—but at the same time I was just as glad she wasn't stretched out there beside me, competing for space on the couch. Her intestines rumbling, and mine rumbling back, in solidarity. Her chest rising and falling as she breathed: just an exchange of gases, moving from one damp, fetid chamber to another. Her boots kicked out across the floor, socks wadded up beside the coffee table, pants and blouse draped over the arm of the couch, stripped off and tossed aside—not in the urgency of passion, only in the hope of some relief from the humidity and heat. From which there was, in fact, no relief. Now, alone on the couch, long after midnight, still steeped in humidity and heat, I struggled to suppress this vision of her nearly naked body on the couch beside me: the white rise of flesh beneath her loosened brassiere; her panties, damp with visible sweat, clinging to her buttocks; the pale thighs so close at hand, textured with heat rash and blotches.

The tribal masks on the opposite wall glowered and leered at me, and on the corner table Kate's collection of wooden figurines and fetishes strutted into the shadows. At times in the daylight I'd thought some of these artifacts beautiful, and others at least compelling in their grotesqueness. But in this light they were only disturbing, and strangely consistent with the revelations of the hour. If they were religious icons they inspired no exaltation of the spirit, but rather tugged at a darkness in the soul; if gods of sex or fertility they expressed only parodies of eroticism, a jeering, nauseating celebration of the flesh.

I didn't fully understand the impulse that inspired Kate to possess these things. Maybe it was just an innocuous, if misguided, nesting instinct. But it wasn't much appreciated by people who came to visit. They'd duck their heads uncomfortably and shy away, embarrassed or even shocked that some-one, even a white person, would hang up these ancient totems with their uncertain powers in her house. But of course, the same rules didn't apply to her; she wasn't mocking or defying *her* ancestors by creating this little museum space in her living room. In fact, it was the tradition of her ancestors to create museums, to admire the beauty and strangeness of the objects they collect and catalogue, and to mourn the lost worlds those objects represent.

For example, the bamboo airplane. Of course, Mavis' desire to possess and display it was absurd, as Pers had taken such pleasure in pointing out. But wasn't he equally deluded? *Mavis recognizes, as you do, that this airplane is far more than the fantasy fetish of a primitive man.* But in fact what I mainly thought was that a fantasy fetish was exactly what it must be. Or at best a convenient metaphor for an impoverished culture, dumbly acquiescing to superstition and perpetual slavery. Or, as Tom would have it, a subversive impulse, some tactical defiance of tradition and the authority of Ndosi's uncles.

But once or twice when we passed beneath it on the motorcycle, I got a different sense of the bamboo airplane. The motorcycle propelled us far across the high open plain, though we never escaped the ground. Meanwhile, the airplane soared out overhead, and suddenly I was mystified and even humbled by it, so that now, with the funeral drums rolling on in the distance and a thunderstorm moving up the valley and my stomach still in the spasms of digesting its first cricket, I wondered if something like this could be a connection, the link or catalyst that Pers was seeking: a few scraps of bamboo and raffia glued together and raised to a provocative sky, as if to claim the invention of flight, a new way of looking for heaven.

1 2

THE NOBLE BUREAUCRAT

The kerosene lamp was low, casting dim shadows in our living room, and the hanging masks and wooden figurines, the books and clothes scattered across the floor, the stains and cobwebs on the dirty whitewash together began to resemble the shifting landscape of a dream. I turned the wick and the light swelled, the dream topography dissolved in the glow. It was a poor light still, compared to the evenly diffused, sourceless illumination of a modern office, or even to the glare of the naked bulb that lit my office at the mill, but at two in the morning in a small house at the bottom of a river valley where darkness was otherwise absolute, the small flame seemed brilliant and strong.

I took up Pers' letter and read through the last couple of pages. It was strange how he'd gone from the bamboo airplane to his odd idea of bureaucratic nobility, an idea that Kate had ridiculed, because it would never occur to anyone in the Kivila Valley to use the words "noble" and "bureaucracy" in the same sentence.

But that might be a failure of imagination. It could be that Uncle Pers was on to something here. His point was that a malevolent bureaucracy only underscored the need for a different kind of bureaucrat. A plodding, methodical hero, grounding an institutional resistance. Building order and regulation in an effort to liberate rather than oppress. Not imposing a bureaucracy from outside, but nurturing one that evolved out of the materials at hand.

Like that fellow with the bamboo airplane, Will, you need a vision. Well, it was a little foggy, and I wondered if it might have something to do with eating that cricket, but I felt like I might be having one. The vision of the noble bureaucrat. Absurd, of course, unimaginable in that place—but the fact that it was unimaginable was what made it so compelling. Because what we needed, more than anything, was a means of liberating our imaginations.

Beneath the scattered pages of Pers' letter, my Consultant's Assessment caught my eye: "Preliminary Assessment of the Ngemba Palm Oil Operation." A responsible document, full of sober analyses and cautious recommendations. Deferential to established power structures; resigned to the ignoble, corrupted bureaucracy embedded in the fabric of the society. A useless document, then, itself corrupt. What was needed instead was a new vision of the mill, a new vision of what the mill could do for the impoverished people who were forced to work in it. What was needed was someone able to articulate that vision. A bureaucrat, armed with the humble, powerful tools of his trade: words and numbers, paper and ink.

Outside, the drumming and thunder continued, but I scarcely heard them. My nausea attack of a few minutes earlier was forgotten. For the next hour or more, transcendent and inspired, I worked on my Consultant's Assessment. Ideas multiplied, new connections and implications appeared, new metaphors and associations crowded to the surface of my mind. But when an hour or so later I read over what I'd written, I saw that much of it wouldn't do. What did the smell of a nightwatchman's fire, for example, have to do with an Analysis of Extraction and Sterilization Mechanisms? How did drums and swaying women figure in the Operation of the Hydraulic Press? All the wrong things had found their way into my report: emotion and personality, aesthetics, ambiguity, fear of the dark. Surely the noble bureaucrat shouldn't be so *dreamy*. The bottom line dropped out of that report; I peered down through shadowy sentences at a gaping empty space.

It must have been the timing, the ambience, maybe even the lighting. A document like that should not be written in the hypnotizing yellow glow of a kerosene lamp. It should be written under humming fluorescent tubes, or even in harsh white daylight. Or better still beneath a broken fan in a stultifying office, when the sun is straight overhead and shadows and textures are washed out of the world. Then it might be possible to write of sterilizers and hydraulic presses in language that never strays from the province of the bureaucrat, never acknowledges the heat and sweat of the night, the drum that is suddenly silent or the sudden wind that blows up the river, bringing the smell of ozone and water.

Thunder and lightning cracked together, and while the house was still rattling, the rain came. I left my Consultant's Assessment on the desk and stepped out to the porch, where Placide stood on the steps in his overcoat, in the shelter of the eaves. On the tin roof the rain boomed. Placide looked up at me, but it was too dark to see his face, and the rain was too loud for talk. I went to the edge of the porch and urinated into the torrent. Thunder cracked and rolled, over and over, and lightning imprinted the scene on my brain and gave it a visual resonance, so that even after I went back inside, undressed, blew out the lamp, and lay in bed listening to the diminished rain and the roar of the flooding creek, I continued to see Placide's small huddled figure, and behind him rainwater streaming off the corrugated roof, trees bending, leaves tossing, and water running in sheets and rivulets through the yard and down the hill to the swollen and rain-blurred river.

Where in that torrent was Kate? It was crazy to be so sanguine about her continued disappearance. When less than nine months earlier, on the interstate outside Tucson, I'd found the prospect of parting with her for forty-eight hours so unbearable that I'd kidnapped her instead. And now she was out somewhere in the heavy darkness of the African night, with the storm rolling off across the valley, the streams surging out of their banks, the muddy earth slipping and the roads washing away; and I lay in bed beneath a tent of mosquito netting, at peace with myself and the world: the noble bureaucrat at rest, savoring a long moment of falling into sleep. The rain had taken the heat and energy from the night. I even seemed to hear Kate breathing, deep and rhythmic as if she lay beside me, but I knew that was only some distant or imaginary sound on the border of sleep. I knew that Kate was crouched somewhere in the darkness, maybe dodging leaks in a crowded hut, shrugging off the discomfort, secure in the company of women who still sweated and swayed from a night of dancing, women who sang now in soft, hoarse voices, urging babies wakened by thunder to return to sleep.

I slept through the passing of the storm and into the cool dawn. I slept through the noise of rushing water, dripping trees, continued drumming. Roosters crowed, children shouted, women pounded manioc, and people talked and sang along the road, on their way to the fields or the river. The cantoniers— the road crew—came out to repair the flood-damaged road. Asleep, I heard them call to one another as they struck their picks and shovels against the heavy clay. The whistle blew at the mill, and once again the old engines coughed and shrieked into life. I heard it all and slept through it all, every sound of the morning absorbed into the calmness at the center of my sleep.

But outside my window a sudden harsh, rattling sound broke into my sleep, followed by a squalling voice, as persistent and unmodulated as a crow's. "Waa-waa-waa! Waa-waa-waa!"

No one could mistake that sound for a baby crying, though outside the window there was also, in fact, a baby crying. But the baby could scarcely be heard, because its cries were drowned out by the *waa-waa-waa*s—the sound of a woman crying *at* the baby, and by the rattling of the tin can filled with pebbles that she shook in the baby's ear.

If the idea was to persuade the baby to stop crying, the wailing and rattling seemed unlikely to work, but if it was supposed to do something else, like make the baby's cries seem insignificant and benign by comparison, then maybe it wasn't such a poor strategy. The can rattled, the woman squawked. "Waa-waa-waa! Waa-waa-waa!"

"Shut up!" I squawked back, struggling to free myself from entangling sheets and mosquito netting. Pulling on a pair of shorts, I stumbled over piles of laundry and lurched out the door.

The woman standing by the gate gave me a look of complete incomprehension when I suggested that she rattle her goddamn can thirty or forty kilometers down the road. I recognized her—one of those mamas who came around now and again looking for Kate. The baby's face was covered with sticky leaves and scrunched up in a sustained howl that effectively communicated distress in spite of being inaudible. "Waa-waa-waa! Waa-waa-waa!" the mother cawed at it, and then explained to me, "The baby's sick"—a neutral statement, not an apology or even an acknowledgment that she had violated my privacy and deprived me of a beautiful sleep. My head throbbed and my guts contracted, as if suddenly recalling the cricket they still hadn't finished dealing with. Over the rattle of her can, the woman demanded, "Where's Mama Kate?" and losing what was left of my composure I launched into a lecture that immediately deteriorated into a rant. What did she think she was doing, wailing and shaking a can of rocks in a sick baby's ear? And why was she doing it in my yard? Was she trying to make me as miserable as her baby? I was finally asleep after being up most of the night, and she comes wailing and rattling into the yard, waking me up and giving me an instant headache; didn't she know what time it was—which of course she didn't any more than she knew how far down the road thirty or forty kilometers was—and how should I know where Mama Kate was any more than she did? That is, those were the things I tried to say. But my discomposure was such that the language completely failed me—my Kituba emerged garbled, my pronunciation appalled even me, I was using the wrong words, and in any case they were jumbled up with English and even Spanish of all things, probably more Spanish than I ever used in a full sentence in Mexico. I raved, and the expression of stupefaction thickened on her face and jelled into profound incomprehension when a sudden watery spasm rumbled through my intestines and I abruptly stopped raving, blanched, and rushed past the gate toward the waysay.

I squatted for a long time on the wooden slats, much longer than necessary, until I heard the woman return up the path and into camp, still shaking her can and wailing at her baby. There were several breaks in the wailing and can shaking, and I could make out greetings and brief exclamations, and imagine the woman muttering to people she passed along the way: "White man's flipped out about something. Check it out."

Which would explain why so many kids were loitering around my gate when I emerged from the waysay. Most of them scattered when they saw my ill-tempered face, and I sent the rest on their way with a brusque command and a wave of my arms. I watched them scurry down the path to the river, some of them giggling, some in real fear. What a collection of ragged, filthy, round-bellied, green-snotted, malnourished runts! You might think I would have felt a sense of self-reproach at scattering them as if they were a pack of skulking dogs, but I didn't. I pitied those children and helped them when I had the energy for it, but that didn't mean I had to put up with them hanging on my gate, waiting to get a look at me coming out of the john.

However, that situation was much improved since we'd gotten a gate for them to hang on. During our first weeks in Ngemba they'd gather in the yard, often right by the porch, and lay siege for hours. They'd wait quietly, staring at our empty porch, and when I'd finally venture out, either to joke around with them or chase them off, depending on my mood, they'd pipe a chorus of greetings and thrust their hands up at me. Fatalistically I'd oblige them, shaking each filthy, luku-encrusted little hand and trying not to think about where it had been.

Though I hated to join the chorus of adult voices that so often seemed to be shooing these kids away, as soon as I could speak the language well enough to make myself clear I told them to stay out of our yard unless we invited them in. "But we don't know where your yard is," they said, and it was true that the boundaries were unclear, since the public path to the road and river led right through our compound, dividing the waysay and garbage pit from the other structures. So we decided to define our territory by having Dimanche, who at the time was still employed by us, build a fence.

Though as expected, Dimanche demonstrated little skill as a fence builder, our fence did spark in him a rare display of energy and even zeal. No, that's not accurate: the fence left him cold, his enthusiasm was all for the *gate*. For about a week he went to the forest every day, returning after many hours with a couple of pieces of bamboo and some raffia string for lashing the fence together. Finally he started building, and by the end of another week he'd finished the gate. He was uncharacteristically proud of his work, and called us out to demonstrate its operation. But his labor seemed to have exhausted him; after that he was sick for a few days, and when he returned to work one excuse led to another and he never did get anything done on the actual fence. By the time we fired him, the project was essentially forgotten.

But the gate, standing alone on the edge of the open yard, was a sturdy if surrealistic structure, and amazingly it worked. It didn't keep the goats from ravaging our garden, of course, but the kids respected it as a border. They congregated there, instead of drifting into the yard and hanging around the porch. On those occasions when we invited them in they never walked around the gate; they opened it, filed through, and carefully closed and latched it behind them.

But now, with my guts still rumbling and my body deprived of sleep, I had no tolerance for these urchins. The last couple of stragglers stood on the path, looking at me. I ran them off with a shout and a fierce gesture, and retreated inside.

. . .

Placide had gone home, as he always did at dawn. The cantoniers had moved off down the road, to the other side of the stream. They probably had a full day's work ahead of them, repairing the road. Even in our yard I could see the storm's impact—deepened rills and gullies in the yard, and new sediment washed against the walls of the cook shed and garage.

The sun was not yet up, but the camp above me was fully awake. Pestles thudding, the drift of laughter and talk, a snatch of high sweet song. The faint cry of a baby, the rattle of rocks in a can, and the answering cry: *waa-waa-waa*—the final *waa* dropping in pitch, as if there were a Doppler effect as Crow Woman and her baby were sucked into the vortex of the camp.

Kate was up there somewhere, supposedly. She may have been out thomping a pestle herself, her enthusiasm was that extreme at times. But I wished she'd give it up and just come home. The interior of the house was still dim, and desolate in her absence. Nothing beneath the mosquito netting but a wad of crumpled sheets. Nothing on the floor but piles of laundry, nothing in the kitchen but dirty dishes. What was I going to eat? I needed some sustenance to have the strength to haul all that stuff down to the river and wash it, which I'd promised myself was the first thing I'd do today. Of course, I'd been making that same promise for days.

Tom told me that as my own boy, I was providing a valuable example to the privileged classes. It's got to make them think twice, I agreed, when they see a rich American boy washing his own underwear. What I'm saying, said Tom, is that you're providing evidence for one of their favorite arguments: that if they raised the slave wages they pay to their peons, the peons would get cocky and lazy. Now they have you to point to—the highest-paid boy on the continent, and your house is a goddamn wreck.

It was true that the job of boy had proven to be more taxing than I anticipated. Today I had to deal with everything—laundry, dishes, food, drinking water, and the general clutter of the place. And at some point I absolutely had to head over to the mission to do some major provisioning. There was almost nothing to eat in the house. We did have some coffee and sugar, a tin of powdered milk and another of oatmeal, which would get me through the morning at least. And I could always pick up something for lunch and dinner at the company store in the camp, though it was hard to imagine eating another meal of sardines or Vienna sausages.

This was the fourth or fifth morning in a row for oatmeal. It was by far the most expensive oatmeal I had ever eaten. We'd bought it in the Lebanese store in Mafemba for an outrageous amount of money, the equivalent of a mill worker's weekly salary for one lousy little tin of oatmeal, but what the hell difference did that make to the richest boy in Africa? I could eat oatmeal every morning if that's what I wanted, if that's what I needed to get my strength up for beating the patrón's clothes on a rock.

I made two cups of coffee, in the hope that Kate would show, but a half hour later I was still alone, working on the second cup and my third or fourth trip to the waysay. Somebody in the camp had to know where she was, but I didn't feel like going up there to ask. That would have been something for Dimanche to do, if he were still around. One problem with being your own boy is that you have to send yourself on every menial errand that comes up. Too bad I'd chased those kids off. I'd forgotten how useful they could be for running errands, gathering information.

There was a certain subdued beauty in the cloudy morning, though, and if I didn't think about the piles of laundry or my interrupted sleep or Kate's absence, I might take some pleasure in the cool air, the wet earth, and especially my still and quiet house. Sounds of the factory and voices of people outside seemed remote: the murmur of a separate life that washed past me. My curiosity about that life was at a low ebb—the peacefulness of my house, the refuge promised by my books, maybe some calming music on my boom box, and the proximity of my waysay were all I required. The laundry could wait. I poured the last of the coffee and shuffled again through the pile of papers and books on the desk. I glanced over the Consultant's Assessment, then read it more closely, and reread it.

What could I possibly have been thinking when I wrote this? Did Pers' letter really trigger this half-baked theory of bureaucratic nobility? Was I the victim of a passing euphoria, an enchantment worked by those nighttime spirits Placide was supposed to be keeping at bay? Maybe it did have something to do with eating that cricket. The report seemed to presume that I understood the Kivila Valley and knew what I could do for its inhabitants.

And that I had the language skills to communicate my understanding to them. The noble bureaucrat! Well, that was last night's visitation. Now in the daylight it was back to being the boy, who could hardly speak the language at all, any language. Back to being a foreign body, a grotesque implant, something large and white and cloddish, weakened by disease and heat and humidity, surviving on sterilized imported food sealed in steel cans thousands of miles from the bacterial breeding grounds of Central Africa. My very presence was absurd, an affectation. Who was I trying to kid, swaying arrhythmically at a funeral dance, sitting out on the porch all night feeding the malarial mosquitos, walking around in the blind dark as if I had the sixth sense of a night sentinel? Eating crickets, for God's sake. Doing my own laundry. Now there was an affectation for you: beating my clothes against a rock!

And what about my wife? My wife! Gone all night and half the morning, and still I had no idea where she was. Wasn't my complacency inappropriate, an affectation in its own right? Shouldn't I abandon these pointless theories and speculations and try to get my hands on some facts? Shouldn't I *do* something? And there was nothing to be done but send out the boy, incompetent, unsociable, and ignoble as he was.

The path I had followed the previous night skirted the edge of the camp and ended at the village that over the years had sprawled beyond the bombed-out brick shells of the original colonial settlement. The village was a congestion of mostly neat thatch houses with well-swept yards, to my eyes less impoverished and desolate than the camp itself. At first I wondered why they called it the "camp," implying impermanence, when those brick and cement-block buildings were the most solid and permanent structures around. But I'd come to realize they weren't so far off the mark. It was true that the village houses, built of flimsy plant materials, didn't last long. But they were rebuilt again and again, so that the village itself was constant, even while its components were in constant flux: rising and falling, built to rot and leak and collapse and give way to a fresh house. None of the huts was more than ten years old, though the villages may have been there for centuries. Those European houses, on the other hand, no one would ever rebuild. In a few decades the tropical molds and acids would finish dissolving the yellow colonial brick, and that would be the end of the camp.

I often used the path on the outskirts because it avoided the main part of the camp, where I was usually at the center of an embarrassing amount of attention. But since the point of this visit was to get information from the people of the camp, it seemed counterproductive to avoid them. So I turned off the path, climbed past the store, and came onto the long dirt boulevard that divided the two rows of company houses.

Almost immediately the first shouts went up. I was expecting them, and I kept walking, affecting a brisk but relaxed gait. Chickens and goats scattered before me, a ragtag procession formed at my heels, and crowds gathered on the porches and yards to marvel at my passing. I waved and smiled, my benevolence as phony as a beauty queen's. I couldn't remember anybody's name, and with dozens of faces staring openly at me a general anonymity settled over the crowd, and I didn't even try to recognize anybody. But they all knew who *I* was. The children began to call my name, and as more and more took up the cry it became a syncopated, mindless chant: "Will, *Will!* Will, *Will!* Will, *Will!*" But they had trouble with the pronunciation, and it came out sounding more like "Wee, *Wee!* Wee, *Wee!* Wee, *Wee!*" Even some of the adults joined in. Others called out that I could find my wife at Matama's house. The children would show me. So I hurried up the boulevard, waving here and there and shaking a hand or two as I passed: the great Monsieur Weewee graciously acknowledging the accolades of his admirers. And remembering, in passing, the words of Uncle Pers: *You deserve greatness, in some form or another. And greatness is actually quite easy to come by.*

Between the camp and the village the funeral dance continued, though the circle of women had grown smaller, the fire was a puddle of wet ash, and the people who'd slept outside or gathered to watch the dancers were gone. The drummer's eyes were closed, his head lolling, but his hands still beat strongly, faster than my eye could follow, and the women still leaned on one another and shuffled, swaying as deeply as ever to his drumming.

In the village the Weewee chant faded, though I still felt as if I were caught up in some strange parade, the Pied Piper with the tables turned, following his retinue of ragged children through a maze of dwellings, waysays, cook sheds, chicken huts, and goat pens to a small thatch house where Matama, a gossipy woman who often visited Kate at our house, welcomed me with a smile and a warm handshake.

Even in the full light of day there was a heavy dusk in her windowless hut, and I could scarcely see the people—several children and another woman— who murmured greetings. From the far corner a white face looked up at me, and my anxiety dissipated.

"Ah! There you are at last! I was almost starting to worry about you."

She said nothing in return, only stared back at me, eyes widening, mouth working—huge pale blinking eyes, flapping bloodless fishmouth, hideous nostrils gaping, emitting snorts and gasping breaths, yet still I moved toward her for a second, in growing horror, before I realized my mistake and stopped. Then she was on her feet with a strangled shriek, upsetting her stool as she fled, a low-darting skitter around the table, a more full-bodied cry as she went out the door: not Kate but an albino girl maybe twelve years old. I'd seen her around before, a lumpy freakish thing, thick-featured, doomed, hiding from the sun that was surely killing her. How could I have mistaken her for Kate? Well, because of the sudden darkness of the hut and the expectation that Kate was inside. But Kate was no longer there, Matama told me, laughing. Matama thought it was a wonderful joke that I mistook the albino girl for my wife, and after explaining that Kate had only just left, taking the back path to our house, she insisted on going over it again, describing my expression and the girl's and the way I greeted her in English and moved toward her, and the way she fled and I recoiled. She introduced me to the other woman—some-body the nurse, whose name didn't even register, because I was occupied with making some excuse and moving for the door.

"What's the hurry? You want to chase the whiteskin?" Matama laughed again, but the nurse smiled and reached up to gently shake my hand. "Stay and eat luku with us," she said.

Matama shooed the children from the hut and out of the doorway, sent a boy to get a basin of water, and pushed a chair under me, keeping up a steady monologue all the time. You're too skinny, Monsieur Will; you're starting to look like one of us; you'd better sit down and eat. The food is ready; Mama Katy has already eaten some and pronounced it delicious. These are Katy's favorite mushrooms; Matama herself went out in the forest to gather them in the earliest light, when Kate was still up on the savanna.

I looked up from washing my hands. "I thought she was at the funeral dance, or visiting somebody."

Matama threw out her hands, lifted her eyes to the ceiling. "Of course that's what you thought! But you know how she is, Will. She has to go everywhere, see everything—the dance, the villages, the truck stuck in the mud on the savanna."

"She went all the way up to the savanna to see a truck stuck in the mud?"

"Well, that wasn't the only reason. And lots of people went—they had to help push it out of the mud."

"In the middle of the night? What mud? The savanna is all sand, everywhere I've been."

"Well, yes. But this truck driver didn't know his way around, and it was at night, and he found some mud, no question. Wait till you see Katy's clothes! Then you'll believe in mud. You had better beg Dimanche to come back and wash those clothes—they won't come clean for you!"

The nurse set a couple of covered pots on the table—luku and a small bowl of rich-smelling Things. We broke off chunks of the stiff, doughy luku and dipped them into the Things—a stew of palm oil orange, floating pieces of meat like some kind of nautical wreckage, hurricane flotsam. And not even meat, for that matter—mostly bone, gristle, and fur. It didn't *look* appetizing, certainly, but it may well have tasted delicious: an intense and mysterious blend of flavors. Palm oil, wild meat, hot peppers, fragrant leaves, wild mushrooms, dirt, what else? The trouble was, I wasn't really in a position to objectively judge the taste, and if it hadn't been for the total inadequacy of my high-priced oatmeal breakfast, I doubt I would have been able to put down more than a couple of token bites. The memory of my midnight cricket snack was fresh, and suspicion and revolt still simmered in my stomach. In any case, mystery is not a quality I value in food. I like to *know* what I'm eating. A stew like that was all guesswork—any number of organisms might inhabit such a sauce. The meat especially made me queasy. Where had it been, and who'd done what to it since it was killed? How long ago was it killed? What was it, anyway? And why didn't she at least take the fur off before she tossed it in the pot?

The women were very intent on their food, but I needed conversation to keep me from contemplating these unanswerable questions.

"So, you're a nurse," I said to the nurse, who couldn't answer, having just stuffed a big wad of luku in her mouth. But she looked straight back at me, clear-eyed and vigorously nodding and chewing. My eyes were growing accustomed to the dim light, and now I remembered seeing her with Kate once or twice—a striking face, flesh and bone in high contrast; hints of deep shadow, hard angles, and pockets of softness beneath her cheekbones and around her mouth.

"A nurse," said Matama, "only she doesn't have a job."

The nurse swallowed her luku, still watching me as she licked the grease from the corners of her mouth. "I used to work in the dispensary at the camp, but the chef de poste fired me."

"Monsieur Will is a great friend of the chef de poste," said Matama.

"We work together," I said. "We get along."

The nurse shrugged, rolling another ball of luku in her fingers. "I got along with him too. The people were dissatisfied. They said there was too much sickness and dying. They wanted more injections. I said, maybe it's the injections that are killing you. But they didn't like paying at the dispensary and going home without an injection. So they told the chef to fire me."

The women nodded, murmured, and turned back to the food. I broke off another wad of luku, took another tentative swipe at the sauce. But what I wanted was to eat like that nurse: out of a hunger in my stomach, with a mouth that kept its dignity and composure even as it chewed, and lips that dripped oil and chili like a shining gloss.

"We heard you went to the funeral, Monsieur Will," said Matama. "We heard you danced with the storekeeper. I wish I'd seen that."

"Weren't you at the funeral?"

"Oh, yes. We came and went. We didn't sleep; we danced half the night, and walked or talked the other half."

I tried to explain how beautiful I found the dance, how simple yet complex, with the circle of swaying women all leaning on one another. The nurse nodded.

"We lean on one another, yes. You're right, it's very complicated. We hold each other up. And at the same time we are pulling each other to the ground."

When we finished eating I excused myself and made a quick escape—down the back path this time, with no escorts dogging me. Back at the house, the kids loitering at the gate told me that Madame Kate had returned and gone inside. They pointed out her clothes, draped on the porch bench, splattered with a black mud.

The shutters were closed in our bedroom, and I peered down through the mosquito netting, where Kate slept heavily in the shadows. The netting was like a veil, and in the unlit chamber beneath it everything was ambiguous and suggestive: the white glimmer of a shoulder or breast or thigh, the entanglement of leg and sheet, the slow abandoned motion of breathing and dreaming. She stirred in her sleep, and a smell, familiar and strange at once, came through the mosquito netting. The smell of her body and sweat drying on her skin, and also something like leaves and soil, clay and water . . . but not like any of those things, really; those are just associations, a description merely evocative at best, like when people try to describe the taste of a wine. This smell was its own smell, something wild and female and not altogether pleasant. Then it was lost, and I sniffed the air to find it again, sorting through the smells that were always there, so much a part of the house that it took an effort of concentration to distinguish and name them: mildewed clothes, kerosene, coffee, bat shit, industrial palm oil.

Kate stirred again, turned, cried out a garbled and meaningless string of syllables. The smell rose again, and blood pounded in my temples, my head buzzed. Had I been sleeping with that in the air, night after night, and never known it? Or was it something new, something she returned with from a night of dancing and roaming the savanna? I lifted the netting, and the uncertain contrast of shadow and limb became more defined. She lay on her back, wearing only a sleeveless top. The bedsheet was cast to her knees. Her breathing only deepened when I put my hand on her leg and trailed my fingers up to the rim of her pelvis. For a moment the world was silenced, except for the rush of the air we breathed, and the pounding of blood.

Outside the window I heard a sudden exuberant song. Kate caught her breath, shook her head, and turned away from me. The smell dissipated. I pulled away, and the mosquito netting dropped back over her. A man's voice rang out—a wandering, improvised melody, a falsetto harmony.

The plane has flown.
The plane has flown.
The sky, the sky, the sky,
The sky has taken the plane.

The singing stopped at our gate. I stood up, smelling only dirty clothes and palm oil, and leaving Kate in heavy sleep and shadows, I went to answer the hoarse shout at the gate. "Madame! Monsieur! Come out! My airplane has flown!"

BOOK THREE

THE DRY SEASON

1 3

THE BOY IN THE HOUSE,
THE MAN IN THE ROAD

The morning he woke to find his airplane gone from its perch on the bamboo pole, Ndosi did not speak with his uncles or the local fetisher. He didn't go looking for a priest or his fisheries advisor or any of the wise old ones of his clan. He came to see me. His consultant.

He stood at our gate, singing and calling. In the bedroom I let go of the mosquito netting, left Kate sleeping, and went out to the porch. The yard was wet and sparkling from the night's rain, and Ndosi opened the gate and walked to the porch slowly, looking up at me with the beatific smile of a man who has been granted some expansive and irrefutable vision. He told me his plane was gone, and asked if I could tell him where it might have flown.

He could not know, of course, that I had just been peering through the mosquito netting at my own expansive vision, confusing and ambiguous as it was. I stood on the porch looking at Ndosi, my pulse racing, my face burning, my brain still struggling to decipher the smells and the contrast of shadow and limb in my bedroom.

"How would I know where your plane is?" I said. "Probably it fell off the pole. Probably it's in the field next to your house."

"No, no, Monsieur Will. It didn't fall. It *flew*. In the night it flew. This was the kind of night when such things happen."

I thought back on the things that had happened to me during the long night: weird conversations with Placide, a meditative trance lying on the ground, the funeral dance, cricket eating, the vision of the noble bureaucrat, and finally the storm blowing in and the pulses of rain lulling me to sleep.

"Wasn't it windy last night?" I said. "It must have blown off its pole."

"No. It was windy before it rained, but I came home late, after the rain had passed and the wind had died. The plane was still there. The wind didn't blow again, and in the morning the plane was gone."

"Maybe it was stolen. Somebody's playing a joke on you. I bet one of your uncles took it."

"No, no, no, Monsieur Will. I asked myself these same questions as I stood in the yard this morning, looking up at the pole where my plane used to be. Did the plane blow off? No: there was no wind late at night, and the plane's not in the yard or the fields. Did someone climb the pole and steal it? No: there's no sign of anyone entering the yard. Did some fetisher fly in and take it? Maybe, but I think this plane's magic is stronger than the magic of my enemies. It must have flown on its own. So I asked myself: where has it flown? And why? And who was the pilot? I asked myself: who can explain this thing to me? And I answered: our consultant. He understands machines and flight; he's actually flown himself, many times, and he's come to teach us how such miracles can become commonplace."

This was not the sort of consultation I had prepared myself for, not a subject that was ever broached in *Products of the Oil Palm*. But maybe it was time to create some expertise out of the materials at hand. I sighed, and looked up at the sky.

"If your plane can really fly, it might have flown a long ways."

"Yes!"

"Beyond the Kivila Valley, perhaps. To Kisaka, even."

"Maybe."

"But why should it land in Kisaka? Why not keep going?"

"Why not? It might still be flying, Monsieur Will. Even while we stand here talking."

"Maybe. Crossing deserts. Crossing the ocean. Flying to Mputu, maybe."

"Yes, yes! Monsieur! That's exactly what I thought—it must be flying to Mputu!"

Ndosi laughed, slapped my shoulder, pumped my hand. I laughed with him. He was so full of joy, and he *was* funny, and *I* was funny. But I had to wonder who was bullshitting whom. If it hadn't been such a hot and steep trek up to the savanna, I might have been tempted to go look over the sight of the miracle myself. But what could I have made of a single bamboo pole standing above fields of knife-blade grass and a yard where old men sat in the shade with a calabash of palm wine, muttering at one another? Anyway, I was not at liberty to play consultant all morning long. Our bidóns were dry, the cupboards were empty, a pile of laundry was mildewing in the corner of the bedroom. It was time to be the boy again.

The morning clouds had rolled away. The sun shone bright and warm but not yet fierce; the night's rain still cooled the earth. I decided to start with the laundry. Ndosi waited on the porch while I went into the bedroom to gather up the dirty clothes. Beneath the mosquito netting Kate's breathing was deep and rhythmic. I put the clothes in a basket and left the room without approaching her. Ndosi took the basket from me, carried it down to the river, and sat high on the bank while I soaped and scrubbed, rubbed and beat.

"You should use more soap," he called out. "You should scrub harder." But he wouldn't come down and demonstrate. Sunlight sparkled on the green river. Kingfishers swooped over the water; hyacinth spun in the bright currents. I worked up a sweat scrubbing and dove in. Splashing and diving in the sun-warmed water, I found it easy to laugh at the tales the villagers told, the myths of old terrors: crocodiles and fetishers and malevolent spirits of the black water.

But Ndosi huddled in the shadows high on the bank, his spirits subdued, and when I splashed him he shivered and moved farther up the bank. I went back to beating the clothes. "You should use more soap," he said again, grumpily, but I'd had my fill of the laundry. The clothes looked distinctly gray, but there was always a chance they would lighten hanging in the sun. Again Ndosi took the basket, and we scrambled up the path to hang the clothes in the sunny yard.

Away from the river Ndosi's spirits revived. He amused himself by pointing out the many stains and smudges on the clothes we were hanging. "You didn't get them clean at all, Mr. Will! All you did was get them wet."

"I only know how to wash clothes in a machine," I said. "I thought you were going to help me instead of sitting up on the bank, pouting."

"I wanted to help you, only you went to the river. But there's no point in hanging them to dry now, still dirty. Put them back in the basket, and I'll take them to the source and wash them."

"What are you saying? They get clean in the source but not the river?"

"No. It's just that for me, the river is dangerous." He began taking the wet clothes off the line and putting them back in the basket. The river was forbidden to him, he explained. If he were to bathe in it or boat on it or fish in it or even eat fish that came from it, he was asking for trouble. When he was compelled to cross it he stood in the middle of the ferry, his eyes fixed on the opposite bank. Seldom did he come as close to it as he had this morning.

His fear of the river, he said, was a thing that had been passed down to him, an inheritance that had something to do with his sorcerer uncle, though it went further back than that, to some history of murder and unconsummated vengeance from the distant past, and a curse still carrying through the years to threaten him. This curse didn't seem to affect other members of his family, some of whom lived in Malembe, their ancestral riverside village. In fact, his cousins the Nakahosa brothers were fishermen, setting fishing lines in the river and standing up in low pirogues to skillfully paddle from set to set. But years ago, some dream or vision or intuitive realization had told Ndosi that he carried this river curse, and he had accepted it and gone up to the savanna to live with his uncles and turn his eyes to the sky.

Now all the clothes were returned to the baskets, but Ndosi made no move to carry them to the source. Instead he stood looking around the yard with a critical eye.

"This place isn't like it used to be," he commented.

"We're fixing it up," I said. "Little by little."

He nodded, but didn't look convinced. He stared at Dimanche's gate, standing in its absurd isolation on the edge of the fenceless yard.

"I'm getting ready to put up a fence," I explained. "And Kate wants chickens, so we'll be fixing up that chicken shed. Also, I'm putting in a big garden. See? We've already started the compost pile."

I pointed to a small mound of leaves and kitchen garbage, but Ndosi's gaze rested on the chicken shed. I studied it with him, and saw for the first time how far beyond "fixing up" it was. It looked more like a compost pile than the compost pile did. Ndosi turned to look at the garden, where a few weeks before I had made a tiny clearing among the vines and saplings. But already it was nearly overgrown again.

"I remember these gardens," Ndosi finally said. "When I was a child they were still beautiful. Terraces, with flowering bushes and fruit trees and vegetables from Mputu. Like the vegetables the sisters at the mission grow. And brick paths between the terraces, smooth yellow bricks. We'd sneak in and steal vegetables to take back to our mothers, or fruit to eat ourselves. But I think already the gardens were mostly abandoned and becoming overgrown."

"Weren't people living in these houses?"

"Sometimes, I think. There were guards, at least. But usually they were drunk or asleep. The whites were gone by then. There weren't any on this side of the river. But to us children it seemed as though the gardens still belonged to them. We called these the Road Builder's gardens, even though we'd never seen the Road Builder."

"The Road Builder. Who was he? I mean, what was his name?"

"I don't know, monsieur. I never heard his name. Everyone just called him the Road Builder."

I remember the names of the roads, Uncle Pers had murmured dreamily at his dining room table. And later he had said, not dreamily at all: *Ask questions, continue the research. But don't mention my name.*

"Tell me how this yard used to look," I said to Ndosi.

He nodded. "Ah, oui. I remember all that. I remember exactly how it used to look."

But he didn't say anything else, he just kept studying the yard, and finally I said I was going inside, figuring he would take up the laundry and go rewash it, as he'd said he would. But maybe I'd misunderstood him; maybe he hadn't said anything about the laundry at all. He left it in the yard and followed me into the house, where he sat at the kitchen table amid the clutter of dirty dishes and pots and pans and books and papers, and looked around with that same critical gaze. I was embarrassed by the mess, but on the other hand I hadn't invited him in. Or maybe I had. Anyway, I had no idea what I was supposed to do with him now.

"I was about to make some coffee," I said. "Would you like some coffee?"

He nodded. Actually, I hadn't been about to make coffee. More coffee was the last thing my nearly empty stomach needed. I'd come inside with the vague idea of finding something to eat, but now that would have to wait until

I got rid of Ndosi, so I wouldn't be compelled to share whatever morsel I might scavenge.

"I need paper," he said, as if the need were obvious, as if I were neglecting my basic duty as a host. "And a pen."

I brought him pen and notebook paper, and shoved the clutter on the table to one side. While I made the coffee he bent over the paper, drawing something. I heard Kate stirring in the bedroom, but Ndosi did not look up. In a moment she appeared in the doorway, blurry and pallid and hung over, nothing like my vision of female flesh in soft focus beneath the mosquito netting. She squinted at Ndosi and shook his hand, gave me a questioning look, shrugged, and said she was going to the river to bathe.

Ndosi poured about half a cup of sugar into his coffee. While he stirred it he showed me his drawing—a diagram of geometric shapes, intriguing little symbols, and neat labels written out in a precise and beautiful hand. At the top of the page he'd written: "The Road Builder's Gardens."

"That's how they were, monsieur," he said flatly, and took a loud slurp of his coffee.

"Come on outside," I said. "You can explain it to me."

I went outside and stood in the center of the yard, trying to orient the diagram. Ndosi didn't follow, but for the moment I was just as glad to have the drawing and the yard to myself. Maybe at last I was on to something. It gave me a little thrill, just holding that paper in my hand, poring over it as if it were a map of buried treasure. In the context of the overgrown yard it really did make some sense. Here was how it all had been laid out: the terraces and the stairways, the lush garden beds with their brick borders, the fountain, the pond. But what a contrast between the entangled wilderness of the yard and the meticulous ordered beauty of the drawing! The drawing was something out of the lost past, a memory that was decipherable, maybe, but no longer attainable. I wandered to the far corners of the compound, pushing my way through the dense foliage, making small discoveries, confirming here and there the accuracy of Ndosi's memory. And wondering all the time if this was a meaningful connection, "research," as Pers understood it: one of his unconformities at last taking on shape and substance.

On the path above the house someone was singing, high and melodic. I emerged from the bushes just as a young woman swung past the gate and came skipping into the yard, all bright colors and exuberant motion and plump, voluptuous flesh. It was the chef de poste's new girlfriend. His dux-ième bureau, people called her. She saw me on the edge of the bushes and abruptly stopped singing.

"Monsieur! You're here."

"Oui."

"They said you were down at the river."

"I was."

"Washing your own clothes, they said! And madame's!" She giggled.

"Oui. I was washing clothes."

"We didn't know you knew how to wash clothes, monsieur." She broke into a fuller laughter, then cocked her head and looked curiously at the paper in my hand. "But now you're out in your garden," she said. "Reading a letter, monsieur?"

"No. I'm studying something. A plan."

"Ah, bon. A plan." She nodded, and looked around the yard. When she noticed the baskets of wet clothes she began laughing all over again.

"Now you're going to have to learn how to *dry* clothes, monsieur! They don't dry if you leave them in the basket. Ça ne va pas! You have to hang them on the line."

She tossed her head, and with a peal of silvery laughter flounced off toward the guest house. I walked up to the open part of my yard and saw her looking back from the door of the guest house, still laughing at me, maybe— a flash of her brilliant white teeth, a final sashay of her round bouncing ass as she slipped inside.

I stayed out in the yard a few minutes longer, but the intrigue of Ndosi's diagram had faded and I found myself glancing periodically at the guest house, where the chef de poste and his duxième bureau met several after-noons a week. Everyone in the camp knew, presumably even his wife, though she was rarely seen on this side of the river.

Ndosi came out of my house, singing, with an empty water bidón in hand. He said nothing about his drawing or the Road Builder's gardens. Instead he called out something about somebody slaughtering a goat and how someone ought to go to the marché and buy meat and how it was too bad we had no onions because without onions it would be difficult to make a truly excellent goat stew. He put the bidón in the basket of clothes and took up the basket and balanced it on his head, then set off down the path, singing again, before it occurred to me to wonder how *he* knew that we had no onions.

I went into the house. The dishes had been washed and put away, and the floor swept. Our small stores of food were neatly arranged on the pantry shelves, and the pots, pans, and dishes were organized and stacked. Shelves, floor, stove, and table all had been wiped down, and the clutter in the living room and bedroom was gone. The cobwebs were swept from the corners, the floor scrubbed and seemingly polished. Books were lined up between bookends, papers placed in orderly piles, and for the first time in weeks the desk was free of rotting garbage. But the change was more fundamental than cleaning and straightening. Each object in the house had been in some way rearranged, and the result was a new sense of balance, proportion, and space: the tiny cubicles seemed to have opened up under the touch of a careful hand, an orderly mind.

I looked again in the pantry, wondering if in organizing the food Ndosi might have found me something to eat. But then I heard voices outside. I went to the window. Ndosi and Kate were stopped in the road below, talking. After a moment they parted, Ndosi heading down the road and Kate ascending the path. Streams of water ran off her hair, onto her shoulders and down her back. She had mastered the African woman's trick of wrapping her wet body in a single pagne after her bath, and she moved confidently, without a hand on the pagne. But I couldn't tell what kept it from falling off. The thin, damp cotton seemed to adhere to her skin, as if held in place by a static charge.

I sat at the kitchen table and watched her come to the doorway. She stopped just outside, wringing water from her hair and looking around the room in delight.

"The house looks so nice, Will! I didn't think it was possible."

"Yeah. It's kind of weird, though. I can't figure out what's come over Ndosi."

"Well, maybe he has a natural aptitude for order. Unlike some boys I know. I can't tell you what a relief it is to see you finally coming to your senses about the boy thing."

"Who says I've come to my senses?"

"Well, you got Ndosi to straighten up the house, and then you sent him off to do the laundry and get water. So it *seems* like you're coming to your senses. Relatively."

"Look, I don't know what he's up to. He volunteered to do the laundry. Then he went inside and cleaned the house. I didn't tell him a thing."

"A coup, then! He probably figures he'll just do your job until it becomes obvious that it's *his* job. Which might not take very long."

"He does seem to be a lot better at it than I am."

"He needs it more, too. He needs money. He's courting that girl up in the camp. You've seen her, haven't you? Just a child, maybe thirteen or fourteen years old, but he's planning on marrying her as soon as he can put together a down payment on the bride price. But now he's lost his fishponds—his main source of income—and he's worried. He really needs a job."

"He lost his fishponds?"

She went into the bedroom, and came back brushing her hair. She moved around easily and never adjusted the pagne, which stayed in place, perfectly wrapped and tucked. "His uncles took possession of them. They filed a complaint with the chef de groupment, a kind of trespassing charge against him. The groupment'll uphold it, since he's a crony of the uncles, and anyway Ndosi doesn't have any kind of hard claim to the land, besides the fact that he's the only one who's worked it in the last twenty-five years."

I asked where she had gone during the night. She had been to the child's funeral, she said, dancing and talking with people, and then they got word that a truck was stuck on a muddy road, and a bunch of them had gone to push it out.

"In the middle of the night?"

"I guess the driver was in a hurry. Boy, it was a long way to walk, though. Of course, they *told* me it was only a little ways. Well, it would have been, if I were driving. I don't see how anyone can expect me to *walk* all over the place like that."

"Who expects you to?"

She leaned against the kitchen table, next to where I was sitting. She set her hairbrush aside and looked down at me. "People have all kinds of expectations, Will. But I hope they're not expecting much today, because right now I'm going back to bed."

"Why was the driver in a hurry?"

"Well, he wasn't supposed to be there."

"What do you mean? Did he have some kind of contraband?"

"Well, sure. Practically everything is contraband around here, if somebody wants to get a fair price for it. That's the reality of it. I guess the question for us is, how are *we* going to deal with that reality?"

She seemed to have edged closer, so that the pagne clung to her thighs only inches from my face, and I was thinking: *No, the question is how are we going to deal with the reality of this pagne, and the curious force that keeps it clinging to your body. How will we deal with the drop of river water caught in the down on the cleft of your lip.* That water sparkled. It bent light, *radiated* light; it alone might have been the source of the potent smells of wet clay and river plants coming off her body. It also probably teemed with *giardia* and *ascaris* and hostile *E. coli,* so I stood and untucked a corner of the pagne and wiped it away before I kissed her.

Carefully I tucked the pagne back in, but I must have disturbed the static charges, because the cloth began to slip. I tried to fix it but Kate only shrugged and pulled me back against her and kissed me again. I tasted river water still on her lips and in her mouth, but fear of microorganisms was already slipping from my mind. When she stopped kissing me and moved away from the table the pagne slid off her breasts, down her back, and hung for a moment on her hips. It slid farther as she walked, and fell away from her legs to the floor as she crossed the doorway into the living room.

It was only a short distance across the living room to the bedroom, but as I followed her I was aware again of the new spaciousness in our house, which in turn seemed to expand the time spent crossing to the bedroom. It gave me a chance to study things. The figurines and masks, expressionless now, mere museum pieces powerless to invoke nausea or fear. The subtle roll and sway of Kate's hips, the arching geometry of her back, the long smooth reach of her leg as she stood in the doorway, kicking off her sandals. There was time to consider a new smell in the bedroom, like a reminder of clean moss, grottos, river rock, and clay. Was that the smell brought up from the river on Kate's skin? Or could it be something liberated from old cement and brick and plaster that had been scrubbed for the first time in years?

She knelt on the bed and threw back the mosquito netting, then waited, still kneeling, for me to come to her. But before I closed the bedroom door I turned away for a moment and looked back on the room we'd just walked through. A sandal lay in the center of the floor, a table was knocked askew, and a pagne lay crumpled in the kitchen doorway. It seemed we required only a brief passage to upset the delicate new order of the room. And when later I lay next to her, listening to her breathing going slow and deep, I saw that in our short and dreamlike occupancy of the bedroom we had already begun to return it, too, to its accustomed state of disorder. The sheets lay tangled beside the bed. Another sandal lay on its side in the doorway. My clothes were scattered from the door to the bedside, and the neat stack of books and magazines on the table had fallen in disarray to the floor.

As I dressed I watched Kate sleeping. She was restless, full of twitching, uneasy motion. Her skin looked so white, accentuating the dirty gray color of our bedsheet. I vaguely recalled noticing how brown her arm once had looked against the whiteness of the same sheet. But that must have been during our first days here; the longer we were in Africa, the whiter we became, and the dimmer our sheets. Perhaps someday Ndosi would be able to wash the gray from the sheets, but there was nothing to be done with the skin except continue to smother it with sunscreen, since unprotected it would only burn under the equatorial sun.

But Kate did have some color now: flushed cheeks and a rosy tinge along those pale arms, color that only seemed to further highlight the essential whiteness of her skin, because it was derived not from pigmentation but from blood flowing in her surface capillaries. It gave her a different look, a different aspect of beauty. Unnatural, you could say, like the extreme heat that had come off her body when she was clinging to me so fiercely a short while before.

I turned to leave. A sound came from her throat, like a cry. She might have been calling my name. She was staring at me, but I wasn't sure she was awake until she began to speak, her voice slow and still hoarse, as if she remained hovering on the very edge of sleep all the time she was telling me, or maybe telling herself, about the dream she'd just woken from.

She was walking at night on a path in the jungle, she said, with a group of women; it was as if they were African women coming back from the peanut field, though most of them were girls she'd known years before in college, girls she was certain would never be found with a hoe in a peanut field even in somebody's dream, yet here they were, walking in the jungle with hoes on their heads, to all appearances much more at ease with the situation than she was, since *her* hoe teetered and slid on her smooth hair and she had to keep shifting her balance and tilting her head and performing graceless contortions with her neck and shoulders (but never reaching up to steady it with her hand) to keep it from falling off, and she kept stumbling on the rough road anyway, getting anxious about the hoe and trying to keep her footing. She didn't really think about the body she tripped over on the road until sometime after she had passed it, and then she suddenly panicked and turned away from the other women and rushed back alone, the hoe bouncing and tumbling on her head but still miraculously not falling, even as she got on her hands and knees to search desperately along the road. In the thickening darkness she could make out nothing, but she found the body by touch. She was filled with dread; she knew she was stumbling on a knowledge she didn't want, running her hands over a man's body and through the warm and sticky fluid that coated it and pooled beneath it on the ground. It came to her that her hands were bathed in a stranger's blood on an African road. She thought of AIDS, she thought of Ebola, and then she realized that she recognized the contours of this face and body. Her fingers knew what her mind still would not acknowledge. She forced herself to think who of all the people in her life she would know by touch alone, and in the instant before she opened her eyes and saw me turning in the doorway, she arrived at the only possible answer.

14

COMPANY STORE

Kate drifted back into a fitful sleep, and I left the room. I gathered up my wallet and a raffia shopping bag, wrote a quick shopping list, and had a drink of fresh water from the full bidón that had appeared in the corner of the kitchen. Then I stepped from the cool interior of the house into full-afternoon sunlight on the porch.

As I crossed the threshold—probably because I'd still had nothing to eat all day but a bowl of oatmeal and a few bites of Matama's mystery stew, and also because I'd just written the word "eggs" on the shopping list, though there was almost no chance of finding any at the company store—I remembered for the first time in years an illustration in a science book I'd had as a kid, dramatizing the temperature difference between the sunny and shaded sides of the planet Mercury: an astronaut knelt in the cold darkness, holding a skillet out of the shadows to fry a couple of eggs in the heat of the sun. At the time I must have interpreted this as a literal illustration of a remarkable but well-established Fact of Science, and so it had stuck with me and now resurfaced, an image so convincing I might have been tempted to try something similar on the porch of my house, except that if I'd had any eggs I would have been inside frying them on a propane stove, and eating them.

In any case, it *was* like the top of a stove out on the porch, or an oven: a wall of heat slamming into me when the door opened, heat and light glaring off the pounded red clay of the yard and the whitewashed walls of the house. But I was prepared for this when I opened the door. In a way, I looked forward to the plunge, to the shock of contrasting sensations: stepping from a dim refuge of books and papers, cool vessels of water, dreaming wife, into that harsh afternoon, with its heat and glare and grinding noise of the palm oil mill.

But the yard was billowing and bright, strung with banners and tapestries as if to welcome dignitaries or celebrate some grand occasion. Actually it was only the laundry, rewashed by Ndosi and now hung out to dry. Still it was something to step into: the brilliant whites, the pastel colors in the sun, curtains of windblown cloth rippling in a clearing above the shining river. It would have made a terrific detergent ad. But there had been no detergent. Like me, Ndosi had used harsh and greasy palm oil soap. But somehow for him the clothes had come clean.

For a moment it seemed that the laundry had changed things in the yard. It billowed in a hot wind, breaking up the light and the open reflective spaces. It seemed to absorb or dissipate the heat, or perhaps despite the humidity there was an effect of evaporative cooling as the clothes dried. Though the truth was that no process of nature—not evaporation, not absorption and diffusion of sunlight, not even shade—could really ease the humid blood-boiling heat of an average Kivila Valley rainy-season afternoon. Yet I remained on the porch, catching the full force of the sun on my untanned face, feeling the sweat drip down my chest and soak into my T-shirt. I understood that I too was absorbing something from the heat, some insight or revelation or pure form of energy. Could that be how it feels to convert light and heat and moisture to carbon compounds, essential sugars? Photosynthesis—a power that comes of surrender, surrender to the sun, the way we surrendered to the rest of it: to the sensuality and the nausea, the rain and the mud and the smells, the waiting and the confusion, the pressure and sweat of bodies, the fevers, the roasted crickets, the fiery orange stews, the hollow insistent anxiety in the belly.

The laundry rippled, and at the end of the line a towel flapped, opening up among the pale colors of the clothes a patch of bright red earth. Wind gusted, and a couple of shirts sailed up, revealing for a second a framed view of the river and the houses on the opposite bank. A sheet blew off the line, and I saw the porch of the guest house, where the chef de poste stood smoking and sweating and watching the same sheet falling, his face contorted a little in what, from that distance, had the look of deep and ironic thought. His gaze shifted to my porch, but neither of us waved though each of us, chef and chef's consultant, stood on his own porch watching the other's porch, framed by the same underwear and towels, each with a house at his back, and in each house a dim room where a woman slept naked on crumpled sheets.

Of course, I really couldn't say where the chef's duxième bureau was or what the two of them may have been doing together. His second office. People called her that matter-of-factly, as if it were a job title. His wife had one job, and her duty station was their house on the other side of the river, and his duxième bureau had a slightly different job, and her duty station was somewhere inside the otherwise unoccupied guest house. I never had entered the guest house myself, and had no way of knowing what it might be like inside. But it was easy enough to imagine well-swept rooms, painted cement floors, sparse mahogany furniture, and long hallways that remained silent and cool even when outside the sun blazed and the mill howled. And deep in the interior a shadowed, muffled room furnished with a single chair, a small table, a kerosene lamp, and a duxième bureau, plump and naked and slumped on the bed, trying to muster the will to wrap herself in her pagne and slip on her plastic shoes.

The chef threw out his cigarette and seemed to laugh to himself. Then he turned and went down his porch stairs and off toward the mill. Finally I too got down from my porch and into the shade, and after cooling off a few degrees I remembered that I was hungry, on my way to buy groceries at the company store.

The company store was a gloomy brick structure on the hillside above the mill, as corroded and mildewed as any other colonial building in the camp. There was no sign to indicate the place was a store, nothing at all to distinguish it from the similar buildings that people lived in. The usual cracked and crumbling cement steps led up to the small porch, though in this case the first step was only a teetering rock. Inside it was dusky even in midday; the only light came through the door and a couple of heavily grated windows high in the walls. At first, before my eyes adjusted, I saw only the larger details: the towering shelves, the huge bare counter. On the raised floor behind the counter the storekeeper stood, blending with the shadows except for the glittering whites of his eyes. The eyes of a couple of despondent customers turned to me as well, and I nodded a greeting to the entire company. At the same time the smells hit me: palm oil and kerosene, mildew, and musty, decomposing brick. But mostly what I smelled was macayabu, salted dried fish, though in fact I knew it was very unlikely that the storekeeper had any actual macayabu in stock. At one time he'd probably had a regular supply, and on occasion he still got a box of it in, and those rare occurrences were enough to keep the smell of it permanently on hand. And the way I felt about macayabu was that the smell alone ought to satisfy any desire for the thing itself.

As my eyes grew accustomed to the dim light I could make out a couple dozen cans on the shelf: sardines, Vienna sausages, corned beef. A sack of salt lay on the floor beside stacks of greasy yellow bars of soap. There were a few bolts of dingy cloth, and a half dozen shirts that had been folded for so long, yellow stains were visible along the creases. The only item that was truly plentiful was skin lightener, which was available in several different brands and filled up an entire shelf. Mostly, though, what I saw was empty: empty shelves, empty bottles, the long empty counter that separated the storekeeper from the rest of us.

The woman ahead of me was buying salt, about a quarter kilo, from the look of it. The storekeeper added a pinch, squinted at his scale, took a couple of pinches away. The woman complained, and the storekeeper, grumbling, brushed a couple of tiny chunks back onto her pile. My stomach growled loudly but no one acknowledged it. This was not a store where people joked and told stories, where men loitered on the benches and talked about the weather or the old times. People kept silent in the company store, at least when I was there. It was the kind of place where you did your business and got out as quickly as you could. But you could never get out quickly.

Like the building he inhabited, the storekeeper was a construction of a ruined feudal estate, a colonial relic clinging with a fool's pride to the crumbling remains of empire. He had a flat and officious demeanor that did not disguise his nostalgia for the days when white people gazed past him at well-stocked shelves and a humming refrigerator full of butter and cheese and beer, or his scorn for the impoverished peasants who now bought from him their salt and soap, palm oil, kerosene, and an occasional bit of cloth.

Probably my presence aggravated these emotions in him. He seemed to want to keep me in his store as long as possible, though we had little to say to each other. Still, he managed to prolong our transactions, because with me he spoke French, and used his machine.

At last the salt was poured into a cone of paper, money was exchanged, and the woman left. The storekeeper went into the back room, and we waited in silence. Eventually the storekeeper reemerged, without explanation or apology. The other customers stepped back against the wall, looking at the floor or at the far end of the room. Perhaps they were not customers at all. The storekeeper turned to me, as if he had only just become aware of my presence. "Ah. Bonjour, Consultant."

"Good morning, Storekeeper."

He bowed toward me. "How can I serve you, Patrón?" With the store-keeper there was no middle ground—it was either a studied rudeness or this exaggerated politesse. Either way, I was always reminded that I was in the domain of a petty tyrant and that it was in my interest to indulge his pre-tenses and affectations. It was best to act as if the store were bustling, the shelves at his back loaded with desirable goods, and the storekeeper himself a central figure in a drama of commerce and prosperity. This meant I couldn't look too hard at the few cans of Vienna sausages, whose presence only called attention to the emptiness surrounding them, and which must have been, come to think of it, the same five cans, in the same configuration, I'd stared at the previous time I was here and thought better of purchasing. But who would buy them besides me? In fact, a good part of the stuff in the store—not just the Vienna sausages or sardines or canned corned beef, but the rice, the sugar, the tins of oatmeal and powdered milk—were things you never saw most local people eat, which maybe explained why they remained in stock in this store.

If the storekeeper grumbled, I sympathized: sure, it's a lot of work for an old man to run this store, heavy boxes and bags to move around, piles of worthless money to count, all those figures to sort out in his head, and no sup-port from the management, no appreciation from the populace. And if he came at me with his mission-school manners, I tried to play the part as well, as if I were a distinguished and discerning client and he a well-bred servant, both of us belonging to a social enterprise secure in its hierarchies and its foreordi-nation. I did whatever I had to: flatter him, indulge him, patronize him—any-body who calls me "Patrón" has got a little patronizing coming. Only I wouldn't speak French with him. His French, with its unnatural nasal tones and strangled guttural r, was a real abomination, even to my abominable ear. And once he went beyond his few stock phrases, his grammar was so muti-lated and his vocabulary so confused that the words lost all meaning, though they did retain a kind of pathos, evoking the image of a colonial schoolroom, where children repeat their French lesson in fearful chorus and the schoolmaster stalks behind the wooden benches, rapping the knuckles of those whose liaisons are staccato, whose *r*s roll off their tongues instead of out of their constricted throats.

But sympathy for the storekeeper's unfortunate education was pointless and in any case would not get me out of the store any quicker. Mostly that was beyond my control, but there were a few delays I could circumvent. I knew, for example, not to request more than one item at a time. "Two kilos of rice," I said in Kituba, and waited.

"Oui, monsieur. Eh, two kilos of rice." He shuffled over to the rice, dished some out in a bucket, whacked his scale with a spoon, dumped some rice back, fiddled with the scale, added some rice, studied the result. Then he looked at me and waited.

"You have no plastic bag, monsieur?"

Damn. Forgetting a plastic bag is a good way to draw out the ordeal. Now the storekeeper had to duck behind the counter, scrabble around, disappear in the back of the store for a while, and eventually come out with a couple of sheets of newspaper, which he folded into cones. He poured the rice in, folded the ends over, and set the package carefully on the counter. "Would you care for another item, monsieur?"

"A kilo of sugar."

After my third request—five candles—the storekeeper heaved a sigh. His politesse was nearly exhausted. He pulled out his notepad and wrote down my purchases and the amounts. Complications were minimal, since most of what I asked for was out of stock. No eggs, no potatoes, no onions, no beer, no kerosene in spite of the fumes. I broke down and bought a can of corned beef. The corned beef was actually quite edible, a big step up from Vienna sausages or sardines, but the price was so extravagant that I was embarrassed to be seen buying it. No one else in town, not even the chef de poste, could afford such a luxury, which made me wonder how long it had sat on the shelves. The storekeeper turned the can in his hand with what might have been a sentimental touch, a gesture of longing—not for the corned beef itself, perhaps, but for the days when it was a common thing to put such a can on the counter in front of a white man.

Now the storekeeper bent over his notepad and studied his figures. "I'll get my machine," he announced, and from an otherwise bare shelf he took down a calculator and began to punch in figures. This machine was not something he used with the average customer—the villager or farmer or mill worker—but only with people of higher status, like me. It was an honor he conferred on me—a tedious and exasperating honor, and the longest part of the entire procedure. By now there were several other people waiting, but the storekeeper did not look up from his machine, and the people themselves did not complain. Going to the store, like almost everything else in life, involved waiting a long time for no very good reason. Finally, with a dramatic flourish the storekeeper punched the total, looked up at me, and, as if he were throwing out a challenge, announced his conclusion. I paid, put my purchases in my raffia bag, and got out. He would have to be off by several orders of magnitude for me to consider arguing with his machine.

Again I stepped out of a dim cool room onto a sunblasted porch. But this time I didn't stop to contemplate frying eggs or human photosynthesis or any of that foolishness. I was too intent on escaping from the company store and all its wretched associations. But in my hurry I took the steps too quickly, and misgauged the distance to the unstable rock that served as the bottom step. I came onto it off balance; the rock shifted, and my ankle, weakened from my tumble into the ditch the night before, gave way. I went down hard. People rushed to the porch of the store, warning me to watch my step, and a gravelly voice boomed from the path below, "Attention, Consultant! Slowly, slowly, slowly! Are you hurt?"

It was the chef de poste, coming up the path with his duxième bureau on one arm and a long pole and tripod tucked under the other. The storekeeper appeared in the doorway behind his customers, machine still in hand, and the chef began to shout at him. The duxième bureau disengaged herself from the chef's arm and knelt by my side.

"Are you all right, monsieur?" she said. "Have you broken your leg?"

I didn't answer, because I was in pain, and also because I was startled to find the duxième bureau suddenly so close beside me, looking not at all as she had looked in the sun-addled vision I'd experienced on my porch, all heavy-fleshed and slumped over in a post-coital torpor. She looked fresh and bright and full of genuine concern, and the hand she laid tentatively on my shoulder was soft, in contrast to this incredibly hard ground I had just smashed into. It was difficult to believe that it had once been soil, now compacted into something like pavement by decades of pounding rain. Or that a substance so solid was capable of eroding—though, judging by the rills and gullies all around me, it still was. And then, feeling the duxième bureau's soothing touch on my shoulder and staring at the gullied red earth and the rock step that had tripped me up, I had my second revelation of the day. I suppose I'd assumed that the original lowest step had somehow been lost or destroyed and subsequently replaced by the rock. But now as I looked at the steps and the earth and the algae-coated foundation of the building, I realized that initially that first step had not existed at all, or rather that the first step had been the earth itself, and during the forty or fifty years of the building's existence several vertical feet of soil had eroded away from the entire surrounding area, exposing the foundation and leaving the steps high in the air, accessible only by the rock that someone had placed below them.

The chef finished shouting, and the storekeeper whined a response. The chef turned to me.

"The carpenter will build a new step this afternoon. I already have the cement. I told the storekeeper to close the store so work can begin. He says he doesn't want to close, what will people eat? Ha! Usually he doesn't want to open when I tell him to, what will people buy? Anyway, what does he prefer, his customers breaking their legs coming out of his store? How is your ankle, monsieur?"

I told him that my ankle was probably going to be all right, but already he had turned away and was shouting again. Two men jumped down from the porch and rolled the rock away from the base of the steps, pushing it off down the hill. Now alone on the porch the storekeeper seemed remote, as if he had finally been set entirely adrift. He stared down at us, then abruptly drew back and disappeared into the gloom. One day he would not emerge from that darkness, but still the torrential rains would keep falling and the denuded soil would wash downslope and the company store would recede farther and farther from the ground upon which it stood.

The duxième bureau helped me to my feet. She and the chef de poste each took an arm and escorted me down the hill, and I leaned against one, then the other, as we descended, not so much for the support as to feel the opulence of their flesh, an antidote to the skeletal poverty of the company store.

"If you planted some grass," I suggested to the chef, "this sort of thing might not happen."

The chef stopped walking, so the duxième bureau and I had to stop as well. He let go of my arm, leaned on the pole and tripod he was carrying, and stared at me in disbelief. "What are you talking about? You want a soft landing? Grass isn't going to help, if people want to be reckless. If people are going to throw themselves off of dangerous heights like that."

"That's not what I mean. I mean, if you planted grass, you wouldn't have erosion. The earth would stay on the same level, and you wouldn't end up with a step a half meter off the ground."

The chef said something to his duxième bureau, and she too let go of my arm. She cooed solicitously at me one more time, giggled, and skipped off up the path toward the camp. The chef and I watched her go. Then he looked at me again, and laughed. "Monsieur Will, how does your ankle feel?"

"It hurts. But it's nothing serious."

"Nothing serious. You throw yourself off a big step, maybe you hurt your ankle a little. But assume we plant grass and there is no erosion, as you say. No big step, no twisted ankle. Instead you come down on the nice soft grass, *where the snake lies hidden!* Zup! You get bit! You now what a snakebite on your ankle feels like? You know what it does to you? Kills you, or maybe worse. So, William, what do you prefer: snakes, or a little erosion?"

"They have grass all over the mission, Chef, and I never hear about people getting snakebit."

"Oh, the mission! You know why there aren't any snakes? Because they kill them so fast. Because the pères pay cash for every dead snake, so everybody's out killing snakes instead of working. They plant grass, the snakes come, they pay people to kill the snakes. This is what the pères call economic development. But I don't have that kind of money, so we just keep the snakes away. Maybe the pères like throwing their money around like that. Maybe they have a use for all those snakes. You know what they do with them?"

"I have no idea."

"Well, you never know with the pères. Any man who hasn't touched a woman in forty years you have to wonder about. That is, if you can believe in such a thing in the first place."

The celibacy of the pères and soeurs was a favorite theme of the chef de poste. In turn he was fascinated, appalled, skeptical, even grudgingly admiring of their alleged abstinence. The practice of foregoing sex for an entire lifetime was one of the most outlandish ideas he'd ever encountered, and he'd spent a lot of time puzzling over how and why anyone would ever do it. He was also obliged to defend himself against the criticisms of the fathers, who condemned his wanton behavior—his duxième bureau and casual infidelities in the villages.

Sometimes he was scornful of the pères' righteousness, probing lewdly for hypocrisy and chinks in their moral armor. "Consultant," he said to me once, chuckling, "you've been inside the pères' house. Is it true that Père Andrés' bed is wide enough for him and two fat women besides?" Or: "Consultant, can you explain why there are so many mulatto children born to the women of Bulolo, the most pious village in the region? Is this a sign of the favor of God?" But now his mood seemed more serious, as if he really wanted me to provide him with some insight into the whole inexplicable question of celibacy.

So I threw out in no particular order whatever explanations occurred to me: it's a form of religious ecstasy, a practical response to the barrage of stimuli and distractions a priest must contend with. It's a purification of sorts. A discipline, a simplification, a way of achieving concentration. A path to a higher plane of spirituality, or something. After a couple sentences of this I lost myself in improbable French cognates and Kituba syntax errors, but the chef de poste bent his head toward me, his face wrinkled in concentration, trying to make some sense of it. He lit a cigarette and took a couple of deep puffs before he answered.

"Well," he said, "maybe it's not quite as crazy as it seems. How could a priest help anybody else with their problems if he had the biggest problem of all in his own house, in his own bed? Married life is just too complicated. You're always chasing around after some problem or another. Priest couldn't do his job with a woman around. Look, Priest is supposed to run off to some village to say Mass, but his wife disappears: he's not going to show up for Mass, he's got to look for her. Or he's hearing confession, and his wife gets in the box and tells him she's been having an affair—he's not going to absolve her, he's got to beat her. You're right, Monsieur Will, it wouldn't work. The way it is now, priests can concentrate on their jobs: say Mass, hear confessions, grow tomatoes, plant grass, read books, drink beer, whatever they want. They don't waste time worrying about what their women are doing, like other men do. Especially white men. Imagine a priest married to a white woman! Trying to keep track of her while she runs all over the country, wondering when dinner's going to be served, probably having to listen to her throw the scriptures back in his face whenever he tells her what to do."

"Well, he might find one who doesn't cause him quite that much trouble."

"You think so? Maybe." The chef smoked distractedly, and then demanded, "Where's Madame Kate? You have any idea?"

"In bed. Asleep."

"In the middle of the day? Oh, right, because she was out all night. You didn't sleep much last night either, I understand. I'm the chef, I know about these things. I have to know. But you don't look so good, William. You're getting skinny. I had a job I was going to ask you about, but now you've hurt your ankle, and anyway I can see you're in no shape for it."

"My ankle's fine. What job are you talking about?"

He held up the objects in his hand. "You know what these are?"

I looked more closely at them. "Sure." The pole was a surveyor's rod, and a brass level was mounted on the tripod—rusty, perhaps slightly crooked, and possibly missing some parts.

"I found them in the warehouse. I bet the Road Builder used this very level when we laid out the Ngasi Road, the Mission Road. But nobody's known what to do with it since. Now, though, my Modernization Project is getting under way, and a rod and level are just what we need. You know how to use them?"

"Not really. I mean, I understand the principles—"

"It doesn't matter. The secretary knows. He wants to start surveying right now, but he needs an assistant, somebody who understands, as you call them, the principles. But maybe you've got some reports to work on. Maybe you've got your own projects. Or maybe you should just go home and spend some time in bed with your wife."

I thought about my Consultant's Assessment, Ndosi's diagram for the garden, the chicken-shed-cum-compost-pile. "My projects can wait," I said. "Let's get going on the surveying."

A half hour later I was out in a sunny field next to the mill, surveying the site that was to become the Place de la Révolution, the centerpiece of the chef de poste's Modernization Project. I was assisting the chef's secretary, or he was assisting me. Perhaps because neither of us knew much about surveying, we quickly established a compatible working relationship. I called him "Secretary"; he called me "Consultant"; and we took turns holding the rod or squinting into the level. We pounded stakes, took notes, fiddled with screws and wing nuts, and discussed ways of compensating for what appeared to be an irreparable tilt in the plane of the instrument. Sweat poured down the secretary's face, but he did not seem to mind the brutal heat; clearly he was enjoying his novel toy and the opportunity to play engineer. I too was greatly taken by the rod and level, understanding that these elegant and mysterious instruments conferred on me a new legitimacy and authority, however illusory. And I took the white-collar-man's pleasure in a day of fieldwork, relishing the feel of mud beneath my boots and sweat running down my neck.

But I was weakened by lack of food, and the heat was getting to me. Bending over the cockeyed level, I suddenly felt dizzy and sick. The secretary was speaking intently to me, but I couldn't concentrate on his trigonomic improvisations and leaps of faith. I excused myself and fled into the shade of the big trees at the foot of the hill, where a small marché was doing a slow business. The secretary, who quickly recruited a couple of kids to hold the rod and move stakes around for him, seemed happy to have the level all to himself, so I leaned back against a tree and watched the marché.

It was a slow entertainment. The weekly marché was the chef de poste's idea, one of the first aspects of his Modernization Project to be enacted, but maybe Ngemba was not yet ready for a marché. There was a kind of tarp for shade, and a few tables of goods, but I didn't notice any actual buying and selling—the few people there seemed occupied mainly with watching the secretary's genuflections with his level. Heavy-lidded merchants slumped behind their tables. Flies buzzed around the severed head of a goat, which had been placed prominently on the table where the meat was sold, presumably to advertise the product but also, the butcher told me when I wandered over, so that customers could judge the quality of the meat by staring into those depthless eyes. Take a look for yourself, he said, see how healthy our goat is. I don't have to look at his eyes, I said, I can see at once that he's not healthy at all. Why, his head's not even attached to his body! This comment sparked the marché: everyone laughed, and one of the butchers stood up to slap me on the palm with his bloody hand. Pleased with myself for having successfully pulled off a joke in Kituba, however lame, I bought a kilo of meat. The butcher recounted my joke to the entire marché while he cut the meat, and everyone laughed again, inspiring him to throw in an extra half kilo for free.

There wasn't much else to buy. A woman sat behind a box of wilted greens, and another tried halfheartedly to entice me into buying one of the hideous-looking roots laid out on a cloth before her. That was pretty much the extent of the marché, except for the flashy fellow displaying a case of cigarettes at the base of a tree. A petit commerçant, who probably sold a few packs a day for a few cents a pack profit. But then, his work was not demanding. When I told my joke he laughed louder than anyone, but his laughter was vaguely annoying: high and ringing, and lasting longer that necessary. Even in the deep shade of the tree his jewelry glittered, and his clashing baggy clothes were jarring to the eye. I turned to the butcher.

"Well," I said, "it is nice to have a little marché in town."

He shrugged. "Not many people here agree with you, monsieur."

"What's the problem? Why are there so few customers?"

"They don't know what's good for them," said one of the women. "People in Ngemba are lazy and backward. They just want to eat manioc leaves all day."

The butcher laughed. "Maybe they're too backward to buy your shriveled greens, Mama, but everybody wants meat. The problem is, they can't afford it. They don't have money."

"Ç'est ça! Ç'est a dire, monsieur: pas d'argent."

A silky voice at my back provided this unnecessary translation. It was the petit commerçant. "Pas d'argent!" he repeated, and laughed, that tinkly false laugh. He swung back around to his cigarette case, and I studied him more closely: lots of plaid, lots of color, a plump soft body. His long fingernails were painted with a red nail polish. He wore several large rings on his fingers, and a watch on each wrist, and one end of the long skinny belt that held up his baggy pants swung down obscenely between his legs. A crumpled derby sat on his sculpted hair, and his eyes were hidden behind sunglasses. He was a strutting, mocking, self-satisfied farceur, and I was amazed to recognize him as my old houseboy, Dimanche.

The last time I'd seen Dimanche he was wearing the ragged clothes of a villager, the stuff that churches in the States bundle up and send to Africa when they can't sell it at a rummage sale. He mumbled, he was clumsy, and he slunk out of our house under a weight of apathy and resentment. That was six months earlier, and we'd heard or seen nothing of him since. Now he was back, glittery, plump, and cocky, full of phony laughter and phony French. But how had he managed this transformation? It was as if getting fired had triggered an internal crisis, causing him to examine his values and finally redefine his personality. As if he had spent the last six months exiled in the wilderness, huddled deep in the forest with his chrysalis hardening, and emerged giddy and arrogant, a grotesque butterfly.

Most likely, though, he'd taken his severance pay to Kisaka and bought some shiny clothes and jewelry and a couple of cartons of cigarettes, and that was enough to overwhelm his old dishrag personality, which would no doubt reassert itself, if that's what a dishrag personality does, once the cigarettes were gone, the clothes worn thin, and the jewelry pawned.

But I didn't ask him where he'd been, what were his plans. I didn't talk to him at all. Not that I preferred my old sullen and cowering houseboy, but I had no desire to strike up a conversation with this version of Dimanche either. For his part, he acted as if we'd never met. He addressed me again as "monsieur," nearly gagging on the r, and commanded me to buy his cigarettes, though he knew I didn't smoke. I turned away without answering, took up my package of meat and purchases from the store, and went up the road to my house, where Kate still lay in bed with the sheets and mosquito netting thrown back, giving off heat, stirring up dreams.

For the next three days she lay there, taking the cure for malaria. This was the third time she'd come down with malaria since we'd been in Africa, in spite of the prophylactic drugs we both took weekly. I was at her side much of the time, nursing her, which is to say fussing over her, since there wasn't much I could do other than make sure she took her medication and fend off the well-wishers who came by with their gifts of peanuts and luku and even palm wine.

Ndosi arrived each morning to sweep the house and yard, fetch water, wash dishes, and prepare a meal. Tom stopped by twice, subdued and serious, to see if he could help. But there was nothing to do, and Kate was asleep both times he came, so he didn't stay long.

Matama and the nurse visited each afternoon. Matama made a big production out of bringing a bowl of mediocre luku and another of grayish Things, which I gave to Placide each night. Not even Kate would be able to face down a bowl of Matama's luku in her condition. But she seemed to appreciate the solicitude of the women, and on the third afternoon, when her fever was at an ebb, she asked me to invite them into her room to talk for a while.

The nurse assured me that Kate was improving and that she soon would be well. I believed her and felt some gratitude toward her, some consolation in her presence. She projected compassion and self-assurance, and seemed to have a real understanding of disease. Perhaps there was a healing quality in her personality. After all, she was a nurse, even if she had been fired, though maybe that was a point in her favor. But I might have just imagined these nursely attributes. I didn't really know anything about her, except that she was, at bottom, a peasant woman whose main concerns were probably her manioc field and her peanut patch. She was literate, had some education, a title of sorts, and probably some kind of professional certificate. All of these things were rare among village women. But what did a professional certificate mean in a place where bribery was the only practical means of obtaining any sort of document at all? Or a title in a place where the word for "nurse" was the same as that for "witch doctor"? Or literacy in a place where there was nothing to read? Context was everything, and it would be wise to keep in mind that the nurse's knowledge of modern medicine was grafted onto deeper beliefs in ancestral fetishes and black-magic superstitions.

As if to confirm my skepticism, when she came out of the bedroom she produced a packet of leaves, which she said was a special tea, and instructed me to brew some for Kate in the evening if her fever came on again. I assured her I would, though I had no intention of medicating my sick wife with a random dose of jungle weed. The nurse said she had to go work in the cornfield now. How is the corn harvest, I asked politely, and she said it was good. I tried to picture her out in the field, bending her back and dripping sweat in a line of singing and jabbering mamas, babies tied to their backs, pendulous breasts swinging among the cornstalks. But the nurse's breasts were not pendulous. At that very moment they were at eye level to me and about two feet away from where I sat at my desk, and their form was clearly discernable beneath her snugly wrapped pagne. Along with the rest of her body, they suggested a certain youthfulness and vibrancy, though as I studied her face I guessed she was close to forty years old. Most village women were old and haggard by that age, having borne at least half a dozen children and worked from dawn to dusk every day of their adult lives that they weren't deathly ill or giving birth.

"How many children do you have?" I asked her, since she seemed in no hurry to leave. The truth is, she was making me uncomfortable, standing so close to my desk and studying with open curiosity the papers scattered all over it.

"Oh, I have more children than you can count. You remember all the children when you came to my house the other morning, monsieur."

"I didn't realize they were all yours."

"Oh yes, all mine! Of course, my sisters are the ones who gave birth to them. But I'm one of their mamas all the same, though I've never given birth to a child myself."

I nodded, and pretended to study a paper I pulled at random from the pile Ndosi had stacked on my desk. The nurse was attractive and there was something intriguing about her, but as usual the conversation had quickly run its natural course. We'd covered disease, farming, and children—what else was there to discuss?

That evening Kate was feverish again, worse than before. I heard her calling me, but when I went into the bedroom she was asleep, breathing rapidly, her skin burning. I woke her to give her some aspirin and tried to cool her skin with wet towels, but she threw them off. Watching her, I began to feel almost feverish myself, and I went out on the porch to get some air. Placide called out, "How is Madame Kate?" A simple and reasonable question, but it gave me a deep chill. That invisible voice, calling mournfully from somewhere out in the darkness, sounded inhumanly patient, resigned to eternal fevers and death. I went back inside at once, without answering.

Kate's fever ran higher. I'd already given her a double dose of aspirin. Now I made a tea from the nurse's weeds and got her to sit up and drink it. Sweaty hair was matted on her forehead; she complained of a vicious headache and seemed almost delirious. It was frightening to see her like that, but also in a way reassuring, to be so obviously *needed* by her, and also to know that the nightmares and body heat that had disturbed me two days before could be explained as the symptoms of a presumably curable disease.

After she drank the tea she fell asleep. I tried to sleep on the couch, but began to have misgivings about the tea. She slept so soundly—what kind of narcotic had I given her? It was a relief when she started talking in her sleep. I stood next to the bed, listening; that is, eavesdropping. What was I hoping to hear? Some clue, I suppose, something about contraband trucks stuck in a black mud, bodies on the road, encounters in savanna villages: something to help resolve the uneasy enigmas she presented me with her dreams and her night wanderings. But I couldn't decode the short cries, the murmured phrases that seemed unlinked to one another, as if to articulate only the arbitrary jumble of her subconscious.

The next day she slept all morning, and spent the afternoon reading, writing letters, and drinking the nurse's tea. And by the following day she was out in the villages again. That was what amazed me about her malaria attacks. Wasn't malaria supposed to be one of those powerful diseases that transfigures the very foundations of life? Shouldn't the malaria survivor, purged of illusion and frivolity, emerge from her fevers with a new understanding of suffering and mortality, a fresh and sober vision of the fragility of life? And wasn't this the kind of harrowing experience you could undergo only a few times in a lifetime, without exceeding so far the normal boundaries of human experience that you become some species of visionary or lunatic?

But I guess these ideas belonged to my own personal mythology of disease. Sheltered and heavily immunized, raised on a bland pathology of chicken pox and measles, colds and mild flus, I was in awe of a famous disease like malaria, and it was hard to get used to the idea of my wife coming down with it as a matter of course every few months. But she acted as if these racking fevers and chills were as inevitable, and nearly as inconsequential, as her menstrual period: just another rhythmic inconvenience in her life. Certainly the experience didn't moderate her behavior. As soon as her strength returned she was out there walking the hot bush again, eating whatever people put in front of her, and staying up night after night fueled on kola nuts and palm wine, careless of the parasites that were once again multiplying in her bloodstream.

THE MAMAS' SUPPORT GROUP

Those sweltering, feverish days proved to be the end of the rainy season. Thunderstorms no longer developed in the afternoons, and soon the misty, stagnant, and slightly cooler air of the dry season—the mushipu—settled over the savannas and forest valleys. Travelers passed more frequently on the road below our house, and it seemed that people were always stopping by to ask for Kate, wanting to arrange meetings, bringing small gifts of food, or just hoping to chat. Work at the mill slowed. Fewer palm nuts were ripening, and now the men were needed to clear trees and brush for new corn and peanut fields, though some remembered urgent business they had in Kisaka and disappeared altogether.

I don't know what brought it on—just the slowdown in work, maybe, or a quarrel with his wife—but in those early days of the mushipu the chef de poste and his girlfriend had a party nearly every night at the guest house. Sometimes other people came and went, but usually it was just the two of them, laughing and drinking, talking and dancing. And always the boom box played at maximum volume, blasting out frenetic music that overwhelmed all other sounds of the night.

This was much worse than when he played his music in his own house, on the other side of the river. There, the music, however obnoxious, was only a single component of the nighttime symphony; here at close range it took on a diabolical presence and power. It still wasn't quite loud enough to completely drown out other night sounds, but it did sweep them up in its confusing rhythms and distortions and render them incoherent and chaotic. Once or twice during this period I tried to indulge in my accustomed evening meditation on the front porch, but I soon found myself shaking with the old fibrillations, driven by the energy of the music but unable to comprehend its meter and structure. I'd sit on the porch with the nerves firing up and down my legs, watching the dark river and the flickering glow of the nightwatchman's coals, and I would begin not to meditate but to brood, obsessed with the chef's music and the delusions it inspired. It was as if the music had gotten inside me, an enchantment or a disease pathogen, and I couldn't shake the idea that these melodies and rhythms that had taken over the night were not the work of one man and a small machine, not just a rude aberration in the night soundscape, but instead something intrinsic to the true nature of the night itself. I was hearing the songs of ghosts that occupied the black spaces: a driving, implacable noise, issued in a spirit of malice by choruses of the still unpacified dead.

From this perspective it seemed almost miraculous when the music broke off. But that didn't mean that the calmer sounds of the night—insects, water, drumbeats from a distant village—were restored to their proper proportion. Instead I found myself listening voyeuristically for the sounds that came out of the hidden rooms of the guest house: the chef's laughter and his rumbling insistent voice, and the duxième bureau's giggle, rising to something like a shriek or a scream, cut off by the sudden interjection of drums and guitars.

I couldn't sit on the porch night after night taking this in. I retreated inside; within the thick walls of our house, in the warm glow of kerosene lamps, Kate and I were removed from night music, ghosts, whatever was going on at the guest house, and whatever was going on in our yard. We abandoned Placide to the front lines, and who knows? Maybe he enjoyed the nightly assaults, the break in the monotonous Muzak of insects and village drums, though I never noticed that he responded in any way to the chef's music. But during this time I hardly spoke to Placide, and when I did glance outside and see him huddled by his fire, or glimpse his shadow moving down by the shed, his solitude seemed to me more extreme than ever, interrupted now only by a greeting exchanged with a rare passing traveler or by the command of the chef himself, stepping out on the guest house porch to call for Placide to wake up the storekeeper and bring down more beer.

It would be an exaggeration, though, to say that the chef's music drove me off the front porch. The truth was I now scarcely needed the front porch. The porch was for dreaming and impressionistic speculation, for casting thought adrift on the ambience of the tropical night. It wasn't for focusing ideas, for organizing arguments and data and laying cold facts down on paper. It wasn't for getting the job done.

The job was my Consultant's Assessment. By day I worked on it in my office, and at night, with the chef's music throbbing in the background, I worked on it in my house. While Kate wandered in the fields and villages or zipped about on the back of Tom's moto, and while Ndosi quietly assumed the boy's duties, I took Uncle Pers' advice and found a niche beyond the porch. I became the noble bureaucrat, and the Consultant's Assessment was my first piece of work.

It was entitled "Assessment on the Operational Status of the Ngemba Palm Oil Mill," and it seemed to me that it was a document of the highest quality, certain to far exceed any expectations my employers might have of me. Never mind that they had expressed no expectations at all. Never mind that I had only the vaguest notion of who they were, or even where to send the report. The confidence I had in the document itself overcame any of these quibbling doubts. It made an irrefutable case for a number of common-sense reforms in the management of the mill and its employees. It was analytical, factual, and scientific-looking: a dense text supported by footnotes and carefully plotted graphs and tables. Some of the most factual parts I had lifted directly from *Products of the Oil Palm,* a plagiarism I could justify on the grounds that, one, it gave new life to the moribund work of Professor Lindquist; and two, there was almost no chance I would get caught. It took some effort to blend Lindquist's writing with mine, but the result, I thought, was perfect: a prose style leaden enough to appeal to the bureaucratic aesthetic yet carrying just a hint of passion, a suggestion here and there of rhythm and wit, and even a phrase or two that for all I knew might pass for eloquence in the sterile and stilted environment where it would be read.

However, I had no way of knowing how much of this survived the French translation. Or maybe it was enhanced by it. It was the secretary's French. Specialized, he said, a "français du bureau." The secretary had volunteered to type the report for me when he saw me in the office, sitting in front of the chef de poste's antique Smith-Corona, trying to extract something from an ancient desiccated bottle of Wite-Out. It never had occurred to me to ask the secretary to type anything or to perform any kind of mundane clerical task. He didn't seem like that kind of secretary. He was more like a cabinet-level secretary, with executive duties to discharge, though after more than half a year of observing him I still had no idea what those duties might be.

But it turned out he *could* type, just like a real secretary. In fact, he had some real typing muscles in his fingers, unlike those of us who have grown up flitting our fingers across electronic keyboards, and was able to whack away for long stints on the old Smith-Corona, making considerably fewer mistakes than I, and getting a remarkably consistent print out of the worn ribbon. But he marveled at the appearance of the written English language and remained unconvinced that anyone would understand such gibberish.

"Well, they may *not* understand it," I admitted. "They may not speak English."

"Then we must translate!" the secretary exclaimed, and I saw at once that he was right. But since the secretary didn't speak English either, I had to loosely translate for him myself, in French or Kituba. He grasped my ideas quickly, or at least managed to extract his own ideas from whatever I was saying. He nodded energetically and let his fingers fly, and when I read over what he had typed, it seemed to me that he had the gist of it, insofar as I could make any sense out of his français du bureau.

The chef de poste, when he reviewed the report, seemed to understand it well enough. He approved of all my ideas, even the modifications I suggested in his Modernization Project. He praised my suggestions for infrastructure improvements—road construction and grading, better ferry maintenance, a more reliable boat for transporting the refined palm oil downriver to market. When he read my tentative proposal for seasonal modifications of factory machinery to process and add value to other agricultural commodities—milling corn, hulling rice, and roasting coffee were among the possibilities I raised—he slapped my hand in delight. He even claimed to like my plan for a more democratic management structure at the mill. "But we don't need to involve people in Kisaka in that," he said. "This democratization stuff we can do on our own. We'll incorporate it in the Modernization Project."

But he was most intrigued by the idea of higher wages. "That's a real good one," he told me. "You should give it a prominent place in the report. Underline it."

"Well, I have emphasized it. It's obviously a central part of the whole concept. If they want to raise production, they need to raise wages. A lot."

The chef laughed. "Of course! But you'd better not worry too much about that! Your job, William, is to write the report. It's the job of our superiors to read the report, approve it, and not implement any of the recommendations."

"Oh. So you don't think they'll pay any attention to this."

"What kind of attention are you looking for? Surely you don't expect them to *do* anything! I can tell you they won't raise wages. And they'll never rebuild the factory or pave the roads or build bridges or plant trees or anything like that. But you should still include all these suggestions in your report. It will make a very fine report. Everyone will be pleased with you."

Against my better judgment, I showed the report to Tom. He sat on our couch and read through it quickly, then tossed it aside without comment. I put it back in its envelope, and he picked up a magazine and started reading.

"Well?" I said finally.

He looked over the top of the magazine and gave a little shrug, as if for once he really had nothing to say. But after a minute he spoke, without taking his eyes from the magazine. "There's something I've been meaning to ask you, Will. A while back I saw you and the secretary running around with a tripod, measuring tape, field notebooks. I kind of wondered what the hell you were doing."

"Surveying."

"Surveying!" He put the magazine down. "Is that in your job description too? I guess it doesn't matter—it's the same thirty or forty bucks an hour whether you're holding up a rod or writing a report, huh? What do you suppose the secretary makes?"

"I don't know, Tom. Not very much, I'm sure."

"You've never talked to him about that."

"It's never come up. We work really well together, as equals, and the money we're earning just doesn't seem to be an issue."

"You *asshole*, Will!" He jabbed at his glasses, scowling. "This is why I say you're naïve. Because you want to pretend that money doesn't matter! Not even naïve—blind, *willfully* blind. Money is *always* at the center of things, don't you see that?"

"What do you know about it? You don't have any money."

"That's how I know its value. Because these goofy romantic ideas that money is peripheral only work for somebody whose pockets are stuffed."

"I know it's a double standard, Tom. Obviously. That's the reality we live in. I wrote a report on it. I recommended a lot of changes."

"Right. It's the fucking reality. You make three or four hundred bucks a day, they make fifty cents. That's the fucking system. Nothing personal about it. What can you do, one guy out in the jungle, surrounded by injustice. Write some reports. Survey. Drink palm wine with the common man. Above all, make recommendations."

I suppose that was more or less the response I anticipated from Tom. And I couldn't really expect that the noble bureaucrat would impress the chef de poste either, whose perspective on all bureaucratic endeavor was hopelessly warped by twenty-five years of subjugation by one of the most corrupt and self-serving governments on the planet. But I did look for a more encouraging response from Kate.

"Well, it is a very genuine-looking report," she said.

"What does that mean?"

"You know—official-looking. Technical. Bureaucratic. Really dull, if you want to know the truth."

"Dull! Of course it's dull! Stylistically dull. I wrote it that way on purpose, with a specific audience in mind. However, it does have meat. The content is not dull."

"Oh, no. New parts for the extruders. Maintenance schedule for the hydraulic press. Palm oil production graphs. It's all so stimulating."

"Wait a second. Palm oil production is what we're *supposed* to be concerned with. That much is clear in our contract."

"I guess. But maybe you shouldn't take the stupid contract so literally, Will. Or at least look at it in a broader context. I mean, all these charts and graphs and recommendations—that's all fine, except, shouldn't they be a little bit grounded in *reality?* The chef de poste is right—Jucht Brothers is not going to raise wages just because some consultant recommends it."

"So what do you want me to do?"

"Well, maybe you should start by asking *why* people get paid so little. And maybe the answer would suggest where more money might come from."

"Who knows where money comes from?" I said, imitating Uncle Pers' voice. Kate didn't smile.

"*Somebody* must know. It would be something for the noble bureaucrat to work on, anyway."

"You don't think much of the noble bureaucrat, do you?"

"I like the noble bureaucrat just fine. Let's just say, I don't think he's living up to his potential yet. I think he's awfully naïve on the one hand, and awfully cynical on the other—you know what I mean? Maybe he's just out of touch."

"Sure. By definition, the noble bureaucrat is out of touch. It's what redeems him."

But she said that what would really redeem him would be if he could get his hands on something solid, like a truck, and she insisted that I attach a cover letter to my report, emphasizing that the consultants in Ngemba were still in dire need of the vehicle they'd been promised. Then she said it might also redeem him to get out of the office, off the front porch, and into the bush and the villages. I said fine, I'd love to go into the bush with you. So the next day she took me back to Telo's farm, to a meeting.

When I'd visited Telo's farm with Tom and Kate, I'd been struck by the poverty and desolation of the place. I remembered a flock of scrawny chickens pecking invisible scraps in the kitchen doorway, old men kicking at mangy skeletal dogs, and listless children lying around in the dirt and the goat shit. But now chairs and tables were set up beneath the veranda, garlands of flowers and woven palm fronds lined the fence, and music played on a boom box. Dozens of women were gathered in the shade of the veranda and around the cooking hut. The place was full of their laughter and bright swirling pagnes, and the old men and children and dogs were scarcely visible beneath this miraculous blooming of color and sound.

Telo led us to the veranda and sat us at a table. In small groups the women came to greet us and shake our hands. I recognized a few of them— the nurse, Matama, Telo's wife. Ndosi was there with his young fiancée, helping to set up chairs.

"So, this is a mamas' meeting," I said to Kate.

"Yes."

"And what's it about?"

"I don't know."

"But you organized it!"

"Sort of. I'm not sure how it happened, Will. I think they organized it *around* me. I'm the magnetic body, or the inert material that the active particles adhere to."

"Is that your official position? The magnet? The magnate?"

"Actually, I'm the animatrice, officially. They elected me. And the nurse is president."

"The animatrice. But you don't know what you're animating."

"Well, so far it's been something like an ad hoc discussion group. A free-speech forum. They have a lot of grievances. It's kind of like a support group, really. Maybe that's what they should call themselves: the Mamas' Support Group."

"Great. You're importing the culture of victimization to Central Africa."

"I don't have to import anything, Will. These are African peasant women. And if anybody's a victim . . ."

"What are they going to do at this meeting?"

"What are *we* going to do, you mean. I'm the animatrice, you're the consultant. Which means we give speeches, for one thing."

"I have to give a speech? Forget it."

"You *have* to. You can't just sit there stroking your beard. You'll have to say something."

"I have nothing to say. And I can't say it anyway. Not in Kituba, in front of all these women."

"Pull something out of your Consultant's Assessment. It doesn't have to be much. They don't expect much. I haven't worked out everything I'm going to say either."

The meeting opened with a couple of songs. Then the nurse welcomed everybody and talked for a few minutes. I couldn't follow her very well, but I recognized the word "consultant." And the next thing I knew I was up in front of a crowd of fifty or sixty women, fifteen or twenty babies, and a half dozen men looking on from the periphery.

My speech was received with polite enthusiasm, though I'm sure no one understood anything I said. I tried to paraphrase a few of the summary points in my Consultant's Assessment, and when my Kituba vocabulary failed me I resorted to French cognates, or French-like cognates. An irrelevant distinction, since few of the women spoke any French at all. In any case, I think several lines may have emerged in Spanish. The women looked up at me with a variety of expressions: incomprehension, indulgence, sardonic amusement, but mainly slack-jawed wonder at the spectacle of this exotic beast blithering on in front of them. It was obvious, though, that the speech itself wasn't holding them. I tried to employ a few standard tricks of public speaking, such as selecting a member of the audience and making forceful eye contact, but I think this only works for someone delivering a semicoherent speech. I could see the women weren't thinking about anything I was saying. They were thinking about how profusely I sweated, how pale was my flesh, how odd I would look naked. I felt naked. I blundered my way to a conclusion and sat down to loud applause and cheering.

Strangely, though, once I sat down I didn't feel much humiliated by this experience, and no one acted as though I had made a fool of myself. Probably Kate was right: they didn't expect to understand me. I was a functionary; and what people want from a functionary is form, not content. If anybody needed content they could work on digesting Kate's speech.

As soon as the applause faded she got up and launched into it. In less than fifteen minutes she managed to talk about contour tillage, nutrition, sustainable development, nutrient cycling, oral rehydration therapy, crop rotation, green manures, biodiversity, climate change, and desertification. She was impassioned and—as far as I could tell—articulate, but I didn't know what she was driving at. She didn't know either. She stopped abruptly and sat down.

"Was I arrogant?" she asked me while the women cheered. "Do you think they feel patronized?"

"No. I'm sure they're too confused to feel patronized."

"I rambled, didn't I? There are too many issues, I don't know what to focus on. Okay, fine, next time I'll stick to talking about the hydraulic press."

But if I had fulfilled my role, she too had fulfilled hers. What was it the women called her? The animatrice? Well, the meeting, which had begun stiffly, was now animated. The women gave testimony, they argued, they shouted and laughed. They quoted from Kate's speech. The nurse jumped up and delivered a speech as rambling as Kate's, going on about road construction, truck transportation, the price of peanuts, the weight of a basket of manioc, the demands of chefs and soldiers, God knows what else. She was a firebrand, and she made her eye contact with *me;* she seemed to be lecturing me specifically, as if she were responding to something I had said, though in fact I had said nothing decipherable.

The meeting gradually broke apart into several separate high-spirited discussions, none of which I could follow, since the women had abandoned Kituba and were now speaking in tribal dialects. Food was served, and a token glass of palm wine.

Kate apologized to the nurse for the disorganization of her speech. "I got carried away. I don't even know what I was trying to tell you."

"You were telling us ways to not be so poor. Telling us how to create money."

"I was? Maybe, sort of. But you see creating money is complicated."

The nurse nodded. "Still, Mama Kate, you're giving us ideas." She pulled Kate away, and I was left to my own devices. I talked briefly with a couple of the women, and others came over and shook my hand before they left. The crowd had thinned out, and the old men drifted back under the veranda. They didn't speak to me. My glass was empty, and there seemed to be no more palm wine. Soon there was no one in the yard but the old men, the children sprawled in the dirt, watching me, and the chickens and dogs scavenging the paltry crumbs of the meal. A dog came sniffing around, and I shoved it away with my foot. So. The Mamas' Support Group had come and gone and nothing had changed on the farm, except that now I was a part of the torpor that once again had settled over it.

I was dozing when Ndosi pulled on my arm. "Where's Kate?" I asked.

He waved vaguely toward the forest. "She's over there having a discussion with the nurse. Talking, talking, talking! I was with them, but she sent me to get you."

"I'm hungry."

"There wasn't much food, was there? Or palm wine!"

"I would have gone home, only I'm not sure of the way. I'd better talk to Kate."

"Yes. Come with me, Monsieur Will."

The air was a kind of white mist, thick with a substance that was something between smoke and water vapor. It seemed to muffle sound, like snow. Ndosi and I walked in silence through the forest, and emerged to skirt the bottom of a cleared and burned hillside. We heard the voices of the women before we saw them, calling to one another high on the hill as they swung their hoes above the smoking earth. We only glanced at their naked backs, damp from mist and sweat, and paid no attention to their laughter or their harsh voices, and they were not aware of us at all, passing along the edge of their field on male business, some abstract mission that did not concern them.

And what did I know of them? They were always in the background, hoeing and cooking and taking children to the mission hospital, swaying in a circle at funeral dances, going out to the fields to hoe again. No wonder I'd had nothing to say when I stood up in front of them at Telo's farm. Telo's farm, but his wife did all the hoeing. Anyway, I could understand why the women were so enthusiastic about the meeting. At least it got them out of hoeing for a couple of hours.

We entered a village. To me it looked like any other village, except for the bamboo pole and the model airplane that towered over it. So I knew it must be Malembe, Tom's village, and now Ndosi's too. It was the village of his father, and he had moved here after his uncles took over his fishponds, though he said it was not the loss of the ponds but the disappearance of his bamboo airplane that had convinced him to make the move. He'd decided the flight of the plane was a sign that he also should fly from the savanna, and so far things were working out well for him. He was close to his new job and to his fiancée, and there was ancestral land, virgin land, available to him in the nearby forest. So he'd built himself a small hut in his father's compound, and erected a new model airplane outside of it, though the village elders, like his uncles, grumbled about the plane.

He sat me down in a low chair at the base of the bamboo pole.

"I guess you never did find your old plane," I commented.

"No, monsieur. It hasn't returned from Mputu yet."

"Oh, right. So, is Kate around here somewhere?"

"Here? No, monsieur. She's over there, talking." He waved his hand in the direction we had come and then abruptly left, promising to return soon with luku and palm wine.

I settled back to wait. I had escaped from the farm, but now I was a victim of Ndosi's hospitality. I never should have complained of being hungry. He wouldn't allow me to leave until he fed me luku, but it might be hours before he got his hands on any, since all the luku makers were busy hoeing or else talking with my wife, who once again had vanished into the African jungle without explanation. It was distressing, but what could I do? I could fret, I could make a scene and demand explanations, or I could allow things to take what seemed to be their natural course: sit back in my chair while numbness and resignation spread through my body and the old men hobbled up from their mats to shake hands and the inevitable rabble of dusty children gathered to stare.

In fact, though, these children were not really paying attention to me. I watched them for a while, trying to figure out the game they were so intent on. They had a couple of toy trucks, hand made from pieces of bamboo and raffia. In the bed of each truck they had crammed a few palm nuts or a piece of manioc root, and a couple of them were pushing the trucks around a little track between the huts. Others crept around the huts, whispering to one another, making quick dashes here and there, converging on the trucks. The albino girl poked her face around the corner of one hut. Lately she had taken to wearing a wig—a hideous, oversized, blondish thing that loomed over her face and drew attention to her every movement, though she ducked away whenever I glanced toward her. She seemed to be giving instructions to the truck pushers, who periodically sneaked around to her. One kid sat on a stool, shuffling through a couple of school notebooks, seemingly oblivious to the activity all around him. On his chin he wore a piece of brown moss held in place by some string attached to his ears. At first I thought this was a kind of fetish or old-time remedy, but as he stroked and patted it I realized it was part of a costume—a beard.

Some of the children noticed me studying their drama and began to giggle self-consciously. I called them over.

"What game are you playing?"

Now they all began to laugh. Most of them seemed to be trying to hide behind one another. Finally one kid spoke up.

"We're playing Smugglers."

"Smugglers! Like pirates or something, huh? And who's he supposed to be?" I pointed to the kid sitting on the stool. He pulled off his fake beard and looked nervous.

"Come on! Who is he?"

An older boy stepped up and looked me in the eye. "Il est le consultant, monsieur."

They squealed and giggled, and one of the old men reared up and dispersed them with a wave of a stick and a violent stream of curses.

There was no telling what the point of that game had been. I could grill them on it, but probably it was beneath my dignity to pay much attention to childish provocations. Perhaps they had been ridiculing me, but so what? Wasn't I immune to ridicule? Hadn't I once again immunized myself, with that ridiculous speech to the Mamas' Support Group? In any case, the children now reverted to more conventional behavior, regrouping silently to simply observe me, keeping a respectful distance. I ignored them and did my best to provide a dull entertainment, sitting stiffly in the chair and looking up at Ndosi's bamboo airplane, which rose straight above me into the white sky.

This forest airplane did not achieve the same effect as the one that had disappeared from the savanna. What caught my attention was not a soaring plane but the engineering that kept it in the air: the long vines stretching taut from the top of the pole to the edges of the village, and the pole itself, a remarkably tall stalk of bamboo planted in the ground outside Ndosi's hut, taller even than the one he had used on the savanna. Yet it did not create a convincing illusion of flight. This plane was not a sky machine; it was a model airplane on a bamboo pole, tied to the huts and jungle and fields of hoeing women below.

I shifted in the hard chair, trying to get comfortable. I had a pain in my shoulder, and a headache. I wanted to get home so I could take some aspirin and eat something substantial. What was Ndosi up to? It was annoying, really, to be subjected to inconvenience and discomfort just so he could fulfill his perceived obligations as my host. Slumping farther down into the chair, I looked almost straight up into the sky and focused on the airplane above me, trying to isolate it from the distractions of its support system. But when I succeeded in shutting out the pole and the vines, the plane too seemed to disappear against the white background, and I found myself searching an empty, dimensionless sky. The children tittered and whispered, and I realized my eyes were closed, I had dozed off. But what difference did it make, asleep or awake, if I saw the same blank expanse in either case?

The children soon fell silent again, and I kept my eyes closed until I felt a light touch on my face, and then another, and another. I brushed a gray speck from my cheek. It was only ash, the first light ashfall of the mushipu. I closed my eyes again, breathed in the smoky air, and let the ash come down—all we could expect of that smoky sky. The children watched a motionless scene; old men lay on their mats in the shade; and out in the forest, amid charred and fallen timber, the women kept hoeing. This was the ennui of an African village; surely there could be nothing stiller and duller than this dead-light afternoon, these silent children, this eternal hoeing. How could Tom have stood it for three years? How could Kate hope to change any of it, or animate it?

Yet somewhere above us was a bamboo airplane, invisible against a washed-out sky. And in my own mind Ndosi's vision taking hold, an anticipation, against all odds, of his plane's transformation and return: a huge airplane roaring out of the whiteness, rippling in its own heat and hanging in the air as if seen through telephoto, with the red sun wavering behind it, warped by the fire of turbines.

16

OIL STAIN

I sat on my porch in the darkness, alone, listening to the silence of the crickets.

At first I couldn't identify that silence. The night was peaceful: no boom box, no parties, the first night in more than a week that the chef de poste and his duxième bureau hadn't rendezvoused at the guest house. Yet the peace was nerve-racking in its own way, like the calm in the eye of a storm or at the uncertain end of a siege. But the night is full of its natural sounds, I told myself: rustling leaves, fussing babies, drums, water, insects. And it was then that I listened harder, and realized there were no crickets singing.

Placide sat with his back to me down by the cook shed, poking at the coals. "Placide!"

He vanished from the firelight, and reappeared a moment later at the foot of the porch stairs. "Oui, monsieur?"

"What happened to the crickets, Placide?"

He nodded solemnly. "Wait," he said. He went back to his fire, poked around in the coals, and then returned. He shone his flashlight on an ash-covered banana leaf that lay unfolded in his hand, cradling several small black objects.

"Here they are, monsieur. Be careful—they're still hot."

I waved the leaf away. "That's not what I mean. What I want to know is, what happened to the crickets in the bush? Why aren't they singing?"

"They're roasted," he explained patiently. "They never sing when they're roasted."

"I'm not talking about *these* crickets. Obviously they don't sing when they're roasted."

"They sing before they roast. Once they're roasted, they can't. The fire's too hot. The crickets make a noise when they heat up, but Monsieur Will, it's not singing."

He was still holding out the banana leaf, so finally I took a couple of crickets, just so we could move on. He turned off his flashlight and wandered down toward the garage, and distractedly I bit into a cricket and began to chew, without really tasting it. Why was it that whenever Placide and I discussed crickets we had such a difficult time communicating? And yet it was through the exchange of crickets that we often were able to establish a kind of intimacy. Crickets are, after all, an intimate kind of food: captured through private stealth and quickness; small cold things made warm by the coals of a low fire; tenderly wrapped in a leaf; cupped in the hand; popped in the mouth. Recently I had even given Placide crickets, which I had obtained through Ndosi, and he obviously had been touched by the gift. Why then couldn't he answer a simple question about the absence of cricket singing? Was it that he just didn't expect me to notice that kind of detail in his night world? Or that while he was concentrating on one form of crickets—roasted—he couldn't switch modes so easily and discuss crickets that sing, or don't sing?

But halfway through the second cricket I made the connection between the cricket crunching in my mouth and the silence of the crickets in the bush. It was suddenly obvious: they were silent because they weren't there, they'd all been roasted, or if they were there they had sense enough not to sing, because singing meant capture, and capture meant roasting. *They sing before they roast.* Placide had understood my question and answered it quite reasonably, and I had only been annoyed with him, waving him off as if he were an idiot.

Now I felt annoyed with myself, for my continued inability to communicate clearly with Placide. It was as if I still hadn't learned his language, as if I had settled into a pattern of interpreting—and dismissing—his remarks: they were obscure, unreal, implicitly paranoid. It was sometimes amusing to elicit these remarks but always difficult to follow them through to a real conversation. And so generally I didn't try. I took Placide's presence for granted now; I hardly noticed him, peering out from the darkness, prowling around all night with his little bow and arrows.

It was obvious he was on some separate plane of being. But once you got past the metaphysical unease he inspired, maybe there just wasn't that much to make of Placide. It was always the same old watch cap, the same tattered greatcoat, the same opaque expression and silent vigilance. Even his remarkable stealth no longer captured my attention, now that I'd given up on ever being able to emulate it. In less generous moments I had begun to wonder if my awe of his inscrutable mental processes was misplaced; maybe he was just stupid. Certainly he was stoical, seemingly saintlike in his acceptance of life, but perhaps that was an expression of apathy and surrender. An expression of the sadness of a man living in isolation from his fellows, always watchful and suspicious on someone else's behalf, always in communion or conflict with the ancestral spirits of the night.

Maybe he just needed a little human company. On impulse, I left the porch and went down to his fire, where he sat hunched on his stool. I squatted next to him. This was unorthodox, but I said nothing. What explanation would make sense to Placide? He took everything in stride anyway. I mean, he stared at me as if he were looking at something that might be a hallucination, but he always looked at me like that. And now that I sat beside his little fire and looked around, trying to get his perspective on things, I had to admit there was a certain hallucinogenic quality to the world he saw every night. My porch looked especially weird to me. How strange I must appear to him, sitting up there in the shadows, dimly illuminated by the lamplight that escaped from the open window of the house, probably muttering to myself as I stared out into the darkness, with the smoke of his fire caught in the eaves of the porch and thickening over my head. Now the smoke hung above my empty chair, and though the night was windless it began to creep along the wall, and then floated off toward the darkened guest house. I followed the drift of the smoke, and Placide watched it too, and spoke.

"The women enter, and later they leave."

"What?"

"They enter the big house. Always at night. I saw them, monsieur."

"I don't know what you're talking about," I said.

"Young women. Women of different tribes. Batuba women. Bakwenga women. It didn't matter to him. Many different women, coming and going."

We both peered off into the darkness, following the drift of smoke. Presumably "him" was the chef de poste, though I'd never seen any woman besides his girlfriend going into the guest house. But who could tell what Placide was getting at?

"Well," I said, "it's certainly peaceful over there tonight. Isn't it?"

Placide was silent.

"Nobody going in and out. Is there?"

Placide stared at the house intently, as if there were important details to be noted, as if in fact people *were* going in and out. "Camion," he said.

"You're losing me, Placide. Anyway, it looks like the chef de poste won't be using the guest house tonight."

"Bringing palm nut." Placide continued to stare out into the darkness. Then, just as I was thinking that we had entirely lost contact with each other, he turned to me and said, "No. Our chef has no need of the guest house. He'd rather be home relaxing with his wife and family."

Sometimes I wished that my conversations with Placide didn't always take place in the dark, so I could make out his expression when he said things like that. But no—as always, he would have no expression, just a set of deadpan features looking out from between a watch cap and a greatcoat. I couldn't match his deadpan, or keep the sarcasm out of my voice.

"And I'm sure his wife and family are grateful for the opportunity to relax with him."

"Excuse me, monsieur, but I don't know what you're saying. I don't speak English."

"I didn't say anything in English."

"It sounded like English." He made some rasping troglodyte sounds in his throat. "Like that."

"I was speaking Kituba, Placide. Plus a little French. *Occasion*. That's a French word."

Placide shrugged. "Oui, monsieur. French, only you said it in English."

"Should I get the dictionary, Placide? Do you want me to *show* you the word?"

"Excuse me, monsieur, but I don't know what that is."

"A dictionary? It's a special kind of book, a list of words."

We were silent. Then Placide said: "A book you read, like other books?"

"Well, you don't usually sit down and just read it. You find words in it, words you might not know. It explains how to spell them, what they mean."

"I see. This special book teaches you words, so you can read them in other books."

"Sort of. I can show you mine later, if you want. Or I can probably even give you one, if you're really interested. Whatever."

"Merci, monsieur." Placide sighed deeply, thanked me again, and shook my hand. Something occurred to me.

"Placide, do you know how to read?"

"No, monsieur. They never taught me to read. That's why I'm excited about this book."

He certainly didn't sound excited. He seemed if anything more somber than usual, to the point of being morose. But why should he be excited about my dictionary, and what did his supposed excitement have to do with never having learned to read? That made no sense, even by Placide's standards of logic. The best explanation, as usual, was that he hadn't said what I'd thought he said. Probably he hadn't used the word "excited" at all; probably we hadn't been discussing dictionaries or languages or women going in and out of the guest house. Now I remembered why I didn't get involved in long discussions with Placide, why I knew so little about him. I felt a sudden desperate longing to communicate with someone, to converse unambiguously with a speaker of the English language. Kate, for example. But Kate was gone, and the best I could do was go to bed and read.

"Good night, Placide," I said, but there was no answer. He had vanished again. I left the fire and saw him standing at the corner of the house, where the smoke crawled off the wall and disappeared.

"Camion, monsieur," he said. "Do you hear it now?"

I grunted noncommittally, though I heard nothing. "Maybe Kate's coming home," I said. "Maybe she got a ride from somebody."

Placide shook his head. "Palm nut truck," he said.

"What would they be doing out now?"

"Collecting palm nut, monsieur."

"In the middle of the night?"

"The coupiers have been cutting a lot."

"Have they? Well, we sure don't see it at the mill."

Now I too heard the truck, and a moment later the headlights flickered through the trees on the other side of the mill. The truck rumbled into the clearing, cut its lights and engines, and coasted to a stop next to the mill. A couple of doors slammed.

"Two people," I said, but Placide was no longer by my side. I went down the path toward the guest house, half expecting to see him skulking around the porch or along the side of the house. But there was no sign of him. A flicker of light came from the garage, and I went over and looked in. Placide was on his hands and knees, shining his flashlight on the dirt floor.

"Placide! What are you looking for?"

"Nothing, monsieur. But there's a problem with the Land Rover."

"We don't even have a Land Rover."

He shone his flashlight on a large oil stain that darkened the dirt floor. "Look!"

I squatted next to him, and together we stared at the ancient oil stain. As if we were studying the spoor of an animal, some fierce feral beast that Placide had been tracking for decades.

"This oil stain's probably thirty years old, Placide."

Placide nodded. "From the Land Rover."

"How many years have you been a sentinel here, Placide?"

"There were many Land Rovers in those days. The director, the agronomist, the chef de poste, the Road Builder—they all had them."

"The Road Builder, huh? Hey, were you here—"

"Why don't you and madame have a Land Rover, monsieur?"

"Well, we do, sort of. Only we don't keep it here. I guess they keep it in Kisaka for us, Placide. Did you know the Road Builder?"

"With a Land Rover she could come home at night, instead of sleeping in villages."

"Do you remember what this Road Builder looked like, where he lived, anything about him?"

"No. The Company should give her a Land Rover, monsieur."

I couldn't get him to tell me anything else about the Road Builder, and finally, so that he would stop pestering me about the Land Rover, I told him I'd be talking with company officials about it very soon, perhaps as early as tomorrow. He shook my hand again and went back to poking around the corners of the shed, examining broken tools and old empty cans of motor oil and brake fluid. I went inside and undressed, listening to the squealing of pulleys on the ferry cable and low voices from across the river: disjointed sounds in a night that had never lived up to the promise of its stillness. Those sounds echoed around in my head, squealing and rumbling, while I lay in bed and tried to play back the conversations I'd had with Placide. It was all so much gibberish, I suppose, just an exchange of voices to help us through the dreary mushipu night. Yet certain things we'd said had resonance, and as I drifted off to sleep events of the night repeated themselves in my memory and took on an unexpected significance, even while their meaning remained hidden. I saw the oil stain on the floor of the garage, spreading and darkening, while the cloud of mosquitos and gnats buzzing in the beam of Placide's flashlight grew larger and darker too, as he swung the light from one empty corner to another. I heard the squealing pulleys and the voices on the water, and I saw the dark guest house and the movements in its shadows. Women going in and out, slipping through the door past the silent sentinel sitting by the porch, padding on bare feet down the long dark corridor and into the shuttered room, where a dim orange light flickered and a voice, low and soft and persuasive, rumbled on through the night.

I awoke to singing and thudding outside my window. At once I rolled out of bed, pulled on my pants, and stumbled out the door.

Ndosi was at the edge of the dirt yard beside the porch, tapping tufts of grass sod into the dirt with his heel. On one side of him was a pile of sod and a hoe, and on the other was a swath of scarified soil.

"It's six o'clock in the morning," I complained. "Why are you singing outside my bedroom window at six o'clock in the morning?"

"The sentinel told me to get you up at dawn. He said you're going to the mission to make a call. To talk to the director about the Land Rover."

"I never said I was going to the mission this morning! And I didn't say to wake me up. He imagines things. He just invents things, all the time. You should have heard him last night." I told how Placide had gone on about the oil stain and the old Land Rover and the women coming and going. Ndosi nodded, but he didn't seem to get my point.

"Yes!" he said. "Yes, it was exactly that kind of night!"

"What kind of night?"

"Things were happening last night. Oh, yes," he repeated, "lots of things were happening, all night long. People were out on the road. Many of us walked very far, Monsieur Will, carrying heavy loads. I myself walked all the way to Kasengi."

"Kasengi! That's where Kate said she was spending the night."

"Oui, monsieur. Because it was so late, and she had no Land Rover to drive home. So she slept in Kasengi."

His grim tone and the dark look in his eyes seemed to imply it was my fault she'd slept there, my fault she didn't have a Land Rover. Or maybe it was just the mention of Kasengi, which always made people nervous and paranoid and accusatory. Kasengi was a notoriously disharmonious village, a hybrid of refugees and different tribes. It was a political creation of the colonialists, who seventy-five years before were moving people around—out of the forest to escape the sleeping sickness, in from another region to break up a rebellion or a clan dispute that had gotten out of hand. But from the beginning it had been afflicted with disproportionate disease and sorcery. Twice it was burned to the ground—once by a savanna fire that got out of control, and again during the wars of independence, by rebels or mercenaries or government soldiers.

I didn't much like the idea of Kate sleeping in the haunted malarial huts of Kasengi either. I also wished she had a Land Rover to drive home, though maybe the Land Rover would bring its own set of problems. I told Ndosi, as I'd told Placide, that I would talk with Company officials soon. "But it's not like Placide seems to think, that I can just go to the mission and call up the director, and voilà, the Land Rover appears."

Ndosi nodded. "People were watching out for her last night, Will. I was there, and Telo. Tom too, for a while. And the nurse spent the night with her."

"What was Tom doing there?"

"He was just there. Anyway, nothing bad happened in Kasengi. Telo and I returned very late to Malembe, and the whole village seemed to be sleeping. But when I went to bed I heard a strange noise outside my house. I went out and saw an old woman climbing the pole that holds my plane. I shook the pole and told her to come down. She stopped and looked down at me. Her face was hooded like a vulture, Monsieur Will, and when I shook the pole harder she screeched and jumped from it. She flapped her arms and dropped like a chicken trying to fly from its perch. But she didn't hit the ground. She flew straight into the open window of a hut, and I ran after her and went in the door. She was lying on her mat pretending to sleep. I shook her and kicked her, and warned her to stay away from my plane. She started wailing, and pretty soon half the village was up. Some people yelled at her, and others yelled at me. I couldn't sleep anymore in that village, so I left again. The moon was bright, and I remembered how you wanted grass in your yard, so I went to a place I know where the wild grass grows in a lawn like at the mission. I harvested the grass, and returned here in the dawn to plant it."

And there he was planting it, carrying on his work of civilizing us—sometimes according to our vision of civilization, sometimes according to his own. I now saw that before Ndosi came to work for us, we had existed in a semisavage state. Living hand to mouth, in deteriorating conditions, we had abandoned the standards of more or less middle-class Americans and tried to survive as grossly incompetent African peasants. We didn't know how to get food, how to wash our clothes or carry water or grow a decent garden or build a fence, or even how to clean our house, apparently. I remembered the piles of laundry on the floor, the dirty dishes accumulating in the basin, and the pantry, empty except for a few imported tins. I remembered the hot bare yard, with its unfenced and untended boundaries, and my goat-ravaged, rain-pelted garden, emblematic of the disordered impulses that characterized our lives.

Under Ndosi's care our small house had become livable, even in some ways beautiful. And now he was doing the same for our yard. The chef de poste would not approve, of course. And Ndosi had agreed that the chef had a point about the snakes, but he said we could minimize that threat by pushing the forest back. So he'd spent a day with his machete, hacking down the grass and scraggly trees and bushes that were encroaching on the yard. I was horrified to see all the lush vegetation laid to waste by his blade, but Ndosi promised he would soon have the garden flourishing, once he had built a fence to keep the goats out.

It took him a couple of weeks to build the fence. I felt some regret that Dimanche's gate should lose its distinction and mysterious power by being joined to an ordinary fence, but this was more than compensated for by the increased privacy the fence provided, and by the prospect of growing an ample supply of fresh vegetables.

Our diet, though, had already vastly improved. Ndosi prepared about half our meals now. He was a decent cook, and a skillful scavenger and barterer. He always seemed to know who had tomatoes or onions to sell, or where he could get mushrooms or fresh fruit or squashes, or who had just slaughtered a goat, or when his cousins the Nakahosas had caught a large fish. He brought us wild game, strange new fruits, and even insects, which he prepared in ways that made them at least palatable and sometimes delicious. He brought produce from his own garden, which he had planted in a forest clearing on the edge of the river. He wasn't happy about having to work so close to the river, with its old curses and hidden terrors. But this was land that belonged to his father's clan, and the soil was rich. Already he was harvesting greens, and late in the afternoon, when the women were resting from their work in the fields, he would put a basket of greens on his head and walk through the camp, calling out the names of his greens and exhorting the women to buy. Those that didn't sell he brought to us, and I was amazed at the diversity and richness of flavor that could be found in a bowl of boiled greens.

But Ndosi enriched and diversified our lives in so many ways. Some of them having nothing to do with material goods or the way he did his chores. This was a rich moment right now, for example: sitting on the porch in the cool morning, describing to each other the way our dreams had merged so seamlessly with the true events of the night. Of course, Ndosi had told his tale as if it *all* were true events, as if all night long he'd never slept a wink. As if the old woman chicken-flapping down from the bamboo pole were not something he had dreamed, any more than he had dreamed the people walk-ing the dark roads at night, converging with their heavy burdens on a haunted village; or the secret place in the forest where the grass grew like a mission lawn; or for that matter these neat rows of transplanted grass he was at the moment so carefully watering. It was all equal in his narrative; I was the one who sorted and categorized as he spoke: this is dream, this is metaphor, this is something that may have actually happened.

But it had been a strange night, and it was a wavering border that sepa-rated our dreams from whatever really had occurred. And dreams and true events alike seemed incongruous with the daylight that followed—morning sunlight on rows of grass and cool cement and whitewashed walls; the innocu-ous daytime presence of the guest house across the yard. Where were my dreams of the guest house now; where was the midnight smoke that wreathed it; what had become of Placide's invocations of women going in and out?

What was the significance of an old oil stain, or a camion cutting its engines as it coasted into the mill yard late at night?

I made some coffee and drank it on the porch, watching Ndosi plant another row of grass. Watching him bring to life, little by little, his abstract diagrams of the Road Builder's gardens. I saw now how selective his machete blade had been in clearing the overgrowth. Below where he was now working, the hibiscus and the bougainvillea were beginning to flower, and papaya, pineapple, and banana were once again open to the sun. Sections of low brick walls and pathways were visible, along with some of the terraced beds where soon a vegetable garden would flourish, as it had thirty years ago, before the whites fled.

"Whatever happened to the Road Builder, Ndosi?"

With his bare heel he finished tapping down the red earth around a clump of grass. Then he wiped the sweat from his face and peered up at me. "I don't know that, monsieur. The old people tell stories, is all."

"What stories?"

"He was a powerful man, they say. But he had enemies. He was going to marry an African woman, before independence, and never return to Mputu. He was going to live like an African chef. But then some people say that he was poisoned. Or that he was killed by rebels in the independence wars, or drowned in the river when they blew up the Mission Road ferry. I've heard that he came under some enchantment and was hidden away in the forest, and still lives in Africa. Others say that he stole the Company bulldozer and drove off to another country. I don't know, monsieur. The old people love to talk."

"Who was he going to marry? Is she still around?"

"I don't know. He had a lot of women, they say, and it was a long time ago."

"He had a lot of women?"

"Oh, yes. That's what they say. Maybe some of us are his children, Will!"

I went down to the office. The mill chugged away, and workers rolled barrels of oil down to the dock, where the old rusty boat waited. It seemed industrious enough, though there weren't all that many barrels. The chef de poste was in his office, studying some plans that were spread across his desk. "The Place de la Révolution," he proclaimed. "The secretary drew these up. You ought to have a look at them, William."

"I will. I see the oil boat got in yesterday. Any news from Kisaka?"

"No, just the usual—empty barrels and the payroll box. What, you're still hoping to hear from our superiors? Well, you know, I don't often hear from them either, William. But that doesn't concern me. They know they don't need to be checking up on me. They know people at Ngemba aren't wasting time with the usual red tape and bureaucratic excuses for not doing anything. That we're out getting the job done."

By this the chef did not mean that we were out inspecting plantations or harvesting palm nuts or processing oil. He meant we were out in the mill yard, working on the Modernization Project. The chef was in his early sixties and planning to retire within a couple of years, assuming there was something left to retire from by that time. He had spent most of his adult life working in the palm-oil industry, rising through the ranks, and as he rose he had witnessed the simultaneous decline of the industry, so that by the time he achieved a position of some importance the industry itself did not seem important at all. "Not important to white people," the chef said to me. "But remember: the whole business was your idea in the first place. You came over here with your machines and factory blueprints; you forced us out of our manioc fields and told us, here's your future, making palm oil for Mputu. And now you've decided it gives you, what do you call it, cholesterol, and you don't want it anymore."

"Saturated fat, you mean," I said. "Not cholesterol."

"That's what I'm saying. You decided it makes you fat. So the skinny Africans can keep it all to themselves, give them something to dip their luku in. You white people!"

He laughed, and slapped me a high five, as if he'd just told me one of his sex jokes. If the chef de poste was bitter he wasn't the type to dwell on it, or let it cripple his spirit and initiative. However discouraging the prospects of the palm oil business, for himself and for his mill he preserved a vision of a higher destiny. That vision was the Modernization Project, intended to be the culmination of his achievements, an act of public service that would establish a momentum of progress in the face of failure and collapse.

I had to keep reminding myself of this context when I worked on the

Modernization Project. Because although the Project was an ambitious undertaking that diverted the labor of nearly all the employees of the mill, there was no reason to anticipate that the modernized mill would produce palm oil cheaper, more efficiently, or more abundantly than the unmodernized mill. The Modernization Project made no effort to improve marketing and shipping, to arrest the declining productivity of the wild oil palms, to replace the antiquated machinery or alter the inefficient methods of operation or repair the crippled infrastructure.

But what could be done about these things? They were dependent on events beyond the chef de poste's control: the continued erosion of the palm oil market, the supply of parts and machinery from Europe, the ongoing political disintegration of his own country. So he came up with the Modernization Project, which transcended, or at least ignored, these grim economics.

We built an employee "break room"—a thatch hut next to the mill, furnished with a couple of benches. We built a hut by the river so people could wait for the ferry out of the rain, and on the terrace above the river we put up a permanent veranda to shelter the weekly marché. We installed railings on the new steps at the company store, and repaired the roof over the porch so that, said the chef, "the mamas don't have to stand in the rain when they're waiting in line to buy macayabu." People praised the chef's thoughtfulness, and no one mentioned that it had been months, maybe years, since any mama in Ngemba had waited in a macayabu line.

There was a shortage of most building materials but we had plenty of whitewash, so every building in the camp got a fresh coat, and then we started in on the rocks. As the river dropped, we even brought up truckloads of river stone to line the roads and paths, and by this means kept the whitewash operation bustling and prosperous.

But mostly we cut trees, cleared brush, and moved a great deal of earth, working to construct the huge Place de la Révolution between the river and the mill. The Place was the centerpiece of the chef's plan. Mainly he wanted something big, and since he didn't have the means to build a big structure, he hit upon the idea of building a big space, which could be created simply by removing the material that now filled up that space—that is, the forest. He wanted to create a sanctuary from the disorder and dangers of Nature. He envisioned a meeting ground where thousands might gather before a monument and a podium, a place where the voice of civilization and order could be heard by all the people.

So for the past month we had worked, moving, digging, cutting, and clearing. I say "we," but in fact the consultant was not expected—or even usually allowed—to lift a shovel or machete. My main responsibility, as far as I could tell, was to lend a certain stature and authority to the project. Also I dabbled with plans and blueprints, made outlines, surveyed, offered suggestions. It was seldom productive work, but I did manage to prevent the chef, in his zeal, from clearing out the most beautiful shade trees in Ngemba. And together the secretary and I perfected our idiosyncratic method of surveying, though in the end he always depended on his eye and his intuition, rather than our trigonometry, to straighten lines and flatten fields.

For the first couple of weeks, work proceeded at a pace that in Ngemba may have been unprecedented since colonial times. The chef wanted to have everything finished by the time the rains started and before the commissaire came for his promised inspection. But before long we started running into problems.

One difficulty was a critical shortage in a basic construction material. The chef de poste's intention was to line all roads and paths and encircle the entire Place de la Révolution with whitewashed river rock, and to "pave" these areas with the broken shells that were removed from the palm nuts during the oil-extraction process. This pavement, said the chef, would serve at least two purposes: it would keep the area from getting muddy during heavy rains, and it would be a great deterrent to snakes.

People, especially women, complained bitterly about the paving plan. It would be painful, the women said, to walk barefoot across that pavement carrying heavy loads, with the sharp edges of the shells pricking their feet. The chef had little patience with such objections. "These women have no sense of progress," he grumbled. "Their feet will get used to the shells. But what about a snakebite? That hurts too, though the snake will prick their feet only once. Let them tell me which pain they prefer, and then we'll decide about the paving."

No one dared to point out to the chef that people never stepped on snakes in the vicinity of the mill anyway, but for the time being these arguments became moot, because we ran out of shells. The shells normally were used to fuel the boilers in the mill, though for some time now the chef had been stockpiling them and sending crews into the forest to gather firewood for the boilers. But when we began to spread the shells, it soon became obvious that we didn't have nearly enough. The truth was we hadn't been producing many lately, partly because most of the mill workers had been working on the Modernization Project rather than processing oil, and partly because the coupiers were supplying the mill with only a trickle of palm nuts.

Work on the Modernization Project slowed for other reasons as well. Enthusiasm for the project waned, perhaps as people began to realize that it was not likely to improve their lives in any significant way. The men began to complain about the heavy work. Absences increased. The mushipu was upon us, the season of sickness and travel and fire, and the men had additional responsibilities and diversions.

Also, the chef was distracted. He spent more and more time up in the guest house with his duxième bureau, but he also crossed the river more often, even in the middle of the workday, to return to his house and his wife. Now as I bent over the secretary's blueprints I saw he already had lost interest, and after a few minutes he left the office and went down to the ferry. I had trouble focusing on the blueprints too. Could it be lunchtime already? And if so, did we have anything to eat? I could ask Ndosi to fix something for me, but then I'd have to listen to him fret about how Kate wasn't home yet and had I gotten some word from Kasengi and what progress had I made in getting a camion. Well, it worried me, too, that she hadn't come home yet. And if I was worried, shouldn't I really do something about the camion? In fact, hadn't I promised to do something about it today? Or did Placide make that up? But that didn't matter, because in fact both Placide and Ndosi were right: Kate needed a camion, and apparently it was going to require some effort beyond a letter or a report to get it for her. It would require, first of all, actually *talking* with someone from the Company. And in the Kivila Valley, if you wanted to talk with someone far away you went to the pères at the mission and you made a call on the ham radio, which people called the phonie.

THE ENGLISH LESSON

Somehow I always ended up visiting the pères around lunchtime. The timing may have been calculated on my part, but if so there was something perverse in it, because lunch with the pères was always a frustrating experience. The food itself was wonderful: platters of meat and potatoes, fruit and garden greens, fresh-baked bread with slabs of butter and cheese, and pastries and chocolate for dessert. The problem was that I couldn't begin to keep up. For the pères, eating was no leisurely affair, no genteel recreation or occasion for refined social interaction. They were intent only on the business at hand. They bowed their heads for a brief blessing and then fell to like starving men, with a commotion of cutting, stabbing, chomping, and slurping that scarcely was interrupted by speech at all. Ill-mannered, by some standards, but their hunger seemed genuine enough. And even as they fed they took turns getting information out of me—asking me brief questions about how things were going at Ngemba, what the chef de poste was up to, how Kate was doing, what I had been hearing about the commissaire's activities. I swallowed my food, held my fork at bay, and made some careful answer. But in the meantime they were mopping the gravy from their plates, and when the servant came in to clear the table I was only halfway through my first helping, which was only a modest part of what I would have eaten, given time. But it seemed there was no time to give at the pères' table, and I could only watch as the still heavily laden serving dishes were whisked off to the kitchen.

But there was always some consolation. Now Père Andrés shoved his glasses back, wiped his fleshy lips, and announced that he would make the call to Kisaka on the phonie. Père Michel ushered me onto the veranda and brought me a tall mug of beer, and also a couple of letters that had just arrived, including one from Pers. I put the letters into my bag, and we settled into our chairs and took long drafts of our cold beer. Père Michel sighed deeply, as if to say: "Now at last we have a little time to relax!" But the pères always seemed to have time to relax when they were drinking beer, which made me wonder why they had so little to spare for eating lunch. I suppose because they were anxious to get to the beer.

In the next room Père Andrés barked loudly into the radio microphone. A blast of static and a relatively subdued voice answered him. Père Michel shook his head and leaned across the table. "I fear he is becoming deaf," he said. "Always I am hearing his voice most painful in my ear. Also he becomes a small bit confused because of not hearing well. It causes, ah, some difficulties for the fathers."

Père Andrés appeared at the French doors and waved me inside. "Okay," he whispered excitedly. "They wait for talking. Les frères Jucht!" And a moment later I found myself speaking French not to anybody's brother but to a woman who said she was the office manager. I had trouble making myself clear to her. On several occasions there were long periods of nothing but static coming over the airwaves, and I wondered if the woman had wandered off, perhaps to complain about this conversation to someone else in the office, or maybe to get a soft drink. Finally she returned with the definitive information that no camion had arrived. "Pas encore," she said several times. "We will let you know." But her "pas encore" did not convince me that she ever expected to have a camion for me, or that she had any idea why I should be asking her for one, or that she even knew who I was or had heard of the place I was calling from. And when I asked her about a response to my Consultant's Assessment, it was obvious I'd pushed her civility and patience with my stammering French to the limit. "I don't know specific details of this report," she said icily. "We process many reports. Perhaps you should come into the office. Avec un interpreter, peut être."

"How can I come into the office," I replied, her rudeness inspiring indignation and an almost heroic French fluency, "when I'm four hundred kilometers out in the bush and I have no Land Rover?"

"Il faut voler," she suggested. "Don't you have a bush plane? If you are a technician in the remote bush, as you say, you should have a bush plane. This is how most of them are accustomed to traveling. The roads, in any case, are not passable."

When I got off the radio Père Michel poured me another glass of beer, and Père Andrés patted me on the shoulder.

"I will advice you something for this country," he said. "You should not never be making some business with the phonie. No. Who will understand nobody talking on this phonie, eh? Much lyings and confusions begin this way, in the phonie."

"This is especially if the hearing is not so good, of course," pointed out Père Michel. "But it is true that we don't really give attention to what we hear on this radio."

"Not for business," said Père Andrés, wagging his finger in my face. "People will like to see you for making the accordance, they like looking your eyes and shaking your hand. They desire first for seeing the person, and follow with making the business accordance."

"Yeah, sure," growled Père Michel. "They got to see. The eyes, the hand, but especially the pocketbook, see how thick is the money."

"Of course, of course," said Père Andrés. "They having to see money, yah, this is the natural. Money is making the business, this is accustomed for all places, eh? You go to Kisaka and show moneys, you will be finding some camion, sure. Ha-ha! Even here at the mission we are making the business sometime, you know? Not for having moneys. Because here we following only word of God. Very simple, very purity, eh? All moneys we are leaving in hands of God. We do not endure corruptions of such regulation, but in the name of God, we are making business sometimes. Ha-ha!"

"Do you know what he is saying?" Père Michel asked me. "His English confuses, don't you think? This kind of English gives me something like a headache."

"Eh? It is the beer making a headache, eh? The same reason for his confuse in English. But I explaining to help you find the camion. Because you see there are many, many camions. Already I tell you, eh? You must make your thinking beyond this only one, that nobody never seeing with the eye! Many camions! In this country all Europeans having them, all Americans, all Indians and Arabs. Even Father Michel having a camion, you know? A Land Rover."

"*Has* a camion, Andrés, not *having*." Père Michel rubbed his forehead.

"Yes! You see they are all places." Père Andrés giggled suddenly. "Hey! You want to buying transport for cheap, maybe you buy that motorcycle of your friend. You know, he is here today, short time before, hoping for selling to the fathers his moto. Selling cheap. Ha-ha!"

"Yah, not sufficient cheap," grumbled Père Michel. "That's a garbage moto."

"Tom was here?"

"Yah. We explain to him, we don't want no machine like this. Maybe we have an interest for a machine to go one place from another, but not one just sitting in the road making the oil puddle. Okay, he says, maybe I try the sisters. Sure, the sisters!"

The pères shook their heads and rolled their eyes, as if to indicate that they thought Tom was crazy but they didn't hold it against me, just because we were countrymen. Then Père Andrés turned to me, serious again.

"So you see this talking on the phonie is nothing. Zero. Better no talk, just showing the proper moneys to the person of competence, as Père Michel is said. Then you make the business accordance! Then, driving the Land Rover."

"I often drive mine," Père Michel said. "It is very useful in my work."

"On the mission," added Père Andrés, "you will see him driving only on the mission."

"Where my work is. Father Andrés works in the bush, I work in the mission."

"He was before driving also in the bushes," Père Andrés explained. "Until the time there is the unhappy accident. A boy is mounting on a bicycle along the road, and Father Michel in his Land Rover does not saw this situation entirely, and bad chance! He drived overtop this boy!"

Père Michel shook his head, glowering. "You understand he exaggerates. The boy, of course, was not truly injured."

"Eh? The boy is broken his leg. But oh, yes, he was fortune, coming under protection of God. But the people of village has very much anger of Father Michel."

"Well, you know, this boy was not watching. He showed no competence for riding this bicycle. He had no balance. He had no steerage ability."

"They wished to kill Father Michel. Oh, yes. They make the offer for burning the Land Rover. I decline this occasion. I offer compensations to avoid this injury. We agree for Père Michel to not again be driving in bushes, passing villages. Only the mission."

"Well," said Père Michel, "this story does not concern you. It was long ago, and everyone has forgiven each other. And in any case I am quite satisfied to drive only in the mission. These roads I myself maintain. Outside the mission the roads are terrible and very dangerous. Do you know that in this country after independence they have gone from having fifty thousand miles of road to fewer than ten thousand? The rest they give back to the jungle. I do not wish to also give my Land Rover to the jungle, so I am most content to remain driving only in the mission."

"But the mission is not large," said Père Andrés. "It is possible for walking."

"I am a builder. I work with my hand, but I must move tools and materials. We are already limited in the purchase of materials. Without transportation, construction will become primitive. The buildings will fall down each five years, like in the village."

Père Andrés pushed his glasses back up on the bridge of his nose. "There are many hands to working. Wagons, in all case. Materials and tools have not so difficult in the moving. He always having way for moving at time his Land Rover has been broking."

Père Michel spread his hands apart. "What is he saying? He has no comprehending of tenses for the English language, if you ask my opinion. This is all very painful for my head. Excuse me, I must make him an explanation." And he turned to Père Andrés and let loose with a torrent of passionate Flemish, which was returned with equal vehemence. Père Michel, still talking emphatically, got up and went inside.

"It is the drinking, eh?" said Père Andrés quietly. "And perhaps also because he is old. His mind going many direction at the same moment, like his Land Rover. But still he has intelligent, sure, and much skills. But this driving of the Land Rover, ach! Now we have something to make a headache!" He pushed his glasses up and shook his head. We could hear snatches of Père Michel's argumentative voice coming out of the rectory. "For myself," Père Andrés continued, "I open the eyes, also ears, as I am walking. And getting off from the road, if I see he is driving. But the sisters are unhappy. There will be coming a terrible accident, they say. I think they are right, eh? But what command can I tell? He is living here forty years, eh? Long, long time. So is a question of making a persuasion, not telling command. A question of making for him a compensation. Like a business accordance, eh? This would be satisfaction for him, this would make no shame for him in giving over his keys."

Père Michel returned to the veranda, reading aloud from an English-language textbook. He put the book in front of Père Andrés, and I drained my beer and excused myself, leaving the two priests on the veranda, opening another bottle and jabbing their fingers at sentence diagrams.

On the way back to Ngemba, I passed a motorcycle parked by the side of the road. Up the slope a dozen or more children stared down at me. Behind them some men sat in the yard outside a group of huts. A white man rose out of the crowd, waving.

"Consultant!"

"Nice haircut," I called up to him. Tom had mowed off most of his hair since the last time I'd seen him. The flattop made him look a little more dangerous, now with his bristling skull to go with the cockeyed glasses and high dusty boots and the raffia bag slung over his shoulder. And his greasy, filthy motorcycle leaning on its kickstand in the sandy yard. No wonder the pères thought he was crazy. He looked like some kind of highwayman. Or something wildly displaced, someone from a forgotten sect wandering out of time, an ancient human phenomenon that no longer had a place in the world.

"Come on up here, Will. Monsieur Consultant. I need some advice."

"What are you doing?"

"Waiting. That's what people do here, isn't it?"

"Are you waiting *for* anything?"

"Not really. There's a guy here who says he wants to buy my moto. I'm sure he's telling the truth. He just doesn't want to break it to me that he doesn't have a fucking cent to his name. He's gone to get his uncle or brother or somebody to look at it. An expert mechanic, you know."

A man gave up his chair, and we sat down with the others. Someone handed me a glass of palm wine.

"I bought a calabash when I saw I was going to end up waiting," Tom explained, "just to moderate the tedium. That's why I got so many friends here now."

"Why are you selling your moto?"

"Well, because I can't take it on the plane. That's right, the plane. I'm out of here, Will. I bought my ticket a few days ago. What, you thought I was going to stay forever? That agoraphobia had me by the balls, and Thanesboro was just a myth? Well, it's real, and I'm going to prove it to you by going there. But don't worry, you'll have time to get used to the idea. I got a lot of hassles, loose ends to tie up, and especially my good-bye fête to put together. A good-bye fête is a very big deal around here. Now everyone is shitting in their pants wondering what I'm going to do with all my stuff, especially my running shoes and this goddamn moto and of course my boom box. There must be at least half a dozen people in Malembe who've convinced themselves they're destined to receive the sacred boom box. But what the hell. I got my plane reservation. Now all I have to do is survive this fête, and in a few weeks the past three years of my life will seem like a weird dream. No, it already seems like a weird dream. Maybe from a distance it'll start to make some sense. But look, Monsieur Weewee, I didn't stop you just to drink palm wine and shoot the idle shit. I stopped you for a consultation."

The men sat silently. Some of them leaned toward us as if they too were listening to Tom, though of course his monologue was incomprehensible to them. All their drinking glasses were empty; Tom had emptied the calabash into ours. The children tightened their circle around us, staring. Now Tom drained his glass, set it down, and looked around at them. "Christ. Do you ever wonder what these miserable little fuckers are thinking when they look at you like that?" He locked eyes with one of the older kids. The boy sucked in his breath and backed away, and some of the others giggled nervously. "Huh? What are you looking at, you stinking bug-eyed scab-head? Fucking freak show? Some kind of fucking paleface juju prince of darkness? What *do* they think, man? If they sit here looking at me long enough I'm gonna— what? Levitate? I'm gonna wave my arms and televisions and running shoes and fucking motos and Land Rovers are going to materialize in front of them? Just watch me, you credulous little bastards, I'll spit on the ground and snakes and crocodiles'll rise out of the slime. Ha! I'll piss on your mama's fire and a geyser'll shoot up, bury your huts in steam and ash." He stared harder, then suddenly lunged toward the children, who scattered shrieking and giggling and regrouped farther away. "Okay, fuck it," said Tom. "You know what

I'm gonna do? I'm gonna sit here and do fucking nothing, kid. Kima mosi ve. You never saw such a miraculously boring white man. Just boring. But I guess I'm in good company, huh. Now get out of here. Katuka! Go on, get! I'm a guest of your father's, I don't have to put up with this bullshit." He waved them off, and one of the men stood and harangued them until they wandered away.

"Are you drunk?" I said. "Or just in a bad mood?"

Now it was my turn to come under that withering stare. "Will, you're so fucking out of touch. What do you mean, am I drunk? Drunk is meaningless in this country. That is, sobriety is meaningless, which amounts to the same thing. But no, technically I'm not drunk. Hung over, maybe. Brutal fucking coupiers' meeting in Kasengi last night."

"I heard you were there."

"I was there, all right. I'm telling you, those coupiers' meetings take it out of you. And your wife doesn't hold back, you know."

"Have you seen her today? Do you know where she is?"

"Sure. She's at your place, sleeping it off. I gave her a ride down on the back of my old pony here, before I went to the mission. Don't look at me like that, man, I let her wear the helmet. And don't worry, she was careful not to put her arms around me. She held on to the seat."

"I wasn't worried," I lied, thinking of them together all night in the darkness of Kasengi, drunk, then in the morning the motorcycle bouncing and swerving down the road, with her face close to his neck, and gravity or g-forces or maybe some other force pressing her up against his back.

"So, piñatas," said Tom.

"What?"

"That's what I wanted to consult you about. Didn't you tell me you've spent a lot of time in Mexico? You must have seen a piñata party somewhere."

"In Mexico? Never. Probably they only have piñata parties in the States, in suburban second-grade classrooms on Cinco de Mayo."

"Okay, I didn't know that. We never had Cinco de Mayo in Thanesboro. We went straight from the fourth to the sixth. We heard of piñatas but we don't know the operational details, the rituals, nothing. That's why I'm consulting you. It's obscure, but as a consultant don't you specialize in the obscure, the far-fetched, the inapplicable?"

"A piñata's a papier-mâché animal," I said flatly, "stuffed with candy and hung from a ceiling or a tree. Kids take turns swinging at it with a stick until it busts open, then there's a mad rush for the candy, and that's it."

"I knew it was something like that. They're blindfolded, right?"

"The kid with the stick is. You blindfold him, spin him around a few times, stand back, and let him swing. You have somebody on the end of the rope changing the height of the piñata too, to really disorient him."

"Yeah. Further disorientation will not be necessary, I think."

"Why do you want to know about piñatas?"

"Just a brain fart. I'll let you know if it amounts to anything. Look, I'm sick of waiting around for those bozos. Come on, I'll give you a ride back to Ngemba."

But I told him I felt like walking, and I shook hands all around and set out alone.

When I entered our yard Kate and Ndosi were sitting face-to-face in chairs under the mango tree. A dozen or so children leaned on the fence, watching. Kate would talk, and Ndosi would watch her intently; then he would talk while she watched him intently. They'd do this for a little bit, and then one or the other would start giggling, and pretty soon they'd both break down in hysterical laughter. After a while they'd compose themselves and go through it again.

So for once the children had reason to stare. But I didn't. I'd seen this odd behavior before, and I knew it was only an English lesson. You might think English lessons would not have been a priority for someone who had no hope of ever finding himself in an English-speaking country, someone with a sixth-grade education who hardly spoke passable French, which was in theory the *lingua franca* of his own country. But Ndosi had gotten fixated on the idea of learning English and somehow persuaded Kate to teach it to him. Probably she had no idea what she was getting into. Probably she expected only to indulge him in a few lessons before the obsession ran its course and the futility of the undertaking became apparent to everyone.

But it turned out that Ndosi had an aptitude for the language. He had exceptional powers of memory and concentration, a sharply tuned ear, a quick and adaptable tongue. And a fluid sense of logic, which allowed him to absorb without resistance the shifting rules and rationales of English grammar and spelling. His rapid progress sparked Kate's enthusiasm, and now she had another project on her hands: to help Ndosi achieve fluency and literacy in a language that no one around him spoke, except us.

You see I was a little sour on that project. Because in the Kivila Valley English was our private language, one of the few private things left to us. In English we could write notes and letters no one could decode. In English we could speak as openly in the public square as we did in the depths of our house. The English language insulated and protected us in this country where we were objects of constant scrutiny and speculation, where so much of our lives was in the public domain, and where domestic servants moved freely along the borders of our most private moments. And now Kate was further compromising that privacy by going out of her way to teach our secret language to one of those servants.

But Kate said that she at any rate had nothing to hide. She said this dichotomy between public and private no longer held, and that in any case Ndosi was not a spy. His motives were pure, she said. He loved learning, he loved language, he loved communicating and deciphering. And he read everything, or tried to, with equal patience and fascination. *Heart of Darkness* or *Products of the Oil Palm*, food labels or newsmagazines, a grocery list or a letter or the page of a journal left open on the desk—there was no boundary to what he would read, and he read not to probe forbidden secrets but simply to exercise his skill, and to celebrate the joy and miracle of literacy.

I waved to them and went up to the house. No one had started dinner. The beer and palm wine were wearing off, my head was starting to ache, and my residual frustration from lunch was building into a more serious hunger. I scrounged around in the cupboards for a snack, settled for a handful of peanuts, a banana, and a couple of aspirin, and went out to sit on the porch and read the letter from Uncle Pers.

Pers wrote that his health continued inexplicably to improve. Mavis was planning a vacation for them, a cruise, and he supposed he would have to go if she actually went through with it, though it sounded like a hellish sort of trip—a ship of fools touring pointlessly along the ruined coastlines of prostituted countries. Actually, what he looked forward to most was reading our letters. That took him into the real tropical world, that didn't even appear on the nautical charts of those floating geriatric motels. He told Mavis that if they must take a holiday, he wanted to go sailing. If only you had the strength, dear, she answered, not to mention the reflexes.

What does she know of my reflexes! She accepts without question that reflexes are slowed by the aging process, as the conventional wisdom tells her. But what of the dying process? The culmination of aging, certainly, but it puts a new twist on it. If Mavis went to the trouble of making her own obser- vations, she might notice something very curious: my reflexes are actually speeding up, they're faster than they've ever been; in fact, it's gotten to the point where quite often my reaction <u>precedes</u> *its catalyst and I find myself responding to an even before it has occurred! Reverberations of mortal trans- formations and impending ghostliness—but perhaps not as dramatic as it sounds, because in truth there's very little to react to around here, and any- way, these prescient reactions are mental and must still be physically processed by a body undeniably in the advanced stages of decay. Well, who would expect Mavis to recognize prescience, though she loves to toy with its imitations? Still, what it amounts to is a literal manifestation of those metaphors of Time she tosses about so carelessly. Here is your circular, nonsequential Time, Mavis, your Time standing on its head! But like most of us, she is comfortable only with metaphor—a cushion from reality, not something anyone expects to take on a life and breath of its own.*

I'm flattered that people in the Kiwila Valley remember me, or at least someone who resembles me. The Road Builder. I like that. Not that I recall ever being called the Road Builder before. And no, I have no memory of any particular building at Ngemba, not even which house I may have lived in.

Of course, you still haven't provided many clues to stimulate my mem- ory, have you? The Road Builder, the Road Builder's gardens, the Mission Road, the independence wars. Mavis loves all that, it's all so vague and mys- tical. She wants to scatter these allusions throughout my book—which is, after all, the work of an engineer, and sorely lacking in mysticism—and then <u>*get the damn thing published!*</u> *I believe she may be on the verge of losing her patience. She's taken to calling my agent (when she thinks I'm sleeping) and plotting strategies to convince me that the book is finished. Well, who can blame her? She's old, and the old have the best of reasons to be impatient.*

I am even older, though, and far more impatient than she. And I no longer give a damn about this book. I'm impatient with its unconformities, impatient for a clue, a discovery, a moment of significance, impatient with years and years of observations, packaged neatly in a book now, and pointing to nothing.

That could be a clue. Observation: some phenomenon recorded by an observer. So couldn't the unconformities represent a time when there was no observer, when the observer became, for a time, the phenomenon itself? When the observer was at last engaged in something of significance.

Maybe. And maybe that's no longer recoverable, maybe mystical allusion is all that's left of it. All that I should expect of you two, in any case. You're young; everything is different now, as you say, Will, and you are caught up in your own affairs, whatever they may be. Katy still running around the jungle, from the sounds of it, planting peanuts, going off with Marlon Brando on the back of his motorcycle, which doesn't seem to make Will jealous at all, somehow. That may be a sign of exceptional maturity, Will, or else just slow reflexes on your part.

This palm oil business seems to have captured your imagination, though, which is something I never would have expected. I'm glad you found my suggestions about your job illuminating, though I wonder if you have taken them very far. This idea of nobility in bureaucracy is not a joke, you know, and not merely a slogan either. I wonder if you've ever thought about what a bureaucrat is actually for. Surely not to be a model of something, to set impossible standards, or even to legitimately inspire people. Inspiration seems to be Katy's responsibility, as I understand it. No, what you must recognize is that beneath all the debris of reports and regulations and forms and recommendations and duplications, the bureaucrat exists for one purpose: to make connections. To join things together in an orderly fashion. Linkage! (Once again I quote Mavis.) Linkage between people, between people and things. The joining of separated remote bodies that need each other but that otherwise would never connect.

No doubt Mavis would accuse me of ambiguity here. Of giving advice that is abstract to the point of being useless. But if you begin to consider your jobs in these terms, you may come up with some things that are very concrete, not at all mystical, which you have the power to join together.

—Pers

I put down the letter and looked out at the yard. Beneath the mango tree the English lesson continued, with the bright river behind and the jungle on the opposite bank going into shadow. In the open sunlit spaces white mushipu light was shifting toward the shorter wavelengths, the orange and red tinges of late afternoon. And all around was the order and abundance of the yard, the swept earth and flowering vines, rows of sprouting vegetables and new tufts of grass in tight irrigated rows, like a scale model of the geometric fields of California. And the English lesson part of the symmetry: Ndosi focused and deliberate, leaning to Kate who sat as intent in her listening as he was in his speech, with her hair washed and brushed and her eyes clear, her summer dress clean and light on her shoulders, no residue left in her of a night in Kasengi on a hard lumpy bed with drunken voices echoing and her own sour palm-wine breath reinhaled in the confines of a sealed guest hut.

In laughter and handshakes the English lesson ended. They walked together to the porch. Ndosi reached up to shake my hand.

"Good afternoon, Mr. Will," he said carefully. "I go now to camp. I go now to make some visit." Then he laughed, as if to say: isn't it a kick, me speaking this English to you! He went out the gate and up toward the camp, and Kate sat down on the porch steps next to me.

"Making some visit," I said. "His girlfriend, I guess."

"Not even. She can't visit anybody, she has too much work to do. He'll sit around and talk with her father." She sniffed the air. "You smell a little— fermented."

"I had a beer at the pères'. And palm wine with Tom on the way home. More your style, I guess, for the middle of the day."

"Please don't talk about palm wine. It was hell this morning, coming down on the back of Tom's moto."

"Maybe you should get your own moto, so you could stop and sleep it off whenever you like. In fact, you could buy Tom's. He's trying to sell it, you know."

"That's what he says. But who would buy it? Not me. I don't even want a moto that *doesn't* break down all the time. I need a truck."

"Well, I spent the morning trying to find out about that. And I got through on the pères' phonie to Jucht Brothers in Kisaka. They say they don't know anything about a camion. But Père Andrés says that means nothing, because only confusion and lies come over the phonie. He says we shouldn't fixate on just one camion, because there are lots of camions in this country. Even Père Michel has one. A Land Rover."

"Père Michel? But I've never seen him driving."

"He only drives in the mission. And Père Andrés says even that's too much. That someday there will be a terrible accident if he keeps driving. He says everyone wants Michel to give up his Land Rover, but it's a question of how to persuade him. A question of compensation. He says at the mission they leave all money in the hands of God. But that in the name of God they do business sometimes."

STEEL AND GREASE

Kate went to the mission three times during the next week. The third time she returned driving an old battered Land Rover, with a crowd of jubilant children running in her dust.

It had required many hours of negotiation, she said, and a diplomatic sensibility not usually required in used-car deals. And in the end she had not made such a great bargain. Père Michel had flatly refused to sell his Land Rover, and after much argument Père Andrés agreed that no title would be transferred. Then Michel withdrew into a brooding silence while Kate and Père Andrés negotiated. Andrés gave little ground, and in the end Kate agreed to lease the vehicle on a monthly basis for what seemed an exorbitant sum. But after all, she said to me, the money didn't mean that much to her. She had no feeling for it, it was just accumulating as of its own volition in a remote California bank. Now she would be paying something like a quarter of her monthly salary for this Land Rover. But how would she even know the difference?

I didn't argue with her. Why not share our wealth with Père Michel, who would use at least some of it to build a hospital wing or a bridge or a school-room? Why not rent a Land Rover with it, and gave Placide a treasure to watch over, Ndosi a trophy to polish, the kids hanging on our fence a miracle to marvel at? And of course so Kate could return from Kasengi on something other than the back of Tom's motorcycle.

But the Land Rover itself left me feeling oppressed. It filled our small garage, and I felt its presence through the darkness when I sat on the porch at night, as if there were stabled within those aluminum walls some living thing that breathed and snorted and stamped the oil-soaked ground. The Land Rover was hard and tangible, a thing made of steel and grease, whatever its actual use and purpose might be. Beside it, my noble bureaucracy scarcely seemed to exist at all. It was still only a concept, abstract or even vacuous. Uncle Pers was right to criticize it. It had *seemed* like an idea with substance and merit, when he first had broached it. But what had come of it? If bureaucracy existed to connect things, as Pers claimed, then this noble bureaucracy was fizzling out completely. So far it was made only of sophistry and euphemism. So far it had connected nothing.

I told Kate I was giving the workers a raise.

"Excuse me?"

"I said the workers are getting a raise."

"Really?" I thought she looked slightly alarmed. "You mean the company's implementing one of your recommendations?"

"No."

"Well, what, then? What did they tell you?"

"They haven't told me anything. *I'm* implementing one of my recommendations. *I'm* giving the workers a raise. I recommend it, implement it, and provide the cash. I figure a thirty-percent cut out of my salary will double the incomes of seventy-five workers."

"Where'd you get an idea like that?"

"From you, obviously. From Tom, who may turn out to be psychotic but who at least knows that money is at the center of things. And from Uncle Pers, who says it's the job of the noble bureaucrat to connect remote things. This is what I came up with: a connection between a palm oil mill in Africa and all this money piling up to no purpose in my bank account."

She got up and went into the other room. A minute later she came back.

"Don't you think you're getting carried away with this noble bureaucracy thing?"

"What do you mean?"

"At first I thought you were being facetious. I thought you were entertaining us."

"Maybe. But being facetious will only get you so far."

"Well, how far are you going? How far have you thought this raise through? The best you can say for it is it'll provide some temporary relief.

Temporary. Because it's just a handout, Will, not a restructuring of any system. People won't comprehend where the money comes from, or why it stops coming when it inevitably does."

"I suppose they won't. I don't comprehend where it comes from either. Except that it's basically a handout to us to begin with. Why do the mill workers deserve a handout any less than I do? Or any less than you deserve a Land Rover?"

"The Land Rover's different. It's going to create work, create wealth."

"Really. What exactly are you planning on doing with it?"

"I'm going to drive it. I'm going to put Uncle Pers' beautiful roads to use. Haven't we been talking all this time about transportation, shipping, marketing? How people lack options, and how crippling that is? The Land Rover's a tool that can help them."

"Well, maybe my money can be a tool too. You need capital to create wealth, right? Maybe this will be an investment in long-term productivity. Maybe it can demonstrate to the Company the benefits of paying their workers a living wage."

The chef de poste was more receptive to my idea, though we had to work out the details. The chef's position was that he should get the same percentage raise the workers got. I didn't think the raise should apply to him at all, since he was already many times more affluent than his workers. But I needed his cooperation, so I agreed to give him a 25 percent salary increase, plus buy a load of cement for the Modernization Project. In return, he would provide the administrative and political cover to implement the raise and make it look like a raise, rather than the handout that Kate deplored.

Shortly afterward we had our first public meeting in the Place de la Révolution. A neat border of whitewashed rocks lent a certain formality to our gathering, though the Place still looked more like a bomb crater than a public square. The shabby crowd of workers stood shuffling before the chef, coughing and hacking, runny noses and tubercular lungs aggravated by the ash blowing off the piles of brush and timber they had cleared and burned during the previous weeks. But they broke into a spontaneous cheer when the chef announced that the Company would now pay twice what it had been paying for a basket of cut palm nuts, and everybody's hourly wage would double as well.

He held up a hand, and the cheering died out. Well, not quite *everybody*, he said. He himself was getting only a 25 percent raise, though he had many expenses that people who weren't in a position of leadership never considered. Sure, there were some benefits, sure he had a big house across the river, but it wasn't that great having a big house; in some ways all that space just complicated your domestic life, which as anyone who was married knew was a huge hassle even if you had nothing more than a chicken coop to worry about. Sure he had a duxième bureau, but think of the trouble created by that—it was hard enough supporting one woman, but supporting two was even worse, worse than twice as bad, because it was impossible to make both of them happy simultaneously. In fact, each woman was pissed off at him precisely half the time, which meant he had to spend twice as much money on whoever was upset to make her happy again, which made the other one twice as jealous. So if you worked out all the math, a 25 percent raise didn't come close to covering it. Still, he was taking only a small raise because he knew the Company was having a rough time, and he was hoping that this raise would get people off their butts and back on the job, working on the Modernization Project so when the commissaire finally showed up they'd have a mill they could show him with pride.

One more thing, said the chef: this raise was largely a result of the tireless work of Monsieur Will the consultant, who had skillfully negotiated it with the appropriate authorities. So everyone owed Monsieur Will a debt of gratitude.

The men cheered me, and some came up afterward to fervently pump my hand. I was a hero, everybody's benefactor, everybody's patrón. But I had no idea what the men were really thinking, because as the mushipu wore on, they collected very little of the raise they had seemed so pleased to get. Most of the mill workers and coupiers stayed in the camp or worked at clearing and burning fields or simply disappeared into the forest, supposedly to hunt or dig fishponds. Some went to Kisaka. The palm-nut trucks made their rounds only rarely, returning only half full, and the pile of palm nuts waiting to be processed dwindled. The mill and its environs had an obvious air of neglect, and the Modernization Project seemed to be entirely forgotten.

.   .   .

"Well, it's not the first time those kinds of incentives have failed in this place," said Tom. "So I'm not surprised. In fact, there are no surprises here. Everything has happened before. The thing with you, Will, is you're working in your own isolation ward. You got a two-dimensional understanding of your situation. And now you're trying to make an arrangement that lets you feel sanctimonious about something, but I can tell you that's not going to work. Look, I had the same problem, until I finally realized I needed to go deeper. That's when I started reading the history. The old wars and grudges, the insane colonial arrangements, the slavers, the missions, the construction of roads and cities. I dug into it all. Now I'm reading the explorers. Stanley. De Brazza. Dr. Livingstone. Captain Burton and General Gordon. Maniacs, you know what I'm saying? Obsessive, arrogant, and with incredible capacities for suffering. And for inflicting suffering, obviously. They began the invasion which we continue today, Will. They set this remarkably fucked-up machinery in motion, and if you want to begin to understand what you're doing here and how far your complicity extends, you have to look back to them."

Other explanations were more to the point but just as unhelpful. Mill workers and coupiers were very pleased with the raise, Ndosi assured me. But perhaps there was no palm nut to be cut right now, in the middle of the mushipu. No, said Kate, there was plenty of palm nut, but the men had other responsibilities, and the chef de poste was having trouble with his women.

The chef de poste sat at his desk not even pretending to work. "There's always palm nut in the forest," he said. "And the coupiers are always cutting. They're just not bringing it here."

"Why not? They brought you more than this when they were being paid half the money."

"Who understands coupiers? Maybe it depends on what arrangement they have with their animatrice."

"Well, I'm sure she's encouraging them to cut palm nut."

"Oh, sure." The chef leaned back in his chair, smoking and watching me, chuckling a little to himself. "Is she still asleep?" he said.

"She got home late last night. Mamas' meeting."

"Right," the chef said grimly. "In Bulolo." He lit a cigarette, scratched at the thick fold of his neck, blew out the smoke. "I know, because my wife went too."

"I didn't know your wife went to those meetings."

"She went this once. I don't think it's going to be a habit. I mean, it's not going to be a habit." The chef kept watching me while he tapped the ashes off his cigarette. "It's not easy on a man, is it? Marriage, I mean. Sure, it's not easy on women either, I know that. Nobody really knows how to deal with it. Particularly white people. Excuse me, but that's my observation. I mean, the pères and the souers have lots of advice, but who's going to believe they know what they're talking about when it comes to men and women? And when you look at white people who've had some actual experience with marriage, it always turns out they've been divorced. What kind of experience is that? The experience of failure. Have you been divorced, William?"

"No. But I don't have much experience either. I've only been married for . . . I guess it's hard to say exactly how long."

"Well, don't divorce her."

"I'm not planning on it. In fact, technically, I'm not even sure——"

"You may think you have good reasons. She's all over the countryside with that Land Rover. She stays out all night. She doesn't cook. No children. But I tell you, divorce is not the solution. No matter what she's doing, don't divorce her."

"She's not doing anything. I mean——"

"Just beat her."

"What?"

"Beat her," he repeated, gazing thoughtfully through the cloud of smoke he blew across his desk. "It's simple. That's the end of it."

Before I could think of a response, there was an awful clattering sound from the mill, and the machinery fell suddenly silent. The chef didn't seem to notice. He studied me, shaking his head and chuckling. "In the old days, you know, you would have been my boss. Before independence, I mean. Can you imagine? You bossing me around, telling me what to do with the palm nut, showing me how to fix the hydraulic press."

We laughed together at the absurdity of the idea.

"I have to remember this," he continued, "when I think what a huge catastrophe our independence was. Oh, yes. I can't say that in public but anyone can see that it's true. You look at anything—the buildings, the economy, the soldiers, the factories—and it's obvious that things haven't gone well during the past thirty years. And now we can't get petroleum. We don't even have oil to lubricate our machines. And the roads! The roads are maybe the worst of it. They've gone completely to hell. Maybe you're not aware of this."

"Oh, I'm aware of it."

"No you're not. I'm not talking about the roads around here. These are the *good* roads, William. Well engineered, very well engineered. Good drainage. The Road Builder put them in, you know. He had a special touch, they say. A special medicine to make his roads stronger than others. That's what people say. Do you know anything about that? No, maybe you don't. Well, it could be they're still in good shape because we take care of them; we pay our cantoniers, and they get out there with their shovels every once in a while. If you go elsewhere in this country, you'll find the roads are entirely washed away. That's what *I* call erosion, William! When I travel on those roads my body suffers, my bones ache, and I find myself wishing the whites would return and do something about the damn roads. But as soon as the trip's over, I come to my senses and remember: if we were still a colony I might not be traveling at all, because I wouldn't be the chef—William would! You and your wife! What kind of a situation would that be? And that wouldn't be the worst of it. There'd be white people everywhere, telling us what to do. Telling us where to put our villages, how deep to dig our waysays, telling us what to eat, even! We'd be eating bread instead of luku by now, if you were still in charge. Though I wouldn't mind as much as some. Sometimes I actually get sick of luku, you know? Not that I want to give it up. But I would like a little variety. In the old days we got rice occasionally, and lots of bread. I developed a taste for bread, though I suppose I don't really miss it. It's not a natural food for us. We can't even grow wheat here, so why should we be eating bread?"

"I guess you shouldn't."

"But we would be if the whites were running things. Spending all our money on flour from Mputu. Sitting on the grass eating bread—you'd make us plant grass everywhere, like at the mission, and we'd all be making our living killing snakes for you! Don't be offended, William. I like bread. I like white people. I like having consultants, technicians, advisors around. Even priests—they keep the place running, I admit that. But what I like is white people giving advice, not making rules. Providing technological assistance, maybe, and then stepping aside. Like the Frenchwoman I saw in a bar the last time I was in Kisaka, giving away English sacs. Ha! She wasn't the kind of woman you usually see in a bar like that, but there she was, talking with everybody, and passing out pamphlets. It was all about AIDS. And then she came around with a box of English sacs for anybody who wanted one. She *gave* me a box—a dozen English sacs! And—I'll have to show you this—on the box it says: 'A gift of mercy from the Sisters of the Ascension.' That's right. Nuns in Mputu, sending me a whole box of English sacs!"

"English sacs."

"Sure. I've been meaning to ask you about them, if you have access, if you can get me some. I can't hardly buy them these days, and if I do find them they're not cheap. But I've always been willing to pay. Not to use with my wife, of course, or my girlfriend. That would be insulting to them. But I always use them with the village women, out of consideration to my wife. I have for many years, even before people were talking about AIDS, before whites started setting up tables in bars and passing them out to whores and everybody! And giving us little booklets about AIDS with each box. AIDS! What do you think about all this, William?"

"About AIDS? Well, it's a terrible tragedy. People need to change their behavior, obviously. They need education. I don't know, maybe the pamphlets help."

"Oh, sure. We could always use some education, though you have to wonder, some of the things they tell you in those pamphlets. . . . You know what they say? They say it started right here. They say we got it from monkeys. Can you believe that?"

"Well, I guess there is some research. . . ."

The chef stared at me. "Sure," he said, "sure, research, but consider who came up with it, William. These scientists who say we got AIDS from monkeys, these are the same people who say we *came* from monkeys. That our *ancestors* were monkeys! What is it, William, about white people and monkeys?"

At midmorning I went back to the house to get a cup of coffee and see if Kate was up. The yard was deserted and the bedroom shutters still closed, though

Ndosi was clattering around in the kitchen. As I approached the door I heard a soft high voice, so quiet it might not have registered on my hearing, except that it was so familiar, and so entirely out of context in the full light of day.

"Monsieur."

Placide rose out of the bamboo chair in the corner of the porch. I seldom saw Placide during the day, and I never had seem him dressed like this: no watch cap or greatcoat, only a clean untattered T-shirt tucked into what looked to be a pair of maternity pants. And shoes. It was the first time I'd seen him wearing shoes—a pair of ancient warped and scuffed wingtips, several sizes too large, no socks or laces. To keep them on his feet, Placide was forced to shuffle. It was painful to watch him shuffle like that across the porch to shake my hand, and it suddenly occurred to me that Placide was one of the very few Jucht Brothers employees not to have gotten a raise, since there had been no provision for giving raises to the sentinels. Yet the sentinels were practically the only employees still doing any work. Now here he was, dressed up and pumping my hand like the rest of them, no doubt having come to humbly petition me for the money he should have received as a matter of course.

I felt terrible. "It was an oversight," I apologized lamely. Placide responded by holding out a small calabash of palm wine. "Matubish, monsieur," he explained. "Cadeau." I took it from him and waited, not knowing what to do with the gift. Was I expected to drink this stuff now, as penitence, at ten in the morning? Ndosi came out with two chairs, and Placide and I followed him into the shade of the mango tree and sat down. Placide sat stiffly, as if his day-time clothes had all the straightening and constricting effects of a suit and tie. I sat stiffly too, with the calabash foaming on my lap and a sweet putrid smell coming into my nostrils.

"I'm sorry I didn't settle this earlier, Placide. We've been distracted. Things get overlooked."

He shrugged. "Tell the boy to get drinking glasses," he said.

I looked up to see how Ndosi would respond to this effrontery from the sentinel, but he had already gone into the house, and soon returned with three glasses in hand. I poured the palm wine, and Ndosi and I sipped ours. It tasted surprisingly sweet, better than it smelled, better than I'd expect palm wine to taste at this time of day.

"I'll go down and work things out with the chef de poste right now," I suggested.

Placide tipped his head back and poured the entire glassful of palm wine down his throat, his Adam's apple steadily bobbing as he swallowed. Then he put his glass down and looked straight at me.

"It's not the chef de poste's affair, monsieur."

"Well, officially, you know, you work for him. He has to make the arrangements."

"But the book belongs to you."

"The book?"

"Yes. We've already made the arrangements. You promised me the book, and now I'm ready to receive it."

"I don't know what you're talking about."

"The book you said you would give me, Monsieur Will. The book I read to learn how to read. This is what I have come to claim."

"I don't remember saying . . . Wait a second, are you talking about my dictionary?"

I tried to recall our conversation from several weeks earlier, when I'd tried to explain to him what a dictionary was. Somehow from that explanation he'd gotten this paradoxical idea that by reading a dictionary he would learn how to read, and I couldn't persuade him that such a thing was impossible. I made fumbling excuses and apologies, and read in his impassive face resentment and hurt. Really, a raise would have been much easier. Stalling for time, I poured us each another cup of palm wine, and he drained his as he had the first, in a single long, undulating swallow. I emptied the rest of the calabash into his glass and asked him about the health of his wife.

"All my life I've wanted to read, monsieur, but I've never had a book."

"Placide, there is no single book that teaches you how to read. It doesn't exist."

"You told me about this book, Monsieur Will. Why have you forgotten?"

Tousled and bleary-eyed, Kate appeared on the porch, brushing her teeth. I went up to her and explained what was happening.

"So give him a book," she said, spitting over the railing.

"He wants the dictionary."

"We need the dictionary. It doesn't matter what book, he can't tell the difference anyway. Just give him one we don't read anymore."

Ndosi was already in the living room, taking a book from the shelf. "This one will be good, Monsieur Will."

I started to object, and then I thought, why not? At least it's durable, and it has pictures. And when I went back to the mango tree and handed it to Placide, I was rewarded with a rare beaming smile. I tried to make a disclaimer, something to modify his expectations, but Placide got up and wordlessly shook my hand with both of his. Then he stepped back, held the book against his chest, and made the longest speech I had ever heard from him. In the night, he said, monsieur came to my fire. We talked of many things, and monsieur told me the tale of a wondrous book the whites have made, a book that is like a medicine for teaching the magic of reading. Monsieur said, this is a book I will give to you, my sentinel. I gave thanks to monsieur for the promise of this gift. Many days passed. Then early this morning I knew that the time had arrived. I left my fire and went to a coupier to buy palm wine. I changed my clothes, and returned to this house. The boy brought chairs. Monsieur and I sat together, we drank palm wine, we had a discussion. I waited in the chair while monsieur entered the house and returned with the book. Thank you, monsieur. Thank you very much. Now our discussion has ended. The palm wine is finished. The book is in my hands. I will go to my house now, and read it for a while before I sleep. Good-bye.

He shook hands all around, picked up his calabash, put the book on his head, and went out the gate. He seemed to stagger a little, as if he were slightly drunk, though it may have just been a new lilt in his step, or the difficulty of walking in those wingtips, with the additional challenge of keeping *Products of the Oil Palm* perfectly balanced on top of his head.

I went up the porch steps a little unsteadily also—maybe from the palm wine so early in the day, or else because I too was adjusting to a shift in the weight I bore. *Products of the Oil Palm* had many failings, but I did owe to it my understanding of palm-oil processing. And after all I was a technician, that was my area of expertise, and I'd just sent Placide away with my only technical reference on top of his head. I wasn't sure why I had done such a thing, but when a few minutes later the mill coughed and choked and chugged back to life, it was clear that something fundamental had changed. I watched the familiar cloud of greasy smoke go up into the sky, listened to the rising howl, and understood that for me this machinery had returned to a state of mechanical gibberish: a random collection of pulleys and flywheels and gears, spinning and grinding incoherently, and it was no longer my responsibility to try to make any sense of it.

Ndosi came out on the porch and asked permission to leave work early so he could harvest greens from his garden and sell them in the camp in the afternoon.

"I bet people in the camp are glad to have you coming around selling greens."

"Oh, yes. People say I have the most beautiful greens in the valley."

"So sales are good?"

"No. They buy very little."

"Oh. I guess because they have very little money?"

"No. Because they have very little intelligence. That is, because of their little intelligence, they have little money. And I tell them this: the reason you have little intelligence is because you don't eat enough greens. Oui, monsieur! They lack protein, they lack vitamins, and this makes them stupid. But because they don't eat greens they're too stupid to understand the need to eat greens. So they don't buy any, and this is a big problem for me. Only you and Kate buy my greens, and look at you—the richest, smartest people in the camp!"

Ndosi slapped my hand, roared with laughter, and went out the gate. It was true that Kate and I ate unprecedented quantities of greens, since she always bought whatever was left in Ndosi's baskets when he passed by on his way home from the camp. But we couldn't eat them by the pound, day in and day out, so we ended up composting most of what we bought. Ndosi pretended not to see the greens in the compost pile, and Kate and I pretended that this situation didn't betray a failure of the intelligence all this greens eating was supposed to promote.

There was sometimes a moment in the dry-season afternoons when I became aware that the day had lost much of its momentum. Things seemed to be going on as before, yet there was a certain diminishment in the world, as if the weight of the mushipu were bearing down harder on its inhabitants. The mill ground on, and a few people moved about: the secretary sitting on the bench outside his office, women and children calling a greeting from the road, maybe a few people milling around the marché, if the marché was even happening at all. Kate in the doorway of our house in that summer dress, brushing out her hair, watching me. A couple of soldiers coming down the road in their fatigues and their high black boots. And across the river the Nakahosa brothers, Ndosi's fishermen cousins, standing to paddle their low pirogues while on the valley slopes behind them thin streams of smoke rose out of the forest clearings and were lost at once in the vast deep smokiness of the sky.

I left the porch and went down to the center of the yard, where I was surrounded by a bright haze, everything indistinct under a dead white sun. For a while there was no one passing on the road, no boat visible on the river. No one in the mill yard except the soldiers poking about in the slag heaps of the Place de la Révolution. No children at the gate, nobody on the porch, the open doorway empty, the house silent and dim, the bedroom windows shuttered, and Kate lying on the bed with the mosquito netting thrown back and her summer dress pulled up to her thighs.

Outside we could hear the grinding of the mill, the rough laughter of soldiers, children playing on the path and the Nakahosas' voices crossing the water. So the static world continued as before. Yet somewhere in the back of my mind I kept thinking how volatile we are. How we must contend with forces we can never reckon with. How on one night, knowing Kate was out in a midnight torrent wild and drunk and sleeping on the floors of huts in villages steeped in sorcery and blood feuds, I could sleep untroubled, secure in the sense of her presence beside me in bed. And how on another night she could drive a Land Rover home and I could wake in the morning with her sleeping beside me and not know what to make of her presence at all. How I could put my hands all over her and never contain her. Never even interpret her. How her skin was full of messages, how everything she was thinking and feeling came through her skin in languages of texture and temperature and moisture and vibration and scent, but that didn't mean I could understand those languages. Or that the languages even kept the same meaning, that they weren't volatile and changeable themselves. How not long ago, lying on the living room couch beneath the leering tribal masks, overcome by sudden nausea and the sensual excess of the tropical night, I'd frightened myself with a vision of her body as a part of that excess—the raw textures of the skin, the interior folds, the scents and secretions, the swellings of fatty flesh on the surface, like some terrible glandular growth. And now I could not take my eyes away as she lay with the sheets thrown back, her body cooling, breathing calmed, her breasts pale and almost luminescent in the dusky light.

"White tits," she said, watching me.

"Well, yes."

"Very different from black tits."

"You think?"

"Some people think so."

She got up and began to dress. "Have you ever wondered what it's like inside the guest house?" she said.

"Sure. But it's never open, except when the chef's in there with his duxième bureau."

She nodded. "Well, I went in the other day. I was walking past and I noticed the door was open. I was pretty sure that nobody was inside, because I'd just seen the duxième bureau up in the camp, sitting on somebody's steps getting her hair done. And not long before I'd seen the chef cross the river to his house. So I went in. I just wanted to see what it was like."

"So what's it like?"

"Well, it was kind of creepy. The light was dim, of course, like this light, only gloomier. There's a lot of stuff in there, unusual stuff, for around here. Old polished hardwood furniture, framed pictures on the wall, a few baskets and vases and even some knickknacky things. And I got this strange sense that I was looking directly into the past, that it had been exactly like that for years and years. That nothing had been added or taken away or even rearranged since the days when people had actually lived there. But there was no clutter, or even dust. Everything was preserved, like a museum. I was looking down the hall, thinking about checking out the bedrooms, when I heard a giggle. This nervous little giggle right at the door. It was the duxième bureau, standing in the front doorway looking at me. Well, I was embarrassed. But before we could think of anything to say to each other, I heard something else: a kind of gravelly rumble coming out of the shadows at the far end of the room. It was terrifying for a second, and I might have bolted if the duxième bureau hadn't been blocking the doorway, still giggling. But the rumble was only some kind of laughter. Because it turned out that the chef de poste had been in the room all along, sitting in the darkness at the far end, and now he came out, still laughing, and said if I was looking for him I should call at the door and not slip inside like a burglar.

"Now I was completely embarrassed. I told him I was sorry and started babbling about how I wasn't really looking for him, I just saw the open door and came in without thinking, because I've always been curious about the house and I didn't think I was disturbing anyone. And he says, oh you still got a hunger for a big house, Mama Kate. You still got your eyes on my guest house. And I said, no, I was just curious about it, and he says, well, it was a curious house, and it had a history. European families had lived in this house. Many different white people had stayed here, at one time or another. Things had happened in that house that we in our time could no longer imagine, he said. He talked on. I think he was getting nostalgic. He followed me out to the porch, talking about the old times, and while we were standing on the porch this woman comes by on the path from the camp, this mama with a basket of manioc on her head and these big old boobs swinging down to her belly button, and the chef stares at her and says to me, kind of gloomily, I must have seen ten thousand breasts in my lifetime. Every one of them as black as the ones that just went by. I didn't say anything—ten thousand seemed like a low estimate if anything. But then he says, I've never seen a white woman's breasts. Really I said. Yeah, he says, and I used to take it for granted that someday I would. I mean, I've worked with whites all my life. There used to be quite a few white women around here, but of course they were always careful to cover up their breasts. Still, I figured one day in the evolution of things I'd have an affair with one of my counterparts' wives, or even with a single white woman, until everything went to hell and all the white women left, except for the nuns. But even then I thought it was just a matter of time. Europe didn't seem that far away, then, and one day I would go to Europe and visit a white prostitute. That's what I planned. But now it's obvious that's not going to happen, either. In my lifetime the world has become very small, they say, yet I can go to my deathbed never having seen a pair of white breasts.

"Well, that was kind of poignant, the way he said it. Yes, Will! As if he were dying with something essential unfinished, something missing from his life. But it was also silly, of course. I mean, what a thing to focus your regret on! But poignant or silly, I was tempted to pull up my T-shirt and my bra and let him have a look."

"But you didn't."

"I didn't. But before I left I asked him if he remembered some of the white people who had lived in the guest house, and he said some of them, and I asked him if the Road Builder was one. Well, yes, he said, he remembered the Road Builder. And was the Road Builder's wife one of those white women, I said. He gave me a strange look and said the Road Builder had come to Africa without a wife. And why were we always asking about the Road Builder, he said. And I said I didn't know that we were. Then he said maybe that wasn't so strange because people talked about him still, maybe because no one knew what had happened to him, he just disappeared during the fighting after independence. There were all kinds of stories about that, he said. There was so much confusion in those days. Rebels and soldiers fighting. People fled their villages, or were driven out. The Road Builder was gone in the middle of it. That was how it was in independence days, the chef said. People disappeared. Everything changed; every day the world was different. You never had time to figure it out, but you got used to being surprised, so now, he said, nothing surprises me, even the sight of you, Madame Kate, coming in without knocking through the door of my house, as if you belonged here."

1 9

FÊTE

"Tragedy or farce, Will?"

"What?"

"That's the question I'm wrestling with lately. The wrong question, of course. Mere taxonomy. But I can't help asking it."

Tom's fête was the highlight of the season, a grand affair of feasting and drinking, music and dance, marred only by the unexpected demonstration of witchcraft or insanity that concluded it. That's how people seemed to remember it. But for me it was a shadowy and dusty affair, a crowd of people shuffling about in a black night, stirring up dry earth. There was a band, pushing a tiny battery-powered amp far beyond the limits of its capabilities, until it mercifully expired in the early hours of the morning, and the partygoers danced on to the beat of drums.

"Some of these people walked twenty, thirty clicks to come to my party, Will. Why? They should be sleeping, so they can work in their fields tomorrow. Some of them are going to be sick, because they got drunk and didn't sleep and walked twenty clicks each day. They'll be too sick to work. Then the rains will be here and they'll be late planting. Crops will fail. Children won't get enough to eat because of this fête, Will. Children will die because of my fête."

Dinner was several hours late, and most of the male guests, including me, were drunk by the time we sat down to eat. Female guests were mostly sober, except Kate. The food was excellent—roast pig, fried tilapia, spicy greens, luku, sweet potato, and rice—but people complained that although Tom had bought plenty of food, there wasn't enough to go around. Someone involved in the preparation must have stolen some. Ndosi, who'd been in charge of slaughtering the pig, came under suspicion. He spent the evening careening from one group to another, offering indignant rebuttals and counteraccusations. Occasionally he came by Tom and me to present a new piece of evidence or an additional convolution to the argument.

"Your boy's awfully fucking animated tonight."

"I guess you can't blame him for being upset. Was there really food missing?"

"How should I know? Who's to say he didn't pack away some bacon on the side? And that he's not enjoying a little squabble and intrigue now? What about you, Monsieur Weewee? You look a little dazed. Are you bored with my party?"

"Not exactly. It's a spectacle, in its own tedious way. It's hard to know what to make of it."

"Sure. That taxonomy problem again. Farce or tragedy? Our problem, not theirs. A problem for the literary mind, the abstracted mind, the technological mind, Will."

Kate and I were seated as guests of honor. We drank palm wine and chewed on kola nuts that old people kept pressing into our hands. They were nasty, bitter things, but I was developing a taste for them, and they seemed to go along with the sour palm wine, the coating of dust on my throat, and the figures lurching past in the dust and darkness.

"You heard anything lately from that old uncle of Kate's?"

"We got a letter not long ago."

"You hear stories about that guy, huh? The Road Builder. People tell some wild stories."

"What stories have you heard?"

"Oh, all kinds of wild shit. I'm sure none of it's true. People just make stories up, that's what they're good at, mainly."

We watched Kate dance with the secretary. Tom hooted and clapped and shimmied in his chair. Kate smiled, but for an animatrice she seemed subdued.

"I been thinking more and more about the similarities between this place and Thanesboro, you know? Also the differences."

"Oh. So there *are* differences."

"Some. This is the fundamental one: here, the processes are all crazy, right? The premises. The cause-effect sequences. They're totally screwball, know what I'm saying? And yet in the end they take you to a place that is rational, that makes sense. This is what draws us to this place, even though we don't understand what's going on. Whereas in Thanesboro, the processes and premises are nothing if not rational. Yeah. And they lead to conclusions that are entirely fucking mad."

I stayed in my chair and drank, but Tom danced frequently, going fluidly from conversation to dance and back to conversation again, as if these were just different aspects of the same activity. He was a good or at least an exuberant dancer, not as subtle and intricate as some but perhaps more interesting to watch, because he maintained such a high level of risk and exposure. He always seemed on the verge of a spectacular crash, the kind of wild drunken spinning collision that could take out half the dance floor. But he never entirely lost control, never followed through on the threat implied by those flailing arms and stomping boots. Nobody got hurt, and people cheered when he careened off the floor, snatched his glasses out of the air as they went flying off his face, and sat down in the dust, panting and laughing.

"You know, I never did pay for that airline ticket."

"What?"

"Never mind. What time do you think it is?"

"I don't know. Late. I'm thinking about going to bed."

"We should all go to bed. But first I gotta finish packing. When are these people going home, Will? When will they let us sleep? The palm wine's gone. The amplifiers are blown. Why do they stay?"

"They stay to honor you, right? That's what I keep hearing. Also I guess they're having a good time."

"Oh, yeah. To honor me. Also to see who gets my boom box. Everybody's got a hard-on for my boom box. They can't help themselves. Every sonofabitch here can find some reason to hope he'll be the chosen one."

"So, who gets it?"

"You want it too, huh? Well, you'll have to wait with the rest of the cargo cult."

The night ground on. Finally I went to Tom's hut to try to get some rest. The hut was nearly empty, and I put my sleeping pad on the dirt floor and wrapped up in a sheet, though after all those kola nuts I didn't expect to sleep. I lay listening to the drums and noise of the party, and sometimes voices passing closer to the hut. I got up to take some aspirin, and again to go behind the hut and pee. I lay back down and pulled the sheet over my head, but my mind was full of shadowy, agitated images, with Tom's persistent, ironical voice echoing among them. When I looked out from under the sheet again, yellow light flickered on the ceiling of the hut, illuminating cobwebs and sagging thatch. Tom sat cross-legged in the corner, next to his pack, winding a piece of duct tape around the frame of his glasses. A candle burned beside him, and Kate sat nearby, with her back against the wall and her knees drawn up, holding a beer bottle on her lap.

"Tom," I said. "What did you mean, you never paid for your plane ticket?"

He didn't look up. He tore off another strip of duct tape and carefully wrapped it around his glasses. "Next time I come to Africa I'm going to bring some superglue," he said. "Life in Africa would be so much easier, if we only had some superglue."

He put on his glasses and glanced over at me. There was a big wad of duct tape on one hinge, but the glasses were reasonably straight.

"Yeah, Will, I never paid for my ticket home. So I guess I canceled my reservation. I guess I kind of changed my way of thinking about the airplane option. The idea of going to Kisaka, getting on a plane, and being done with this place started to seem anticlimactic. Too easy. An evacuation, just an escape. The next thing I'd know I'd be back in Thanesboro, freaking out, and the *next* thing I'd know I wouldn't be able to remember *why* I was freaking out, and pretty soon it'd be just like I never left Thanesboro at all, except the terror of the place would be a little closer to the surface."

"So why are you having a good-bye fête, if you're not leaving?"

"Oh, I'm leaving. I have to leave. I got a very powerful urge to get out of this place, Will. Like an instinct, you know? I think I've stirred up an ancient human drive. Tapped into some primordial genetic coding. The old migratory urges, Will. The urge to move on. To follow the great herds. The urge to get the fuck out of Africa. But I'm not flying. I'm going by moto."

"Whose moto? Not yours."

"Who else's? Don't worry, I'll fix it up first. I'm short on cash, but Kate just made me a small loan. So I'm going to stop in Mafemba on my way out and get a complete overhaul."

"Mafemba isn't on the way out. Mafemba is to the east. That's farther in."

"Absolutely, Will. But sometimes the only way out of a place is to go farther in, you know? Remember that Michelin map of Central Africa I used to have on this wall? I practically memorized it—the names of hundreds of little towns, most of the rivers and lakes and mountains between the Kivila Valley and Dar es Salaam. The roads. Primitive roads, the key says. No shit, primitive. Well, it's not often done, but it's possible, especially on a motorcycle, to ride those primitive roads across the continent, over the mountains, all the way down to the Indian Ocean. And that's what I'm going to do. Because another urge I have is to circumnavigate the globe. I want to sneak up on Thanesboro from the *west*. Just to rattle them. To go around the world is an unsettling concept for people in Thanesboro. In Thanesboro they don't much like the idea of a big round world. I mean, the whole town's got fucking agoraphobia, right? Why else would they stay there, huddled together inside the city limits? People in Thanesboro want to widen their horizons a little, they don't leave town, they just build another subdivision on the outskirts and fucking incorporate it."

He took his glasses off again and wiggled the hinges. He laughed. "They don't generally go to a place they've never heard of, and live there for three years. Or if they do, you never see them again. So it'll blow them away when I come home. I'll be more of a freak in my own hometown than I am here. Kids'll gawk at me, worse than they do here. I'll be quarantined. They'll study my microbes, behavioral aberrations, flush out my blood, sterilize me, lobotomize me. Then they'll push me out on the street and give me a fucking ticker-tape parade."

He studied his glasses for a while in silence, holding them up to the candlelight and turning them slowly in his hand. I thought Kate had fallen asleep against the wall, until she lifted the beer bottle to her lips. She put the bottle back down on the floor, and Tom tore off another long strip of duct tape and began to slowly wind it around the wad of tape already in place.

"And after the parade?" I said.

"What? Oh, well, the future is a little blurry after the parade. But you know, I'll have seen a bit of the world by then. I'll be another explorer. I'll have a fucking pedigree. Old Stanley, septic and starving, the forced-march champion of the jungle. Burton and Speke, lost in the Mountains of the Moon, obsessed and feverish and terminally pissed off at each other. Dr. Livingstone, a pickled corpse carried out of the mountains down to the consulate at Zanzibar. They're my predecessors, man. So who can say what I'll be like by the time *I'm* done, what genetic coding will be catalyzed?"

He talked on, and Kate drank her beer and sometimes responded to him, but soon their voices were just murmurs in the background, mingled with drumbeats and the cries of dancers. I must have fallen back asleep, because when I opened my eyes the diffused light of the early mushipu morning seeped into the silent hut. Tom and Kate were gone, and I wondered if I hadn't dreamed his fantasy of a canceled airline ticket and an eastward overland journey into the myths and terrors of the nineteenth century.

The village was still and empty under a cold fog. Cooking pots hung untended over smoking fires. Dogs skulked beneath racks of drying manioc. Even the chickens seemed listless and disoriented. It was as if some alarm had sounded and the place were suddenly abandoned and awaiting destruction. I shivered, and felt for the first time a genuine equatorial cold, the penetrating, pathogenic cold of the mushipu.

I almost walked past the old man, though he was talking on and on, and there was no one to hear him but me. But his voice hardly broke the silence; it was the kind of muffled, monotonous sound the fog itself might make. He blended into the earth around the fire where he huddled, all bones and old skin, the color of Kalahari sand ground up with the ash and charcoal of ten thousand cooking fires. He held out a trembling claw for me to shake and pointed down the path and all the while his rasping whispering voice uttered its incantatory words, beyond the purposes of intelligible language.

I left that voice behind in the smoke and fog. In the center of the village dozens of people were gathered around a tree, and as I drew nearer I saw Kate on the edge of the crowd, squatting on the ground like a peasant woman, staring off toward the river. Everyone else looked toward the tree, where Tom stood beside his motorcycle. Behind him his boom box hung from a branch, slowly twirling on a long rope.

The fog, the silent abandoned village, an old man who would be dead before the first rains. And now the boom box hanging from a tree, and my wife looking away from it all, washed up on the high ground amid the other wreckage of the party, her beauty surviving dishevelment and drunkenness but seemingly out of reach to me. Behind his heavy glasses Tom's eyes glittered. But his voice was calm, even warm, and his usual detached and ironical tone seemed subdued. In fact, what he was saying was gracious and reasonable. He was thanking people for all they'd done for him, all they'd taught him, and I began to think that my premonitions of disaster were exaggerated; fog and a sleepless night and a touch of a dying man's hand would make anyone imagine signs and portents, though the boom box hanging from the tree was disturbing, no question about that, and then I heard him thanking me, the consultant, for technical advice in regard to the piñata party we were about to have, and I knew there was going to be trouble.

"The piñata party is an ancient ceremony in Mputu," Tom said, "as the consultant himself will tell you. Though the wisdom of our ancestors is largely lost to us, we can still glimpse it in some of the old traditions that have been handed down through the generations. Like the smashing of the piñata. And we can adapt these traditions to modern situations. Like the radio situation."

He was silent for a moment, turning to stare at his boom box as if mesmerized by its slow rotation on the end of its rope. He sighed. "I know that after three years of looking out for me, of patiently listening to my advice, you figure the least I can do is give you my radio when I leave. One radio. Maybe a pair of shoes. Big deal. Well, I need the shoes, since I'm going to be on the road for a while. And I'm sorry, but I need the radio too, to help me give you one last piece of advice. One last demonstration of appropriate technology. Maybe you won't understand it. I don't know how to explain to you why I'm not just giving you the radio and washing my hands of it. I could tell you the radio would only make you poorer, but you won't believe that. You think you're already as poor as you can get. Look at us, you say, we have nothing; just give us your radio, Monsieur Tom, and quit screwing around.

"But it's not that easy. If I give one of you the radio, then nobody else gets the radio. So I don't know. Maybe one radio doesn't matter much, one way or the other. There's about a billion radios in Mputu. And billions of other beautiful, magical machines. The radio will tell you about them, promise them to you. But that's a false promise. Nobody intends for you to have these things. A few of them will wash up on your shores. Not really a gift, just thrown out by the people of Mputu, who have such a glut of possessions they can't possibly keep track of them all, let alone put them to use.

"Like me. Mr. Sticky Tree will tell you, I've hardly been listening to this radio lately. I've been reading a lot of old books, the words of my ancestors. I've been sitting outside a lot at night, listening for the voices of your ancestors. Maybe I got the idea for this piñata party from them.

"This is what you do. You take up a big stick." Tom turned to Sticky Tree, who had stood beside him throughout this speech, holding a stout branch and looking small and uncomfortable. Tom took the branch from him and gripped it between his knees, leaving his hands free. "You wear a blindfold." He took a handkerchief from his pocket and tied it around his head, over his eye. "Somebody spins you around in circles." He held the branch above his head, and Sticky Tree uncertainly spun him around a couple of times. I began to push my way through the crowd, calling to him to stop. Blindfolded, he stabbed a finger at me. "Fuck you, Will!" He seized the stick with both hands. "Then you get everyone to stand back. Stand back!" he roared. "You swing the stick! You smash the guts out of the fucking piñata!"

He swung wildly, missing the boom box by a foot. People screamed, and angry men came out of the crowd to stop him, but couldn't approach as he spun and swung. He got in a couple of glancing blows and then connected, and a cry went up from the crowd as the plastic cracked. Now that he had the range he smashed it again and again, and each time the same involuntary cry issued from the crowd. But when he stopped swinging there was silence. Tom pulled off the blindfold, tossed the stick aside, and climbed on his moto. Then people began to shout again, and the crowd pressed in on him. I'd pushed my way in close by now, and Tom looked up at me.

"Sorry you didn't like it, Will. Okay, I misrepresented the piñata tradition, and a piñata party isn't really *my* cultural heritage, but screw your nit-picking distinctions. Europe, United States, even Mexico: it's all the same fucking Mputu for my purposes."

"That wasn't my objection, Tom."

"Oh. You object to me being a self-righteous Luddite sonofabitch, is that it? I guess you got a point. But I can't discuss it right now, because I gotta head out before some of these hotheads try to rewire that radio with my intestines or something. I know this ain't gonna make me popular here, Will, but see, that's *good*. I don't need that kind of popularity, and they don't need that kind of hero."

People were shouting angrily. Some grabbed at Tom's clothes and at his pack, while others seemed to be trying to pull them away. A man had picked up the branch and was pushing his way through the crowd. Tom kicked the starter pedal, revved the engine, and let out the clutch. He skidded, swerved, and nearly went down in the deep sand. Several men jumped toward him, and I ran out with them, I'm not sure why. I felt for a second the blind passion of the lynch mob, though I'm sure I intended only to defend Tom. But he regained his balance before we were on him, and rode off through the village and out onto the main road.

The adults in the crowd watched him go, and none of us moved or spoke until he was out of sight. Kate watched too, from the outskirts, never looking at me. And the children scurried about in the early morning fog, already intent on a silent game, combing the red earth for shards of plastic, strands of wire, batteries, shattered circuits.

NIGHT WALK

At night four men came to my house. From the road below they called softly to Placide, who met them at the corner of the fence and then came to the porch.

"Monsieur, they want you to come with them."

"Where?"

"I don't know."

"Who are they?"

Placide shrugged. "Men from Malembe, and from the camp. Palm nut cutters. Fishpond men. The boy."

The men passed through the gate and followed Placide to the porch. One by one they reached up to shake my hand. In the dim moonlight I recognized Ndosi and Telo.

"We have something to show you, monsieur."

"Do you have to show me now? I was about to go to bed."

"Yes, now. You need to put your boots on."

"Where are you going?"

"Not far. Three, four kilometers. You'll want your boots."

Above the trees across the river, half a red moon hung in a smoky sky. Drums rumbled in the far distance—probably another funeral—but in Ngemba the night was very quiet. Even the chef's house across the river was dark and silent; even the insects by the river, and the babies in the camp, seemed subdued. The river was only a low murmur of moving water, and the trickle flowing in the creekbed was inaudible. We hadn't seen rain or heard thunder in months.

"Mama Kate is gone?" one of the men asked, or maybe it was just a statement.

"Yes. She went up . . . " I waved my arm vaguely toward the eastern savanna.

"Kasengi," Ndosi said. He drew the *s* out, hissing, and I thought maybe I did remember her saying something about Kasengi. I felt drowsy and thick-headed, and my curiosity was only slightly piqued by this enigmatic invitation. The point of it was probably something trivial: some intrigue that meant nothing to me, or an entertainment likely to provide more discomfort than amusement—a hunt, for example, which as Tom described it was usually a disorganized and confusing scramble through trailless brush in pursuit of some tiny, elusive, and possibly imaginary antelope or rodent.

But there was no urgency about getting to bed, either. During this last month of the mushipu I'd been sleeping nearly ten hours a night, though it wasn't as if I needed the rest. In those cool, hazy, and identical nights, my imagination had dulled. How long had it been since I'd joined Placide by his coals for a little enigmatic repartee; how long since I'd stayed up past midnight, lost in dreamy speculation on the porch? And in the ten months we'd been in Africa, I'd never gone out in the forest at night.

The men were quietly jubilant when I agreed to come. As I laced my boots Placide squatted impassively in the yard, plucking at a clump of grass. Did I only imagine his disapproval? He didn't speak again to the others, but before we left he reminded me to get my flashlight.

"We have flashlights," said Telo.

Placide ignored him. "You don't know where you're going, monsieur. There may be hazards. There may be a lot of ditches."

I grabbed my flashlight and joined the men on the road. In silence we walked a few hundred yards along the road, over the trickling creek, and then followed a path skirting the village of Malembe. The path was very dark, but when I turned on my flashlight Telo hissed at me to extinguish it. He walked ahead, holding fronds and branches to the side so I could pass more easily, and behind me, Ndosi—seamlessly blending Kituba, French, and English into what had become his signature patois—kept up a low jabber of encouragement and advice: "Malembe, Monsieur Will, slow-slow; watching, watching, keba, monsieur, down please, très bien, merci, oh yes, attention le pont, oh yes, the bridge now, the log falling, step please here, step-step, ç'est ça, oui, oui, très good, we are arrive!"

Where we'd arrived was nowhere very distinctive, as far as I could tell: a section of narrow path in the deep forest, much like any other section of narrow path in the deep forest. The men told me to wait and slipped away into the brush. They soon returned, two of them carrying full burlap sacks on their heads, the others a heavy raceme of palm nuts across each shoulder.

"Okay, monsieur, let's go." Telo grunted.

I continued up the trail twenty yards or so before coming to a stop so abrupt that Ndosi bumped into me, staggering under his load.

"What's the matter, Monsieur Will? Did you see a snake?"

"Of course not. I can't even see the ground. What's going on, Ndosi? Look, I have to know where we're going."

"It's just a place. It doesn't have a name."

"But I need to know where you're taking these palm nuts. These are supposed to go to the depot. You know that. We need them at the mill."

"Oui, monsieur. The forest is full of palm nuts for the mill. Please, monsieur, keep walking, this load is very heavy. It's okay to use your flashlight now."

I turned on my light. But the batteries were low, and in the faint light I could scarcely see the rough path. I asked Telo if he really had a flashlight.

"Oh, yes! Absolutely."

"Can I borrow it?"

"You can. But I must warn you that the batteries are dead."

"Why'd you bring it if the batteries are dead?"

"Ndosi wanted me to bring it because he thought you would like a flashlight. Maybe you would have batteries for it. Myself, I would like to buy batteries, but do you know how much palm nut I would have to cut to earn money for batteries?"

Already I had no idea where we were, though I was certain I'd never before been on that particular path. Unlike most jungle trails it was straight and open, lined by grass and low shrubs, with large trees set back several yards on either side.

"What is this trail?"

"It's an old road," Ndosi explained.

"Do you know what it was? An ancient highway? A trade route of your ancestors?"

"*Your* ancestor!" said Telo gravely. "And not so ancient. The Road Builder put this through when I was a child—his last great work, they say."

"The Road Builder!"

"But yes, a sort of highway," said Ndosi. "We call it the Mission Road."

"It doesn't seem like we're heading toward the mission. At least, I've never gone this way."

"No one goes this way. The Mission Road doesn't pass near a village. It doesn't go to the mission either. Of course not, Monsieur Will. That was the point of it."

The men laughed. The joke, and the significance of the Mission Road, completely escaped me. But Ndosi could explain that later. Right now I was just trying to keep up. The trail seemed to have left the old roadbed, and now we were climbing through forest hills, though the pace hadn't slackened. Hurrying to keep up, I tripped on a protruding root and fell to the ground.

"Attention!" The men sang out. "Keba! Attention, monsieur!" Telo helped me to my feet, and behind me Ndosi murmured reassuringly, or reprovingly, and then let fly with a couple of furious machete whacks, excising the offending root from the path.

Of course, they fully expected me to fall down on the trail. I'd tried to convince them that I wasn't as clumsy as they made me out to be, but the fact that I frequently stumbled, walked into things, or simply fell down for no apparent reason made it difficult for them to believe my claims that in America I crossed rushing rivers on narrow fallen logs, leapt over deadfall with a chainsaw in my hand, and sped down snowy mountains with my feet fastened to a couple of boards. They responded to such tales not so much with disbelief as with polite incomprehension—what I was telling them clashed not only with what they knew of me but also with their idea of Mputu: a fenced-in, paved-over land. Only Placide took my extravagant boasts in stride. "You fall down a lot," he explained to me once, "because here you are walking on different earth."

The trees began to thin out, and the path steepened, following a narrow gully toward the top of the escarpment. But still the pace didn't slow. If anything, the men seemed energized by the climb, scampering up the slope and talking loudly about Tom. They seemed to be openly comparing him to me. Monsieur Tom, *he* never fell down on the trails. Even at night, even drunk, or high on marijuana, skidding and plunging down the steepest trails, Monsieur Tom kept his feet. Though on his moto it was a different story. Frequently he crashed his moto, especially during his first year here. Laughing, the men recounted stories of his most drunken, most spectacular crashes, and the improbable gymnastic contortions, quick reflexes, and strokes of bald luck that enabled him to survive them.

"Ah, Monsieur Tom."

Their laughter faded into sighs, and they were silent for a minute, before moving on to an animated discussion about the chinois, the Chinese man who ran a development project 100 kilometers downriver, growing rice and buying and shipping agricultural products. They seemed to find the chinois remarkable, hilarious, disturbing; his very existence confounding, distorting the stark polarities of their worldview.

Telo stopped to wait for me and cleared his throat. "Pardon, Consultant, we would like your opinion, please. Is the chinois considered a white man, or is he not?"

When I didn't immediately answer, Ndosi elaborated. The chinois was like a white man in that he came from a far-off land and exhibited many inexplicable behavior patterns. Also he had powerful magic. Yet he seemed to have little money, he associated with whites as rarely as with Africans, and he had a taboo about going to bed with African women.

I told them not to worry about classifying the chinois or anybody else, though the truth was I didn't know what to make of him either. The only time I talked to him, when I went with Tom to buy a sack of rice from him early in the dry season, I couldn't even tell what language he was speaking—French, Kituba, English, or Chinese. His interpreter laughed openly at the chinois' attempts to converse, and admitted that his translation was impressionistic, since he was also uncertain which language he was translating from.

The men laughed. "Monsieur Tom, he said the same thing about the chinois."

"That's right. But he still liked to talk to him. He was always trying to get the chinois to buy from us—fish and coffee and manioc."

"Ç'est ça! The chinois pays good money, they say."

"He pays well, citizen, but he's too far away. Who wants to carry a sack of coffee all the way down to the chinois? Jamais!"

"Monsieur Tom, he talked to the chinois for an hour or more, one day."

"Did he understand anything he said?"

"Rien! Like you, Monsieur Will, he said he didn't know what language the chinois was speaking. And he didn't even know what language he himself was answering the chinois in! But they talked, they had a long conversation. Monsieur Tom said the chinois was lonely, he just needed to talk. He realized he was never going to learn the language, and if he wanted to talk, he had to talk without knowing it."

"Ah, Monsieur Tom."

The men sighed deeply again, fell silent, and picked up the pace. I lagged behind. The path leveled off and joined a sort of road or two-wheel track. We seemed to be emerging onto the savanna plateau, still following a watercourse, with the land sloping up gently on either side, blocking our view of the larger valley we'd just climbed out of.

The moon was low in the sky, and as the track turned to the east, its diffused light shone from behind us. Beneath the sacks and racemes, sweat streaked the necks of the men who walked ahead of me, and soaked their tattered shirts. The moisture reflected the moonlight, and numbly I followed this small light, this glimmer of sweat, along the long and desolate road. I was weary but resigned, and the resignation was like a second wind, a fatalism that had something in common with the fatalism that powered other migrations of the mushipu. The season of sickness, the season of walking. Those days the roads were full of travelers moving between village and city, and from village to village. It was a good time to travel—paths and roads were dry, streams easy to cross, and you didn't get caught out in the rain. And people had to travel a lot during the mushipu, in order to attend funerals. As the season dragged on, with its cool nights and days of stagnant dry air, food stores dwindled and deteriorated, and people—especially children and old people—began to sicken and die. Then it seemed that a strange cycle of self-destruction ensued. Since the dead required the honor of a well-attended funeral, as the frequency of funerals increased more and more people were obliged to travel, to neglect their farms and gardens, and to stay up all night dancing, often drinking, but seldom eating much. This made them sick; some of the sick ones died, obliging more people to go to more funerals. . . . And so the pace of death quickened. Fortunately, the mushipu lasted only three or four months; otherwise, the population might have been entirely decimated.

The track left the shallow valley and skirted the edge of the escarpment, with the Kivila Valley in darkness below. The men put down their loads and leaned back against the embankment, complaining of the cold night, though they all were dripping sweat. Telo coughed incessantly, a harsh and phlegmy sound, unnecessarily loud, it seemed to me. On such a still and silent night that sound might carry for miles through the forest, down to the sleeping villages and the camp, crossing the river to disturb the trusting sleep of the chef de poste. All distances seemed equally close; every place occupied an equivalent shadow: river, villages, fields, fishponds, and mill all as black as the unbroken forest. Kate too occupied that shadow, maybe, a night creature moving unseen somewhere beneath the canopy.

But to the south there was light: a red glow on the horizon, faintly pulsing or flickering. "Fire, monsieur!" Ndosi, close by my side, spoke softly, but with an edge of excitement in his low laughter. "Ç'est la saison du feu, monsieur!"

The season of fire. New fields had been cleared in the forest, and before the rains returned the slash would be burned. But already the savannas were in flames. In the wilderness grasslands to the south, beyond Mafemba, the grass fires would burn huge and uncontrolled for the next month, until the fuel was exhausted or the rains began to fall.

In these final weeks of the mushipu the daytime sky was white. Each morning a red sun rose, swollen in the smoke of the fires and the haze of the dust that blew off the stripped land. There was a palpable weight to the smoky air, pressing down on the land and its inhabitants. I recalled the persistent illusions of the rainy season, when distance and perspective were distorted by the clarity of light and the sheer immensity of the landscape. Those were gone, replaced by a different order of illusion. Light was bent, objects magnified by the heat and thickness of the air. The eye strained to make out what lay at the edge of a contracting field of vision. Nothing happened—the weather was unchanged, the earth slowly dried, pieces of ash drifted down from the sky—yet there was somehow a sense of nervous anticipation. I found myself peering into the opaque sky, as if waiting for all those neutral molecules to coalesce into something. . . . But nothing came out of the sky except ash. I felt, or imagined I felt, the light touch of the ash now, as I too leaned back against the embankment and turned my face from the glowing horizon up to the night sky: just a few blurry stars and a hazy quarter moon, seen through a thick layer of smoke and dust. Telo coughed, a hoarse, racking sound from deep in his lungs. The other men responded with their own coughs, hacks, sniffles, and nostril blasts. As the mucus settled, one of the men cursed.

"This damn cold. What can God's purpose be in allowing such a season on His earth?"

"It's not for us to question God's purpose, citizen," said Telo weakly—a prudent position for someone with a tubercular cough to take, maybe.

The other man leaned toward me. "Monsieur. Do people in Mputu have to put up with a mushipu like we do? Does the air get like this—*cold* like this?"

Without raising my head I answered him. "No, not like this. Oh man, nothing like this. A different kind of cold."

No one knew what I meant. Who could explain high-latitude cold to equatorial men, shivering and sickly on a 60-degree night? How could they comprehend a sky full of frozen water instead of ash, or imagine a Canadian cold front, a hard October freeze, pushing Indian-summer air away in a matter of hours? That is a cold that would kill you, I could tell them, faster than your heat is going to kill me. What would you make of God's purpose then, with ice cracking on the river and snow squeaking under your feet, on a long sub-zero night in a northern mountain valley?

But the conviction might be absent from my voice. The memory of ice was remote now, and I could hardly explain a northern winter to myself. Placide was right: it was a different earth there. And I was a different person, with no malaria in his bloodstream, no *ascaris* in his guts, no crickets in his belly. The air was different too: clean, free of ash, circulating—nothing like this stagnant weight of gases pushing me toward the ground.

The men hoisted their burdens once again, and we resumed our wearisome trudge along the sandy road, through a world obscured by haze and darkness. I tried to recall the details of winter: what was it like to go out to the shed for firewood and enter a blizzard, or to skate onto the lake in a flat light, an immense whiteness, with nothing to separate the earth from the sky? What was it like to glide over snow, unweighted, accelerating? I remembered the rush of air, the sensation of weightlessness, a surrender to gravity that was also a release from gravity. But the memory was vague and included no details of place: no specific mountain, no specific snow, not even the feel of skis on my feet. But I held on to the image nonetheless, and as the voices of the men receded, along with their sniffling and coughing and shadowy movements, the memory turned into a kind of sleepwalking dream. Though in the dream I was no longer walking, just *moving*. I moved through winter air, a torrent of clean, cold air. I could see a vast distance, but there was no object to focus upon, no way to measure velocity or direction or the passage of time, nothing to tell me whether that rushing effortless motion was freefall or flight.

"Attention, monsieur! Where are you going?"

The shadow of a man loomed suddenly ahead of me. The voice and the shadow belonged to Ndosi—a small man, really; it was a trick of dim light and perspective that made him seem so huge—but the face faintly lit by a diminishing moon seemed unfamiliar, and the soft voice came from a great distance away, an insistent murmur, like the sound of the wind in a sparse dream of flight and winter.

"You turned the wrong way, Monsieur Will. You're out in the field." A firm hand closed over mine. "Are you tired? I have something to give you strength."

I gripped his steadying hand, leaned against his small sturdy body. He took a banana-leaf packet out of his bag, unfolded it, and offered me the contents. It was too dark to see, so blindly I reached in and pulled out the damp, sticklike objects, with their tiny appendages. . . .

"Crickets!" Ndosi laughed. "Protein, Monsieur Will! Vitamins! Crickets to give you strength!"

"Merci. Crickets may be just what I need." I bit into one, then accepted the entire packet.

"The sentinel gave them to me," Ndosi explained. "He caught them last week up by Bulolo, and he told me to give them to you."

The cricket—the first I'd tasted in over a month—was stale and desiccated. "It'd be nice to have something to drink with this."

"Or some sauce, monsieur. Crickets taste better with a sauce."

"Maybe. Placide doesn't do sauces. You need a pan to make a sauce."

"Someday I'll cook crickets in sauce for you. With luku, or on rice, if you like."

He handed me another, and we walked on, nibbling our crickets in silence. Then Ndosi stopped, and pointed across the valley that fell away at our feet.

"Kasengi," he said softly, with that ominous hiss.

I couldn't see much: the glow of fire on a distant savanna; the sudden tiny flicker of flame; and closer to us, shadowy clumps of trees on the edge of a dark point of land, above the deeper darkness of the valley. That valley seemed steeper and narrower than most valleys here, more like a cleft or a ravine, and Kasengi—if that was what that clump of trees was—sat above it on a peninsula of savanna, in isolation. Could Kate be there now, part of that sleeping shadow? It seemed impossible: I had no sense of her presence, felt no connection. Instead there arose from the valley a vaguely malevolent sound: rumbling and humming, strange tones and murmurs, the inarticulate voice of the night. Down there, in air trapped beneath a closed canopy of trees and vines, an unknown and inhospitable world teemed. I shivered from a deep chill, and Ndosi too seemed to shudder involuntarily.

"Eat your crickets, monsieur," he urged me, and we continued walking, more quickly now, passing a clearing and a dark compound, a scattering of huts. A dog barked, a baby coughed and cried, and Ndosi further quickened his pace. But it was not until we were well past the compound that I realized it was his old dwelling. So the valley we were looking into must have been the valley of his fishponds. Nothing about it looked familiar, but it wasn't hard to imagine his fetisher uncle down in that deep hole, casting spells in a swamp of snakes and crocodiles.

Ndosi hiked in and out of that valley nearly every day for two years. He put more sweat and muscle into those fishponds than I had put into anything in my entire life. But now as the road turned away and I stopped to look down into the valley one last time, he told me he didn't even turn his eyes on the place anymore. "My work is with you and Kate now, and for myself in my garden, in another valley. If I tried to eat a fish that came out of those ponds, I would choke."

Ahead of us we heard laughter and voices. Ndosi whistled, and an identical whistle answered him. "Finish your crickets, Will," he said. "We're very close now."

Close to Kasengi, I thought, hissing the word in my mind. But I must have said it aloud. "Oh yes, Mr. Will," Ndosi said, laughing softly. "Close to Kasengi, but not the same. This place we are never calling a name."

He handed me another cricket, and we turned away from his old valley and the sinking moon, and followed the others down the road into a heavy darkness of grass and sand.

21

THE PLACE WITHOUT A NAME

The moon was down, and both the forest and the savanna were lost in the same darkness. Out of that darkness came small bands of women, drawn into the light of the kerosene lamp burning on a box beside the truck driver's scales. Reflected off particles of ash in the air, the light of the lamp intensified, and the ash itself seemed to emit a pale glow. The surrounding sky of ash further reflected and contained this light, creating a bubble of ash light illuminating a small depression at the end of a spur track in a field of burnt grass on the Kasengi savanna.

The Place Without a Name. Of course it didn't have a name—what would anyone call it, with nothing at all to distinguish it from the surrounding, featureless savanna? But now the ash light made it a specific place. The light, and the big Mercedes truck I leaned against, and the dozen or so men milling around near the back of the truck next to their sacks of coffee and racemes of palm nut, and now these hard-breathing, sweat-glinting women coming out of the darkness with baskets and basins of manioc and dried corn and peanuts and coffee on their heads. As they helped one another lower their burdens to the ground, they laughed and called out to the men, who laughed too and returned the teasing of the women. Everyone was jostling, expectant, caught up in the suppressed excitement and wildness that had drawn us all out of the villages and through the forest and over the interminable savanna roads until at last we stumbled into a nameless place under a light glowing out of all proportion to the size of its flame.

Ndosi was more excited than anybody. He moved from one group to another, erupted in laughter, pulled someone aside to whisper urgently in his ear, whirled away to a peripheral conversation. Then he fell silent, watching the truck driver weigh palm nuts. After a minute he stepped up and began a fierce argument. He seemed to be accusing the driver of having rigged the scales, and the driver, after a strong denial and an exchange of insults, threw out his arms and pretended he was about to gather up the scales and leave. It was hardly worth it for him to come in the first place, he said, just to pick up a few half-filled sacks of produce and some shriveled palm nut. This run wasn't working out for him: in the rainy season he got stuck in the deepest mud in the province, and in the dry season people had nothing to sell. And then to be accused of dishonesty! But calmer voices soothed him, reminding him that this was the mushipu and the fields were producing little everywhere, but he should be patient, because more was coming, much more. Telo and some others pulled Ndosi away, and almost immediately he seemed to forget his argument and was again talking and laughing, darting from group to group, everywhere pushing the conversation up a pitch, as if seeking some collective passion or fever of language, or at least another argument.

He also seemed to have forgotten me. Out on the edge of the ash-light bubble, I warmed myself on the radiator grill of the truck, and no one paid any attention at all to me. Well, I was too tired for conversation, and certainly I didn't share in the spirit of animation inspired by the occasion. Also I had a stomachache. How many crickets had I eaten in that brutal hike across the savanna? I think Ndosi just kept shoving them at me, as if an abundance of roasted crickets would make me as strong as an African, as if the mechanics of munching crickets were linked to the mechanics of walking, and by this means he could catalyze the reaction that would move me along the road to this night rendezvous.

The truck driver and his boy chauffeur were busy at their scales, and all around them people talked and moved about. I caught only the ragged edges of predictable talk and noise: the usual coughing and hacking, teasing and laughter; the usual serious exchange of money and goods; the usual speculation about who poisoned somebody's fishponds, when the rains will begin, what malevolent power might have infected Monsieur Tom. Ndosi darted manically in and out of the light, now dragging his racemes of palm nut up to the scales, now joking with the boy chauffeur and a couple of women. Even in the near darkness I recognized Matama, by her voice, and the nurse's familiar gestures: slapping Ndosi's hand, rocking back in laughter, pushing him playfully in the chest. Languid and fluid, all motion linked, equalized. The language flowed out of her too, a sharp, rippling repartee of words and laughter, like a counterpoint

to the story Ndosi was telling them: *then I said this, and he said that, and I said,
but Monsieur Will.* . . . Oh. They were talking about *me*. Ndosi laughing so hysterically he could hardly get the words out, telling how I barely made it up
here, how I walked off the road into the field, and how the crickets revived me
enough so I could stumble on. Not like Mama Kate, said Matama, laughing
with him, *she's* strong, she walks this far every day and thinks nothing of it. Even
now that she has a Land Rover she still walks all the time.

The boy chauffeur laughed too, but his laughter was harder to read. Was
he mocking the white man who sleepwalked in the road, or these crude villagers with their unhip language and ignorant peasant tales? He strutted, he
leered at the women. It seemed he had recently returned from Kisaka, with
freshly sharpened disdain for provincial life. Under Ndosi's urging, he condescended to demonstrate the latest urban dance steps, which Ndosi and some
of the others tried to imitate as well. But the boy chauffeur looked away from
them, straight at me, though I'd thought I was invisible to them in the darkness at the front of the truck.

"Monsieur! Vous dancez!" he commanded.

"No, merci."

"Tout le monde dance. Vous aussi." His tone was slightly belligerent, but
maybe that was just the boy-chauffeur style. "Allons, monsieur!" He stepped
up to me like a playground bully, but Ndosi moved between us.

"Monsieur Will can't dance," he explained, as if it were one of Newton's laws.

"Yes he can," said the boy chauffeur. "Give him some beer, and watch
him dance!"

"No, no, he can't dance at all," explained Matama patiently. "We've seen
him. We've tried to teach him. It's no use."

Several people murmured in agreement, but the boy chauffeur only went
further out on the limb. "He's a great dancer," he insisted.

"No, he's not," said Ndosi firmly, with some annoyance.

"I saw him dance, and he was good. He was great."

"Where'd you see me dance?" They all turned at the sound of my voice, as
if surprised I was still capable of speech. I was sure, for a second, I'd never
seen the fellow before, but as he spoke I suddenly remembered that cocky,
lilting head, the look of smirking complicity, the fat joint twirling in long
painted fingernails.

"At the truckstop. In Mafemba. You should have seen him, man." The boy chauffeur whistled and flapped his hand. "He was fantastic. Monsieur, he got right up to this woman—a good-looking woman! And he was like—" The boy chauffeur ground and slithered his hips, dancing obscenely. I doubt I ever danced like that, but everyone hooted and laughed and I could see there was no point in denying anything. Let them believe that Monsieur Will is a cricket-gobbling weakling who can't stay on the road. That the consultant is a farceur who dances with crotch-grinding women in a public square. That the noble bureaucrat is a charlatan who joins in nighttime smuggling operations that undermine the pious platitudes he spouts by day. Let them draw whatever conclusions they liked, while I sat silently in the darkness drawing my own ill-informed and speculative conclusions about whatever it was *they* were doing.

I could have just asked someone what was going on. I could have asked the nurse, who watched now from the edge of the light, no longer laughing with the others. But surely she wasn't the one who owed me an explanation. It was Ndosi who had dragged me up here. Mr. Dream, who was always gently interpreting for me, smoothing my path, hacking off the roots that tripped me up. And who now seemed content to let me dangle, sulking in the darkness, while he flirted and teased and made jokes at my expense.

"Ndosi!"

He came spinning over, reeling palm-wine breath and grinning and slapping my shoulder and jabbering on again about the crickets. But he turned serious when I demanded that he tell me what was going on and why he'd brought me up here. He nodded, sighed, and assumed a grave and weighted expression, though when he answered me in his pidgin English, the effect was largely spoiled. He said the reasonings for walking me over here were indeed superior reasonings, and he began to count them off as if they were distinct and orderly as well. But it all came out in a jumble. Something about the consultant and the animatrice, the solidarity and the education, the useful knowledge, the technology and the self-sufficiency and the sustainable and the expertise and on and on, an impressive vocabulary trapped in a tangle of prepositions and confused tenses and inventive conjugations. The reasoning may well have been superior, but the syntax was making me crazy. I cut him off. I'm obliged to report all smuggling activity to the chef de poste, I told him straight out. Oh yes, he nodded enthusiastically, and pointed out that I had other obliges I would first place regard. I said my only oblige was to give advice, and my advice was to take the palm nuts and the rest of it back to Ngemba and sell it to the Company like they were supposed to, before the mill closed for good and everything went completely to hell. And Ndosi said this was strong and superior advicing and with full respect no one must regard it because there was gone too great a work in the rising of palm nut up from the forest to the savanna and not possible for returning the same palm nut in the forest for a pay from the hand of the chef de poste so much lesser from the pay coming off the hand of the smuggle man. And I told him that if I understood him correctly what he was saying couldn't be true because as he knew we'd arranged for a very big raise, and he said yes at this time everyone was making raises which will include the smuggle man who made the raise that became the bigger money of it all. And by then I'd about had it with Ndosi's English and his superior reasoning and especially the long confusing night, and my voice was getting loud and breaking in pitch but I didn't care. I was thinking that if Ndosi was looking for an argument and superior reasoning I was ready to give it to him, and it came down to this: we were talking about a bush smuggler, Ndosi, and *palm nuts,* for God's sake, and who would believe that a bush smuggler was paying that kind of money for a product without value in the modern economy?

But Ndosi held up a hand to silence me in mid rant. "Shhhh," he soothed. "Shhhh, Mr. Will. Do you listen?"

A smile spread across his face. "You hearing, Mr. Will?" I was hearing nothing yet. But beyond the ash-light bubble the sky was lit by a faint wobbly light, growing stronger. The light pulsed erratically, splintered beams flashed into the sky and illuminated the haze, and a dim sort of light simultaneously began to fall on the hazy expanses of my brain. Ndosi slipped away, distracted by some minor commotion over by the scales, but in any case our argument had already lost its edge. Sipping the palm wine Telo brought me, and savoring the bitter taste of the kola nut the nurse pressed into my hand, I considered what those diffracted beams revealed. I considered that same boy chauffeur, crouched in an alcove of manioc sacks in the back of a Mercedes truck, rolling a joint and watching me dance while his driver leaned out the window, discussing trucking routes with my wife. I considered Kate leaning back against our kitchen table, a pagne clinging to her river-damp skin and a drop of water glittering like a diamond stud in the cleft of her lip. *Everything is contraband, Will. The question is, what are we going to do about it?* I considered her nightlong absences, her obsession with having a camion, and her disapproval of my raise for the workers. I considered her support groups and animation and muddy clothes on the porch, and I considered the continuing failure of my raise to have any effect on the dwindling piles of palm nuts outside the mill.

I knew more than I had seemed to know. I wasn't just a blind walker in a dry-season fog that obscured reason and causality. Some things could be seen through the fog, and some things I knew without seeing. I knew, for example, that when the splintered beams broke over the horizon, they would reveal themselves as headlights; and I knew that within two minutes, Père Michel's old Land Rover, stuffed with sacks and baskets and piled high with racemes of palm nut, would pull into the Place Without a Name. I knew that people would swarm around the Land Rover to unload the cargo, the truck driver would work his scales and count out money, and the boy chauffeur would jump up on the back of the truck, prancing and jeering and stacking the palm nut and the sacks of produce. And I knew that Kate would swing out from behind the steering wheel of the Land Rover, ready to join in it all, the sack throwing and the counting and the handshaking and the laughter and the arguments and the sexual jostling, and I could imagine her standing for a moment on the running board, looking over the scene she had helped to create. But I didn't know, I couldn't imagine how she'd react, whether with dismay or satisfaction or indifference or guilt or righteousness or something else, when her gaze was stopped by the sight of my white face looking back at her from out of the darkness at the hood of the smuggler's truck.

BOOK FOUR

THE SMUGGLER

22

MALARIA LOGIC

I don't remember ever in so many words agreeing to become a smuggler myself, though I suppose I never explicitly said I *wouldn't* do it. Maybe I even admitted there was a certain logic to smuggling, on that mushipu night when Ndosi and the others took me for that long cricket-fueled hike and we met the smuggler at the Place Without a Name and Kate, driving us down from the savanna in the early hours of the morning, finally got around to telling me that she and Père Michel's Land Rover were part of a smugglers' network. The Smugglers' Support Group. Or maybe I never did admit this was logical. Maybe I just couldn't put my finger on what was *illogical* about it, though I do remember saying to myself: this whole thing's crazy. I remember flying down the mountain in a Land Rover full of noise and sweating bodies, Kate leaning across the steering wheel shouting explanations at me, and I remember thinking: keep your eyes on the road, please goddamnit Kate; this night is too warm, too loud, too strange; I need some air; whose head is this on my shoulder; please slow down; whatever she's saying is terrifyingly rational, but isn't it crazy that this woman piloting a careening Land Rover down an African mountainside is my wife? My thoughts, you see, were already spinning out of control, because as it turned out I was feverish with malaria. So perhaps my memory of that evening is unreliable, and I may well have made some commitment I was later obliged to honor.

At first I was thinking that the head on my shoulder belonged to Kate, because she was talking to me and because it felt so natural there, but that just shows how disoriented I already was, because Kate was on the other side of me, driving, and there were two or three people on the seat between us, as well as another six or eight crammed in the back. Most of them had worked up a sweat earlier in the evening hiking up from the valley. Their clothes were damp, and they howled about the mushipu cold when I tried to roll down the window to let some fresh air into the suffocating interior of the Land Rover.

Not long before, I'd been soaked with cold sweat and deeply chilled myself, leaning on the hood of the smuggler's truck. Now I was hot and sweating again, but it didn't occur to me that malaria might be stirring in my bloodstream. The crush of human bodies, the short supply of oxygen, the crickets and kola nuts I'd eaten, the palm wine I'd drunk, the miles I'd trekked through forest and savanna, the events I'd witnessed at the Place Without a Name, and especially the current terror of this Land Rover ride—wasn't all that enough to explain my discomfort and disorientation and fear and obsession?

One thing I was obsessed with was the likelihood that the Land Rover, stuffed with people and swaying wildly in the ruts of a curving road, would finally tip too far and plunge off the road into the dark valley, snapping off trees and bushes as it tumbled down the slope, scattering bodies all the way to the bottom of the gorge, maybe even coming to rest, for all I would ever know of it, in the haunted dark mud of Ndosi's old fishponds. It seemed a precariously balanced vehicle, rocking and swerving in the sand as we descended the steep winding road. It was too narrow, its center of gravity too high—what had those English engineers been thinking? And what was the driver of the Land Rover thinking? The driver, who not so many months before had dreamed of running her hand over a blood-drenched body on a dark savanna road. Well, why shouldn't Kate turn out to be an agent in the fulfillment of her own dream? Inattentive at best, perhaps feverish and obsessive herself, she seemed oblivious to danger, shouting over the laughter and talk of the other passengers, taking her eyes off the road for long seconds to lean toward me, though in the darkness she couldn't see my face.

"This smuggling has been going on for years," she said. "It's the only alternative in a feudal economy, where prices are fixed so artificially low. Where one company—our company, Will—runs the place like its own private fiefdom. Jucht Brothers buys low out here in the bush, where everybody is forced to sell to them, and sells high in the city. Of course, the government chefs get their cut, and send their soldiers around to deal with people who try to buck the system. Every once in a while somebody gets beat up, thrown in jail. Stuff gets confiscated, people are fined, a house burns down. But the smuggling goes on; the black market's as solid an institution as anything else. It's haphazard, though, and disorganized. Communication is difficult. It's hard to know exactly when a truck will be coming through, and the drivers don't dare come down into Company territory in the valley. So everything has to be taken up on foot to the savanna, which means nobody can sell much at a time. And that means there's never any guarantee of a large enough purchase to make the trip worthwhile for the truck driver. So the trucks only show up irregularly, and infrequently."

"Slow down," I said.

"Sorry," she said. "I guess it's a lot of information to digest all at once."

"No, I mean *slow down*. Don't drive so fast. Don't *swerve* so much."

"Oh. I know what you mean. It feels like it's going to tip over, doesn't it? That's just how it is. I don't even notice anymore. Anyway, remember at that mamas' meeting at Telo's farm, the woman who came up to me and said I could help them create money? You know her, the nurse. In fact, she's sitting next to you right now."

This is the nurse sitting next to me? With her head on my shoulder? Was she asleep or awake, then? Oblivious, or conscious of the body she was so intimately pressed up against? But the nurse was accustomed to being pressed up against people; she grew up sleeping skin to skin in a mound of bodies on a rough bed in a thatch hut. Maybe she still slept like that, in a bed full of other women's children.

The Smugglers' Support Group was the nurse's idea, Kate was saying. The nurse was a natural organizer, and she was the one who'd drawn Kate into the whole thing. She and Ndosi. They'd come to her asking for help with financing and transportation logistics, and Kate had agreed. She talked to Tom, and in Mafemba he introduced her to a truck driver who wanted to develop new contraband runs. At first there were problems: the driver didn't know the roads, the roads were a mess, he got stuck in the mud. The first couple of times people didn't bring him much, and Kate had to pay him off in order to ensure that he would return. But soon people became more committed, and when she got the Land Rover things really came together. For every sack or raceme people carried up on their own, she agreed to carry one in the Land Rover for them. Tonight there had been a lot of participation. People were starting to really believe in the Smugglers' Support Group.

"What I can't believe is that you'd really call it that," I said.

The name wasn't her idea, Kate said. The smugglers voted on it. But it was a natural evolution—the coupiers' and mamas' support groups pointed the way to it. In fact, lots of things had pointed the way to it, going all the way

back to Uncle Pers' study and the stories we'd made up and deleted sitting at
his computer. And going back even further, to the cab of my truck on the
road to Mexico, when I'd told her tales of smuggling trinkets and blankets
under the eyes of the customs police. Then I'd turned around and abducted
her; she herself had become contraband for a while, in a sense. That had been
the genesis of it too, she said.

Contraband. The word had a broader meaning than I'd thought, if it could
be applied to Kate, spirited away over the Tehachapis, past the desert windmills in my truck. Maybe it was a good word for the nurse too, then, with her
head resting on my shoulder in the dark. Or maybe not. My head ached, and
I couldn't think whether or not that made sense. Kate downshifted, and raised
her voice over the whining engine.

"You inspired me, Will. Remember what I was like then? An academic, a
theoretician. You're the one who's shown me how to apply the theory."

What theory was she talking about?

"The nurse, too. She shows me. And Ndosi. And Tom, of course."

"Of course."

"But you're still my main inspiration, Will. And other people's, I might
add. They wanted to know what you thought of all this, and I told them, well,
we hadn't discussed everything yet, but this kind of thing was in your blood.
So I had to tell them about your Mexican smuggling days. That made a really
big impression. They don't just see it as a coincidence. Because, you know,
they don't really believe in coincidence. Things don't just *happen.*"

"No." *Things don't just happen. Things are in your blood. Blood makes things
happen.* Kate turned the wheel, the Land Rover tilted, the nurse's body
pressed up against me, hard. Her breath was on my cheek, and her bare
shoulder, soft and cool, pushed against my arm. The road straightened again,
and her weight rocked back, seeking a new equilibrium.

Kate was talking about risk. Technically, there was no risk, she said. Technically, we were not even smuggling. It was supposed to be a free market. The
law said you could sell to whomever you wanted to.

*Technically, there is no risk. Technically, the nurse's body is a neutral mass,
responding only to immutable laws of physics: gravity, momentum, centrifugal force.*

But laws are easy to write, she said, particularly when nobody intends to
obey or enforce them. And the commissaire had made this status of the law

clear enough, issuing proclamations promising to deal severely with smugglers or any other criminals and provocateurs trying to sabotage the established economic order. But the commissaire was remote, and for the time being, things seemed reasonably safe. Political power, such as it was, remained in the hands of the chef de poste, who wasn't about to interfere in the smuggling, even if it went on under his nose. *Right* under his nose, in fact.

Technically, the suffocating heat inside the Land Rover is a consequence not of any one particular body but of all the bodies present, consuming oxygen and giving off metabolic heat in equal measure. I cracked the window again. A rush of wind carried away Kate's voice and the protests of my fellow passengers. I stuck my nose out, sucking in the cool, smoky air. We rounded another curve, the Land Rover tilted, and a bare foot swung out in front of my face. The Land Rover righted itself, and the foot swung back, nearly brushing my nose. I rolled the window part way up. "There's a foot out there," I said to Kate, but she was talking again.

"So you can see," she was saying, "why I was so upset by the noble bureaucrat's idea to give everybody a raise."

The foot swung out again, swung back, disappeared. "What about this foot?" I said.

"It changed the price dynamics, just when the smuggling connection was coming together. We finally had a marketing outlet tied to the economy and incentives of the real world, and your raise—which is just a subsidy, Will, a bribe, really—threatened to destroy it, without addressing in any permanent way the inequities of the situation. I had to do something about it."

How could a foot change the price dynamics? I rolled the window back down, ignoring the open hostility of the other passengers, and stuck my head out the window. The foot rested precariously on the rain gutter above me, attached to a leg that extended off of the roof rack.

"There's somebody on the roof!"

"There are at least half a dozen people on the roof, Will. That's the trouble—you give one person a ride, you have to give fifteen people a ride. But what difference does it make? Anyway, it seems to me I had no choice but to match your raise. Nobody else knows about it, but now I'm making a direct payment to the smuggler—a price support—so he can boost his payments high enough to stay ahead of the mill."

"What do a half dozen people on the roof do to this thing's center of gravity?"

"They raise it, I'm sure. On the other hand, all the people inside probably balance that out. So there's still a chance that we won't crash."

In fact, it was beginning to look as though we might make it home safely. We were off the escarpment now, driving through hilly terrain on a straighter road, and though the Land Rover still swayed unsteadily, at least there weren't any hairpin curves or mountainsides plunging away into nothingness below us. Kate was quiet and now appeared to be paying a reasonable amount of attention to the road. Big trees flashed in our headlights, and the engine roared back at us off the jungle that walled in the road. We stopped near dark huts or villages to let people out. Conversation died as the truck emptied, and the nurse snuggled down to nestle her head in the crook of my elbow. Her weight cut off circulation to my forearm, and I shifted position, so that her head settled into my lap. My hand was stranded awkwardly above her, and finally I rested it on her head. Her calm breathing did not change, and in the darkness my fingers traced the smooth parts in her plaited hair, brushed her temple, touched the side of her face.

Her skin was cool, and soft like a young girl's. For the rest of the journey I left my hand on her cheek, my fingers pressing lightly against the unfamiliar contours of her face. Through the open window I smelled mushipu smoke, forest humus, river stone, dry leaves of the uplands. Heat and cold, moisture and dryness, decay and renewal. The air was loaded with strange scents and oppositions. I smelled faith and betrayal, engagement and detachment, order and chaos, resignation and terror. I smelled the lawless smuggler and the sanctioned mill; the manic energy of Kate and the seductive oblivion of the sleeping nurse. Every scent had its opposing scent, with widening gaps between them, and no middle ground on which to stand.

I didn't recognize it at the time, but of course it was the malaria in my blood that made me sense these radical contrasts, that caused me to sit caressing the nurse's face though my wife sat on the seat beside us. It was a malarial mind imagining those smells on the wind, perceiving everywhere only conflict and irreconcilable opposites. And it might even have been the malarial vision of the world, with its affinity for huge irrationalities, for sudden grim ironies and contradictions, that eased the awkwardness of that mutation: from consultant to the mill to consultant to the smugglers.

Not to put too much on the malaria, because the truth is that the reality of the disease cured me completely of any lingering romantic notions I might have entertained about it. It was all headache, nausea, double vision, aching muscles, and fever, and all its revelations were unpleasant to contemplate. In the midst of it I took the malaria cure, a brutal blitzkrieg therapy, an overdose of all the prophylactic drugs that hadn't worked in the first place. They provided no immediate relief but only seemed to horribly amplify all symptoms of the disease. So I swallowed handfuls of aspirin, and when the nurse came with her potion of forest weeds I swilled that down too.

The pain and delirium receded, leaving in their wake a few lingering effects: exhaustion, a certain unsteadiness in my vision, and a vacuum at the center of my thought. I recalled my old belief that malaria might have a purifying power, a power of renewal. I thought maybe I felt renewed, or at least altered. And weren't things different, once again, between Kate and me? A new balance, as we sat together on the porch. She'd materialized out of the mushipu darkness and confusion, and now she was so attentive and close at hand: a clean, smooth, solid body; a clear and rational voice. The more she talked, the more the Smugglers' Support Group began to make sense to me. Perhaps, as Kate suggested, up until now I had simply been in the wrong frame of mind to consider it. Several times, she said, she'd tried to tell me what was going on, but I'd always seemed not very curious. Sort of distracted, and I tuned her out. I was so wrapped up in my own scene, with the mill and the noble bureaucrat and the Modernization Project, and then when I gave everybody that raise it seemed like she and I were working at cross-purposes.

"It's not that I'm against the idea of giving the mill workers a raise, Will. God knows they need a raise. They need to keep the mill going, in spite of everything. Maybe they even need Jucht Brothers. It gives them some kind of institutional structure, at least—an alternative to the Church and the government. The roads get maintained, it breaks up their isolation a little. So yeah, mill productivity is an issue. But the picture is much bigger than that. I mean, the reason we came to Africa was not to boost mill productivity, whatever our contracts may say. We had other reasons for coming."

"Well, sure," I said, though I couldn't, at the moment, think what those reasons had been. The way I remembered it, the reason I had come to Africa was because she did.

She sighed. "I know, they were vague reasons. We couldn't even explain them to ourselves, maybe. But isn't that how lots of things go? You stumble around, you bump into things. Blinded by the light, holding on to somebody in the dark. Only what if you suddenly look around and discover that whether through accident or design some things have actually come into focus? What if you realize you're in a position to *accomplish* something, to deal with an injustice, to make a difference in people's lives? Instead of just going around powerless and appalled and grateful as hell that *you* weren't born to be a palm-oil worker in Central Africa. And if you have a realization like that, then maybe you ought to consider that *that's* why you came, and act on it."

I nodded, wondering if she was talking about a realization *she'd* had or one she thought *I'd* had, or ought to have. Wondering if my mind, so recently scorched by malarial fevers, was still too empty to nurture anything so substantial as a realization. Still, what she said seemed mainly reasonable. In fact, the whole world looked very rational, and tranquil, seen from the front porch through a soft mushipu haze. Even the occasional postfever optical bounce wasn't really disconcerting. At the same time, I was aware that things were mutating furiously all around us, and I was thinking how naïve it would be to assume that an empty mind would necessarily fill with reasonable thought, clear and enlightened thought. Rather any sort of thought at all, including useless thought, stupid thought, vile thought, might flow into the vacuum and occupy it. Random thought, like random mutation. No doubt Kate and I were undergoing another mutation right now. Our marriage was evolutionary, as she first had characterized it. Even sitting on the porch staring into the flat mushipu glare we couldn't be sure of what we were becoming. But this was not necessarily an orderly progression toward some higher, more refined state. Evolution was scarred by millions of dead ends, broken branches, grotesque mistakes. Most mutations *were* mistakes. Not that the mutating organisms themselves were aware of this. They struggled on, doomed, woefully ill-adapted, and only with historical perspective, only in the deep genetic record, did it become apparent that they were failures, that evolution had in fact abandoned them and chosen a different path.

OFF THE MAP

By the end of the mushipu the earth was dry and cracking in blackened fields. The river ran clear and low; the streams only trickled; and even in the densest jungle leaves crackled underfoot. Now travelers often passed by on the river road. Some stopped to stare up at our house, and from the porch we heard the rhythms of unfamiliar languages as they continued on their way. Soldiers appeared, alone or in pairs or small groups. No one could say what their business was.

Each day the sky grew whiter, the red sun weaker, and each starless night we fell asleep to the beating of funeral drums. In the morning people who looked as if they had not slept all night huddled around their cooking fires and ate pasty white luku and unsalted saka-saka. The children were listless, the old people skeletal and ghostlike in the smoke and the fog. Often we heard the crying of sick babies and the wailing of mourning women, sometimes close at hand, sometimes faint and far away, coming from the hills across the river or some fever-racked hut deep in the forest. But even these sounds blended into the background. At times we were unaware that we'd been hearing them, until for some reason they stopped and there was only the silence ringing. It was a tenuous, threatening silence, and there was no peace in it, but rather the sense of the same wailing and crying continuing, on some inaudible frequency or in some distant village just beyond the range of human hearing.

We waited for the first big storm that would liberate us from this grim season, but in fact the end of the mushipu was an excruciatingly gradual process. Along with that half-imagined wailing, we began to hear a low rumble. Thunder, yet a long way off, and still it did not rain. In the featureless sky, in a shrunken hazy world, the thunder as much as the wailing seemed to come from no particular direction and no definable distance. It was hard to believe that within a few dozen miles, on some savanna plain or in some other forest valley, rain was falling, flushing the smoke and dust from the sky.

Our own sky only grew denser, slowly going from white to gray. But each day the thunder was louder and sharper, no longer just a rumble coming from an unimaginable source, but now a crack and a long roll up on the nearby savanna. The sky thickened further, the red sun was blotted out, and finally it began to rain—barely more than a mist at first, but slowly gathering strength until great muddy drops fell from a black sky, and then at last a steady clean rain poured down. People stopped in the road and began to laugh, or came outside their huts and stood in the dust that was turning to mud, and Kate and I stepped off the porch onto our clumpy brown grass, laughing like everyone else, our faces turned up to the sky while the warm rain soaked our clothes and streamed off our bodies.

Rain broke the spell of torpor and defeat that had settled over the Kivila Valley. Corn and manioc and peanuts sprouted in the fields, the coupiers returned to the forest to cut the quickly ripening palm nuts, and the chef de poste resolved his stalemated meditations on sex and marriage by deciding to wed his duxième bureau. It was too much trouble maintaining her separately, he said, and too undignified for him to be sneaking off whenever he wanted to spend time with her. Anyway, the guest house was supposed to be reserved for guests. Any day now the commissaire would show up, and what kind of impression would that make if the commissaire had to wait on the porch while somebody changed the sheets on the bed he was supposed to sleep in?

So the chef would just take the girl into his household. Naturally his wife wouldn't like it, but she'd eventually adjust. The bride price was steep, since the girl was plump and lively and he was considered a wealthy man, but what better use could he make of his new raise? Polygamy was, after all, the traditional way of his people and still considered appropriate, almost an obligation, for a man in his position. This idea of a single wife was something imposed upon them by the missionaries, and what qualified the pères, of all people, to dictate how men and women should live together?

Once the chef made this decision, his mind seemed to clear. Again he concentrated on his work, directing the final preparations for the commissaire's imminent arrival and the first public meeting to be held in the Place de la Révolution. Rumor had it that the commissaire, displeased with developments in the Kivila Valley, was planning some sort of crackdown. But the chef de poste said the commissaire knew nothing, his informants were fools, and these were merely the standard veiled threats politicians always felt obligated to deliver. Still the chef seemed fueled by a sudden burst of energy. And whether through the force of his authority, the contagion of his enthusiasm, or the fear inspired by the commissaire, he managed to get the Modernization Project moving forward again. Although much of the palm nut the coupiers cut was delivered in secret to the smuggler, some still went to the mill, and enough of the shell accumulated to finish the paving project. After that, the chef mandated a slowdown in oil processing so that a large pile of fresh palm nut would accumulate outside the mill, creating the impression of harvest bounty.

Naturally the mill consultant counseled against such a transparent and cosmetic gimmick, as I had counseled against most of the Modernization Project. But sometimes I walked to the edge of the Place de la Révolution and gazed at the new signs and painted rocks and geometric pathways, at the stage and kiosk slowly taking shape, and at the vast plain of palm nut shells raked into smooth, striated patterns by otherwise idle mill workers. At these moments, in spite of my better judgment, I felt a flush of pride. Whatever might be said about the practical benefits of the chef's projects, no one could deny that a great deal of work had been done, and that I had played a crucial role in it. For better or worse, Ngemba Station had been transformed, and maybe that achievement—a transformation in a place where nothing ever changed—was enough to justify all the frenzied, absurd activity of the Modernization Project.

In any case, the noble bureaucrat was in no position to condemn an endeavor on the basis of its absurdity. Acting on the recommendations of my Consultant's Assessment, I had prodded the chef de poste into forming "Democratization Committees," whose purpose was to make management of the mill less autocratic and give workers a voice in the decision-making process. We established four committees: Beautification, Human Rights, Production, and Safety. The chef resisted the idea initially but soon became an enthusiastic advocate of democratization. He ordered people to participate, punished them for missing meetings, and sat on each committee himself. Claiming a particular appreciation of beauty, he appointed himself chair of Beautification, which quickly endorsed every initiative of the Modernization Project, and (invoking the snake terror) rejected my suggestions to plant flowers and grass in a few spots.

Even at that, Beautification was more dynamic than Human Rights. No one with a sense of self-preservation would openly discuss such a politicized subject. There were long silences at Human Rights Committee meetings, and when people did speak they focused on peripheral issues: petty attacks on small-time authority figures like the storekeeper, or complaints about wives and girlfriends, the very people whose human rights were most frequently violated.

Production mainly occupied itself debating unworkable or barbaric proposals, such as a suggestion to revive the early colonial practice of chopping the fingers off laggard coupiers. The problem with this committee was that everyone knew the question of mill production could not be addressed apart from the question of smuggling, and at such an official forum the question of smuggling could not be addressed at all.

Only Safety had any really solid accomplishments to point to. As a direct result of Safety Committee directives, loose boards were nailed down here and there, and some particularly rickety supports shored up. A rule requiring periodic breaks for workers was passed and occasionally invoked. But most of the rules and recommendations were pipe dreams: protective clothing, respirators, remodeling that amounted to a rebuilding of the mill. Safety passed a rule requiring all mill workers to wear shoes, but many workers complained, claiming they didn't even own shoes. So the committee persuaded the chef de poste to create a "safety fund" and purchase a half dozen plastic shoes. But then it came out that nobody used plastic footwear in the mill, because it was much safer climbing oily ladders and traversing catwalks in bare feet. The shoes weren't a total loss, however, since whenever a mill worker had to cross the Place de la Révolution to tend to some business in the office, he would slip on a pair in order to protect his feet from the sharp edges of the palm-nut-shell pavement (unanimously endorsed by Beautification) that now entirely covered the yard.

Episodes like the plastic shoe fiasco, I had to admit, reflected poorly on my noble bureaucracy paradigm. Surely a traditional bureaucracy could have achieved a similar result. Still, at least we had put some new structures in place, and possibly something substantial would come of it. In the meantime, though, palm nuts continued to ripen, people needed money, and the Smugglers' Support Group held a secret meeting to discuss how the palm nuts would be sold and where the money would come from.

We met in a place unknown to the commissaire's soldiers and informants: a thatch hut by the river, on the edge of the clearing where Ndosi had his vegetable garden. Several dozen people crowded into the hut, many of them smelling of palm wine and marijuana, and I anticipated a chaotic and confusing argument. But each person calmly waited his turn to make a statement, and though many of the statements were contradictory, by the time we finished it seemed we all agreed on everything. We agreed that the Company exploited the people and that the smuggler's black market provided the best opportunity for fair compensation. We agreed that this black market was an unstable and unreliable outlet for their production, and that they should never become entirely dependent on it. We agreed that although the Company was corrupt and decadent, it did provide some level of financial security, institutional organization, and infrastructure support. We agreed, in summary, that for the time being both mill and smuggler were necessary and that it was the responsibility of all coupiers and farmers to strike the right balance and sustain each with an adequate supply.

But we didn't discuss how that balance might be struck, and in the weeks that followed, the smuggler continued to receive the great bulk of palm nuts and produce. After the meeting Kate quietly dropped her subsidy, which should have made the mill a more attractive market. But in fact no one seemed to notice that the price had changed. The smuggler said this was because of hyperinflation—prices were constantly rising anyway, and people could no longer keep track of how much anything was worth. They kept selling mainly to the smuggler, even when the mill (subsidized by my raise, which remained in place) offered an equivalent payment. So maybe it didn't even come down to economics, Kate suggested. Maybe people just liked smuggling more than they liked selling to the mill, because the mill was dreary and oppressive, and smuggling felt like an act of liberation.

With the paving finished and little work to be done in the mill itself, the chef de poste now turned his attention to the kiosk and stage. He reminded me that in exchange for his permission to give the workers (and him) a raise, I had promised to supply the cement for the foundation. When he put it in those terms I saw I hadn't struck much of a bargain, but I was pleased to have so tangible a task to perform, so I got in the Land Rover and drove off to the mission.

Père Andrés took my money, and Père Michel supervised the loading of the cement. He folded his arms and scowled down his long nose at me.

"So. You working as some kind of chauffeur for that fat chef de poste now? Running his crazy jobs with my camion? We sell you cement, but I tell you to the face, this is not something I approve. You know what he builds with this?"

"It's a kind of a stage for the new public meeting place."

"No. He calls it meeting place, maybe, but I tell you what is the truth. It is some kind of monument. Sure, a monument to himself, like the African dictator always gotta build. You expect it in Kisaka, but out here? Well, maybe. It's a crazy construction, but not the craziest we ever see, maybe. Only we don't see nothing so crazy since a long time. You have to go lotta years back for a construction so crazy. Probably all the way back to the Road Builder."

"You knew the Road Builder?"

"Your people tell you about that man? Yah, sure, I knew him. We work together, little bit, because we are both engineer, and at first he builds some pretty good road. But always there is difficulties. Maybe he is not so crazy, in the beginning, but always he has many prejudice, about the fathers and other things too. And in the end, he forgets himself, he doesn't want to be European no more, no God, no wife, no morals, no rational thinking even. He goes off building his road with no plan, making the plan in his head but nothing on the papers, just going into the jungle with the bulldozer, sending the man in front to wrap the little red cloths on the trees for showing the way. I am engineer, yes? I build many constructions: bridges, roads, buildings. I am saying to him: look, it is necessary for first to have the blueprint, in advance of bulldozering through the jungle. He answers to me: Father, we have no time for blueprints. We are building different kind of road this time. This time, we build a road for trapping. A trap for rebels and cannibals, Father. Priest-eating cannibals! This road is for saving your life, to permit you for staying in your rectory and drawing more blueprints! This is how he talks to me. Then he is back on the bulldozer and crashing through the jungle again. And he builds a kind of a road, leading until nowhere, only to the river, and stopping."

"Is that what they call the Mission Road?"

"You hear about this too. Yah, the Mission Road, they call it. Making a joke, you see. They show you this road? Nothing there, eh, only the jungle overgrowthing it again. And someday, thirty, forty years away, the jungle will overgrowth also whatever this foolish monument your fat chef de poste is building with my cement."

While we were pouring the cement the first letter from Tom arrived. Ndosi came down and told me that a boy was waiting at the house with a letter he would deliver only into my hands.

But the boy clutched the letter to his chest and handed me a note. The note was unsigned but I already guessed it was from Tom. It said to pay the kid for bringing the letter to us. I gave him some money but he just stood there and looked at the ground. "I walked a very long distance," he said. "Look at my feet." His feet were dry and cracking. I gave him more money, and he handed me the letter and went away.

Dear Kate and Will

Is my name still poison in the Kivila Valley, or what? Look, I admit I was an asshole about the boom box, but what do you expect? You knew I lacked social graces. And it was an intense night, I sort of got my perspective skewed. Don't take this as an apology. I was still acting on my beliefs, however clumsily—I may not have said what I meant to say, but I meant what I ended up saying.

And my feelings about all this haven't really changed, except in the sense that the whole incident seems way overblown right now. I just couldn't see getting worked up about a boom box one way or the other anymore. I mean, I spend my days in the shade of a broken-down truck here in this scrub-savanna wilderness, and some of those days a boom box may be playing and some of them it won't, and in the end how much fucking difference can it make?

Now a fuel pump is another story. A fuel pump is a piece of technology you don't just hang on a tree at a piñata party and casually beat into oblivion. A fuel pump has real value, and when it breaks you have to send the boy chauffeur hitchhiking back down the road to get it fixed or replaced, while you set up a gypsy camp in the miserable thorn trees and sit around slapping gnats and telling dirty jokes and watching the damn fool white man write letters.

The piñata party might not have worked out like I hoped, but it was definitely a good feeling to blast out of Malembe and not look back. Screw the radio. Screw my legacy in the Kivila Valley. I stopped off at Kilala Mission and had a drink with that crazy old priest before I went on to Mafemba, where I spent the money you loaned me, Kate, getting my pony spruced up. New piston, cylinder rebored, new plugs and rings, a new front wheel. Then I headed out on the highway.

This country beyond Mafemba makes our old tournées seem like suburban Sunday drives. And out here you don't necessarily feel linked to anything by the roads. For the first couple of days every time I came to a crossroads I'd pull out my Michelin road map and try to figure out where the hell I was, but eventually I realized I was being way too literal with that map. Do you remember the network of squiggly red lines the map shows all over Central Africa? "Primitive Roads." I planned my trip around those roads. It turns out, though, what they really represent is only an _idea_ of primitive roads. The mapmakers never expected anybody to try to correlate any particular squiggly red line with any particular washed-out track or rutted mud wallow. The more I tried to use it, the more I saw that this map I'd been fantasizing over for the past couple of years was just a cartographic fantasy itself—the work of fanatical Germanic minds bent on imposing order and structure on the natural chaos of the world.

But I couldn't fault the mapmakers for the inadequacy of their map. They were entrepreneurs, running a business, responding not to physical reality but to a marketing imperative. They were selling road maps, which meant they had to put roads on the maps they made. But they weren't road builders—it wasn't up to _them_ to put roads on the fucking ground.

I stopped to ask directions in this truck-stop town, a dive like Mafemba only on a smaller scale, not with any hope of getting a coherent answer but just to give people something to argue about for the rest of the afternoon. The usual gang of runty kids was staring me down, and—call it an impulse or a revelation or whatever—I traded the map to one of them for two oranges and a leafful of peanuts. God knows the skinny little fucker needed the food more than I did, but even more he needed the illusions that map can provide. A kid like that, growing up in a shithole like that, needs something like a vision of a macadam strip laid down across the savanna, waiting to carry him an infinite distance away from mud and dust and whores and drunks and the smell of piss and diesel.

Without the map I felt better—like I had some chance of getting to a real place, or at least a possibility of seeing which way I was headed, because I'd be looking directly at the land, not filtering things through some schematic theory of the land. There were only two rules of navigation now: (1) travel in a vaguely easterly direction, and (2) whenever two roads diverge, choose the most fucked-up—the deadliest ruts, the unfathomed potholes— the idea being that only trucks do that to a road, big overloaded trucks going someplace that can be found on a map.

But I found myself wishing at times that Kate's mysterious uncle had taken his road-making magic out this way. Because eventually all the bouncing over bumps and slamming down in ruts and coasting through potholes to the top of the fenders took its toll on the bike, and the sonofabitch broke down. I never figured out the exact problem. I pushed it many hellish clicks through the sand and finally put it on a passing truck and got to the nearest town, where a guy who said he was a mechanic ripped it apart and decided the magneto coil was "reverse magnetized"—a problem, he said, not for a mechanic but for a fetisher.

Maybe I could have found another mechanic. Or what the hell, a good fetisher. But I needed to maintain the momentum of travel, and this town I was stuck in was really grim, a three-star shithole (I give Mafemba two). In a big town I could get the bike fixed, but it was a long way to the next big town. So I negotiated and put in some time and eventually got me and my busted bike on an eastbound truck, which is where I am today—eastbound, which is to say, pointed easterly. Just not moving anywhere.

It's just a regular truck. The driver's a no-holds-barred, head-up-the-ass farceur, the boy chauffeur's a huge wildman who sells dope and diamonds on the side and wears a bandanna on his head that doesn't quite cover the machete scar on his forehead, the truck's outrageously overloaded with people, goats, chickens, manioc, and now a motorcycle, all riding on top of a payload of beer and, if you can believe my luck, a few stinking cases of macayabu, and the engine sounds like it needs the attention of both a mechanic and a fetisher. And sure enough, 50 clicks into my journey with this outfit, we've broke down. It's no big deal, though, only a fuel pump. Shouldn't take more than a week to fix.

But fuck it, you just have to get into it—the rhythm of the breakdowns, the timelessness of the waiting, the infinity of the distance. After all, waiting is what Africa is all about, huh? And assuming we do get rolling again, at least I won't have to ride in the back, on top of the macayabu with the shitting goats and the suffering babies and the dustcoated women. Under the evil eye of the Road Warrior boy chauffeur, who hasn't liked me ever since I suggested that his diamonds may have originated in a Coke bottle smashed on a sidewalk in Kisaka. I paid extra—a lot extra—to ride in the cab, with the commandant. That's what the driver calls himself, I have no idea why. Maybe he was a mercenary in a former life or something. "Mois, je suis commandant!" he snaps, if he senses anybody questioning his authority or competence. Since he appears to be a psychopath and our lives are in his hands, we indulge his delusions, though when we get to the end of the road we may decide to kill him.

Three or four other people are crammed into the cab, including the commandant's girlfriend, Tsimba, who sometimes makes an effort to talk to me and who is dangerously beautiful and, though maybe I'm only imagining this, provocative. It's awfully crowded in this cab, so maybe she's only trying to get comfortable when she slithers around and rubs herself against me and ends up half sitting in my lap. But then she shoots me this sideways sloe-eyed look and does this smirky thing with her lips, and the commandant snorts and snarls and jams it into a higher gear and I start thinking that maybe the next time the arrogant sonofabitch sticks his nose in the engine pretending he can fix whatever's wrong I'm going to step up there and slam the hood down, throw Tsimba over my back, and run off hooting and slobbering into the thorn trees.

Keep in touch.

—Tom

I stood in the kitchen doorway, waiting for tea water to boil and looking out at a steady dripping rain. Ndosi sat at the kitchen table behind me, flipping through the dictionary. He studied an entry for a while, then picked up Tom's letter again and studied that. He'd been doing this in his spare time for several days now, going back and forth between the letter and the dictionary, occasionally shaking his head and breaking into an odd little chuckle. As if there were some personal joke he and Tom shared, as if the letter actually evoked for him some fond memory of the exiled Monsieur Tom. Well, maybe it did. But I didn't believe he understood even a quarter of what he read there. Sure he had the dictionary, but that only further confused things, since he couldn't understand more than a quarter of what he read in the dictionary either. And when I questioned him about the letter, his answers, when they weren't hopelessly vague, indicated that he had hopelessly misread it. He seemed to think that Tom was attempting through deceit or magic to take over the commandant's truck; that Tsimba was a sorceress trying to lure Tom off into the wilderness and abandon him; and that Tom too had turned out to be a smuggler, carrying a stash of diamonds beneath the salted fish and the beer.

"That's not what the letter says," I told him.

"Mr. Tom is capable of remarkable things," he countered.

"The most remarkable thing about that letter," Kate called from the other room, "is that it arrived at this house. How did a letter make it back through the country he's describing to a place like Ngemba, that's not even anywhere near a trade route?"

"Mr. Tom is capable of remarkable things," Ndosi repeated.

"Tom didn't deliver that letter, Ndosi," Kate said. "It was passed from person to person; it probably went through half a dozen hands or more before it got here."

"Maybe." Ndosi shrugged and turned back to the letter, as if to say it didn't matter how it got here, what mattered was that it was in his hands and that it was full of strange and wonderful accounts, waiting to be deciphered.

2 4

THE DELUGE

The rain came down, and Ndosi read on. More often than not, he could be found sitting at our kitchen table with the dictionary and a letter or a book, a pamphlet, a magazine. It took him a full day to finish with Tom's letter. Then he worked his way through a *Newsweek* magazine, and afterward started in on the Bible. He made it through the story of Noah but bogged down in the genealogies that followed. Immediately he was on to some FAO documents Kate had picked up from the sisters: studies of laterite soils, agroforestry systems, high-yield tropical agriculture. For sheer technical dullness this stuff was on a par with *Products of the Oil Palm,* but Ndosi sat down at the table and plowed through it doggedly.

It was good weather for reading, I had to admit that much. We were in the heart of the monsoon now. For three days a hard rain fell without stopping. Gullies and streams swelled, whole fields washed away, and the river ran reddish-brown, breaking dirty, foaming waves over its upper banks. A flow of mud blocked the forest road and up on the savanna several bridges washed out. For several weeks we were cut off from Kisaka and the principal travel routes, though you wouldn't expect that to make much difference to anyone, since the roads carried almost no traffic even when they were open. But the pères couldn't run their usual errands to Kisaka, and the smuggler couldn't get through, and after burying her Land Rover up to the axles in mud the animatrice quit trying to go anywhere either. Even travel by foot was limited by high water and washed-out bridges. But the palm oil boat came upriver once, bringing empty barrels, the payroll, and a few items for the Company store. It brought some local people who had been stranded downriver by the road washouts, a message from the commissaire explaining that his visit was once again delayed, and a long, convoluted letter from Uncle Pers.

We each read the letter the evening it arrived, and kept going back to it the next day, when torrential rains and flooding kept us in the house. It moved with us from room to room, insinuating its observations and opinions into our lives. There it was on the desk, or lying open on a porch chair or on the kitchen table, moving restlessly about in a confined space, as if it had arrived with a case of cabin fever to match our own.

It is a lovely summer afternoon on the bay. Following a morning's sail, we've anchored for lunch in the calm water in the lee of Angel Island, and now Mavis has gone below to nap, while I sit on the deck to write. No circumstance can prevent her from taking her midday nap, and she always sleeps exactly one hour and fifteen minutes, as deeply as a corpse. As for me, I scarcely sleep at all, though in other ways my resemblance to a corpse is much more striking.

Earlier the fog was dense, but by mid-morning it had rolled back offshore, and there's been enough breeze to push us about in the bay. We sailed to one side, and back to the other. I was at the tiller, nominally the captain, though there is little steering to be done. Mavis fusses with the sails and does whatever else she damn well pleases. When she suggests that we come about, I always wait a few moments, then I say, "Coming about!" and we come about.

I am not complaining. I never expected to get my hands on a sailboat tiller again at all. But during the past month it has been determined that I am "in remission," which is apparently not the same as being "in denial," and so I am permitted to come out and pretend that I am once again captain of my own ship.

Kate sat cross-legged on the floor of the living room with scissors and crayons, making a poster for a discussion on fertility cycles for the next Mamas' Support Group meeting. "Fertility of what?" I wondered. "Human beings? Soil? Chickens?"

She smiled. "All of the above. They're linked, you know. But I'm ready for a coffee break. Go make us some coffee, and we'll sit on the porch for a few minutes."

In the kitchen Ndosi sat at the table, flipping through the dictionary. He stopped flipping and read for a minute, following the words with his finger. Then he picked up one of the FAO pamphlets beside him and studied that.

"What is that?" I said. "What are you reading?"

He didn't look up. "I don't know yet, monsieur. I won't know until I read it."

I looked over his shoulder, then left the coffee dripping and went back to the living room. "'Basic Principles of Stone Wall Construction,'" I reported to Kate. "I guess the first principle is, find a stone. I mean, there aren't any around here, right?"

She didn't look up from her poster. "I guess not. I guess all we have is dirt."

"I have to say, your ESL curriculum is fairly haphazard. If you're going to go to the trouble to teach him, couldn't you at least find a decent text?"

She made a face. "I don't like that word 'text.' Implying a bunch of academics dissecting real books, theorizing and abridging and anthologizing. What's wrong with haphazard? That's the way children learn, the way we learned language to begin with. Can't Ndosi read whatever he wants, whatever he finds on the table? Will, he already speaks four languages. Let him follow his instincts on this one."

Fine, let him. I guess I didn't really care, so long as the clothes got washed and the floor swept. Of course, lately the floor didn't get swept all that often, and on several occasions I'd had to interrupt Ndosi's reading to ask him to fill the water jug or wash the dishes. And since the end of the mushipu, his various outdoor projects—fence maintenance, chicken-shed construction, the renovation of the Road Builder's gardens—had been entirely abandoned.

The weather has been fine, and I have persuaded Mavis to take me sailing twice this week. You must be getting well, she says, if you can sail so much. Obviously I'm not well, I'm dying; one doesn't get out of it so easily, just by going sailing. As if sailing, of all things, could postpone the final voyage. The final crossing. I don't know what you mean, she sniffs, the final crossing! Why do you say "sailing, of all things"?

Naturally Mavis—though she fancies herself a Jungian—is not attuned to the dark metaphors of boats and water. It would never occur to her to smell this air for the presence of Death. She can't see the black waters lapping

*the silent shore, or the hooded Boatman, with his long oars thudding on the
gunwales. For her on a day like this, there is only the blue bay, shining hills,
white sails filled with air. The metaphor hides behind this mirage. Meanwhile
the tide sucks on our hull, pulling to the open sea, and we sail in silence across
the bay and never speak the name of the river we are crossing and recrossing.*

"He seems so remote to me," Kate said loudly. We nearly had to shout to
hear each other on the porch, with the rain pounding on the roof and pouring
off onto the compacted ground below. She sipped her coffee and peered
through the screen of streaming rainwater, as if searching for something out
on the brown river. But of course there was nothing to be found there, only
logs and brush and clumps of uprooted hyacinth swept along on the flood.

"Because he's in his own world," I said, "reading all the time."

She looked annoyed. "I'm talking about Uncle Pers, Will, not Ndosi.
What I'm saying is, his letters make me realize how we've drifted away from
each other. The memoirs brought us together, but now that's finished, I guess.
Now there's nothing left for him to do except get older, and then die."

We sipped our coffee, watched the rain and the river. "Were you thinking
he should be out gardening or something?" she demanded.

"Where'd you get that idea? Anyway, Mavis is the one who does the
gardening."

She sighed, exasperated. "Not Uncle Pers, Will! I mean Ndosi. You were
complaining that he's just sitting around reading, as if you thought he should
be out working in his garden."

I didn't, if only because the rains had already pounded his garden into
oblivion. When the rainy season first began, he had dug some channels and
built a few little thatch tepees and lean-tos to protect his plants. But then the
heavy rains came, ripping his plants to shreds and washing his beds of fragile
soil into the river, and he abandoned the project, with little apparent regret
for his lost labor.

"I guess people don't garden much in the rainy season," she said. "I mean,
look at it come down. When was the last time you weeded our tomatoes?
Anyway, right now Ndosi's garden isn't much use to him. He couldn't sell
much, now that people are beginning to harvest from their fields and with so
much forage available in the forest."

"Sure. Of course, we're still foraging corned beef and sardines in the company store. Remember all the great stuff Ndosi used to bring home to eat? And all those greens we used to compost? But that was before he had so much reading material to get through."

You will perhaps have guessed that this sailboat tiller in my hands is essentially a reward. Or compensation, for my surrender. I have informed my agent—and more importantly, Mavis—that my memoirs will be ready for the publisher within weeks, unconformities and all. I have acquiesced to all her demands, included all the myths and rumors and allusions she wants to hang like gaudy ornaments on the dull facts of my life. Let her make whatever she will of the Road Builder and his Mission Road. The truth, apparently, is already out of reach. You say that the jungle has now entirely overgrown this Mission Road. Well, let it vanish! I'm sure you are quite right to concentrate instead on these new clearings—this Place de la Révolution and this Place Without a Name and whatever other Places emerge out of the placeless African wilderness.

"The truth is, he's kind of pissing me off lately," Kate said.

"Well, yeah! He's hardly done a lick of work all week."

She set down her coffee cup and glared at me. Apparently I was pissing her off too. "I'm trying to talk about Uncle Pers, Will. I mean, we just got this intense letter from him, and you want to bitch about Ndosi not mopping the floor."

"Sorry. What was it you wanted to bitch about?"

"Well, the way he talks about Aunt Mavis, for one thing. He makes a caricature out of her, and just assumes that we're on his side. But she's not half as kooky as he makes her out to be, you know. And now he's acting like we haven't come through for him, like we're the ones who've dropped the whole thing about the unconformities and filling in the gaps in his memoirs."

"Well, it's true we haven't gotten to the bottom of anything."

"Maybe there isn't any bottom. A place of no significance, right? Or maybe getting to the bottom just takes a lot of time. Anyway, he told us to be discreet. Why do you suppose he said that? Do you think he had an idea that we'd be better off keeping our distance from him?"

I must say, your lives seem to be opening wider and wider. It seems that nearly anything might happen to you. I am prepared to read that the ominous commissaire has at last appeared and ordered his soldiers to seize you, but just in time you were alerted to the ambush and fled into the mountains to join a band of insurgents. Or that Will has fallen entirely under some enchantment and cannot be moved from his front porch, where he sits gazing toward the river, breaking the hypnotic silence only to exchange an occasional non sequitur with the night watchman. Or that the two of you have finally dispensed with civilities and skirmishes and had a real argument, with violent words and accusations and insults and recriminations. And it ended with Will bursting out of the house and driving off in that Land Rover and not coming back for days. Or with Katy jumping on the back of a motorcycle and riding off into the wilds with her piñata-smashing anarchist.

"Do you think we'll ever see Tom again?"

"We could, Will. Or just as easily not."

"Okay. Do you think you're ever going to see the money you loaned him again?"

"It wasn't very much money, Will."

"That's not the point."

"What is the point?"

"I don't know. I guess the point is we never talked about that night. Tom's fête."

"It was a shitty night. Who wants to talk about it?"

"Well, I thought you might have some insight. Into the piñata thing and all."

"I don't have any insight. I'm going to get more coffee now. Do you want more coffee?"

"I guess not. I guess I'll go inside for a while and work on some stuff."

"Tom flipped out, Will. That's all. He flipped out, gave a speech nobody could make any sense of, beat his boom box into oblivion, and ran away. In hindsight it seems totally predictable. He'd been on the edge all along, wasn't that obvious to us?"

"And now?"

"Oh, he's still flipping out, I'm sure. I don't know, you read his letter. What do you think?"

"I don't know. There's a lot of tough talk. But I think he sounds vulnerable."

"Everybody's vulnerable. But Tom has his own resources. Tom surprises people."

"Ah, oui. 'Mr. Tom is capable of remarkable things.'"

"Well," said Kate, "maybe he is."

Amid the news of your adventures and discoveries, I note no mention of your dissertation, Katy. Well, no wonder—it must seem absurd, in that context. Still, it strikes me as an unfortunate waste. All that time spent creating something so intricate, so meticulously plotted out and quantified. All that fantastic numerology. There must be a way to draw upon it in your current circumstances. Because it is a resource, you know. One of the materials at hand. . . .

"What are we having for dinner, Ndosi?"

He raised his eyes from the pamphlet, but not enough to meet my gaze.

"I don't know."

"Is there any way to get some meat? Some vegetables?"

"No."

"We could have beans. Why don't you cook us some beans?"

"There isn't enough time."

"It's that late? What time is it?"

"I don't know. My watch battery's dead. But beans take a long time."

I could have ordered him to cook some beans, regardless of the time. But he wasn't really obligated. Sometimes he cooked dinner and sometimes he didn't. Lately he generally didn't. I rummaged through the pantry, if you can call it rummaging when the pantry is essentially empty.

"We could have some popcorn right now. How does that sound?"

"I'm not hungry," Ndosi mumbled without looking up.

"Don't make any popcorn for yourself then. Just make it for Kate and me."

I guess I was snapping at him, though maybe it sounded okay in Kituba, an admirably blunt and unapologetic language. But when I turned from the pantry to look at him he was staring directly at me. I can't say for certain what I saw in his face in that brief instant before he lowered his eyes, but it seemed like a violently hostile look, as if to say: "make your own stinking popcorn, asshole." I'd never before seen such an expression on his face, and of course that was not the kind of thing Ndosi had ever said to me. On the other hand, he would have had a point, saying it—I was perfectly capable of making my own popcorn, and it probably didn't seem as if I had anything better to do. But he sucked in his breath, let it out in a heavy, Dimanche-like sigh, and got up to make the popcorn.

Usually Ndosi liked making popcorn. With the *ping!* of the first popping kernel, a smile would spread across his face, and by the time most of the kernels were popping he would be laughing helplessly, contagiously. We'd taught Ndosi about popcorn, and he in turn taught us how intrinsically comical the stuff is, particularly when he would take the lid off at the moment of the most climactic and frenzied popping and go down on his knees roaring with laughter, popcorn zinging about the room, caught in his hair, showering down on his outstretched arms.

For Ndosi the transformation of popcorn must have been a kind of magic. Not black magic but something more playful, like the magic of his bamboo airplanes. Of course, the airplanes were more enigmatic than popcorn, and less frivolous. It wasn't clear exactly what the airplanes did, but they weren't slapstick, and the laughter they inspired was serious and defiant. Their novelty alone gave them a radical, even subversive aura. Especially now that there were so many of them. Other young men had followed Ndosi's lead, and there were now six or seven airplanes swaying in the wind above the village of Malembe. Like a village in Mputu, Ndosi had told me, laughing. And it was true that with all those erect poles and slanting support lines the young men of Malembe had captured something of the chaotic geometry of a modern city, suggesting a skyline dissected by power lines and telephone poles and rigid reflecting buildings.

I am not quite satisfied with your noble bureaucrat, Will. It's nice of him to give the workers a raise, but still the fellow is not exactly breaking new ground, as far as bureaucrats go. I suppose a bureaucrat, even a noble one, must write reports, but why not put a little life into them? Look around you! Once again, use the materials at hand. Your villagers and farmers—how do they accomplish their ends? As I understand it, mainly through the use of magic. Why not put some of that in your report? Not their magic, but your own. Using the alchemies and transformations and fetishes that are familiar to us, and that are convincing to the sort of people—administrators, bureaucrats, technocrats—who will read your report. For that audience I recommend the magic of quantification and mensuration. Numbers! They have many advantages, Will. With numbers you can present something entirely ambiguous and make it appear to be very exact. You can start with almost nothing and end up with a great deal. Properly processed, numbers can convince people of anything. Because we all believe that numbers reveal things as they truly are.

The heavy smell of hot palm oil filled the house. The oil sizzled, louder than the sound of the rain, and the first tentative popping kernels hit the lid of the pan. But it was a somber popping, not the usual manic burst of joy at all. Ndosi himself was silent, though his sulkiness seemed almost audible. Today not even the slapstick antics of popcorn could lighten his mood.

It was hard to reconcile the laughing, enthusiastic Ndosi of the bamboo airplanes and the popcorn showers with this resentful fellow now serving up popcorn in the kitchen. He left the two bowls on the counter and returned in silence to his reading. I carried the popcorn into the living room and set one bowl on my desk and the other on the floor beside Kate, who didn't even glance up from her poster.

I envied her that concentration. The possibility that I would ever become so absorbed in my reports seemed remote. The sight of my latest draft on the desk was merely depressing. "Annual Report," I'd entitled it, as if the noble bureaucrat were already an institution, anticipating a long bleak future of churning these things out. Pers was right about that anyway: this report was a collection of tedious and lifeless words, existing in isolation. It needed something to connect it to the world. The "magic of numbers" was his suggestion. But numbers by themselves were nothing, mere arithmetic. They needed the power of statistics behind them. A numerology, as he said. Yes, a numerology for the Age of Science.

I went to the bookcase and quietly slipped Kate's dissertation out from beneath papers and books on the bottom shelf. No one had opened it in well over a year, since that day in my truck crossing the Nevada deserts when I read a few pages and felt it trigger some sense of inadequacy in my life. But now as I took up a handful of popcorn, I was thinking that maybe I did have a use for this sort of thing, for the irrefutable magic of two-tailed T tests and multivariate regression analysis.

I chewed the popcorn, and choked. Dropping the dissertation, I fled to the kitchen for a glass of water.

"My God, Ndosi, you must have put half a cup of pili-pili in this stuff!"

"Pili-pili?" said Ndosi vacantly. Unsmiling, he looked up from the dictionary. "Oh, yes, a little pili-pili. Extra vitamins, monsieur. Protein!" I glowered at him, poured a tall glass of water, and returned to the living room.

"I think all this reading is doing something to his sense of humor," I remarked. "He used to laugh a lot more."

"Oh, I bet he's still laughing," Kate said. She was on her hands and knees with her crayons, coloring in mysterious shapes on her fertility poster. Fallopian tubes? Earthworms? "A few tablespoons of pili-pili in the patrón's popcorn, who wouldn't laugh? Anyway, he's entitled to his moods. Probably his life is more complex than we imagine. He'd have to be an idiot to keep laughing as much as we'd like him to."

Tentatively I chewed on a kernel of popcorn, wondering if she might have a point. Ndosi was uncommonly industrious and creative, an insightful and considerate person who cheerfully transcended the ongoing adversity of his life. But clearly he had a darker side, and it wouldn't do to ignore the various demons that haunted him.

Lately he'd been complaining more and more about his problems with the old people of his village. They entered his hut at night, he said, threatened him, harassed and tempted him. He'd told of one old crone who'd taken the form of a young girl and crept up beside him as he lay sleeping. She knelt by his head and murmured in his ear, ran her hands across his chest, pressed her breasts against his face. He sat up in bed, sniffed the air, and knocked her across the room, sending her screeching from the hut.

How do you know it was an old woman? I teased him. Maybe it really was a girl. But Ndosi didn't smile. I know the smell of a witch, monsieur. He turned away, and once again I didn't know what to think: was he describing a dream vision, or did he actually believe that a young girl who was really an old woman had knelt by his bed and traced flesh-and-blood fingers across his chest in the night?

Nighttime visitations were becoming commonplace in Ndosi's hut. His dead uncle the crocodile fetisher had appeared and told him to reclaim his fishponds near Kasengi. But he would have to form alliances, the uncle said; since his own uncles had turned against him, he would have to join with another clan. So he had stepped up the pace of his courtship of Kitoko, the girl in Ngemba. He asked us for an advance on his wages to make a down payment on the bride price. Immediately Kate said no, we wouldn't give him money to marry a thirteen-year-old child. Ndosi said he wasn't exactly marrying her yet, only formalizing a contract with her family, and he wouldn't sleep with her for at least a year.

"You mean you'll wait until she's fourteen," said Kate.

"We die young in Africa," Ndosi said. "So we have to grow up young. Especially women have to grow up young."

"Especially women die young, maybe because you make them grow up so young. Anyway, Kitoko's not a woman. She's a girl."

"She has breasts."

"Little pokey things."

"No, madame! You look again. Besides, they're growing all the time. And already she has the buttocks of a woman."

"You're imagining things. Anyway, there's more to it than breasts and buttocks."

"It's true that she's young," Ndosi sighed. "Which means she has no history of love. That's a great virtue in a wife, in these days when a woman's embrace might lead to death."

For once Kate seemed to lose patience with Ndosi. "What about your history?" she demanded. "Have you considered what risks she might be running, embracing you?"

"I'm healthy, madame, I'm clean. En tout cas, some things we must leave in the hands of God. We can't anticipate and fear every disaster."

"No. But you can certainly create one, marrying a child."

"Well, the older women are already taken. And I'm telling you, madame, experience is a dangerous thing in this time of the world."

But Kate pressed on. "What about the nurse? She's single, she's beautiful and intelligent. She likes you. And I think you like her."

"I would never marry the nurse."

"Why not?"

"There are many, many problems with the nurse, madame."

"But you get along with her. You're always kidding around. And you're already partners."

"That's not the question. She's intelligent, as you say. She's very beautiful, oh yes. But what is the origin of her beauty? Why doesn't it fade with time? Many people ask this question. And to what use has she put her intelligence? She has no husband, no money, no children, no job. Anyone who considers marrying the nurse had better ask himself why this is so."

I'm intrigued by this Dream fellow doing your dishes. I must say he seems capable of more complex tasks. Did you give him a bonus for excavating your garden? That was some feat, wasn't it? Anghor Wat rising out of the jungle! And now you stroll among flowering vines, and pluck your breakfast from your little orchard. I always had bananas growing in my yards in the tropical countries, and ate them as a staple. Nowadays I scarcely touch them, out of terror of constipation. Mavis, however, requires a banana every morning, for regularity. If there is no banana in the house, someone must make a trip to the grocery, or she won't have a bowel movement and soon will sicken and die. Like many old women in Europe and America, she feels very strongly about this. In this way do the little countries, banana republics, sustain our matriarchy, the old wives and widows of the powerful states and empires. A great industry revolves around this, plantations and packing houses, flotillas of freighters steaming north, their hulls stuffed with bananas to stimulate the bowels of old women.

It occurs to me that palm oil may have similar properties. Why not? And if properly publicized—first the medical journals, then the supermarket tabloids—couldn't such properties restore your disreputable oil's appeal to the fickle stomachs, or intestines, of the affluent world? Something for the noble bureaucrat to investigate, perhaps.

I looked out the window, thinking, my God, how long can it rain like this, and as I watched it rained harder. The room darkened. The pounding on the roof overwhelmed the little house, obliterating the sounds of pages turning and crayons squeaking and the front-door hinges creaking as I stepped out, unnoticed, onto the front porch.

Water poured off the eaves and flowed across the yard, scouring small gullies between the clumps of grass Ndosi had planted. The Road Builder's fruit trees rose out of a thickening understory above brick paths and walls. But beyond this little orchard the paths vanished. Ndosi had torn down the old chicken shed, and the pile of rotting thatch and boards had already nearly disappeared beneath the spreading vegetation. The small vegetable garden we'd planted was indistinguishable from the weedy growth that surrounded it. But perhaps the weeds were necessary, to shelter the tender hybrids from the crushing rain.

However, protection from the rain was largely a moot point for these garden plants. While the uncultivated plants in the yard flourished, the garden vegetables had scarcely grown at all. The few that had shown vigor had been snapped up quickly by the goats, who periodically managed to batter and worm their way through Ndosi's fence, and any plants overlooked by the goats had mostly succumbed to disease and pests when the rains began. In the beginning Ndosi had made some effort to keep the fence in good repair, and I had gone down there a few times to mulch and pull weeds, but gradually and without acknowledging it, we had abandoned any effort to save the garden.

When you are old, though you may lose entirely whatever convictions you now hold about God, love, friendship, duty, honor, you too may develop strong convictions about bananas. Such is the wisdom of the aged. Perhaps you see it happening already: over the years, the forms of the larger world blur, but the details of one's own physical comfort become specific, obsessive—comfort becomes the entire focus of our lives. Our specialized beds and chairs, our elaborate rituals of sleeping and eating. And the medicines, the pills and salves and potions, that we require! Not to mention the food— bananas are but one example, and not the most extreme, of the fierce ideology we bring to the table.

I contrast this with the old people you describe in your letters. "All bones and sagging skin," huddled in a little piece of cloth around a fire, going out to

work in the fields until the day they die. But I suppose they too have their
obsessions; I suppose they too find something to fuss about.

Beyond the garden, the strip of forest Ndosi had cleared out six months
earlier was growing back with surprising speed and vigor. It was like a wall
going up, closing us in again, though there were still gaps through which I
could have seen the chef's house across the river, if it hadn't been invisible behind the rain. Or maybe it wasn't only rain obscuring the view. Maybe Ndosi
was right about the lateness of the hour, and the sudden equatorial night was
already upon us. Could the day have passed so quickly? No, not quickly—the
day had dragged on and on, but with nothing to mark its passing, only the
swelling and diminishing rain, the rustling of pages, the drift of fragmented
conversation and thought. The repeated cups of coffee, too much coffee. The
gradual gnawing of hunger. The popcorn, the fiery, cheerless popcorn.

I looked again toward the garden. None of the fruit was ripe, but beneath
the weeds and vines some vegetable might be found. It wouldn't take much—
a few tomatoes, a handful of greens—to blend with a can of sardines and
make a palatable stew.

The rain intensified, the garden further dimmed, and I stripped down to
my undershorts and went out into the yard. That was a cold shock, but almost
instantly I was as wet as I could get, which gave me some immunity from the
downpour. Carefully I moved down the slippery path to the garden, mindful
of the chef de poste's warnings about snakes. It was easy to ridicule his obsession, but certainly it had some foundation in reality—there were, after all,
deadly snakes in the African jungle, and here I was moving barefoot and bare-
legged through thick wet undergrowth. And hadn't I heard that snakes were
attracted to overgrown clearings, and especially active in the rain?

When I guessed I'd come to the vegetable garden I stopped and began to
poke around gingerly in the undergrowth. Yes, here were vestiges of agriculture under the weeds: neat rows of short shriveled stems, all chewed off an
inch above the ground, and a few blighted tomato and squash plants sprawled
limply here and there. And here, miraculously, was something to harvest: one
half-ripe tomato, a couple of hard green ones, and several stunted round eggplants. Something, anyway, with which to dilute the intensity of sardines.

But at least your old people over there, however miserable, are not invisible. In fact, they are honored, aren't they, sometimes even feared? And however they may suffer, they can look forward to being dead and to the exalted status and power they will then possess. Whereas I am dying in a country where ancestors have no citizenship. Where the dead simply vanish, sucked into the ground or consumed by fire, with little wisps of spirit-matter carried at the exact moment of their passing into some unreachable fastness of heaven or hell.

In such a country, one must expect to encounter a variety of pathetic, futile efforts to achieve immortality. A memoir, naturally, is one of these. Though the best the memoirist can hope for is a brief extension of his life into the memories of his descendants. What if millions do read his book? Then it will merely require a generation or two to entirely forget him, rather than a couple of years.

Beneath a dense cloud the rain came at me in waves, a monsoon pulse. But out in the garden the gray light was less oppressive. Perhaps after all, night was not yet falling; perhaps this was only the dimness at the thick center of the cloud.

"Will!"

It was a little bit ghostly, standing out there in a garden gone to ruin, with the rain coming down. The world retreated, hunkered down, before that kind of rain. I hunkered down myself, and pulled at the weeds surrounding the surviving tomato plant. It wouldn't take all that much work, really, to clear the garden out, give it some air and some light. The question was, would it do any good? You have to consider the kind of air and light you're giving it—in this case, hot infested air, fierce light.

"Will!"

Still, these weeds were no alternative. No one could claim this was a real garden growing here. But how do people grow food in a place like this? I pulled another weed, then stood and shook the muddy red soil from my hands. My skin looked whiter than ever, glaring back at me as the soil fell away, reflecting disproportionate light from the surrounding cloud. Rain came down all around me, falling in waves, blurring the trees and fences, roads and pathways, the shuttered guest house down the hill and the darkened company store on the slope above, nearly invisible now within the deep shadow of trees and behind the curtain of rain. I wondered if I looked as dim and gray and blurred by rain as everything else, or if with all that shining white skin exposed I wasn't glowing a little, a freakish beacon rising out of the red earth, a whitewashed scarecrow in the rain.

"Will! What are you doing out there? Are you okay, Will?"

I wiped the rainwater out of my eyes. Kate was on the porch, waving at me.

"I'm fine!" I shouted. "I'm just getting some air! I'm just—weeding the garden!" And I bent down to pull a couple more plants out of the red mud.

Her nap was invigorating, Mavis announced when she came up to the deck, and on such a day no doctor could object to an old man spending more time on the water. Her enthusiasm was so forceful I didn't try to argue, and so we took a long westward tack toward the open ocean.

As we approached the Golden Gate, Mavis kept glancing at me—her way of issuing a command to come about. But I liked that tack. The sea is larger out there, and from the top of a swell one can see the breakers at the point, and beyond the bridge, the bay opening to the ocean and the waves rolling in toward the Marin headlands.

"Look what I found, Ndosi. An eggplant. Some tomatoes. We could have a stew."

Still reading, he didn't seem to hear me, though you'd have thought he might have taken some notice, since I stood in my underwear dripping water on the kitchen floor. I put the eggplant and tomatoes on the counter, and went into the bedroom to get a towel. Kate was lying on the bed, looking up at the roll of mosquito netting. I asked her what she was doing.

"Nothing. Sometimes this place does seem just like Uncle Pers described it. You know. Insignificant. Dull. A lot of rain. You pick a strange time to garden."

"It was refreshing. More reasonable than gardening in the sun, anyway."

"Well, you didn't look reasonable. Mud dripping from your hands, wandering through the pineapples in your skivvies. Just another white man losing his marbles in the equatorial rain. That's what you looked like. How's the garden?"

"I harvested something. Tomatoes. A couple of spherical blobs that may be eggplants."

I stood drying myself and looking out the window toward the guest house, which was still dim and rain-shrouded but not yet, I decided, fading into the darkness of night.

"I was thinking it was almost night. But I guess it isn't."

Kate laughed and sat up. "It's barely mid-afternoon, Will. But maybe you are a crazed jungle explorer. Maybe you did catch some kind of fever, running around in the rain in soggy underpants." She tugged on the elastic. "How can you stand wearing these things?"

"If they bother you," I said, "you can take them off."

"Okay," she said. And she did. Then she took the towel and sat drying me, while I leaned on the windowsill and looked out at the rain. It was coming down harder again. Again the guest house blurred, the world darkened a little—not the fast-falling darkness of night but rather the twilight of rain, the only equatorial twilight that endures. We could lie in that twilight for hours, if we wanted. We could escape from cabin fever, escape from Africa, even, into that slowly deepening shadow, which was lie a shadow falling on a bedroom in a northern country at the slow end of a midsummer's day.

The waves gather momentum, water sweeps to the shore. Of course, that's an illusion. In reality the water remains out at sea, churning in circles and swept along in the great currents, independent of waves. So it is more or less the same water rising and falling in place to form each wave and trough, the same water crashing again and again on the rocks. But if not the water, then what is it moving so resolutely toward shore? What sort of progress is this, where the material moves in repetitive circles and only an idea of forward motion is carried into the land?

We ventured farther to the edge of the ocean, sailing in heavy chop, funneled winds and currents below the orange bridge. The water was dark there, in the shadows of towers. The boat seemed small. Mavis shouted at me, and I looked down at her, expecting some stem admonition. But she was smiling, with a look in her eye that I didn't recognize at first. A look from 40 years ago, maybe.

"You see!" she shouted. "Old men should be explorers!"

*The wind was blowing her hair out of its bun, and the salt spray show-
ered over her. And she was laughing. Oh yes, we should be explorers. But
after a moment I called out, "Coming about!" We came about, and took a
long tack along the Marin shore before crossing the bay a final time and
returning home.*

—*Pers*

Kate said she dreamed of the molecules in the waves. The molecules were
dense and intricate, but she couldn't get a fix on them because they were tumbling, swirling, spinning, and there were millions of them: a tremendously
complex and beautiful motion, she said, and then the wave rode on and it
all collapsed.

I couldn't see her face. It was dark, really dark—this was unmistakably
night, no trick of the monsoon cloud. But at last it had stopped raining, and
the night sounds of the house and valley were again audible: cicadas, rustling
bats, flooding creeks, the rise of drumbeats and pestles in the camp. I lit the
lamp and got some clothes off the shelf.

She had dreamed Pers' sentences, Kate said: the waves sweeping to shore,
and the realization that nothing tangible was moving in that direction. In the
dream she dissected waves, gazed with magnified vision at molecular motion.
Water molecules tumbled in the wave; the wave itself was just an idea heading
for land; and Pers was at the tiller of a boat skimming over it all, heading away
from the waves, out to sea.

"And Aunt Mavis?"

"I never saw her. She got ditched, I guess. Or she ditched him." Kate sat
up and threw back the covers. "Where the hell are my pants? Boy, that was a
weird dream. But now I'm famished. You don't suppose Ndosi made dinner
before he went home?"

"I don't. I'll go put rice on. We can make a sauce with sardines and
vegetables."

The kitchen table was empty except for a lamp, burning with a low flame.
I measured water and rice and lit the stove. Kate came out and started cutting
up the eggplant and tomatoes. She let out a cry and dropped the knife. I
thought she'd cut herself, but when I turned around she was staring into the

living room, where Ndosi sat in a chair in the darkness, lamplight glinting off his cheek and the sclera in his eyes.

"Ndosi! We thought you'd gone home."

He shook his head, barely. Maybe he didn't move at all.

"It stopped raining. We fell asleep. You should have gone home a long time ago."

Still he said nothing. Kate sat down, keeping her eyes on him. I picked up the knife and finished cutting up the vegetables. Then I opened a can of sardines. Ndosi sighed, and Kate and I both jumped at the sound. He stood up and came into the kitchen. In his hand he had Uncle Pers' letter. He put the letter down on the table, got his bag, and went to the door.

"That letter is from the Road Builder," he said quietly. "You are the Road Builder's children. Now we know this." Then he opened the door and went out into a darkness of roaring streams, dripping trees.

TWO ROADS

The silence in our kitchen held for a long while, after Ndosi laid Uncle Pers'
letter on the table and carried off into the postdeluge night the revelation
that Monsieur Will the consultant and Madame Kate the animatrice were
children of the Road Builder. Eventually Kate looked up from the bubbling
eggplant-sardine stew. "Okay, you were right," she said. "I should have found
something else for him to read."

"Yeah, you should have. But they would have eventually found out in any
case. Didn't Tom warn us? That you can totally fucking depend on people to
root out a connection like that. And it will totally fucking freak them out
when they do."

Within twenty-four hours the connection was known to everyone in the
Kivila Valley, and we were already becoming aware of the consequences. That
revelation changed everything, instantly altered all relationships and percep-
tions. It mutated, infected, interbred. It spawned other revelations, and
opened new clearings and pathways in the tangled brush.

The children pushed homemade bamboo trucks along a narrow muddy trail
winding among the tufts of grass in our yard. Along the length of the trail
they smoothed and packed the dirt down, excavating and filling and lining
the dirt with twigs and pebbles.

"Hey, be careful you don't dig up the grass!"

"Oh, no, monsieur, we don't touch the grass. We're very careful."

"Playing Smuggler again, are you? Don't let the soldiers catch you!"

"Not Smuggler, monsieur. We don't play that now. Now we play Road
Builder."

"Oh. Road Builder. Well, naturally."

They looked up at me, grinning, arms and faces streaked with mud.

"You see, Mr. Will? We are building the Mission Road!"

"Be careful of mercenaries, Mr. Will!"

"Watch where you step, monsieur. Dynamite!"

Matama stopped by the house to ask for a loan, because the price of kerosene had suddenly risen and she was short of cash. "The storekeeper says you still have three empty beer bottles to return. I'll take them back for you when I buy the kerosene, if you are able to make this small loan, merci. People are talking. They say the chef de poste has gone to Kisaka for business, traveling on the savanna road. His old wife went with him, his new wife stayed home. They say the Yambezi bridge will be repaired after the rains stop. They say that the next time the river rises, the Road Builder will ascend the flood on a great barge, loaded with shining new equipment to restore the Ngemba mill."

Placide lay on his cardboard bed with his hands folded over his chest, staring up at the nighttime sky. His little column of smoke went up into the blackness, and he spoke without turning his head.

"They say the Road Builder will soon return to complete his work among us. That you are here before him to prepare the way. They say the Mission Road will at last be finished, and covered with a surface of smooth black rock, like a highway of Mputu."

They say he is coming by convoy on the river road, or flying in at night on a silent airplane as swift as a falling star.

They say the chinois downriver is working for him, supplying equipment and stockpiling stores for his workers.

They say his agent has been seen at the Kilala Mission, a white man preparing to raise an army of mercenaries to hunt down the old rebels in the southern savannas.

They say the consultant and the animatrice are smuggling weapons to supply the Road Builder's army.

They say that out of fear of the Road Builder, the commissaire post-
pones his inspection of the mill, and sends more spies and soldiers into the
Kivila Valley.

But the chef de poste said that in the Kivila Valley this kind of hysteria
was nothing new, though there was no telling where it would lead. He said
that Kate and I had set this in motion and now there was no denying these
rumors, or dictating the course they would take. Even he, the chef de poste,
could not control this, though *he* knew these were the superstitions of a backward people and that we had no powers of this sort, that the Road Builder was
only a feeble old man dying in a bed in Mputu, and that the commissaire was
not afraid but had been delayed only by the normal disruptions in the life of
a politician—recalled to Kisaka, in this case, for a consultation.

The chef looked at me warily, and added some comment about the futility of keeping secrets from him; he was the chef, after all, and it was his business to know these things. If there were a connection to the Road Builder, he
was bound to learn of it sooner or later; such things could not be hidden from
him for long. He went on in a similar vein for a couple more sentences, but it
was obvious his heart wasn't in the lecture. He had his own worries. The soldiers made him nervous too, and he was feeling increasing pressure from the
director in Kisaka, as well as from the commissaire. Also, his domestic life was
still out of balance. In the aftermath of his recent wedding, his first wife
remained bitter and angry, unaccepting of the second, and now it seemed the
new wife was unhappy too, just moping around the house, her sparkle tarnished, her giggly plumpness gone heavy and lethargic.

He lit a cigarette and sighed. "Don't believe what the old men tell you
about polygamy, William. In the old days it must have been a fine idea, but in
the modern world it just doesn't work. I hate to say it, but maybe those old
priests are right about this. Though it's mostly their fault it's no good anymore—it *used* to work, before there were missionaries meddling everywhere,
stirring the women up and confusing the men."

"Well," I said, "the world is changing everywhere—"

"Sure it's changing, William, but don't be so dispirited about it," he said
glumly. "I know—these changes make life emptier. They take away a young
man's ambition, make the future small. But it's best to resign ourselves to this.

One single wife, for as long as you live . . . It's not as bad as it sounds, maybe. There are always the girls in the villages. I imagine it's the same in Mputu, eh? My advice to you is: go with the village girls now and then—don't forget your English sac!—but come home to sleep in your wife's bed. That's the way to have a tranquil marriage."

Strangely I found this conversation reassuring. Whatever his misconceptions, at least with the chef de poste I stood in a recognizable place, a being governed by needs and desires grounded in the physical world. Which is not to say he was immune to superstition himself. But in his eyes I remained a more or less comical figure, and he just couldn't take me seriously enough to attribute to me these mystical powers and complicated intrigues.

At the smugglers' hideout things were different. Whatever image the smugglers once had had of their consultant was forgotten in the freewheeling metamorphosis of Road Builder myths. Now I had become both a professional smuggler of Mputu *and* a secret agent of the Road Builder, and my innocence as mill consultant was irrevocably lost. Before, the smugglers had accorded me the respect and deference demanded by my position, but, like the chef de poste, they hadn't *expected* much of me. Now they must have wondered what else I was hiding, and they watched me, and Kate, more carefully. They were more subdued in our presence, and fatalistic, waiting for us to reveal something. And eventually it became apparent that what they expected, in one form or another, was nothing less than the Road Builder himself.

The nurse got up in front of them in the smugglers' hideout and told them flat out that they all were in trouble, that the smuggling thing was out of hand and they needed to come to some kind of agreement about how to manage it. Because now as we entered the most productive agricultural season, business for the smuggler was booming, but deliveries of palm nut and other produce to the mill remained low. Someone would have to answer for this situation. Already, the nurse said, answers were being demanded of their chef de poste. Everyone had heard how on his recent visit to Kisaka the chef had been summoned before the director, and how upon his return he'd received a letter from the commissaire, promising investigations and reprisals in the absence of an immediate boost in production at the Ngemba mill.

With one voice, the smugglers reaffirmed their intention to supply the smuggler and the mill equally. But beyond this, the discussion deteriorated into accusations and insinuations. Ndosi came under attack, then the nurse. No one dared accuse us directly, but it was obvious that suspicion—of fraud, embezzlement, and especially witchcraft—fell most heavily on Kate and me.

Telo stood and launched into a long, rambling harangue. He kept mentioning the consultants and at first I thought he too had turned on us, but then he began talking about the price of a tin of sardines in the company store, comparing that to the price of a liter of palm oil. For fifty years they'd been focusing on the wrong product, he said. Fifty years, citizens! He soon lost me entirely, but Kate said as she understood it he was proposing a plan to convert the mill into a fish cannery, an industry that would combine the aquaculture taught by Monsieur Tom with the marketing genius of the animatrice and the technological expertise of the mill consultant.

A few of the smugglers seemed intrigued by this idea, but others went off on their own tangents, and soon three or four separate arguments raged simultaneously. Over the din Telo kept shouting, with increasing urgency and passion: "Sardines! Citizens, consider sardines!"

Ndosi sat off to the side, silent. When I asked him to explain what was happening he shrugged and said there was no explaining. They argued like this because they were poor and ignorant, he said. Because they'd done so much work in their lives with so little compensation, because all choice and opportunity was denied them, because their entire lives they'd walked such narrow paths. He looked hard at me. "Maybe you think we are resigned to this path, monsieur. That we have no argument with this life that everyone tells us is all we can have. But here you see that isn't so. We have an argument that can go on for days."

I'd judged the smugglers fatalistic, but now I saw a reaction—a sense of injustice so incoherent they could only lash out at themselves. Maybe it was a process they had to work through, and given time they would have come up with a solution on their own. But to Kate and me it seemed that the Smugglers' Support Group was falling apart, maybe on the way to becoming a kangaroo court or a catalyst of clan warfare. "Sardines, citizens!" Telo shouted one last time, and Kate suddenly stood up, whistled loudly, and called for silence.

She said they were talking of their own fears and nightmares, but the time had come for her to speak of her dreams. She'd had a dream she didn't fully understand, which concerned them. She had dreamed of the Road Builder coming to her across a great water. He stood paddling a small pirogue, and when he came ashore she greeted him, but he said nothing, only gazed at her, stern and sad. She followed him into the forest, and he stopped beside a palm tree. The paddle in his hand had become a machete. He climbed the tree, disappearing into the fronds. She heard him chopping, and then the two largest racemes of palm nut she'd ever seen fell from the tree. He climbed down and lifted one of the racemes to his shoulder. She bent to pick up the other, but he stopped her. "One stays on the forest road," he said. "By day they'll take it to the mill." They walked on through the forest until they came to the intersection of the Kasengi Road. The Road Builder put his raceme down along the side of the road. "At night they'll carry that up to the savanna," he said. Then he lay down on the grass and called Kate to his side. "Long ago I built two roads, one through the forest, leading to the mill, and one along the savanna, bypassing the mill, leading out into the wider world. Let everyone use the two roads in equal measure, each according to its own purpose."

Then the Road Builder closed his eyes and spoke no more, Kate said. The dream left her, and she woke at dawn in her own bed beside her sleeping husband.

Some people said they'd never heard of a white person having a dream like that. Others pointed out that while the Road Builder had actually constructed a number of roads, the savanna road was not among them; it had been put in a number of years before his time. But these small notes of skepticism were soon overwhelmed by the positive response to Kate's dream. Here, after all, was the return of the Road Builder, crossing the water with a message of undeniable wisdom and utility. A message people took to heart. In the next several days there was a large increase in the quantity of palm nut and other produce sold to the mill, and this new level was sustained during the weeks that followed. In the meantime, somewhat reduced amounts were sold to the smuggler, who complained but made no credible threat of abandoning his run to the Kivila Valley.

So the smugglers' dilemma was resolved by a dream. "A fake dream, right?" I said to Kate. "Calculated, premeditated."

"Not premeditated, Will. I was improvising. People were at an impasse, they were going to destroy things. They needed something, and that dream is what I came up with on the spot."

"I just can't believe anybody's that gullible."

"I don't think gullible, exactly. I mean, they believe it because they want to. They need to. It provides a solution to their problem. I don't know why. I mean, why should Uncle Pers have such influence over them? They haven't seem him for more than thirty years."

"Maybe that's why. He's a ghost. And a ghost is way more powerful than a man."

"But now it's kind of freaking me out, you know? It's *spooking* me. I meant it as just a story, a parable. I guess I figured, they've been making up all these stories about him, and about us, so why can't I make one up too? But now I'm sorry I opened my mouth. Because it's not my story anymore. It's taken on a life of its own."

2 6

THE ROAD TO ISTANBUL

I went by the rectory at Bumba Mission, because I'd heard that the pères had received mail for us. Père Andrés nodded, and ushered me into the foyer. "No mail isn't coming from Kisaka many weeks now," he said. "But we hear something of your motorcycle friend."

It was nearly noon, and the house was full of delicious food smells, but Père Andrés left me standing in the foyer and disappeared into the back rooms. My relationship with the pères had chilled considerably in recent months, maybe because of my involvement with the smugglers or else because I had aligned myself too closely with people they disapproved of: the chef de poste, Tom, now the Road Builder. It had been some time since I'd been invited to share their gourmand lunches or to sip a leisurely beer on the patio. These days I couldn't get past the foyer. But in the foyer, no longer distracted by food orgies and goofy mannerisms and bachelor squabbles, I began to notice details that formerly had escaped me.

There was nothing of Africa there. I might have been waiting in some bourgeois drawing room in Antwerp or Ghent, surrounded by lace and painted porcelain, objects of finely cut glass, framed pictures on the wall—a Vermeer print, a map of Northern Europe, family portraits, a photograph of a brick abbey in some medieval village of Flanders. The foyer was a shrine, preserving some memory of the native country they'd left so long before but never forsaken. It was testimony to the purity of their devotion, or at least the tenacity of it; to the burden of a forty-year exile in a country never embraced.

Père Andrés emerged from the hallway. He handed me a letter, nodded a curt farewell, and showed me to the door.

Dear Consultants,

Le commandant, in his infinite arrogance and stupidity, has presented me with another opportunity to write a long letter. "On ne peut pas marcher," he explains, as if he's talking to an idiot. "Le camion il est rompé." Well, yes. In fact, Commander, you patronizing sonofabitch, no one can march, because your truck is blocking the entire transfuckingcontinental highway. Ça va, shrugs le commandant. We are all accustomed to the inconvenience of breakdowns.

Oui, Commandant. The inconvenience of breakdowns. Except this isn't exactly a breakdown, is it? This is more of a colossal egotistical fuck-up on your part, yes? Just admit it, you prick, and we'll tie your waterlogged transmission around your neck and drop you in a crocodile lagoon and be done with it.

But why should I be so angry with our commandant? I don't actually mind being here. Other people may have places they need to go, business to attend to, but I don't. I'm the First Tourist, and I can't for the life of me remember why I'm here. To gaze around blankly, I guess, take in the sights, and send off an occasional postcard to the folks back home.

And this is a relatively nice spot the commander has selected. In the shade of big riverside trees I sit gazing out on the village on the opposite bluff, the little river shining in the sun, the pirogues crossing back and forth, the ferry stranded in mid-current, and the commander's truck with its rear wheels on the edge of the bank and its hood submerged in six feet of river water.

When we arrived at this ferry crossing yesterday afternoon, the ferryman told us our loaded truck was too heavy for his ferry. We would have to unload, and he'd take the cargo across on one trip and the empty truck on another. But the commander said that was just a scam to make him pay for two crossings. The big trucks always unload at this ferry, citizen, says the ferryman. Vraiment? says the commander ominously, and Road Warrior crosses his arms and stares at the ferryman while the commander explains that other drivers might do as they please but he is not about to unload his truck for some shitbreathed jerkoff ferryman on a whorepiss river. Mois, je suis commandant, etc. Eventually the ferryman throws up his hands and goes to sit in his hut, and the victorious commander drives onto the ferry, which sinks under the weight of the truck and then shoots out from under the tires into the middle of the river, leaving the front end of the truck buried in water and mud.

So now, a day later, there are crowds of people and a dozen trucks on either side of the river, waiting for the tractor that's supposedly coming from a mission somewhere to pull our truck out so they can cross. It's quite an encampment, an impressive gathering that the commander, in his pighead-edness, has convened. The other drivers ganged up on him and demanded compensation for lost time, and the commander ended up having to give away a good deal of our beer. You'd think such an experience would be humbling for him, but experience doesn't generally affect our commandant in this way. __All__ experience only confirms his own superiority and the failings of the miserable scumbags he's forced to associate with. I guess he's feeling a little frustrated, though, because his insults and recriminations are getting more frequent and more obscene, if that's possible. At first even my ears were burning when he'd go off on one of his ugly little riffs, in front of the ladies and all, but then I noticed none of them paid much attention, except for his woman, Tsimba, who just answers him back in kind. Tsimba, with her graceful and delicate limbs, deep rich voice, baby-soft cheeks, eyes of a doe . . . well, a doe in heat, maybe. She can match that foulmouthed old commandant, scat for scat.

A few days later . . .

You've probably got the impression now that our commandant is just a blowhard and a buffoon. True—but a buffoon with a sharp sense of business and a very profitable gig. You could see his business mind working when the priest showed up with his tractor and winched the truck out of the river. He was a young priest, a little naïve-seeming. While the engine was drying out, the commander sidles up to him and makes himself ingratiating and suggests that we come recuperate at the mission for a few days. The priest looked dubious, a little put off by this unctuous chauffeur and more than a little uncomfortable in the presence of all these good-looking women, hitching up their pagnes so boldly and strutting around in front of him as if they really didn't give a damn for priestly vows. I'm sure he had an inkling that some-thing was wrong, but he couldn't put a finger on it, and he probably figured he had no choice, because after all the House of God is open to all.

Well, he should have let us founder in the river. Because it turns out the commander's truck (and I didn't know this at first, though I figured it out some time ago) is a kind of traveling sin-wagon, peddling beer and sex to the repressed populations of these mission towns. The ladies are all hookers, the men are pimps and hustlers and dealers, and the commandant—well, I guess the commandant is the biggest pimp of all.

It generally takes us about 24 hours to shred the fabric of mission life. Here the town soon divided into two factions: the scandalized faithful and the apostate heathen, who may have been sober and pious when we arrived but were soon spinning deliriously in our carnival of alcohol and whores and music. There were a couple of nights of this, culminating in last night's fête, when the préfet got roaring drunk and staggered through the crowd with his arm around one of our girls and a Primus bottle in his other hand, alternately pouring beer down the girl's throat and sprinkling it out on the crowd with a papal blessing.

This morning the préfet is nowhere to be seen, and the commander has decided we've exhausted the local business opportunities and it's time to hit the road. It looks as though I'm continuing on with him. There's a machine shop at this mission, and when we first arrived I spoke with one of the frères about working on my bike, but now my guess is the opportunity has passed.

A couple of days later we broke down again, outside this abandoned-looking village a long way from any mission. A long way from anybody's God, I guess. The women set up camp, the commander and the boy chauffeur went under the hood, and I walked into the town for no particular reason. Except that's what a fucking tourist does, right? Takes in the sights, whatever they may be. Maybe I was hoping to buy a postcard. Only it turned out that this town was too exotic even for the First Tourist's jaded sensibilities. It stunk, some vile smell of disease and death beyond anything I'd smelled before in Africa, which of course is way beyond anything I ever smelled in Thanesboro. The houses were a bunch of rotting sticks, the yards were unswept and filthy, and everyone was just lying around, as if the best they could do was drag themselves from one piece of shade to the next. SIDA, somebody hissed at me. It was an AIDS village, the whole town sick and dying. I don't know why one particular village would get like that—maybe they were so isolated that everybody was just screwing everybody else, or maybe they had some weird blood-transfusion rites or something.

Back at our camp the women were tending the cooking fires. They didn't look much like the titshaking beerswilling missionshredding harlots of a few nights back. They looked like poor barefoot peasant women who get pregnant, nurse babies, fetch firewood, cook luku, and bury dead children. They looked like they were wondering what kind of life they could hope to salvage out here, and they kept glancing over at SIDAtown like it was some kind of omen, the village of the future waiting to absorb their young, prostituted gypsy flesh. And for them of course it is the future. For us, something else. AIDS is nothing to us, right? It ain't Ebola, anyway. We used to be afraid, but now we got a handle on it. We can dodge it, or confine it. We just turn away from that specter, or roll on an English sac and figure we'll probably be fine.

What we fear now are the unknown viruses or protein shards, the lifeforms, death-forms that might not even have a name yet. Waiting in a place like this for something to come along and stir them up, bring them to the surface and carry them to a crossroads somewhere. Some mindless or stupid force, like le commandant raging at the wheel of his truck, plowing into the jungle and churning up air and soil that hasn't been disturbed for eons. Or these women riding in the back, churning up the savagery of men weakened by piousness. Or the First Tourist, some chump passing through on another frivolous journey, and slamming up against, of all things, a sense of destiny. He could amount to something after all. He could be—a vector! A vector of some new, more horrible disease, contaminating everything he touches: a woman, a piece of currency, the envelope he moistens with saliva to seal a letter.

Before dark the commander had half the engine spread out on the side of the road, and I was thinking about trying to flag down another truck, but the next morning he put it all back under the hood and to everyone's amazement the truck started right up. He hooted and crowed and laid onto the horn, and Road Warrior yelled at everybody to get their ass in gear and break the fucking camp, which we did, grumbling, while the commandant strutted around haranguing us. By that time he felt so good that just when we had it all packed up he decided to drag Tsimba off into the bushes for a self-congratulatory piece of ass, while the rest of us sat in the sun and waited. And that made him feel so good that a few kilometers down the road he suddenly swerved off onto *a side road, announcing that this was the <u>true</u> transcontinental highway, now a shortcut that few drivers had the skill and courage to take, but for him it was nothing and would save us a hundred kilometers, at least.*

That was two days ago, and we still haven't seen the main road. We pass a couple of villages, and the villagers stare at us in wonder and fear. We come to a fork in the road, and the commander never hesitates, but chooses his road with confidence and a great show of disdain for the road not taken. We descend into jungle, the track narrows, vines close over the cab. We can't see the sun, or tell which direction we're headed. But what does it matter? Where are we trying to go? And how do you save a hundred kilometers if you don't have a destination to begin with? The fragile rationality of this enterprise begins to disintegrate completely. But we drive on. We don't need no rationality. We ford rivers, we navigate ruts that spread like chasms, potholes gaping like craters, outsloped roadbeds that put us up on two wheels and leave the commander sweating bullets and the women in the back screaming in terror. We plow through long stretches of pure, creamy, surreal mud. We skid, we slide, we seem to float. Here and there pieces of wood or metal protrude from the mud. In the flashing light and shadow we glimpse exhaust stacks, pieces of railing, rusted hood ornaments. Slowly, dully, we come to realize that the oozing roadbed that supports us is built out of the vehicles that have sunk in the mud before us.

Most surreal of all is our reaction. No one seems upset by our predicament. Why should they be? The commander's insane, and the rest have entered an altered state, a catatonia of waiting that for the African traveler is like hibernation. But that's not an option for the tourist. I have no choice but to fall back on the instinctive idiocy of my kind. Whenever the weirdness and hopelessness start to overwhelm me, I remind myself: "you're just a fucking tourist, man. You don't have to pass judgment or understand anything. All you have to do is gawk." I only wish I had a postcard to send.

Well, I wouldn't mind some news, but I guess it's obvious there's no address where you can reach me here. You could send me a letter in Southern Europe, and I'll pick it up before I set out across Asia. Try General Delivery in Athens, I think Athens would be a good starting point, or Constantinople. Constantinople is good—a crossroads, gateway to both the East and the West. Though I guess they call it Istanbul now, come to think of it. I've been reading too goddamn many of these 19th-century explorers, probably. They called it Constantinople, and they went there to raise private armies or buy camels for their expeditions or to smoke hash and fuck concubines. But the world has changed since then, I understand. Istanbul it is. General Delivery.

For the moment we've emerged from the jungle mud. Another mission beside another river, another opportunity for business. We brought out the Primus and the boom box, people got drunk, and the priest came over this morning and told us to move on or he was calling the gendarmes. I guess the girls could deal with the gendarmes too, but we're just as glad to move.

I'm going to seal this up and wander over to the rectory. I'll apologize and make an offering and try to disassociate myself from this traveling circus of depravity, and hopefully that priest will consent to forward this letter to Bumba Mission. Though I'm not sure he can do that even if he is willing. It may be that even the mission networks are broken down out here, and we random vectors are the only connection left. In which case mailing this will be like putting a message in a bottle bobbing out to sea, but if the winds and currents are such that someday you find yourselves reading it then please give the vector who brought it to you a handful of money for his trouble, and the circle of miracles will be complete.

—The First Tourist

2 7

A FLEMISH THING
FROM THE MUDFLATS

"It's hard to picture him," said Kate. "You know, sitting back against a truck tire on the side of the road and writing a letter like that."

"Mr. Tom is capable of remarkable things," I reminded her.

"I have trouble with the part about driving on top of trucks sunk in the mud."

"I think maybe that was supposed to be a metaphor."

"Maybe the whole thing's a metaphor. But at least he's moving. Going *somewhere*. I suppose he could come out on the other side, I don't know— somehow redeemed."

Ndosi's response was less ambiguous. He thought we should go after him.

"Go after him! What do you mean by that?"

"He's in trouble, Mr. Will. You should go in the Land Rover and rescue him."

"I can't rescue him. Besides, Tom's always in some kind of trouble. He's in trouble here, for that matter, so what would be the point in bringing him back?"

"He shouldn't have traveled into the East. That country is full of dangerous people. Mercenaries. Highwaymen and prostitutes. Fetishers. Cannibals, monsieur!"

"Oh, cannibals! Come off it, Ndosi." I shot Kate an exasperated look, but she was pretending to read a book. Pretending she wasn't involved, wasn't the English teacher, hadn't continued to insist that no harm could come of allowing Ndosi to read Tom's letter. It was totally different from letting him read Uncle Pers' letter, she'd said, because Ndosi knew Tom and had a more intimate relationship with him than we did, in some ways. And his English was better now, so he was less likely to misinterpret things.

"If we can't bring him back home," Ndosi said, "we should just take him farther east ourselves. Across the Ruwenzori, to Lake Victoria if we have to."

"Why not all the way to Constantinople while we're at it?" I said. "Look, we're not going after him, okay? We'd never find him, the Land Rover wouldn't make it, we'd probably never come back ourselves. It's a ridiculous suggestion, actually. Stupid."

Kate closed her book and glared at me. Ndosi sighed and stood up from the table.

"You're right, monsieur. Ridiculous. Stupid. A stupid idea I had."

"Well, I didn't mean that. Not stupid, but—"

"No, you're right. A stupid idea from stupid bush people. Un broussard. En Afrique."

"Look, Ndosi—"

"The Land Rover belongs to the pères. We can't take it across the savanna, looking for Tom. Mpila ve! The savanna is as big as the sky. We'd never find him."

"Right. But that doesn't mean it's a stupid idea, Ndosi. Just . . . impractical, okay?"

"This letter is about something happening far away," said Kate. "We don't even know how much to believe, and there's nothing we can do about it anyway."

Ndosi shook his head. "We can do what Tom requested, madame." And he asked for pen and paper, sat down again at the table, and began to write a letter.

It took him two days to compose a four-page letter, in English. He used the dictionary extensively but refused all offers of assistance from Kate or me, except to ask for some postage stamps when he was finished. Then he sealed the letter in an envelope addressed to Tom at General Delivery, Istanbul, Turquie.

"Tom won't get this, Ndosi."

"You don't know that, monsieur. I can only send the letter, and hope."

"I *know* he won't get it."

"This is the address he gave. If God wills, he and the letter will both arrive there."

"That address was a joke, Ndosi. You can't take what Tom says at face value. He exaggerates. He makes things up. Sometimes his meaning is the opposite of his words."

"I've known Tom a long time, monsieur. Longer than you have. And just because we don't always understand him doesn't mean we shouldn't answer."

Ndosi refused to tell us what he'd written in his letter, but I watched him write it, and I could guess by the dark fury of his concentration the tone the letter must have taken. I'm sure it was full of complaints, omens, resentment, and suspicion. He must have told of his continuing skirmishes with the old people of Malembe, his nighttime visions of persecution and deceit at their hands. How mistrust and criticism of his bamboo planes was mounting, though they remained in flight in the sky above Malembe. No doubt he mentioned his upcoming marriage, explaining how he was persevering in his suit in spite of his employers' refusal to assist him. And I'm sure he told of the mysteries that had surfaced regarding Monsieur Will and Madame Kate, whom many people now regarded with suspicion and even fear. And how by association some were now suspicious of him, Ndosi, though it was he who uncovered the deepest deception and revealed to the people the blood ties between the consultants and the Road Builder. Now everywhere one heard talk of the Road Builder, everywhere one saw evidence that his long disappearance from the Kivila Valley was at last ended. Madame Kate herself had encountered her old uncle, harvesting palm nut in the forest, though lately she'd begun to act as though she'd forgotten the encounter.

Who knew what Tom might make of such a letter? Maybe he'd only laugh, sitting at a café in Istanbul reading these outlandish stories, told in Ndosi's outlandish English. Or he might still know how to extract the glimmer of fact and truth that lay behind them, the meaning hidden in the heart of the story. But he probably would never sit at a café in Istanbul, and certainly he would never read Ndosi's letter. If I thought there was a chance of that, I might write him a letter myself. And I would have an entirely different interpretation of the situation.

I would point out first of all that Kate had encountered Uncle Pers not on a forest road but in a dream, and that furthermore the dream was a fake. Yet dreaming a fake dream, it turned out, was more productive than smashing a radio and riding off into the eastern darkness. Yes, people were mistrustful of us now, afraid, as Tom himself had predicted. But their fear was what gave power and credibility to Kate's dream. And largely because of the dream, oil production at the Ngemba mill was higher than it had been in years, and the smugglers' black market also continued to prosper. Wages were up also, thanks to the noble bureaucrat's efforts—which Tom had ridiculed—to distribute wealth more equitably.

Actually I wouldn't have tried to explain this in a letter. I would have just mailed Tom a copy of my Annual Report, which I had recently sent off to the Jucht Brothers office in Kisaka (after the secretary translated it into his *francais du bureau*), and which told the tale with economy and clarity far beyond the power of a letter. Because a letter communicated with words—imprecise, subjective, undisciplined words—and the Annual Report spoke a language of numbers.

The magic of quantification and mensuration. Graphs, charts, formulas, and tables, all showing significant increases in palm-oil production, mill revenues, and worker income during our eighteen-month tenure in Ngemba. Reading over them even I was convinced, forgetting the weakness of my original numbers, the fragility of my many assumptions. There must be some theorem or rule of mathematics—the Law of the Statistical Mirage—dictating that the perceived infallibility of the data increases as a square of the number of times it is manipulated. Which is not to say that the Annual Report was a complete snow job. Production, sales, income—these really had increased, and the trend was upward. There *was* some correlation between my wage hike and the increase in production (though not nearly as strong as the correlation between Kate's dream and the increase in production). But these trends had not been in place for long. Most of the time we'd been on the job, the trends had been flat or downward. Of course, in my presentation I'd managed to disguise this fact, though a careful reader might raise a question or two. Also, there was a fundamental problem with the numbers themselves. Mostly they represented quantities of money, and that was not a black-and-white issue either, since the actual value of the currency was erratically but precipitously declining. Naturally I adjusted my figures for inflation. However, this was no ordinary inflation but rather an extreme hyperinflation, requiring a surrealistic calculus that was more art than science.

But the truth is all that was a bit over my head. In fact, ultimately the math had entirely defeated me and I'd leaned heavily on the statistical analyses in Kate's dissertation. Several graphs and charts I'd copied almost verbatim. She said I could do whatever I wanted with the dissertation, she had no use for it, didn't even want to look at it, though she did glance over my Annual Report before I sent it off, and said that she guessed it looked okay.

But later, after the director had returned it to me, she read it again, more carefully, and wondered how I could have gotten so carried away. How I could have taken out of her work some complex idea that I didn't understand at all, crossed out some numbers here, filled in some numbers there, and arbitrarily plugged it into a report. And how, even just skimming the report, she could have missed such obvious non sequiturs. Though I must have known myself how absolutely nonsensical some of this stuff was.

I told her I supposed I did know that but I must have figured that the flaws in the mathematical reasoning would be overwhelmed by the greater empirical logic of my argument. She said, *that's* what you figured? And I said, or else maybe I figured that no one would look too closely at that sort of thing. That they'd read the introduction and the conclusion, flip through the pie charts, and decide, well, the details may not be perfect but it is an impressive presentation, and at least things appear to be looking up in Ngemba. Or, I said, maybe I was thinking how I'd already sent in several reports and gotten no response. Nothing. And that working in that kind of vacuum gave me if nothing else a tremendous freedom to experiment, to play with alchemies and transformations and fetishes, as Uncle Pers had suggested. That I felt free to mess around with my own magical numerology, because these reports were apparently immune to approval or rebuttal. Maybe that's what I figured, I said.

Well, said Kate, you figured wrong.

By then the director had come and gone and it was obvious I'd figured wrong. The director made it obvious right from the beginning. She arrived unannounced one afternoon in a chauffeur-driven Company Land Rover. The mill was not running, and the secretary greeted her sleepily in the office doorway. The chef de poste, when he heard of her arrival, left his house and crossed the river in a panic. But the director spoke to him only briefly. She was just passing through, she said, on other business; another time he could tell her about his mill and show her his Place de la Révolution. For now, she would just have a short discussion with his white people. So the secretary was sent up to get us, and the director and the chef de poste went into his office to wait.

"Madame Stuyck," said the chef. "Our director."

We shook hands. The director didn't smile. Maybe she never smiled. She was pale, chinless, droopy-eyed, and she looked hot and uncomfortable in her wrinkled khaki skirt and jacket. Maybe she always looked hot and uncomfortable. The chef bowed nervously and left the room. At once, the director reached into her briefcase and pulled out my Annual Report. She put on a pair of reading glasses and flipped through the pages. Eventually she looked up over the rim of her glasses, at me.

"I read it all," she said. "I wouldn't have taken the time, except that we kept hearing about you. Complaints, mainly. So I read it. It's a strange document. I keep thinking it must be some idea of a joke. Only, not so funny, eh? It does reveal a certain naïveté, a certain ignorance of the way things are. And most of the charts make no sense at all. As for the text: well, you might have saved us all a good deal of trouble and written it in English. But I do want to acknowledge the effort you put into this. It's difficult in this environment to be so . . . self-motivated. However, that's another issue I should like to discuss—the self-motivation, as opposed to an effort encouraged and supported by the company whose interests you are supposed to represent."

She took off her glasses and handed me the Annual Report. She wanted to make sure we understood our situation, she said. We seemed to have forgotten that we were only contractors, in no position to establish our own policies or alienate local officials or stir up trouble by interfering with wage and price structures that had evolved over a long period of time, in response to difficult historical and economic constraints. Perhaps we were under the influence of romantic or literary ideas about what it meant to be a white person in an isolated post in Central Africa. It was true that the palm-oil mill at Ngemba was a throwback to an earlier age, a historical relic that could not possibly turn a profit, given the nature of the commodity and the terrible operating conditions in the country and the competitive advantage of Asian and South American producers. It followed that the continued operation of the mill could not be much influenced by anything the workers themselves might do, or by any of the usual localized production or economic factors, and that certainly it would not be influenced by unauthorized interference with established Company wage scales. Rather, the operation of such a mill depended on arrangements that governments and corporations made with one another, often for reasons that might have nothing to do with the mill or anything that touched it. Sometimes these reasons might be purely political. Sometimes they might be influenced by humanitarian, even sentimental, factors: several Company directors were old Africa hands who'd gotten their starts in places like this. And of course, on some level or another there were always economic reasons—even in a mill like this, a negligible enterprise in the portfolio of a global company.

"You mean, it's a place of no significance," said Kate. "We knew that."

"So why bother to send us here?" I asked.

"Indeed," answered Madame Stuyck.

"Somebody thought it was important enough for that. They hired us. They pay us."

"We did not hire you. Your generous salaries are not provided by us."

"You don't have to be so mysterious," said Kate. "We understand that these arrangements might be complicated. But that shouldn't mean that nobody takes responsibility. That everyone pretends we just materialized here, and the money to pay us just falls out of the sky."

"Who knows where money comes from?" I asked rhetorically, thinking of Uncle Pers and his ironic, cryptic smiles. But for some reason, maybe because I was staring at the Annual Report in my lap, I said it in French, *Qui sait d'ou provien l'argent?* Is that right? Possibly my syntax was garbled. But Madame Stuyck understood, and had the sense to keep speaking in English.

"Well, certainly money is becoming abstract these days. But it is still possible to determine its source. Only sometimes you need to ask questions. If you don't know where your money comes from, then perhaps you haven't asked enough questions. But don't ask them of me! I'm not being mysterious, I simply don't know the circumstances of your employment. It was an arrangement made in Brussels, and I had nothing to do with it. No one in this country requested consultants for this little mill. We merely received a directive to accommodate people who were working on a contract for—what is the name of your employer? World Inter . . . Interwhat? Inter something or other."

"Global Interconnect."

"Yes, Global Interconnect. I'm afraid that's the sort of name one just doesn't remember. Nobody I know has ever heard of this company. Well, there are thousands of little companies. They exist for all kinds of reasons."

"Well, whatever their reasons were for sending us here, they managed to get people at Jucht Brothers to cooperate with them."

"Yes. Perhaps someone in management had his own reasons too. Many of our directors are old men. At times their strategies and motives are not so easy for those of us in the field to understand. I see you have some idea of what I'm saying."

"We know people like that," Kate admitted.

"You see! Now *you* are being mysterious! But I don't care about that. Your mysteries are your own business. But you should be careful about trying to rearrange other people's business, especially when you haven't studied the history."

But we have, I wanted to tell her. The problem is, the history is full of unconformities. But she was already standing up, shaking our hands again. She spoke once more as we moved toward the door.

"You should also remember that while Jucht Brothers does not employ you, you do occupy this property at our discretion. You seem comfortable here. Maybe you feel secure. But this is perhaps another situation you don't understand. Because there is no security here. The law means nothing. This isn't really even a country, you know. You have a thief who calls himself president, you see a flag and soldiers on the road. But it's only an idea of a country, some lines drawn on the map a hundred years ago in Berlin. Occasionally the world still finds this idea useful and pays attention, but more often, people prefer to look the other way. Soon, though, they will be forced to pay attention again. Already they are beginning the official warnings to leave. At some point there will be a panic. It will become difficult to get out. I suggest that you arrange your affairs now, when you can do it with some presence of mind, in relative calm. While the color of your skin still opens doors for you, and hasn't become a liability."

"I feel like somebody's just threatened to break my kneecaps," Kate said when we got back to the house. "Who does she think she is, telling us to 'arrange our affairs'? As if she's just diagnosed us with some terminal illness. What a bitch, Will. Madame Mud. A Flemish thing from the mudflats. Coming out of the lowlands with her insinuations and threats."

"Well, she had some information too, Kate. Apparently nobody knows where the money comes from or who Global Interconnect is. Apparently we're entirely on our own, more than we'd imagined we were."

That was interesting information, Kate agreed. It seemed to change things. But we didn't have much of a chance to consider all this, because the next day a boy from the mission brought us a telegram, and things were changed in a more fundamental way.

Pers lost in sailing accident. Memorial service scheduled. Come at once Katy.
                                                                    —Aunt Mavis

I had a kind of anxiety attack the morning Kate left. I'd offered to take her to Kisaka in the Land Rover, but it turned out Père Andrés was going in on some business of the diocese and she could catch a ride with him. So we were in the kitchen having a cup of coffee, waiting for him to show up, when I felt a panic similar to what I'd experienced a year and a half before on the highway south of the Tucson airport. Only now I wasn't at the wheel of any vehicle and I had no power to abduct her, and no possible justification for it anyway. This was just another mutation, I told myself, and hadn't we survived many mutations already? Starting way back in Idaho with my small, impulsive deceit on a hotel register. *Mr. and Mrs. Will Haslin.* Which eventually brought us together into Pers' sickroom for my first introduction to Kate's family. *Will Haslin. My . . . my husband.* I still wasn't sure how serious she'd been. But that first mutation had led us into others—in Pers' study and at Mavis' dining table and in the skies over Africa and eventually on this porch in Ngemba. Yet it was worth remembering that one mutation we had skipped was the actual definitive act of getting married. Maybe that wasn't important. We *acted* married. We referred to each other as "my husband" and "my wife," though what we literally said, in Kituba, was "my man" and "my woman"— terms of possession that don't require even so much as the sanction of common law.

But now Pers was dead and Kate was dressed to travel and Père Andrés would arrive at any moment to take her away. We had a few moments together on the porch, and I asked her if she ever saw us having a real wedding.

"Well, gosh, Will, I don't know. I'm not an oracle."

"I'm not asking for a prophecy. It's not like a wedding's something totally out of our hands, like the Second Coming. People just *decide* to get married, and then do it. If they want to."

"Why would we want to?"

"I don't know. I'm just speculating. Feeling insecure, I guess. Sometimes my faith in purely random mutations wavers a little."

"Sure. You're having a crisis of faith. Madame Mud's visit was demoralizing, and now I'm leaving and Uncle Pers is dead and everything. But I don't think a wedding would help."

"It could. Weddings do make a difference in people's lives, Kate."

"Some people's lives. But a wedding is only a ritual, Will. Symbolic. Which is fine. But it's not necessarily substantive. It doesn't require anything of you. It's too easy. That can't be the way to build faith and security into your life."

"Okay, what is the way?"

"Well, you have to do something real."

"Like what?"

"I don't know! I guess just try something and see if it works. Slay a dragon. Bring me the head of the evil commissaire. Take Père Michel's Land Rover and smuggle something."

2 8

DAY OF BOUNCING VISION

The palm-oil boat came up the river in a heavy rain, churning steadily against the brown flood. Seen from the porch, it appeared to shift suddenly in the current, lurching forward, like a film that skips a few frames. But I knew that in fact the boat moved steadily upriver, and the lurching only meant that it was Monday, the Day of Bouncing Vision. Bouncing Vision was one of the side effects of the chloroquine Kate and I took every Sunday night as a malaria prophylaxis. The drug was only marginally effective in preventing malaria but I could count on it to distort my sight every Monday, imparting random jolts and jiggles to the visual world.

Perfectly credible jolts and jiggles, in this case, since you'd never expect a boat that looked like that to make steady headway against such a current. You wouldn't expect it to be out in the current at all. You'd expect to come across it half-sunk in the reeds and mud of the river, with hyacinth crowded in its eddy and holes in its hulls, a home for squatters or river pirates, for rats and river birds. Only the ramshackle forecastle retained a trace of its last paint job, a peeling coat of dirty blue, surely decades old. The rest of the boat was the color of rust and mud. There were few adornments on the deck or hull: a railing extended for a few feet along one side, and a kind of a mast, really only a stick, rose for no clear purpose out of the foredeck. There was no registration number on the hull, or even a name, and as usual no sign of a crew. Behind the blurring rain, even the pilot house had a look of abandonment.

But almost every week that boat came upriver, and whenever I saw it I felt a similar thrill. I understood that I was privileged to stand on my porch and watch this rare and evocative vision: a rusting old wreck of a steel boat powering up a flooding river, with a high jungle wall rearing up behind and the rain thundering down. A vision that in much of the world could be understood only in the context of a theme park or a movie, or maybe a fashion ad. A prop, intended to evoke a clichéd past or set the stage for an implausible adventure, or to make some oblique and ironic marketing statement.

But probably no one else watching it shared my sense of privilege. They might even have been feeling something more like *humiliation,* thinking: what a shitty boat we've got; what a bitch of a jungle we live in; what a monotonous goddamn rain keeps falling on us. Thinking what it would be like to live someplace where the boats are big and sleek and fast, or at least painted. Where the river is lined with buildings and docks and electric lights instead of only trees, someplace with more than one miserable rusted boat, anyway.

But they didn't have that choice, as Tom so heavy-handedly pointed out to them at his good-bye fête. They might dream of fancy watercraft, like they dreamed of Land Rovers and radios and running shoes, but for some time to come they weren't likely to see anything on their river but their own dugout pirogues and that decrepit boat.

Still, they too had reason to exult. The boat rode high in the water coming upriver, because the big payroll strongbox and the empty 200-liter barrels didn't weigh much. But going downriver, its gunwales would be near the waterline and its hold and deck stacked with full barrels of palm oil from the Ngemba mill, bound for the warehouses and marchés of Kisaka. And soon another large shipment of produce would leave the Kivila Valley. Any night now, up on the savanna near Kasengi the smuggler's truck would take on its cargo: sacks of corn and peanuts and manioc and coffee; and raceme after raceme of palm nut, some carried out of the forest on the backs of sweating coupiers, an equal amount brought up the forest road in Père Michel's Land Rover, which most likely would be driven by me, consultant to the mill and now to the smugglers as well.

This shabby boat, then, represented new hopes for prosperity in the Kivila Valley, new links forged between farmers, coupiers, the smuggler, and the mill. Yet it also provoked in me a strange unease. There was something a little ghostly about its implacable progress up the river without a visible crew, the pilot obscured behind a blur of rain. And I wondered if we in Ngemba hadn't become something similar: a shabby apparatus making improbable progress against a rising current. Propelled now by nothing but inertia, with our engines losing power and our doomed craft about to falter and turn downstream, spinning helplessly in brown currents.

Still, whatever my misgivings, I liked watching the boat go past. And I loved that rain, the booming, obliterating rain. I loved those monsoon storms, building off the powerful heat of the early day, a heat that toward the end of morning would drive humans out of the open to seek an inadequate refuge in the shade. Still steaming and sweating, we'd sit and contemplate the contrast between our own consuming lethargy and the humming vitality of the rest of the world. Heat and light and water mixed in a potent brew, the rising electric chorus of insects and birds, fish driven to riots of feeding and breeding in the hot, swampy pondwaters. The silent chemical frenzy of plants, building carbon structures, pumping huge quantities of water out of the ground into the upward rushing air. And finally the great cracking rush of electrons, and then the long rain, and cool damp air moving down the valley with the rising river.

And solitude. No one would come visit me when it was dumping like that. There would be no voyeurs or petitioners, no consultations or animations, no English lessons or house chores. All of it would have to wait. Not even Ndosi—not even Matama with her little pot of rancid luku—would venture out in a deluge like this. Though as soon as the rain let up they'd all be there: Matama and Ndosi and the children and coupiers and smugglers and mamas descending on the white man alone in his house by the river, wifeless, to relieve him of his terrible solitude.

It *was* terrible, if I stopped to contemplate it: Kate truly *gone,* not merely a brief disappearance beneath the jungle canopy or into a village hut or a milling crowd of smugglers at the Place Without a Name, but absent from my life, incommunicado, carried away indefinitely to the far side of the earth. Yet I found far more comfort in the solitude than in the prospect of visitors. I left the porch, closed the door, and settled down on the couch to immerse myself in the hypnotic noise of the rain and the far-off, private world of a book.

Waves of rain pounded the tin roof, obliterating all other sound, but during one of the brief lulls a separate banging intruded. Maybe a piece of tin on the roof was loose and flapping in the downpour. Maybe the bats were pushing one another around in the rafters. Or maybe I was wrong about my immunity to visitors, and somebody was knocking on my door. When the rain built again the banging too seemed to increase in volume, and I got up and opened the door.

The albino stood on the porch, rearing back with a fist cocked to pound on the door. She gasped, and dropped her fist. She stared at me wide-eyed and stepped back, half turning, muscles tensed for flight. I greeted her, though I couldn't remember her name. Lowering her head behind her ghastly wig, she mumbled something inaudible.

"I can't hear you," I shouted at her, and she jumped back, her eyes darting from side to side as if looking for an escape. I invited her into the house, and she flushed and trembled but stepped into the doorway. There she ducked behind the protection of her wig, confronting me with a dense mat of nearly dreadlocked synthetic hair, looming asymmetrically over her face. No doubt this wig was originally intended only to protect her hairless pale head from the sun, but now she wore it constantly, indoors and out. She must have been aware of how much it transformed her. Maybe beneath the wig she had a different sense of herself: someone less afflicted, no longer terminally childish and genderless, though to my eyes it made her look less like an actual woman than a drag queen.

She looked at the floor and began to mumble again. I bent down to hear her better, and she took a sharp breath and blurted out, "Matama says can you lend her an onion."

I should have been ready for that. Even a hundred-year flood wouldn't stop Matama, who couldn't let a day go by without asking us for some favor, or some "loan" or gift from our pantry. For years before we showed up, she got by without onions most of the time; why couldn't she at least wait until the rain stopped before she hit us up for one now? There aren't any onions, I told the girl curtly—though in fact there was a ten-kilo sack of them in the pantry. Yet I wasn't exactly lying. She knew I didn't mean definitively that I had no onions but rather that regardless of whether I had onions, there was none for her. "Matungulu ikele ve," I repeated. There are no onions. How I loved those passive, impersonal constructions, so abundant in the Kituba language! Absolving me of any responsibility, describing a situation simply presented to us, beyond the realm of human volition. And leaving the albino with no option but to nod, back away, and go home. But she refused to cooperate. She stood in the doorway, terrorized and shivering and giving out these little gasps and convulsions, though I wasn't certain about the convulsions, maybe that was just another trick of chloroquine vision. Tell Auntie Matama there are no onions, I shouted. Good-bye! But the girl kept mumbling and sucking air and swinging her head around, my God, I couldn't believe it but she was starting to *hyperventilate*, something I never believed I'd see in rural Africa, of all places. Isn't hyperventilation like bulimia or anorexia: endemic to affluent, neurotic Mputu, an affliction of teenage girls in the first bloom of suburban angst? But the albino was doing it for me, her freckled cheeks puffed up and her ghostly skin turning an ugly raw red as she desperately sucked air. I didn't know how to deal with it. Aren't you supposed to put a paper bag over their head or something like that? But that was out of the question with this albino girl, who would go totally psychotic if I tried to cram a paper bag over her head, who'd probably never even *seen* a paper bag before. Well, I didn't have one anyway. But something had to be done.

"Wait here," I told her, leaving her gasping and trembling in the doorway while I went to look around in the pantry. There was hardly anything in there *except* onions. The simplest thing would have been to just give her one, but that would have damaged my authority and credibility and ability to tell white lies in the future. Anyway, I wanted to stand up to scheming Matama for once, and demonstrate to her that it didn't pay to send out her panhandling minions even in the middle of a downpour.

In the darkness among the onions my hand squeezed a couple of shriveled potatoes. Potatoes were a sort of delicacy too, scarce and expensive like onions, imported from the high southern savannas and considered a white man's food in this hot wet climate, hence probably also coveted by Matama. Maybe they would have the desired effect on the girl. I pushed the potatoes into her hands, explaining that there were no onions but maybe potatoes would serve Auntie Matama's purpose as well. She grabbed the potatoes and made her escape, ducking beneath the shelter of her wig as she hustled down the steps into the rain.

I closed the door behind her and returned to the couch, but the mood of tranquil solitude had been destroyed. An albino girl had just hyperventilated all over my living room, and I had to ask myself: what could this strange episode mean? Was it just another random slice of Africana, incomprehensible to a Westerner? Was it another mutant hybrid, some unforeseen result of the unlikely chemistry of our interaction? The work of a fetisher? Something out of somebody's dream world, some warning, some sign?

The rain eased off, and after a few minutes I heard the sound of children's voices in the yard, and then a timid knock on the door. This time there were three wet kids on the porch, a couple of shier stragglers at the foot of the steps, and several more standing in the downpour along the fence line. The albino was not among them. The oldest child handed me a note.

Dear Will

Greetings How are you I hope you're well Do you hear from Kate I hope she's well We're all well but it's raining very hard I sent the girl down to borrow an <u>onion</u> but she returned with no onion only potatoes Thank you for the potatoes but they are not an Onion and also are very small though we'll eat them for dinner anyway Will we're confused by the meaning of this potato not onion which doesn't answer the very important question we asked when we sent the girl down asking for an onion.

Stay well, Matama

It *was* a sign. How could I have forgotten? It was *the* sign, the Sign of the Smuggler, part of the Smugglers' Communication Network, which I admit I didn't take all that seriously when we'd discussed it at the last Smugglers' Support Group meeting. The idea was to secretly let Kate and me know when a smuggling run was scheduled. Drum messages informed most people when the smuggler's truck was about to come through, but Kate and I weren't tuned in to the language of drums. Claiming that with so many spies and soldiers about it was too dangerous to simply send a written or spoken message, Matama came up with the idea of the albino/onion code, which was supposed to work like this: when she got word that the smuggler was going to be at the Place Without a Name, she would send the albino down to borrow an onion. If we sent an onion back up with her, it meant everything was okay, the Land Rover would be available for transporting smuggled goods. If we didn't send an onion, it meant there was some kind of problem, and further discussion was needed.

Matama said the albino girl was a good code because she didn't work in the fields and was always available, and because she was white, like us—she would serve as a reminder that we were needed. And I knew why she'd chosen onions. She was aware that we'd recently bought a large sack of onions, and this was a way of insuring that she'd get at least a few of them, no matter how stingy we were feeling. If we ran out of onions, she said, she'd just ask for something we did have.

I was a little put off by her presumption that she would always know just what was in our pantry, but I'd said nothing. In fact, I hadn't given the albino/onion code another thought until now, my first opportunity to put it to use. Maybe potatoes would work, though I doubted it. I left the kids waiting on the porch while I wrote an answer.

> *Dear Matama,*
>
> *Greetings to you and your family. I am well. But there are no onions. This is why I sent a potato. But the meaning of the potato is the same as the meaning of the onion, which I certainly would have sent if there were any.*
>
> *Stay well, Will*

I sealed this letter and sent it up with the kids. Soon there was another knock on the door, easily audible now, with only a light rain falling. One of a half dozen children on the porch handed me another note, while a larger audience watched solemnly from the yard.

> *Greetings to you Will We received your letter also the Potatoes you sent before and we thank you for both but remain confused because of your failure to send an onion which you remember was the plan we made in the Smugglers' Support Group meeting last month For myself I think I understand but others question do the Potatoes really have the same meaning as the onion they want you to answer the question directly avoiding the use of all vegetables will you be driving the Land Rover to Kasengi tonight? The nurse needs to know She is coming with you to Guide and also M. Ndosi to be Boy Chauffeur. Thank you.*
>
> *Stay well, Matama*

> *PS it is still possible to clarify this by sending an onion if you find one you might have overlooked in your pantry where Kate has always located one in the past.*

I'd thought my note was clear enough: *the potatoes have the same meaning as the onion.* Maybe the punctuation threw her off. If I'd had more potatoes I might have just sent them up to her. Perhaps with enough potatoes I could entirely disable the Smugglers' Communication Network, and disassociate myself from this dangerous business in the bargain. But it was too late for that. In fact, I surrendered. It was obvious that Matama would get her onion, because her mind was set on it; the Land Rover would be transporting smuggled goods, because that was why we had it; and I would be driving it, because the regular driver was ten thousand miles away. So why not let people know? Why not let the whole camp know?

I got an onion from the pantry, and scribbled a quick note:

Dear Matama:

    After a difficult search I managed to find an onion. Like the potato, the onion means Yes! I will be taking the Land Rover to Kasengi tonight. Tell <u>*everyone*</u>.

                                                    —*Will*

◎

I stood on the porch in the evening and looked down on a devastation of fallen trees, ravaged brush. And above it my vegetable garden, still untended and unproductive, but now opened to the air and sun. A couple of weeks earlier a band of workers had fanned out on either side of the river road, and with machetes, axes, handsaws, and one small smoking chainsaw cut down the majority of trees and bushes between the road and the river. This deforestation was of course mandated by the chef de poste, who called it "Le Nettoyage"—an essential component of the Modernization Project. The mill consultant had instinctively objected to such a wholesale cleansing, but the chef had responded with his standard argument about snake control, and added that the commissaire, whose visit was imminent, wouldn't have much respect or sympathy for the administrators and consultants of a place that looked like a nineteenth-century outpost half-reclaimed by the primitive jungle. And the chef's arguments, naturally, had carried the day.

I had to admit that both the view and the quality of light had improved, especially in the evening, with the air purified by the day's rain. Before Le Nettoyage the yard lay in deep shadow at that hour, and the forest was closing in rapidly on our view of the river and the hills beyond. But now the fading light fell abundantly, highlighting relief and illuminating new detail, both close at hand and across the valley. In the garden the fruit trees stood out sharply against the pale sky. The river flowed high and green, and at the half-sunk wharf the palm-oil boat that had come upriver a few hours earlier swayed and rocked gently in the current. In a field above the chef's house one of his women—a daughter or a wife—gathered up the laundry she earlier had spread out to dry. A couple of women were walking down the road to the river for their evening bath, and several men moved about in the mill yard or stood talking on the edge of the Place de la Révolution. Even on the desolate Place the light fell softly, filling in the harsh spaces surrounding the men, smoothing the jagged edges of palm-nut shells at their feet. Everyone moved gracefully and unhurriedly, as if they were passing through water, as if, down on the shadowed road and the fields of laundry and the artificial desert of the Place, time were available in exact proportion to the needs of their lives.

There was an occasional sudden movement, a jolt that momentarily upset the tranquillity of this scene: the women on the road jerking as if panicked or surprised; the boat tipping violently as if by a weight suddenly shifting in its hold. But at the end of a Day of Bouncing Vision I was accustomed to such illusions. I knew that I inhabited a separate medium from that of the people I was watching. There was nothing fluid about *my* movements, and rather than grace I felt the pressure of panic—a panic that had been rising in me all afternoon, since I deciphered Matama's albino/onion code and understood that tonight I was obligated to drive a Land Rover full of contraband up on the Kasengi savanna to the Place Without a Name.

I had to check the oil and tire pressure, fill the fuel tank, gather the ropes for tying racemes of palm nut and sacks of produce to the roof rack. Even such simple tasks seemed daunting, maybe because I had to perform them out in the open, where the whole world could see the mill consultant making preparations for a night journey. It would have been better to work under the cover of night, but I needed daylight to organize things. The nurse and Ndosi would arrive shortly, and we'd leave as soon as it was dark.

Somewhere in the garage was a piece of clear plastic tubing to siphon the diesel fuel out of the fuel drum and into the Land Rover's tank. I should have looked for it earlier, but I hadn't thought it would be so dim in there. The evening light faded so quickly; it still caught me by surprise. But I might not have found the siphon hose even in the full light of day. You'd think Kate would have taken ten minutes to put things in order in this garage before she left. The ground seemed to be covered with empty oilcans, the used oilcans of an entire colonial era, with just enough wire and old engine parts scattered around to prevent a person from satisfactorily kicking the goddamn cans out of the way. I kicked a couple anyway, though a couple more just rolled in to fill the void. Maybe the siphon hose would have to remain permanently buried beneath a sea of shifting oilcans. I kicked a few more cans, more violently. A shadow in the doorway further darkened the interior of the garage.

"Placide!"

"Bonsoir, monsieur. What are you doing?"

"Just looking for the stupid siphon hose, Placide. Do you suppose Kate took it with her to Mputu, or what?"

"I don't think so, monsieur. In Mputu you have machines for siphoning fuel. Did you look in the back of the Land Rover? That's where she usually keeps it."

I knew that. There it was, curled up neatly beside the tool kit. I uncoiled it, opened the fuel drum, put one end of the tube in, and carefully sucked out the air. But it was too dark in the garage to see the diesel moving up the hose, and my timing was off. Diesel gushed into my mouth. Spitting and coughing, I stuck the hose in the fuel tank, but there must have been an air bubble in it, because the siphon flowed for only a couple of seconds, then slowly trickled dry.

"Monsieur, that stuff is poisonous. You shouldn't drink it."

"I know that, Placide. Okay? I know that. For God's sake, I'm not drinking it." I spat a couple more times and got ready to suck again. Placide took the siphon hose out of my mouth.

"It isn't necessary to suck the hose, monsieur. Let me show you."

Exactly as if he knew what he was doing, Placide pushed the hose further into the drum and, grasping the upper end, thrust it up and down a number of times, pumping diesel into the tube on the downward thrusts and preventing it from flowing out by quickly capping the top end of the hose with his thumb when he raised it. When the hose was full he took his thumb off, and diesel flowed into the tank of the Land Rover.

We stood together beside the Land Rover while the tank filled. The sun was behind the ridge, completing its plunge to the horizon, and Placide and I watched in silence as a few streaks of color came into the western sky. He shuffled nervously and cleared his throat, no doubt working himself up to ask me why I was making these preparations and where I might be going at this hour. Just a place, Placide. It doesn't have a name. I forestalled him with a question of my own.

"How's the cricket hunting these days, Placide?"

"Crickets? There is no cricket hunt now, monsieur."

"What happened? Did you catch them all?"

"No one can catch them now. There are many crickets, but no one catches them."

"Why is that?"

"This is the season when the crickets change. They become very small. Who can see to catch them when they're so small?"

"I certainly haven't seen any."

"Because they're so small. You're looking at them all the time, monsieur, but never seeing. And even if you see one, you don't know it, because they change in other ways."

"What ways?"

"They change shape. Sometimes they flutter in the air, like small black moths at night. You feel them brush your skin, but you can never see them. And sometimes they're round and hard, like a tiny stone, and they roll deep into the earth. If you put your ear to the ground you'll hear them singing, the same song they sing later in the year, when we catch them. And eat them."

I didn't know much about the life cycle of crickets, but that didn't sound plausible. You'd think somebody like Placide, who spent so much time with them, would be able to tell me what the crickets were really up to, instead of giving me a natural history as full of fantasy and mysticism as his ideas about books or jet airplanes. As usual, though, I couldn't completely disregard the possibility that he was pulling my leg.

The siphon gurgled and went dry, but the tank was nearly full, so I removed the hose and tossed it in the shed. Placide coiled it and returned it to the back of the Land Rover while I gathered a few pieces of wire and rope that were hanging in the shed, to use for tie-downs. Placide followed me up to the house, stopping at the foot of the steps.

"Monsieur, I was reading my book today. The reading book you gave me."

I turned, half inside the door. "Oh, right. Well, how is it?"

He shrugged. "It's not easy. The book doesn't work as well as you said it would."

"Listen, I never said—"

"I have trouble with the language. When she comes back from Mputu, I'm going to ask Madame Kate to teach me your language, the way she's been teaching your boy."

"I suppose you could ask her, but—"

"In the meantime I keep reading. Today I read for a long time. I'll show you what I learned."

"Fine. But right now I have to go inside."

"I left the book at my house. I'll go home and get it."

"I'm kind of busy tonight, Placide."

"I know, Monsieur Will. But you'll still be here for a few minutes?"

"Sure, I'll be here. Fine, Placide. Run home and get your book."

I poured a short glass of rum and stood on the porch, watching the light go out of the sky, dusk settle down on the river. The pulleys on the ferry cable squeaked, and the ferry swung away from the mill dock into the current, crossing to the opposite bank. I could just make out the figure of the chef de poste descending the darkening path from his house to the ferry dock.

The chef boarded, and the ferry crossed back to our side. But why was he coming over here so late in the evening? Did he have business with me? If so, why now, why tonight, the night of the smuggler? Might he have heard some rumor of my involvement, sparked perhaps by those ridiculous notes that went back and forth between Matama and me earlier in the day?

But the chef didn't come up to my house. I heard voices down by the mill, then banging metallic sounds, and men grunting. Doors slammed, and a truck started up and pulled slowly out of the mill yard, bumping up the steep road leading away from the river.

The chef won't interfere, Kate had said. *Even when it happens right under his nose.* What she meant was that his nose was in the middle of it. That he kept his own night assignation with the smuggler. Selling him barrels of processed oil rather than raw palm nuts, judging from the muffled clanging sounds that had come from the mill yard. Well, he had to do something to support a couple of wives too proud to work in the fields, a half dozen children, and a steady stream of relatives seeking favors from the most prosperous member of their family. And now a bride price to be paid. He couldn't possibly meet all those obligations on his salary alone.

The truck rumbled out of sight, and I went inside, lit the lamp, and tried to rinse the diesel residues out of my mouth. After a quick supper of cold rice and beans, I laced a cup of coffee with another shot of rum and settled down on the couch with a book, to wait for Ndosi and the nurse. But I couldn't concentrate. It wasn't so easy to escape from the night that now had fallen, pushing me closer to the driver's seat of the Land Rover and a series of secret rendezvous all along the river road. Under the cover of night people now were beginning to move toward the appointed sites, slipping out of their little huts and villages with heavy burdens on their heads and backs. Some already were waiting patiently for my arrival, squatting in the darkness beside their sacks of manioc and coffee and peanuts and their racemes of palm nut.

What else might be stirring? What spies and informants, what soldiers spreading out along the forest road in their hot fatigues? What information or rumor, what impulses of dream and myth moving from hut to hut, from village to village through the not yet sleeping night, diffusing as of their own volition throughout the Kivila Valley and beyond? I myself belonged to such an impulse: a child of the Road Builder, returned to Africa for a purpose that remained unknown.

I jumped at the sound of a soft knocking at the door, though I was, after all, expecting visitors, even if I was more than half hoping they wouldn't show up. However, it wasn't Ndosi and the nurse standing in the darkness on the porch, but Placide. Only a momentary reprieve, but still I was relieved enough to invite him in.

He stepped inside and stopped. It occurred to me that he hadn't been inside the house for weeks. Slowly he looked around, and though his face remained blank his disapproval was obvious. Of course, things were in some disarray, but what business was that of his?

"The boy isn't coming to work, Monsieur Will?"

"Ndosi? He still comes. But he's been . . . occupied elsewhere."

Placide set his bow and arrow down in the corner. "Monsieur. This is what I read."

From his overcoat pocket he removed *Products of the Oil Palm.* Carefully, as though he feared it might disintegrate, he laid it on the table and began to slowly turn the pages. Suddenly he stopped, let out a little whistling breath between his teeth, and motioned for me to look.

The book was open to a black-and-white photograph of a riverboat. In the photo workers were rolling barrels down a ramp onto the boat. The workers were Asian, and a white man leaned on the boat's railing, watching them.

"You see?" Placide leaned close to the lamp, looking up at me, his eyes glittering more brightly than ever.

"See what?"

"Monsieur! It's a picture of the Road Builder!"

"No."

"Yes! The Road Builder!"

I couldn't help but laugh. It was so absurd, and so *predictable.* Ever since Ndosi had made the connection between Uncle Pers and us, visions of the Road Builder had become a cheap hallucination in the Kivila Valley. People constantly recalled his prophecies and counsels, showed us places where he supposedly worked or ate or slept or made love, found new resemblances between him and Kate or me, and discovered evidence of his continued presence in their lives.

Indulging Placide, I leaned over to look at the picture more closely. A shiver went down my back. Maybe it was only a trick of the orange lamplight, but as I studied the fuzzy photograph I saw in the face of the man leaning on the rail the beaked nose and hooded eyes of Uncle Pers. He was about my age, and seemed to be looking not at the workers on the dock but straight out of the photo at me. His expression was familiar: bemused, ironic, and slightly condescending, as if already he knew more of my weak and capricious nature than I ever would perceive myself. I could even trace the faint outlines of modern wrinkles, the crevasses and canyons that forty years ago were just beginning to incise in his face.

But what a lot of foolishness to read into an old and blurry photograph! I blinked, and looked again. The man leaning on the rail could be anyone: his features were indistinct, the details lost.

"You see?" whispered Placide. "The Road Builder!"

"It's an old picture, Placide, out of focus. Just a man leaning on a railing. You can't tell."

"It's the Road Builder," he said with assurance. "In a boat. Not in a bull-dozer or a Land Rover or an airplane. On a boat!"

"Why not a boat? He traveled on boats a lot, right up to the end, in fact. He was a sailor. But that has nothing to do with this picture. This is just . . . a guy on a boat. Not the Road Builder."

"He travels on boats. We didn't know. We didn't remember. It's something else to consider."

More material for the construction of myths and hallucinations, is what he meant. He touched my arm and pointed to the caption.

"These words are difficult for me to read, monsieur."

I imagine they were. "Loading crude palm oil in Panchor for shipment to a refinery in Bandar Maharani. In the palm-oil industry, delivery of both raw and processed material is often tied to river transportation."

Placide nodded enthusiastically while I translated roughly, as if the pro-saic words confirmed his vision or even expressed some further revelation. The whole thing was ridiculous, and I pushed the book aside, repressing the urge to look closely again at the photograph. I must have looked at it many times before and noticed nothing remarkable, back in the days when I was studying *Products of the Oil Palm*. If I now could see some resemblance to Uncle Pers in the face of an anonymous colonialist leaning on a boat's railing, it meant only that I was one more victim of mass hypnotism, my powers of reason weakened by anxiety over the impending smuggling run, by the night-watchman's haunted whispers and glittering eyes, by the awareness of conti-nents and oceans rising up between me and my wife.

Again there was a knock on the door. Placide started, and reached for his bow and arrows. "I'm expecting visitors," I told him, moving to open the door.

The nurse was alone on the porch. She shook hands with Placide and me, and explained that no one knew what had become of Ndosi but that Telo had agreed to substitute as boy chauffeur and would be down shortly. There was a moment of awkward silence, then Placide gathered up his bow and arrows and slipped outside, leaving the nurse and me looking at each other in the faint lamplight.

The nurse didn't appear to be dressed for a night of traveling muddy roads and moving heavy sacks. Her hair was done up in tight braids, and a small purse swung from her shoulder. Her lips glistened, her earrings glittered, and her pagne rippled darkly. She'd drenched herself in some cloying perfume, a cheap and artificial scent that struck me, in my confused and nervous state, as strangely harmonious with the chemistry of the equatorial evening. A smell in perfect balance with the cooling breeze blowing off the river, the glimmer of light reflecting from the sky onto the water, the rustling of light cotton fabric against her legs. I inhaled deeply, and the nurse watched me, a faint smile on her glossy lips.

"I'm almost ready," I finally blurted. "I'll be out in a minute."

I closed the door in her face, which was rude, certainly, and anyway I was lying—there was nothing left to do to get ready. But the truth was I didn't think it would be a good idea to invite the nurse, looking and smelling as she did, into my house. I returned to the kitchen and poured another swallow of rum. *Products of the Oil Palm* was still open on the table. Again I studied the photograph. It could be Pers on the deck of the boat; it could be anybody. You could look that far back into the past and see anything at all. Everything blurs, all details wash out, and when you look long enough at such a picture you begin to see not the past as it really was but as you might imagine it. As you might derive it from the present. And now as I stared at the photograph I had the distinct sensation that I was not looking across a gulf of forty years at a still photograph of a place irrevocably changed and a man who had ceased to exist. That instead I was looking at something happening *now:* at sparkling eyes, a rocking boat, a head nodding slightly (another familiar, ironic gesture) toward the drums of palm oil rolling down the ramp.

Oh, but of course it was all in my head, a trick of the light, an imbalance in the neurochemistry processing what I saw. Again I reminded myself that it was Monday, the Day of Bouncing Vision. Again I reminded myself that none

of this really mattered. An old picture was just a curiosity; whatever its revelations, events had overtaken it. *Pers lost in sailing accident.* I closed the book
and pushed it off to the side. It may well have been a picture of Uncle Pers in
Placide's book. Pers may well have done some of the outlandish things attributed to him. And he may well have sent us here with some secret purpose in
mind. But what difference did any of that make? It all was dead history now,
no matter what people might choose to make of it, and the picture in the
book was at best only a small coincidence in a story whose ending was already
told, written bluntly in a single sentence in a telegram.

CONTRABAND

"I have a new plan, Monsieur Will."

The road wound through deep jungle. Headlights swept past huge buttressed trees, looming walls of vines and branches, cutbanks oozing mud and water. Peripheral objects, crowding the edges of the hurrying light.

"A plan for self-improvement. For a better way of life."

I kept my eyes steady, resisting the lure of the periphery, focusing only on the strip of illuminated road ahead, with its ruts and gullies and clay surfaces still slick from the day's rain. My eyes were steady, but my foot shifted uncertainly from accelerator to brake and back to accelerator again, sending the Land Rover into then pulling it out of another little fishtail slide. I found the fishtails nerve-racking, but the nurse liked them. That was the only thing she'd said since we got in the car; after the first fishtail she laughed quietly and said, "I like that." Her hand seemed to fishtail in the air between us, and on the seat beside me her hips may have fishtailed too. But it was dark and I couldn't really see these things. Since then she had been silent, and Telo had been talking nonstop.

"Oui, monsieur. This plan will change things for me."

"Well, what is it, Telo?"

But instead of answering, Telo began to cough. A couple of shallow hacks at first, and he tried to keep talking, but then he was seized by a great spasm of pulmonary coughing, a cough wretched beyond the chronic hacking I had come to expect from him. It spoke of TB or pneumonia or one of those unnamed infections that Tom wrote of, some pathogenic monster not yet emerged from the microbial breeding grounds to gain the attention of science.

Between Telo and me the nurse too stared fixedly at the road. She leaned against me as I turned the wheel to the right, unweighted as I turned to the left, pressed back against me when I turned again to the right. The choking scent of her perfume welled up, then was swept away by forest air rushing in the open window, smelling of leaves and water and saturated clay.

"Oui, monsieur." Telo's coughing finally subsided enough to allow him to speak again. "A new plan: I've decided to start an exercise program."

In spite of myself I glanced toward him, but his face was invisible in the darkness.

"Like Monsieur Tom. I always admired Tom for his exercise program. Did you know that in the mornings he used to jog five kilometers along the river road? He did calisthenics. And weights, he lifted weights! I want to follow his example."

We rounded a tight corner and began the descent to a narrow bridge. Storm runoff had eroded treacherous gullies in the steep section of road, and the Land Rover tilted precariously as I struggled to keep the tires up on the drier, smoother sides of the gullies.

"I hope to persuade other farmers to join me," Telo said. "Some of them already have the running shoes. This is the problem for me: I don't have the proper shoes."

The headlights illuminated a bridge made of two parallel logs, roughly planed on the top. Moss and algae glistened on the logs, and the full-running stream splashed on the underside. These small bridges, built to handle palm-oil trucks, were a bit widely spaced for the wheelbase of a Land Rover. You had to line your tires up on the very inside edge of each log, Kate had warned me, and there wasn't much room for miscalculation.

"Do you think you could loan me a pair of running shoes, Mr. Will?"

The important thing was to keep the vision steady. Everything else would follow: steady hands, steady feet, the steady coordination of eye and muscle and nerve. The problem was, I couldn't trust my eyes. An attack of Bouncing Vision is one thing when you're sitting on the porch watching palm-oil boats and market-bound women go by, or looking at an old photograph of a man leaning on a railing, and it's another thing entirely when you're driving a skittering Land Rover over a slippery log bridge on a narrow wet road at night.

"Pardon, monsieur. I repeat my question: is it possible you have a pair of shoes I can borrow? Or if it's too much trouble to make the loan, I would accept them with gratitude as a gift. For the sake of reviving my strength and my health."

It felt like we were *sliding* down the grade to the bridge. I cursed the bald tires, pumped the brakes, and tightened my grip on the steering wheel, resisting the pull of the tire-swallowing ruts. And I never took my eyes off those two narrow logs, with the stream boiling up in the wide open space between them. The front tires bumped onto the planks leading to the bridge, and I stomped the accelerator and closed my eyes. A second later we bounced down safely on the opposite shore, and I opened them again.

"Monsieur. . . ."

"No. I'm sorry, Telo. Bazapato ikele ve. There are no shoes."

"No matter." Telo sighed. "I can jog without shoes. Mambu ve. Or I can wait until some come my way. Chance. But it's a pity Monsieur Tom left without giving me his." He sighed again, and gave himself over to another spasm of lung-racking coughs.

The next bridge I managed to cross with my eyes open. Perhaps I'd exaggerated the difficulty. Kate drove across these bridges all the time, I'd driven across a few of them myself, and to my knowledge even a driver as famously unskilled as Père Michel never landed in the creek. And neither Telo nor the nurse seemed to share my anxiety. I guess my reputation as a cool-headed professional smuggler of Mputu carried more weight with them than my manifest jittery incompetence. The nurse remained silent and relaxed, her body rocking with the movement of the Land Rover, almost as if she were asleep. Her perfume continued to swirl around the car, carried in eddies and whirlpools of air. An elusive scent, without fixed qualities. First a gaggy overpowering stench in my nose, and the next moment something wild and earthy: complex and shifting bouquets that were sour like luku, acrid like palm wine, bitter like kola nuts. A strangely disturbing, strangely familiar blend, and then it changed again or was swept up suddenly in the smells of flooding streams and dripping jungle carried in on the night wind, and lost.

Meanwhile Telo kept his monologue running. He was indisputably a good-hearted man, hardworking and dedicated to his family and full of virtues that are sorely lacking in this world, but he was also a stupefying bore. To be born into an oral culture with a voice like that! He seemed to have no use for inflection, no use for the occasional lilting cadence or emphatic interjection or even, God forbid, the sudden meaningful silence. He just plodded on and on, persistent as the flow of mud. An exercise program! What an idea! His whole life was a brutal workout, a constant battering of a body only minimally supplied with calories and besieged by infections his immune system could scarcely stalemate. And now he wanted to go *jogging;* he thought jogging would renew him, fill him with the vitality of the modern world. I guess that's what he thought. Actually, I hadn't been paying very close attention to his explanation, because the delivery was so tedious and because, after all, I had my own preoccupations.

"Turn here," said the nurse.

I turned onto a spur road, which ended in a clearing a hundred yards into the forest, where a half dozen people waited beside sacks of produce and racemes of palm nut.

This was our third collection point of the night, and I was familiar with the routine. The nurse hopped out with her flashlight, her list, her tags. She put a tag on each sack and recorded a name on her list, while Telo supervised the loading. Later, when the goods were delivered to the smuggler, the nurse would record the amount paid for each item, collect the money, and subsequently reimburse the owner. This was a serious business with a lot of opportunity for mistrust, corruption, and error. People watched closely, and spoke only in short sentences and low voices.

"We waited a long time for you, Nurse. We got cold and tired out here, waiting."

"It takes a long time, Uncle. Monsieur Will drives much slower than his wife."

"Well, we're used to waiting. And we don't wait alone. The Road Builder's with us, eh, Mr. Will?"

"The Road Builder is dead, Papa."

Everyone knew that the Road Builder was dead. They knew about the telegram from Mavis, and about Kate's journey to San Francisco for the memorial service. They knew the name of that city in Mputu where the Road Builder died, where the news of his death originated and began to make its laborious way halfway around the world to us, as slowly as if it had crossed the ocean on a sailing ship and struggled up the rivers in a mailbag tossed in the hold of an ancient steamer.

The telegram was unequivocal: *Pers lost in sailing accident.* Though I had to wonder how accidental a death could be when a person had spent so much time and energy anticipating it. In any case, Pers was now at the bottom of the bay, or eaten by sharks, or washed up on the sand to be discovered by a beachcomber or a surfer. His possessions would scatter, his wife would move on, the events of his life would lose their tenuous structure. His memoirs might be published and even read by a few, but San Francisco would hardly register his passing. His death would be ritually acknowledged by a small group of people and then forgotten.

But in the Kivila Valley the news of his death had a deeper, stranger resonance. Here, in a country that accommodates all of its dead, even those who die far away, who vanished decades before, Pers' death had at last made his presence real.

I shone a flashlight beneath the Land Rover as the sacks and racemes were loaded on top. "These springs are flattened out! We can't put much more weight on this thing."

"It's all right, Monsieur Will. The road to Kasengi is smooth."

"Exactly how the Road Builder built it, citizen! He knows our Land Rover will be heavily loaded."

"Ç'est ça! One hand filling the camion of the mill, citizen, one hand filling the smuggler's Land Rover."

As we climbed to the savanna, Telo's voice continued to drone away, filling the Land Rover with repetitive musings: his exercise program, his sardine enterprise, the usual talk of black magic and ghosts. He mentioned a couple of minor Road Builder sightings, and a rumor about the flight of a bamboo airplane near Kasengi. It was this rumor that caused Ndosi to walk up to the savanna in the heat of the afternoon, Telo informed me, leaving him to accompany me as boy chauffeur. Kasengi. That reminded him of a kangaroo trial held there recently in response to the distant death in a truck accident of one of the village women. A trial, because someone had to be at fault, *n'est pas?* Things don't just *happen.* Some old uncle must have evil in his heart. After a long deliberation, the tribunal decided which of the old ones had to pay up—a goat, a few chickens, some palm wine. A small price for a fetisher to pay, in exchange for the public recognition of his power to send his spirit a great distance and change the course of events. And these days, said Telo, such spirit traveling is increasingly common, even among whites. He pointed to Madame Kate's dream, to the many other appearances of the Road Builder, and to the sighting a few days ago of a white man's ghost rising out of the overgrown gardens of Kilala Mission. The ghost of a young frère, people said, killed by the rebels when they razed the mission back in independence times.

The road was smooth and straighter now, and the nurse had stopped swaying. Her body pressed only lightly against mine, just enough to communicate the rising and falling of her chest as she breathed, and the residual fishtailing of her hips. We hit a sudden piece of rough road, and the Land Rover bounced and swerved. I stiffened, wrenching the wheel, and Telo grunted a warning. But the nurse remained silent and languid, unaffected by the jolts. Like the women walking earlier in the evening on the road below the house, she seemed to move in a separate medium, as if she were drifting in water, responding to the currents and the tides, like Uncle Pers sinking slowly into the bay while on the receding surface above him his capsized boat drifted away. Presumably, though, he was wearing a life jacket. Unless he was *trying* to drown. But probably he didn't drown at all; probably it was a heart attack or hypothermia that did him in. *Pers lost in sailing accident.* I wished I had more to go on. If I knew exactly what had happened, if I could visualize his last moments, I might have had a sense of finality about his death, and a conviction strong enough to deny the ghosts and visions of a superstitious people.

"Kasengi," murmured the nurse.

We'd come out on top now, following the narrow spine of the ridge. Kasengi was off to our left, a shadow of trees on the savanna peninsula. A village of fire and violence upon the crest of the world, where all the land was wild, dark, ungovernable. Unless a government is a roving consortium of uniformed thugs and bandits, backed by a network of betrayers and rumormongers and spies and extortionists. Unless a government is a bamboo pole lowered across the road, and soldiers coming to the window with heavy guns slung over their shoulders. *Your papers, monsieur. Attestation, quoi.* But my papers were blank. I had no authorization, no alibi, no protector. And I was at the wheel of a Land Rover swaying with the weight of contraband, pitching and yawing like Uncle Pers' boat cast adrift on a black rising sea.

. . .

But there was no roadblock waiting at the Place Without a Name, no midnight ambush of soldiers. Only the smuggler and his boy chauffeur, along with a crowd of people who'd carried produce up from their villages. Immediately people crowded up to the Land Rover and began unloading. I found myself on the edge of the jostling crowd, as disoriented and superfluous as I'd felt on my first visit there. Once again I was stumbling around in the dark while anonymous people pressed sweaty kola nuts into my hand. Over the muted babble of the crowd I recognized Ndosi's excited, argumentative voice, insistently repeating something about his airplanes. I couldn't tell what his story was, but several other voices were raised in disbelief or refutation. As before, the kerosene lamp burned on a table near the back of the truck, but with no mushipu haze to trap it the light was scattered, and served only to emphasize the vast reaches of darkness all around it. Moving along the edge of the crowd, I stumbled over a sack of manioc, and someone shone a blinding flashlight into my eyes. "Attention, monsieur!"

Why was I wandering around? I asked myself. Because I was looking for the nurse. But when I found her she was engaged in an argument with the truck driver, and I couldn't think what business I might have had with her. I moved away from the crowd, toward the purer darkness at the front of the truck. Someone standing on the bed of the truck hooted at me, and for a moment I had the idea it was Dimanche, in some new incarnation. But no; it must have been the boy chauffeur, and I wandered by without responding. I leaned against the front bumper, toying with the idea that this was a dream that was supposed to represent my time in Africa: a time spent stumbling around in the dark randomly colliding with people, plucking fragments of intelligible language out of a stream of babble. A time of blood infestations, of malarial logic revealing the contradictions that eat away at the foundations of things: failure built into success, intimacy constructed on deceit, longing for my wife mixed up with some fatalistic attraction to the nurse. The clean smells of the wet savanna, yielding to the corrupt odors of diesel, rotting produce, industrial-strength palm oil.

At the table the nurse and the smuggler weighed produce in the lamplight. Each watched the scales intently, and the nurse recorded numbers in her notebook. The boy chauffeur tossed sacks onto the bed of the truck, and the smuggler went to the cab, unlocked it, and brought a suitcase back to the table. He unlocked and opened the suitcase, revealing thick stacks of currency: red, pink, violet, and chartreuse bills, each with a reproduction of the president's puffy, bespectacled face. I'd never seen the chartreuse ones before. In the dim light, looking over the smuggler's shoulder, I couldn't count the zeros lined up on them.

The nurse showed the smuggler her figures, and they argued for a while. Eventually he threw up his hands and, complaining all the time, counted out a big stack of bills for her. She began to call out names and dispense the cash, and the smuggler rearranged his bills and closed his suitcase. He looked up at me.

"Do you have something you want to sell, monsieur? You see I'm prepared to buy."

"That's a big suitcase. I've never seen so much cash before."

"No? But it's worth nothing, you understand. Here. You can have it all. Give me your wallet, with a little money from Mputu, and I give you the entire suitcase. Ha-ha!"

"Most of those bills look brand new."

"Oh, yes. The people complain they have no money, so the government, in its generosity, provides us with more. Larger denominations, too! We have no education, monsieur, but we are learning to count very high. Still, the big bills can't catch up with our inflation, so, as you have noticed, I trade in my little attaché case for this suitcase!"

"Well, at least the mint is working. Printing money. That's one government agency still doing its job, huh? One production line that's still moving."

The smuggler laughed scornfully. "They print this in Mputu, monsieur. We buy it, import it, pay interest on it, like everything else. The only difference is, maybe the tariff is waived. Ha-ha!"

At least fifteen people crowded into and on top of the Land Rover for the return trip. This time Telo hung on the back railing, but once again the nurse was beside me in the front seat. I felt much better driving back. The unknown dangers of the night had melted away. The soldiers did not materialize. The gaps between bridge logs were not so wide as they had seemed earlier. And the Land Rover didn't handle so badly, once you were used to it. I could see how a person might come to like the feel of it, once he got a few smuggling runs under his belt.

I was a little ashamed, though, thinking back on my faintheartedness of a couple of hours earlier. It was a good thing Kate wasn't there to see me, trembling and whimpering and squeezing my eyes shut as I plunged across bridges. Her dragonslayer! *Bring me the head of the commissaire. Get in the Land Rover and smuggle something.* She was making a joke, of course. One of her ambiguous jokes that might or might not be serious at the core, like her original joke of introducing me to Pers and Mavis as her husband. Though maybe the smuggling really was working in the way she suggested it might—something real, strengthening my faith and security. I did feel stronger, perhaps more secure—but I couldn't say more faithful, with Kate an ocean and a continent away and the nurse so close beside me.

I suppose the nurse never noticed how anxious I was. She was in her languid trance, not paying that kind of attention. But now she was alert, and I sensed the tension in her muscles. She too was riding the adrenal surge of the moment: the secret mission accomplished, the Land Rover speeding into the jungle night, a sudden fishtail on the rain-slicked road, warm bodies pressed against each other. Or maybe she was just balancing figures in her mind, still sorting out what she knew of exchange rates and commodity prices. And she did seem to know something of those things. She cut an authoritative figure, dispensing wads of cash, planting herself in front of the smuggler to argue on behalf of the Smugglers' Support Group. Which was one explanation for her fancy clothes, her earrings and coiffure and mascara and perfume. She'd made herself up not as the seductive nurse but as the treasurer of the Smugglers' Support Group, a position that required dignified dress, something to distinguish her from the illiterate peasant women who knew only how to bend their backs over a hoe.

Of course, once the treasurer had discharged her duties, she was free to do as she pleased. To be as seductive as she pleased. Certainly a person might just as easily be seduced by a treasurer as by a nurse. Only it would be absurd to imagine that person would be me. Yet now at the end of this long drive we found ourselves still together, and alone. The Land Rover slowly emptied out as we wound through the forest, stopping at Telo's sharp whistle on the edges of sleeping farms and villages. At last only the nurse and I remained, no longer squished together by the crowd in the front seat but remaining close to each other, much closer than necessary, sitting for a moment in front of the garage with the engine silent but still echoing off the walls of the guest house behind us. An echo that didn't fade, even when I stepped down and stood in the darkness, listening, until I realized that the echo was the sound of insects once again buzzing and humming and throbbing like an engine driving the night.

Who could sleep through a night like that? Surely there were other adventures to seek out. Myths to invigorate, commodities to smuggle, dragons to slay. But already the nurse and I were walking toward the gate, where we would say good night to each other. She'd turn up the path to the camp, Placide would rise out of his cardboard in the glow of his coals and tell me that everything was peaceful, nothing had changed, and I would enter the dark empty house and in defiance of the insects and adrenaline and jumbled smells and pheromones of the night lie down on my bed and try to sleep.

The nurse stopped at the foot of the steps. "Good night," she murmured, holding out her hand. We shook, then stopped shaking. But we didn't let go. She moved, or I pulled her, almost imperceptibly closer, and I inhaled in a sudden wave the fullness of her scent. My voice sounded unfamiliar to me, a hoarse, low whisper as if from some other man's throat.

"Remember the day I first met you, in the house with Matama the morning after a child's funeral? Remember how you told me that someday you'd teach me to dance?"

"Oh yes, I remember. But you said you didn't think you could learn."

"I did? Well, tonight I feel like maybe I could."

I must have pulled her even closer, because now her face was only inches from mine, and I could feel her breath, coming harder. "Listen, Will!" Her hand suddenly squeezed mine, and at the same time it occurred to me that Placide had not yet come out of the shadows to greet us and that the darkness down by the cook shed was unrelieved by even the faintest glow of his fire. But from under the door of the shuttered house a little light escaped, and with it a human voice, faintly raised over the buzzing of the insects.

"Who is it?" the nurse whispered again, still close by my side, though her hand had slipped from mine.

"I don't know." Though I did know that voice, or felt that I should. And when I went up on the porch and opened the door it really was like a dream: the small sealed room, the sudden orange light, and Placide looking up from the opposite side of the table with his bow and arrows at his side, his machete on the table, and his bright nervous eyes darting from me to the nurse to the man sitting with his back to us at the table. Wisps of white hair gleamed in the lamplight, and mottled hands left the tabletop as the man shakily turned. His voice too was something out of a dream: thin and trembling but not, as I had thought, lost forever to the world of the living.

"You keep late hours, William."

He spoke my name but his eyes passed over me and rested on the nurse, who stood in the doorway calmly returning his gaze, as if she too recognized him but did not share my disbelief at seeing him: the Road Builder, whom I knew to be in California, dead, sitting with his white hair shining at my kitchen table in the center of Africa.

BOOK FIVE

THE EXPLORER

3 0

BORIS

His hair was thin and white as luminescent smoke, and in the high contrast of the lamplight the textures of his face, the pits and crevasses and collapsing excavations, were like the scars and tailings of an abandoned mine. Skin hung from his neck and arms in pale flaps, toneless and colorless except for blotches of melanoma and spidery networks of blood vessels. The nurse stopped in the doorway behind me and sucked in her breath, muttering something about a ghost. On the far side of the room Placide sat tense and coiled, his machete lying on the table in front of him. The battered blade faced the old man, but the nightwatchman gripped the handle tentatively, as if he doubted the steel's capability to cut flesh and draw blood.

For me, though, the smell soon spoiled any ghostly effect. Mainly what Pers smelled like was the dark crusted bowels of a palm-oil mill, and for a moment I thought that he must have been spewed from the chimneys during the night, a nocturnal emission of the bubbling vats and glowing furnaces, or else a spirit taking shape out of the unquiet dreams of the chef de poste, or the industrial hallucinations of the chef's consultant. But then I became aware of other smells, beneath the palm oil—an unwashed, aging body festering in filthy clothes—and I knew this was no dream or spirit, that a ghost would not give off such a mortal stench.

I must have recoiled a little when he reached up to shake my hand, because he wrinkled his nose and said: "Excuse the odor, William. I didn't remember it being such a damn strong smell. And one doesn't get used to it, I've noticed, or are you by now? Well, I just spent two days wallowing in the stuff in the hold of that boat, and I'm not used to it yet."

"What boat," I said weakly.

"Why, the *only* boat. That's what I understood that Chinese fellow to be saying, at any rate, when I told him I would just wait for another one. He said there wasn't another one. People get out to that place on trucks, he said, if they go there at all, which they generally don't. Not that he put it in those words, exactly; in fact, I'm not certain he was using any words at all. But I understood him, and he understood me. I told him my bones are already crumbling and I can't ride in the back of a truck. So he put me on the boat. I was a stowaway, essentially—I don't think the pilot knew I was there, down in that hold slicked with palm oil and filled with empty greasy barrels. Better than a truck ride, maybe, but still not pleasant!"

"We heard you were dead," I said. "We got a telegram."

"Well, yes. You received a telegram, did you? Well, it's true, old Pers Merlicht is dead. Your information was correct, as far as it goes. Ha-ha!" He gestured at the suitcase propped on the chair next to him. "Move my suitcase and sit down, Will. It's good to see you."

I left the oily leather suitcase on the chair and leaned against the wall.

"There *was* a funeral, right? That's what the telegram said."

He was looking at the nurse, who still stood in the doorway.

"You haven't introduced me to your companion, Will."

"Oh. Well, this is the nurse. We've been . . . out making some deliveries."

"Deliveries, eh? The nurse, you say? 'Nurse' is her name?"

"We call her the nurse. Her name is—"

"Masayatia." She smiled, stepping forward to shake Pers' hand. He rose from his chair and bowed unsteadily.

"This is Pers," I told her in Kituba. "From Mputu."

"Not Pers!" Pers said. "I tell you that old fool is gone. You have a telegram, don't you? Believe what you read, and forget old Uncle Pers. Let me show you something."

He began to fumble with his belt. Placide stood too, his grip tightening on his machete as if he expected Pers to draw a weapon. Instead the old man undid his belt and, to my distress, began to unbutton his pants. But it was only to pull up a money belt and take out of it a United States passport. Holding his pants up with one hand, he flipped open the passport and showed it to me.

"Boris Vestor? Boris?"

"Yes! I am Boris. Well, it isn't my favorite name either. Of course I wouldn't have chosen it, had I been given a choice. But I wasn't. It was the best they could do at the time, they told me, and I would just have to get used to it. And so I have."

"You're telling me you got into this country on a fake passport?"

"Yes, this is what I'm telling you! Well, no. Not *fake*. A *new* passport. A new identity. This is *me* now, you understand. Boris Vestor. I bought Boris. He came with all the accessories, eh? Social Security number, birth certificate, a short biography even, though I can't remember the details very well. Actually, we have been acquainted for some time. I knew something of his character already. Ha! You see, I bought him several years ago, as insurance. A hedge against mortality, one could say. And he has done a little work for me, in the past. But now I had to bring him out of the shadows, because I was disposing of Pers. He is dead, as you were informed. A seizure, drowned, eaten by sharks. Very dead."

He put his passport back in the money belt and buttoned his pants. "Excuse me," he said, turning again to the nurse. "Mata——"

"Ma-sa-ya-tia."

"Ah." He smiled again and held out his hand. "I am Boris."

"Enchantée," said the nurse.

"I watched that boat coming upriver this morning. I had no idea you were on it."

"Of course not. I was down in the hold, where the oil is thickest, and I didn't emerge until night. Is it not the custom in this country, Will, to offer a guest a drink?"

"Do you want a drink?"

"Yes, thank you. Red wine, I think. I believe I still have enough liver to metabolize a glass of red wine. My liver escaped from those medical people in the nick of time. A few more biopsies and the entire organ would have simply disintegrated, vanished from their radar screens. That would have been a disappointment to them as well, because if they perforated it out of existence they wouldn't be able to extract it with a more complicated procedure, which is what they were after with all the perforations. They're always looking for an excuse to cut a person open and remove something. What was it they got last? Gallbladder, piece of a kidney, something like that."

"We don't have any red wine. No wine at all."

"What's that? No wine? I'll have gin then. On the rocks."

"There's no gin. We have rum. And no rocks. There's no ice here, Pers."

"Excuse me, remember your telegram, William. Pers is dead, do you understand? I am Boris. Give me some rum, then, if that's all you have. Vile stuff. It's *rum* they drink here?"

"No. Mostly they drink palm wine."

"Yes, of course. Palm oil, palm wine. Well, it's not as bad as rum, is it? I can't remember. Do you have any? You should keep some on hand, to welcome visitors."

"It doesn't keep. You have to drink it right away. And I wasn't expecting visitors."

"No. I suppose not." Pers glanced again at the nurse, and took a grimacing sip of the rum I had poured. "Neither was your man here, I might add." He nodded genially at Placide, who was seated again, a hand still on his machete, his eyes fixed on Pers. "He was nowhere to be seen when I first came into the yard. No one answered when I called at your door. So I went in and lit the lamp. Then this fellow appears in the kitchen. I believe his first inclination was to shoot me with one of his exquisite miniature arrows. I had the devil of a time persuading him not to. We had a difficulty understanding one another. I suppose my French is creaky, but then, he doesn't seem to speak French at all, does he? Well, he didn't need to say much, sneaking out of the dark with an arrow set in his bow. I understood him well enough! Ha-ha!"

"I have a lot of questions for you," I said.

"Oh, yes! And I have some for you as well. For example: what have you done with my niece? What are these 'deliveries' you are making in the middle of the night? And why are you bringing your lovely young nurse into your house at this hour?"

"It's not like you think—"

"Well, I don't think anything at all! I don't speculate; it's a waste of time and I haven't the imagination for it. These are only questions, inspired by an innocent curiosity. You have your own questions, as you say. And the answers will come in good time. But for now, perhaps we should speak of other matters and simply enjoy our visit—though I may be offended, if I traveled all this way and Katy isn't even here."

"Well, she isn't. She's in San Francisco, at your funeral. And if she wasn't there you might be offended too."

"Yes, I see what you mean. The offenses contradict one another, don't they? It's hard to know what position to take. Well, one can't expect to change identities without having to confront a few dilemmas, eh?"

"Monsieur." Placide stood formally before me, expressionless as always. But his voice trembled. "For two years I am your sentinel, monsieur. All night long for two years I never sleep. The house is safe, because everyone knows I'm watching. But tonight this old one appears, and I hear nothing, see nothing, until the lamp is lit in the kitchen. Why, monsieur? Because I'm lazy, a sentinel asleep at his post?"

He paused, waiting for my obligatory denial. I grunted, and he continued.

"Or because he's not an ordinary intruder? Because an enchantment closed my eyes as if I were sleeping? Because this is the Road Builder, fulfilling the prophecy of his return!"

"Yes!" said the nurse. "We recognize him, Will. The Road Builder!"

"Well, I don't remember any *prophecy*, exactly," I said.

"What are they saying?" said Pers.

"They say you're the Road Builder. I guess they remember you, somehow."

"Ah, yes. The Road Builder, eh?"

"But they were also under the impression that the Road Builder drowned. It's confusing for them. And for me. What should I tell them?"

"Tell them what you like. It doesn't matter. But technically their Road Builder did not drown. The drowned man was Pers Merlicht. As for Boris Vestor, he's flexible. He might as easily be the Road Builder as not." He rose and bowed again to the nurse, who smiled, and to Placide, who did not.

By dawn everyone in the camp knew that the Road Builder had come back. Early in the morning a crowd of children gathered by the gate, but the first adult visitor was Ndosi, already waiting on the porch when I stepped outside at sunrise. He was ready to go to work, he told me, and he wanted to meet the Road Builder.

He didn't look ready for work, or in any condition to meet somebody. He was mud-splattered, exhausted, hung over, and still drunk. He smelled of stale sweat and smoke and metabolizing palm wine. But there was a fire burning in his eyes. It had been a night of miracle and consummation, he said. On this night Monsieur Will had successfully evaded the commissaire's soldiers and for the first time delivered the smugglers' contraband. The Road Builder had at last returned to the Kivila Valley. And he, Ndosi, had held in his hands the bamboo airplane that had flown from its savanna perch more than a year before.

Yesterday afternoon, Ndosi told me, a woman had come across the airplane half buried in her manioc field. She was afraid to touch it, but when word reached Ndosi he immediately set out walking, and though it was night by the time he reached the field, he searched by moonlight and found the plane. It was unmistakably his. All night long he walked from village to village, showing others the plane so that the miracle might be witnessed and confirmed. Before dawn he returned to Malembe, where people were also amazed at his discovery but said that a wonder of far greater magnitude had occurred in Ngemba, at the house of his employer.

So it was natural that he hadn't slept on such a night. It was natural that he had walked incredible distances and that everywhere people had given him palm wine and kola nuts and marijuana. Now he squinted his bloodshot eyes at me. "You didn't sleep either, did you, Will?"

In fact, I hadn't slept a minute, with Pers—or rather, Boris—sprawled on my couch, snuffling and snoring and stinking up the house. I'd already decided that the first priority of the day was to get him bathed. But when he woke the old man refused to go down to the river. So Ndosi called to the children who were lined up along the fence, hoping for a glimpse of the Road Builder. He set them to work shuttling buckets of water up to the raffia bathhouse, which Kate and I never used, since we bathed in the river. Then he sent the children away, took Boris gently by the arm, and ushered him down the porch steps. At the door of the bathhouse he gave him a bar of yellow soap.

"What is this substance?" said Boris.

"Ah, yes," Ndosi replied. "Substance of soap."

"Soap. Smells terrible."

"Terrible," Ndosi agreed. "Very cleaning substance."

"Awfully dedicated man you've got here, William," Boris called over to me. "Reporting to his post, performing duties in his condition. And he seems to speak some English as well. But this is questionable soap, you know."

"It's produced locally. Made from wood ash and palm oil. You get used to it."

"One gets used to all sorts of paradoxes. But palm-oil soap to wash away palm oil? This is a quixotic undertaking, William." But he stepped into the bathhouse and took some kind of bath. Afterward, he put his filthy, oily clothes back on.

"I guess bathing *is* quixotic," I said, " if you don't bother to change clothes."

"You're speaking to a refugee, Will. The fact is, I don't have a change of clothes."

"No? Well, what's in your suitcase?"

"Ah, my suitcase! Not suits, I can tell you that! Not even a change of underwear!"

We put him in a chair in the shade of the mango tree, where he was occupied greeting the many people who came to welcome him. He shook hands, nodded and smiled, accepted gifts of kola nuts from the men, peanuts and pineapples from the women. He said he didn't remember a word of Kituba, so Ndosi stood by his side, eating the kola nuts and translating the questions and observations of the villagers into impressionistic English. Boris ignored my efforts to clarify the translations. The secretary and the storekeeper tried out their French on him, but Boris just smiled genially and bobbed his head and turned to Ndosi for a translation.

Matama and the nurse arrived. Boris greeted the nurse like an old friend, and hurriedly passed the luku Matama gave him on to Ndosi. Old people hobbled up, mumbling incantations and benedictions that Ndosi made no effort to translate, and Boris bowed deeply over and over. He performed a coin trick to entertain the children; he fumbled the coin and the trick failed, but the children were impressed in any case; and everyone was amazed when, during a lull in the introductions, he produced a small electric shaver and began to run it across his stubbly chin.

No one seemed to have a problem accepting the Road Builder's presence. He used a different name now, but that was not unusual; names were notoriously fickle in that place. And remarkable as it was, his arrival only fulfilled a general expectation, a prophecy, as Placide had said. Even the telegram announcing Pers' death had prophesied it, in a way, though of course in another way it contradicted it. But the contradiction could be easily shrugged off. It was only a piece of paper that said he was dead, some people pointed out. What are you going to believe, a piece of paper, or the Road Builder himself coming out of the sky into a sunlit clearing? Others conceded that he may well be dead in Mputu, but it was clear enough that he was still alive here in Africa. And others said, so what if he's dead? It's not the first time the dead have walked among us.

What was confusing and contradictory to me, then, they saw as an opportunity for multiple explanations. A being might manifest itself in different forms, or speak in parables that are not easily understood, and in any case the point was that here was the Road Builder in our midst, with his white hair and pale wrinkled skin and sunken burning eyes, smelling like a god of palm oil and stroking the convoluted landscape of his face with a small humming machine. And that was cause not for doubt and nitpicking distinctions but for wonder and celebration.

At midday the chef de poste crossed the river with both his wives. The chef was wearing his formal suit, and the wives wore expensive pagnes and fresh coiffures. They sat flanking the chef in the shade of the mango tree, and Ndosi and I stood beside Boris. A crowd pressed against the fence, straining to overhear the conversation. Boris was beginning to tire, though he still seemed to be enjoying himself.

"I remember you," the chef said, "from when you were building roads, in independence days. I worked in the mill then."

Ndosi translated this more or less accurately, and Boris smiled blandly and said: "Well, I don't remember him! These elegant ladies do look slightly familiar, though. They are his wives, you say? Two of them, I see."

"It was long ago," Ndosi translated for the chef. "And he's built many roads since. His arms tire, remembering the earth they moved in the Kivila Valley. His eyes blur, but they haven't forgotten the faces they gazed upon here, as if only yesterday."

The chef nodded, and leaned to whisper first to one wife and then to the other.

"A fat one and a skinny one," said Boris.

"He compliments you on the beauty of your wives," said Ndosi.

"And where is *his* wife?" said the chef.

"He asks for your wife," Ndosi translated.

"What's that? He wants three of them? Fine, he can have her. That is, he could, if I had a wife. As it is, I'm a bachelor. Ha-ha. Boris the bachelor."

"His wife remains in Mputu," Ndosi told the chef.

The chef had brought a calabash of palm wine, which he now poured into glasses. Before we drank, he tossed a little out of his glass onto the ground, "for the ancestors."

"Would he be offended if I were to toss mine out for the ancestors too?" Boris said after he took a sip. But Ndosi was already assuring the chef that Boris loved the palm wine.

Only at one point did Ndosi permit an unadulterated exchange. Breaking a short silence, the first wife leaned forward and asked the Road Builder what he intended to do, now that he had returned to Ngemba. Perhaps because he was wondering the same thing himself, Ndosi translated accurately.

Boris said that he had come because he was an explorer, and it was the nature of an explorer to continue exploring and to return to the places to which he had set out in his youth. And now in his old age he was writing a book about his explorations of long ago. He planned to travel again upon the roads he had built, and explore the memories of the people who had used those roads. The stories he uncovered he would put into his book.

"He's writing a book," Ndosi announced, and let it go at that.

Everyone nodded and seemed satisfied with this answer. A book might be anything, contain any sort of knowledge and power, encode the deepest mystery. To write one was the perfect mission for the enigmatic Road Builder. Also his answer effectively shut off further inquiry, since nobody could think of a question to ask about a book.

"I came by boat," Boris told them when they asked how he'd arrived, and I heard him repeat it several times in the days that followed. But nevertheless the belief took hold that he had come by air, perhaps because he had materialized so suddenly in our midst. Or because people seldom heard a coherent translation of his story about the palm-oil boat, and it was more satisfactory to imagine a transformational being like the Road Builder swooping in on a night flight rather than slogging upriver in the hold of their own sorry boat. But the most persuasive evidence that he had flown in was the aircraft itself: Ndosi's lost bamboo airplane that had appeared in a remote savanna field the day of the Road Builder's arrival.

There was no obvious explanation of how the plane had come to be in that field, I thought. But most people were convinced that the explanation lay in a juxtaposition of miracles too compelling to be dismissed. So the miracles were joined: it was determined that the Road Builder had returned in Ndosi's plane, which a year before had flown off to Mputu to find him. Ndosi himself championed this theory, and seemed to think that it vindicated his obsession, representing a triumph for him and a defeat for his uncles and the suspicious elders of Malembe, who had hated his planes.

The plane was heavily damaged. A wingtip was gone, the tail broken off, and the fuselage crushed and charred. People interpreted the plane's condition as evidence of the great speed with which it had plummeted out of the sky to crash-land on the rugged earth. And this was what seemed to most amaze people: not the idea that the Road Builder had somehow flown in on a miniature bamboo plane, but the wonder of an old man surviving unscathed a landing that had so damaged his aircraft.

"You're becoming a skeptic, William! But you must admit that I am hard to kill. If you are not persuaded of this, I'll tell you another story. For your ears only, of course. Let the people here believe I plummeted out of the sky. Far-fetched, but so is the truth: that I crawled out from under the water. Not once, but twice! You know about the second time, when I emerged from the bilges of that oil boat. Beneath the surface of the water, but not immersed. Well, the first time I was completely immersed."

We were in the living room, at night. Boris sat on the couch beneath a pile of blankets, gesturing widely as if to a spellbound crowd, though his only audience was me and the leering masks on the wall. "A couple of weeks ago," he began, "I went sailing, alone. This was, of course, forbidden—or would have been, had anyone suspected I was capable of it. But no one did. My condition had improved, but still I was a frail, dying old man. Ha! And capable of activities much more strenuous than sailing a boat about the bay, as it turns out!

"Anyway, Mavis had gone for the day to some kind of ladies' affair down on the peninsula, and I packed my suitcase and took a cab to the bus station, where I left the suitcase in a locker. I took another cab to the marina, got the boat ready, and went out on the water.

"I sailed about for an hour or so, permitting old Pers a final look at his beloved, ruined old bay. An indulgence, yes, but one benefit of arranging one's own death rather than leaving it in the unindulgent hands of the gods. At least they indulged me with a bit of wind, even as night was coming on! It was nearly dusk when I approached the Golden Gate, sailing close to shore. Anyone watching would have noticed nothing unusual, at first. They might have wondered why this small sailboat was pushing out into heavier seas at nightfall, and where was the captain, but as the boat approached the bridge they would have seen me come up from below.

"Probably no one was watching. But if they were, they would have seen me suddenly tremble violently. I staggered, and leaned against the railing. Then I tumbled off. Yes, I tumbled! This wasn't easy—really, an old man ought not to have to perform his own stunts. But there I was. I had arranged everything else, and there was no acceptable way around it. If I had an audience, I needed to give them a convincing performance. It was convincing to *me:* for a moment I wondered if I might have a real stroke, lurching off the boat like that into the cold black water. There are sharks in it, and on the shore water was crashing against the rocks; and beneath the surface it was already deep night. But I wore a wetsuit—because, you see, I had changed down below—and I stifled my panic and made it to shore. No one saw me crawl out of the water, like some emerging terrestrial life form. Among the rocks I changed into my clothes, which I'd brought in the dry bag on my back, you see. I put the wetsuit into the bag, walked underneath the bridge, and found my way up to the streets. I rode a bus into the city, recovered my suitcase at the station, took another bus to the airport, and picked up a plane ticket that had been reserved in the name of Boris Vestor. When I changed planes in Chicago, I put the dry bag in a garbage receptacle. And that covered the last trace of Pers Merlicht's passing."

Some part of this story, at least, was true. At any rate, Boris was here, and that was a miracle in itself, whatever the details of his journey. Still, I found his self-satisfaction galling. "What about Mavis?" I said. "She's mourning you, and you're not even dead. Doesn't that bother you, tricking her like that?"

"Don't waste sympathy on Mavis, Will. My insurance policies, my pensions, my will—they're all in order. She's fully prepared to enjoy her liberation. But yes, if you must know the truth, the deceit does bother me a little. It's the sort of thing that nags at one's conscience. But what does one's conscience know of such matters? I ask my conscience: in what sense have I wronged Mavis? And the only answer is a stammer and shrug. In fact, I should have been dead and out of her hair long ago, instead of lingering, fussing interminably with those memoirs."

"But you finished the memoirs. You told us they're about to be published."

"Well, yes, they were. Old Pers was on the verge of giving them up. That was another reason to kill him off. And now, Boris shall deal with the memoirs!"

He laughed, a sharp barking sound. He didn't quite meet my gaze but seemed to be looking past me, glaring defiantly at one of the masks on the wall. "Oh, yes. I tricked Mavis, Will, but you see it was in her interest as well as my own. I have no regrets. Except I felt bad about turning my old boat loose on the open sea. It may have been lost, or smashed up on the rocks somewhere. It was a shame to risk the destruction of such a serviceable boat merely for dramatic effect, but then, if we don't have dramatic effect in our lives—and more so in our deaths—then what have we got?"

I told Boris about Madame Mud's visit, and prodded him to explain the relationship between Global Interconnect and Jucht Brothers, and his own role in arranging our employment. But his answers were vague and uninformative. He'd settled into the living room, taking over the couch and desk and becoming increasingly self-absorbed, though not to the point of paying attention to his personal appearance or hygiene. He brushed off my suggestions to bathe, and slept on the couch in the same filthy clothes he wore day after day. He said he hadn't brought a change with him because he was afraid Mavis would notice if clothes were missing, and anyway there wasn't room in his suitcase. He'd stuffed in a pair of pajamas at the last minute, that was all.

Finally I convinced him to wear the pajamas for a day, just to give Ndosi the opportunity to wash his clothes. But when the clothes were dry he decided not to change back into them. Pajamas were more appropriate for the climate, he said. So now he wore pajamas day and night, in private and in public. He wore them without embarrassment, and possibly they looked odd only to me. As an alien creature whose ways were inscrutable, he might as well wear pajamas as anything else.

Though unencumbered by personal belongings, Boris somehow managed to clutter up my house. He obviously wasn't accustomed to doing housework. I wasn't either, for that matter, since I had Ndosi to do it for me, so I guess the problem was with Ndosi, who was more energized than he'd been in months but not much interested in cleaning house or buying groceries or building the long-promised chicken shed. What interested him was Boris.

By day Boris mainly conducted interviews, sometimes in our living room, sometimes in the houses of his subjects. Accompanied by his translator (and wearing his pajamas), he cross-examined people about their recollections of events thirty and forty years in the past. The imprecision of Ndosi's translations was amplified by the fact that generally Boris was interviewing very old people, who tended to ramble and even rave. But Ndosi always managed some more or less rational-sounding interpretation of their words. Boris scribbled furious notes and sat up in the evening going over them, studying and transcribing and cross-referencing. He wrote intently, frowning and grimacing, tongue darting in and out of his mouth, lips moving constantly, jowls working independently of his lips. He sighed and wheezed and groaned and rumbled and farted; he wrote rapidly for a while and scribbled out what he had written, and then suddenly dropped his pen and shuffled madly through his papers. He blew his nose viciously into long strips of toilet paper pulled off the roll he kept on the desk, and gave himself over to harsh coughing spasms, depositing in the toilet paper whatever was yielded up from his lungs.

After a few nights of this I felt as though I were becoming infected with his manic energy. But in me it was corrosive, mere agitation; I wasn't crazy enough to know what to do with it. So I took the bottle of rum and fled to the porch steps, hoping the energy would dissipate, that Boris would go to bed, that Kate would come home. Maybe she would know how to deal with her uncle, sitting at my desk so obsessed and self-absorbed that he had no sense of how out of place he was there, how much he upset the balance of things. But nobody in the Kivila Valley seemed aware of that, besides me. I sensed that his presence required something of me, but I had no idea what, though what I kept thinking was how that story of his arrival here—the fake drowning, the new identity, the trip upriver in the hold of a palm-oil boat—was like one of those sensationalized fantasies Kate and I had made up in his study, disposable fictions to cushion the unconformities in his memoirs.

Returning from her evening bath, the nurse climbed the steep and slippery path up from the river and paused at my gate. Watching from the darkness of the porch, I probably only imagined that for once her pagne was carelessly wrapped, that as she climbed it slipped lower on her breasts, and that her dark legs glistened in the shadows behind a widening gap in the cloth. I was certain I just imagined it. Such a provocative, disorderly image was merely a product of my own provoked and disordered state of mind. It was best to ignore it and let the nurse pass unacknowledged. She climbed with her eyes on the path, as if intending only to return to the camp. So she surprised me— maybe she surprised herself—when at the last second she hesitated at the gate and suddenly entered our yard. Just inside she stopped to greet Placide, who was laying a fire in his brazier.

The nurse's beauty seemed more striking than ever, these days. There was something elemental about her, as if a superfluous exterior had been stripped away and the underlying structure of beauty revealed. Maybe she was just getting thinner. But didn't this thinness only emphasize—in her lips, her breasts, and where her pagne was drawn tightly across her buttocks—a slight but breathtaking extravagance of flesh? And how erect and slender was her neck, how compelling the arch of her cheeks, the silhouette of her skull against the sudden fire flaring up in Placide's brazier!

"You're sitting on the porch, Will."

She stood at the foot of the steps, looking up at me.

"You've just bathed in the river, Nurse." I was comfortable now, using these statements of the obvious as a form of ritual greeting. I offered her a chair but she sat on the step below me. The smell of the river was on her, and soap, and another faint smell: her perfume, pheromones, whatever it was. Her dangerous smell. She sniffed the air herself. "Whiskey," she said.

"Would you like some?"

To my surprise she said yes. I went inside and got her a glass. Boris, still bent over the desk, seemed unaware of my presence.

The nurse made a face, swallowing the rum. I was a little sorry she was drinking it—it marred her cleanliness, the purity of her smell.

We talked briefly of work in the fields. She said if the prices held there would be a lot of produce for the smuggler, next time. Mama Kate would be pleased.

"Let's hope she gets back in time to help deliver it," I said.

"If not, you will," said the nurse. "We'll go together again."

Already the twilight was gone. I couldn't see Placide in the darkness, or read the expression on the nurse's face. "They'll miss you in the camp," I said. "They'll think a crocodile got you."

She shrugged. "No one is waiting for me in the camp, Will. I come and go as I please. And I'm not concerned about crocodiles. Crocodiles who eat people are fetishers. And fetishers are old men. What do I have to fear from old men?"

"I don't know. Nothing, maybe. What about young men?"

The nurse laughed, and so I laughed too, and poured a little more rum for us. My hand trembled. The smell of rum was fierce in my nostrils, and so was that strangely familiar smell of the nurse. Suddenly I knew where I'd smelled it before: here on the porch, and in the shadows of my own bedroom, rising up through the mosquito netting off the body of my sleeping wife. A smell that even then had evoked in me a disproportionate sense of longing, as if I'd come close to something desired and within reach but not possessed, and ultimately lost.

The nurse breathed deeply too, drawing in her breath like a long sigh.

"Where's the Road Builder, Will?"

"He's inside. Why . . ." I stopped, uncertain of what I meant to ask her. Why do you care where the Road Builder is? Why have you come here at night, after your bath, to sit on my porch and shift your thighs beneath your pagne? Why do you smell exactly like my wife when she's returned from a night of wandering the savanna and the forest, when she's naked and dreaming and shrouded in mosquito netting?

Now the nurse wriggled her shoulders in time to the music on the chef de poste's boom box, though to tell the truth, up till that moment I'd been unable to distinguish any rhythm at all and had wondered if the cassette were double-tracking. "The chef de poste is having a party," she said. "We're too quiet on this side of the river, Will! We should be having a party too."

"You think?"

"We should have music. We should dance, Will! I still mean to teach you to dance."

She stood, and turned to face me. She was on the low step, half an arm's length away, smiling faintly. I could have put my hands on her waist and pulled her to me. She might have swung her leg across to straddle me; she might have leaned into me, her hands gripping my shoulders, her pagne falling open, the soft pressure of her breasts coming down on my face. But I didn't move. I watched her, and after a moment her smile turned and her eyes broke away and she slipped past me, a swirl of light rustling cotton and bare feet and fading smells. She opened the front door and stepped inside, and I got up and followed her.

Boris looked up at once, beaming. He pushed his papers away and stood, bowing. "We should have music," the nurse announced. "We should be dancing!" She spoke in Kituba, but he seemed to understand her exactly, because when she turned on the radio he took her in his stiff arms and, though he hobbled a bit, managed to twirl her across the living room floor.

An hour later I was back on the porch. I still had the rum bottle, and I was drunk. The chef's boom box was silent, but inside my house, where Boris and the nurse were maybe still dancing and maybe not, my own boom box blared the music of Radio Afrique.

I had to admit they danced well together. In fact, they looked entirely charming, at first: the old man serious and intent, holding the laughing younger woman in his arms, moving as he had not moved in years. He showed her some ballroom steps and she was delighted. "Why have you never shown me these dances, Will?" she called out as he swirled her around. "I thought white people only danced le Jerk!"

Of course, in my case, that's true: le Jerk is all I know. Boris would see that as a typical failure of public education. Since our education consists of the vulgarization of culture, he would say, of course we learn only a vulgar form of dance.

But after a while his own dancing lost its appeal. The nurse began to dance in an African style, and he followed her. He moved stiffly, yet somehow the rhythm went slithering through his body too. But it wasn't a pretty sight. In the dim orange light his face was like one of the wooden masks that hung on the wall: all shadows and promontories, terribly worn and ravaged, and the movements of his body seemed a grotesque parody of youth and sex. And the parody stripped the veneer of youth from the nurse. Her eyes receded into their sockets, her laughter went shrill and thin, and her slenderness now suggested disease and the wasting of flesh. She clung tightly to Boris, and when her hips began to pump against him I had a chilling revelation. The music went on, the obscene rhythm shimmied down their bodies, but I couldn't watch any longer. I took the rum and went out on the porch.

Was this still the same song playing, or was it two or three songs later? I couldn't tell. But at last it ended, and over the voice of the DJ I heard people moving in the house. Boris came outside. "There you are, William," he said. He teetered to the edge of the porch and peed over the rail, humming snatches of melody—an easy-listening version of the driving souka tune that had just finished playing.

"A remarkable woman." He chuckled. "The nurse."

"People say she's a witch."

"Excuse me?"

"They say she's a witch." Suddenly I felt very drunk.

"I see. And what do you make of that?"

"I don't know anything about it. But I do think you ought to use a rubber with her. The chef de poste has some. He'd be delighted to share."

"What are you saying, Will?"

"I'm saying you should use a rubber, Boris. A condom, you know?"

Boris finished dribbling on the rail. He fumbled with his fly, peering at me through the darkness. "What a ridiculous idea. You must be drunk. Your assumptions are offensive, to speak frankly. Anyway, what possible purpose would that serve?"

"I think she has AIDS."

"What? AIDS? Well, she may. That would be sad. But many people here do, I understand."

"You have to protect yourself."

"Protect myself? From what? I'm a dying man. And a great advantage of dying is that, in practical terms, it confers immunity to fatal disease. I have nothing to fear, William. From a beautiful young woman I have nothing to fear at all."

He went inside. The music continued for a while, and then was silent. Once or twice Placide rose from his cardboard bed and poked at his fire. I dozed, though I had a chill. The mosquitos buzzed lightly in my ear, almost a soothing sound, and landed with a touch too light to feel on my arms and on my neck.

JET LAG

Kate returned sooner than I expected, flying in one day from San Francisco via Chicago and Paris straight into the rising turmoil of Kisaka, where almost immediately by pure good luck she met some medical-relief workers who were traveling far to the south and stopping in at Bumba Mission on the way. So within forty-eight hours of leaving Mavis' house in San Francisco she got out of a truck in our driveway, and Sticky Tree set down his broom on the porch, flung open the front door, and announced, in the imperial manner of a professional servant: "Monsieur. Madame, elle est arrivée."

By the time I held her in my arms the crowd of children was already gathering at our gate. Sticky Tree carried her bags up to the porch, shooed the children off, ushered Kate inside, and bowed again. "Madame, vous êtes fatiguée. Je fait du café."

"Pas de café, merci," said Kate, staring at Sticky Tree, then at me. "You shouldn't treat jet lag with more coffee, should you? You look different, Will. But that's probably just the jet lag too. Or culture shock, or something. I should probably just go to bed. But I doubt I could fall asleep. You have to tell me the news, Will. The ferryman was full of gossip. He said something about a plane crash, and a white man walking out of the wreck without so much as a bruise or scrape."

"Well, the plane crash part is basically an invention. But the white man is real."

"Will. Is it Tom?"

"Tom? No!"

"Good. I was afraid . . . I dreamed about him, on the plane from Paris. Well, the dream wasn't really about him. It was this shadowy dream I don't really remember, except for the part about Tom. He was making a fire in this manioc field. Staggering around all sweaty and wild-looking, and flinging things into this fire that was roaring up behind him, flame and smoke every-where and then it all shifted and we were in these old brick ruins and the fire was somehow contained in this huge stone incinerator thing, like the furnace in the palm-oil mill or something. I don't know what it was all about. But when I woke up it seemed so *real*, like a premonition, and then on the ferry they were talking about this white man appearing and I was sure it must be Tom."

"It's not Tom. How was the funeral?"

"Well, there was no funeral. Will, what's Sticky Tree doing here? Where's Ndosi?"

I explained that Ndosi wasn't really working for us anymore. He'd arranged for Tree to fill in for him—to *subcontract*, Ndosi had said tri-umphantly, after he spent about an hour looking the word up in the dictio-nary. But what are you talking about, I said, no funeral, and Kate said that Mavis had canceled it. She said that Mavis had proven herself very adaptable and resilient in the face of losing in one afternoon the two things she'd focused all her energy on for years: her husband and his memoirs. Both of them vanished without a trace: Pers' body over the side of his boat, appar-ently, though the divers had found nothing. They assumed at first that the tide had carried his body out to sea. And they assumed his papers must have been on board with him, and gone down with the boat when it broke up on some rocks and sank near the mouth of the bay. Mavis and Kate and Pers' agent had searched the office and found nothing—no memoirs, no journals, no notes or computer files. But some things didn't quite make sense. Mavis started asking questions, and when she got some of the answers she began to redirect her energy. She canceled the funeral. In fact, said Kate, she rearranged her entire life. With a lot of help, of course. Pers' agent was very helpful. So were the insurance adjusters, detectives, lawyers, financial coun-selors, publishers, even. Money people. And of course her usual assortment of body workers, spiritual advisors, psychics, whatever. With all those people involved, Kate said, there wasn't much for her to do. All that time in San Fran-cisco she was basically on her own. Which was fun, except for the part about not having any money.

"I thought we had plenty of money."

"Well, it turns out we haven't been getting paid for the last three or four months. When I found that out I decided it was time to call Global Interconnect. Only it turns out you *can't* call Global Interconnect. There's no place to call, and nobody to answer the phone anyway."

"So they'd skipped town."

"The question is, who's 'they'? I did some detective work. I talked to people at the bank, the Better Business Bureau, the IRS, even the State Department. I penetrated bureaucracies, Will! You would have been proud of me. And it turns out that G.I., Inc., is about as shady as Madame Mud suspected. Nobody's ever heard of them. They were incorporated less than two years ago—shortly before we came here, actually. They never had an office, only a P.O. box that hasn't been paid for in months. And their bank account was closed over a month ago."

"I see. So we really don't have jobs anymore."

"Well, we don't have an *employer*, anyway. You can still be the consultant if you want, just don't expect to get paid for it. But listen, that's not all. In Kisaka, on the way back, I went to see Madame Mud. And we had a pretty good visit."

"I thought you said she was a bitch."

"She is, she's a quintessential bitch. But I decided I like that about her. Anyway, she'd been looking into G.I. too. And she found out that one of the directors of the Jucht Brothers board was the one who'd set up our contract with G.I., and nobody else had paid attention because it was such a minor project and there was so little money involved. But now some kind of accident had befallen this director and it was no longer possible to ask him any questions. So Madame Mud got other people in Brussels to look into it. They confirmed everything I'd learned about Global Interconnect, and also found out that there were only two people on their board of trustees, and one of them was the same Jucht Brothers director who had arranged the whole scam in the first place."

"I see. And that director turned out to be Uncle Pers."

"Right. Uncle Pers."

"And who was the other?"

"I didn't recognize the name, I can't remember. Something like Bruno or Igor somebody or other, one of those kinds of names."

"Boris? Boris Vestor?"

"Yes, I think that was it. It was. How'd you know?"

"I know Boris Vestor."

"You know him?"

"And so do you."

Jet lag, culture shock. Easy, feeble labels; ways of naming a shift in circumstances so sudden and wrenching it can't be assimilated or reconciled. "Culture shock," Kate could mutter to herself as she once again dragged her body up the rutted boulevard of the camp in the unlivable heat of the sun, thinking how only twenty-four hours ago she'd been weightless, hurtling through the sky in a long metal tube. She'd been anonymous in crowded streets and airline terminals, and now here were all these people streaming out to greet her and this straggling mob of children at her feet, mindlessly chanting her name. She'd slept in cities where the earth was beyond reach, buried under acres of steel and glass and synthetic rock, and now she walked on an eroding path between rows of houses whose soft mildewed brick was already crumbling back into the soil.

Impossible to reconcile, yet these are now common circumstances, the clichés of the global village. These jarring contrasts are the *norm*, and by now we ought to be used to them. We ought to have learned to move easily, unamazed, among fragments of separate worlds bound together by nothing: no common religion or integrating philosophy or Unified Field Theory, only theories of chaos, which make no predictions but can easily accommodate all the fragments. There are no surprises here, Tom said. So you go away to mourn your dead uncle and when you return there's the same uncle in his pajamas, sitting in the sun with old men who don't understand a word he says but who believe he came to them out of the sky in a tiny bamboo airplane. Everyone believes it: your former houseboy who waits on him and the children and farceurs who shadow him and the albino girl who skitters around him like an uneasy spirit. And even your friend the nurse, who spends the nights with him in her little mud hut on the edge of the camp.

"It's a bit of a shock, then, seeing me here, eh, Katy?" said Boris.

We were sitting in the nurse's yard, after dinner. We'd eaten inside her hut: Boris, Kate, Ndosi, the nurse, and myself crowded into a dark room that smelled of smoke and earth and mildewed thatch, breaking off chunks of *luku* with our hands and dipping them in a sauce of forest mushrooms and *pili-pili* and palm oil. We sipped a cloudy, effervescent palm wine and listened to Boris tell Kate the story of his staged drowning and the journey that brought him to Ngemba, where the people had accepted him and taken him into their hearts and filled his mind with a powerful history. And in the face of this openness and acceptance he found it impossible to live under the old rules of separation, in the house by the river where generations of white men had brooded and plotted in ignorance and isolation.

I felt an odd sense of dislocation as he spoke. As if I were back in Pers and Mavis' dining room, intoxicated by red wine and the old man's webs of irony and aphorism and the gravelly low-country inflections in his voice. As if here among the rough furniture and musty darkness we had again fallen under the spell of his house of artifacts and mirages above the glittering bay in San Francisco. But then we went to sit outside in the African twilight, and Kate laughed softly and told Pers no, it wasn't such a shock, after all, seeing him here, and the spell was broken.

"But after attending the funeral and so forth. Your old uncle Pers' funeral. Ha-ha! I hope it was a suitably somber occasion?"

"They didn't have a funeral."

"No funeral? Well, I suppose it doesn't matter. The funeral is only a formality. Ceremonial. And lacking a body, I suppose the ceremony must have seemed as hollow as his coffin. Ha!"

"Not hollow so much as false."

"Eh? What are you saying, Katy?"

"It seemed false to them, having a funeral for a man who wasn't dead."

"What do you mean by that? He tumbled off the boat, didn't he, straight into the bay? A sick old man, suffering a heart attack, a stroke, something like that, lost in the icy bay—that's not dead enough for them? Who said he wasn't dead?"

"Well, the coroner, for one. And the police, and the insurance people, of course. They all agreed there was reasonable doubt. And Mavis, especially Mavis. She had her doubts right from the start, she said, and eventually she became quite certain you weren't dead. I thought she was just in denial, at first."

"Katy, the woman's been in denial for years."

"I guess that's true, Uncle Pers. But it turns out denial was a reasonable place to be, wasn't it? And she convinced me too. Because actually there was quite a lot of evidence. So no, it's not a shock, exactly, though I didn't *expect* to find you here. Well, I did have kind of a premonition. Of course, nearly everyone here has been having them, I understand. Maybe even Will."

"What sort of 'evidence' are you referring to?" Boris asked stiffly.

"That you weren't dead. Everywhere we turned there was another clue. Do you want to hear some of them? Well, to begin with, there were people watching from the shore the evening you disappeared. And they said what they saw was a man lowering himself down the ladder over the side of a boat. Not 'tumbling off,' Uncle Pers! And somebody else claimed to have seen you later that night, on a bus, in town."

"That's not possible. I was in disguise, Katy."

"You were acting very strangely, apparently. You seemed disoriented. But the witness was old himself, and probably drunk, so no one paid much attention. But then when Aunt Mavis was going through your things she noticed that a pair of pajamas was missing. She got all worked up about that, though at the time I thought she was blowing it way out of proportion."

"The pajamas! Of course Mavis would notice that."

"But the detail that really nagged at her was the disappearance of the memoirs."

"Why, what did that prove?"

"It didn't *prove* anything. But it brought home to her a sense of permanent loss. She felt as if she really had nothing left of you, as if forty years of marriage had simply disappeared."

"Yes, well, Mavis always has lacked a reliable means of gauging the falseness of her own sentiment."

"We looked through your computer files. We couldn't find anything. Everything Will and I had worked on for you was gone."

Boris, now slumped in his chair, brightened momentarily. "Yes, I erased it all. Delete, delete, delete! There is something to be said for that damnable technology after all. I like deleting, at least. That horrendously efficient machine, with its diabolical memory, is vulnerable after all."

"But you kept a hard copy."

"A hard copy?"

"On paper. You printed it before you deleted it."

"Oh, yes, I see what you mean. Well, perhaps. I could have."

"That was the piece of evidence that really bothered Mavis. The fact that there was a hard copy somewhere."

"But why should she think that?"

"Because when we checked out the computer, naturally we looked at the printing history, and discovered that the day before you disappeared, all the files Will and I had created—the files containing your memoirs—had been printed."

"Damn. You mean to say the thing remembers everything it's ever printed? This is worse than I imagined. It's evil, literally, this idea of documenting every detail of existence! What use do human beings have for such a stockpile of data?"

"Well, this particular data was useful to Mavis. And now her suspicions were fully aroused. She thought, why would he print this, in secret, a few hours before he went sailing? So she undertook an investigation. She went to lawyers, private detectives, forensics people. She even went to a professional medium. To give you an opportunity to prove you really were dead, she said. But the medium could make no contact. This is what she said to Mavis: 'No one on the other side knows of this man.'"

"My God, Katy, we'll all end up characters in a ghastly farce before Mavis is through with us! How could you listen to her? A professional medium! As if the dead would respond to such pandering! As if the dead had as little self-respect as the living!"

"I think she was just making a point. I don't know that she really believes that stuff."

"Oh, she believes it. And she may be right, eh, how should I know? I only cling to the belief that the dead, being dead, must have acquired some of the wisdom and dignity so manifestly denied to the living!"

Boris fell back in his chair, wheezing. The nurse came around the corner of her hut. "It's not good for him to get so excited," she told us. "He's very tired. Tell him that I'll make him his tea, and then he must lie down."

Kate watched the nurse duck into her hut. "Is she your physician now?"

"I'm not sure 'physician' is the right word," Boris said. He looked at me. "She's a beautiful woman, eh? Men desire her. Young men, following desire blindly and stupidly. Over the precipice, across the desert, into the sea. And old men too, who no longer remember what they mean when they say the word 'desire.' Ha!"

There was a silence. Kate looked from Boris to me and back to Boris again. Finally she said: "Well, you must have some difficulty living together, without a common language."

"We communicate very well. Much better than Mavis and I used to. In any case, my man is generally available to interpret."

"Your man."

"Yes. Um, your man also, of course. Ndosi. I'd be lost without him, Katy. He's rather a brilliant linguist, have you noticed? Whereas I—I no longer have a head for languages, I'm afraid. Even English tires me now. Have we finished catching up on things? Because I think she's right: I ought to lie down."

"We haven't finished. I still want to know, why did you set this whole thing up?"

"Excuse me?"

"Why go to so much trouble to send us here? Why all the lies and secret arrangements?"

"I helped you get jobs, Katy. You needed jobs. An opportunity presented itself. That's it."

"No, it isn't," she said. Then she told him what we had learned about Global Interconnect. She said that it now was clear to us that we had never been employed by a legitimate company, that our whole situation in the Kivila Valley was an extravagant plot Pers himself had concocted. And she wanted to know what his motive had been.

Boris laughed softly. "My motive! Your aunt would accuse you of relying exclusively on the left side of your brain, Katy. It's true that I made some unorthodox arrangements on your behalf. But a motive? That's a reductionist sort of concept, eh? It's quite possible that the whole thing began in a spirit of play. A spirit of exploration. Possibly I was already mulling over the need for field research, and hoping that you could do some of it."

"But why the elaborate deception? Why not just send us over here to do whatever it was you wanted us to do?"

"Because that wouldn't have worked. Something like this you can't approach so overtly. You have to come at it from some other direction. That was one of Mavis' insights, do you remember? *You must go with an open mind, an empty mind. So you don't take hold of the wrong things.* She didn't fully understand what she was saying, of course. But the idea has merit. She often has good ideas, it's just that it's necessary to take them away from her before she goes to work on them, stripping them of all sense. What else was it she said? Something about, what was it . . . going on a journey for which you could never prepare. I saw at once that was exactly what you were ripe for: an open-ended adventure. A quest. Which is rarely so cut and dried as people imagine. Still, it was no good to just let you wander off to Mexico, according to your own inclination, you remember. You needed more structure than that. This situation was the best I could come up with on short notice. It was an improvisation. I didn't think it through very far. Such a complex undertaking is impossible to think through."

"I don't think I'd call this a quest," said Kate. "It's too contrived, for one thing."

"Certainly it's contrived! You can't expect a quest simply to happen of its own volition. We have to contrive these things just to get them going—but once they have momentum, you see how they take on a life of their own. A purpose of their own. You think you are coming for a job, or to get some information for my memoirs, or simply for a tropical interlude. And then you find out you are here for very different reasons, for something else entirely. Just as I worked so long on those memoirs, believing I was writing a particular story, until I realized that no, that was not the story I was after. So now, like you, I must improvise!"

"But you're still writing," I said. "You told people you're here to write a book."

"Yes, but in fact, lately I write very little. Not at all since I moved up here to my new quarters. I'm on to a different stage of *my* quest. If there's any writing to be done, someone else shall have to do it."

"That's something else I should tell you, I guess," Kate said. "Someone is."

Boris looked up sharply. "What do you mean? Who?"

"Mavis. Yes, don't look so alarmed. Why shouldn't she write something? She's perfectly literate. And when she realized your memoirs had truly vanished, she had another idea. Or rather, she and your agent had it together. They decided that in the absence of your memoirs, *she* should write her own. Telling much of the same story that had just been lost, only from a different perspective, of course. And using the vanished memoirs as a kind of allegory for her life with you, or something like that."

Boris glared at her, indignant. "This is absurd. Who would read Mavis' memoirs?"

"Apparently several publishing houses were interested. Just before I left, the agent was negotiating a contract, with a substantial advance, supposedly, and the likelihood of excerpts, or even a serial, appearing in some national magazine."

"What are you saying? An advance? How long has she been writing this thing?"

"Only since after you left. But she's made a lot of progress. She works quickly, and she's motivated. I guess she's structuring her book around quotes—paraphrases, maybe—from your journals, which she uses as a kind of counterpoint to her own reminiscences."

Boris snorted. "Paraphrases, is it! She can't know my memoirs so well as that, Katy. Not well enough to just regurgitate them, at least in any sort of coherent chronology."

"Well, she's not that concerned about chronology, I guess. She never was, remember? What was it she told Will and me? That sequence is the least important connection between things."

"Yes, that does sound like something she would say. She's quite adept at cooking up formulas for complete chaos and unintelligibility."

"Well, she told me that what she's after is a feminine perspective on the death throes of a very masculine enterprise: colonialism. With the disappearance of you and your journals woven into the story—not revealed as a plot twist at the end, she said, but embedded into every event, somehow. So there's this tragic sense running through it, a sense of intrigue and betrayal and the futility of ambition. The agent said this gives the story the drama and focus it always lacked. That it will make it more marketable. Those are their words, Uncle Pers! I'm just quoting."

"I see. Well, they can call it whatever they please, but what she'll write is nothing but trash. Pure speculation and mysticism. I assume you tried to dissuade her."

"No. I figured it was a way to salvage something of your stories. And I thought you were out of the picture. I thought it wouldn't matter to you anymore."

"Well, that's true. It doesn't matter to *me*. Old Pers Merlicht *is* out of the picture, dead, and the dead have no defense against the fictions and fantasies of the living. But do you really think people will be so taken with the prattlings of a deluded old woman? You wouldn't expect there'd be any general interest in something like this, but I suppose if she can play up some scandalous aspect, people might want to read it."

"You do still have a copy of your memoirs, don't you, Uncle Pers?"

"Eh? Boris, Katy. Not Pers."

"What are you planning on doing with them?"

"Ah, well. That's one of the things I haven't thought through all the way. The quest evolves. The improvisations continue, Katy!"

"You could just publish them. If you're concerned about Mavis, that might take some wind out of her sails."

"Oh, no. I won't let her bluff me. Which may well be her strategy—to rush me into publication. She's a clever woman, and clearly my agent—that double-dealing bastard!—has got her stirred up. He may be trying to instigate a public argument, a literary sideshow. That's how they market these trash fictions, you know. So now, if I were to publish, it would only seem to prove that something titillating and scandalous is going on. Which of course would just give rise to nastier speculation. That fool of an agent would probably spur her on to a sequel! My God, she'll probably appear on talk shows! Another victim of the colonial patriarchy is how she'll come out of it. It's ridiculous, a joke. You see how it is—characters in a farce, if we permit ourselves to be drawn into this. Still, she oughtn't be allowed to print whatever she pleases. If you can't dissuade her, Katy, then you must at least denounce her. Expose her memories as false, her speculations as absurd!"

"Oh. You want me to go on the talk shows too?"

"No. I see your point. It would only fuel the hysteria. It would only sell more copies, of course. Never mind. The thing to remember is this: Mavis' book means nothing to me, Boris. None of this does: the old man's scribblings, whether he climbed off his boat or fell into the water, the printing history on that computer he was fool enough to buy. It's all less than meaningless to Boris Vestor."

The nurse came around the hut again and took him by the arm.

"This is too much excitement," she said. "Your uncle is old, he needs to rest. Visiting is over." And in a few seconds she had us out of our chairs and was shooing us all from the yard, as if she were scattering chickens.

In the camp the children were playing one of their inexplicable games, and Kate and I stopped on the road above them to watch. The albino girl stood before the others with a stick, hitting something—it looked like a wad of rags and leaves—that hung from a tree branch beside her. Suddenly she flung the stick at the other children, and with a scream took off running. The children rose up shouting and pursued her through the paths of the camp. Shrieking and laughing, the albino led them weaving among the company houses and the shantytown huts and the row of waysays in the back, and then broke out sprinting down the rutted surface of the main boulevard. Several adults yelled at them, and the albino ducked into the side door of the open-air chapel. The children milled around, then disappeared beyond the far side of the chapel. Kate and I, still unnoticed, drew near and looked inside.

The albino knelt by the altar with her eyes closed and her hands pressed together. Her face was raw and sweaty, and she panted and coughed as if on the verge of hyperventilating again. Behind her, the other children filed in the main door and knelt by the benches that served as pews. The albino opened her eyes and stood. She looked nauseated. When she saw Kate and me watching she shrieked and rushed outside.

"All right, we'll leave," said Kate. "But first tell us what game you're playing."

"We're playing Nyata," a girl answered.

Nyata is a little insect, a gnat. "I don't understand. What are you doing? Who's the nyata?"

"We'll show you, Mama Kate."

The children took us back up the boulevard and pointed to the wad of rags.

"Why do you call it the nyata?"

The children shrugged. "We don't know. We call it that—because that's what you called it, madame. You and Monsieur Will and Monsieur Tom."

3 2

GOD'S FAULT

That year the heat and humidity persisted up to the very end of the rainy season, but the rains themselves ended early. The river began to drop, and the water cleared. Thunderheads still built up over the savannas in the afternoons, but only scattered rain fell in the Kivila Valley, not enough to cool the humid air. Those nights were too hot and still for sleep, and sometimes, while thunder rumbled faintly and the sky pulsed with distant lightning, Kate and I came out of our stuffy house to sit on the porch. As long as we weren't trying to sleep the oppressive heat was not so bad; in fact, it was energizing, in a way, though we seemed to be able to do little with the energy besides sit on the porch and watch the electric sky.

My muscles quivered, nerves pulsed down the backs of my legs, images pulsed through my head—erratic bursts, random as heat lightning. Or maybe not random, maybe just one more pattern that was indecipherable to me. Maybe my muscles and nerves understood something my conscious mind could not yet grasp: that the darkness had its own drama, that powerful events were unfolding deep in the recesses of the night.

Or maybe my level of anticipation was once again wildly out of proportion to anything that was likely to happen. Yet over the radio we'd heard news of protests and sabotage in the capital, of genocide and rebellion in the eastern provinces. And the unrest now was spreading into the hinterlands. Word came from the smuggler that he would pick up one last load of contraband, then no more. Every day now small bands of soldiers passed by on the river road, and once I saw them escorting a prisoner—a shirtless, bruised-looking man, hands bound behind his back, eyes staring straight ahead up the already dusty road.

You had better arrange your affairs. It will become difficult to get out. Perhaps Madame Mud had been right, though not because soldiers were rampaging or the airport was closed or rebel armies were at last rising out of the jungles. For me and now even for Kate, it was becoming difficult just to get off the front porch.

It must have done me some good, Kate said, taking the Land Rover up to the Place Without a Name. When she'd left for the States I'd been anxious and tense, and now I was maybe the least anxious person around. I seemed connected in some way I hadn't been before, she said; tapping into some richer vein, yet still somehow uncontaminated by the tide of suspicion and fear rising slowly all around us.

Uncontaminated, maybe, because there was still no real substance to that tide. Those pulsing and stifling nights, fuller than ever of plots and rumors and imagined evil, were still mainly empty of actual events. Beside the shed a shower of sparks went up into the sky. Placide's small silhouette stood out for a moment against the glow of his fire, then dissolved again into the shadows of his cardboard. It was so timeless, so inevitable and repetitive, and so beautiful in its repetition. You could not count the nights that had been exactly like this, and the identical nights to come. A dark tableau composed of constant thunder, pulsing sky, drumbeats, nightwatchman, mosquitos, river. And Kate and I were a part of it too: creatures of the front porch, highly evolved, fully adapted.

Her voice came out of the darkness beside me: "How familiar are you with the inside of her house?"

"Whose house?"

"Well, the nurse's, of course."

Why 'of course'? We hadn't mentioned the nurse all evening. Kate was just self-absorbed, distracted, thinking out loud. Shifting the puzzle pieces around in her mind: Uncle Pers and his memoirs, Boris Vestor, the nurse, Ndosi. The Mission Road, the bamboo airplane. But why would she think that I knew anything about the inside of the nurse's house? Had she heard a rumor of infidelity; was she perhaps brooding over her uncle's words? *Men desire her. Young men, following desire over the precipice . . .*

But in fact I *hadn't* gone over the precipice, though it was not virtue that had saved me but only circumstance, the unexpected presence of Boris in my house in the middle of the night. Still, as infidelities go, my affair with the nurse was fairly benign. And it wasn't as if I now dreamed of her in Kate's place beneath the mosquito netting, or that the source of my agitation was some burning image in my mind of her coming up from the river wrapped in a wet pagne, pausing in the dusky shadows at my gate. In fact, it seemed that my infatuation had run its course. The nurse's mystery and sexual allure had been rooted in her exoticism—which is to say in my ignorance of her ways. And now, watching the development of her relationship with Boris, I was learning those ways. I was seeing her as a *real* nurse, a person whose business was with the secretions and bedsores and stiffening muscles and rebellious organs of an old man's failing body. There was nobility in the sordid drudgery of her profession, and I admired her more than ever. But if in certain moments she still gave off that mysterious scent I was barely able to detect it, smothered as it was by the smells of cooking fires and medicinal teas, palm oil and luku and sweat from the fields, sickness and old age. And although there had been no confirmation of my intuitive revelation that she had AIDS, I now could see her only in that context: stricken and doomed, like her patient. She never complained of being sick. But once or twice visiting Boris, I heard her behind her hut, coughing and spitting. Her body seemed always to grow thinner, and in certain lighting her face could turn suddenly macabre, the same death mask I'd noticed the night she danced with Boris.

"I've been inside her house a couple of times," I said to Kate. "I'm not *intimately* familiar with it, if that's what you mean."

"I *know* that. Wait a second, what do *you* mean, 'intimately'?"

The conversation was making me crazy, with its unarticulated subtexts and undercurrents. Maybe if we weren't talking in the dark, invisible to each other, our meaning might be more explicit. I took a deep breath.

"*Not* intimately is what I said, Kate. Because we could have been intimate, in theory. She's very attractive. She gives off a certain vibe, or whatever. So I am attracted, on one level. Or I have been."

Kate was silent. I had no idea how she was taking this. Finally she said: "Fine, Will. Men desire her. So why should you be any different? The only thing that saves the rest of them is, they're all afraid of her. Because of the witch thing, you know. But maybe that's not a problem for you."

"Oh, don't worry, I'm afraid of her too. For one thing, I'm afraid she has AIDS."

Kate sighed. "I'm afraid of that too. She's sick so much, though she doesn't talk about it. I know she's had a lot of lovers. I asked her if she's been tested for HIV, and she said no, but it doesn't matter, because there's nothing to be done anyway. And she's not endangering anyone else, because she's finished with sex. She's focused on other things now, she said."

"What do you mean, she's finished with sex?"

"Well, she's celibate."

"The nurse is celibate? Since when?"

"Oh, for the last couple of years, I guess. Anyway, that's not the point. What I was wondering is, if you know your way around her house at all. If you know where things are kept inside her house."

"What things? She doesn't have any things."

"But Uncle Pers does. He has a whole suitcase full of things."

Boris had continued to refuse to talk about his suitcase, or admit what seemed obvious: that it contained his memoirs, and probably his old journals as well. Kate kept badgering him about the suitcase and the memoirs, and finally Boris told her it was getting tiresome, and hadn't we moved beyond those dusty old artifacts? Kate said *she* hadn't, and Boris said he and his biographer certainly had.

"Your biographer, meaning Ndosi? Ndosi, who worked for us until you showed up?"

"Yes, I stole him from you, didn't I, Katy? Which wasn't difficult to do, since you'd been paying him such a miserly salary. And wasting his talents in the bargain. What's a fellow like him doing washing somebody's clothes and dishes? A man with such extraordinary ability to synthesize information, to master language! Weren't you aware of his tremendous literary aptitude?"

"But he's never even read a book," I said.

"Exactly my point," Boris answered. "His genius is innate, pure and uncorrupted."

"Every time I've seen him lately, he's been scribbling something in his notebook," Kate said. "One of those cahiers like schoolchildren carry."

"Yes, we're doing research. We conduct interviews, and he translates, records, interprets. We've done dozens of interviews now, Katy. Yesterday we even interviewed those two old priests. You should have seen the expressions on their faces when they saw us coming up to their porch. Because *they* remember me, of course."

"What do you mean? Did you walk to the mission?"

"Of course not. I took a boat with my biographer. A fellow paddled us up in his little canoe. One of Ndosi's relatives, I think. Anyway, there we were at the mission. We spoke briefly with the nuns at first, but they are impossible to interview. Fierce women, actually, and they don't reveal much. Whereas those priests love to hear themselves talk. They went on and on, interrupting and contradicting each other, and in the end my biographer and I returned with a portion of a coherent story. I'm not saying it was a pleasant interview. One can't expect pleasantries from a pair of old fanatics who've spent three or four decades alone in the jungle, stewing in their own self-righteousness. One can expect hypocrisies and incessant moralizing. One can expect the affectations of privilege and aristocracy."

"Well, aristocracy, I don't know. They don't live so extravagantly. I mean, sure, if you compare them to people in mud huts—"

"I don't compare them to anyone! I merely consider their treatment of my biographer, whom they tried to dismiss as if he were one of their chattel servants. But I insisted that he stay, to take notes. How can the boy take notes, they grumble at me, when we are speaking Flemish, and naturally he can't understand a word of Flemish? The hell with Flemish, I tell them, the man understands *language*. So I'm going to speak English, and you can use whatever damned language you like. Which shuts them up for a minute, though soon enough they are squabbling with each other and with me, out of habit rather than any conviction, I think. They bring me a glass of beer, and they begin to talk. About the Mission Road and other things. Their recollections are enlightening at first, but as we approach the end of the story, they become less informative, more dogmatic. The formula is simple enough with them: their zealotry increases in proportion to their ignorance of the facts. They argue in the style of medieval theologians: all hypothesis and theory; they have no use for the physical evidence! And they are *bitter*, Katy. And afraid— they know their luck might not hold a second time, if people get in the mood again for massacring priests. So soon enough the old animosities overwhelm these feeble shows of civility, and they forget they still owe the Road Builder a debt of gratitude. The interview deteriorates, the beer goes flat. They begin to abuse, and then to preach. It's a reflex with them: when they don't know the facts, they preach! But at my age, I don't have to listen! Thank you for the beer, fathers, now we are leaving. I return to the riverbank and the little canoe. That boat is unsafe, they call out to me. We will give you a ride in our car. And it is my great pleasure to refuse."

Kate visited her uncle daily in the camp, and when she came home she fretted about his behavior and health and living situation and his attitude toward his memoirs. But she didn't know what to do about any of this. She continued to go to farms and villages and attend various support-group meetings, and soon after she returned from the States she took the Land Rover on another smuggling run. But her enthusiasm was diminished, and no one could claim that she animated any of these activities. People were too nervous for animation, and her presence only increased the tension. They didn't know what to make of us anymore, she said. There was a story she kept hearing about Monsieur Will: how I'd exchanged threats or insults with a group of soldiers passing on the river road, and then stood up on the porch and reached out and pointed a pistol at them. The soldiers, four men cradling automatic rifles, had stared back at me, then backed away and continued down the road.

People didn't tell this story in an admiring way, Kate said. I wasn't a hero opposing the tyranny of soldiers, but just another aspect of the violence they were importing to the valley.

I couldn't think where such a story had come from. Maybe someone had seen me from a distance, standing on the porch and pointing at something. But the truth was, my life was more mundane than they could imagine. I still went down to my office now and then, though I could think of little to do once I got there. Sometimes the chef de poste would wander in and talk about how he should deal with the commissaire, who was said to be more and more displeased with developments in Ngemba and who was likely to show up at any time to express his displeasure. Perhaps he would have me write another report. And when the time came for the Dedication Ceremony for the Modernization Project and the Place de la Révolution, I, as a representative of Jucht Brothers—of all Mputu, for that matter—would be asked to say a few words, and perhaps help escort the commissaire on a tour of the renovated mill, and assure him of the Company's continued cooperation and support.

I refrained from pointing out that in fact there was no renovated mill. And what did he expect me to say in commemoration of the Modernization Project, which had cut its final swaths of destruction without anyone bothering to solicit the consultant's opinion? None of the democratization committees had met for weeks. Oil processing and smuggling each blundered along on their separate tracks, independent of any input from me, other than my continued subsidy of the workers' salaries, which now would have to be dropped, since the income that supported it had vanished.

My noble bureaucracy was a chimera, then, devoid of purpose, mandate, or any link to a larger organization. And the noble bureaucrat, isolated and marginalized, was an oxymoron and a non sequitur. The lone bureaucrat. What sort of creature could that be? Hardly a creature at all, but more like a sloughed-off cell. More like the lone ant: removed from the colony, an amputated and now useless component of the larger organism, performing meaningless labors that are little more than reflexive twitching.

So while the noble bureaucracy foundered in the swamp of its own inutility, I occupied myself gardening, reading, and helping Sticky Tree build our chicken shed. Perhaps that was the object of my quest: a chicken shed. From my seat on the porch I could see it in the darkness of the yard, or thought I could: a shadow among shadows beneath the papaya trees on the far side of the cook shed. The chicken shed was a solid accomplishment I could point to—an exceptionally sturdy, well-made, and useful structure—and Kate and I were looking forward to putting chickens in it. A steady supply of fresh eggs would improve our diet, and the chickens themselves would be a positive influence in a number of ways: by day pecking about in the yard, recycling garbage, controlling insects, providing a much-needed sense of domesticity, purposefulness, and calm productivity. And by night perhaps they'd have a sedating effect on the place—locked in their secure refuge, soft clucks and coos fading into a sleep undisturbed by superstition or radio news or village rumors or the paranoid prowling of the nightwatchman.

"Will." Kate's hand reached out and found my arm in the darkness. "Do you think if I staged a diversion you could get inside the nurse's house and find the suitcase? In the dark, you know, if I got them all away from the house?"

"Oh, boy. No. That's a really bad idea, Kate."

"Never mind, then." She stroked my arm softly. "It's just that the suitcase is making me crazy, you know? If his memoirs are in there—and they must be—I want to get my hands on them. I don't trust Uncle Pers. Who knows what he's thinking, hanging around with deranged old men and making Ndosi follow him around scribbling down everything they say. He makes me nervous, the way he'll hardly talk about the memoirs or even admit he still has them."

"Well, he likes his little intrigues. But I'm not going up there, Kate. I couldn't steal them anyway. I can't even see in the dark. You'd need a real cat burglar for that job."

"A cat burglar," she murmured, sliding her hand over mine.

"But I doubt you could find anyone around here willing to sneak into *that* house. They've all got too many weird ideas about the nurse." The mysterious, solitary, changeable nurse. The aromatic, erotic nurse. The celibate nurse. That was a different way of thinking about her, definitely. It seemed counterintuitive, but really it made sense. All that sexual power restrained, or harnessed for some other purpose. What purpose, then? What was she doing with Boris? Certainly the idea of celibacy between them was easier on the imagination than the idea of sex. The idea that death rather than sex was the force that had brought them together.

Down by the cook shed Placide rose again from his cardboard and took a few steps toward the gate. Kate called softly to him, and a moment later he appeared at the base of the porch steps.

"How are things tonight, Placide?"

"Bien, madame," he answered unconvincingly.

"Wait a second, Kate," I said. "You aren't thinking—"

"Hush, Will. So everything's peaceful, Placide? The camp's peaceful?"

"Peaceful, yes," said Placide. "But the nights have become dangerous."

"What do you mean? It seems quiet to me."

He shook his head. "The world is changing, madame."

That was true, of course, but it struck me as a particularly odd thing for Placide to say. Everywhere the world was changing, *except* for here; hadn't I just been thinking that the nighttime world of Placide was the most constant thing that I knew?

"The world is turning over on itself," he explained.

"You mean, spinning around? It's always done that, Placide."

"We're going back to an earlier time. We go around, but we're not the same." His high-pitched voice was flat and expressionless, and he looked straight ahead and spoke as if he were in the schoolroom, called upon to deliver some recitation of incontestable fact. "We watch the sky, we watch the earth move. We watch the falling river. The soldiers are out on the road again, and the white people are coming back."

Kate let out an exasperated sigh. "Right, the Road Builder came back. But look, Placide, that's getting to be old news. Listen, I need to go up to the camp for something. And I want you to come with me."

"Oui, the Road Builder. And you too have come back to us, madame."

"That's old news too. And I always expected to come back. Anyway, I have a job for you. You can earn some extra money."

"White people have returned to Kilala Mission, coming out of the old killing rooms."

"Well, but that's not exactly the same thing, is it? That's just a ghost that people are talking about, right? The ghost of a dead frère, supposedly."

Placide hesitated. He began to speak and then broke off, listening. Suddenly he was absolutely still. Perhaps he'd heard some faint sound that didn't quite fit into the night. I'd heard nothing unusual myself. But now Placide had vanished, and Kate and I were again alone on the porch. I started to say something, but her hand slipped out of mine and gripped my leg.

"Shh!"

There was a little scuffling sound beyond Placide's fire, over by the gate. A dog, maybe, I would have thought, only it was followed immediately by a sharp thud and a brief strangled cry. I was off the porch in an instant, heading toward the fence. But I could see nothing in the dark yard, and I slowed, weaving blindly. Eventually I stumbled up against the fence. My hands searched along the rail for the gate. Fast ragged breathing came from the blackness on the other side, but no voices.

Kate came out of the house with a flashlight. We went out the gate together, and her light shone on Placide, straddling a man on the ground. A boy, actually, making soft whimpering and gagging noises. He was larger than Placide, but his arms were pinned beneath the nightwatchman's wiry legs.

Placide gripped the boy's neck with one hand, and held an upraised machete in the other.

"Placide! Let him up."

Slowly Placide stood and backed away from the boy, keeping the machete raised. The boy sat up and put a hand to his neck.

"Who are you?" I said. "What are you doing here?"

"An intruder, monsieur!" Placide said grimly. "A thief, sneaking through the gate."

"I'm doing nothing!" the boy whined. "Just walking down the path and this man attacks me."

Placide suddenly leaned over and snatched something off the ground. Triumphantly he held up a tattered envelope. "He was carrying *this,* monsieur."

The boy looked at the ground. "I was trying to deliver a letter," he said. "That's all. And this man comes out of the night, wanting to kill me."

"Shall I turn him over to the chef de poste now, monsieur?"

I took the envelope from Placide and looked at it under the light. It was from Tom.

"The chef de poste requires that all intruders be brought before him."

"The chef de poste is asleep, Placide. Don't bother him."

"Are you hurt?" said Kate. The boy shook his head. "Next time," she said, "call out a greeting before you try to come in the gate. Our sentinel is vigilant."

"What shall I do with the intruder?" said Placide in a particularly flat voice.

"He was only delivering a letter, Placide. He's done nothing wrong. Let him go."

Dear Kate and Will,

I wish I still had my old road map. I know—I cursed it, ridiculed it, traded it for a handful of peanuts and thought I'd cut a pretty good deal, because after all it was a totally useless map. For purposes of navigation, anyway. But navigation isn't really part of the picture anymore. To navigate you need to move, and we in the commander's truck have definitely stopped moving. We've come to a final dead stop here on the southern fringes of the equatorial forests, where, because that seems to be the only choice, we are founding a new settlement. Kaka Nzambi. Christened by the commander himself, in his final act of leadership.

That's why I need my old map. I want to check out this theory I've been formulating, and see if Kaka Nzambi is on the map. Okay, I guess it's more superstition than actual theory. But I was thinking that maybe there was more to that map than clutters of misnamed villages and tangles of road nobody's ever seen. That maybe those German cartographers were aiming for something greater than cartographic accuracy, something along the lines of the First Tourist Memorial at Kivila Falls, only even more ambitious. Cartographic prophecy.

Close your eyes. Picture some inhuman corporate/industrial place in Bonn or Hamburg. Anonymous technoids punching a time clock, filling coffee cups, shutting themselves into a windowless room full of computers and scanners and satellite photos. And when the door closes, a transformation— they're a kind of mystical cabal, it turns out, they believe in their souls that the world is flat, that Africa is terra incognita to the white man, and that the way to understand it is through prophecy and dreams. They invoke occult powers, intone the ancient spells, and gaze into their stereoscopes, transfixed by futuristic visions. Revelations hit them like seizures. They see the roads shift, the jungles fall, the borders dissolve. They see the migration and annihilation of villages, the shantytowns rising, deserts expanding, lines of fire moving into the rain forest. The new jungle overgrowing the old roads, and the new roads cutting through the old jungle. They see a refugee village rising in the wilderness. And they sit before their monitors in a trance, converting these visions into digital data.

I don't know where I got such a sweet lunatic idea. Okay, I suppose it's just as well I don't have my old map. It couldn't stand up to these expectations either. But it does feel like the fulfillment of a prophecy, to be here in Kaka Nzambi.

I can't believe we drove a truck down this road. Even the commander would've turned back, once he saw how bad it was, but there was no turnaround. Finally we hit a pothole so deep, and we were riding so low and heavy, that we just submerged, with no spring to carry us through. There was an ugly sound, and the truck lurched over on its side. When we got it jacked up we saw that an axle had broken, and the drive shaft was going off at a cockeyed angle. "Kaka Nzambi." The commandant shrugged. The Hand of God. You know how they say that. A complete abdication of human responsibility. It's not our doing, it's God's will. Or, put another way, God's fault. Anyway, the name stuck.

Some days I walk to this settlement up the road. See, this is a wilderness, but not like your wilderness out in Montana or wherever, where they don't build roads or let people live. People live here without making it any less wild. This place has a few shacks, a store with nothing to buy, a restaurant with nothing to eat. I ate there anyway, and the restaurant girl hung around and smiled at me.

Do you like her? the old men asked when I paid for my meal.

Sure, I like her. She's—very nice.

Nice? She's beautiful, monsieur! Of course you like her. You want her.

Well, in a way, sure, but—

Take her then, man! Give us some money, and take her into that hut.

Oh, no. I couldn't do that.

They laughed. Of course not, monsieur. A man like you must marry her instead.

Ha-ha, too bad my circumstances wouldn't permit marriage right now.

Who cares about circumstances, monsieur? Look at hers. Just take her out of this place. Un petit cadeau pour nous, and you bring her home to Mputu.

Well, I'm not actually going to Mputu right now. And anyway, I don't think she'd be happy there. A remark which sent their laughter over the edge into bitter hysteria, and ended our hollow repartee. Yes, her happiness is here in a scum-pit restaurant on the outskirts of Kaka Nzambi: hoeing manioc by day, truck-stop whoring by night, popping a baby every year or so and turning into a crone by the age of thirty, if AIDS or malaria or childbirth or just exhaustion doesn't kill her first.

God's fault. What a place for an agoraphobic tourist to end up, the most remote, disconnected place in the world. What was I thinking, trying to travel overland across this country? Probably nobody's done that since the slaving days. Who would try it without a whip at his back? Though there may have been a time, between the distant Age of Exploration and the com-

ing *Age of Tourism,* after the roads were built and before they started disappearing again, when an overland trip across this continent seemed like a more reasonable undertaking. What's happening now is we're completing the circle. The roads return to the jungle, people return to the tribe, and the cartographers return to the map of Pliny the Elder: draw a couple of gargoyles in the blank center of Africa and slap on a footnote: "Your guess is as good as ours what the fuck is out there, Jack."

But the First Tourist isn't guessing now. I <u>know</u>. What's out here is Kaka Nzambi. Though maybe even here there's still some room for heroism and myth, myth drained of all glory. The First Tourist: hero of mud on a mythic scale, ruts and potholes, banal discomfort, wretched waysays, breakdowns, ineptitude, stupidity, futility, and resignation. All on a mythic scale.

Yet an incredible creative force is also at work here. And the flip side of resignation and futility is stoicism, endurance. Kaka Nzambi really is a kind of miracle: a refugee civilization taking shape out of the jungle, out of the wreckage of the commander's dead truck.

There isn't much left of the truck now. They built a little forge, and if they don't have a use for something metal, they melt it down and make something else out of it. The truck's mostly been recycled, reincarnated as various implements of survival: houses, shoes, cooking pots, spears, monkey snares . . . The commander snarled and raved but couldn't stop it from happening. Now he sleeps in what's left of the cab, alone and irrelevant, and Tsimba shacks up with Road Warrior, that big evil brute of a boy chauffeur.

Maybe you're thinking this was an opportunity for me. That Rube Goldberg shit I liked to build back in Malembe—here was a situation where people could really use it! But actually I felt a little irrelevant myself, and like the commander I was humbled. At one time I'd written my companions off as whores and farceurs, but now I saw that those roles too were improvisations, survival adaptations. As for me, I was less adaptable. I lacked patience, that finely tuned fatalism. I was freaked by the hopelessness of the situation. Not that anyone was optimistic—they were just better at dealing with a hopeless situation.

I tried to be useful. I built a fuel-efficient clay oven, which took twice as long to heat up as the oven they made out of the muffler and tailpipe. There's plenty of firewood, so I couldn't get anybody to see the point of fuel efficiency.

Also I tried to start an aquaculture project, an idea that had entertainment value but never made it to the shovel-toting stage. Obviously nobody with a 20-year supply of goddamned stinking macayabu needs to break a sweat building a fishpond.

I like macayabu, actually, but when I looked at all those crates and thought about how many meals of stinky fish a guy sitting on a dead moto in Kaka Nzambi could end up eating, I got a very bad feeling. I remembered how Dr. Livingstone's servants made a kind of macayabu out of him, when he finally wasted away after wandering around in circles for years up on the Zambezi. They pickled and salted him and packed him out for a proper Christian burial. They loved their white man, and also they were covering their asses, because they knew there'd be hell to pay if they showed up back on the coast without him.

Well, I knew nobody was going to bother making a macayabu pickle out of me. Nobody had to answer to anybody about what happened to me. It was starting to look like my agoraphobia, which I'd taken for a neurotic syndrome, had in fact been an instinct of self-preservation. An instinct I'd defied, and now all these grim-faced motherfucking chickens were coming home to roost.

So I scuffled around Kaka Nzambi, wondering if in the final analysis it meant anything at all to be the First Tourist. Well, maybe. I had nothing productive to do, yet I wasn't at all like the commander, a useless being now scorned and cast aside. I still had stature and a certain power. Why? Because the First Tourist, by default, is also something much more significant: the First Advertiser.

In Kaka Nzambi I'm the poster boy for: shoes, clothes, stereos, cell phones, airplane rides, cigarettes, booze, software, hardware, you name it. I'm connected to Mputu, so all those things are connected to me, and when people look at me it's not a bereft confused white boy they see, it's all this shit. Shit they don't have, obviously. So that's my purpose: to remind people how poor they are, and instill in them the rabid insatiable desires of consumerism.

That's exactly the role I set out to reject at my piñata party, you'll recall. A crude attempt, I admit. What I regret, though, is that pious little morality speech I gave, not the actual smashing of the radio, which really wasn't a

*statement about them or their needs and desires but about _me_, me fed up
with being an unconscious advertisement, a blazing neon logo for Mputu
and all the garbage it disgorges on the world.*

*I know—you're thinking I'm overreacting again. You're thinking: how
can _you_ advertise anything, Tom? You're wearing rags, you smashed your
fucking radio and your boots are rotting off your feet. But even in squalor I
send out a powerful marketing statement. Look at my effect on Tsimba,
who's made it clear that it's not her ambition to pioneer a new rathole village
at Kaka Nzambi. She met me in the forest on the outskirts of the settlement
to tell me this. Kaka Nzambi! She spat on the ground. Then she licked her
lips and smiled at me.*

I hate this place, Tom-Tom. I want to go to Mputu.

*She gets up real close to me and puts her hand on my leg, a very desta-
bilizing physical presence and a total invasion of my personal space which no
woman has occupied for some time, you understand. She makes this sound in
her throat. I want to wear jewelry and perfume and shoes with a pointed heel
about this long. I want you to drive me around in a car on paved roads, Tom-
Tom, and we'll play American music, Madonna, Spice Girl, real loud on
the stereo and you'll drive very fast and . . .*

Oh. What about the boy chauffeur? I thought—

*Boy chauffeur is shit, breathes Tsimba, her lips right up in my face and
her hand finishing its run up my leg.*

*Right. Boy chauffeur is shit. Boy chauffeur advertises Kaka Nzambi,
while Tom-Tom, in spite of his current shitlike appearance, advertises
Mputu. And yes, in some ways I would be willing to strike a deal with
Tsimba and exhaust my depleted stores of virtue on her delectable ass. But
I'm very sick of being the First Advertiser, and of course I know that the
glossy picture of Tsimba fondling me in a convertible is a lie. So I turned
away from her and went back to Kaka Nzambi. I put my clothes in my bag,
slung it on my back, and pushed my bike on down the road, all the time feeling the heat of Tsimba's hand at the top of my thigh. At the restaurant the
girl watched me from the doorway. I went in and talked to the old people, and
they told the girl what to do. She wrapped up a few things and put the bundle
on her head. We shook hands all around and left the folks admiring their
new motorcycle and set off down the road, heading west.*

That's about all my news. Her name's Sukadi. We've been together two weeks now, doing what humans evolved to do—walk in the forest, eat, sleep, screw, and talk, a little. We don't share much language. But it's obvious little Sukadi's been around the block a few times. "Man that was good, Sukadi," I whisper as we lie beneath the thorn trees. "Sure, Tom-Tom." She shrugs. These gals all call me Tom-Tom, I don't know why. Better than Weewee, I guess. "I fucking beaucoup chauffeur before you come around, Tom-Tom. Beaucoup soldat." Well, Tom-Tom knows what that means, in Central Africa in this time of the world.

We're emerging from the forest now, into the savanna. Maybe eventually we'll come to a refuge of some kind. A mission might take us in. We might head for the Kivila Valley, settle down for a while, do a little farming, a little fish culture. Sukadi would put some life into the Mamas' Support Group, for sure.

Of course, I know the First Advertiser can't abdicate so easily. What Sukadi wants is what Tsimba wanted, though she might not have as many of the details worked out. Or she's just not as crass about it. But I think she assumes that going to Mputu is part of the deal. I could just take her back to Thanesboro, settle down, get a job in real estate or software hell, drive around in the convertible with her *. . . she'd put some life into the fucking Thanesboro Junior League too, I guess.*

I haven't forgotten the loan, Kate. Another reason to swing by Ngemba on our way to Thanesboro. I'd send you the cash, but obviously you can't just send cash around here. For that matter, how do you even send a goddamn letter?

—Tom

Kate read the letter first. She went to bed while I was reading it, but she was still awake when I crawled beneath the mosquito netting an hour later.

"Can you picture him kicking back against a truck tire writing *that* letter?" I said.

"There aren't any more truck tires," she said dryly. "They've all been turned into sandals."

"I wish I hadn't told Placide to let that kid go. I'd like to ask him a couple of questions. I'd like to get a look at him in a good light."

There had been something familiar about the tone of the boy's voice: insolent and apathetic at once, even when he was overpowered and looking up at Placide's machete blade glistening in the flashlight beam. There was a connection somewhere I had missed. An opportunity missed. Placide was right, I should have interrogated him. Though of course I had no stomach for interrogation, and even with the intruder pinned beneath him I still didn't entirely believe Placide, always interpreting the night through a filter of superstition and hallucination. *The nights have become dangerous.* What had he meant by that? What primal sense or clue or quirk of reasoning had compelled him to say that? How had he known that danger was so close at hand— a dark figure on the hill above the house, waiting and watching, creeping down to the gate when he thought we were asleep? And then the dark figure had turned out to be a scrawny kid carrying nothing but a letter from Tom. Placide may have been disappointed—what, this whimpering creature lying flaccid beneath his machete, *this* was the terror of the night made manifest? But he had not been entirely surprised. He'd known *something.* Perhaps I should be interrogating Placide, who could smell a threat in the night, who knew the world was changing and the ghosts of the whites were returning. The ghost of a young frère, returning to Kilala Mission. *Rising out of the old killing rooms.* But everyone knew that; even the children were obsessed with these ghosts, in their innocent games acting out the ignorance and prejudices of their parents. Chasing the albino girl, whiter than any of us and something of a ghost herself, away from the nyata she'd been beating on, pursuing her through the camp until she found a secure refuge huddling in the chapel— the mission, they called it in their game, though they hadn't said which mission. And why did they call the game Nyata? *Because that's what you call it, madame. That's what Monsieur Tom called it.* That is, that's what they heard him call it, or misheard him, when he beat on one himself.

Nyata, a small gnat—or a small word hidden in a larger word. A childish game, full of absurdities and the shadows of adult superstitions but containing as well pieces of fact and knowledge, unnoticed or invisible in the real world, yet seen with sudden clarity in the context of the game. A dream was like that too, or could be, working in the mind of a powerful dreamer. A dreamer like Kate, asleep now beside me, her mind already untethered, sorting through the jumbled information of the day and the night. And maybe producing, out of nonsense and random juxtapositions, a single image that seemed to be true. Like that image in the dream she'd had on the plane: Tom weaving through rows of manioc, skin gleaming with sweat or water, coming out among the ruins of brick buildings where a great stone fireplace blazed like the wildfires of the mushipu or the furnaces of the oil mill.

At dawn I was drinking coffee and rereading Tom's letter when Placide knocked on the door and said that the prisoner was asking for a glass of water. I got the water and followed Placide down to the chicken shed. He untwisted a stiff wire on the latch and opened the door. The boy was sitting on the dirt floor, blinking in the sudden light but otherwise looking at us without expression. Placide handed him the glass of water.

"I thought I told you to let him go, Placide."

"Oui, Monsieur. But you didn't mean let him go in the night. You meant let him go in the day, when we can watch him."

Placide said something to the boy, and he came out of the shed. I studied him while he looked past me toward the river.

"That's not the first letter you've brought to us."

The boy just kept looking at the river. He said nothing.

"Aren't your feet sore this time? It's a long way to walk—all the way from Kilala Mission. Don't you want me to pay you this time too, after walking so far?"

After a few seconds he spoke, still without looking at me.

"The frère already paid me. But he said if the white people saw me I would have to give all the money back."

"How much did he pay you?"

The boy told me, and I went into the house, got some money, and came back out. I didn't look at Placide while I counted the bills into the boy's hand.

"Give the frère his money. Tell him you failed, but it wasn't your fault. He knows we have an exceptionally vigilant sentinel."

The boy's face was still impassive, but now his cheeks glistened with tears.

"Why are you crying?"

"The frère said if I told where the letter came from there would be a curse on me. He said it would bring me suffering for the rest of my life."

"Don't worry about what he told you. That frère is the most famous liar in Mputu."

We left for Kilala Mission that day. Kate hadn't wanted to go, at first. She said that if Tom really were hiding out at Kilala Mission like a cloistered monk, a possibility that seemed totally outlandish but not inconsistent with the rest of his behavior, then maybe we ought to just leave him alone.

"He doesn't want to be left alone," I said. "That's what those letters are telling us. I think Ndosi was right after all: Tom's in trouble, and we have to go after him. Especially you, Kate. He always just raved at me. You were his . . . his confidante."

"Oh, his confidante. Well, that didn't stop him from raving at me too. Anyway, I don't know what you think you might achieve by going there."

"I don't know either. But it's not a situation we can just ignore, hoping it will resolve itself."

"Why not? If he goes away it's resolved, right? And he might still just go away. Maybe it's not even really an abnormal situation. Everything takes a long time here, Will. Maybe it's just taking him a long time to go away."

I went to fuel the Land Rover. I had filled the tank and was running the siphon into the spare cans when Boris, supported by Ndosi, came shuffling down the path and into the yard. Ndosi carried his schoolboy cahier under his arm and Boris' suitcase in his free hand. He greeted me and said something about preparing for the journey.

"How do you know anything about a journey?"

"Everyone knows, Will. Since early morning, when we hear this news of Mr. Tom."

It was hard to imagine silent Placide spreading gossip so quickly. Though of course in the camp gossip required nothing but a few muttered words, a spark to dry tinder. Maybe the boy himself, traumatized by his night in the chicken-coop prison, had blabbered his secret as he fled through the camp.

Ndosi opened the passenger door of the Land Rover, put the suitcase in the backseat, and boosted Boris in after it. I asked them what they thought they were doing, and Ndosi said they were coming on the journey. But it's not a journey for an old man, I told them. The road was a disaster, and we had no idea how long we'd be gone or what we were getting ourselves into. Ndosi shrugged and said the Road Builder needed to get the research and take the interview with the priest and look with his own eyes on the disaster road, and the Road Builder grunted and said old men should be explorers, shouldn't they?

It was because of Boris that Kate decided at the last minute to come. She couldn't just let her uncle take off across the savanna with only Ndosi and me to look after him, she said. It wasn't her fault he was in Africa and behaving so strangely, but still she felt some responsibility for him. After all, she had dreamed him coming here, almost as if she had willed it to happen. Well, in fact you *didn't* dream it, I said. You made up a dream about him coming. Yes, she said, and that was what made it willful. A person bore no responsibility for her real dreams. But a fake dream was bad faith, and she was responsible for it. She was also responsible for the père's Land Rover, and besides, she wanted to keep an eye on that suitcase. And since right from the start this expedition had the feel of an unmitigated disaster in the making, she had better do what she could to protect those things, even if she couldn't control the self-destructive urges of people under the sway of delusions and crazed agendas. Tom, Uncle Pers, now even Ndosi—all these clever and charming men were coming unhinged, apparently; they were turning out to be *cranks*, and you had to wonder how intelligent and original minds could be so easily subverted to crankiness and why that was such a *male* phenomenon, in her experience at least. She threw a change of clothes and a sheet and sleeping pad in her pack, looking up now and then to glare at me, so that I had to wonder if she was including me in that category of men. But by the time I ventured to ask that question her mood had turned silent and sulky, and she just climbed into the driver's seat and gave me an exasperated look and didn't say anything for most of the drive, except for the occasional unconvincing apology when she slammed us with particular vehemence into a rut.

It wasn't enough to say that Kate's not a morning person, though she isn't. Even under the best of circumstances you want to give her some extra room the first couple hours of the day. And these were not the best of circumstances. Yet as we left the Kivila Valley and began to cross the high savanna, I noticed that, stressed and irritable as she was, for some reason she was looking exceptionally beautiful. Her head in profile, framed by the sparse steel interior of the Land Rover, while behind her an immense green country turned slowly in the heat of the sun. Heat and water rose off the land into a blue sky, and the sky went to indigo and then black as it absorbed them. Damp green earth, thick humid sky—still the landscape of the rainy season, but inside the Land Rover Kate's hair and skin and eyes reflected the color and tones of the mushipu. Of course, they were the same color and tone they'd always been. Familiarity eclipsed the full power of their beauty, except in brief moments of passion, or moments like this, when the strangeness of certain settings overwhelmed the familiarity. But what if you saw her like this in every setting? What if you saw her beauty as alien and inaccessible, the way I had seen the nurse's beauty, steeped in an exoticism that carried an extra erotic charge? It would be possible to see her like that, for someone who felt too acutely the strangeness of every setting. Or for someone dreaming of moments of passion, and never achieving them.

"Why do you think he's still hanging around?" I said. It was the first anyone had spoken since we started driving.

"I don't know, Will. Does he need a reason? Agoraphobia, that's the reason he keeps giving."

"Which explains nothing."

"Right, nothing. Fear of motion; fear of being out in the open. That's an awfully broad phobia, when you think about it. Really, that's broad enough to include a whole spectrum of fear."

"This was the road they took," said Boris. "After the Kilala Mission massacre, on the way to the ambush in Kivila Valley." We had been driving in silence for some time. Now he suddenly announced that it was time people heard the real story of the Mission Road: actual unarguable facts, distilled from the old myths and vague anecdotes that up until now everyone, from the most superstitious peasant to me and Kate and apparently even to old Mavis, had been content to believe and repeat. He and his biographer had done the research, and out of it this true story had emerged, a story forged from living memory, as opposed to the dry archaeology you might get from somebody's journal. A story Kate and I might have uncovered ourselves, if only we'd allowed the biographer the freedom to exercise his remarkable abilities instead of putting him to work fetching water and scrubbing pots.

In the back of the Land Rover the biographer sat stoically beside Boris, clutching the suitcase in his lap and bracing himself against the jolts and sudden swerves. In the front seat I had to brace too, at the same time leaning back and half turning in order to hear Boris. The conditions were not conducive to conversation, but then this was not really conversation, only Boris talking without encouragement or provocation, clutching the top of my seat and bobbing his head and shouting his story at us over the wind and engine noise.

Of course, much of the research was contradictory, he had to admit that. Yet in each contradiction one sensed a further revelation of the truth. Each witness contributed to the truth, no matter how untrustworthy his memory or implausible his story. The research had been exhaustive, and out of it emerged a clear picture of those days: the country in chaos, no government to speak of, the overseers abdicated, and the country swept by war and rumor of war. Though in the Kivila Valley everything was extraordinarily peaceful, for a time. The rebellions were elsewhere. People here had no weapons, and no coherent articulation of their grievances. The name Karl Marx meant as little to them as—what? The name Adam Smith! And they were busy building things, mills and ferries and roads. Under white supervision, of course. They were clearing the forest for a road to open up new palm-oil lands downriver; that came to be called the Mission Road, though not everyone remembered that original purpose. Even with all the uncertainty, they continued to produce great quantities of palm oil—much more palm oil than anyone seemed to be producing nowadays. But eventually the work slowed, as materials and fuel became difficult to obtain. The war drew nearer and with it news of brutal massacres, the genocide of villages, the slaughter and mutilation of missionaries. Word came of a great rebel army marching, or marauding, out of the east. By then nearly all the whites had left. European society was reduced to two components: the priests and nuns on the one hand, and the Road Builder on the other. And that of course was no society at all, since they scarcely spoke to each other. But the Mission Road brought them together.

For the first time in years, the Road Builder visited the priests. They refused to invite him inside, so he stood on the porch and proposed his strategy to save their lives. The rebel army was heading their way. From all accounts it was a blood-maddened mob, and its strategy and the course of its march were unpredictable. But the European missions and factories were the main object of its rampage. If they arrived in the vicinity of the Kivila Valley, the rebels would surely descend upon the mission and the mill. However, these rebels were mainly an eastern tribe. They would know only the approximate location of Ngemba and Bumba Mission, and would find them only by following the road. But what if that road deceived them? What if somewhere in the forest the true road were blocked and obscured, and a new road constructed, turning away from the mission and the villages and the camp and the oil mill, and leading instead deeper into the jungle, across the river, out of the Kivila Valley, and onto the highway to Kisaka? Where the rebels would be caught up in new strategies, doing battle with soldiers and mercenaries, while the Kivila Valley remained forgotten, at peace, no matter who came to rule the country.

At first the priests told him his plan was crazy. But eventually they decided to cooperate with him—maybe because their only other option was blind faith and prayer, which clearly wasn't working at the missions to the east, unless the objective was martyrdom. So to the Road Builder's unworkable dream they contributed fuel and equipment and manpower, and one of them—the engineer, the drunkard—even showed up for a while to operate the grader.

The Road Builder and his crews worked day and night turning the rough track that was the Mission Road into a phantom highway. They cut and filled, graded and compacted, built bridges over the large streams and fords through the smaller ones. They even carved ruts and gullies and washboard stretches into the surface, and drove trucks up and down until it looked like a well-used road, traversing the uninhabited jungle to arrive at a river crossing. There they poured cement and built pilings and stretched a steel cable across the river. They put up a sign that said "Bumba Mission Ferry," floated the ferry from Ngemba downriver and attached it to the cable, and ferried the road-building equipment to the other side of the river. They built another bit of road on that side, and joined it to a seldom-used but already existing track connecting to the main road to Kisaka. Then they crossed the river again and returned to the beginning of their new road. All around the original road to the mission and the mill they cut down the jungle and left the great trees and the slash lying thickly over the road surface, so that this section of the true Kivila Valley road now looked like a clearing cut to make way for a farmhouse or a cornfield, with wild jungle beyond it.

It was at this point that the news arrived of the massacre at Kilala Mission and the rebel mob swarming west, only a day's march away, chanting for the blood of Christians and whites. The priests returned to Bumba Mission to pray, and the villages emptied out, everyone fleeing upriver and into the hills. But the Road Builder drove his bulldozer back along the new Mission Road to the ferry crossing, where in the roadbed approaching the crossing and within the cement piling and the steel hull of the ferry itself he planted great quantities of explosives.

"And it is also at this point," said Boris, leaning farther over the front seat, "that the stories diverge and become hopelessly contradictory. There are many opinions and secondhand accounts, but no eyewitnesses. At the ferry crossing on the Mission Road it was only the Road Builder, waiting for the rebels to arrive and crowd the landing and the ferry and swarm across the river. Then he would detonate the explosives, the crossing would exist no longer, and the rebels that still lived must follow the only roads left, all leading away from the Kivila Valley.

"He waited, alone, after two weeks of constant work and almost no sleep. He had a few scouts on hand too, or thought he did. Maybe they too had fled upriver, as night fell and the rebel army drew near. But nobody can tell of that march, or the battle that was fought at the end of it. People know that villages went up in flame, that there was gunfire, that government troops finally appeared on the roads. They know that somewhere on the plain helicopters descended from the sky and spilled out bellyfuls of mercenaries. And they know that an explosion destroyed the new ferry crossing on the Kivila River, obliterating the memory and the evidence of the Battle of the Mission Road. The Road Builder and his bulldozer vanished, and the rebel army broke apart, its soldiers killed or skulking back to their villages in little bands. And eventually the priests and nuns at Bumba Mission stopped praying and emerged from their chapels into the daylight with their throats unslit and their vision of martyrdom retreating with the rebels and soldiers into the east."

THE PISSING CONTEST

"I'm glad to see you, Will. I expected you, actually. I kind of thought my mail-man wouldn't be able to keep his mouth shut."

Tom popped the cap off a bottle of beer and poured two glasses. We were sitting between the church and rectory, in a patio area that opened on out-buildings, the père's garden, and above the garden a manioc field. Beyond the tilled land a field of drying grass rose to a low ridge that cut off further view.

"That kid didn't say anything, Tom. We just figured things out, finally. For months people have been talking about a white man at Kilala Mission, an invalid or the ghost of a monk or something. I don't know why it never occurred to us it was you."

"Well, it was. Frère Tomás." Tom chuckled, and stroked his patchy goatee. His shaven skull glistened with sweat.

"I guess your letters threw us off. I guess we're suckers. I mean, we figured you were exaggerating, but we did believe the basic premise: the trip across the continent and the dead moto and the truck breakdowns out in the wilder-ness and so forth."

"'Course you believed it. You are kind of gullible, Will, but don't feel stu-pid. Most of what I put in those letters was true, or mostly true. My moto really did break down in Mafemba. A transmission thing. I tried to get it fixed, because I was psyched to go. But I had to send off for new parts, and wait around in a hotel until they came."

"You stayed in one of those hotels in Mafemba?"

"Yeah. One of those hotels. I didn't get a lot of sleep, and the new trans-mission didn't come. And then the moto got ripped off."

"Didn't you have it locked up? Wasn't somebody watching it?"

"It was in fucking Mafemba, man. What kind of security do you think there is in a place like that? Locks don't hold. Watchmen don't watch. People's attention spans are very short in Mafemba. So the moto disappeared. Okay, fine. It was a shitty moto, you couldn't drive it or anything. Somebody probably threw it on a truck and carried it a thousand miles to find a transmission, or just to strip it for parts. That's how things work in this unbelievably shitty country. I was so disgusted I just got on the first truck heading east. And that was the commander's truck, just like I wrote to you. A fucking bar and whorehouse on wheels. I rode with them for weeks, but as it turned out we were just going around in circles. I figured out we never got more than three hundred clicks from Kilala Mission."

"You must have known the truck wasn't going where you wanted to go."

"Hey, when I got on they said they were going east. I never asked again, and after a while I sort of lost my sense of direction. How was I to know we'd eventually end up back in Mafemba? At that point I didn't even have a map. At least you still had a map, Will. *You* should have figured out I was just going around in fucking circles."

"I guess I did, eventually. Anyway, I figured you probably weren't walking across Africa with a girl you'd acquired in a trade for a brokedown moto. Not just any girl, either. Sukadi, the noble nympho savage."

"Yeah, okay. Sukadi was a weak character. A failure of imagination. But she was real, sort of. I modeled her after a girl I knew in Mafemba. We had a pretty superficial relationship, so I never really knew what to do with her as, you know, a literary character. All that stuff probably seemed pretty adolescent to you, Will. Guy trades a busted moto for a beautiful girl, they set out across the jungle, can't keep their clothes on, nobody so much as gets a mosquito bite on the ass . . . but what do you expect from a guy who's in a goddamn cloister, hanging out with an old lunatic priest? You got a sexy wife, or whatever she is to you. It probably wouldn't occur to you to trade a moto for a girl like that."

"What's my wife got to do with it? What do you mean, whatever she is to me?"

"Never mind your wife, then. Your woman. I mean, you aren't exactly *married*, are you? Forget it. You want some more beer? How are things going, otherwise? Anybody throw any more piñata parties? Smuggling parties? Hey, how's the noble bureaucracy working out?"

"We've made some progress. We've got some structures in place."

"Good. It's good to know somebody's putting structures in place. God knows they need some fucking structures."

"People appreciate us, Tom. They can see we're doing our best to help."

"Of course they appreciate you, man! You're paying a little attention to them. Nobody's paid attention to them for thirty or forty years, not since the Cold War almost stumbled on them, by mistake. The Kivila Valley's missed out on all the big world events, you ever think of that? Slave trade, great white explorers, world wars—everything skipped over them. Even the missionaries only came as an afterthought. Now they got AIDS, but not as bad as some places, so still nobody pays attention. They're skinny and sick, the kids are malnourished, but they'll never get a real headline-making famine because it rains all the time and manioc, at least, grows like a weed in this shitty dirt. They're oppressed by their government, but the government's the same color they are, so nobody notices that either. They don't have anything anybody wants. Only thing they got is palm oil, and a long time ago they gave up hoping anybody would pay attention to their palm oil. Then you and Kate come along. You don't know shit, but you hold meetings, you put people on fucking committees, you act like their fucking palm oil means more to you than anything else in the entire fucking world. Of course they fucking appreciate you, Will."

He poured the last of the beer into my glass and called to one of the children who stood at the edge of the patio, watching us. "Get us another Pilsner, Maurice." The boy ran off with the empty bottle into the rectory. Tom stood and looked toward the garden, where Kate and the old père were moving slowly through a tangle of squashes and tomatoes, talking. Tom watched them for a moment and turned away, shaking his head and laughing softly.

"What's so funny?"

"Funny? I don't know. Actually, there's nothing at all funny about Père Leo, believe me. We need some more beer, huh, Will?"

"You just sent a kid for beer."

"That's right, I did. He's taking his sweet goddamn time, isn't he? Or maybe not. Maybe he's hustling his skinny little ass, hoping that Frère Tomás will reward him with a Fanta or something. I'll give him thirty seconds." Tom paced to the edge of the patio and looked out across the field. He sucked in his breath. "Now, this guy," he said. "This guy's a fucking wild card, isn't he?"

Boris appeared, shuffling slowly along the edge of the manioc field. He was shirtless, and over his pajama bottoms he wore a pagne as a long shirt, in the fashion of the elders of the country. Concentrating on the path, he did not look up until he stopped at the corner of the field. Then he gazed about, intent and quizzical, though he didn't seem to notice Kate and the père in the garden, or Tom and me on the patio.

"The vraiment Road Builder, huh? You're telling me he just showed up, no warning? Look at him. Is he a fucking wildman, or what? Why did he come back?"

"Nobody knows why he came back. That's one of the darkest secrets of darkest Africa, though not as dark as the secret of why you haven't left."

"And fucking Mr. Dream. Can you tell me what the hell he's doing with that cahier? Did you know he's sitting in the library as we speak, *writing* in the damn thing?"

"That's what he does with it. He writes. God knows what. Another dark secret, I guess."

Maurice returned with a dusty beer bottle. Tom took the beer and thanked him, though he seemed to have forgotten about Maurice's Fanta, and after waiting a minute the boy returned slowly to the other children. I sat back with my fresh beer and looked around for Boris, but he was no longer in sight—he must have turned back the way he had come, or vanished among the thin foliage of the manioc field.

"Your old fish farmers keep asking about you, Tom. Telo had a real good harvest not long ago. He was pretty excited, if you can imagine Telo excited about something. He got about fifty kilos out of his smaller pond."

"Fifty kilos, huh? That's great. Seriously. You know, I really liked doing the fishpond thing, screwing around with the appropriate tech, the sustainable ag. But it couldn't last forever. You gotta be straight with yourself sometimes; you gotta look with a cold eye at where you're coming from, what you're moving toward. What you're *accomplishing*."

"So, what are you accomplishing now?"

"Now? Not much. Or not a goddamn thing, you think? Well, I'm hanging for a bit. Maybe I told you I needed some time in a quiet place to sort things out, reflect on the past few years. I'm getting that time here. I guess I was thinking of a tropical beach, but really a mission, a comatose fucking mission, is much better."

At the corner of the patio a nun appeared. She stopped as if she sensed something amiss, though she didn't look directly at us. Tom took no notice of her.

"It's real quiet here, Will. There aren't the constant interruptions, like in Malembe. People aren't so meddlesome. So *needy*. In Malembe everybody seemed to need so much *maintenance*. Here, they go their own way, and I go mine."

"Have you been writing letters to anyone besides us?"

"Oh, sure. Family and friends in Thanesboro. But those letters were boring compared to the ones I sent you. I told them I got involved in a new sustainable-development project at a local mission—which is true, only it's mainly on a level of personal sustainability. But I've been doing some other shit too. Père Leo's appreciative of just about anything—he's like everybody, starved for attention. I made a new compost system for his garden, and he got off on that. I don't know why. My own feeling is, one pile of rotting shit is about like the next pile of rotting shit. Now he wants me to help him build a fishpond. I told him it won't work. The fish won't grow, and they won't reproduce. The soil here is nothing but peat, way too acidic for tilapia. But Leo doesn't look at it like that. He doesn't really have a use for a concept like acidity. He's coming at it more from a standpoint of prophecy and miracle, a multiplication of loaves and fishes kind of thing. Which is cool with me. I mean, I don't give a damn if his fish grow. Maybe they will. I told him we'd dump a bunch of ash in the pond, try to neutralize the pH, and he liked that, it had a good mystical aura. Biblical connotations. Apocalyptic. He likes ash."

The nun was gone. The garden was now empty, though I hadn't noticed Kate and the old père leave. I took long draughts of warm beer. In the middle of the field a woman bent over, hoeing. I hadn't noticed her arrive either. Tom apologized for the beer. You shouldn't have to drink warm beer at a mission, he said. If there was one thing a Catholic mission ought to be good for, it was cold beer, but Père Leo had not started the generator for several days. He did that periodically—shut down the generator for as much as a week or so. Maybe it was to ration fuel, though Tom suspected that it had more to do with the père's complicated accounting of sin and penance, and his need to practice some further self-denial.

But the beer went down easily; my body seemed to crave the stuff, if for no other reason than to keep the sweat glands primed. The afternoon was muggy, Tom talked on and on, and the best response seemed to be to sit as motionless as possible while pouring a steady stream of beer into my body.

While he talked I studied the beer in my glass. Bubbles broke away from the side, floated to the surface, vanished. I held up the glass, and looked through it at the fields beyond the père's garden. The beer enhanced the light, warping it in a pleasing way, coaxing a bit of color, something like a glow, out of the listless afternoon. It was pleasant to sit there, I decided, looking out on fields where people appeared and dropped out of sight with equal abruptness. It was pleasant to sip warm beer and it was even pleasant to listen to Tom, though the ceaseless irony of his tone was starting to oppress me. That irony washed the meaning out of everything he said, made him seem deep but featureless, like the mushipu sky. Listening to Tom was like looking at that sky and knowing there's a great fire burning somewhere, but seeing only the trapped and stagnant smoke.

Kate joined us on the patio. "We saw you talking turnips with Père Leo," said Tom.

"Actually, we talked history, mainly. He seems to know a lot of history. Local stuff, colonial-era stuff. Though he didn't remember Uncle Pers."

"No, he wouldn't. He doesn't have a memory for faces. Well, unless they've been disconnected from their bodies." Tom made a slashing gesture at his throat.

"He was caught in the middle of some terrible times. I heard all about what the rebels did, and the soldiers that came after them, and what *they* did."

"No. You didn't hear all about it. You just got the tip of the iceberg. The *Reader's Digest* version. The *Cliffs Notes*. You didn't get the detail, because there wasn't enough time. He's got infinite detail. He remembers it all, see. And what happens is, he's always looking at it with a more powerful lens, so each time he comes up with more precise detail. You can never hear it all. Of course, everything he says is probably true, I'm not saying it isn't true. But he's definitely mad. Fucking King Lear, raving in the African heath. Speaking his mad truth."

"So, what kind of a mission is this? I mean, is there a congregation? Does Père Leo hear confession, preach, that kind of thing?"

"Sure. That is, people come around on Sundays to hear him mumble the Mass. I wouldn't call them a congregation or anything. I mean, they don't *congregate*. They wander in, and they wander out. But it's a real mission, with all the accoutrements. There's Leo's sidekick, young Frère Tomás. There's nuns. 'Course, they're a different kind of nun than the ones at Bumba Mission. More removed from the earthly sphere. I guess you could say that these nuns represent the gothic tradition of the Church. The obsessive-compulsive tradition. But I have no idea what their obsessions are. They don't talk, for one thing."

"So, you mainly hang out with Père Leo?"

"Well, 'hang out,' I don't know. Père Leo doesn't exactly hang. But we get along okay. And he really does call me 'Frère.' Maybe he truly believes I'm a monk. Do you think it's my haircut?" Tom grinned, rubbing his smooth skull. "But actually I don't understand him very well. He mumbles, and he doesn't like Kituba. And my French, you know, sucks. Lately he breaks down sometimes and speaks Kituba to me, but for the longest time I had almost no idea what he was saying. Which was one of the things that intrigued me about the place. When I first came, I told him my situation and asked him if I could rent a room for a while, and he gave this speech about his guest policy, I could tell that much. Either he was telling me he loved guests and I was welcome to stay, *or* I wasn't welcome, it wasn't that kind of a mission."

"So you took a chance and stayed."

"I stayed. I figured he'd clarify his meaning, and he has. We've come to some kind of accommodation. I do the Frère Tomás gig, follow the rules of the order as best I can make them out. Speaking of which, do you have any money?"

"You need another loan?"

"Look, I just need beer money, okay? We've been drinking Leo's beer, and Leo, he's not one to give away beer, not in the quantity Will's been putting down."

I gave him some money. He and Kate went inside to look for Boris, and I stayed on the patio to finish my beer. The hoeing woman was gone from the manioc field. The kids on the edge of the patio had disappeared. There was only the empty garden, the worn, ash-stained patio, and the horizon closing in. Though the mission was set in a wide savanna valley there was no sense of openness, because the buildings were in a depression, and the slopes of this smaller valley cut off the larger horizon. That must have been why people didn't seem to approach or recede, but instead simply appeared and disappeared, as if the horizon, or the walls of the mission itself, delivered them up and snatched them away instantaneously.

Far away, the dry thunder rolled. Beneath the cloud night was falling early, but the heat of the day was trapped on the earth. I was still sweating, and the beer was gone. There was no glow or color left, no way to bend the light to disguise the terrible restriction of that close horizon. For more than thirty years this had been the old priest's world, and now he shared it with Tom. Enclosed, they could imagine whatever they wanted about the larger world. The horizon hid the open dangerous spaces beyond, but it also made the sudden apparition commonplace. And so the apparitions of the past were no longer remote or inconceivable. It was easy to imagine the swarm of rebels rising from the grass, and the sudden column of soldiers already breaking formation as they sweep over the crest of the ridge above the smoking fields, the abandoned village, and the fresh shallow graves in the cemetery behind the church.

Inside the building a weak bulb lit the sitting room where Kate and Tom were talking.

"You must be important guests," Tom said. "We get kilowatts tonight. We'll be able to see what we're eating. Not necessarily an advantage, you understand. We'll be able to see each other too. Which means we'd better rustle up a change of clothes for your uncle. I don't think old Leo'll be able to handle that outfit he's got on now."

A door creaked open down the hall, followed by slow footsteps and the rustling of cloth. Père Leo entered the room. Tom stood, and the père laid a hand on his arm.

"Good evening, Frère." He spoke Kituba, chopping the vowels harshly.

"Good evening, Père." Tom bowed his head slightly. The père mumbled, and shuffled out of the room. At the doorway he stopped.

"Frère Tomás!"

"Yes, Père?"

"Your visitors aren't planning to spend the night, are they?"

"Well, yes, I think they were hoping to. It's late for traveling on. Is that all right?"

"The Lord's house is always open to travelers," the père said without conviction. "Did you show them the guest rooms?"

"Not yet."

"Perhaps you should show them now."

"They're only spending one night, and the guest rooms aren't really prepared. I was thinking to maybe fix up a place in the library."

"The library! I don't think the library is appropriate, Frère, for lodging guests. That's the purpose of the guest rooms, no? Will they be joining us for dinner?"

"Yes. If that's okay."

"I'll tell Mukasa. I hope they don't have extravagant tastes." Mumbling to himself, he shuffled off down the hall. A minute later we heard radio static, and then the voice of a newscaster.

"I'm sure the guest room will be fine," said Kate.

"Are you?" said Tom. "I'll show you one." He led us down the hall and wrenched open a door. The bulb in the hallway illuminated the room enough to give a general impression of boxes, furniture, machinery, tools, and clothing, covering the entire floor and reaching to the ceiling in places. There was also a peculiar, unpleasant smell that I couldn't identify.

"Formaldehyde, naphthalene, mouse shit, and cat pee," Tom announced. "The scent of Kilala Mission. All the guest rooms smell like that. I don't know why the formaldehyde. Anyway, you don't have to sleep there. Nobody's ever going to sleep there again, until another mob comes along and burns the place out. You can sleep in the library."

"We'll sleep in the Land Rover, Tom, if there's a problem."

"There's no problem, Kate. He turned on the fucking generator, didn't he? So I guess he's glad you're here. Don't worry, he never goes in the library after dinner. He just gets shitfaced and listens to the radio some more and goes to bed."

And that's what happened, though "shitfaced" seemed a glib description of the père's drunkenness, which was at least as lugubrious as his sobriety. In the stuffy, dimly lit dining room he said grace, invoking "the spirits of departed souls, whose sufferings and ultimate victory give us strength as we battle the same forces of darkness." When he finished he peered around the table, for the first time looking directly at his guests. His gaze was unnerving, and I ducked my head and mumbled something amenish. But Boris stared right back. At least he wasn't wearing his pajamas and pagne; Tom had found him a shirt and a pair of pants, and somehow persuaded him to wear them.

The père drank a good deal more than he ate, but then the beer was a good deal better than the food. Tom spooned great blobs of pili-pili onto his plate, and offered the jar around. "Better take more than that, Will. You're asking a lot of your pili-pili when you dump it on shit like this. And you pretty much have to wash it down with beer. Just pay Mukasa for the beer."

The dinner conversation began stiffly in Kituba, struggled briefly with English, and finally settled on French. The père gave a summary of the day's news: an Italian journalist kidnapped and murdered in a northern city; curfew and looting in the capital; ethnic violence in the east. The kind of news this country had heard before, he said, and everyone knew where it would lead. Kate tried to turn the conversation to questions about local agriculture, the work of the mission, village customs and beliefs. But somehow all Leo's responses led to recollections of the massacre that had taken place at the mission thirty-five years before. By the end of the meal it was clear that those apparitions of the past were real, and for Père Leo what was substantial was not the day's news or the lack of rainfall or even the glass he kept raising to his mouth, but the memory of dry cornstalks rustling, hiding him from the rebels razing his mission below.

He still could *see* the two rebels running from hut to hut around the perimeter of the mission, throwing fire. Behind them the thatch huts flamed quickly, and heat and smoke rushed upward, rippling the sky. Villagers fled into the fields, and rebels with filed teeth and painted faces pursued them. They ran down a woman at the edge of the cornfield. While he watched they raped her, and when they were finished they cut her belly open. Hands drenched in her blood, a rebel turned his glazed and wild eyes on the cornfield. He looked straight at Père Leo, but his eyes didn't seem to focus, and he moved on.

The people inside the mission began by singing hymns, and ended with screams and gurgling cries. By dusk, the rebels had built cooking fires and slaughtered the goats and chickens of the mission. Patrols went through the fields, ripping up manioc and corn and looking for people hiding. They slashed the cornstalks six feet from Père Leo, and he sat in silent prayer, waiting for the blow on his neck, but again they passed him by. So he understood that the cornstalks conferred invisibility, that as long as he stayed in the cornfield he would be safe. He remained there praying all night and the next day, long after the rebels departed, taking the road toward Bumba Mission and the Kivila Valley.

"Where we were waiting for them."

Père Leo stared down at Boris, as if stunned to find that this old specter poking at his food at the far end of his table was capable of any speech at all.

"*You* were? Who are you, monsieur?"

Ndosi cleared his throat and spoke for the first time. "This is the Road Builder, Père. Who lived in the Kivila Valley years ago. Who built the Mission Road."

"Que'st-çe que ç'est ça?" the père demanded. "I never heard of any of that."

So once again Boris told the story of the Mission Road. He spoke French, though it was difficult for him, and when he paused to search for a word Ndosi interjected clarifications or suggestions, in French or Kituba or even English. Boris told of his desperate idea to move the road and divert the rebel army. He told how the priests at Bumba Mission had reluctantly assisted him; how the old road was obliterated and the new road and ferry crossing constructed and the crossing mined with explosives; and how he had waited, exhausted, with a fog in his brain, for the rebels to come down into the valley. How through the fog he heard the heavy marching, the trucks rolling past, the ferry cable creaking with innumerable crossings. And how in the early morning a great explosion rocked the Kivila Valley and left the ferry a twisted mass of metal, the road near the crossing a series of muddy holes, the air smelling of smoke, and particles of ash precipitating out of a cold fog. The war passed over the valley, and there was no massacre at Bumba Mission. The rebel army disintegrated, straggled home; the Road Builder disappeared, and with him the details of the story.

"Events pile up," Boris said. "Along with rumors, myths. Memory fails. Witnesses vanish, and testimonies diverge wildly. 'There is no remembrance of former things.'"

The père glowered. "Those who cannot remember the past are condemned—"

"Father, please!" Boris waved his fork in the air. "Those old aphorisms are always misleading. We are condemned to repeat the past in any case, sooner or later. All the more likely the past we remember most vividly. Ha! 'What has been is what will be,' eh, Father? As you were saying. 'There is nothing new under the sun.'"

Père Leo glared across the table at Boris. His stubble vibrated, betraying the tight quivering of his jaw, and he leaned forward, gripping the edge of the table. Boris held his fork in front of his eye and squinted through it at the père, as if he were looking down a gunsight.

"The details are lost," he repeated emphatically. "But this much is known: those rebels were coming down a road paved with ampho. Ammonia nitrate and fuel oil, Father. Explosives. And that was where I put my faith. You put yours in cornstalks, I put mine in explosives. So we both stayed where we were, eh, and waited."

The père was silent for a long while. Finally he said: "I put my faith in God, monsieur. Not in cornstalks or anything else. I don't know anything about this story you are telling. But I do know that the rebels returned here the next afternoon, in flight. They had met up with mercenaries and soldiers, out on the plain. There was a battle, a slaughter. The rebels had primitive weapons, and the fetishes they wore to deflect bullets failed, of course. They died in great numbers, or fled. They came back through here in disarray, with nothing left of their army."

He stared fiercely down the table at Boris, who returned his gaze, still sighting through his fork tines. But Kate raised her head sharply.

"How long did you say you were in this cornfield?" she said. "I mean, between the time the rebels left and the time they returned?"

"It was the next day. They left one morning, and returned the afternoon of the next day."

Kate looked at Boris. "That wouldn't give them time to get to the Kivila Valley, Uncle Pers."

Boris lowered his fork and looked away from the père. "There must be some confusion about the time sequence," he muttered.

"Confusion?" Père Leo seemed to rear up in his seat, eyes flashing. "These were the only clear and significant moments of my life, monsieur. I was witness to these terrible revelations; I was Paul, watching the nightmares unfold. And this is my penance for having witnessed but not otherwise suffered: I remember everything, exactly as it happened. I remember it daily, in my prayers and my dreams, as if it were passing again before my eyes. And I am given this understanding: out of pity and mercy, God places a fog in our minds, the gift of forgetting. To punish us, and to provide us with a means of atonement, He gives us memory."

After dinner the père shuffled off to his rooms, and the rest of us retired to the library, the largest room in the mission besides the chapel. But still it was hot and stuffy, and gloomily lit.

Boris sat brooding in a chair at the far end of the room, and Ndosi stood nearby, staring vacantly into space. Kate and I sprawled on a couch in front of a huge rock fireplace, while Tom ranged about by the bookshelves, his glasses and his skull glittering.

"It was this fireplace," Kate said to me abruptly. "It wasn't the furnace at the mill."

"What are you talking about?"

"In my dream on the plane, when Tom made a big fire. The fireplace was like this."

"What's that?" Tom veered toward her. "You want a fire, Kate? Yes, that would be nice and cozy. What do you think, they used this place as a fucking sweat lodge, or what? It makes you see why this missionary thing didn't work out the way it was supposed to. I mean, what sort of success do you expect from people who come to one of the hottest hellholes in the world, and first thing they do is build a fireplace big enough to heat a goddamn medieval cathedral?"

He drained his beer glass and went to the table to refill it. Ndosi wandered down to join us, and Tom stopped pouring beer and watched him. "Fucking Mr. Dream," he commented, poured him a glass as well, and continued talking. "But the thing to remember is the effect they were after, right? Atmosphere is the whole point. These Catholics understand theater, they always have. And to a degree it works. Even the fireplace works. I mean, it puts you in a certain mood, doesn't it, makes you feel like you're in a real library. Settling down in an armchair with a little Aquinas and a snifter of cognac, huh? Except there isn't any. Cognac, I mean. I guess it has to do with the asceticism of our order—all we got to offer is the same old Pilsner. At least it's cooled off a couple of degrees, though. Did you enjoy your dinner?"

"It wasn't as bad as you made it sound."

"Yeah, old Mukasa was in rare form. And the conversation was amusing, for a while. I dig your uncle, Kate. Did you catch Leo's expression when the old man told him in so many words that history is bunk? Throwing fucking Ecclesiastes in his face? He'll be stewing about that exchange for a long time. It'll give him some new material. He doesn't get much new material. I'll probably be hearing diatribes against your godless blaspheming uncle months from now."

"You're still going to be here, months from now?"

"Don't be so fucking literal, Will. But yeah, maybe I will. Or I might leave tomorrow."

"You could come with us. Then go on to Kisaka, take a plane home like you first planned."

"Go back to Ngemba? With you two? I don't think that would work. Do you think that plan would work, Kate?"

Kate said nothing. She slouched low on the couch, staring into the cold fireplace.

"Well, I guess I don't really understand what you're doing *here*," I said.

"What the fuck are you doing here, man? You just get a wild hair? Is the noble bureaucracy expanding its sphere of influence? Or did you just come to give me the third degree?"

"I guess I don't know why we came. I guess we shouldn't have."

He leaned back against the fireplace. "Well, this isn't exactly a fucking crisis, Will. In fact, nothing's changed since the last time you saw me. Okay, I lost my moto. But otherwise I'm still going with my original plan. Still heading overland. I just need a vehicle. But it's not like I can just check the want ads, cruise down to the used-car lot. Or wait around in Mafemba, aggravating my agoraphobia. I'm better off hanging here until something develops."

Kate sat up and turned to him. "Nothing's going to develop, Tom. Okay? So quit making excuses. Quit talking about agoraphobia. You can leave if you want. If all you need is a vehicle, then buy one. You can always find a vehicle to buy."

She stood, got her toothbrush, and went outside. Tom glanced at me, raising his eyebrows. Then he looked at the floor and tugged on his goatee for a while, and finally went to join Boris at the other end of the room. When Kate came back she laid out her sleeping pad in the corner, took off her boots and pants, and lay down beneath her sheet. Within a few minutes she seemed to be asleep.

I moved to an armchair in the other corner, below the bookshelves, and looked around at the library, trying to take myself back thirty-five years and imagine the massacre that might have taken place in this room. I couldn't come up with a convincing image. Thirty-five years was not long enough. Somehow the room seemed much older, an artifact not of recent history but of a more remote and unremembered past.

The fireplace loomed above me, grotesquely out of place and proportion, with its wide hearth, huge slabs of flagstone, and thick overhanging mantelpiece. Maybe at one time it really had heated a cathedral somewhere. Maybe the fathers had imported it, packed it out of some great stone room in Northern Europe, where for centuries it had shed a flickering light on gloomy spaces and warmed the sluggish blood of monks. A crazy idea, but it made a little sense, because where in this stoneless land would they have found flagstone? They must have hauled it a great distance, but why, when they could have built the fireplace, like the building itself, out of brick from the local clay?

Above the mantelpiece a crucifixion painting hung in a peeling gilded frame. Jesus twisted in agony, pierced by nails and thorns. Blood streamed from His wounds, drawing the eye down the painting to the mantelpiece, onto the hearth, out to the stains on the unvarnished hardwood floor. I hadn't followed Père Leo's story well enough to recall the details of the rebels' rampage through the mission. Had there been bloodshed in the library? Or maybe the stains were only spilled wine, a souvenir of the days when the mission served some beverage other than beer. The floor seemed off-color in places, and sections of the wall were replastered. Had a fire burned here once? In the dim unsteady light I couldn't tell whether the edges of things—furniture, tapestries, books—were charred or simply worn and dirty. A thin layer of dust and ash coated everything and seemed even to hang in the air, stirred up by our presence and slow to settle out of such a dense and stagnant medium.

Old portraits and photographs, mostly of priests and nuns, lined the walls behind me. They were unreadable, anonymous faces, and there was nothing that definitively linked them to the bloody history of Kilala Mission. But I couldn't help but feel that I was looking at dead faces, at people who had died violently in the service of their God. Of course, everything in the room was heavy with that kind of implication, everything was a clue, and no doubt if pieced together all the clues would only corroborate and further refine the infallible memory of Père Leo.

"Monsieur Will."

I'd forgotten Ndosi. He was sitting in the shadows by the fireplace, watching me.

"The priests are always telling us about God," he remarked.

"It's their business."

"They say they taught us about God. That before they came we knew nothing of God. But that's a lie, Will. It's true we didn't know the stories of Jesus or Abraham or Moses. Because we had our own stories, which they want us to forget. But we've always known about God."

Outside, the generator droned on, almost drowning out the slow heavy breathing of Kate and the low murmur of voices from the other end of the room. Ndosi stood up slowly and went to join Boris and Tom. At random I took a book from a shelf and began to read. It was in French, with thin, almost translucent pages and tiny archaic print. I skimmed a couple of pages, then looked up at the great bookshelves towering on either side, crammed with thousands and thousands of volumes of similar books. The knowledge they contained seemed fantastically remote and arcane. An ancient ordering of the universe, preserved in this obscure library yet nonetheless lost to us. Here was the lifework of thousands of learned, thoughtful, even brilliant human beings, yet who would ever again have the patience and concentration to read any of their books? The best I could manage was several pages before I began to doze off. The book slipped from my hands, yet I dreamed I was still reading, and the dense arrangement of words was somehow made comprehensible as it was fragmented by my dreaming mind.

But when I woke I remembered nothing of what I'd read or dreamed of reading. My neck was stiff, and I had a chill, and an urgent need to empty my bladder. The warmth had gone out of the air; sweat was cold on my skin; and the fireplace, cold stone and gaping pit of ash, towered over my sleeping wife and the dark corner of the room.

The generator was silent now, but Boris, Tom, and Ndosi talked on at the far end of the room. I couldn't make out anything they were saying, but their tone was urgent and impassioned and somehow consistent with the logic of my dream and the medieval aura of the place—as if they were ghostly philosophers and theologians, chipping away with axioms and syllogisms at the persistent conundrums of existence.

I went out the side door. Half asleep, I stood on the edge of the patio and urinated into the flower bed.

"Pissing on Leo's dahlias, Will? He hates that, you know."

Tom was suddenly beside me, fumbling with the buttons on his pants.

"Sorry. I didn't feel like risking a fall into the waysay."

"Oh, sure, it's not a risk to take lightly. In fact, I think I'll piss on his dahlias too. If he sniffs it out in the morning, I'll just blame it on the guests. He already has an idea of what heathens you are. But you won't have to take any abuse from him, because you'll be long gone."

"We haven't talked about when we're leaving."

"You'll be gone. Kate can't wait to get the hell out of here. Isn't that obvious, Will? It's obvious to me. But Boris would like to stay, I think. He likes the ambience."

"Did he say that?"

"I don't know, maybe the interpreter said that. Fucking Ndosi, he puts his spin on everything, you know? It can get confusing. Still, we're having a great conversation, between the three of us. We're getting at some of the dark secrets, Will. I even found out why Boris came to Africa."

"Why?"

"Fucking immortality."

"What?"

"I'm serious. Those weren't his exact words, okay, but I understood what he was saying. 'Course, there are some communication barriers that just aren't coming down. Ndosi keeps wanting to know why I smashed the boom box. I can't seem to explain it to him. I tried, in three fucking languages I tried—Kituba, English, finally I even threw my French at him, talking about the scourge of technology and media hype and consumerism, the whole cultural imperialism rap—and every time I get done explaining he looks at me and says, that's interesting, but Tom, why did you smash the boom box?"

We both were still peeing. I'd been going for some time, but I felt like I could last forever—side by side with Tom, arcing powerful streams of beery urine into the darkness, as if we were locked in some adolescent pissing contest. Who could pee the farthest distance, the greatest quantity, the longest time?

"You usually can't explain yourself to people anyway. Obviously I can't explain myself to Kate anymore. Which is kind of depressing, because at one time we were on the same wavelength. If things had played out a little differently, we really might have gone somewhere with it."

"What are you talking about?"

Abruptly we both stopped peeing. A tie, then. Simultaneously we shook off, zipped up.

"At my piñata party," said Tom. "She had some kind of fever that night. You were pretty much out of it, Will. Maybe you didn't notice. But she was definitely in synch with my migration vision. And she always liked riding with me on the moto. Whenever we climbed out of the valley, crested onto the savanna, she always wanted to just keep going."

"She likes to keep moving, Tom. She likes road trips."

"Whatever. But that night . . . something was into her, Will. I may as well tell you. She kept kissing me. She held my face in her hands and she kissed me. That's what happened, okay? You aren't thinking of hitting me, are you? Père Leo has a zero tolerance of violence around here. Anyway, nothing else happened. We just talked, held hands, kissed. We kind of fell asleep together. Then it was morning, you know, and I busted the piñata and left. And I don't think Kate liked the piñata part. And I guess she didn't like my letters either. I guess maybe she's decided she doesn't like *me*. She's right, nothing's going to develop now. So don't get all worked up, Will. People are always getting pulled in different directions, know what I'm saying? We're always doing things we didn't expect to. Maybe I was out of line that night. But I felt so fluid, you know? Like I wasn't fixed in a single place anymore. Like none of us were locked into anything, and there were more possibilities than we might have imagined. And one of them was that we could shift positions, move into very different configurations. Because it's not as if any particular configuration is inevitable, cast in stone. Okay? 'Scuse me, I gotta take a leak."

"You just took a leak."

"I did, didn't I? I must not have finished. I must have got interrupted. I keep getting interrupted. Like, I never finished telling you about Boris, did I? The immortality thing. A little while ago he picks up this old suitcase. You know that old suitcase he's hauling around? Well, he opens it."

"He opened it?"

"Yeah. It's just totally crammed with papers and money and old notebooks and shit. A mess. You know what these are? he says to me. These are the facts. A record of things as they happened. Then he goes off on this riff about how recording things as they happened is not necessarily a meaningful endeavor. How a history can be meticulous and exact and still go absolutely nowhere. How in Mputu everything is recorded and nothing is remembered. Everything is put in a book, and everyone reads, and the books are instantly forgotten. He kept talking. He says, in this country almost nobody reads, but if you give them a book they absorb it, the story endures. Memory is pure, it's live, not a recording of memory. Look at Père Leo, he says. I can't remember what else he said. I was just looking at him talking and talking, standing there in that old pagne next to that mess of papers, with Ndosi looking on holding his ridiculous cahier, and it hit me: old Boris, he just wants to be an *ancestor.*"

I left Tom peeing in the dahlias and went inside. I lay down near Kate and slept fitfully into the early morning, slipping back and forth between claustrophobic medieval dreams and the claustrophobic reality of the library, with its steadily dimming light and rumble of intent voices. Just before dawn, a sound I couldn't incorporate into a dream broke into my sleep. I woke up enough to identify it as a diesel engine coughing to life, and to tell myself that it must be Père Leo, journeying off to some distant village to minister to parishioners. I drifted back to sleep, and the medieval walls and shadows loomed again. But the engine intruded, winding through gears, receding down the long driveway. Then I remembered that Père Leo had neither distant parishioners nor a vehicle, that our Land Rover was the only vehicle in the compound.

I threw back my bedsheet and got up. A lamp burned in the far corner of the room, where Boris lay sleeping on the couch. I crouched by Kate's sleeping pad and felt in her pants pockets. The Land Rover keys weren't there.

He had driven south, the nightwatchman said. Frère Tomás, speeding off in his new Land Rover. Full of joy. He said he was going on a long trip. Do you like my new car? he had asked several times. Then he gave the nightwatchman money to buy clothes for his wife and presents for his children. And he gave him an envelope to pass on to the white people who had delivered the Land Rover.

We took the envelope inside and opened it by the lamp. Inside was a thick stack of traveler's checks, countersigned by Tom, and a note:

This was the only vehicle I could find, so I bought it. You were right, Kate: it's not that hard to do. But there wasn't time to haggle about the price, so I'm just leaving you most of my cash. I guess it will have to cover that loan too.

34

RETRIBUTION

In the empty quarter south of Kilala Mission the savanna grasses had not yet turned brown, and the road Kate and I walked along was damp and firm in the early morning hours, a rainy-season highland road. But the air smelled of mushipu fire and by afternoon our throats burned and tasted of ash and the road had dried out and softened into something like a sand wallow, a path of friction and resistance through a green wasteland. We walked for thirty kilometers, all day beneath the monotonous sun, and saw no one, except for a truckload of soldiers that went by in the early morning, heading north. They watched us silently as they passed—no greetings, no catcalls or taunts or demands. Then the road was empty. For the first time in Africa we felt completely alone, traversing a truly uninhabited place.

"This isn't how you imagined it, is it?" I said to Kate.

"What do you mean?"

"Crossing the savanna like this. Trudging along, all sweaty and dirty. With me."

"Well, no. I've imagined us in all kinds of circumstances, Will, but you're right. I never imagined this."

"What you imagined was the motorcycle humming along, the wind in your face, your legs wrapped around Tom's thighs."

She kept walking, looking straight out at the road ahead. A long silence passed between us. When she finally spoke her voice was quiet, and still she didn't look at me.

"You pick a hell of a time to start acting jealous."

"I'm just thinking about what he was telling me the other night. Pretty much the last thing he said to me. He was talking about his fête. How wild you were. How you kept kissing him. Tracing your finger all over his map, and going on about how you wanted to leave too. But I don't know, maybe he was just making that up too."

"Well, yeah." We walked on for a while in silence. Then she stopped. I stopped too, and we looked at each other. She said: "Tom has an overactive imagination. You know that. So I don't know why you would *believe* him. But no, he wasn't making it all up. Because, you know, I have an overactive imagination too. And I guess we stimulated each other's imagination. I'm sure we weren't good for each other. Well, obviously. But look, Will, I imagine all kinds of things. Fantasies, right? And let's face it: Tom always gave off—how did you put it, talking about the nurse? A certain vibe."

"Sure. Women desire him. Look at what's-her-name, Tsimba, that predatory gold-digging bitch. Or the other one, sweet little obliging Sukadi, romping naked among the thorn trees. So why should you be any different?"

"I was kind of drunk that night, Will. And I was intrigued with his idea of crossing the continent. I was excited for him. It's true that I kissed him. But not over and over, in the way that you're thinking. The way Tom was thinking, apparently. Fantasizing. But the reality is, I'm out here with you, trudging through the sand. Sweaty and dirty. And Tom is . . ."

She didn't finish the sentence, and we started walking again. With each tedious step the sandy road gave way a little, dragging us back. It might feel like that to walk on another planet, subject to a more repressive gravitational field. A large soft world that keeps its inhabitants on a short tether, close to its surface, denying them all quickness and grace.

For years Tom might have felt a similar oppression of gravity, a constant drag on all his movements. And that was the physical sensation of what he called agoraphobia. Then yesterday morning he suddenly broke free of it all: agoraphobia and tradition and superstitious fear, debt and commitment and taboo. Free of the huge gap that separated his imaginary deeds from his actions. With one decisive act—the theft of his friends' car in the remote bush—he had liberated himself.

And paralyzed us. Though we wanted to pursue him at once, we had no means. Père Leo made some calls over his phonie, trying to notify the authorities and locate a vehicle for us to rent, but he had trouble establishing a clear connection and getting people to understand what he was talking about. The nightwatchman set out with his ancient bicycle for Mafemba, promising to return with a bush taxi and driver. But he was walking and pushing the bicycle, because the chain was too dry and rusty to turn the sprockets. When he came to the ferry crossing, he said, he would steal a bit of grease from the pulleys; that would free up the chain and he would be able to ride, and he hoped in this way to arrive in Mafemba by nightfall.

Soon after the nightwatchman left, word of a child's death and a violent altercation involving Tom and the Land Rover began to filter into Kilala Mission from the south, and by evening we'd heard the story often enough that we no longer could dismiss it as mere rumor. If it were true, it meant that all urgency had gone out of the pursuit, but nevertheless Kate and I couldn't wait any longer. We left Boris and Ndosi at the mission and set out the next morning before dawn, walking. We took food and water but mainly our long march on the sandy road was fueled by adrenaline, the chemistry of anxiety and dread, which kept us moving across the empty savanna until we reached the first settlement south of Kilala Mission and saw a hulk of blackened metal lying on its side in the charred grasses below the road. A vehicle, fire-seared and battered and stripped, but still recognizable as Père Michel's Land Rover.

A fire also had burned around several low cement buildings along the road, without affecting their long-term state of filth and ruin. But beyond these buildings, in what had been the village, there wasn't a structure left standing. Just black stubble where the huts had been, and among the stubble half-burned chairs and pallets, shattered mirrors, melted plastic shoes and bowls. A few wisps of smoke still rose up here and there, but already the heat had gone out of the fire, already the contoured ash was marked by the prints of bare feet. People had come back to salvage; probably they'd been poking through the cooling ash in the moments before they saw us approach.

Kate gripped my elbow. "Look, Will."

On the edge of a manioc field below the burned village, somber children stood watching us. Suddenly I remembered passing through this place on tournée with Tom. At the time we'd hardly slowed down, but now as I looked at that silent gathering of children I had a clear memory of unsmiling faces watching from beside those cement blockhouses, and a desolate collection of huts sloping off into the valley. And now that place was only smouldering wreckage and stubble. Somehow it seemed a logical and inevitable succession, from the huts to the mounds of ash, and the children still staring.

We followed the retreating children down through the fields. In a scattering of thin trees we came upon an encampment: cooking fires, sleeping mats, clothes laid out to dry. A woman pounded manioc in a mortar; another bent over an enamel tub to wash a baby. A village, but without any real shelter. We heard conversation and argument and even the muted play of children, but the camp fell silent as we drew near. People stared, but no one came forward to greet us. Finally Kate asked for a glass of water.

A girl was sent to fetch a bidón. After we drank, Kate spoke again.

"Why are you living down here in the trees?

You saw what the soldiers did to our village, madame. We can't live there now."

"Did the soldiers arrest anyone?"

"There was no one to arrest. We knew they would come, since it was a white man, so we hid in the forest. They didn't come down. They burned the village and left."

"What about the white man? And the child? Why did you . . ." But once again Kate broke off, leaving her question unanswerable, and the villagers said nothing, though several made vague gestures, as if to appeal to the vastness of the grasslands themselves, or the depth of the sands, or as if to say: who can tell what has become of this white man we didn't know, or this child who lived with us every day of her life?

"We didn't send for the soldiers," I said. "We're sorry about your village."

"They're soldiers. They did what they're expected to do."

"But how will you live now, with no houses? What if it rains?"

"It won't rain. The mushipu is already here."

It all was incontrovertible, with no place for argument or discussion. A speeding Land Rover, a child in the road, and everything else followed inevitably. The villagers did what had to be done; the soldiers came as everyone knew they would; now the villagers would live where they had to live. And it wasn't going to rain, any fool could see that. So our conversation had run its course. But when we turned to go a woman touched Kate's arm, and said, "The child's mother wants to see you. You have to come to her—she can't leave her place."

Of course—a mourning woman must stay in her house, and when her house is burned to cinders, I suppose she must choose a piece of ground and stay there. Just one of the countless taboos and rituals of death and mourning. How could people keep them all straight? Through practice, maybe. They mourn a lot, because they die a lot.

The mother sat beside her belongings on the edge of the encampment, naked from the waist up, her body coated with a red paste of mourning. Large red breasts hung down over the fold in her stomach, and the paste on her swollen face was streaked with tears.

They said she had wanted to see us, but now she looked at the ground and said nothing. A man in the crowd spoke for her. He told how the Land Rover had come speeding through town, early yesterday morning when the children were crossing the road, going to the spring for water. The white man didn't slow down. He seemed to expect the children to fly out of his way like chickens, but this one was always slow. She couldn't hear well; she was soft in the head. The Land Rover slammed into her, sent her flying through the air, into the ditch. And the white man stopped. If he hadn't stopped he still would be alive. Later he could have signed a confession, paid a fine, given money, goats, cloth to the girl's family. Instead he got out of his camion and came running back to where the girl lay dying on the roadside. But in the village anger and sorrow were too powerful to tolerate his presence. Even the women took up machetes and clubs and went out on the road to kill the reckless man with his glistening white skull. Afterward, his camion was drenched in its own fuel and someone put a match to it. When the fire was dying the camion was pushed into the grass and the white man buried. We could take the body if that was what we had come for. But if we were here to claim some further vengeance, we would find they had nothing left to sacrifice, the soldiers had destroyed everything.

The man was sad but not remorseful. No individuals could be held accountable for Tom's death. The village had been punished, but the villagers themselves were immune from personal responsibility, protected by an anonymity conferred by the mob, and by an understanding that they had acted out of a collective passion, fulfilling a collective obligation.

We spent a sleepless night lying in our clothes on raffia mats in one of the hollow cement buildings. These once must have been warehouses, though it was hard to believe that sterile land had ever produced anything to store in them.

The next morning we walked back to rejoin Boris and Ndosi at Kilala Mission, and the following day the investigators arrived. Officials from the American Embassy and the Peace Corps, and detectives from the government police, accompanied by a half dozen soldiers. One of the detectives doubled as undertaker, in charge of exhuming the body and preparing it for shipment home. As friends of the deceased, one of the embassy people told us, we ought to accompany his body back to the States, for the sake of his family if nothing else. Of course, once we left it was unlikely we could return; it had become almost impossible to obtain an entry visa. Not that there was much demand for them. Better to get out now, before the country went entirely to hell. But Kate said we weren't prepared to leave on such short notice, if we couldn't come back. Well, said the official, are you prepared to stay? After seeing what happened to your friend? This sort of violence is becoming commonplace, he said. And you shouldn't necessarily expect a rescue when things get tight. This far out in the bush, you shouldn't even expect people to keep coming out and retrieving bodies.

They asked us questions about Tom, and listened skeptically to our answers. They had particular trouble with the idea that since he'd left the Peace Corps Tom had been unattached to any organization. They wanted to know what he'd *done*, what position he'd held.

"He didn't actually have a position," I said. "He just lived here."

"No one just lives here," said the police investigator impatiently. "'Just lived here' is not a category. He has to *be* something."

"Well, sometimes he liked to say he was a tourist. So I suppose you could put him down as a tourist."

"Out here they don't get any tourists," said the police investigator.

"Not many," I said. "Not yet. Tom was the first."

The embassy people offered to give us a ride back to the Kivila Valley, but Père Leo asked us to stay another day and attend the Mass he was saying for Tom. So we stayed, though as it turned out, the Mass was actually for Frère Tomás. I suppose it was appropriate that in this place where Tom had dreamed up a fictional life for himself, we should pray for the soul of a fictional character. Père Leo spoke of a pious and selfless young martyr, delivered into the arms of God. But the eulogy was remote and clichéd, dense with doctrines of predestination and a sense of déjà vu, as if the père had already mixed Tom up with the people whose photographs hung on the library wall.

Then there was nothing left to do and we were free to go. But we had no transportation. If we hadn't been burdened with Boris we might have set out walking again, though Ngemba was 100 kilometers away. As it was, we waited passively two more days at the mission. Père Leo didn't seem to mind, or even notice—all day he spoke to no one, and went about his activities as if he were moving among ghosts. In the afternoons he retired to his quarters and listened to the news, which he summarized for us at dinner, speaking in short, flat sentences underlain with a grim satisfaction, as if it weren't news at all, only a confirmation of his beliefs and expectations.

> *Another prime minister has fled to Brussels.*
> *The rebels have captured more towns in the eastern provinces.*
> *There are reports of cholera in the refugee camps on the border.*
> *An American tourist has been killed in an uprising at a remote location in*
>   *the south.*

I began to get a sense of how Tom could have stayed on in that mission. This kind of isolation amounted to sensory deprivation; you began to feel insubstantial, as if the core of your personality was something indefinite and impermanent. *You could shift position, move into different configurations. There were more possibilities than you'd ever imagined.* You could become Frère Tomás. You could become a traitor to your friends, a highwayman, a fugitive. You could become an American tourist, killed in an uprising at a remote location in the south.

How was it Tom had described the African travelers in his letters? *They enter an altered state, a catatonia of waiting* . . . That was also an option at Kilala Mission, apparently. It described Ndosi, who had cried openly when he heard of Tom's death but now mostly just sat staring, only occasionally rousing himself to write something in his cahier. It described Boris, who sat in the library for long hours, silent and unreachable; and Kate, who slept most of the time. A dead sleep, she said; no dreaming at all.

I couldn't sleep. I roamed the mission grounds, browsed in the library, drank the warm beer, watched the sky close in on the manioc field. I felt strangely calm. A sterile, bloodless, dead calm, the product of a few moments of passion and violence: the girl's body flung up across the road, the mob converging, a skull smashed, bones cracking, blood flowing out into the infinitely absorbent sand. Like in your dream, I said to Kate. A long time ago, you had a fever and you dreamed of a body in the road at night, remember? You touched it and felt blood and realized it was a man's body and you knew him. When you woke you looked at me and said there's only one man whose body you'd know by touch alone. And later you said, a dream like that is more an expression of fear than a prophecy. But I guess you were wrong on both counts.

She looked at me dully, and shrugged. I have thousands of dreams, she said. A few are bound to end up looking like prophecies.

Everyone seemed to have forgotten the nightwatchman. It was five days since he'd set out, pushing his bike toward Mafemba, promising to return with a bush taxi so we could pursue Tom. Then, in the middle of another hazy formless afternoon, an old two-ton Mercedes flatbed truck came roaring down the driveway, with its atonal horn blaring and thick clouds of diesel smoke trailing behind and the nightwatchman leaning out the passenger window, waving triumphantly.

He was upset to learn we had pursued Tom on foot rather than wait for the bush taxi he'd promised to bring us. He acted as if our faithlessness and impatience were responsible for the tragic turn of events. Ndosi wanted to argue with him, but Kate said never mind, we still need a taxi. She thanked the nightwatchman, gave him some money, and began to negotiate with the driver about taking us to Ngemba.

While they haggled, Boris came out of the building and shuffled around the truck. He asked Kate how much the driver was asking, and when she told him he said it was extortion.

"Well, we have to pay it. We don't have any options, Uncle Pers."

"There are always options." He made his way around the truck again, squinting at the interior of the cab, bending stiffly to peer at the undercarriage. It was the first time in days he'd shown an interest in anything. Kate watched him apprehensively and resumed her discussion with the driver.

They were coming to an agreement when Boris leaned against the hood and said that one option was to buy it.

Kate arched her eyebrows. "Well, that would be an impulsive purchase, wouldn't it?"

"No," Boris said, "it wouldn't." He called to Ndosi to bring out his suitcase. "Ask him how much it would cost, Katy."

"Père Michel would not consider this old clunker an acceptable replacement for his Land Rover, Uncle Pers."

"I'm not buying it for Père Michel."

"I hope you're not buying it for me, then."

"Of course not. It's not something you need."

"It's not something anybody needs, Uncle Pers. It's at least thirty years old. Every moving part has been jerry-rigged a dozen times. I bet it rides like a jackhammer."

"Yes. It was built to carry weight, Katy. To transport cargo! Which is exactly what she needs, what she requested, and what I now understand I'm obliged to buy for her."

"Who the hell is 'she'?"

"Well, the nurse, of course."

"You're joking."

"I'm not."

They'd been speaking quietly, but now Kate got excited. "Uncle Pers. You *can't* buy a truck for the nurse. She doesn't even know how to drive! Where will she get fuel or parts? Who'll keep it running for her? These roads are incredibly dangerous. How will she pay the bribes and deal with soldiers and protect herself from bandits? What if she gets in a wreck?"

Boris shrugged. "Someone will have to teach her to drive. As for the rest of it, certainly there are risks. Believe me, Katy, I've considered them all. It may well be a bad idea for her to have a truck. But I'm in no position to judge these things. For me, it's merely a question of settling an old account. Of making restitution."

Ndosi returned, lugging Boris' old suitcase. He put the suitcase on a bench, and Boris sat down and fiddled with the combination lock. He opened the suitcase a crack and slid a hand inside. "Tell him I want to buy his truck," he told Ndosi. "Ask him how much he wants."

THE OCCUPATION

It was only a half day's drive home from Kilala Mission, but by the time we dropped off the escarpment and began the long rutted descent into the smoke and haze that obscured the Kivila Valley it seemed as if we'd been riding in that jackhammer two-ton for weeks, and when Ndosi muttered something about how it was too early in the season to be burning the fields, so where was all the smoke coming from, no one had the energy to answer. Who cares where smoke is coming from when you're bone-rattled and dust-parched and completely exhausted, when you feel like you've just traversed an entire continent on the truck-swallowing lost highways of Tom's imagination?

We expected to create a commotion, riding into Ngemba not in Père Michel's Land Rover but instead four abreast in the cab of a skeletal flatbed truck no one there had ever seen. But people hardly seemed to care about the truck. They were subdued and withdrawn, and when at last we jolted to a stop in our driveway the exuberant, curious crowds we'd expected did not materialize. A few children somberly watched from the gate, and Sticky Tree and Telo hurried down from the house, and a young man wearing sunglasses and a black beret and a military shirt slouched off the porch of the guest house and stood by the fence with his arms crossed, watching us.

There was no commotion, Telo said, because a commotion already had been created. The night before, a group of soldiers had surrounded the smuggler as he drove his loaded truck out of the Place Without a Name, on what he'd said would be his final smuggling run to the Kivila Valley. They shot out his tires and smashed his windshield, confiscated his suitcase of money and the produce he had just bought, beat him and his boy chauffeur until they were bruised and bloody, and set grass fires all around the Place Without a Name. The fires burned all night and spread to Kasengi by dawn, where they consumed several outlying huts and fields. Meanwhile, the soldiers went down to Ngemba and met the commissaire de region, just arriving with another contingent of soldiers. The commissaire immediately issued a proclamation stating that the lawlessness and acts of sabotage that had become commonplace in the Kivila Valley would no longer be tolerated. Then he summoned the chef de poste and retired to the guest house.

Later that day soldiers appeared in Malembe. They pulled down and destroyed the half dozen bamboo airplanes that had been set up above the village, and searched the village hut by hut for Ndosi, identified by the commissaire's agents as a ringleader and chief saboteur. When they couldn't find him they burned his hut and the huts and fields of his family, requisitioned corn, manioc, and chickens from the villagers, and returned to Ngemba, where they set up a barracks in the break room of the palm-oil mill.

By the time Telo finished telling us all this Ndosi had slipped away, and when the soldiers arrived to question us we could honestly say that we had no idea where he might be. The soldiers stood around for a while looking at the two-ton and talking in the language of the river tribes to the north. Finally they wandered down to the Place de la Révolution. A few children showed up to look at the truck, but the nurse did not come down to inspect her new possession. Boris insisted on returning to her house. He asked me to carry his suitcase, but when I reached for it, Kate told me to wait.

"Uncle Pers, why don't you just leave the suitcase here? We can lock it up for you. It'd be safer than in the nurse's hut, don't you think?"

"Safe from what, eh? There's no money in it anymore. Just a lot of old papers. No one would want them. I'm thinking of turning them over to my biographer."

"It's no use playing games, Uncle Pers. We all know what we're talking about. Will and I have been involved with your memoirs for a long time, remember? We're qualified to look out for them. Unlike Ndosi. His English is inadequate, for one thing. And he's uneducated. What does he understand of historical or social context, even the basic geography of your life? He doesn't know Indonesia from Patagonia, or Sukarno from Ché Guevara. Maybe it's amusing to call him your biographer, but the fact is he'd make a complete hash of your biography. Worse than anything Aunt Mavis could do. I think you should just leave your papers with me. If you don't want me to publish them, I promise I won't. But at least I can preserve them."

Boris looked at her gravely. "Do you really think so?" He took her arm and hobbled toward the gate, barely turning his head to address me. "Bring the suitcase up, Will."

So I got the suitcase and followed them up to the camp, and we left him in the nurse's yard with a couple of other old men, though there seemed to be no one to care for him. Both the nurse and the albino girl were very sick, people said, and of course no one knew where Ndosi had gone.

That night Kate and I tried to sit on the front porch, but that refuge too had been violated by the occupation of the guest house. Occasional music and laughter escaped the house; not particularly loud or obtrusive, except in contrast to the unnatural silence of the camp above. Somewhere a generator was running, and the weak electric lighting next door seeped like a contaminant into the darkness of our yard. It didn't quite illuminate our porch, but still I felt exposed up there, visible to the scrutiny of the soldiers and the man with the black beret. Kate finally just went to bed, but I sat up and read in the kitchen, where the thick cement walls preserved the old silence. Late at night, I turned on the radio and listened to the world news on the BBC. Though for me it wasn't really *news,* because when you're sitting in a small house in the dark center of Africa the day's newsworthy events have no urgency; they might just as well have happened last week or last month or last year. "This is London," the newscaster announced, then recited her litany of threats and disasters, a confirmation of the shifting disorder and volatility of the world. But what amazed me was how London could be so summarily spoken for. As if a single clipped, modulated voice, beamed across the black spaces, could reaffirm the place of London at the center of the world. As if there really existed that kind of London: a city of order and permanence, where the Churchillian jaw is set in opposition to the rising chaos, where the Prime Meridian is anchored, slicing out through darkness and walls of static to link a lost valley in Africa with an empire that encircles the globe.

Such are the delirious effects of radio, late at night in remote corners of the world. But the news itself was only the usual disasters: stories of terrorism and slaughter and corruption and political intrigue, the bitter nightcap we require to ease us into our troubled sleep. Major events, affecting millions of people. Whereas what had happened that day in the Kivila Valley was nothing, the mildest form of terrorism. In a terrorized world it would register on no one's scale. A handful of soldiers, a beating, a bit of broken glass, a few smouldering huts, and to top it off, a half dozen toy airplanes ground under a boot, and the splinters tossed in a pile and burned. Imagine such a story coming over the airwaves, the newscaster's voice precise and bland and neutral as always, as if presenting us with an equivalent example of human savagery and evil.

In Central Africa this morning, a man was beaten by soldiers, who then proceeded to ransack another man's model aeroplanes. The authorities have been unable to confirm . . .

It would play like a parody of the barbarism that is the usual subject of the news. But here where it had happened, there was no irony in it at all. It *was* barbaric, and somehow portentous, opening the way to far bloodier and more newsworthy barbarisms to come.

I turned off the radio and went out on the porch. The generator at last had been shut down, and the guest house was silent and dark. No light glimmered off the river; no fire glowed in the blackness of the yard. There was only the dim inconstant light of fireflies, which illuminated nothing. I peered into the darkness, trying to find Placide or at least recognize some familiar shape: the cook shed, the chicken coop, even the two-ton. But the shadows were strange, outlines of a world where all the balance has shifted. Yet I could *see* things: a vision of what the flashlight and the moonlight had obscured, and beneath the familiar insect sounds of the night I could hear low voices, articulating the dreams of sleepers and plotters.

The vision began with points of orange light streaking in the darkness beneath the trees and along the river road—not fireflies now but cigarettes, glowing in encampments where soldiers drank and laughed, celebrating the camaraderie of rape and genocide. Below them the river scarcely seemed to flow, reflecting and multiplying the lights of the camps like the surface of an oil-slicked lake. A harsh light came into the sky, as if from an artificial dawn, and on the road I saw the checkpoints that had gone up during the night, and the chain-link fences stretched across fields to mark new borders and divisions on the land.

The ferry and the pirogues and the palm-oil boat were gone now, but helicopters flew over the water, sending a great noise and a destructive wind down on the camp and drowning out the calls of birds and the voices that rose from the huts and company houses. Out of that confusion of noise and wind fleets of trucks and earth movers materialized, churning furiously beneath the forest canopy. River water lapped close to my porch steps, but the vision expanded to take in all the rigid alien geometry that was now a part of the valley. I could see the wide straight road that bisected it, and the massive dam of red earth that clogged the narrows far downstream. Dark reservoir waters were flooding the old river road and still rising, moving toward the now-abandoned camp. But at the dam a new and modern camp appeared, to service the turbines and transmitters and the power lines strung from the dam to the great towers that cut another swath through the forest and across the savanna. The villages themselves remained huddled in darkness and poverty, still coveting radios and sneakers, but at last the valley was wired into the grid of the world, connected to the electronic pulses of money and power.

Yet other, older connections were now severed. The ancestors receded, silent and unreachable. The elders wandered blindly into a companionless darkness, while the younger generation, aware at last of its own swelling numbers and empty prospects, rose up in an incoherent rage of destruction. And that captured, for a moment, the attention of the world. Staccato images were fed into the networks: fire and guns and bloody, rusty blades; faces frozen in hatred or fear or grief or anger; waves of soldiers and mercenaries and guerrillas; infinite reprisals; bodies spinning off in the river eddies, caught up in the logjam clogging the dead water at the top of the reservoir. And in the smoking stillness that followed silent lines of refugees moving out for the higher, infertile ground, fleeing the diseases and massacres and famines that finally had given the Kivila Valley its place on the evening news.

The next morning I went with Telo into the forest and along the Mission Road to visit Ndosi, who had evaded the soldiers and fled to the smugglers' hideout. Telo was morose enough to suit my mood, grimly intoning the various omens, among them his own dreams, that had predicted both Tom's violent death and the attack on the smuggler. His racking cough sounded especially hollow and foreboding as we pushed through the drying brush on the Mission Road, and I wondered what he would make of my apocalyptic vision of the night before. But its imagery was literal and brutal and required no interpretation, so I kept it to myself. Still, it had left me shaken, and I feared we would come out into the clearing by the river to find the smugglers' hideout burned to the ground and Ndosi captured by soldiers, or murdered. But the hut still stood, and Ndosi was alone and in good spirits, cutting brush in the little valley above his garden. He'd decided to build fishponds here, he said; Tom had always told him this valley would be an excellent site. So these ponds would be a memorial to his old fish consultant, as well as a means of livelihood and a source of food for the village—one the commissaire and his soldiers would not be likely to plunder.

He seemed almost blasé about the destruction of his airplanes. But how could he just shrug it off, when he'd put so much into them, and expected from them a miraculous flight that would open the world to him? In fact, they hadn't flown at all; they'd just been pulled from the sky, crushed to splinters, and incinerated in the fire that consumed his hut. Yet this did not seem to weaken his conviction that they *could* fly, that at some time they had flown, and that they would, when he built more of them, fly again.

Such a belief could be based only on superstition and delusion: the blind faith of the pretechnological mind. Yet as blind faiths go Ndosi's was remarkably flexible, perhaps even compatible with the scientific facts that seemed to contradict it. As blind faiths go his was easy and graceful, even, you might say, aerodynamic: a faith built of tungsten and cobalt, titanium and plastics, hollow bones and feathers, and modeled after the physics of jets and soaring birds.

I had no faith, only a skepticism that might have been forged of unyielding iron and set in cement on the ground. I made a distinction between technology and magic, and I would never believe that crude bamboo airplanes could fly. Yet I was so upset by their destruction that I extrapolated from it a vision of total devastation. And it was Ndosi who counseled moderation, who seemed to understand my reaction at the same time that he rejected it as extreme.

"We all feel sorrow at the death of Monsieur Tom," he said, flinging a branch onto the slash pile on the edge of his clearing. "But as for the planes, we'll build more, when we have time, maybe when we get a new commissaire who isn't afraid of them. Now we are occupied with other things."

"Ç'est ça," Telo agreed. Then they both gave me an odd look, as if to say, well, *we* are occupied with other things. But what are you occupied with, Monsieur Will?

Nothing so tangible as a fishpond, I might have answered. In fact, what occupied me was entirely intangible, which was one reason I couldn't explain myself to the commissaire when he summoned Kate and me to the guest house that afternoon. We followed a soldier past the small crowd waiting on the porch and in the foyer: people with exhausted and vacant expressions, as if they'd endured a wait so long and tedious it had dulled even the anxiety of appearing before the commissaire.

We were given no time to dull our own anxiety, or even to bring it to a head. The soldier brought us at once into the living room. There was no interior lighting, and the shades were drawn. The soldier left us in the middle of the floor, and the chef de poste emerged from the obscurity of the room and told us to come forward. He introduced us to the commissaire, who was sitting at a table in the front of the room. We shook hands, or rather the commissaire extended a hand from the shadows for each of us to grasp in turn. It felt soft and damp and bloodless, like something that has been underground for a long time. The commissaire asked for our passports, which he examined at great length with a flashlight.

Finally he returned the passports and began to talk. He slouched in his chair and spoke softly without moving his body, except to lift a hand every few minutes and with meticulous delicacy brush invisible pieces of lint from his black suit. His teeth were very straight and white but I glimpsed them only a couple of times, when he drew out a word for emphasis and his soft fat lips curled away from them. There wasn't much to be seen of his eyes, either—just little slits above his puffy cheeks, revealing opaque pupils and a glint of yellow sclera.

He began by speaking of the importance of palm oil to the economy of the region and to the industries of the world. A study of history revealed, he said, that in this very valley, government soldiers had turned back the barbaric attacks of Communist rebels and Boer mercenaries who sought to sabotage the mills and gain control of the vital flow of palm oil. Soldiers still would fight, if necessary, to preserve that flow, against interior sabotage as well as exterior attack. But the people themselves were undisciplined. Every-where laziness, corruption, and incompetence threatened the progressive policies of the government; everywhere the signs of cults and conspiracies could be seen; everywhere was the meddling hand of the neocolonialist, the provocateur, and the saboteur. Even the exploiters of old, driven from the country during the wars for independence, now felt emboldened to return. His agents were currently investigating substantive allegations linked to one of those exploiters, an old man whose documented activities included espi-onage, bribery, economic blackmail, and a long history of subversion, pro-fiteering, and agitation, activities that could lead only to . . .

He talked on—a muttering, low-key sleepy-voiced rave, but a rave nonetheless, and in French, so eventually he lost me. My gaze began to drift around the room. The place seemed deathly quiet and desolate, but in fact it held dozens of people, becoming visible now as my eyes adjusted to the low light. Mostly they were strangers to me, soldiers and chefs and bureaucrats and officials from elsewhere, sitting stiffly in straight-backed chairs lined up against the walls, looking bored but nervous. I recognized a few local chefs, and the fellow in the black beret, who slouched against the wall a few feet behind the commissaire, with his arms crossed. Something about that slouch nagged at me. I guessed he was some kind of bodyguard or aide-de-camp, standing close to the commissaire in a trim khaki shirt decorated with a few medals and insignias—not the usual soldier's uniform, but it did give him a quasi-military look. Then I recognized the insignias—first-class stripes, merit badges, Troop 4. It was a Boy Scout shirt. Probably a rummage-sale leftover, and now it had made its way to a place in Africa where no one had ever heard of the Boy Scouts, where a farceur seething with resentment and aggression could put it on and suddenly feel like he had the authority to break windows and kick people and smash airplanes and set fire to fields and huts.

The room was silent. The commissaire had stopped talking, and everyone was looking at me. Kate nudged me and muttered, "Answer him, Will. He wants you to explain why you're here."

He had no idea what a wide-open question he was asking. Or that he'd asked it just when my anger toward his black-beret flunky was surging, short-circuiting all my instincts for diplomacy and self-preservation. So instead of an appropriately bland and cautious reply, I answered the commissaire's rave with one of my own.

I told him that the reasons I was here were far too complex to summarize in the sort of answer he was expecting, and under circumstances that were not conducive to open and honest dialogue but seemed more like an inquisition or a witch-hunt. But one thing I was *not* doing was beating people, breaking their possessions, and stealing from them. So the more relevant question was, what was *he* doing here? The people of the Kivila Valley had suffered vicious and arbitrary attacks at the hands of soldiers under his command, and until he issued an apology, made restitution for damages, and gave assurance that such attacks would not be repeated, I would categorically refuse to cooperate with him.

This was a bold speech, if not very smart. But I was saved from its consequences by the French language. Because the truth was I didn't have the skill to say these things off the cuff, in French. Beside me Kate swallowed hard, and the chef de poste stared in amazement. But the commissaire wore a blank look. He turned helplessly to his Boy Scout, who leaned over and spoke into his ear, presumably offering some kind of translation. But when the Boy Scout stepped back the commissaire still looked confused. Finally he just shrugged and waved his hand in the air, as if to obliterate the entire episode. There was a moment of awkward silence, then he focused on me again. His lips twisted into a grotesque, unnatural expression that I understood was intended to be a smile, and he shifted the tone of his inquiry entirely. "Merci, monsieur. Ça ç'est tout. Mais, did I mention"—and his hard little eyes bored in on my feet—"how much I have been admiring your excellent shoes?"

"My shoes?"

"Such shoes aren't possible to obtain in this country."

"Surely in Kisaka—"

"In Kisaka they are looting the shoe stores. I'm wondering if you could obtain a pair for me. Perhaps you might even sell me those. Or make a gift, if you like."

"These are kind of worn out. Anyway, I need them. They're my only pair."

"I see. Well, perhaps you should look through your things again. And if you should happen to find an extra pair, I would very much like to own them."

. . .

Kate squeezed my arm as we walked back to our house.

"That was an incredible speech, Will. Of course, nobody had any idea what you said."

"That's probably a very good thing."

"But they were impressed. You said it so confidently. Somehow you even charmed that snake of a commissaire. But oh, God, isn't he horrible?"

"Well, sure. But you know, for some reason it's his flunky who really sets me off. The Black Beret. The Boy Scout. It scares me how intensely I can dislike somebody when I have so little to go on, just a slouch and a sneer and a Boy Scout shirt. Well, and the way he wears his beret and his sunglasses. And of course his association with that snake of a commissaire."

She gave me an amused look. "You have a lot more to go on than that. It's Dimanche, Will."

"Dimanche!"

"Sure. How did you think the commissaire knew about your extra pair of sneakers? His agent told him. It looks like Dimanche has grown another new skin, Will. But I bet you anything that underneath it, he's the same boy he used to be."

At dawn the next day Kate walked to the mission to visit with the sisters and discuss the question of the destroyed Land Rover with the pères. When she returned at midday she was flushed and excited, the first time since Tom's death that I'd seen such a spark in her. She put her arms around my neck and kissed me.

"I have good news and bad news," she said.

The bad news was we had practically no money left. It turned out that Tom's traveler's checks had covered only a little more than half the cost of replacing the père's Land Rover. She and the père had gone over the lease, which clearly stated the value of the vehicle, as well as her obligation to replace it in the event of loss or irreparable damage. There was no insurance. So she'd written them a check, and now we were almost broke.

"Maybe it's time to seriously consider getting out of here, Kate. Before everything goes completely to hell and we end up destitute besides."

"We can't leave without Uncle Pers. Or his memoirs. And how would we get him to go with us?"

"What *are* you planning to do about the memoirs? Still hoping for a cat burglar?"

Well, lately I've been thinking that maybe we don't need to do anything at all. We just have to be patient, and something will happen. I have this feeling about it, that it's all going to fall into place. Right now Uncle Pers is just separating himself from the memoirs, step by step. He's separating himself from everything. And when he's distant enough we just move in and take them, and he never even knows it. In the meantime I don't want to act rashly, because there's no telling how he'd react. But Will, you haven't seen the good news yet. Come on outside."

I followed her off the porch and into the garden. We barely glanced at the soldiers watching us from the porch of the guest house. Kate went to the chicken shed and opened the door. She clicked her tongue, and three chickens emerged, softly clucking and pecking about in the dirt. The chickens were beautiful: fat, fluffy laying hens, twice the size of the stringy village chickens we were accustomed to seeing. Kate squeezed my hand. "We'll eat eggs three times a week, Will! Plus, it's just going to be so much *homier* around here with chickens. You can tell they have distinct personalities. I already named them: this one's Fricassee, the red one's Cacciatore, and the white one is Pot Pie."

"Good. So they'll know they have a future besides pointlessly laying eggs that never hatch."

"Oh, they have a bright future. Pot Pie is very feisty, but Souer Anne says once she settles down she'll be the best layer of the bunch. It was quite an adventure carrying them back here. They're not good travelers. Boy, you should have seen those soldiers eyeing them, though, when I brought them past the guest house."

"Yeah, well, you have to remember that those soldiers are on a mission to eat every chicken in the Kivila Valley."

"They'd better not come chicken-stealing around here. Pot Pie'll peck their eyes out, right through their sunglasses. And Monsieur le Consultant will stand up on his porch and deliver one of his famous speeches, so spectacularly incoherent they'll drop those chickens on the spot and go blabbering back to the barracks with their hands over their ears."

The she put her arms around me and started kissing me again, right out there in the yard in full view of the chicken thieves up on the porch of the guest house, so that I became very confused and couldn't tell what had gotten her so excited: the idea of my spectacularly incoherent speeches, or the thrill of finally owning chickens.

The mushipu was well advanced by the time our chickens laid their first eggs. Everywhere the fields were burning, the rivers shrunken, the earth dried and cracked and clotted. Food was scarce—because the drought was so severe, people said, and the soldiers had taken so much, and because so much had been sold to the mill and the smugglers. Then people began to die. Tom's death had been the first, though the dry season had not officially begun when he died. But it was nonetheless a mushipu death, associated with smoking skies and burning fields, and followed soon after by deaths that could be attributed directly to the deprivations of the season. Several children we knew died, and two old men who were Boris' companions in the nurse's compound. The albino girl died, and Matama wailed and shrieked and then went silent for days.

The day after the albino's funeral Kate and the nurse, now recovered from her fevers, went out in the two-ton for a driving lesson, and I walked up to check on Boris. He was alone in the nurse's yard, sitting on a mat with his back against the wall of her house. His condition was obviously deteriorating. He had that gaunt and unreachable look, the look of a man removed from his physical surroundings, occupying some shifting, shadowy ground between two worlds. How long could it be, I wondered, before he rejoined the old men so recently buried? But he roused himself to reach up and close his hand over mine. Which felt very strange. All the hours we'd spent together, and this was one of the few times we'd actually touched, skin to skin. The brittle weakness in his hand was palpable, but at the same time it gave off a tremendous heat.

"You have a fever."

"Yes. You come to Africa, you get a fever, you die, or wish you were dead. That seems to be the pattern."

He let go of my hand and leaned back against the wall. He was trembling, perhaps shivering from the fever. A rasping, gagging sound escaped his throat, and, alarmed, I reached for him again. But he waved me away, and I realized he was laughing.

"All right," he said. "All right, Will. Perhaps old men *shouldn't* be explorers."

"We can make you more comfortable, Boris. You don't have to live like this."

"You couldn't make me more comfortable. Well, you could get me some water."

I went inside the house, found a bidón by the door, and got a drinking glass out of a small cabinet. But after I filled it up I left it on the table and didn't go outside at once. A mud wall divided the nurse's house into two small rooms. This outer one was the public room, which I had been in several times. But the inner room was private, and I knew of no one besides the nurse, and perhaps Boris, who had been there. I tugged on the padlock that was on the door, and to my surprise it came open. I removed it from the clasp, and the door swung open.

The nurse's bedroom was cool and dark, with a musty, earthy smell, like a cellar. There was a small wooden bed in one corner, and a straw mattress against the wall on the other side of the room. Unframed photographs and pictures cut out from magazines hung on the wall, but it was too dark to see any detail. I felt my way around a chest of drawers and along the wall, brushing against some clothing that hung there: mainly pagnes, but among them something lighter and silkier—a nightgown, maybe, or a slip. I ran my hands down the length of the material, and pressed my face against it. At once I was engulfed in the complex smell of the nurse. The enchantress nurse, the fish-tailing nurse, the seductive, passionate, afflicted, celibate nurse. I wanted to stuff that flimsy diaphanous garment into my pocket and keep it forever, sneaking into dark corners to press it against my face and give myself up to the power of that scent. But then I shifted my weight and my foot hit something behind the hanging pagnes. Letting go of the slip, I reached down and felt the worn leather of Boris' suitcase.

Something will happen, Kate had said. *Everything will just fall into place, and we'll move in and take them.* And now here I was inside the forbidden room, with the house and yard empty, Boris too weak and distracted to know what was happening, and my hand closing around the handle of the suitcase that held his memoirs—just a lot of old papers, or else a unique history, a life-work, the object of a quest.

It would have been easy to slip the suitcase out the door unseen, set it down behind the hut, bring Boris his water, and then pick up the suitcase when I left. But I couldn't move with it, I don't know exactly why. Maybe I had a feeling that it was too personal a theft, perverse in a way, like stuffing the nurse's slip into my pocket. That until he was dead, or relinquished the memoirs of his own will, I had no right to them. That in spite of everything he was still not entirely finished with them, and it wasn't my place to decide what was to become of them.

I let go of the suitcase, brushed against the nurse's slip one last time, and left the room. I replaced the padlock, got Boris' water, and went back outside. He glanced at the glass I set beside him, then peered up at me and sighed.

"You can go ahead and ask me some questions now, Will."

"Excuse me?"

"I know there are things you've been wanting to ask. Now would be a good time."

"What do you mean by that?" He looked incredibly frail, leaning against the wall in the weak smoky sunlight. "Are you saying that . . . Look, should I get Kate, Boris?"

He frowned. "Those aren't the kind of questions I mean. You're wasting your opportunity."

He sat up and drank some water, wincing and swallowing with difficulty, then leaned back against the hut, breathing shallow, hard breaths.

"Can't I get you something?" I said. "We have medications. Are you in pain?"

He sighed. "Those aren't very good either, Will. No, there's nothing you can get me. Yes, I'm in pain. Of course. Pain is the central preoccupation of age. I'm trying to make room for it, like I make room for everything else. To open up enough to make room even for pain."

He moved away from the wall and lay back down again. "I'm going to rest now," he said. Then his gaze went distant and abstract, and I could get nothing else out of him.

That afternoon a boy came to the porch with the news that Telo was dead.

"Telo dead? But I didn't even know he was sick!"

"He was always sick, Mr. Will."

"What happened? How did he die?"

The boy shrugged. "Someone killed him. People are jealous, monsieur. And we have so many fetishers. It's easy to send a fever, a bad cough, to kill somebody."

"But Telo's always coughing. That's just the way he is."

"Yes," the boy agreed. "That's why it was so easy. He just coughed a little more, and then he died."

The morning after Telo's funeral Ndosi followed the Mission Road deep into the forest. He made his way far down the river to the grove where the oldest bamboo grew, and when he returned in the evening the longest stalk of bamboo anyone had ever seen was balanced on his shoulder. The next day he built a new bamboo airplane, and with the help of his cousins the Nakahosas raised it high above his garden and the fishpond he was building at the smugglers' hideout.

"From that height he can see the soldiers coming," Ndosi said. "Maybe he can warn us, or do something to divert them."

Of course, Telo's plane was an act of defiance as much as a warning system. But it was a calculated defiance (and a warning system that was unlikely to be tested), since the people Ndosi was defying would probably remain unaware of it. Though the plane was higher off the ground than any of the planes in Malembe had been, because the smugglers' hideout was so secluded it was not visible from any road or trail. Still, it served as a response to the commissaire and his soldiers. And it preserved and celebrated the visionary aspect of Telo's spirit, while downplaying the impracticality of his visions, and the plodding and phlegm-choked personality that had helped keep them grounded. Also it was incorporated in another vision—one that might, in spite of everything, bear fruit.

I squatted on the steep open slope above Ndosi's pond site and watched him work. Stripped to the waist, he hacked at the forest with a small ax and a machete, and redistributed the raw red soil with a cracked shovel and a wooden wheelbarrow. That was something to see, from the distance and height of my hillside perch: the small bright gash in the rain forest, the bamboo plane suspended above it, and the great buttressed trees rearing up behind, dwarfing the wheelbarrow, the man, and the pitiful little mound of dirt he was piling up. But he kept moving back and forth in his ragged shorts and his bare feet, excavating from one end, building up a dike on the other. And out of this, the labor of one man in the forest, a fishpond was taking shape—another miracle, as astonishing as the miracle of a bamboo airplane in flight.

He dumped a load of dirt and pivoted his wheelbarrow. "What do you think, Will?"

"I think it's an incredible amount of work." I skidded down the slope to join him on the dike.

He laughed. "In the old days—before Mr. Tom—it wasn't so much work to build a fishpond. The ponds were shallow, the dikes were low, and we didn't bother to clear away the trees. But we harvested only a few fish from those ponds, and the dikes were always failing when the streams ran high. Now, if we build the ponds the way Tom taught us, yes it's a lot of work. A lot of work! But if the work doesn't kill me, I'll get real fish out of it, God willing."

"Aren't you worried you'll lose this pond to your uncles, the way you lost the others?"

He shook his head. "That won't happen. I have a title to this land."

"A title! How'd you manage that?"

"The only way such things are managed: with money! I'm buying it."

"From whom?"

"Well, that's one problem. From everybody! This was common land, you know, which means everybody thinks it belongs to them. So I have to give something to my uncles and something to the village chefs and to the chef de collectivité and the chef de poste and the surveyor and the agronome. Eventually I'll have to give something to the commissaire too, after I stop hiding from him."

"How can you afford that? I guess the Road Builder's been paying you a pretty good wage."

Ndosi shrugged. "He pays well. And he's hired me for a lot of different jobs: his boy, his translator, his biographer. But the biography is very difficult! He thinks I should be finished, but he hasn't finished telling me what happened. So it's not easy to come up with the right story."

"I'd like to read what you've written."

"I want you and Kate to read it when it's finished. You read his old biography, which he wrote himself and which he says is all wrong, not worth reading. So maybe you can tell if this time I got the story right."

At midday, Ndosi's fiancée, Kitoko, appeared on the path above the pond site, two serving dishes balanced on her head as she descended the slope. She walked proudly, with an erect and swaying gait, and it occurred to me that Ndosi had surely forgotten his promise to wait several years before sharing a bed with her. And in fact such a promise seemed pointless now, impossible to honor—the girl had so quickly turned into a woman. She was too young for it, her girlhood had ended abruptly and prematurely, but maybe she would weather the shock. She seemed to have grit and intelligence and, like Ndosi, a large capacity for joy. Maybe that joy would be strong enough to survive endless hard labor, pregnancies, miscarriages, births, diseases, and deaths. I wondered what the central themes of Ndosi's life—the fishpond and the garden, the bamboo airplanes, his defiance of the authority and the power of the elders—meant to her, and if she would come to understand and even share the dreams and ambitious visions that seemed to come to him intuitively. Or maybe she had dreams and visions of her own, and these in some way might moderate the more extreme and destructive impulses of her husband.

"I asked the Road Builder," said Ndosi, working a wad of pale luku into a ball, "why he wanted to write another book for Mputu. Why does Mputu need another book?" He dipped the luku into the little bowl of Things—caterpillars, in this case, gathered by Kitoko in the morning and now floating limply in a thin green sauce—and stuffed the dripping wad in his mouth.

"You have so many books already," said Kitoko, shifting on her haunches beside her husband. "How can you read them all?"

"We can't," I admitted, and contemplated my own small, smooth ball of luku.

Ndosi, already seizing another fistful of luku, talked and chewed at the same time. "I said to the Road Builder: you want to give the story of the Road Builder to people in Mputu. Maybe they'll be entertained, but what will they understand of it? The Road Builder is ours. Why don't you write his story for us?"

"The Road Builder thought my husband's suggestion made sense," said Kitoko.

Tentatively, I dipped my luku into the bowl of Things and held it up. Sauce dripped down my fingers. Pasted to my glob of luku was a single deflated caterpillar. "It's sensible," I agreed. "Only, most of you can't read."

"That was his objection!" Ndosi cried. "And I said, true, people can't read. We have no books, so why should we read? If we had books that we wanted to read, maybe we'd learn."

"Didn't Placide already try that?"

"Well, that book you gave him was very dull. Also, it was in a foreign language."

"Well, Boris can't write in your language either."

"That was also his objection! And I answered, true, you don't know our language, but you do have a translator. And then he said to me, yes, you could translate, couldn't you? But I have a better idea. Perhaps *you* should write the book."

The caterpillar clung to my glob of luku, or the luku clung to the caterpillar. Sauce dripped down my wrist. It was awkward: I had to do something with it, and I could think of nowhere to put it but into my mouth. I bit off the caterpillared half, waited a couple of seconds, and decided, well, it was a far cry from roast cricket but still caterpillar was not the *worst* thing I'd ever tasted. Figuring to just get it over with, I scooped up another couple of caterpillars with the rest of my luku and sent them in after the first.

"We didn't know you liked caterpillars, Mr. Will!" Kitoko laughed. I waved my hand and managed to issue a grunting sound of denial from the back of my throat, where the luku was dissolving like a wad of papier mâché, stranding the three unchewed caterpillars in my mouth.

"We need water," said Ndosi. I held the caterpillars between my tongue and the roof of my mouth while Kitoko rose to get the water pitcher. Looking at her in profile, I noticed for the first time, beneath the tuck in her pagne, a small swelling low in her belly. I took a big gulp of water from the glass she handed me, and the caterpillars all went down at once, still intact.

"I'll bring you some more caterpillars," said Kitoko. "Enough for Kate too, though I don't think she likes them as much as you do."

"I thought you and Kitoko had a heart-to-heart about birth control," I said to Kate that evening.

"We did. But maybe she didn't really want birth control. Or maybe she's just so incredibly fertile there's no stopping it. Anyway, it's probably for the best. If she wasn't pregnant, she probably would have been invited to spend the night down at the guest house, or at the barracks, like most of the other young women."

"Does the commissaire order them down there, do you think? Or maybe do they consider it an honor?"

"I can't imagine. Maybe there's financial incentive. But probably they feel they have no choice. Which makes it rape."

Every evening there was music and laughter at the guest house. Sometimes when we sat on the porch we heard a knock on the guest-house door, and then women's tentative voices, absorbed at once by lower tones and easy male laughter. I thought of a night more than a year before, when smoke from Placide's little fire crawled along the wall of our house and drifted off toward the deserted guest house. Placide had watched it for a long time, as if he were seeing something other than the dark shuttered windows of a long-uninhabited house. Then he had muttered something. *The women enter, and later they leave.* Had that been a prophecy, then, or was history once more repeating itself, this time with the commissaire rather than Uncle Pers occupying the seat of provincial power and claiming the privileges and sexual tributes owed him by his subjects?

No visitors at all came to our house. Dimanche and the soldiers kept their distance from our compound, and strangely, no one from the camp stopped by to see us either. People sometimes called out a quick greeting as they hurried by on their way to the road or the river, but even the children did not linger to talk or to look for more than a few seconds upon our house and yard. Now that the river was low they passed by often, going down to fish or swim or play with the boats they made from empty tin cans—sardines and Vienna sausages and corned beef—they had scavenged from who knows where. Occasionally Matama would send a kid down to ask if our chickens were laying yet and if so could she borrow an egg, because there was so little food to be had in the village. But the chickens weren't laying, and the kid, who hadn't even entered the gate, turned at once and fled back to the camp.

Sticky Tree said it was because of the nightwatchman that no one came near.

"Placide? Why, what's he up to? I've hardly noticed him lately." In fact, it had been days since I'd even spoken to Placide. He seldom came near when we sat on the porch in the evenings, and he no longer kindled a fire in his brazier, in spite of the coolness of the nights. I was rarely even aware of his arrival in our yard; he just appeared, standing suddenly at dusk among the papaya and the bougainvillea below the chicken coop, or moving through the thick shrubbery along the fence line separating our yard from the guest-house compound. Then when darkness fell he would vanish entirely.

That's why everyone was afraid of him, Tree said. Because they hardly noticed him. Because he had become practically invisible. By day no one saw him, and at night—well, even he, Sticky Tree, had no wish to encounter Placide at night. It was said that ever since the commissaire had occupied the guest house, Placide had been spending the nights constructing booby traps and hanging fetishes in the yard. Naturally no one would want to enter such a place. Sticky Tree himself was careful never to stray off the path or go near the fence lines. Especially he stayed clear of the chicken coop, which Placide had barricaded with a dense fortification of snares and fetishes. I pointed out that Kate visited the chicken coop several times a day, to feed the chickens or let them run free for a while, and no harm had come to her. And Tree said yes, because they were her chickens, and as a white woman and a foreigner she was mainly immune to sorcery, but even so she ran a great risk.

I went down to the chicken coop to see for myself. From a distance it looked unremarkable enough, just a simple thatch hut, but a closer inspection revealed small hanging bundles of hair, bone, rock, and feathers. Two old medicine bottles hung on raffia strings beside the doorway, one filled with roots and leaves, and the other with some thick bile-colored liquid. I remembered the fetish someone had put in Ndosi's old fishpond. *Just hair and feathers, madame. Sticks.* He'd claimed he didn't believe in its power, but still it kept him from working on his pond. And now this made me a little nervous too, brushing past the encrusted bottles to open the door and look in. The chickens clucked and squawked and flapped down off their perches. They hopped over as if expecting to get fed, and I saw two fat brown eggs in the straw.

Kate was ecstatic when I brought her the eggs. She wanted to scramble them up at once with the last of our potatoes and onions, though there wasn't quite enough to make a meal. If only we had something else to go with it.

Potatoes, onions, eggs, and . . . I thought of the kids going down to the river with their flotilla of empty tin cans. "Corned beef hash!" I said. "Start boiling those spuds, Kate. I'm going up to the store."

Along the dusty path between the dispensary and the store, the children lay crumpled and still. Piled atop one another, arms flung back, small faces ground into the dirt. And the mid-afternoon world silent, as if, like me, the camp could not yet comprehend the meaning of these small bodies scattered along the path.

A high voice broke the silence. "That's enough! Beno ke zenga diaka! You can live again!" Four or five children emerged from behind the company store, carrying sticks that were roughly whittled into the shape of guns.

The bodies stirred, squirmed, disentangled, giggled, and rose to brush themselves off. Discussion and negotiation followed, wooden guns were exchanged, and the children with guns slipped off into the brush. The others formed a tight group and began to move up the path. A boy in front made noises and movements as if he were turning a wheel, shifting gears. The children with guns reappeared on the path, and dropped a bamboo pole in front of the others. The procession stopped. One boy, about eight years old, pointed his gun. "Attestation!" he squeaked. "Cadeau!" Some of the children handed him scraps of paper. He studied the papers briefly, then stepped back and shouted something. Those with guns raised them and made firing sounds, and the children in the path screamed and fell to the ground.

The eight-year-old grinned up at me. He was all bones and belly, with the thinning reddish hair of a kwashiorkor child. "We're playing Checkpoint, monsieur. We're soldiers!"

"And who are they?"

"Them?" He glanced at the bodies slumped along the path or rolled into the ditch beside it. "They're just the people we kill."

The storekeeper sat on a stool on the porch of the store. I stopped on the newest cement step and greeted him, but he looked at me darkly and made no move.

"Are you open?"

The storekeeper shrugged. "I'm at your service, monsieur. Comme toujours. If you like I can be open, why not? Ouvert, fermé, c'est la même chose, n'est pas?"

"Well, I'd like you to be open."

The storekeeper heaved a huge sigh and got to his feet. We entered the store, and a moment later he was staring down balefully from behind the counter while I peered into the shadows behind him, trying to see the cans on the shelf.

"Cloth or salt?" demanded the storekeeper.

"Excuse me?"

"Salt," he said slowly, with great exasperation, "or cloth?"

As my eyes adjusted to the dim light I saw that cloth and salt were all that were left on his shelves, except for the still abundant selection of skin lighteners. "No corned beef?" I said. "No sardines, even?"

"Ha! The sardines are the first thing to go. They love sardines."

"Who loves sardines?"

"Donc, les soldats. No one else shops here nowadays, eh? Just soldiers."

Of course. By now the villagers had learned to hide their chickens, and the soldiers had to look elsewhere for their plunder. Which explained how the children had come into possession of all those cans.

"The soldiers just come in and take whatever they want?"

"Oh no, monsieur, they don't *take*. They *pay* for everything. Let me show you how they pay." He went to his cash register and took out a bundle of small cards. "Requisition cards," he said, "to be redeemed in the currency of the Republic. It says so right here. Only, it doesn't say where we redeem them. But what does it matter, eh? Everyone in Ngemba is rich now. Everyone has a fortune in requisition cards."

A familiar gravelly voice called my name as I descended the steps of the company store. It startled me, because the place seemed so deserted, and also because I had hardly heard the chef de poste's voice for weeks. My head jerked up and I almost lost my balance—or maybe it was just an instinct for déjà vu that nearly hurtled me off that first step onto the brick-hard ground below, where I might lie waiting for the chef's duxième bureau to kneel beside me and envelop my bruised body in the generosity of her flesh. But I kept my footing—and my head—and made it off the steps upright. I went down to meet the chef de poste, who was coming up the path from the guest house. The duxième bureau wasn't with him, of course. In fact, she wasn't even the duxième bureau anymore. She was the chef's second wife, and nowadays she hardly crossed to our side of the river, and then only in the company of his first wife, whose aristocratic dignity and beauty had lately sharpened, while the second wife was losing her color and buoyancy and taking on a sallow and insubstantial look.

The chef de poste looked at me curiously while he shook out a cigarette.

"The secretary and I were talking," he said. "It's been a long time since we've seen you at the office."

"I don't have much to do at the office," I said.

"We were saying that maybe we should think of something for you to do. Something for the Dedication Ceremony, maybe. It's coming right up, you know."

I waited.

"That was an interesting speech you gave at the guest house a while back."

"You mean you understood what I was saying?"

"Oh, no. Not at all." The chef lit his cigarette and took a deep drag. "But the secretary said he understood a little of it. And he told me that with a little coaching, he thought you could deliver a speech that people might understand."

"The secretary is very flattering."

"He said he wasn't sure, but he thought you were *insulting* the commissaire."

I said nothing. The chef smoked, and scratched at his ear.

"It's a bad idea, William, to insult a man like the commissaire. It's necessary for all of us to treat him with respect."

"He beats people up, Chef. He steals things. He breaks things. He doesn't deserve respect."

"I don't like having him around any more than you do, William. But there's no point in insulting him. You have to consider why he acts like that."

"Okay, why?"

"Well, because he's not getting what he needs. He's the commissaire, William. So naturally he has a lot of expenses. But he's having trouble generating income around here. Also, he's nervous. You and madame make him nervous. And the Road Builder! He doesn't know what to make of the Road Builder."

"Who does?"

"All right, nobody does, maybe. But in any case, you won't influence the commissaire with insults and threats. A man in his position is only influenced by one thing."

"Well, I don't have any money, if that's what you mean."

The chef laughed. "You can't convince me of *that*, William. Not when you drive away in one truck, lose it, then turn around and buy a bigger truck to drive home in."

"It's not my truck, Chef. The Road Builder paid for that."

"Oh, yes. The Road Builder, again. He has all the money, eh?"

"He *had* money. I don't think he does anymore."

The chef smoked thoughtfully. "In some ways it doesn't matter," he mused. "As long as the commissaire *thinks* he has money and is committed to investing it productively, that's all that matters. I don't think it would be hard to convince him of that. The best thing would be to get the Road Builder himself to say a few words—except he doesn't seem to be talking at all these days, does he? So I think you are the one to do it."

"Do what, exactly?"

"Deliver the speech, of course. At the Dedication Ceremony. In French."

"Ha-ha. You know, Chef, these French jokes are getting kind of stale."

But the chef insisted he wasn't joking. I listed a few of my objections to his scheme: I lacked the authority and credibility to deliver such a speech; my French, however improved, was obviously inadequate; and it was a blatant lie to claim that the Road Builder or anyone else was about to make large capital investments in the Ngemba palm-oil mill.

He gave me one of his squinting, skeptical looks, blew out a cloud of cigarette smoke, and laughed at me. "I'm just telling you what the commissaire wants to hear, William. He's the commissaire, right? If what he wants to hear is a lie, it's our duty to tell him a lie."

I left the chef without making a commitment, but for some reason I found his words inspirational. Empowering. Maybe because he was finally asking me to *do* something. Here was the noble bureaucrat, isolated and powerless, a frail shadow of his former ambition, but at least he had a concrete task to perform. And maybe that task was not as outlandish as it seemed. Isolated and powerless, yes, the lone ant twitching—but what if the commissaire didn't realize that? What if he had a completely different idea of my position and importance? And what if I used that idea to create a new persona for the noble bureaucrat? Exiled to a remote station, but *connected* to important institutions, to the complex networks of power. Communicating with the exterior world, and exposing the obscure Kivila Valley to the realm of visible light.

At dusk Kate and I noticed Placide slipping through bushes at the far corner of the yard. I called him up to the porch.

"I just wanted to see how you're doing," I said. "We haven't talked much lately."

"It's not the season for talking, monsieur."

"Well, it's always good to talk to each other. Especially when times are difficult."

Placide shook his head. "It's the season for watching. For listening. But not for talking, because others are listening too."

"You mean, like, spies? Do you think someone's listening to us now?"

Placide shrugged. We all were looking toward the guest house.

"Why don't you ever make a fire anymore, Placide?" Kate asked. "These are the coldest nights of the year, and you have no fire."

"It's not a good season for fire."

"Well, I like seeing your fire at night. I miss it."

He looked up at her. "If you'd like to see a fire, madame, you should go up to the camp. There's a very big fire in the nurse's yard."

"Really? Like, a bonfire? In the nurse's yard?"

"I saw it on my way to work. The Road Builder was tending it."

"You're kidding. Tending a bonfire, all by himself?"

"But if you want to see it you should hurry. His fire was big, but it won't last long."

"Why do you say that?"

"Because he doesn't have any firewood. He's making it out of little sticks, and paper. Lots and lots of paper."

Kate and I stood at the nurse's gate and watched the old man emerge unsteadily from the darkness by the huts and toss something on the smouldering fire in the yard. He poked at it with a stick, and a cloud of thick smoke went up. He jabbed it again, and the fire flared suddenly, illuminating his intent eyes and exaggerating the shadowy topography of his face. He was like Placide, a huddled figure poking at a little fire, releasing into the atmosphere mysterious odors, distilled essences.

Another figure appeared in the doorway of the hut and moved out into the yard. The nurse, skirting the edge of the firelight and disappearing into the darkness by the corner of the fence. I took Kate's hand and we went through the gate and stepped into the circle of firelight. Boris glanced up and then began to scrabble around with his stick on the dark edges of the fire. Already the flames had died again.

"What are you burning here?"

"Old things," he muttered. "Trash. Old papers and whatnot."

The nurse murmured a greeting to a passerby at the gate, then moved off into the shadows at the far end of the compound. I flipped on my flashlight and shone it on Boris' suitcase, which lay open and empty beside the fire. The beam moved across smouldering embers, charred corncobs, the blackened ends of small sticks, and hundreds of sheets of paper that were now black and gray ash, their edges curled and glowing as the last of the fire went out of them. They trembled in the wind of the fire but held their form, and I could make out neat rows of printed text on some, and thin, densely scrawled handwriting on others.

The nurse appeared again, moving along the edges of the fireglow. Like an orbiting body going in and out of the darkness, shifting the gravitational fields in complicated ways. I grabbed the stick from Boris and nudged the papers, trying to push them out of the flame, but they crumbled into little pieces of ash and rose up with the heat of the fire into the sky.

"We're too late. He's burned everything." Kate's voice sounded flat and exhausted, but she pressed close against me, and her hand gripped mine with unnatural force.

Her uncle glanced up from the embers. "Every word," he said. "It took so much time to compile them all, and so little to be rid of them. Ha! Humans have created so many ingenuous devices, eh, but fire is still our most valuable tool."

The nurse moved in and drew Boris away toward her hut. It was late, she explained; the old man was tired; it wasn't a good time for a visit. Boris himself said nothing else. In fact, he remained silent for days, until the morning the Nakahosas beached their pirogues by the ferry dock and came running up to the camp with a story of a submerged tractor catching stray rays of light in a silt-bottomed pool at the end of the Mission Road.

3 6

THE RELIQUARY

That was the worst mushipu anyone remembered—the longest, the driest, and the deadliest. For almost four months there was no rain. Leaves fell thickly from the trees, the ground cracked and crusted, and in the sandy uplands the streams flowed a little and then sank away underground. The sky thickened with smoke and haze, but the river, people said, had never been so low and so clear. Young men and boys paddled pirogues along the shore, setting nets and lines, and in the afternoons they came to the door selling strange prehistoric-looking fish. Trapped for millennia between falls upstream and down, evolutionary anomalies swam in the deep pools of the Kivila River. Secret fish, unknown to science, and now these boys were yanking them out of the water and flopping them on my porch for a quick sale. But we ate the fish with little misgiving. Science was remote from us, and meat was scarce.

Lately the fishermen had been bringing their catch to the guest house and showing it to the soldier on the porch. Often he waved them off, but sometimes he called inside, and the commissaire himself would come to the porch, squinting in the sunlight, scowling with disgust at the fish that were offered. In his homeland, he said, the rivers ran full of fat silvery fish, and no one would eat these creatures that were more like evil black snakes than fish. But he'd order the soldier to buy some anyway, and to send them up to the camp to be prepared for dinner.

Today the camp seemed practically deserted, choking under a red dust and a smoky sky. A few children chanted my name as I entered the village beyond the company houses, but their enthusiasm was dulled—partly by familiarity, mostly by the ravages of the season. They no longer had the energy to sustain their fascination with me, any more than they had the energy to run and sing and invent intricate and mysterious games. Like everyone else in the camp, they were preoccupied with conserving their dwindling strength, and waiting for the rain.

But something was happening at the nurse's place. Dozens of people crowded into her yard, where two young men were talking excitedly. As I entered the yard a few people nodded a greeting and made way for me, and a couple of old men rose to greet me, wrapped in pagnes so filthy the pattern of the material was no longer discernable. They gripped my hand, muttered their blessings or curses, fixed me with their lunatic stares. Then they returned to their raffia mats and the company of other old men, all looking out on the world with some similar expression on their faces: as if they were in pain, but at the same time detached from their pain. As if they were living simultaneously in two separate worlds, fully connected to neither. Which is merely to say they were dying. Who among them would finish the business before the rains finally came? And who would linger, dying for months and even years, making dying a way of life? Who, just when you thought he was about to suck his last shallow breath, would rise up again from the mat to grip our hands? Because he was so hard to kill. *Because he has reason to live. Because he has work to finish!*

The young men—barefoot, wearing ragged shorts and T-shirts—were Ndosi's cousins, the fishermen Nakahosa Un and Nakahosa Deux, just returned with an amazing story from a fishing expedition downriver. They floated down many miles, they told us, to a place where the river deepened, bubbling and eddying in a long green pool. An old ferry barge lay half sunken and decaying along the shore, and the trail that once had been the Mission Road emerged from the forest above a beach of black sand and was lost in a landscape of brush-covered red hummocks, like an abandoned and overgrown termite colony. While their pirogues circulated in the long eddy, the Nakahosas peered down into the slow swirling waters, looking for fish, but when the currents parted and the bubbles dissipated they saw instead a great glimmering machine like a tractor, bright and yellow as if it were freshly painted, resting in the silt almost beyond the reach of sunlight. They caught a glimpse of it and then the currents welled up, the light shifted, their boat spun up the eddy. They went around the pool a half dozen more times but didn't see the tractor again, and finally they returned upriver, beached their pirogues by the ferry dock, and came running up to the camp to tell people of their discovery.

"I want to see it," said the Road Builder, rising from his mat and breaking the longest silence of his life.

I sat hunched on a low stool in a dugout pirogue in the middle of the river, staring into the fog that still obscured the banks on either shore. The Road Builder and Kate sat on similar stools in the other pirogue. It was probably as irresponsible to let Boris come on this journey as it had been to bring him along on the trip to Kilala Mission. But it was his old tractor we were going to see, supposedly, discovered by the Nakahosas after lying for thirty-five years at the bottom of the river. Once again he insisted on coming, and Kate said let him come, maybe we'll learn something, maybe we'll salvage one story at least. Clinging to Ndosi's arm, he made his laborious way down through the camp to the Nakahosas' pirogues. Then Ndosi, who would not get out on the river in a pirogue, took up his cahier and set off along the Mission Road to meet us downstream.

I had a better understanding of Ndosi's fear of the river, now that I was out on it myself, bobbing around in an inadequate little boat. A Nakahosa stood with his long paddle in the stern of each pirogue. Both the upright paddlers and the stools elevating the passengers seemed ill-advised to me, unnecessarily raising our center of gravity and increasing the instability of these low, wobbly canoes. Though after a mile or so I saw the purpose of the stools: if we sat lower we would be immersed in the rising brown water that sloshed in the bottom of the boat.

"Nakahosa. I think there may be a leak in your boat."

"Monsieur Will, there are many leaks. This boat is a tree, made to grow in the forest, not float on the water. If you'd like less water in the boat, use the bailing can."

I'd have liked less water in the boat, but I would not have liked to bail. Bailing would require movement, and movement would almost certainly tip the boat and dump us in crocodile-infested water. It was preposterous that we hulking creatures should be seated in such an unstable craft, gripping the gunwales and teetering in the middle of the river. Why did we have to drift so far from shore? Why did the Nakahosas have to paddle standing up, as if to further court the inevitable disaster? I agreed that the log should have stayed in the forest. It wasn't even a very big log. The hull was far too round, and the gunwales were dangerously low, with only an inch or two of freeboard. We were losing even that as we took on more water. The choice seemed to be to bail and capsize, or to not bail and merely sink.

"Excuse me, Nakahosa."

"Monsieur?"

"Do you ever capsize?"

"Capsize? Oh, not yet. Never. Because when I capsize I'll drown."

Over my shoulder I saw him leaning far out over the water, making a long sweep of his paddle to propel us close to the other pirogue.

"I'll sink to the bottom of the river, monsieur. Like the Road Builder's tractor. Because I can't swim."

Elsewhere the countryside seemed permanently damaged by the severity of the drought, combined with the damage wrought by human beings trying to extract some kind of living from it. Yet along the river flowing through the heart of the valley a narrow strip of land was preserved from the harshness of the season, and little of this desolation was visible. Here the Kivila Valley was still native rain forest, wild and unfragmented, rich with its primordial promise. At first we saw a few women on the banks, washing clothes, and a couple of boys fishing, but below the village of Malembe there was hardly a human presence. We passed a thatch shelter in a small clearing, and only far downstream, looking back through the fog, did I notice above the jungle a small airplane riding on a tall pole, almost invisible against the blank sky. Except for the plane I wouldn't have recognized Ndosi's riverside garden and the smugglers' hideout, where we plotted a modest new economic order and where cow-eyed Telo laid out his futile dreams of a modern world. *Sardines! Citizens, consider sardines!*

The river turned and narrowed, and the valley closed in. Huge trees loomed on the banks, indistinct and hazy in the low white sun. They hung over the water, weighted with vines and epiphytes, and we peered up into the tangled branches, hoping to see a monkey or a sloth, or even a wild cat. But the Nakahosas said those were rare sights. The animals had become very few, they said, and although they carried a gun on the river they seldom got a shot

at anything. There were birds; a great noise of invisible birds emerged from
the trees we floated beneath, but in flight we saw only a pair of jeweled green
kingfishers swooping upriver low over the water, and a single heron lifting off
heavily far downstream and slowly beating its way into the rising fog.

As the fog lifted visibility improved, though the fog was not really gone,
only assimilated by a higher cloud. But when we rounded a broad bend in the
river we looked out across the entire valley. A swollen reddish sun hung over
the hazy savanna escarpment. Columns of smoke rose up from the savanna
and became indistinct, absorbed like the fog into the thickening sky. Our two
pirogues drew near to each other, and I saw that the old man also was watching the smoking horizon.

"Kasengi," he muttered, only the second time I'd heard him speak that
day. "They're burning it to the ground."

The river narrowed again, and we glided through more long corridors of
trees. The boats rocked gently in the current, and we sat as if in a trance, mesmerized by still air, heavy green shadow, shafts of pale light. We drifted into a
deep pool with a long eddy on the inside of the turn. In the shallow water
where the pool tailed out lay a half-sunken barge, trailing cables and pieces of
twisted metal, and all along the eddy shore the giant forest trees were gone.
Here were only saplings and shrubs, and the form of the shoreline and the
land behind was altered—the bank broken up into hummocky slopes, with
sloughing red earth exposed, and baked like shards of brick by the sun. This
was a newer, rawer geology, telling a different story from that told by the worn
contours of the earth elsewhere in the valley.

"Here is the pool," Nakahosa said. "Beneath us is the Road Builder's
tractor."

We circulated for a long time down the pool, up the eddy, down the pool
again, leaning precariously over the sides to peer into the green depths. The
water was clear, but in the shifting currents the diffuse mushipu light did not
penetrate deeply. The Nakahosas couldn't remember exactly where they'd
seen the tractor, so we looked everywhere along the pool, now and then calling out: "There!" or "Look!" or "Stop!" But there was no stopping, no fixed
place out in the great circulating pool, and whatever the currents momentarily revealed was at once left behind, or obscured again behind a vortex of
swirling water. At one point I saw something taking shape in the deepest

waters, some shadowy mass that seemed to have the ordered form of machinery, but immediately the image shifted and was lost, dissolving into some abstraction of moving light and water.

The old man's attention soon wandered; he trailed his hand in the water and stared off downstream at the sunken barge, across the eddy at the disrupted shore. But the rest of us kept looking, circulating eight or ten times before I noticed the man on the shore, sitting on the remains of a cement piling overgrown with low bushes and the fraying strands of rusty cable. Had he been there all along, or only just that minute risen out of the unsettled earth? I gripped the gunwales, feeling exposed and vulnerable out on the open river, passing slowly before this strange shoreline. Then, just as I was about to shout out that we were being spied upon, I realized that of course it was only Ndosi. I waved to him but he made no response. We went round and round in the pool and he never called out to us; and when at last we gave up and paddled to shore he didn't greet us or ask if we'd spotted the relic we were seeking. He helped Boris out of the pirogue and seated him on the piling, then squatted against a hummock while the Nakahosas took out a bowl of luku and some cold fried fish. Kate and I ate with them, though I felt queasy after the pirogue ride and had only a few bites. Both Boris and Ndosi ignored the food. Boris stared into the brush and Ndosi watched him, clutching his cahier against his knees and squatting there, among the scrub and the laterite at the end of the Mission Road.

The Nakahosas packed the leftover lunch and bailed their pirogues. "Let's go, Uncle Pers," said Kate, but he didn't move. She stood in front of the piling and looked at him. "Come on," she said gently, reaching out to touch his knee.

"The Mission Road," he said to her. "Did you suppose the name was merely ironic?"

She waited, watching him, and Ndosi and I drew nearer also, because his voice was so soft, as if weak from disuse, or as if he were talking only to himself. Ironic, he repeated, because of course one couldn't get to the mission on this road; that was the point of it. Yet more than any other it was literally a road with a *mission*. A road of salvation, built by the Road Builder to save the Kivila Valley from the barbarians. The Road Builder. A mythical name, the sort of name that might be given to a hero. He had a hero's strategy, surely, to build a road that was like a Trojan horse, drawing the rebels into the wilderness, where it would explode behind them, leaving them isolated. A clever plan, and it might have worked. Except the rebels never set foot on the Mission Road. They didn't have time to get there; they were back in the old priest's cornfield the day after they left. Their witchcraft failed them out on that savanna, and when they encountered mercenaries and soldiers they were reduced to men of flesh and blood, carrying primitive weapons, and they were routed.

None of this was written down anywhere, Boris said. But it was in the memory of the place, and the collective memory of the people. He'd listened to those people, and to Tom, and to the old priest at Kilala Mission. He'd come back to the Mission Road and looked into the waters of the Kivila River, and now he understood that part of it was in his memory as well. Or rather, in his memory alone. An unconformity, we'd called it, thinking there was nothing there. Because it wasn't like something in his memoirs—solid, dense matter, thick layers of detail, memorabilia. Sediment. This memory was a thin, pure layer. Transparent—invisible, even—unless you looked at it with the right sensors.

He possessed those sensors now, and he was looking at it. Now at last he remembered what it was like for the Road Builder, waiting for the rebels at the end of Mission Road. All his workers had fled into the hills, and he was left with only himself and the road he had built. The rebels were up on the savanna somewhere, howling and blood-crazed, but the road remained empty, and for hours he sat staring at his own hand on the detonator and thinking about what a road was and what it meant to be a road builder.

Night fell. The rebels receded, distant, irrelevant. The road, winding deep into the jungle, seemed to come alive. At first just small lights glowing along it, fireflies. Then the lights took on a pattern and grew in size and intensity until he saw headlights, an infinite line of headlights moving toward him. A convoy, carrying a vision of the things his roads would bring into the valley: soldiers, to enforce new dreams of empire or merely to plunder; disease, spawned in foreign lands or in the heart of the continent itself, hidden like contraband in the blood of travelers, diffused into the population along the veinlike roads and rivers; and goods, of course, but not wealth—only images of unattainable wealth, and trinkets and cast-offs, a commerce of envy and bitterness.

The convoy rolled on. But now the directions seemed to shift, and the vision showed him what the roads would take away: the oil and the coffee and the peanuts and the wild animals and whatever was produced by the forest or the soil or human sweat. The forest itself, carried on log trucks off to distant mills. And finally even the impoverished people, displaced by the politics and economics and temptations of the road, piled like refugees into the backs of the trucks. Masculine strength drained away to mines and slave camps and army barracks and cities of empty aspiration. Feminine strength exhausted or given over to promiscuity and prostitution. The migrations continued, the convoys straggled on, and all along the road the monuments to its failure proliferated. The rusting wreckage of trucks that had crashed or rolled, leaving bodies strewn across the road and the ghosts of dead travelers haunting a barren roadside far from their native soil. Worn-out, broken-down vehicles littering the shoulders and turnouts, and huddled beside them the living passengers, becoming ghostlike too in their waiting and the waste of their lives.

By dawn, the Road Builder, sitting in his tractor with his hand still on the detonator, understood that his road was not what he nor anyone else had imagined it to be. People dreamed of a road that would open the world to them, bringing them opportunities and knowledge and wealth. The Road Builder had shared that dream, and also had dreamed of a heroic road exploding in glory, driving the evil invaders from the valley. But now this vision had shown him what the road really would be, and what the Road Builder really was: not a hero nor a benefactor but the invader himself, building roads that were the link to forces that are absolutely destructive.

Boris stopped talking and looked up. Ndosi leaned forward, gripping his cahier, and watched the old man with bright narrowed eyes. He gave a short impatient jerk of his head. "But what happens to the Mission Road?" he said.

Boris' voice was suddenly harsh. "I blew it up. I drove the tractor into the river. I disappeared."

3 7

THE EXPLODED ROAD

Nous sommes arrivés au couer de la saison seche. La terre dors, revant des rêves seches et stériles. Les rêves d'une saison pauvre . . .

High on the dais overlooking the Place de la Révolution, I reviewed my speech, mumbling to myself but imagining my voice booming out over a hushed and amazed crowd. I was amazed myself: a speech like that was a remarkable achievement for someone lacking all natural affinity for the French language. Although, lacking natural affinity for the French language, perhaps I was in no position to judge.

Before me was a great sweltering crowd, waiting in the midday sun for the Dedication Ceremony to begin. A few had umbrellas for sun protection, and those who'd arrived first found chairs, but most were unshaded and unseated. Probably there weren't enough chairs in Ngemba to accommodate such a crowd. People streamed down from the camp, straggled in on the river road, and gathered at the ferry dock on the other side of the river, waiting for a truck to arrive or for a charitable impulse to seize the ferryman, so that he'd get off his stool and take them across. Meanwhile, the Nakahosas paddled back and forth in their teetering, leaky pirogues, providing a ferry service for those with less patience, more money, and a fair amount of courage.

On the outskirts of the crowd, at evenly spaced intervals, the soldiers stood in the full sun with their guns and ammo belts and heavy clothes, their sweat and sunglasses glinting. As if the heat were nothing to them, as if they only derived more power from the heat. While up on the dais we seemed to grow weaker in the protection of the shade, under the soldiers' impassive gaze. We sat in a long row of wooden chairs under a thatch awning: chefs, consultants, officials, and elders. The secretary ran back and forth in front of us, tapping the microphone and fussing with speaker wires and connections. Flower garlands and woven strands of palm frond decorated the dais, and the pathways were lined with whitewashed rocks and strewn with bougainvillea and hibiscus. The paths radiated out symmetrically from a point just below the dais, where in the middle of our row one chair remained unoccupied, waiting for the palm-oil truck to bring down the commissaire, who had not yet emerged from the guest house.

Naturally the Dedication Ceremony could not begin without him. Though in a way it already had begun. This was part of the program too: the stiff line-up of waiting dignitaries and the patiently suffering crowd, the ring of soldiers in the sun, the prominently empty seat, the palm-oil truck idling its engine in the driveway above us, and the invisible commissaire, keeping us in our places while he finished his lunch or his nap or his business with a subordinate or a supplicant or a girl sent down from the camp. What could be more orchestrated, more ceremonial, than these familiar rituals of hierarchy and subservience?

We've arrived at the heart of the dry season. The earth sleeps, dreaming the barren dreams of the poorest season—a time of brown fields, empty bellies, sick children, dead friends. We wait, but the sky only darkens; no rain falls.

As I looked beyond the crowd to the treeless, bushless, weedless expanse of the Place de la Révolution, these opening lines struck me as particularly apt. The crowd itself was a spectacle of color, dazzling bright pagnes and umbrellas and rich, dark skin tones. But the splendor was lost to the austerity surrounding it. Anyone who turned from the crowd to face the Place de la Révolution would feel in his wilting bones that he had arrived at the absolute heart of the mushipu. If the chef de poste had set out to build a monument to the aridity, barrenness, and deadly monotony of the season, he could not have done better than this great lifeless plaza, paved with broken palm-nut shells and evoking on the banks of an equatorial river the expanse and desolation of a desert.

So the opening lines were good; even better than I'd thought. But I felt good about the entire speech. I mean, I didn't feel *physically* good. In fact, I felt sick to my stomach. Stage fright, I suppose, or the old miasma of African waters, a hangover of that long pirogue trip the day before with the Nakahosas, which ended with Boris sitting on a piling, describing his vision of the Mission Road: the fireflies mutated into headlights, revealing the true nature of the road—his own monster winding into the jungle, evil and snakelike, not a trap for enemies but the enemy itself. All the time he was talking I couldn't shake the feeling of circulating in that eddy, with the water lapping at the top of the gunwales, whirlpools sucking at the hull, the yellow tractor not quite visible in the emerald depths below us. It gave me a terrible vertigo, and rather than ride back upriver in the pirogue I elected to return on foot with Ndosi, following the track of the old Mission Road. As we walked I tried out my speech on him. He was ahead of me on the faint path, his head cocked to the side a little to listen. When I finished he kept walking, and didn't turn to face me.

"Well, what do you think?"

He continued walking in silence. Finally he gave his answer, barely audible, as if he weren't even addressing me.

"I don't like it."

"What do you mean? What don't you like about it?"

"I just don't like it."

This blunt assessment shook my confidence a little. But Ndosi pursues his own agenda, I reminded myself; he had no use for the strategies of the chef de poste, including this Dedication Ceremony, which he wasn't even attending. Anyway, I mainly agreed with him: purely as a matter of personal taste, I didn't much like my speech either. But still I felt it was a good speech, in the sense that it would do the job it was supposed to do: please the chef de poste, and placate the commissaire.

Under our feet is ash, but beneath the ash the soil is fertile, the earth still moves. That small, strong movement is the stirring of hope, the movement of people working. Working on the Modernization Project at the Ngemba palm-oil mill.

However, this speech was diminished from its original version. When I took it to the secretary to proofread and edit, he went at it brutally, throwing out entire sections. Keep it simple, the secretary insisted, your audience knows what they want from you, they'll fill in the details.

So the speech would be short and sweet—a few blatant and provocative lies, then the commissaire could draw his own conclusions, start counting his own chickens, if that were his inclination. And now, coming down to the moment of delivery, short and sweet was looking sweeter and sweeter. Relatively sweet, I mean: the prospect of getting up in front of hundreds of people and giving any sort of speech at all still gave me a sour stomach. One consolation was that few of them understood more than two dozen words in French, so my true audience would be much smaller. And if such a thought could settle my stomach—and I wanted to settle it further—I could consider the possibility that once again *no one* would understand me. Practicing alone, I'd felt increasingly confident. The language flowed, more or less; the words began to sound natural. But when I rehearsed with the secretary it seemed he cut in every few words to nitpick about pronunciation, or to claim that he couldn't understand me at all. He drew uncomfortably close and opened his mouth very wide. Look, he said, this is what a person speaking French is supposed to do with his tongue. Then he made me imitate him, poking and tugging at my lips as I spoke, and pulling open my jaw to analyze what was going wrong inside. We went over some words in such anatomical detail that I began to get skittish about saying them at all. And now on the dais I was conscious of the crude mechanics of my jaw, and the words of my speech evoked nothing so much as an image of the secretary's gaping mouth, with its broad pink tongue and flapping tonsils.

We are here to celebrate the transformation of the Ngemba palm oil mill. How did this miraculous transformation come about? Through your own strength, energy, and self-discipline. Through the vision and perseverance of the far-sighted chef de poste. And through the guiding wisdom and intelligence of the great commissaire, following the selfless example of the president himself.

A cloud of red dust rose up on the river road. Over the noise of the crowd I heard an engine revving and gears grinding. The red dust swept toward us, and out of it the two-ton emerged, swaying and bouncing. A half dozen soldiers clung to the railing in the back.

"Look, Will." Kate leaned across Boris to put her hand on my knee. "The bush taxi."

The two-ton stopped abruptly on the edge of the Place de la Révolution, and the soldiers staggered against the railing. Several were knocked off their feet. They cursed and dismounted and began to walk away. The two-ton's horn squawked, and the nurse leaned from the driver's window, shouting at the soldiers. One of them turned, reached into his pocket, and counted a few bills out into her hand.

"Did you see that, Kate? That was real money, not requisition cards."

"She told them she won't take their requisition cards. 'If you don't pay, you don't ride. Or maybe I'll just drive over your thieving ass.' That's how she talks to them. And they laugh and make obscene jokes, and pay."

Kate glanced at the notes in my lap, then turned away. She didn't think much of my speech either. She just looked tired and pained when I read it to her the night before. "I suppose you can say whatever you want to about Uncle Pers, Will. He burned up his past, so I guess he's a clean slate, if you can think of a man who's essentially dead as a clean slate. But I don't see how you expect anyone who sees him now to believe that he has the power to do anything for them."

I can assure you that your efforts have not gone unnoticed. Important and powerful people are now watching the Kivila Valley closely, and the Company will continue to march with you as full partners on the road to progress.

A few of the dignitaries were getting restless. They coughed, shifted in their seats, whispered, and glanced at their watches. I couldn't imagine what point they were trying to make. It wasn't as if any of them had ever in their lives been to an event that started on time.

But others remained composed, as if waiting was what they always had done with their time and what they expected to do with the rest of it. As if on the scale of the Wait they endured, another fifteen or thirty minutes was absolutely without meaning. And of these Waiters, the most composed and patient was the old white man beside me.

But patience isn't really the word for the stillness that had settled over Boris. That stillness had an inhuman, even inanimate, quality, like something existing apart from time as experienced by living creatures. He gazed on the crowd, or beyond the crowd, blinking now and then, his chest rising and falling in regular breaths. Except for that motion he might have been hacked out of stone, a specimen not of humanity but of geology. His face was marked with fissures and folds and deep wandering cracks, with blue veins and hard bulging glands, black moles and laser scars and pores that gaped like craters. Each feature was a clue, a revelation of the processes that had formed it, together telling a history of radioactive decay, bursts of subcutaneous heat, the slow grinding tectonics of muscle and bone.

Except for the eyes. The eyes glinted lifelessly in their hooded sockets, like meteorites burrowed into the terrestrial surface, stones so remote and cold they told of nothing that had ever happened on the earth.

Yet his voice was still alive in my ears, low and rough as I'd last heard it.

I blew it up. I drove my tractor into the river. I disappeared.

That was the Battle of the Mission Road—or rather, the Battle Against the Mission Road. But what had been the point of it? You couldn't stop those forces with the explosion of a single road and ferry. Anyway, taken on their own terms the road and ferry were neutral, not evil at all—just a means to cross the river, to get the palm nuts out of the forest. It was absurd to make them bear the weight of so many larger events. What had happened to the distinctions Pers had prided himself on making—between metaphor and reality, between symbols and the thing itself?

He'd blown up a symbol, that was all. The roads themselves still existed, converging on the Kivila Valley, linking us to all that Pers had envisioned: the AIDS highway, the migrations of soldiers and refugees, the litter of broken vehicles and human bodies, the commerce of envy . . . Even his vision still existed, a thin, pure layer of memory that we all shared. *Don't take all the credit for your own hallucinations,* Tom once advised me. *Don't assume they're your personal property.* The Road Builder's hallucination was also mine. From my seat on the front porch I had seen it take form again, out of the shifting light of fireflies, wrenching familiar objects into new configurations, still laying out the future of the road.

Over the years, one of the Company's senior executives—the man you call the Road Builder—has invested substantial energy, technological expertise, and financial resources in the Kivila Valley. And this afternoon he's asked me to tell you that he has decided to dedicate the remainder of his personal fortune to capital investment in the expansion of the Modernization Project, in order to develop new industries and new public works.

What industries and public works could I possibly be referring to? The only things that came to my mind were the sardine canneries and jogging track of Telo's imagination. The things that would come to *his* mind, if he could have heard my speech, and in that sense I was thankful that he couldn't. Because he wouldn't have been able to just let it go. Telo was too literal-minded for a speech like this; he would have had to corner me afterward, and eventually I would have been forced to admit the obvious: that I was not talking about real money, real machines. That there never would be a sardine cannery, and that to expand the Modernization Project meant only to expand its delusions.

Some boys approached the foot of the dais, dancing self-consciously and singing a kind of nursery rhyme.

Papa Road Builder,
See how light is my skin.
Perhaps I'm a child of Mputu;
Perhaps you remember my mother;
Perhaps this is your blood
Flowing beneath my brown skin.

A couple of the boys giggled, but behind their posturing and teasing was a tone of genuine supplication. However, they all were very dark-skinned, and the Road Builder was oblivious to them. They chanted again and again, until the secretary came along and scattered them.

With capital, the Road Builder told me, everything is possible. There are no limits, once you are caught up in the great flow of commerce.

Actually, what I remembered the Road Builder saying, with evident sincerity, was this: *Who knows where money comes from?* A witty and cryptic phrase, I thought at the time, and it stuck with me, though of course as it turned out he was lying—he knew perfectly well where the money came from. He was comfortable with that kind of lie, and he never expressed any regret for telling it. So I ought to have been comfortable telling an even more extravagant lie on his behalf, without his consent or even comprehension.

You've labored a long time in obscurity, but now the eyes of the world are turning toward you. And this Modernization Project is destined to flourish and expand, reaching far beyond this valley to bring its benefits to the entire region.

Thank you. Merci. Matondo.

Did that mean we would make the entire region look like the Place de la Révolution? Make the entire region look like the heart of the dry season, and let the noble bureaucrat stand up and commemorate the disaster with a detestable speech?

A small band—a couple of horns, drums, electric bass—struck up a jittery tune. No one moved spontaneously, but a dozen women performed a tightly choreographed dance at the foot of the dais. The women were dressed in identical green pagnes, which praised, with a collage of slogans and pictures, the strength and glory of the president. A man wearing a loose-fitting shirt and pants of the same material suddenly bounded in front of the women and began to shout at the crowd. A cheerleader, an animator, and so the crowd, up to that moment unnaturally solemn and still, was instantly and equally unnaturally animated: swaying back and forth, clapping their hands, booming out a chorus in response to the singsongy challenges of the animator. The tinny little band played on, the green pagnes rippled and swirled, and finally, up on the hill by the guest house, the palm-oil truck revved its engine.

Blasting its horn, the truck came bumping down the hill, swung around the edge of the crowd, and pulled up beside the dais. The engine revved again, sending black clouds of diesel smoke into the crowd, and the horn blared once more, as if to emphasize the power and size of the truck and distract our attention from the ridiculously short distance it had just carried its passenger. The commissaire emerged, wearing his stiff black suit and sunglasses, and looked us over with his customary displeasure. He mounted the dais, and we lesser dignitaries stood as he moved down the line, perfunctorily shaking our hands. His scent lingered on my skin after he passed—a sharp, stinging cologne smell, tempered by something more organic, like mildew.

A group of Company employees filed down one of the pathways. They lined up before the now-seated commissaire and began to sing a song of welcome. It was a beautiful song and well sung, better than you might expect, looking at the chorus that produced it. Even freshly bathed and in their best clothes, the workers were a shabby lot. Though at least the coupiers, in spite of a tendency toward sagging and sallow features suggestive of chronic alcohol poisoning, projected a certain dignity and fierceness, like wild forest animals that had not been entirely domesticated and corrupted. But the mill workers just looked beaten down, blinking stupidly in the glaring sunlight as if they'd been herded out of a dungeon.

When the workers finished their song, the chef de poste stepped to the podium as if to begin his speech. But instead he turned to face the mill, raised his arm, and brought it down sharply in some kind of signal. There was a moment of expectant silence; then, with a great groan and a rising howl, the mill came to life. The band played on, but the music was drowned by shrieking machinery. Out of the high chimney came a blast of thick orange steam and smoke. Most of the crowd had seen this sight a thousand times, but for some reason they now began to cheer wildly, as if it were the first time those old engines had ever fired. The mill shuddered, and more orange smoke followed the first, the acrid cloud settling out over the Place de la Révolution. The howl of the mill moderated, and the chef de poste turned back to the crowd, fists clenched, arms raised exultantly. But behind him the commissaire was seized by a paroxysm of coughing and retching. At once the chef de poste turned again to face the mill, waving his arms, urgently signaling the operators. But several more clouds of smoke descended on us before the demonstration was abruptly cut off. The chef leaned over the commissaire, the secretary dashed off in search of a glass of water, and the crowd, presumably oblivious to the commissaire's predicament, cheered wildly. Meanwhile, the mill hissed, and vapor condensed out of the air: a thin layer of yellow oil, lubricating everything.

"Hsss! Will! Over here, Will!"

From the back of the dais, the nurse beckoned to me. For a moment she looked beautiful again, even desirable, smiling and leaning toward me into air tinted pale orange by smoke and refracted sunlight and mists of vaporized palm oil. I slipped out of my chair and went to her.

"Ndosi asked me to give this to you."

She pressed his cahier into my hands.

"What am I supposed to do with it?"

"He wants you to read it to them."

"To who?"

"Everybody. He says this is the biggest audience the Road Builder will ever have. He says that speech you are planning to give is a waste. Nothing but useless lies, he says. And very boring. He wants you to read us something we'll enjoy hearing."

"You're saying Ndosi expects me to read this now? To the commissaire and the chef and all these people? That's impossible. I have no idea what it even says."

The orange light faded, and suddenly the nurse looked skeletal again, hollowed out by disease. I tried to force the cahier back in her hands, but already she'd turned away, arms wrapped tightly inside her pagne. I returned to my seat. Kate glanced inquisitively at the cahier, but there was no time to explain anything; the commissaire had stopped coughing, and the chef de poste was making his opening remarks.

I wasn't sure what the chef's speech was about. A certain amount of it was rote, the usual patriotic exhortations and invocations of the president's name. He bragged about all the work we'd done. He threw in something about the snake danger, and ridiculed the mamas who preferred to trod on the fangs of snakes rather than the shells of palm nuts. The commissaire began to cough again, and the secretary ran up with another glass of water. The chef de poste rambled, veered off suddenly into oil-production statistics, threw out some numbers. I wondered vaguely where he'd gotten them—from me?—but then he was on to some story I couldn't quite follow, a folk tale or fable, something about an antelope and a python, then back to the Modernization Project and agricultural production, and again to the antelope and python, building to some dramatic denouement. I didn't get the point of it, but I admired the way the fable was woven into the texture of his speech: it distilled his meaning, somehow, and hypnotized the crowd, leaving us impervious to counterargument or skepticism.

It suddenly hit me that this was what my speech needed: a fable of its own. Ndosi was absolutely right: people don't want to hear a speech that is merely a lecture, an exposition of facts (or, as the case may be, lies). What we hunger for are fables. Little engines that could, boys with their thumbs in the dike, sorcerers and witches and spirits who break the silence of the dumb beasts and animate the seemingly lifeless objects of the world.

Kate reached across Boris to squeeze my knee. "Are you paying attention?" she whispered. "You're about to go on."

The chef de poste turned my way, gesturing and smiling broadly. Somehow the fable had brought him around to introducing his white man. But I'd lost the flow of the story, and the allegory eluded me. Was I the antelope, or the python? The crowd cheered as I rose and stepped to the podium. Before the applause died away I leaned into the microphone.

"Nous sommes arrivés au couer de la saison sêche."

I glanced down at my notes, then back at the crowd. They were quiet now, waiting for me to continue. A great sea of color at my feet, swirling like the river whirlpools at the end of the Mission Road. The vertigo seized me again, and I gripped the podium and looked down, staring at my notes. Underneath them was Ndosi's cahier. I pushed the notes aside, opened the cahier, and began to read the Kituba words, drowning the chef de poste's indignant protests and the commissaire's feeble coughing with my amplified voice.

"Here's the story you've been waiting to hear. The story of the day of the Mission Road blowing up into the sky.

The people remember two explosions. So long ago, they were children crossing the river in early morning, the pirogues going back and forth all morning because the ferry was gone. And some of them crying for the ferry, little children afraid to cross the big water in pirogues, and the mothers saying hush! The Road Builder is saving you, taking your ferry away down

the river for the rebel crossing. The children don't know what that means;
nobody knows what that means.

 Everyone going across the river to hide in the forest, and all morning
silence in the valley, but far away guns shooting. Smoke coming off the far
savanna, so they knew Kasengi burns, and they fear rebels marching into
the valley, coming to tear out their hearts and eat them still beating out of
bloodsoaking hands.

 The first explosion quick and hard, BAARACK! Like a great forest
tree hit with lightning, ripped apart. The people watching smoke and dust
rise over the Kivila, while the silence comes again, until the second
explosion, a sound they felt with their bodies, coming to them through the
earth. BARUM! BAROOOOM! On and on, still shaking in the earth
even when the sound is no longer in their ears.

 But they saw nothing, and when at last they have courage to leave
their hiding places and go into the valley, they found nothing—no rebels,
no Road Builder, no bodies, no bulldozer. Only the Mission Road ferry,
swallowed in the river mud, and the Mission Road blown apart at
Kivila crossing.

 No one knew what happened. They listen for the story in echoes and
silence, and around the valley finding little pieces of a story, like pieces of
the road blown apart. They told each other the story pieces, but never see a
way to bring them together in one story. Never see a way to put back
together the exploded road.

 Only the Road Builder himself could do that."

These Kituba words, with their improvisations and free-form syntax,
flowed out of my mouth like music, polyrhythmic and strangely melodic,
rippling into the microphone as if off the tongue of a native speaker. Behind
me the commissaire continued his sporadic, ineffectual coughing. The chef
de poste had fallen silent, though I could feel the heat of his mortification
burning at my back. But for the moment that didn't matter. What mattered
was the rapt attention of the crowd. What mattered was what happened to
the Road Builder, hiding in the forest with a detonator in his hand, waiting for
the rebels to come down to the end of the Mission Road.

"But they never do come down. The Road Builder listens to faraway gunshooting, then silence spreading on the valley. At last he goes from hiding and returns to his road-building machine and begins the argument with himself.

You built that road for nothing, he told himself. It goes nowhere.

Anyway, now we got a road. He laughed. Maybe next we build the destination.

But he answered himself, not laughing. Impossible to build a destination, here. All the roads go nowhere. There's nowhere to go. Only the river goes somewhere: to the ocean, and then, to Mputu. That is a destination!

He shook his head. In Mputu people are lost. They fill their hands but their hearts are empty. They destroy, and don't remember the things they destroy.

In Mputu, he answered, there's progress. But in Africa tomorrow is always the same as today. The ancestors stay on, like guests never leaving the party, forcing everyone to make repetition of our lives. Lives that lead nowhere!

And so on Kivila shore, at the end of the Mission Road, the Road Builder had this argument with himself, going back and forth—Africa or Mputu, Africa, Mputu, Mputu, Africa—and that is too big an argument to contain in one man, so at last with a great crack the Road Builder split in two: the first explosion the people heard. Then in the cab of his machine two Road Builders, one white and wanting to go to Mputu, the other black and wanting to stay in Africa. They got down from the cab and began to fight, and that was the Battle of the Mission Road, that the people told stories of afterward, without knowing what they were saying."

I read without looking up at the crowd: not an orator now, just the voice of Ndosi's story. He told how the two Road Builders fought on the banks of the Kivila, and how at last the black Road Builder gained the upper hand and would have won, until the white Road Builder remembered the detonator in his pocket and pressed the button. In the explosion the black Road Builder and the bulldozer were blown into the river, and the white Road Builder escaped. He made his way down the river and eventually crossed the ocean to Mputu, where he married a rich woman and became a powerful chief, with a great house in the city. But he had no children, and in that country of stone and cement and asphalt he never built another road.

Meanwhile, the road-building machine sank into Kivila mud, and the black Road Builder became a creature of the river bottom—a long black worm, blind and silent, burrowed into silt, forgetting the sunlit earth. When at last he emerged from the mud he was like an eel, hiding in crevasses and caves at the bottom of the river. Slowly he made his way upriver, always meta-morphosing. He became a swift fish with a snapping jaw and sharp teeth, and a great swimming lizard, larger and faster than a crocodile. He became a walking catfish, venturing out of the river at night, dragging his belly as he pushed along on fins from creek to creek, from fishpond to fishpond. And far from water he took the form of land creatures: a snake, a leopard, a wild dog. And sometimes a man, standing in the doorway of a young woman's hut at night, like a shadow in her dreaming mind.

During this time strange children were born in the country. Albinos, savants, changelings. No man would claim such creatures for his own, and the mothers said they had no memory of the fathers. These children heard voices; they saw things in the forest that no one else saw. But often they were weak and sickly, and before long most were dead, or lost in the forest, or run away to Kisaka. Only a few grew to adulthood in their villages.

Meanwhile, in a cold stone house in Mputu, the white Road Builder was living in sorrow and confusion. He no longer could see a purpose in his wealth, or remember why he had married his beautiful wife. He wrote a book of his life history, but his memory was thick and he didn't know why he was writing. At night he dreamed of the black Road Builder, still alive on the Kivila shore. By day on the city streets he caught glimpses of small dark children with big round bellies and fever eyes. He began to imagine treachery and assassins everywhere, and at last he called his niece and her husband before him. Go to Africa, he told them, to the Kivila River, and search for a black man they call the Road Builder. When you find him, I want you to kill him.

I stopped reading and glanced up. The crowd waited, frighteningly silent and intent. But surely they weren't taking this *literally*. Surely they recognized an extravagant allegory when they heard one. Surely they drew *some* distinction between metaphor and reality, memory and imagination, symbols and the thing itself.

But whatever Ndosi's fable might have meant to them, it was too late for me to back out. Too late to edit, too late to obfuscate or omit or euphemize. The noble bureaucrat had become merely a mouthpiece, a connective tissue. *The bureaucrat exists to make connections.* And to be absorbed into something infinitely larger than himself. His personal intrigues, opinions, ambitions were nothing. The fable was everything.

"But in Africa the niece and her husband live fearless and careless. Swimming together always in the river, with the eel and the diving lizard and the crocodile. And the black Road Builder spied on them and listened to their loose talk: of the Road Builder, of the woman's uncle dying slowly in a great house in Mputu, and of an airplane flying on a bamboo pole high above the savanna.

So the black Road Builder goes his way up to the savanna. A walking catfish, a snake, an antelope. A small black monkey climbing a bamboo pole. And the next morning the bamboo airplane is gone, and the black Road Builder, flying all night, is halfway over the ocean to Mputu.

In the white Road Builder's great house he lived for days in secret, eating the rich food, sleeping in the soft bed, making love to the beautiful wife. The white Road Builder saw his food disappear, felt the impression left by another body in his bed, heard the soft pleasure cries of his wife, but he says nothing, he thinks only of his own sadness and fear, he becomes more and more the ghost in his own house. So when at last they met face-to-face the black Road Builder saw there was no need to fight again, only to open his great arms and embrace the white Road Builder. Who is shrinking, shrinking. And when the embrace is over, he is gone—back into the black body, and the wound that opened so long ago on Kivila shores is healed.

But to the Road Builder the wealth of Mputu is like dust, and the memory of Africa always burning. So he returned to his bamboo airplane. Flying back over the ocean to Kivila Valley, walking through the camp before the eyes of the people who hadn't seen him thirty years. At first the people saw a white man—how they remember the Road Builder, how they imagine he still must be. But longer they look and longer he lived among them, the more the imagination failed them, and in the days before his dying they began to realize they are looking at something they hadn't seen before: a man with no color, no skin—the Road Builder, returned to Africa as one man, to repay his debts and die whole."

BOOK SIX

THE BORDER

38

FLIGHT

Inside pressurized chambers fuel ignites. Spinning turbines eject the hot gases, and the plane thrusts forward, turning motionless air into wind. An engineered wind, channeled by cantilevered wings into a precisely calculated flow: high pressure beneath, a vacuum above. And so the plane lifts, a huge, heavy object hurled into the thin sky.

This is flight, as opposed to dreams of flight. Nothing like the levitation of spirits and magicians that Ndosi imagined. No soaring freedom, no exultant rush of air; in fact, there's no sense of motion at all, and in my aisle seat I've already lost sight of the receding, expanding earth. Only a few feet away explosions and windstorms propel us at fantastic speeds through the sky, but inside this long metal tube that noise is muted and unreal. Already we ignore it, hearing instead the small sounds of our insular world: the reassuring voice on the intercom; the gentle beeping as the seatbelt light goes off; the whirring of little fans, blowing a synthetic atmosphere down on our faces.

This is a sterile and artificial place, controlled by switches and microscopic circuits, uninhabited by ghosts. It's also the most secure and orderly place most of us passangers have seen for some time. We are still basking in the relief that flooded the plane when we lifted off in Kisaka, breaking away so inexorably from the panicked airport and the anarchic city. On the ground it had been cutthroat—a long sleepless night guarding possessions and a bit of territory on the crowded lobby floor, followed by a morning of negotiation: bribing, threatening, pleading, jostling, pushing, and scratching to get on a plane. Kate and I, arriving at the airport with no reservations, missed the first two flights out this morning. We're seated half a plane's length away from each other on this one, but we know we're lucky just to be on board.

Slowly the anxiety of departure subsides, the reality of escape sinks in, and we begin to relax. My seat companion, a well-dressed, middle-aged

African, glances at me and wearily smiles a greeting. I make a modest over-
ture at conversation, and he responds warmly. Now that we are no longer
competing for these precious seats, we passengers can let our guard down a
little. We can indulge this unexpected empathy we feel for the strangers
beside us. No matter that all we really know of one another is that we have
escaped from a hellhole together. No matter that all we may have in common
is this reenactment of the ancient human diaspora: flight from the hothouses
of pestilence and mutation, from the disease-spawning, conflict-ridden forests
and savannas where we evolved.

If I lean out over the aisle and strain my neck, I can see what I'm guessing is
the back of Kate's head, twenty or thirty rows away. I concentrate my gaze and
beam a telepathic communiqué toward her: feel my eyes on you, Kate; turn
around; wave at me; smile; blow me a kiss! But it doesn't seem to be working.
She might well be sleeping; neither of us has slept for the last thirty hours. Or
maybe her receptors are already weakening, unable to home in on incoming sig-
nals amid all the neurological feedback and static in this plane. Or else I'm the
one who can't home in. Maybe my aim is bad; it could be that's not even the
back of her head I'm focusing on. I want to get up and see for certain where she
is, talk to her, touch her. But it's too late. Now the flight attendants are pushing
their drink carts down the aisle, blocking the way and deflecting whatever weak
electromagnetic impulses may be issuing from my brain.

What a device for instant anonymity and separation an airplane is! No
wonder I abducted Kate two years ago in Tucson rather than let her get on
one of these things by herself. And now we've both been abducted, in a sense,
only forced to get on a plane rather than kept off of one. Flying away into an
uncertain future, joining the great mobile human swarm that could so easily
push between us, absorb us into separate configurations. *Because it's not as if
any particular configuration is inevitable, cast in stone.* That much, I guess, Tom
was right about.

And so once again I'm struck by the tenuousness of our connection, the
inexplicit nature of our commitment to each other. Still, I suppose reconfigu-
ration is not an immediate danger, and I don't have any particularly urgent
reason to communicate with Kate. Why not just sit back and instead converse
with my seat companion, who seems so open and willing to engage me,
regarding me now with a penetrating and intelligent expression that I would

find intimidating, if he didn't at the same time seem so *relaxed*. Whatever tumult and sorrows are left behind or await us on the ground (his eyes and his smile are telling me), here on the airplane, at least, there isn't any urgency about anything. And he's right. On the one hand we're blasting over the Gulf of Guinea at 600 miles per hour, wrenched away from one set of circumstances, accelerating into the next, but on the other hand we're sitting absolutely still, a few hundred humans packed into tight formation, and for the next six or seven hours nothing whatsoever is going to happen to us. The airplane is a dangerous instrument of dispersal and disconnection, but it is also useful for temporarily holding people in place. Nervous, overstimulated creatures that we are, we seldom achieve a *stillness* like this. When are we so free from distraction and responsibility; when are we able to examine the world from a distance, and bring it into focus and perspective?

That's what Tom was after, when he left the Kivila Valley in search of a quiet place to review the events of his life. *To sort things out, reflect on the last few years.* That was what *his* quest amounted to, perhaps: to push beyond the equatorial jungle and the Mountains of the Moon and the East African high savanna, and arrive at some meditative spot on the desert coast or an empty island beach in the Indian Ocean. And then, when all these places turned out to be inaccessible, he tried to convince himself that he had found what he needed in the unnatural seclusion of Kilala Mission.

He would have done better if he'd just gotten on an airplane. He claimed to have an aversion to flight, but if he'd given it a chance he might have found that the cabin of an airplane is the sort of calm and timeless place where an objective accounting of the past is within reach, where it becomes possible to distinguish what really happened from what someone imagined happening. To finally delineate the boundaries that have blurred so much, those distinctions Uncle Pers once listed so concisely: *between metaphor and reality, between memory and imagination, between symbols and the thing itself.* And I would now add to his list: between technology and magic, between history and fable.

History: intricate and cluttered, subject to constant examination and revision yet still riddled with dark holes, resistant to the probes of memory and research. Holes we fill with fables: small contrivances of moral or practical instruction, lacking the force of revelation, the resonance of something true. Because of course they aren't true. Who could believe the fable of the Road

Builder? A man who split in two, took the form of river creatures, migrated slowly upriver, fathered changelings and albinos, and crossed the oceans in a bamboo airplane to reunite with his other half. On some metaphorical level, fine. But obviously none of this really *happened*, though in the days following the Dedication Ceremony people were acting as though it had, as though they'd already incorporated Ndosi's wildly imaginative biography of the Road Builder into their belief systems. Acting as though, because I'd stood up on the dais and read that biography to them, I shared their belief. Even Kate, who by that point didn't seem to care what anyone believed, told me that by reading it I'd completed the incineration of Pers' memoirs—the actual history was gone now, she said; the fable was everything.

Of course, the history wasn't really gone. The history was something real that had happened, and the fable was something impossible that had not, and I assumed people understood the difference. I assumed their enthusiasm for the fable was only a kind of act, but of course I couldn't tell. After all, the causal mechanisms of their world are beyond my apprehension. For two years from my seat on the porch I studied that world intently, but I rarely saw beyond the ripples and reflections in its surface. At times on the porch I was on the verge of believing what the rest of them did: that flying machines were swooping past me low in the night sky, unseen and unheard; that on the edge of the forest invisible beings murmured in the language of wind and leaves; that in the shadowed interior of the mill the same beings shrieked and hissed and rumbled with the voices of extruders and compressors and boilers and belts. That the old men and women who reached for my hand as I passed them in the villages, their flesh burning with the fevers of the living, were at the same time moving into the spaces that seemed unoccupied, already making their way through the territory of the dead.

On the porch, it all had seemed possible. Old assumptions and explanations were obviously inadequate, and we were receptive to new ones, to the collective dreams and hallucinations carried on the night sounds drifting down from the camp and interpreted by the nightwatchman rising out of the darkness down by his brazier. But here on the airplane those enchantments have dissipated. The fables that nourished them seem artificial and absurd, easily refuted. No one can swim back against the downstream current, Ndosi. The world doesn't turn over on itself, Placide. Our lives don't rotate, Uncle

Pers, on some kind of perpetual wheel, allowing us to obliterate one version of the past and replace it with another.

Our ancestors are already remote. The dead recede, quickly. The dead don't linger, watching over our shoulders, compelling us to perpetuate their follies and their ignorance. The rivers flush everything down to the oceans; the airplanes, built not of bamboo but of steel and grease, lift away from the earth; and the past, with its old companions and familiar rooms and well-loved pieces of ground, is fixed in an inaccessible place, disfigured by memory and smothered with the dusts of antiquity and left behind forever.

THE BUSH TAXI

The day after the Dedication Ceremony the rains began. It rained every day for a week, and by the time we left the Kivila Valley the mushipu world had been transformed. The river ran high and muddy, and the earth was green with sudden growth. In the clear mornings people roamed the forest, gathering mushrooms and the fresh shoots of plants. At night, in the aftermath of thunderstorms, the insect voices multiplied, and Placide stalked the singing cricket in the darkness. And a week after the first storm, with the creeks roaring beneath narrow bridges and the muddy roads slick and freshly gullied, the nurse left her patient under the care of Sticky Tree and Matama, and drove her two-ton on its first smuggling run to Kisaka.

Kate and I were in the cab with her, not fellow smugglers this time but paying passengers, traveling to the capital to try to sort out our finances and extend our visas. And maybe also to break out of our isolation a little, escape the fear-driven cycles of rumor and myth and see what was really going on in the country. Ndosi rode atop the sacks of produce in the back, a subdued and watchful boy chauffeur. In Kisaka food prices were spiraling out of control and agricultural goods could be sold for several times what they were worth in the provinces. But there were great risks associated with transport and delivery. The roads were infested with highwaymen and police and soldiers, and of course we had to defy the local authorities just to get out of the Kivila Valley. That, however, was much easier than it would have been a week earlier, since the commissaire and his soldiers no longer occupied the guest house. As soon as the Dedication Ceremony ended, the commissaire had left the valley and moved to the government offices at the collectivité up on the western savanna. He said he'd sacrificed his health long enough to the bad air of Ngemba, and now he had other business to attend to. And in any case he had accomplished his goals, he said: subversive elements were pacified, and order and discipline reestablished.

Most of the soldiers left also, but Dimanche stayed on, claiming, as an agent of the commissaire, the right to occupy the guest house. But after two days the chef de poste told him he was closing the guest house. Dimanche, complaining bitterly and threatening to return with soldiers, had gone up to the collectivité and not been heard from since.

But even with the commissaire and his entourage gone, the nurse wouldn't leave openly in the loaded two-ton, in broad daylight. She came to our house before dawn, on foot, and we locked the door and took up the knapsacks we had packed for the journey and went down to the river, where one of the Nakahosas was waiting beside his pirogue to paddle us across. Placide walked with us, and when he shook our hands he gave Kate and me each a small banana-leaf packet. "God go with you," he said, and slipped away back up the hill. We put the packets into our knapsacks and Nakahosa helped us into the pirogue and stood in the stern to paddle us out into the black flood.

It was a different river from the one we had descended a week earlier, looking for the Road Builder's tractor. In the darkness we could feel the power of the flow against the hull, but we couldn't see the swirling waters or the vegetation ripped loose from the banks or the great branches and trees swept along by the current. But we made it to the other side without incident, coming up suddenly against the nearly invisible shore. Nakahosa helped us out and showed us the path leading up the bank. He gripped my hand hard before he got back in his boat.

"All right, Mr. Will."

"We'll see you, Nakahosa." Un or Deux, I didn't know which.

The nurse led us along the path, barely visible in the predawn light. We came onto a two-track road and followed it until we arrived in a clearing where the two-ton was parked, loaded with cargo to above the top of the rails. Ndosi climbed down from the load to murmur a greeting and softly shake our hands. Kate walked around the truck, looking up at the cargo.

"Coffee, palm nut, manioc, of course. Are all these sacks of corn? Up there, I guess that's peanuts. Where'd all this stuff come from? The mushipu is just ending; I thought people had nothing. I thought people were practically starving to death."

Ndosi nodded. "Ç'est ça, Madame Kate. These are their last stores. But now that the rains have begun, they're willing to sell. Because they can find things to eat in the forest now. And they can put up with a little more hunger, if they get a good price for their produce. In Kisaka, the prices are higher than they've ever been before."

"I guess that's true," Kate said. "Though next week they'll probably be higher than they are today."

"Yes, but today is when they have to sell," said the nurse, "because today is when I'm going to Kisaka. The smuggling could wait, maybe, but the passengers need to go today, n'est pas? And this is a bush taxi too, not just a smuggling truck."

"I hope you're not going today just for our sake," I said.

"Oh, no. Not just for you."

"Look at this!" Kate called out from the far side of the truck. "Barrels of palm oil!"

"Oui, barrels of palm oil," said the nurse.

"Four or five of them."

"They belong to the chef de poste," said the nurse. "Some of the produce, too, belongs to him."

Kate came around the front of the truck to join us. "So now the chef de poste is a member of the Smugglers' Support Group too?" she said.

The nurse shrugged. "I've made an arrangement with him. He provides the fuel for my camion, for one thing."

"Why are we sneaking off like this, then," Kate said, "if even the chef is an accomplice? Who are we hiding from?"

"It's for the chef's sake that we're sneaking," the nurse answered. Then she got in the truck and started the engine, while we considered the nature of her arrangement with the chef de poste. Did she mean that now the only purpose of the smuggling was to help the chef keep up appearances? So he could seem to be standing firm by the commissaire's side in support of the established economic order, while in reality he was stealing palm oil from the mill (oil supplied by the sweat of underpaid coupiers and mill workers), selling it at true market rates, and keeping the profit for himself? And the smugglers—that is, the underpaid coupiers and mill workers—were facilitating the theft.

Ndosi scrambled back up on top of the cargo, and Kate and I got into the cab with the nurse. I sat between the two women, and we rode in silence up the winding road that climbed out of the valley. The nurse had trouble with the gears at times, and the nearly treadless tires slipped and skidded on the wet clay. Once on an outsloped curve we lost traction and started to slide toward the edge, and Ndosi cried out a warning or a protest from atop the load. But the nurse remained calm and never locked the brakes or swerved rashly. She turned the wheel with tight-lipped assurance, pulling us out of each slide. She didn't seem nervous, only serious and intent, and gave no indication that she remembered the last time she and I had sat next to each other on a smuggling run, when I gripped the steering wheel with sweating hands while on the seat beside me she squirmed in delight, as if fishtail slides in an overloaded truck on a slick clay road were just another form of sexual innuendo passing between us.

But now the wheel was in her hands, and I was the one enjoying the fishtailing, and the innuendo, at least a little. Centrifugal force pushed me against Kate as we skidded toward the edge of the road, then back against the nurse as she corrected the slide. I was comfortably hemmed in, a soft female presence containing me on either side. I felt secure there, confident in the nurse's ability to keep us on the road. Or maybe it was just my rising sense of fatalism, a surrender to the force of events, sleepy resignation. I even dozed for a while, aware in my sleep of diminished fishtailing, the curves becoming less frequent, the truck winding through gears, accelerating, speeding along a straight stretch of road. Then decelerating, downshifting.

I opened my eyes on a great bright open space. The first rays of the sun slanting long shadows across the savanna. New shoots of grass, a pale green plain bisected by roads of dark sand. And ahead of us, at the bottom of a long grade, black figures at the crossroads, waving their arms and stepping up to the side of the road.

The nurse downshifted again. "What are you doing?" said Kate.

"Picking up passengers. This is a bush taxi, n'est pas?"

"But there's no room."

"In a bush taxi, there's always room."

Not until we had nearly come to a stop did the two men at the crossroads stop waving. "Oh, my God," said Kate. "Will, it's Dimanche! And the commissaire!" She turned to the nurse. "Don't stop for him! He'll arrest you. He'll have us deported."

The nurse shook her head. "He can't deport anybody, Kate. Don't you see his circumstances have changed? Anyway, I have an arrangement with him also."

The commissaire spoke to Dimanche, who dragged a couple of suitcases and three burlap sacks out of the grass and lifted them up to Ndosi. Kate made me switch places with her when she saw that the commissaire was going to get in the cab and that the nurse wasn't going to stop him. Dimanche climbed atop the cargo with Ndosi, and the commissaire hoisted himself up and eased his bulk onto the seat next to me, compressing the rest of us and flooding the cab with the smells of cologne and mildew.

The nurse leaned in front of Kate to address the commissaire. "Is the boy coming?"

The commissaire shrugged.

"He wasn't part of our arrangement," said the nurse. "If he comes, he has to pay."

"I don't pay for him."

The nurse put her head out the window and called up to Dimanche.

"You have to pay."

"I don't have any money. My patrón will pay for me."

The commissaire sat with his arms folded, looking straight ahead.

"If you can't pay, I'm not taking you," the nurse called up to Dimanche.

After a minute Dimanche got down. He stood at the commissaire's window, pleading, but the commissaire didn't look at him. Ndosi tossed his bag down, and we drove off in silence.

After a while, the commissaire remarked: "That boy smells bad. Did you ever notice?"

He seemed to be addressing me. I shrugged.

"Besides, he's lazy, eh? A parasite."

He turned his head to look at me. I nodded slightly.

"Alors, monsieur. We can no longer be responsible for parasites, eh? The situation is too difficult now in this country. We have so many troubles. The political situation is very bad. In Kisaka, especially, conditions are difficult. Yet you and madame are traveling there. You must have some critical business. Or perhaps you have decided to return to your own country?"

"No. We have . . . personal affairs. We need to renew our visas, for one thing."

"Vraiment? All the others are fleeing, because they think we are preparing to cut their throats, but you are planning to stay longer. So. You must be enjoying yourselves. You must like us."

"We've met many people we like. Some we admire very much."

"In spite of the poverty of our existence. Or perhaps our poverty doesn't affect you directly. Perhaps you are in a position to prosper in any case."

The commissaire was still looking at me. I tried to stare back at him, but my gaze just reflected back at me off of his sunglasses. "Our affairs aren't profitable," I said. "Not in the way that you're thinking."

"Myself, I have only three sacks of peanuts. You saw them. Mais vous, monsieur, you're shipping a big cargo."

"It's not theirs," said the nurse. "I'm responsible for it."

The commissaire nodded, still looking at me. "Ç'est bon." Some of the stiffness was going out of his body, and as he relaxed he seemed to take up more space on the seat. He stretched his arm out behind me, which gave me a little more room but also allowed him to bring his face very close to mine as he spoke. "Vraiment, ça ç'est bon. The free market at work. This woman is practicing the kind of self-reliance we have been teaching, eh? An entrepreneur. It's gratifying to see someone finally following the lesson, n'est pas?"

Kate heaved an exasperated sigh. She was still staring straight ahead and hadn't looked once in the direction of the commissaire. I had no choice but to look at him, with his face only a few inches away from mine. His sunglasses glinted, his lip curled. Sneer or smile, who could say? Perhaps he was making an attempt at irony, some kind of bitter joke. Or trying to entrap us, extract a careless confession, confirm his theories of sabotage and espionage. Or was it possible that he believed what he was now saying about free markets and self-reliance, and that he'd simply forgotten all his speeches and threats, the soldiers he'd deployed to ensure that the market remained unfree, the self-reliant entrepreneurs he'd beaten and jailed?

"I wasn't sure you were an advocate of the free market," I said carefully.

"Mais, oui. Free trade, market-based incentives—these have always been centerpieces of the president's economic policies, which I have supported wholeheartedly. But it's difficult in this country to get people to follow the rules of a free market. Bush people, broussards, they don't understand such things. They don't like to take responsibility for their own welfare. They don't like to do the work."

Kate leaned forward to look around me at the commissaire. I thought she was going to argue with him, but instead she spoke quietly, her voice controlled. "And what about you, commissaire? Why are you traveling to Kisaka?"

"Ah, *oui*. Because I have been . . . summoned. I am part of the political instability we were speaking of. It isn't common knowledge yet, but because we are companions in this small space I will share a secret with you: I am no longer commissaire of the Kivila region. I have been transferred, madame."

"A promotion?"

He sighed. "Je ne sais pas, madame. Mais, une promotion, je ne crois pas. But who can tell? Politics is very unpredictable under the best of circumstances. And nowadays . . . let us say that consistency is lacking. Let us say that sometimes it is difficult to know which path to choose, what is required to advance one's career. Let us say that loyalty and dedication and sacrifice are not rewarded as they once were."

We didn't expect that from him either—the news that he had fallen out of favor, but more than that the self-pity in his voice. But why shouldn't the commissaire have his own resentments and see himself as another victim? To me he had seemed a caricature of the petty despot, dangerous but depthless, a black sheen that reflected back my own fears and preconceptions. And now the sheen was tarnished, the reflection broken up, and we had this glimpse of something else: a tinge of bitterness, a revelation of impotence, a guy in a mildewed suit hitchhiking to Kisaka with a couple of old suitcases.

I had little sympathy for him, but I did begin to feel that we had something in common. He was like the noble bureaucrat—deriving authority and power mainly from his isolation, from the provincialism and insignificance of the place he ruled. In the Kivila Valley the commissaire might have said, fairly enough: "L'etat, c'est moi." But now his isolation was ending, he was leaving his small fiefdom, and his stature and fearsomeness were shrinking in proportion to the decreasing distance between him and the capital city.

All day long we rolled across the savanna plain, descended the slow slippery roads into the river valleys, waited for ferries, and scattered the goats and chickens in countless unfamiliar, identical villages. Here and there we encountered roadblocks: military checkpoints, soldiers engaged in their state-sanctioned piracy. They seemed more insolent and threatening than ever, as if they felt fewer constraints. And now I saw the point of the arrangement the nurse had made with the commissaire. She had agreed to give him a ride in exchange for his influence with the soldiers. This strategy paid off, at least during the first part of the trip, while we were still close to the Kivila Valley. The commissaire spoke briefly with the soldiers in his own language, flashed some papers at them, and they waved us through. But when we came out to the paved highway, where the checkpoints were more frequent and more heavily manned, the commissaire's influence diminished and soon vanished entirely. When he showed the soldiers his papers, they jeered and brushed him aside. Here, so close to the center of power, a provincial politician was merely an object of ridicule. Or maybe there no longer *was* a center of power, and the object of ridicule was the government he claimed to represent.

Kate bought a pack of cigarettes at a roadside stand and offered them around to the soldiers. "It'd be more effective if you'd do it, though," she told me. "It's supposed to be a male thing."

"I don't like kissing up to those pricks."

"They're just illiterate kids. They don't know anything. They don't even know I'm doing my best to kill them, bribing them with cancer sticks."

The soldiers accepted the cigarettes, but they seemed to be jeering at us too. It was a different attitude from the one we had seen before. Some balance of power had shifted in the country. The soldiers eyed us with menace, pushed past us to stare proprietorily into the cab, swung themselves up on the rails to poke through the cargo. Ndosi watched them impassively, and the commissaire, no longer bothering to get down from the cab, closed his eyes and appeared to fall asleep.

So it was left to the nurse to maneuver us through these checkpoints. She jumped down, suddenly animated, and got herself right up into the soldiers' sullen, leering faces. She wheedled and flirted; tugged on their uniforms and shoved them teasingly, audaciously, in the chest. She argued, and taunted them when they tried to argue back. And of course, she bribed them too, though her bribes were minimal, mere tokens of corruption—the soldiers might well have considered them an insult. But in the nurse's hands this offer of money became a further tease and flattery, no longer the crass purchase of a favor but a tool of seduction. I never saw exactly how it happened, but it was the same at every checkpoint: she mingled with the soldiers, talking and laughing and pushing them around, and after a while they were in disarray, dreamy and disoriented, as if they'd all been injected with the same venom.

She gave them a little money, climbed back into the cab, revved the engine, and the soldiers got out of the way. They all were under her spell, their usual banal visions of lust and extortion giving way to something more powerful and rare—some hopeless, disconnected longing that would last only as long as it took our truck to disappear from their sight.

By late afternoon we were driving through the shantytowns on the outskirts of Kisaka. Despite some modern amenities—power lines, TV antennas, patches of asphalt and cement, a few motorcycles and cars—these settlements seemed more squalid and desolate than the most remote bush villages. The commissaire stared out the window, brooding.

"These people are so poor. They have nothing, they know nothing. How can you govern people like that?"

"You mean, how can you tax them?" said Kate, openly jeering now, like the soldiers.

"And why would anyone want to extend their visas to remain in such a place?" The commissaire spoke quietly, still looking out the window. "A place your people have already destroyed." *Your people*—he listed some of them—internationalist speculators, neocolonialist profiteers, mercenaries and missionaries, corporate slave traders, Indian bourgeois merchants, socialists and communists and capitalists alike, all the allied forces contriving to contaminate the African with the confused values of Europe. And this city was the natural product of their efforts, with its open sewers and shantytowns and armies of glue-sniffing, murderous urchins. The ignorance and destitution of his countrymen, and their passive acceptance of this condition, were natural products of these efforts. These rutted potholed roads, the freeway that led nowhere, the unfinished monuments that squandered the resources of the state—what international agency had provided the funding for that? Why hadn't they patched up a road or two instead?

Now the commissaire turned to address us directly. "Why are you here? Because Africans are poor and destitute, and we need your help? Or because it's so easy to make money and advance your careers here, and the job is so entertaining—indulging ignorant people in their delusions. Oh, trés amusant, ces delusions! Here in the city you indulge the decadent fantasies of dictators, and out in the bush it's the self-destructive superstitions of peasants. Les superstitions des broussards! But we don't need your indulgence. We need to reject the old superstitions as well as the new infatuations and weaknesses. We need to be doing real work, learning to make real planes that fly, not willful imitations, childish toys. Your attitude is still colonial. Patronizing and condescending. The African is still a child to you, I can see that. Tell me, why did you love that man's toy planes so much? Why did you get up in front of all of them and read his foolish story? Your African fairy tale, charming and powerless. You admire very much the Africans, eh? So childish, so innocent and ignorant. So powerless."

He got out of the truck on the edge of the downtown area, without giving us a chance to respond or defend ourselves. Ndosi handed down his suitcases and sacks of peanuts, and we left him on the roadside, waiting for a cab, I suppose, while the jostling, directionless, powerless crowd flowed around him. He was as disenfranchised as any of them now: an itinerant politician, fallen out of favor and lashing out bitterly in all directions. No longer the commissaire but something else entirely. And exposing more of himself than the shadow-lurking, lip-curling commissaire had ever revealed.

But in the cab Kate and I sat stunned as the nurse pulled back into traffic. Finally Kate spoke. "Well, no one's going to mistake *him* for a child. There's nothing of the child left alive in him—no humor, no joy, no trust, nothing."

"Yeah. Except . . . he turned out to be . . . not as shallow as I thought. I mean, he was raving again, but it was a fairly articulate rave. I guess he has a point, in a way."

"Don't start getting empathetic with *him*, Will. So what if he has a point? Every evil sonofabitch in the world has a point."

"I'm not saying he's not an asshole, Kate. He is, he's an asshole. All I'm saying is, well, that he has a point. That maybe we're assholes too."

As we approached the center of town the thoroughfare we'd been traveling on splintered into several smaller streets. These in turn were blocked by barricades and excavations, and we soon found ourselves out of the main flow of automobile traffic, negotiating a maze of narrow streets crowded with pedestrians, mostly young men. When they saw Kate and me in the cab sometimes they shouted obscenities at us or made hostile gestures in our direction. Once, Ndosi cried out a warning, and a bottle shattered against the side of the truck. The nurse accelerated, scattering the crowds ahead of us, finally pulling out of the network of narrow streets onto a wider boulevard. Here we could travel faster, though the traffic was heavy and there seemed to be no rules of the road.

Kate touched my knee. "Can you tell where we are, Will?"

"No."

"I think we're traveling west still. Away from the central city." She turned to the nurse. "I thought you were going to sell this stuff at the central market. And Will and I need to go to the bank, and the embassy. That's all downtown, back that way."

"Ndosi and I will go to the market later," the nurse answered tersely.

"Then where are we going now?"

The nurse clenched the steering wheel, glancing out the side windows and into the mirrors. She was jockeying for position with a truck immediately to the left of us, only about a foot away, not really in a lane because there weren't any lanes. The nurse downshifted suddenly and accelerated, swerving to cut the other truck off. Behind us a horn began to sound.

"To the airport," she answered finally.

"Why the airport?" said Kate.

"Because," said the nurse, "that's where the airplanes are. And that's how you'll get back to Mputu, on an airplane."

"But we're not going back to Mputu now. That's not the plan."

"The plan is different now. We had to change it."

"Who's we? Not Will and me."

We were hemmed in on all sides by fast-moving disorderly traffic. Black clouds of foul diesel smoke swept through the cab. The horn behind us wailed on and on, an angry and futile and maddening sound. But all around us there were horns sounding, sirens in the distance, a background tumult of human voices and a ripple of explosions like gunfire. And in the cab of the two-ton the nurse's voice, tense and straining to be heard over it all. "It was the chef de poste's plan. He was getting nervous, having you around. Being responsible for you. With the soldiers and the smuggling and more and more trouble everywhere. And then, after the Dedication Ceremony, he saw he didn't really have any control over you anymore. So he was afraid something would happen to you, and then he would be in trouble too. And the rest of us agreed with him. The secretary, Ndosi, Sticky Tree, everyone, we all agreed that it's time for you to go. And now you should agree too, and stop arguing. It's too dangerous for you to stay here anymore. Look around—people want to kill you. We can't stop them. They want to kill us too, just because we're with you. Anyway, your work here is finished."

"I can't believe this," said Kate. "And I was worried about the commissaire. I didn't think we'd get deported by our friends."

"We don't have any choice. We waited for you to decide to go, and you never did. So now, we've decided for you. We're taking you where you need to go."

"We need to go to the embassy. We don't want to go to the airport! Will, tell her to turn around!"

I hadn't been pulling my weight in the argument, partly because I was considering the possibility that maybe I *did* want to go to the airport, if not necessarily on such short notice, and partly because this conversation, nearly shouted over the noise of engines and horns and sirens and the rush of a hot carbon-monoxide wind through the cab, had such a strange quality of reverberation: words rushing back at us, only slightly rearranged, from out of the past. This was not the first time I had been with Kate in the cab of a truck that was taking her somewhere she didn't want to go. Only at that time, heading north from Tucson, the truck had been taking her away from the airport instead of toward it, and the driver, rather than anxious to get rid of her, couldn't bear to part with her. Also she'd had a plane ticket in hand, that just went to waste, whereas now, of course, we had no tickets at all.

"Look, you can't just drop us off at the airport," I shouted across to the nurse. "We don't even have any plane tickets."

"That's not a problem. You have money. In the airport you buy tickets."

"I doubt that we can. I'm sure all the flights are booked, overbooked. Anybody who can get out is getting out."

"You're a consultant, Will. From Mputu. You have special dispensation."

We turned onto the road approaching the airport. Traffic slowed, and we were besieged by soldiers, vendors, hawkers, scalpers, hustlers of all stripes. "Roll up the windows," said the nurse. We did, and the noise and wind diminished, though immediately the heat and stuffiness were nearly unbearable. Kate was still trying to argue with the nurse, the way she had argued with me on the freeway north of Tucson. But already those reverberations were weakening. She was having trouble sustaining her righteousness, and there wasn't much fire in her indignation. She kept getting distracted by the mob gathering along the road to the terminal, the pleading and taunting and threatening faces surging toward the two-ton as we moved slowly through the heavier traffic. If they could get at us they'd strip us of everything. They'd trample us, suffocate us, rip our limbs off. Special dispensation, indeed. So what *had* we been thinking, that we could stay on indefinitely in a country like this?

Of course, it wasn't like that on the front porch at Ngemba. If we got back to Ngemba, we still might be able to retreat to the front porch, for a while. But eventually the same faces would close in on us there, or at some point we'd have to emerge again, and the mob would have only grown larger, more crazed with frustration and hopelessness and blind lust for retribution.

"But what about Uncle Pers?" Kate's voice was hoarse from shouting, and tears glistened on her cheeks. "We'll never see him again. I didn't even say good-bye. We can't just abandon him."

The nurse glanced at her, her expression softening. "I'll take care of him. He's where he wants to be. And *he* won't feel abandoned. Kate, he won't even know. He can't tell the difference anymore. Haven't you heard him? He calls *me* Katy now."

We stopped at the terminal, and immediately people swarmed around us, shouting offers to exchange money, to sell things, to carry our luggage or buy it or steal it. Ndosi handed down our bags while the crowd pressed at our backs. Ndosi apologized for sending us off in this way. But everyone had agreed it was best, he said. He himself had wanted to tell us so we could make the preparations, but in the end the chef de poste and the nurse and Sticky Tree had convinced him that it was better if we didn't know we were leaving. We might refuse to come, for one thing. And Sticky Tree especially was fearful that if we had the time to arrange a good-bye fête, we would repeat in some way the circumstances of Tom's departure. That we would feel compelled to have another piñata party. No one appreciated that tradition, Ndosi said; no one wanted to see another boom box smashed to bits, or worse.

He rummaged around in the cargo and pulled out a duffel bag. "Sticky Tree packed some things for you," he said. "So you wouldn't have to leave everything behind."

A crowd had gathered around us, edging closer all the time. I didn't dare open the bag to see what was in it. It felt like mainly clothes, plus a few books. "We had a lot more stuff than this."

"Sticky Tree packed the bag, monsieur. He may have forgotten several items. He didn't have a lot of time."

"I don't think my extra pair of sneakers is in here. And what about the boom box?"

Ndosi sighed, glancing worriedly at the crowd. Now I saw real fear in his eyes, and when he spoke his voice was strained and impatient. "Can't you just buy another boom box in Mputu, Will? And more sneakers, and whatever else you want? But in the meantime there will be arguments about what to do with the things you left behind. We need you to make a testimony for us. To write a list of what we are to do with the rest of your things. Who will inherit them."

"A list? You mean, a will?"

"Ç'est ça! A will."

So, while the nurse and Ndosi guarded our bags, Kate and I, aware that we had been nakedly manipulated but seeing no alternative, sat in the cab and wrote out our will, trying to recall each of our possessions that had been left behind. The boom box and cassette tapes to Sticky Tree. The dictionary and my sneakers to Ndosi. Clothes, cooking pots, food stores, propane stove, all distributed as evenly as we could among our friends and acquaintances.

"Oh God, there's one more thing," said Kate. "My laptop! What are we going to do about that? My entire stupid dissertation is on that thing. The machine's worth $3,000, Will."

Of course, she had copies of her dissertation back in the States, if it ever came down to working on her dissertation again. And what did it matter how much the machine was worth? It was gone, unless we wanted to defy these deportation proceedings and make our own way back to Ngemba to reclaim it. But what would be the point of that? Already Kate was resigned—no, fully committed—to our departure. So we added a line to our will and gave the laptop to the secretary. Maybe he would figure out how to use it, in the same way he had figured out how to survey: through intuition and improvisation. Or maybe it would just sit on his desk, an undeniable manifestation of progress and affluence, of Modernization.

THE SEAT COMPANION

High above the Gulf of Guinea our plane throbs along, following a straight and level trajectory through the monotonous sky. Ndosi and the nurse are tiny and fragile specks somewhere on the ground behind us, beneath the clouds, beyond the curve of the earth. There are a thousand malevolent forces that could destroy them there. That may have already destroyed them, for all we would ever know of it. There's no longer a connection between us, no sorcery or technology powerful enough to transcend the physical distance and the isolation of their circumstances.

The flight attendants make their way down the aisle, passing out peanuts and drinks. I ask for a beer, and my seat companion joins me. "After all, we have reason to celebrate, eh? As well as to mourn!" Well, sure. I don't know exactly what reasons he may be referring to; we each have our own reasons, no doubt, our own compromises, contradictions, ambivalent rationalizations. Still, it's an easy statement to agree with, and once again the sense of camaraderie swells. Soon we are huddled over beers like old friends, speaking English, then French, with seemingly equivalent fluency. Trading jokes and allusions as if we share a vast acreage of common ground, or some fundamental identity. But in fact, for all his talk, he's revealing very few personal details. I haven't found out where he lives, what he does, what family he may have, where he's going. He seems somehow to deflect any question that probes at such information, instead veering off on tangents. Now he contemplates his unopened bag of peanuts and begins to muse about the history of peanut cultivation. Did I know the peanut was endemic to America? Brought to Africa by the slave traders, actually, perhaps offered as compensation for the human product they were extracting from the continent. Not that the slavers saw much value in the plant. "An American plant," my seat companion tells me, "but a distinctly African food. You only learned to eat them from us. You were afraid to eat them at first, because they came out of the dirt. From under the ground."

"The underworld, I suppose."

"Ç'est ça, the underworld! But things change, the fears of our ancestors are forgotten. And now where are we? Far from the underworld, high in the heavens, in fact, and everyone—European, American, Asian, African—is tearing open these foil packages and eating little beans from under the ground. So we have progress. Such things reconcile humanity, eh? The airplane, and the little peanut. Only I don't much like to eat them myself. They disagree with my digestion. You can have mine."

I slip his bag of peanuts into the pocket of my knapsack, for later, and my hand brushes against some strangely smooth object in the pack. Instinctively, I recoil from the touch—an unexpected and foreign thing: pliant, waxy, almost alive. While my seat companion watches, I pull the object out and set it on the seat tray next to my beer.

It's the banana-leaf packet that Placide gave me yesterday morning, tied up with a strand of raffia twine and smelling of smoke and red earth and chlorophyl. Exotic, maybe even forbidden smells in this synthetic place. I carried it right onto the plane, not knowing what was in it, and somehow the customs police going through my bag never even saw it, though someone must have asked me the usual question: if I had ever left my luggage unattended or accepted any packages from another person. I suppose I automatically answered no, already forgetting—or dismissing—the nightwatchman and his parting gift.

I loosen the twine, unfold the banana leaf, and release an even wilder, unnameable odor into the plane. Beside me, my seat companion lets out a long tense sigh, gazing at the open banana leaf as if I have just revealed a thing of immense and forbidden value: smuggled diamonds, heroin, rhino horns, or ivory. Or an object of immediate deadliness and danger: the hijacker's gun, the terrorist's bomb that will make of us all a shower of shrapnel falling on the rippling Atlantic. But what the banana leaf contains is contraband of a different order: Placide's standard offering, a half dozen roasted crickets.

I carefully shake the crickets onto the seat tray. They are battered and charred but essentially whole, and off the banana leaf, isolated on the clean white tray, they look like specimens in a laboratory or museum case, displaying the terrible rigid beauty of arthropod design, the precise matching of form with deadly function. But these fierce pincers and cruel crunching mandibles and powerful legs are now limp and useless, and the wild crickets, like the foil-wrapped, domesticated peanuts, have become merely an airline snack. I offer one to my seat companion.

"Do you like cricket?"

"Well, I don't know. I used to eat them in the village, when I was small. Before we moved to the city. We'd catch them in the grass, and roast them over the cooking fires. They were a delicacy for us."

My seat companion chews his cricket with great concentration, making little sounds of obvious delight. He swallows and reaches for another. "May I? It's been so long since I ate cricket. And now, to eat them on this airplane, with you, an American . . ." Again he exuberantly pumps my hand. But actually I'm having some trouble matching his enthusiasm. My cricket doesn't taste quite right. In fact, it's making me feel queasy, almost the way I felt the first time I tasted cricket, that night a year and a half ago when nausea overwhelmed me on my porch and I fled inside to the couch while the thunderstorm raged. Maybe because it's not so fresh. Or because already we've come too far from the African earth, too far from the insect-crawling bush and the nightwatchman's brazier where the cricket was singed by the coals. Because we are too enclosed in a space where roasted cricket is simply an untenable concept.

A passing flight attendant leans over to see what we're up to, and quickly retreats. Several passengers stir and begin to murmur among themselves, darting glances at the arrangement of insects on my seat tray. One woman turns pale and looks away in distress, perhaps contemplating her airsickness bag, and my seat companion reaches over to fold the remaining crickets back up in the banana leaf. "If you're finished," he says, and when I nod he slips the packet back under the seat, into my knapsack. "People seem to be offended." He shrugs. "So. We see that the cricket is not yet a food of human unity. But remember, once they were also offended by peanuts."

I manage only a weak smile, grateful to him for managing things but no longer in the mood for repartee, thinking of reaching for an airsickness bag myself. I push my seat tray up, recline my seat, and close my eyes. Slowly the nausea drains away. Actually I'm exhausted, in no condition to challenge anyone's cultural constructs or dietary prejudices, least of all my own. I don't need to be crunching crickets *or* peanuts; I just need to sleep. And I do man-age to doze a little, aware of the murmur of conversation around me, the occasional beeping of call buttons, my seat companion rising and gently brushing past me to make his way to the bathroom. Fans whirr, engines throb, a thin wind wails along the fuselage. Rhythm sounds, motion sounds—but the motion doesn't feel like propulsion so much as precarious balance. Sway-ing, teetering. As if our airplane, rather than rushing forward in space, were rocking on a bamboo pole tethered to the distant surface of the earth.

My head lolls, swinging to one side, then the other, then rolling out a little too far, losing its fragile equilibrium and dropping over against something hard enough to jolt me awake. I open my eyes, and find my face squished against the surprisingly bony shoulder of my seat companion.

"Excuse me."

"It's quite all right. Make yourself comfortable, Will."

What does he mean by that? That I should snuggle up against his calcified shoulder and give myself over to sleep like a child? Instead, I pull myself erect and lean back against my seat. I don't want to take this passenger-affinity thing too far, too fast. I'm not all *that* comfortable with him, not to the point of allowing myself to drool on his shirt. In fact, I wonder if we've already pushed things a little with the cricket eating, which rather than strengthening may have actually weakened our bond, like the premature disclosure, in the first intoxicating flush of intimacy, of a personal secret one now regrets revealing.

Still, my head is so heavy, my neck weak, and it's not affinity for my seat companion but the gravitational pull of Earth, six miles away and seemingly stronger than ever, that draws my head down even farther, against his arm, practically all the way into his lap.

I jerk myself upright again. "Hey, I'm sorry."

"Don't apologize, William. You're asleep. Dreaming. Free to do what you never permit yourself when you're awake."

His voice has become more guttural, frail-sounding—perhaps he's on the verge of falling asleep himself. Yet there's something that disturbs me in those gravelly tones. Something uncanny. Something *familiar*. Perhaps it's only the universal voice of civility, of polite discourse and good breeding. Though if he's so well bred, why has he begun making all these unpleasant noises, snuffling and wheezing and gagging a little, and even, for God's sake, loudly farting in this closed space, crowded with people? Apparently those crickets didn't agree with his digestion either. Or else eating them, in defiance of the rigid etiquette of the airplane, has liberated him from the normal constraints of civilized behavior. But come to think of it, didn't he just now go off to the bathroom? And why has he suddenly begun to speak English again, when we were doing so well with our French? And how come he's calling me William, when I don't remember ever telling him my name?

Forcing my heavy-lidded eyes open, I turn to look at him. And what I see is not the well-dressed, dignified gentleman who was sitting there a short while ago but a ragged, wrinkled, gurgling, pale specter of an old man. A horribly ancient and decrepit creature, as out of place in a modern jet airplane as a handful of crickets wrapped up in a banana leaf. But I recognize him—the voice, yes, and also the fissured and blotchy flesh, the shock of luminescent hair, the pajama bottoms, and the rag of a wretched pagne wrapped around his waist. The way he turns his head away from me, vaguely dismissive, vaguely sardonic.

It's Uncle Pers on the seat beside me, gazing out the window at the distant earth.

"The world is made of fire."

His voice is barely audible. Leaning forward to hear him, I too look out the window. In the horizontal distance the air is clear, indigo blue, but below us the surface of the Earth is obscured by a dense white haze or cloud. We must have crossed the Gulf of Guinea and come out over the African continent again, and now are looking down on smoke from the dry-season fires of the northern tropics. Or perhaps we are already flying over the southern Sahara, or the Sahel, where the sandstorms of the advancing desert meet the slash fires of the retreating forest.

"People understood this once." His words are whispered, spoken to the window and not to me, and I have to lean close in order to hear. "They knew to worship fire. To fear it, and to welcome its destruction. The renewal and the cleansing. The fertilization, the germination. They knew fire is the end and the beginning of things."

Is there any sense in offering up a response? I could elaborate on his metaphor, and acknowledge the link between burning fields and burning memoirs. I could point out that, judging by all the smoke below us, people have not yet abandoned the ancient gods of fire. But why try to argue with a man in his condition? Who has no business being here in the first place, who got here by what means no one could say. Deposited by the nurse and Ndosi, artful smugglers beyond the imagination of the disoriented consultants they were also deporting? Or else . . . could it be that at last I'm witness to a bit of unequivocable magic, an incarnation of spirit matter and myth: the ghost of the Road Builder, muttering only to himself now, his last revelations lost to the labyrinth of airplane sounds that rises all around us, amplified and distorted. High-pitched, hysterical sounds, as if in imitation of his wheezing, gurgling, rattling breaths. As if the little fans are suddenly whirling in a vacuum, bearings gone dry, oxygen dissipated into space, while the whining engines shred themselves, and the fabric of the wings erodes in the unnatural turbulence of the air.

The plane shudders, and once again I force my eyes open and turn to look at Pers. His head has fallen back on the seat, leaving his neck grotesquely distended. His mouth gapes, and a trail of bloody spittle, already drying, runs down his chin. The color is drained from his face. There's no movement in his thin chest, no pulse of the artery in his neck. He can't possibly be faking it this time. The Road Builder is dead on the seat beside me.

The other passengers remain oblivious, asleep or seemingly half dead themselves. I push the call button, close my eyes, and wait for the flight attendant to come. Though if she was so offended by a few roasted crickets, what's she going to think when I present her with a corpse?

"Did you call for something, monsieur?"

She hovers over me, cocking her head, solicitous and suspicious at once. But there's no fear or horror in her expression. I glance at the seat beside me. Empty. No corpse, no Uncle Pers, no indication at all that he was ever sitting there.

"Are you feeling all right, monsieur? A little queasy, maybe, après votre petit hors d'oeuvre? You would care for something to drink?"

She makes it sound like a command. I decide not to put up a fight. "Sure, something to drink. I guess, what, a ginger ale. Merci. S'il vous plait."

"Bon. A ginger ale." Suspicion, definitely. Icy professional courtesy, and beneath it suspicion, distaste, and yes, maybe a little fear. "Autre chose, monsieur?"

"No, merci. Attend. Well, yes. Autre chose. A whiskey, please. Bourbon. Two bourbons."

"Excuse me? *Two* bourbons with your ginger ale? Are you sure—"

"Yes. S'il vous plait. Two of your little bourbons. To settle my stomach. I would like that very much, please."

My seat companion returns from the bathroom, and I draw up my legs so he can slide into his place. I'm very glad to see him again. In fact, I'm thinking that I like this seat companion more than anyone I have met in a very long time. He sits down and smiles at me, as if nothing has changed on the airplane, as if he expects our pleasant conversations to continue, obliterating nightmares, transcending even the morguelike atmosphere that has now settled over the cabin. And of course, he's right. In spite of everything, we must continue. I pull myself together and try to smile back.

"You look pale, monsieur."

"I'm fine. I just . . . I had a dream. A very strange dream. I saw . . . a ghost."

"Vraiment! What sort of ghost?"

"Well, a human ghost. An old man I knew well. We left him behind, en brousse, day before yesterday, I think. But he was right there, in your seat, just a moment ago."

"How extraordinary."

"He spoke to me. He said: 'The world is made of fire.' And then . . . he died. He was lying right there, dead."

My seat companion stares at me. "You saw him die, monsieur? In this seat?"

"I called the flight attendant. But when she got here he was gone, and I realized I must have been sleeping, that it was only a dream.

"Only a dream? What do you mean?"

"I mean . . ." I mean a dream, and therefore not a ghost. My seat companion keeps staring at me, as if to say, what sort of distinction is that? As if to say, what is a dream but the natural habitat of a ghost? The *only* habitat left to this ghost, in any case. And how could the dream not be real, when it's left me with the certainty that Pers is finally dead, when I hear so clearly his ragged exhausted voice still resonating in the plane?

The world is made of fire.

I lean over and look out my seat companion's window. Indeed, the world below is smoke-shrouded, as it was the last time I looked, when Pers' ghost sat muttering beside me. When I was dreaming. Yet this waking moment seems no less dreamlike, and these somnolent and dazed passengers surrounding